OTTER CREEK PRESS

CALIFORNIA GHOSTING

APPROACHING THE RESORT

Blasing was just about to ask a question when he heard hoarse yelling, clattering hoofbeats, and the metallic jingling of harnesses. As he watched the phantom stagecoach approach, he heard the squeaks and groans of shifting boards, the wagon protesting as if running over rutted ground.

Two spirits, one driving and one cradling a shotgun, sat up front with an iron-banded chest between them. The bearded driver lashed the ethereal horses with a whip, then yelled, "Outta my way, lady!"

Blasing glimpsed what he thought was frilly lace and a Sunday bonnet in the coach window. Green eyes suddenly appeared, piercing him, then they were gone as the stage jockeyed past. "I don't believe all this! This has to be a trick, some technical wizardry, like... like the Haunted Mansion at Disneyland."

Suddenly, a black Ferrari and a second, but more ornate stage-coach, raced alongside them. The entryway was instantly over-crowded and cacophonic—the thunder of hoofs on pavement and the yells of encouragement to go faster blending together.

"Dammit! The Ferrari is racing it! Of all the stupid...."

The flagman turned around, his eyes wide and his expression con-fused. He began waving at a truck backing into the street, then at the Ferrari and then the oncoming horse-drawn stage. Finally giving up, he jumped aside.

Angela braked, the pedal going all the way to the floor. "No brakes!"

TITLES by WILLIAM HILL

Fiction for the Young in Spirit:
The Magic Bicycle
Stealing Time *

Fiction for Young Adults:
The Vampire Hunters

Fiction:
The Wizard Sword *
California Ghosting
Dawn of the Vampire
Dragons Counsel *
Hunting Spirit Bear *
Vampire's Kiss

* Forthcoming

CALIFORNIA GHOSTING

WILLIAM HILL

OTTER CREEK PRESS

3154 Nautilus Road
Middleburg, FL. 32068

CALIFORNIA GHOSTING

Copyright © 1998 by William Hill
All rights reserved.

Published by Otter Creek Press
P.O. Box 416 ◆ Doctors Inlet ◆ Florida ◆ 32030-0416
Toll Free 800/326-4809

Library of Congress Card Catalog Number: 97-068139
Cover Art by Mandy Davis and Rod Volkmar
Manufactured in the United States of America

Quality Books, Inc. has catalogued this edition as follows:

Hill, William, 1959-
    California Ghosting/by William Hill—1st ed.
    p. cm.
    ISBN: 1-890611-01-8

    1. Ghosts—California—Fiction   I. Title.

PS3558.I43C35 1998   813'.54
                            QB197-40636

Printed in the United States of America.

DEDICATION

To my wife Kat—my heart and soul.

ACKNOWLEDGEMENTS

Thanks to everyone who has made California Ghosting the best it could be: Kat, Mom, Dub, Lynne, Owen, Jon, Siobhan, Dr. Steve, Susan, Butch, Richard and Jim E. Special thanks to Lewis Adler for all those phone calls and letters.

GHOSTAL SHORE'S
VISITORS, SPIRITS, AND MURDER SUSPECTS

ANGELA STARBORNE – Mac's beautiful San Francisco lawyer seeks the truth about his murder, his heir, and why rogue spirits are drawn to the resort.

BLASING MADERA – The widowed father of two, handsome heir to Ghostal Shores and fearless thrill-seeker, is intrigued by Angela and unnerved by the ghosts. Should he run the resort or sell it?

SEAN HELLER – The ill-tempered, Scrooge-like co-founder of Ghostal Shores treats people like the origami he folds and runs the resort the way he's always wanted, now that Mac is dead.

PETER "Mac" MacGUIRE – The murdered co-founder of Ghostal Shores was an alcoholic and a ladies' man. Does his spirit haunt the resort?

RICTOR – This menacing spectre has a mysterious link to the co-founders' past.

BRODERICK – Mac's former spirit valet and the resort's stiffly formal British majordomo keeps the ghosts organized and efficient.

DR. GEOFF LANDRUM – The flirtatious in-house physician is interested in Angela and life after death.

CANDY WHITE – Angela's friend is an astrologist, computer whiz and unabashed, too-cute, California blond.

EVA DARE – The sexy French marketing manager was fired after her affair with Mac, then rehired by Heller after Mac's murder. Blasing is her next challenge.

EFREM XANTINI – The Bostonian psychic and master mentalist is a man who reads minds and finishes sentences.

MADAME ZANADANE – Now that Mac is dead, the new in-house psychic from Vancouver finally has the prestigious job she has coveted for years.

CANNON – This "bull of a woman" spirit is the resort's alchemist extraordinaire.

EARL CASH – The assistant manager clashed with Mac over turning the resort into an extremely profitable interval ownership vacation resort.

CHIEF PORTER – The stout head of security lacked authority while Mac co-managed the resort.

MEG CASSIDY – Mac's illegitimate daughter hated her father and now seeks her share of the inheritance.

GRANT ROBERTS – The Texas financial wizard and lecherous spirit is an opponent of Heller's regime.

CALIFORNIA GHOSTING

ONE

With blond hair flying and blue eyes sparkling, Angela Starborne was enjoying the windy drive along the narrow coastal road. Driving fast helped her escape, and after the terrible news of Peter's murder, she could certainly use an outlet. Although leading a guided tour through a haunted hotel wasn't her idea of catharsis.

Still, racing along the twin lane blacktop that snaked through the undulating hills north of the San Francisco Bay was just what she needed. Angela's smile was slight and just a little tight. Her soul was still heavy, but the radiant sun and clear skies seemed to promise better times ahead.

The stark beauty of Point Reyes stretched out before and all around her. The small humps and hummocks along the peninsula appeared to be migrating southward, descending along the finger of land toward the endless expanse of the Pacific. Numerous coves and bays were snugly nestled among the knolls and white-cliffed beaches.

Scattered copses of cypress trees and fields of high grass brown from the winter covered the rolling slopes. Cattle were abundant, grazing in the dairy pastures, near historically preserved barns, white-washed cabins, and miles upon miles of fencing. Angela could understand why the Scots, Swedes and English had been reminded of their homelands, especially when the fog rolled ashore.

All in all, not a bad place to conduct business, Angela mused, if you didn't mind ghosts. She didn't feel like working, but a promise was a promise. Peter had asked her to help his heir assume partial ownership of the resort when such a time arrived. Unfortunately, that time was now.

For what must have been the hundreth time, Angela looked at her sleeping client. Blaise "Blasing" Madera's wavy black hair was tousled as if someone had been running their fingers through it. For some reason that thought nearly made her flush.

Unlike last night, Mr. Madera's handsome face was unlined, making him appear younger than when she'd met him. Angela never would have guessed that tall, dark and handsome was in his late thirties and widowed with two kids. Slim, fit, and dressed in gray slacks and a white turtleneck, he looked at least a decade younger.

If his smile could charm women as well as Peter's, then Mr. Madera would attract plenty of attention. Angela suddenly recalled his dark eyes—the way his gaze pierced her as if he could read her mind.

Angela was glad Mr. Madera was asleep. Not only did he obviously need it, but she was tired of dodging reasonable questions. Angela had told him what little she knew of Peter's murder—how he'd been shot in Heller's office, in a case of mistaken identity during a robbery attempt—but she felt awkward stonewalling his inquiries about Ghostal Shores.

Peter had been adamant; she wasn't to tell his nephew anything about Ghostal Shores until he'd set foot on the resort's front steps. But why? And why the stipulation Mr. Madera must arrive at the resort as soon as possible after Peter's death?

After a moment's reflection, Angela finally admitted what was really bothering her: Was Mr. Madera a good fit for Ghostal Shores? He and Peter had been estranged for a long time, and Mr. Madera probably didn't care about Peter's dreams. He just might sell to the highest bidder. Or even to Sean Heller. Angela shuddered at that thought.

As she pulled her attention back to the road, a red Porsche 911 skidded around the corner, weaving drunkenly into her lane. "Sonuvabitch!" Angela yanked the wheel right, jerking the 4Runner onto the low-sloped shoulder.

The car skidded, spraying gravel everywhere. Rocks clattered loudly underneath. The 4Runner suddenly hit a rut. The front end nose-dived with a screech of metal. Angela and Blasing were thrown forward.

"Hey!" came Blasing's groggy voice "What's...."

The 4Runner bounced airborne. It landed cockeyed, threatening to whip around. Angela fought to keep it from careening into the wooded hillside.

With a rickety slap, tree branches smacked the windshield, then clawed across the roof. Angela jerked the 4Runner back onto the pavement. The car bounced awkwardly, then landed hard. Tires squealing, it fishtailed into the wrong lane and skidded around the blind curve. The fence posts and tall grass blurred into a wall of green, brown, and gold. Angela prayed nobody was coming.

Nearly halfway through the turn, she wrestled the car into the proper lane, then cast a withering glance in Blasing's direction. "Damn Californians! If it's not at least four lanes wide, bone dry, and straight, they can't drive it!" she snapped. Her coppery face was livid.

Blasing didn't respond. He recognized when simply saying anything could provoke a confrontation. Blasing saw something out of the corner of his eye. "LOOK OUT!"

Angela looked back to the road and slammed on the brakes. An old man and his mule were in the road! Angela cringed, awaiting the bone-crushing thump and the sight of bodies flying.

Instead, the pack animal and its master passed through the hood, then the windshield. The ethereal prospector smiled a toothless grin and doffed his dusty cap as he sliced through the interior of the 4Runner. The ghostly mule was less accepting, its eyes wide with panic. The rank smells of old sweat, dust, and unwashed mule suddenly overwhelmed them.

After the 4Runner squealed to a stop, Blasing whirled around, eyes popping wide. "What the hell is that?!" He pointed at the grayed and somewhat translucent miner dressed in worn clothing.

As if desert mirages, distorted background shapes could be seen through the spirit. The ghost was obviously angry, cursing and tugging on his mule's bit, trying to convince it to move. The pale beast was amazingly overloaded with transparent boxes and bags bound together as if caught in a large spider's web.

"Is that a ghost?" Blasing whispered incredulously. "Ms. Starborne, I...." His lips worked silently.

Angela watched Blasing struggle with the concept of wandering spirits, his handsome face a mask of confusion and his eyes unsettled. He ran a hand through his hair, then his dark gaze met her unwavering stare; he seemed to have composed himself quickly.

"I don't believe in ghosts." He didn't sound convinced.

"You will," Angela said cryptically, no longer looking at Blasing but feeling the weight of his stare. "Maybe he's...wandered away." According to Peter, this wasn't supposed to happen.

"Wandered away? From where?"

"I'll ask," Angela said trying to sound casual as she rolled down her window. Her heart was pounding, her palms were damp, and the urge for a cigarette was strong.

"Isn't that dangerous?" Blasing asked. The near accident was not a big deal, but she was acting as if this were an ordinary, everyday experience.

"It might be."

The ghost spat, wiped his mouth. "Lillybell! Dang it ya floppy-eared varmint. If I had my stick ya wouldn't be actin' like this!" The mule appeared offended, setting its ears back in preparation for the forthcoming struggle.

Angela cleared her throat, started to speak, but was stopped by the ghostly prospector. "This is your fault, purdy lady. Why I oughta...." He stalked toward the car.

The mule snorted, then nosed its master, almost knocking him off his feet. The miner staggered, then whirled quickly, yanking off his hat and slapping his unruly companion. "Think you're cute, do ya?" Lillybell bared her teeth, then began hee-hawing and rocking back and forth. Madder than a hornet, the prospector threw down his hat and began hopping back and forth.

"You know, I've never heard of a ghost being this far away from the resort," Angela said tightly. Then she realized she'd let important information slip.

"You mean the Ghostal Shores Resort really is haunted?" Blasing asked. "Not just a gimmick like Disneyland?"

"This makes no sense, at all," Angela continued uneasily, trying to ignore Blasing's hot stare. "Spirits are supposed to be tied to a person or place, not wandering around looking for food and lodging."

"Ghostly hitchhikers. Right."

"Believe it," Angela replied.

"I wish I'd stayed in Tahoe instead of letting you drag me here. All I have to deal with there are drunks, jealous boyfriends and confused teenagers in hormonal overdrive."

Angela's eyes flashed, then narrowed; she bit back a retort, along with a childish urge to stick out her tongue.

It was probably wise to drive away, but Angela found herself morbidly fascinated. The old miner had moved behind his mule and was leaning against its rear, grunting loudly and pushing as hard as he could. The mule took two quick steps forward, then another sideways. The prospector fell on his face, partly disappearing into the ground.

Angela almost laughed but didn't, sensing the miner might turn his wrath on her. "Are you going to Ghostal Shores?" Angela didn't recognize him, so he certainly wasn't from the resort

The miner didn't reply, instead he hauled himself to his feet and dug into a pack. "Ya win, ya ornery beast." He gave Lillybell a sugar cube. "Lady, will ya kindly get your new-fangled whatchamacallit out of the way? The first carriage that went by really shook up Lillybell, but you scared the hell outta her!"

Angela's anger swelled; she started to say something about walking in the middle of the road, then realized it was pointless. When you were dead, you didn't care about getting run over.

"I said get the hell outta here!" He walked menacingly toward them. "Nobody messes with J.P. Johnson!"

"Ms. Starborne..." Blasing began.

Without another word, Angela stomped on the gas pedal and the 4Runner raced away. She glanced over at Blasing who was staring back at the receding spirits. Angela had seen a similar expression in the mirror during her introductory visit to Ghostal Shores.

"Now that we're almost there, I think you can tell me about Ghostal Shores and its ghosts," Blasing said, nearly choking on the last word.

"I'm going to pull over and see if anything is damaged," Angela said, ignoring his statement. She slowed, then pulled the 4Runner onto the side of the road. After turning off the engine, she walked around the car, removing a leafy branch from under a windshield wiper, then checked under the car. "Not too bad," she informed him as she climbed back into her seat. "Just a bent bumper and some minor scratches."

Blasing jingled her keys in his left hand. "I'm tired of this cat and mouse game. Talk to me." For a time, they just sat staring and challenging each other to give in. "What happened back there?"

Angela's expression stiffened, then colored as anger overwhelmed her. "What happened?! I'll tell you what happened!" Her irises lightened to almost white hot, ready to melt anything holding her gaze. "Some moron in a little red sports car cut a corner, and I almost hit a tree!"

Blasing said nothing. Angela Starborne was a hard person to evaluate, especially in such a short time. He was usually good at quick character judgments—a necessary trait in the security business.

Yesterday she'd been calm, collected and measured—the consummate lawyer in a power suit that concealed all but her slenderness. Even without makeup or an ounce of jewelry, she'd been arrestingly attractive.

When he'd seen her this morning, she'd undergone a significant transformation. Angela was still dressed simply in a cobalt blue blouse, white blazer and skirt, but now she was heavily adorned in Southwestern-style jewelry. Nearly a dozen bracelets hung from her left wrist, and rings of varied styles adorned every finger. Each was accompanied by a simple blackish-silver oval. Her silver necklace was artfully inlaid with turquoise, and her earrings were large white feathers.

Angela caught him staring and said, "They're gifts, mostly from my grandmother. This one is from your uncle." She raised her right hand and showed him an ornate gold ring with a rose stone. She seemed to hear his unspoken question. "I don't normally wear jewelry while working because it can give people the wrong impression, but now I'll fit right in at Ghostal Shores."

She bit her lip, and some of the anger left her face. "Besides, I always feel better for their company." She absently stroked a feathered earring. "During my last trip a few weeks ago, Ghostal Shores felt...different." She said nothing else, simply staring ahead and wondering why she'd picked this month to stop smoking.

"Nice performance, but you're stalling," Blasing said. "Talk to me." He rattled the keys again.

Angela tried staring him down, but that didn't work. Blasing wondered what she'd try next. Would she bat her eyes coquettishly or act dumb? And either would certainly be an act.

Finally, Angela said, "If you'll give me the keys and let me keep driving, I promise to tell you all about Ghostal Shores."

Blasing had a feeling she wasn't giving in, but simply using a negotiating form of jujitsu. "If you talk as we drive, deal."

Angela nodded. Blasing gave her the keys.

Without a word, she started the engine and continued driving. After some time, Angela finally said, "I'm sorry Mr. Madera. May I call you Blaise?"

"Blasing, if you would, please," Blasing said more coldly than he intended; he was mad at her, but this wasn't a good reason to jump on her case. "Only Uncle Mac, my parents, and Jennifer called me Blaise, and they're dead." He paused, then continued on more softly. "My friends call me Blasing. It was a nickname that stuck."

Angela smiled broadly, magically transforming her face; it was radiant, her smile touching her eyes, now the color of the sun-dappled waters of the Caribbean. Her cheekbones seemed less angular than before, no longer hard and stony. Even her nose seemed pert and sassy, upturned as if lifted by brighter thoughts.

"Oh, I am sorry, Blasing. We've gotten off on the wrong foot, haven't we? Peter's death has been traumatic. He was the first person to treat this once neophyte lawyer with respect. Sometimes I almost thought of us as father and daughter. I can't believe he was shot and that his murderer escaped.

"Not long ago, when he seemed so obsessed with the future of his estate, I asked him if he'd had a premonition about his death. He chuckled, and said, yes, in a sense. That after all this time spent around the spirits, he could sense the Grim Reaper's closing hand." She bit her lip. "I hope Sheriff Middleton has made some progress on the case."

"I have a feeling we should be talking about...ghosts instead of the recently dead," Blasing said coolly.

"You weren't very close, were you?" she asked coldly.

"Once, long ago," Blasing said. "But as always with Mac, nothing was more important than a beautiful woman. He used to say that a smile from a pretty lady was a blessing from God—like the sun shining specifically for you. I wouldn't be surprised if something to do with a woman got him shot."

Angela bristled. "He treated me well."

"I don't doubt it," Blasing replied sardonically.

"And he was loved by all the employees and spirits of Ghostal Shores."

"Don't get me wrong, Ms. Starborne. Mac wasn't interested in women just for sex. He truly loved women, but he rarely saw past their smiles and beauty, and that often got him in trouble."

"And you're different?"

Blasing held her gaze. "I learned not to follow in his footsteps. But that's not what we agreed to talk about. You may resent the fact that I inherited Ghostal Shores, but I didn't ask for it." She bristled, starting to retort but was cut short, " Now tell me about the resort and its ghosts."

Angela was quiet for long moments, absently stroking a feather, then said, "To be honest, I wasn't sure I believed in ghosts before visiting Ghostal Shores, but then over fifty percent of the populace do, which could be why the resort is so popular."

"There really are ghosts at this place?" Blasing asked, still disbelieving despite what he'd seen only minutes ago.

Angela nodded vigorously. "Most definitely. Haunt aficionados talk about going ghosting—searching out haunted places and exploring them—and this has become their favorite spot. I've heard people refer to it as California Ghosting.

"Ghosts. Hard to believe."

"Maybe so, but be ready. This experience might shake you. Even challenge your beliefs."

"We'll see. You know, I thought you were going to speak to that ghost like he was a person."

"After some time at Ghostal Shores, you too may find yourself talking to ghosts as though they were real people."

"Ghosts," Blasing said flatly. "A haunted resort. That's very hard to believe. Very hard." He was silent for a long time, and she could almost hear his mind working. "How many?" he finally asked.

"About a dozen or so," Angela told him. "I'd hoped to gradually introduce you, but that's sort of out of the question now."

"So, let's say there are ghosts; if so, what was one doing way out here so far from the resort?" Blasing asked. Angela shook her head, and he had the feeling she was hiding something. " I thought you were going to tell me all about Ghostal Shores."

She sighed, then began, "A couple of years after the earthquake of 1908, Thomas Heller purchased the land north of where the lighthouse had been built. Sean Heller inherited the land and a great deal of money from his uncle. Heller mentioned wanting to run his own resort to Peter, who was managing a resort in Palm Springs. Peter had a crazy dream." She paused for dramatic effect. " He wanted to build a benevolently haunted resort. Can you believe that?"

"Sounds like something Uncle Mac would dream up. Beautiful ghosts would always be timelessly beautiful."

Angela frowned. "In hopes of moving some of the spirits, Peter wanted to build the place with old brick from deserted Nevada 'boom towns.' They purchased the Goldfield Hotel with the intent of re-building it on Point Reyes. Later, they bought brick from a lady who needed to sell some of the Aurora buildings to reduce her tax liabil-ity. Other material contributions came from Gold Hills, Silverdale, and even Virginia City." In the distance, Angela could now see a pair of white buildings against the seemingly endless blue of the sky and the Pacific Ocean.

"The building of Marin Shores," Angela continued, "was de-layed more than a decade by Nevadans attempting to pass protec-tive legislation to keep people from removing historical landmarks. The law was passed, but Mr. Heller and Peter were grandfathered."

"Is this going somewhere, Counselor," Blasing asked, "or is this just more of your stalling tactics?"

Angela gave him an annoyed look, then continued, "During all the legal hassles, Peter and Mr. Heller decided not to reconstruct the Goldfield, but build a first class resort with the materials. A lot of people thought they were crazy—using brick in an earthquake area."

"I thought I saw a couple of brick buildings in Point Reyes Station," Blasing said.

"You did. They're specially reinforced, just like Ghostal Shores, to handle tremors and shaking. Anyway, over the years, Mr. Heller had another cash windfall and began purchasing antiques to stock the place. Ah, here we are."

Behind low bushes on each side of the entrance, square pil-lars of white brick were connected by a wrought metal archway above the open gates. "Ghostal Shores" was written in white script across the black arch and seemed too bright in the sunlight. As they drove forward, Blasing shivered. He couldn't help but think "abandon hope all ye who enter here."

The circular strip of asphalt cut a dark path through the lush green lawns before splitting around a flower garden and heading toward the white columns of the stately portico. Compared to the winter-weathered lands outside the dark metal fencing, the grounds of the resort appeared to be an oasis. Many of the trees and bushes had been painstakingly trimmed into a topiary of horses running, rearing, and standing proudly.

"Construction of Marin Shores finally began in 1981 and took a little over three years to complete," Angela continued. "There were some one hundred rooms, a large garden, indoor swimming pool, library, restaurant and much more. When they built the southern wing they added the second hundred rooms and tennis courts."

Blasing leaned forward to get a good look at Ghostal Shores; it appeared to be a blend of southern charm and the Old West. The main building was three stories high with a grand portico spanning much of its front. The columns' shadows cut across the facade, striping the entrance with dark, diagonal lines. A green cloth canopy covered the stairs and balustrade from the porte-cochere to the entryway. The windows above the double doors were tall, at least two stories in height, and designed to let in eastern sunlight.

A two-story wing lined with balconies had been built to the south, its uppermost wall green and wavering as though made of netting. Blasing figured the tennis courts were on the roof. Next to the wing was a parking garage surrounded by low buildings. A second wing was being constructed to the north. The foundation had been poured and a few brick walls covered wooden framing.

"Marin Shores officially opened June 1, 1984 with some local fanfare. At the opening day party, the spirits made their surprise and yet hoped-for appearance. To make a long story short, after the shock had worn off, the spirits were an instant hit, just as Peter had surmised. Word spread far and wide. News crews and psychics flocked to Marin Shores.

"Professors from U.C. Berkeley performed para-psychological studies. Just about anybody who could did a story on this place. The publicity died down quite a bit when they discovered they couldn't film the ghosts. Most people ended up thinking it was just a marketing scam. Still, it was all the rage that summer. Didn't you hear of it?"

Blasing shook his head. "At that time, I was spending summers in Argentina and winters in Switzerland teaching skiing."

"I see. As you can imagine, with that much PR, especially with the rave reviews and the uniqueness of it all, Marin Shores became

Ghostal Shores and drew incredible crowds. They went from hoping to break even to a surefire success in about four months."

Blasing was just about to ask a question when he heard hoarse yelling, clattering hoofbeats on pavement, and the metallic jingling of harnesses. As he watched the phantom stagecoach approach, he could hear the squeaks and groans of shifting boards, the wagon protesting as if running over rutted dirt roads instead of smooth pavement. Two spirits, one driving and one cradling a shotgun, sat up front with an iron-banded chest between them. The bearded driver lashed the ethereal horses with a whip, then yelled, "Outta my way, lady!"

Before Angela could respond, the ghostly stage passed them on the left. The phantom horses were lathered and laboring, white froth pasted to their pale muzzles and strewn across their colorless flanks. Steam trailed from their nostrils as if they were boiler-powered, and sparks from their iron-shod hooves danced above their knees.

Blasing glimpsed what he thought was frilly lace and a Sunday bonnet in the coach window. Green eyes suddenly appeared, piercing him, then they were gone as the stage jockeyed past. Blasing had the fleeting impression of someone coldly beautiful, almost regally disdainful.

Angela and Blasing suddenly began coughing and choking. Blasing couldn't see any dust, but he smelled it, and his teeth felt covered with sandpaper. He blinked, then rubbed the grit from his eyes. The ghostly stage quickly left them behind and ran through a stunned construction flagman.

"I don't believe it," he muttered.

"Just relax," Angela smiled warmly, wiping away her gritty tears. Despite all her visits to Ghostal Shores, she'd never seen or heard of such a sight. "Don't let it overwhelm you. Just remember, people pay good money to see this, and now part of this is yours."

"I don't believe all this! This has to be a trick, some technical wizardry like...like the Haunted Mansion at Disneyland."

"Believe and relax. And remember this: even if you don't show emotion, the ghosts can sense it. Just pretend you're skiing off a cornice." She smiled. "I know that doesn't scare you."

Angela nodded toward the flagman. His back was to them, watching the phantasmal stagecoach head for the entrance, rushing through luxurious cars, international guests, and the green-uniformed staff.

"I'm sure everybody will be happier when this construction is completed."

Angela tried not to let Blasing see her shiver; what was it that unnerved her? Was it the sight of the wandering ghost? Or the stage? Peter had never mentioned them.

Suddenly, a black Ferrari and a second, but more ornate stage-coach, raced alongside them. The entryway drive was over-crowded and cacophonic—the thunder of hoofs on pavement and the yells of encouragement to go faster blending together.

"Dammit! The Ferrari is racing it! Of all the stupid...."

As the second ghostly stage passed them, Blasing saw inside the coach. A big, bony spirit was waving his fists and exhorting the driver to go faster. He suddenly turned toward them. From the shadow of the ghost's stetson, yellow eyes like a cat's caught in the bright lights stared at Blasing. A sense of dread overwhelmed him, and he had to turn away.

The flagman turned around, his eyes wide and his expression confused. He waved at a truck backing into the street, then at the Ferrari and then the oncoming horse-drawn stage. Finally, giving up, he jumped aside.

Angela braked, the pedal going all the way to the floor. "No brakes!" The truck hauling brick continued to back up. The Ferrari swerved left, lost control, then slammed into a parked car across from the resort. The sports car careened back into the driveway, almost hitting a diving valet, then slid directly into the 4Runner's path.

TWO

"Damn" Angela jerked the wheel to avoid the spinning Ferrari. The 4Runner moved sluggishly, the wheel resisting her efforts. Something popped painfully in Angela's left shoulder. A hot wire burned down her arm, and the wheel slipped from her grasp. The 4Runner whipsawed, the back end suddenly sliding around. "Please Great Spirit!" Angela prayed as she re-grabbed the wheel. She was too late; they were heading for a man loading a luggage cart.

The bellman dove aside as the car clipped the cart, scattering bags and sending a lady's feathered hat flying. Angela finally managed to right the 4Runner. The 4Runner shot between two parked cars, then bounced over a curb, plunging through a short fence and plowing through the garden before sliding to a halt.

Angela slowly regained her senses, counting herself lucky that only her shoulder ached. Glancing over to Blasing, she saw he was a little dazed. Thank Great Spirit she hadn't killed anyone.

Suddenly her anger flared. Where had the ghostly stages come from? Better yet, where had they gone? And who was that idiot driving the Ferrari?!

"Counselor, I think I'll drive next time," Blasing said, gingerly touching his head. "WHAT???!" Blasing recoiled from the transparently pale face poking through the windshield. Hackles rose on his neck, and it tingled maddeningly.

"Oh dear, oh dear. Is everybody all right?" the ethereal figure asked, then bit his lower lip. The ghost's eyes were wide, and his handlebar mustache twitched nervously as his gaze darted back and forth between Blasing and Angela.

Blasing was disconcerted, his mouth working soundlessly for a time. When he finally managed to speak, his voice was hoarse. "I've survived worse, thank you." Blasing unbuckled his seat belt, then glanced at Angela. She had a pained look in her eyes but appeared unharmed otherwise. Somehow she looked even more stunning disheveled than she did composed. "How about you, Counselor?"

"Counselor? Miss Starborne? Oh my!" the crestfallen spirit cried, his ethereal hands fluttering about as though a flock of birds.

"Besides a sore shoulder," Angela said as she rubbed the spot, "I think I'm okay. I can move everything that's supposed to move. How about you?"

"I'll...be...fine." As though the ghost's disembodied state was contagious, Blasing was leaning away from it.

"I tried to warn you. Barney, meet Blasing Madera, Peter's heir and now part owner of Ghostal Shores."

"A pleasure indeed, sir." Barney bowed, the tip of his head disappearing into the dashboard. Blasing was glad the ghost didn't offer to shake hands. "I apologize for such an inauspicious beginning to your inaugural visit to Ghostal Shores. We try diligently to ensure that our guests have an enjoyable stay. Though recently it seems that has become more difficult."

"Why do you say that?" Angela asked. Unfastening her seat belt with shaky hands, she shoved open the door and crawled unsteadily out of the car. Blasing was already out and stretching.

"Ever since Mr. MacGuire was murdered, things seem to have...well...soured. We have had numerous accidents, enough that the doctors, I mean the METS or is that EMTS" he rolled the acronym around in his mouth, "certainly know their way here from Point Reyes by now." The ghost sagged as if he had never had a bone in his body. Even the bars and jacket tassels on his shoulders drooped.

"How many accidents?" Angela asked.

"Nearly a dozen," Barney replied.

"Are people dying?" Blasing asked, suddenly alarmed.

"No! No! Nothing quite so severe, good sir," Barney explained. while curling and stroking his mustache. " Just broken bones, cuts and the like. They tell me it's the usual kind of accidents, just a very large number. Some believe it's our fault, but I assure you it's not. Mr. Heller believes someone is trying to sabotage the construction. Maybe the same person who tried to kill him and murdered poor Mr. MacGuire by accident."

"Hey, is everyone all right?" a stout young man clad in a green bellman's outfit asked.

"They're fine, Anthony," the ghost concierge replied, then gave instructions to take good care of them.

"I want to discuss driving with the owner of that Ferrari," Angela growled. She didn't see him anywhere. Anthony promised to get his name. "Thank you," Angela said, her smile feral.

"I imagine the sheriff will want to talk with you folks," Barney said, then sighed, his chest puffing up like a balloon. "At least he won't have far to go."

"What do you mean by that?" Angela asked; she didn't like what she was hearing.

"Sheriff Middleton is staying here while he continues to investigate Mr. MacGuire's murder." The ghost looked critically at Angela, who was leaning on Blasing, then smiled apologetically. "But enough. I believe you should rest awhile. Just ask any ghost— after it's all said and done—a near death experience is more frightening than actually dying. Go relax. We'll check in for you."

"Is this it?" Anthony asked, holding up Blasing's overnight bag and both of Angela's suitcases. They nodded.

"What about those ghostly stagecoaches?" Blasing asked Barney, who had stopped at the curb. Anthony also halted, waiting for a limousine to pass. It was followed by a burgundy Mercedes 450 SL, then a classic white '65 Jaguar with gold wheels and trim.

"A very odd sight," the ghost bell captain replied, his brows knitted together. The three of them looked around at the crowd. People were talking excitedly and pointing toward the front entrance as if the stage had raced up the steps and through the main doors.

The customers were a melting pot of various nationalities and cultures. By their clothes, jewels, and mannerisms, many were obviously well-to-do. A few patrons looked stringently studious. Others were eccentrically attired with crystals to match. Regardless of their background, each one appeared thrilled as if something miraculous had happened to change their lives.

"The first stagecoach to arrive at the Goldfield Hotel in over a hundred years," Barney told them.

"I thought I was at Ghostal Shores," Blasing said, now very confused.

"You are at Ghostal Shores, but I have—had—worked at the Goldfield for so long, that it just slips out sometimes. Mr. MacGuire said he understood. You see, the spirit of the Goldfield lies within

Ghostal Shores—a fine establishment that welcomes all and spoils most." He winked.

"The essence of the Old West is here, wrapped within Ghostal Shores' grandeur, beauty and spirited service." He smiled broadly, then made an elegant, sweeping gesture toward the front entrance. "If you like, I will ask around and see if any new spirits have checked in."

"Thank you."

"Take good care of them, Anthony. Mr. Madera is your new boss." The bellboy straightened as if he'd been starched. "You'll be checked in so fast you'll think the express line is run by snails." Anthony headed across the driveway. " Yes sir, ma'am, I'm your man, Tony Swift that's me." Angela and Blasing followed him. Barney just floated along lazily apace.

"Thank you, Barney," Angela said. "You always take such good care of me. How is Broderick handling Peter's death?"

"He has been rather withdrawn, I'm afraid."

"I'm not surprised."

"But I'm sure your presence will brighten his day. I'll let him know you're here."

"Who's Broderick?" Blasing asked.

"Mr. MacGuire's personal valet," Angela added.

"If I may be so bold," the host ghost began, "might I suggest you ring the house doctor? While you wait for him, might I also suggest you visit Cannon? It might help you relax."

"I'll take your advice," Angela replied.

"Then good day, madam and fine sir." The ghost floated off to greet others.

"Who's Cannon?" Blasing asked Angela.

"The bartender. Are you sure you're all right?"

"Come tomorrow, it'll probably feel like an awkward ski fall. My guardian angel takes good care of me."

"You believe in guardian angels?" Angela asked with an arching eyebrow.

"Ms. Starborne, you're talking to the only survivor of a private plane crash at age six. I felt I was unlucky then, but when I survived a commercial airplane wreck at age thirteen, I just knew I was hard to kill, and for the next dozen or so years, I was determined to prove it.

Isn't youthful wisdom wonderful?"

"Blasing, please explain to me how believing in ghosts is stranger than believing in guardian angels?"

Blasing was thoughtful, then admitted. "Good point, Counselor. I'll try to be more open-minded. How are you feeling?"

"I'll survive," Angela replied as she gingerly moved her shoulder. "Blasing, if it isn't too much trouble, could you call me Angela? I am your lawyer now, and we could have died together."

"Sure, Angela," Blasing replied with a slight smile. "I wonder where the stagecoaches went?"

"Let's ask," Angela said. A lanky bellman with red hair and a droopy mustache told them that the stagecoaches had raced through the side of the building. Her thank you and smile made him beam.

While Anthony was grabbing a luggage cart, Angela and Blasing paused at a forest-green carpeted stairway. One set of steps headed upward to the portico. The other and a ramp led down into a modern-looking lobby where the green-suited staff tried to guide and organize the guests and their islands of luggage on the sea green carpet.

A Hispanic priest was standing back and appeared to be studying the crowd. An overdressed and heavily jeweled woman carrying a poodle was harassing her husband and a stocky bellman. An elderly Asian gentleman, with the aid of his valet, counted and then recounted his black trunks. Coming up the ramp, a group of bald men dressed in brown robes were departing. They were followed by a thin man dressed in a tweed suit, smoking a pipe and reading the *SAN FRANCISCO CHRONICLE.*

"Anthony, do you need anything else from us?" Angela asked.

He promised to check in, then take their baggage to their rooms. "I assume you have reservations?" Anthony asked.

"I'd better have," Angela said grimly. " My office was supposed to have called yesterday."

"Just like last night?" Blasing asked.

She shot him a sharp glance. Her office had forgotten to notify him of her visit, leading to several awkward moments; Angela had been the first to tell him of his uncle's murder. He'd been upset; a week had passed since the murder, and no one had notified him. She'd been out of state, but that didn't explain why no one else had contacted him.

Anthony asked, "Where should I bring the keys? To the bar?"

"That sounds like a good idea." Blasing handed him a twenty.

Beaming, Anthony thanked him, then carted their luggage down the ramp into the bustling lobby.

"You certainly know how to make a good first impression."

"I live in a resort town, remember? Almost everybody lives off tips," Blasing reminded her.

"Even bodyguards? What kind of tips do they get?"

"I wouldn't know. Rich handles the bodies," Blasing replied blandly, "I handle the equipment. I'm not certified to handle bodies."

"How do you get certified?" Angela almost laughed. When she saw his serious expression, she decided otherwise. "Let's go this way." Angela waved toward the front steps. "You'll get a better feel for the place than by entering through the lobby." Throwing him a smile, she headed up the steps.

Blasing watched her lithe movements, trying to convince himself he should be paying more attention to Ghostal Shores than Angela. But in all honesty, he wanted to be distracted. The ghosts had unnerved him more than just a little —and that couldn't be said about too many things.

After a deep breath, Blasing steeled himself and ascended the stairs, running his hand along the ornate balustrade. Angela was waiting at the large double doors. Hanging above her was an elegant crystal chandelier.

"We're actually on the second floor, but they call it the first. The bedrock prevented much digging." Angela took his arm, guiding him inside. "This is the Pacific Overlook, but I call it the Cathedral to the Coast, for obvious reasons."

"Impressive," Blasing agreed.

Across the cathedral-like chamber, a panorama of blue water and sky was framed by a large bayview window. It was as if he hadn't stepped indoors at all. The mammoth chamber was airy, the ceiling over three stories tall with arched windows stretching toward a bright, domed skylight. The second and third story walls were mirrored, adding depth and space by reflecting the sky and sea.

To their left, three sets of double doors stood between pairs of fluted gold lamps, and the dark wood furnishings were situated as though small talk, cards, or backgammon were required. None of the furniture looked very comfortable—more to be looked at than sat in. "The furniture is from the late 1800's, most of it Victorian, and was part of Peter's attempt to capture the mood of the past."

"And half of this is mine?" Blasing asked, sounding amazed.

"Yes, but don't be surprised if Mr. Heller contests the will," Angela replied. "The signed copy of the final will never reached my office, and oddly enough, it wasn't found among Peter's effects either. We'll just have to deal with it. Earlier versions are signed, and I don't foresee a serious problem. A delay at worst."

"The Pacific Crest Restaurant and the Clifftop Bar are this way. Come on." She finally released his arm and headed for the steps and ramp. Murmuring voices, some light laughter, and the clinking of glasses and silverware drifted down toward them. As they ascended the stairs, they passed a descending security guard.

"Quite a place," Blasing said.

The bar was part tea room and part arboretum, full of potted trees and plants surrounding dark tables and comfortable-looking armchairs that might have been removed from a favorite uncle's lavish study. A massive set of windows faced westward, ready to capture a Pacific sunset and the migration of any whales.

The lounge was busy but not crowded, the twenty or so tables occupied by an unusual mix of people. A young couple dressed in matching sweat suits of bright magenta were drinking Mimosas. Nearby, a foursome of African-American women dressed in black with their hair piled high sat close together, whispering between them. Across from them, a tall, thin man wearing a bowler and white cardigan was smoking a large pipe and reading Friday's WALL STREET JOURNAL. A few tables over, an elderly, salt and pepper-haired lady clad in a robe and shawl interwoven with crystals was talking excitedly with a pretty, young blond woman.

In contrast, the copper-topped and horseshoe-shaped bar was very crowded near the coastal windows. Hustling about, a short, amber-haired young man was busy mixing and blending drinks. Bright sunlight glinted off the mirrors behind him and splayed through the smoky haze. Near the apex of the horseshoe, the restaurant could be seen through an archway.

"Come on," Angela laughed, "there's someone I want you to meet."

With the ease and familiarity of a couple who had been together a long time, Angela took his arm and led him toward the quiet end of the bar. She was surprised at the girlish tingle of excitement she felt and told herself to get a grip.

The bar was made of a rich, dark wood; but the footrail and countertop were polished copper. Suspended above the bar and bending around the horseshoe into the restaurant were racks of glasses. The pillars behind the bar were chainsaw-cut wooden bears that held a low shelf of liquor bottles. Above them were three mirrors etched with scenes of the ocean—one at sunset, another during fog, and the last at night under a full moon.

Blasing took a moment to check his reflection; he looked tired and frazzled. He glanced at Angela. She was quite striking—seemingly windblown and wanton but somehow composed at the same time.

"What would you like?" she asked.

"Something stiff. A B&B, I think."

"And a glass of merlot," Angela said to no one in particular.

At the far end of the bar, the bartender was working feverishly in an attempt to keep up with the laughing and yet demanding crowd. There were over a dozen patrons, with nearly an equal number of men and women of varied nationalities. Except for a few brilliant ties and a couple of strikingly short skirts, they were dressed in conservative business attire and smoking like dragons with serious indigestion. Drinks rarely sat idle, either rapidly consumed or sloshed with every gesture.

From what Blasing could overhear, the group had the air of wheedling street merchants. "I'll have another Tequila and Grape." "Come on bud, step up to the pump. I bought the last round." "Isn't it your round?" "Can I borrow fifty bucks? I'll pay you Friday."

Angela noticed where Blasing was looking and said, "They remind me of salespeople."

Before Blasing could ask his question, a brandy snifter and a wine glass drifted from the glasses rack. He felt the hair on the back of his neck rise as he watched a brown, genie-looking bottle float from a nearby shelf. The cap spun off, then the bottle inverted to pour.

"Cannon, please show yourself. Mr. Madera is looking skittish," Angela teased, trying to relax Blasing. It didn't work. "Please, Cannon."

The air behind the bar wavered as if above hot asphalt, then a gray mist appeared, coalescing into a very large ghost. Cannon was a broad, bull of a woman. Her hair was short, her nose crooked, and her double chin added creases to her dimples. Cannon was dressed in a white cotton shirt, bow tie and dark pants.

Laughing, the ghost said, "I can see why ya wouldn't want this one ta run off, Angie!" Her smile was mammoth, extending from ear to ear.

Angela blushed but said coolly, "Unnerving a person is not an appropriate greeting, especially for Peter's heir apparent. Liberty Cannon, meet Blasing Madera, nephew of Peter MacGuire. Blasing, meet the Ghostal Shores spirit bartender extraordinaire."

"Alchemist, I say. Not bartender. Not mixologist. Alchemist! My drinks are as much magic as mix since 1860. But don't think I'm out of date, behind the times or livin' in the past, no siree! I'm up ta date on the latest trendy concoctions, like the Bullwhip, the Mustache Ride, and the Extreme Creme." She rolled her eyes, then said, "Blame it on Orgasms, Sex on the Beach and a Sloe Comfortable Screw. Hey, what's a hair parent?"

"An heir," Angela said, rolling her eyes. "Peter left his half of Ghostal Shores to Blasing."

"Did ya say new owner?" Cannon asked.

Angela nodded.

"Praise the Lord!" Cannon threw her ethereal arms into the air. The glasses in the rack jumped, performing a quick jig in celebration. Cannon suddenly grew serious, scrutinizing Blasing as if sizing him up.

"Pleased to meet you, uh, Liberty," Blasing managed. Under her stare, he felt pierced to his soul, as though the ghost had pushed aside the veil of flesh to reveal his true spirit. Curious about what would happen, he offered to shake hands.

Liberty Cannon looked at his hand, then his face, then blew him a kiss. She "tsked" him twice, then in an accusing voice said, "Ya know the rules."

"No, he doesn't," Angela said. "He was just informed about Peter's death last night. We just drove in from Tahoe."

The other bartender stopped behind Cannon, whispering something. She nodded and he left, heading toward the restaurant.

"The rules?" Blasing asked.

A pair of bright yellow rubber gloves floated to Cannon and she slipped them on. With a smile, she shook his hand "None of the ghosts are allowed to touch a guest flesh-ta-flesh, so ta speak. It ain't proper, nor easy. Not like moving things around, though that takes lots of practice too. And touching people...feels strange, does something ta both the ghost and the person being touched. I did it while at the Goldfield once or twice. Anywho, blame the rule on Fawn."

"Fawn? Who is she?" Blasing asked, looking from the ghost bartender to Angela, who appeared disgusted.

"Hey, Cannon," someone at the end of the bar yelled, "the Blues for everybody."

Cannon didn't look at him, or at any of the others crammed around that end of the bar. "I used ta do this at the Goldfield late at night when it was busy and the customers were really drunk."

A large glass, a steel shaker and a bunch of ice suddenly jumped together. Somewhere below the bar top, a refrigerator opened and a dark bottle flew out. It inverted as it drifted over the shaker, then the top fell off letting schnapps slowly drain out. At first the liquid flowed normally, then it changed, spiralling before finally performing loops as though pumped through an invisible tube. The shaker snapped together and rattled about.

"And what are the other rules?" Blasing managed.

The glass half of the shaker suddenly popped off, and the concoction surged back and forth over a few feet, never spilling a drop.

"If any of the ghosts are caught stealing, harming a guest, or anything prohibited to a regular staff member, that ghost would be cleaned out." She appeared perturbed.

"Cleaned out? How?" Blasing asked.

"They call in a psychic or a priest, then they try ta exorcise ya," Cannon replied. "Not that they need to call one anymore. We have one on staff now."

"You do?" Angela asked. "Who?"

"A Madame Zanadane from Vancouver. She used to be a frequent visitor."

"I know her. She was always asking Peter for a job. Why did Mr. Heller hire her?"

"Hellraiser doesn't confide in me, but I think it's ta keep us in line. Not that it's needed. Fact is, the rest of us ghosts might do the cleaning first, kicking out the offending party. But there's never been any trouble. We like it here, I'll say, and the others agree. I sure miss Mr. MacGuire, though. I sure do."

"Me too," Blasing said, suddenly feeling low about not staying in better contact with Mac. If these spirits and Angela cared for him that much, he must have changed. "Why Cannon, instead of Liberty?"

Cannon laughed raucously. "I'll say times have changed, that's fer sure. In my living days—and I've been tending bar since I was fifteen—a woman with the name Liberty put fool ideas in a man's head, if ya get my meaning. Might have been better if my mamma had named me Faith, but then they'd probably say, I just gotta have Faith! Or, I need a Faith healing! But, as ya might suspect, Cannon puts them off. Bombastic, that's me! At closing time, I can yell over any crowd.

"Want ta hear?" She had a mischievous gleam in her eye.

With a loud smack, the shakers clamped back together. Leaping out from a stack on the back counter, a group of on-the-rocks glasses air-danced, then lined up with military precision. A strainer joined the shaker and the pouring began. " Sure ya don't want to hear?"

"I get the feeling that's not a good idea, Cannon," Blasing replied.

The ghost winked at him. "Ya can call me Liberty, if ya want."

"Uh," there was some stifled laughter from behind Blasing, "excuse me. Mr. Madera, Ms. Starborne. You're in Suite 351."

They turned to look at Anthony.

"That's Peter's suite," Angela said, then realized, "You mean we'll be staying together?"

Anthony quickly grew serious, apologizing as he hastily explained about the booking problem. "Besides, where else would you want to stay? Mr. MacGuire's suite is fantastic, with a huge lounge and two bedrooms with their own baths. It's loaded like no place else with a TV, stereo and bar." His excitement faded as he remembered why the suite was available. He told them their luggage had been delivered, and if they had questions to ask Mr. Cash—the assistant manager. Then he handed them each a card key.

"I also took the liberty," Anthony suddenly chuckled, " of bringing you these." He handed Blasing a bottle of ibuprofen. "If you need anything else, just ring. Anthony at your service."

Before he could move, Blasing tipped him again. "The room will be fine. I don't bite," he said, glancing at Angela.

Anthony gave her the information about the Ferrari driver, then said, "I also took the liberty..." He chuckled again, barely able to finish, "of telling Broderick that you were here."

Blasing could feel his hackles rise when Cannon leaned over the bar. "Ya'd better get outta here before ya become a ghost bell boy, Antonio," Cannon said in a low voice filled with menace. "Remember, I'm not meek and kindly like most of my fellow spirits!"

The bellboy quickly thanked Blasing again, then departed.

"Cannon," Blasing started.

"Call me Liberty," she said.

"Would you remember I was talking to you if I did?"

Cannon blinked quickly several times, then laughed loudly and said, "You're a quick one, I'll say. Liberty, dear, bring me a beer!" Tears came to her eyes. "I'd say probably not! I might think I had a relative of Patrick Henry's at my bar! Cannon it is!" The large ghost nodded then wiped at apparent tears.

Blasing glanced at Angela. She appeared surprised as though she'd never seen Cannon cry before. If he touched her tears, would they be wet, Blasing wondered?

"Cannon, was Broderick Mac's personal valet?" Blasing asked. She nodded. "Good, he might be able to answer some questions."

"He can if ya can tolerate his British superiority."

Blasing sighed. "Have you seen any new ghosts around? Somebody who might've just come in on a stagecoach?" Cannon shook her head. "You're sure? Big man with a bony face and a scar? Or a bearded man with a shotgun? Even a beautiful woman in a frilly dress?"

"A stage ya say? That's odd. Don't know the gents, but the filly might have been Charity, or one of the other ladies of the evening. They're all pretty. If it wasn't one of them, this might be fun. I haven't met any new spirits in a while."

"Not even Mac's?"

"Nope, and we searched, I'll tell ya. New ghosts just don't come to Ghostal Shores by stagecoach or horse."

"How do new ghosts arrive?" Blasing asked,

"This ain't no old folks home for wandering ghosts, you know! We don't want no vagabonds! We got a good crew, I'll say. Toe the line, ya know. Besides, ghosts don't just wander around. We're tied ta something—a person or a place. I died of a heart attack while bartending at the Goldfield. Anyway, so ya see a stagecoach from Gold Hills or Virginia City don't just pull up."

"Two just did," Angela and Blasing said simultaneously.

"I believe ya! It's just that we ghosts are usually bound where we died, someplace very familiar, or near somebody for some reason. I could never think of anyone I wanted ta be around that long, ya know." She winked at Angela.

"So there's never any new ghosts?"

"That's not what I said," she sounded exasperated. "We picked up about a half-dozen newcomers from Aurora when they built the south wing." Before either Angela or Blasing could say anything, Cannon continued, "And none new from the north wing yet. It's probably not even haunted. S'okay. Plenty of us already. And we all get along together, nice and family like. Well, except fer Marsh, as ya know." She shrugged.

"So there aren't any scarred or beautiful green-eyed ghosts at Ghostal Shores?" Blasing asked, wanting a definitive answer.

"Not unless they're newcomers."

"I've got a headache." Blasing popped the top off the bottle, took two pills, then gave the container to Angela. As Blasing glanced through Cannon at the mirror, he said, "I'll be back in a minute. I'm going to clean up. Where are the bathrooms?" The ghost pointed to the left. "Thanks."

Angela watched him go, then in a resigned tone muttered, "And I'm going to call the doctor, then the front desk about our rooms." Cannon laughed heartily.

Blasing passed a loitering security guard, then rounded the corner into the hall. He spotted a house phone and remembered he'd forgotten to call Patrick and Kelly. Blasing dialed the front desk, billed the call to his room and spoke to Mrs. Wilson and his kids.

When Blasing hung up the phone, he felt a tingling sensation as the hair stood on his neck. Scraping sounds, like boots across planks, came from the hallway. He warily turned to face the noise.

Standing against the wall between the bathroom doors was a ghost from the stage. He was clad in a starkly white leather jacket that hung to his knees and a black cowboy hat with a red band. His face was shaded darker than a moonless night, leaving little visible but the spirit's blocky jaw, the outline of a bony face, and bright yellow eyes like flames deep within dark pits. Again Blasing felt as if something terrible were going to happen.

"Can I help you?" Blasing asked, managing his fear.

The ghost pointed at him, made an hourglass gesture with both hands, pointed again, then slashed its finger across its throat in a slitting gesture. Its head suddenly rolled free, falling through the floor. As the headless body turned around and disappeared into the wall, there was the fading sound of laughter.

THREE

Still a bit stunned by the obvious warning, Blasing wasn't sure what to do next. Why would a ghost want him dead?

Blasing paused outside the bathroom door, listening carefully. What sounds did a ghost make? He knew it was all right to be frightened, but he refused to let it dictate his actions.

As Blasing pushed open the door, he again felt a tingling along the nape of his neck, then it was gone. Had something fled? There was only one way to find out. Blasing took a deep breath, then entered cautiously.

The bathroom was deserted and elegant, done in black and white marble with silvery fixtures. Feeling a bit ridiculous skulking about, Blasing moved to the sink.

No matter how hard he tried, Blasing couldn't shake the sense of being watched, nor the expectation that something strange was going to happen. He stuck his hands under the faucet, and it came on automatically. While Blasing washed, he kept an eye on the mirror. Blasing couldn't help but wonder if a ghost would suddenly stick its head out of the mirror, jump out of the drain, or drop from the ceiling.

Blasing was even less certain than before about spending several days at Ghostal Shores. He'd already had more close shaves than he appreciated. That's what age could do to you. Until he'd met the ghosts, the only thing he truly feared was leaving Patrick and Kelly parentless and penniless; according to Angela, this venture would secure their financial future. Wondering if he had imagined it all, Blasing left the bathroom.

As he reclaimed his chair at the bar, Angela was handing the house phone to Cannon. "Maybe he'd rub ya down?" Cannon laughed.

"Cannon, we have a professional specifically employed for that very purpose," came a stiff voice laden with a heavy British accent. Cannon shook her head in disbelief. Angela sighed; she knew better than to bandy words with Broderick. " No sense in leaving such a mundane task to rank amateurs."

"Mundane ya say, Broderick? Ya always been a ghost?"

Blasing hadn't noticed the tall, thin ghost at first. Probably because he was standing on the other side of Angela with the copper bar top cutting him in half just below his ribs.

Broderick was formally clad in black and whites with a bow tie. The ghost's thin hair was steely gray, matching his eyes, and slicked back in rows, giving the impression every hair was neatly in place. Even the spirit's mustache was meticulously trimmed. Broderick's features were angular with a sharp nose perfect for looking down on others and a pointed chin doubled by age. He appeared even older than Barney, maybe in his sixties judging by his deep wrinkles and the crow's feet around his eyes.

"Ah, Mister Madera," the ghost said, his eyes lighting up as he slid out from the bar. "I am delighted to finally make your acquaintance. Master MacGuire, God rest his soul, spoke of you often. I am Broderick Hayden, at your service, sir." The Englishman bowed deeply, his knees not bending the slightest.

"E's from England, iff'n ya can't tell," Cannon said, exaggerating a cockney accent.

"My heart and soul are England's, and the Queen who rules such a glorious land that it rose at Heaven's command out of the azure mist."

"Loyal, isn't he?" Cannon said with an arched eyebrow and telltale smirk.

"Please call me Blasing." He instinctively extended his hand. When Blasing suddenly remembered the rules, he felt embarrassed.

"Blasing. Hmmm," Broderick said, his expression stony except for the twitch of his nose. "As you wish, Mister Madera. Due to Master MacGuire's passing, you are the new master of the grounds and I am your valet. My loyalty to you is second only to the Queen."

Blasing looked quickly at Angela. "Is he kidding?"

"I never joke sir," the Englishman said stiffly.

"Never," Angela agreed.

"Queen's honor," Cannon snickered.

Broderick looked a little annoyed, his mustache quivering as he sniffed. "If I may say so, Master MacGuire, God bless his departed soul, found me extremely capable and exceedingly efficient."

"Indispensable, I believe he often said," Angela added, smiling as Broderick straightened even further.

"And sometimes a royal pain in the butt," Cannon added.

Broderick frowned slightly, then his perfectly patient expression returned. "Sir, I must apologize for not meeting you promptly upon your arrival."

"You didn't know we were coming."

"Quite right, but Anthony informed me of your arrival. As is every day, it has been very busy. Today though, I endured an encore performance of discord between two draggle-tailed maids. Century old grudges are so tiring, and boorish besides. Some people simply cannot let go of the past."

"Relax," Blasing said to Broderick, then took his own advice and sat down.

"He can't," Cannon laughed. "Too much starch in his britches from when he was alive."

"I was wondering if there was anything you require?" Broderick asked, blatantly ignoring Cannon.

Blasing asked for a tour after lunch.

"It would indeed be a pleasure, sir."

"He knows more about this place than anyone else," Angela told Blasing. "And he's better company than Mr. Heller or Mr. Cash."

"Oh please, miss, you do me a grievous injustice."

"I'm sorry," Angela said. Broderick bowed in response.

"Since Uncle Mac is dead, why aren't you Heller's personal valet?" Blasing asked.

"A simply ghastly suggestion. I would rather endure a cleansing by Madame Zanadane," he replied, then amended, "or suffer the rest of my existence in France."

"It sounds like you don't care for the in-house psychic?"

Broderick shook his head. "Maybe you will see fit to change that, sir, as well as other things. Master MacGuire never treated us as though we were diseased, thereby seeing no need for an intermediary. Nor do we need the guillotine blade of a cleansing held over our heads. Between Madame Zanadane, the guards, and the new security system, one would think Ghostal Shores a cesspool of illicit activities instead of a prestigious establishment."

"New security system? Interesting. I'll have to look into it," Blasing told him. "Who's in charge?"

"Chief Warren Porter," Broderick said dryly, his expression hinting his displeasure.

"Thanks. Broderick, were you with Uncle Mac when he was murdered?" Broderick nodded. "Would you tell me about it?"

"Sir, though it grieves me to be uncooperative, this is neither the appropriate place, nor the right time, to recount such a grisly tale." Broderick's gaze swept over the room. "Later, I will address that tragic night just a week past."

"All right. Know anything about a stagecoach or new ghostly arrivals?" Blasing asked. Broderick didn't. Angela and Blasing took turns explaining the events surrounding their arrival.

"Fascinating. If you have no objection, sir, I would like to complete my duties and poll my compatriots about said stagecoaches, before guiding you and Ms. Starborne around these lovely grounds."

Blasing didn't say anything until Angela nudged him, then he realized Broderick was asking permission to leave. "Fine. Meet us in an hour at the restaurant."

Broderick bade them good-bye, bowed, and then suddenly dropped through the floor.

Blasing jumped back. "I wish he wouldn't do that. It makes my skin crawl."

"Then just tell him," Cannon said. "He'll stop."

"Is he really my personal valet?" Blasing asked Angela.

"He comes with the place," Angela replied. "The only way to get rid of him is by selling Ghostal Shores."

"Don't let 'em drive ya to that!" Cannon exclaimed. "I already know ya're better looking than the current owners, so I sincerely hope you're also smarter than those zombies."

"Zombies? Excuse me?" Blasing said.

"It's a drink. Lots of rum and fruit juices. Makes ya loopy, like Hellraiser and Cash—our dynamite team of bosses. Ask me now, money don't mean spit. I just like ta mix and pour. Everybody's gotta have a talent or joy, even a minor one; says something or another like that in the Good Book. Anyway, just ask Jessie now about selling her body for cash, and she'd say no way, but she can't do anything different because that's what she did until the day she died. Now she just can't stop— like a bad habit ya want ta quit but can't.

"Ya see, Cash and Hellraiser don't care what we think, and we're their main attraction," she said indignantly, big fists balled on broad hips. "They didn't ask us about no expansion. And didn't ask us about making this a crimeshare," she snorted, "instead of a top class resort. Different people come from all over the world to Ghostal Shores. It's like travelling but stayin' home."

"She means a timeshare," Angela interjected.

"I mean what I say I mean."

The din at the end of the bar had quieted down as if a few of them were listening. "Hey Cannon, a round of bartender's helpers!"

"I know. I know. Everything depends on who manages it, and who he hires," Cannon said, jerking her head toward the group at the end of the bar. Cannon made a disgusted noise. "Mac was devoutly against Ghostal Shores becoming a crimeshare. That's what he called a time-share."

"Do you think he was killed because of it?" Blasing asked.

"Don't know. All I know was that if Mac were here, I wouldn't be so worried. Just look at the parasites Heller hired." She waved to the crowded end of the bar.

"He hired them?!" Angela exclaimed.

"They're all reincarnated vultures, I say. Well, except for one or two. But like knows like and attracts like. They have no idea what an honest day's work for an honest day's pay is."

Cannon adopted several different facial expressions and postures as she began imitating salespeople. "Hey Cannon, how about an extra shot in this? Can you make this a double? Or really special? Wanna buy some vacation property in the Everglades? Hey," she looked at them critically. "Where are the Everglades anyway?"

"In Florida," Blasing said. "Swamp land."

"Well, maybe Blasing can be of help. We'll just have to see," Angela said guardedly. "Right now, I suspect he doesn't have enough information to make a decision. He hasn't taken a tour of Ghostal Shores or looked at the finances yet."

"Carefully chosen words, Angie," Cannon said. Angela colored.

"Look Blasing, I see ya're a good guy and a smart one too. Trust me, ghosts know these things, and I think that after ya meet and speak with all the spirits and employees of Ghostal Shores, y'all see the light and do right by us."

"Thanks." Blasing looked down the bar. Several of the timeshare salespeople were walking toward them. They didn't get far before a stunning black woman called out to them. She was statuesque and tastefully dressed in a beige pin-striped business suit that drew attention to her long legs. She spoke to the group and, after a bunch of grumbling, they downed their drinks and left.

"That's Eva Dare," Cannon said, "the manager of marketing. Hired, fired and rehired. Makes my head spin."

"I remember her," Angela said. "She and Mac were an item once. He claimed she was using drugs, something he wouldn't abide."

"She's French born and has marketed some of the most exclusive resorts in the world," Cannon continued. "She's a looker who seems ta know her business. Broderick describes her as a silk hammer."

Eva watched the salespeople leave, then turned and walked toward Blasing. Her stride was fluid, the sway of her hips almost hypnotic.

Angela glanced at Blasing. His face was stony, but his eyes had a gleam to them. Angela felt outclassed by the woman who might have just stepped out of Vogue magazine, clad in shoes by Gucci and a dress by Adrienne Landau. Angela despised women like Eva.

"Bon jour, Cannon," Eva said coolly, her voice rougher and deeper than Blasing would have imagined.

"Afternoon, Ms. Dare."

"Angela, I see you have returned, probably in association with the tragedy. So much like a lawyer, living off someone else's misery." She smiled sweetly to Blasing. "Mac was a good man. He will be missed by many."

"What're you and these sales people doing here?" Angela asked, too upset by Eva's air to indulge in banal pleasantries and meaningless condolences.

"All business and no pleasure is what Mac used to say about you, mademoiselle," Eva said cattily, then her expression became one of tolerance, as if she were speaking to a child. "I was rehired by Sean. As for the latter, I will let him explain." She looked inquisitively and somewhat hungrily at Blasing.

"Blasing Madera," he said, offering her his hand.

She took it gently, then surprised him by kissing it, her lips lingering. "A pleasure." She continued to hold his hand. "You are Mac's nephew, no?" Blasing nodded. "He spoke about you often, but I never imagined you to be so..." Her gaze undressed him. "I would never have guessed you were related."

"We're related through my mother. My father was Argentinian," Blasing replied. He gently extracted his hand from her grasp.

"Dark, hot-blooded and romantic, oui?" she asked.

Blasing blushed a fraction, surprising Angela. She figured he'd be used to this kind of attention. "And what do you think Heller will have to say about having a new partner?" Angela asked.

Eva's glance was blank for a moment, then surprised. "Partner? Oh, you mean, Blasing is...his heir? Mon dieu!" Her gaze suddenly sharpened. " Sean will certainly be... surprised."

"I'd be glad to tell him," Angela said.

"He is booked with meetings. I'll have to tell him. He has so many plans in motion."

"This may put a crimp in them," Angela said.

"Too true. Sean will be surprised. He doesn't even know you've arrived. Earl told me, and I thought you should be greeted properly. I am so glad I did. I will ask Sean to give you a call, but don't expect to see him today."

"Too bad," Blasing said. "I was looking forward to meeting him."

"I will be in meetings with the salespeople most of the day," Eva said. "But tomorrow, I'll be glad to help you in whatever way I can."

"Thanks," Blasing said, "that's very kind of you."

"It is no trouble. I will call you. Au revoir." Eva Dare sauntered off with every male and a few jealous females watching.

When Eva was out of earshot, Blasing shook his head and said, "Just the kind of woman who always got Uncle Mac in trouble."

Cannon and Angela burst out laughing. "I knew ya were a good judge of character!" Cannon boomed.

"But sales people!" Angela exclaimed. "What does Heller think he's doing?! Even if there wasn't a will, the courts freeze the estate during probate. Unless there's something I don't know."

"Excuse me," a voice from behind them said, "but are you Angela Starborne? I'm Dr. Geoff Landrum."

"Hello, Doctor." Angela turned to find a handsome man smiling at her.

Dr. Landrum was in his late thirties with dusky coloring as if his family origins might be Middle-Eastern. He had a full mustache, wore wire-framed glasses and was athletic in the same way as Blasing, but a bit more middle-age solid.

"I must say, you are in very good spirits for someone just in a car wreck. But if you don't need a doctor now, you will soon if you keep hanging around the bar. It's the salespeople's favorite spot," Dr. Landrum told them. "Watch them. They're very contagious. I'm not sure which goes first: your mind, your wallet, your lungs, or your liver. In fact, I'm surprised they're not here." Dr. Landrum looked around, then at Blasing. With a wry smile he said, " You sir, already look dazed."

Angela introduced Blasing. "I'm not sure if the accident is at fault or the company," Blasing told him.

"I can understand." The doctor's smile was dazzling.

Something told Blasing that the doctor was a man who could take care of himself. In many ways he reminded Blasing of an EMT friend of his—a former medic in the Marines.

Dr. Landrum noticed Blasing's scrutiny and seemed to return the appraisal. "And how do you feel?"

Blasing shrugged. "Sometimes I wonder if I'm having hallucinations, but I could probably blame it on the ghosts. No offense intended, Cannon."

Cannon and Dr. Landrum laughed together. "Well, I should be able to tell you in a minute, but ladies first. Where do you hurt?" Angela touched her left shoulder. He told her to relax, then gently maneuvered it around. She winced. "Sorry." He poked, prodded and pressed, then announced. "Just a simple sprain. Take an anti-inflammatory to reduce the swelling and ease the pain."

"Times haven't changed much. Take two aspirin and call me in the morning," Angela said, looking serious.

Dr. Landrum smiled. "Next." He moved to Blasing, asking where it hurt. Blasing pointed above his right ear. Dr. Landrum examined and palpitated the spot. "Quite a contusion."

With an otoscope, he peered into Blasing's ears. "There's no blood behind your eardrums." He felt along the back of Blasing's neck and asked about pain and tenderness. "Move your neck around in a circle." Blasing did, without any trouble. "Any blurred vision?"

"A little."

Dr. Landrum examined Blasing's eyes with an ophthalmascope. "Did you lose consciousness?" he asked. Blasing said no. "Your pupils are symmetric with normal light reflexes, and I don't find any retinal hemorrhages or other abnormalities. Now, holding your head still, follow my finger with your eyes." As the doctor moved his hand, he said, "You know, Blasing, ghosts can unnerve you enough that psychological trauma leads to physical dysfunctions."

"Are we talking about stress?"

"Yes. It might even account for the accidents we've been having." Dr. Landrum thought for a moment, then said, "I think you might have a mild concussion; nothing to worry about, but no more alcohol today. Have someone check on you every four hours over the next day or so. Let me know if you're vomiting, feeling lethargic, or having any change in your vision or difficulty speaking." Blasing promised he'd call if any of those problems arose.

"Was anybody else hurt in the accident?" Angela asked.

"Nothing reported," Dr. Landrum replied.

"What do you think of Ghostal Shores?" Blasing asked.

"This place is fascinating! I've even been able to discuss medicine and treatments with some of the ghosts. To tell the truth, I don't think I would've been able to get a room if the regular physician hadn't gotten sick. The hotel is booked solid."

"That's good news," Angela said to Blasing.

"Were you working when my uncle was murdered?" Blasing asked.

"No."

"Did you see a report on it?" Blasing asked.

"I'm not at liberty to discuss anything."

"I'm Mr. MacGuire's attorney, and this is his nephew," Angela said. "Does that help, Dr. Landrum?"

"Not really. You'll need to talk with Sheriff Middleton. He's staying in room 155. He should be able to tell you everything you want to know. But I can tell you this: Mr. MacGuire died very quickly, and probably painlessly." Dr. Landrum's beeper went off. "I wonder what now?" Before he left, he said, "A little bit of advice for you, Mr. Madera, if I may: I found that thinking of the ghosts as people helped me cope with the alienness of the experience. And all in all, the spirits seem to be very good 'people'. Enjoy yourselves."

"What now, Blasing?" Angela asked. "Should I see if Sheriff Middleton can be found?"

"Sure. Let's invite him to lunch," Blasing said, looking over at the dining room. Over half of the tables were now occupied.

"You want to talk about Peter's murder over lunch?"

"I'm starving. Mac would understand. He loved to eat. In fact, he always claimed he'd arrange a big, catered wake when he died."

"He never mentioned that, but you're right about his love of good food and wine, second only to women with long legs. Still, how can you be hungry?"

"I read somewhere that near death experiences do strange things to people," Blasing said. "Often times, when I've tested my mortality, I've ended up getting very hungry. Besides, I didn't have much for breakfast. Someone was in a hurry, remember? And eating settles my stomach."

"Really, I thought that would make it worse," Angela said." I could sure use a cigarette."

"Well, what do you think?" Blasing said,

Angela gave in, agreeing to call Sheriff Middleton. When he didn't answer, Angela left a message.

"Let's eat before I starve. Cannon, it's been a pleasure. I'll return to see if I can stump you on a drink recipe or two. We protect several bars in Tahoe, and I know a few very creative bartenders."

"My heart might stop thunderin' by then," Cannon laughed jollily.

They walked through the archway near the bar and past the fronds into the two-tiered Pacific Crest Restaurant, which also overlooked the shore. Serving tables lined the far wall, steam drifting from the stainless steel serving dishes. The wealthy were here in force, but so were professors, foreign travellers, scholars of one venue or another and two security guards surveying the area.

To the right of the food line was a small stage. Blasing thought he saw a piano through the narrow gap in the curtains. Just below, a group of rough-looking ghosts wearing cowboy hats and smoking cigars were crammed around a table, hunched over hands full of cards. The sound of rattling coins and the clink of bottles seemed to come from everywhere as if an echo still reverberated from a time long past.

At the podium, an attractive Asian hostess with long, jet-black hair and almond-shaped eyes looked at them expectantly. She arched an eyebrow while she took in Blasing, then welcomed back Angela. "Table for two, or are you expecting someone else?"

"Two, Chian," Angela said coolly.

"Broderick said you would be stopping by. I have your favorite table ready, Ms. Starborne."

They followed Chian through the maze of tables. With a smile, she seated them near the ghostly poker game, then handed them menus. Chian lingered near Blasing, mentioning the specials, making recommendations and touching him lightly, then she departed reluctantly.

The table was formally set with elegant silver, glistening crystalware and fine china of beige and green tones. A vase held a white rose.

"This is your favorite table?" Blasing asked, nodding to the game in progress. The cigar smoke was heavy and rank.

"I know. I'd really prefer a view, but this was Peter's favorite, so I often sat here. This group of ghosts are the most entertaining of any in the place."

"Really?" Blasing asked. He rubbed the back of his neck, then studied the ghostly poker game. The table, chairs, chips and cards were real, but the players were ethereal—six male ghosts crowding around a table. Because of the blue cloud of smoke, the ghosts seemed a bit out of focus. The ashtrays had overflowed, and the collection of bottles easily outnumbered the glasses.

Sitting closest to them in a reversed chair was the roughest-looking ghost. He had a long, droopy mustache and wore an eye patch. Matching his teeth, the spirit was dressed from hat to toe in black and silver. His hat was pulled low, and he was chewing on a cigar while he smoked it.

Next to him was a mountain of a man. Muscles rippled underneath his white shirt whenever his black body moved. He smiled at Blasing, his teeth brightly white and just a bit crooked, then tossed a chip into the central pile. The Blacksmith ran his hand across his bald pate while he contemplated his cards.

Directly across from him sat a blond, blue-eyed pretty boy sipping from a shot glass. His suit was freshly pressed, and his western tie was perfectly knotted. Even through the smoke, Blasing thought he smelled his aftershave.

The spirit at the far end might have been a banker once; the elder statesman of the poker players had thin, clay-gray hair, burly sideburns, a double-chin and round spectacles.

On each side of him were twin brothers, square-faced cowboys straight off the back of a horse. Their large, close-knit brows and their narrow noses made them appear rather dim-witted, but their eyes were sharp and calculating.

"Say, partner," the man with the patch called to Blasing. His one-eyed stare was so riveting, Blasing felt pinned. Angela glanced back and forth between the two, but before she could say anything, the ghost spoke again. "You wanna join us? Room for one more, and I know a ruthless poker player when I see one."

Blasing was surprised, holding his tongue until he was composed. "Thank you. I'm lucky, but lousy at cards."

"Suit yourself. Samuel's easy money," he said unsmiling.

"Only you, Dirk, would rather be playing cards than dining with such a ravishing vision," the smooth-faced man said.

"You know this...gang?" Blasing couldn't believe he was talking about ghosts so casually, but Dr. Landrum and Angela had said the same thing: treat them as if they were real people.

"Peter used to join them once in a while. You should get to know them. Don't worry, they'd rather play poker than anything else. There's rarely any problems, and if so, the malcontent Sly Marsh is at the root of it."

"I SAW YOU DEALING FROM THE BOTTOM OF THE DECK, YOU DOUBLE-DEALING SWINE!" Samuel shouted. He jumped to his feet and drew. The Colt .45 suddenly looked very real— solid and shining coldly.

"What's going...." Blasing started to rise.

Dirk was faster than Samuel, grabbing the underside of the table and throwing it. Chips and cards scattered as the table passed through Samuel.

The brothers were just drawing their guns when the banker smacked their faces with his cane. They reeled backwards, their chairs brushing a nearby table. The frightened couple dove for cover.

The Blacksmith grabbed the banker's arm, forcing him to drop his cane. Dirk's hand flashed toward his holster and a gun appeared in his grasp. As Samuel recovered, both ghosts fired, and thunder filled the air.

FOUR

While guns thundered, Blasing pulled Angela behind the table. Somewhere nearby a woman screamed. As others fled, chairs were overturned and glasses broken. "We've got to get out of here!"

Angela was composed, calmly watching Blasing who was holding her close and shielding her. Strong. Caring. "Blasing, listen ...."

Their Colt .45's spitting fire, Samuel and Dirk fired again and again. The restaurant shook, glasses and dishware chattering. The pretty boy grabbed his chest, looking down at his once fine jacket now riddled with holes. Samuel's form seemed to waver, then he staggered back, stumbling into an empty table and knocking it over before collapsing against the wall. Samuel feebly tried to raise his pistol. "You redskin lover."

Angela bristled.

"You always were too slow, pretty boy," Dirk said, then spat out his cigar. "Worried about style and flash instead of just stayin' alive." His silver teeth gleamed as he pulled the trigger.

"Angela, let's go," Blasing said and began to slide backwards.

Gun blasts ripped the tense silence once more. Dirk jerked, his one eye widening, then he collapsed onto a pile of chips. They rolled and bounced across the carpeted floor in every direction as though a horde of scattering mice fleeing a cat.

One of the brothers held a smoking gun; the other wrestled the banker, a chair held high over their heads. They struggled for a while, then the banker kneed the cowboy in the groin. When the ghost crumpled, the ethereal banker slammed the chair onto his back. More gunfire, and the banker's spectacles shattered. Clawing at his face, he collapsed.

Blasing had stopped moving. Angela couldn't help smiling as realization dawned on Blasing's face. His hand dropped away as though she no longer needed protecting. Angela discovered she missed his touch.

Blasing turned to her, his face stony. Embarrassment and anger gleamed in his eyes. "We're not in any danger, are we, Counse-lor?"

Angela smiled sweetly, batting her eyelashes. His expression changed little. "No, it's just part of the entertainment."

"Nobody can get hurt?" he asked. She shook her head. "Be-sides a heart attack, maybe."

She winced. "Most people know about this. It's one of the rea-sons they visit. These were—are—real western gamblers having a shoot-out. Those who don't know about this kind of entertain-ment don't know because their friends want to spring it on them."

"Thank you for sharing this with me," Blasing said flatly.

Angela would have preferred if he'd yelled at her. " I would hire you as my bodyguard." That got her an unreadable glance, but she could tell he was still angry. "I am sorry. With all that's happened, this sort of slipped my mind. They don't do it on the hour every hour."

"What else has slipped your mind?"

She didn't think that was fair, but she said, "Probably a lot. I'd hoped to discuss Ghostal Shores with you when Heller was around; but since he's busy, let's do it now."

"What about the mess?" He waved toward the two overturned tables surrounded by scattered chips, playing cards, broken chairs, and smashed glass.

"Watch."

The two brothers helped Samuel to his feet. Then like a theater troupe, they linked arms and bowed. Dirk, Mason, and the banker stood, brushed themselves off, then joined the trio. The applause was hesitant at first, then grew until raucous. The ghosts were smil-ing and seemed brighter—more substantial than before.

"See, they loved it," Angela said. "This is what makes the place popular. I was here one night when they performed card tricks and had a dagger-throwing contest. Obviously, they can do things other entertainers can't."

Most people hadn't budged from their chairs but were talking excitedly with their companions and fellow patrons. One couple dressed in country and western outfits were still on their feet applauding. Looking sheepish, a few guests were slowly coming back to their tables.

"So you're telling me that this is for show? That the spirits won't touch or harm any of the guests or staff?"

Angela nodded and said, "Everything but the ghosts are props. The guns are even made to appear ghostly. They brush the flour off just before they begin shooting blanks."

While the clean up was underway—the furniture mending and righting itself, broken glass being swept up as though tended by invisible servants, and the chips gathering and the cards stacking by themselves—Dirk came over to Blasing. The ghost's smile was broad, although it didn't reach his cool, dark eye. "Hope we didn't scare ya, tinhorn."

Blasing said nothing; he just stared back, looking mad enough to bite a nail in half. "No, I guess we didn't. Good. If I'd moved that fast when I was alive, I might've lived longer." The ghost glanced at Angela, then said to Blasing, "You keep good company, but if you want a change of pace, you're always welcome at our table. Enjoy lunch. See ya Ang." And then, as though nothing had happened, the six spirits began playing poker again. "Ante's a dollar."

Blasing was startled when the curtains parted and a piano began playing. Nobody was sitting on the bench. The tune was Elton John's "Saturday Night's All Right For Fighting."

"Blasing," Angela said, putting her hand on his arm, "the first time I was here I actually dove under the table, snagging the tablecloth and dumping shrimp fettucini all over me." She laughed, then touched his hand. "You handled it as well as anyone could. And thank you for protecting me; I was serious about hiring you."

"Sorry. I'm just mad at myself; I saw and heard danger, but didn't really feel any. In fact, if I'd listened better, I would've noticed there wasn't widespread panic. I guess my nerves are stretched too taut." He paused as if a thought had come to him, then said, "Besides, you don't really need protecting, do you?"

Angela felt pinned; she didn't know what to say but was saved by the waitress. She rattled off the specials, then they agreed on the buffet for lunch.

As their server departed, a ghostly figure wearing service black and whites slowly came into focus. The spirit was mammoth, almost seven feet tall, and very barrel-chested. His upper arms could have been confused with hams. Despite this, he was neither looming nor intimidating, his friendly face full-cheeked with a beaming smile.

"Is everything all right, Ms. Starborne?" His hair was carefully combed back, and he was neatly groomed, in contrast to their table. Some of the silverware and crystal had been jostled out of place during Blasing's actions. The arrangement suddenly changed as a salad fork, soup spoon and a wine glass apparently moved themselves into the proper positions. The spirit's smile was so broad even Blasing smiled.

"Everything is fine, David," Angela said.

"Might I recommend trying the salmon quiche or spicy shrimp quesadillas?" The ghost looked at Blasing, chuckled softly, then gave him a knowing look. "Is there anything I can do for you, sir? You appear to have a touch of ghostitis."

"Nothing I can think of, David," Blasing told him. "I imagine I just need time to adjust."

"Just remember, I want your dining experience to be simply perfectish." The ghost glanced at Angela, then added, "But with such a lovely companion, how could it not be? If I may say, you two make a fine looking couple." With a bow, he faded away.

Through gritted teeth, Angela said, "As I mentioned earlier, it helps to think of the ghosts as people with personalities and histories. Some are helpful, some are arrogant, and others like to talk a lot, like Cannon and David."

"But they're not living," Blasing said. "They can walk through walls and move things without touching them. They don't bleed or get hurt...." He made an exasperated sound.

"I know, but I also know they can sense and feel," Angela told him. "Did you notice how they brightened with the applause? From what Peter told me, I believe the main difference between us and the ghosts is that they can't change. If you come back and visit them in a hundred years, David and Cannon will be the same— same perspective, same views and same interests. They're stagnant as well as dead. Or maybe being stagnant is death." She was thoughtful for a moment, then said, "They're hard to slap, too."

"Really? You've tried?" Blasing asked, surprised. Angela explained about slapping Allen, the barber. "Can I ask why?"

"He had lecherous eyes," Angela replied. "His gaze seemed

to ... stroke my legs." She shivered. "Then he began to visually undress me, so ... I tried to slap him."

"What did Mac say?"

"That hormones were hard to control, and that he didn't understand why women expected men to control their hormonal urges when they couldn't control their hormonal moods."

Blasing laughed, "I would think that a lecherous ghost would rule out hormones as an instigator," he said tongue-in-cheek. "Not fleshly delights, but lusty spirits."

"Funny, I never thought of it that way," Angela replied with a wan smile. "Maybe it starts out hormonal and becomes a habit."

"I've always wondered why people let past actions rule their lives," Blasing said thoughtfully.

"Do you mean influence?"

"No, I mean rule. Influence I understand. Some people live in, or for, the past because of something or somebody. I know, I've been looking toward the future. I have young ones depending on me."

"And have to keep going?"

"Yes. And it's better than dwelling on what's been lost. I finally realized I didn't have any control over the past, just the present. I don't want to end up as a lecherous ghost." He smiled.

"You mean you were lecherous when you were younger?"

Blasing ignored her stab. "You know, I keep thinking about what you said—about the ghosts being stagnant. Cannon said she was up-to-date on the latest concoctions."

"That she did, and Peter said he had a heck of a time getting her to change. But then pouring new drinks is not really a ... personal change. Is it?"

"It migh be for Cannon," Blasing said. "Besides, after their mid-twenties, most people don't change unless there's some kind of traumatic event." Blasing paused. He felt an itching along the back of his neck and smelled a cloying waft of perfume. "Do you...."

A shapely ghost suddenly appeared in his lap, a stunningly beautiful spirit with a smoothly rounded face and a cavalcade of dark curly hair. Her eyes were brown, very large and locked onto Blasing's. His pulse quickened so fast his head swam.

Two other ravishing female spirits appeared; both were clad in long, frilly western dresses that were cinched tight at the bodice, waist and hips. All of the "ladies" were more vivid and colorful than any of the other ghosts. The piano tune changed to "Bump and Grind."

"Hi, we're the welcome wagon," the ghost in his lap said. She suddenly became coy, looking down and plucking at her white dress. "I'm Fawn. This is Amber." Fawn motioned toward the petite young woman with a wealth of golden curls, smoky gray eyes and a pert nose. Amber's full, red lips parted with an inviting smile. "And Missy," a tall, young spirit with waist-long brown hair, green-yellow eyes and an unlined face full of an innocence not matched by her eyes. Blasing cleared his throat, looked at Angela who was fuming, then tried to find his voice.

"As soon as we heard of your arrival, Mr. Madera—may I call you Blasing?—we came to meet you. We wanted you to feel..." Fawn emphasized "comfortable" at Ghostal Shores. Think of it as your home away from home." Her look was reminiscent of the cat who was going to take its time eating the trapped canary.

"We are at your beck and call," Missy said sweetly.

"Or any other way you'll have us," Amber said wickedly.

"Hussies," Angela breathed.

Blasing didn't trust himself to speak. A scarf suddenly appeared in Fawn's hands, one end of it draped around his neck.

"Fawn, would you mind standing please?" He'd had enough of being...handled. Although he hadn't felt anything physically, he'd sensed... something—sensed her desire.

"I'm not too heavy am I?" she asked innocently.

" No, I'd just like to get a better look at all of you."

Fawn rose to her feet, her clothing unweaving then re-weaving quickly, becoming a dark, shoulderless one piece miniskirt. In heels her legs appeared unnaturally long. "We're familiar with modern fashions, too. Changing one's clothes is part of the fun of... theater and acting." Blasing managed to hide his expression, but Fawn smiled knowingly.

Angela had been looking away and missed Fawn's transformation. The male customers' reactions alerted her. When Angela turned around, she was relieved to find Fawn simply fawning instead of doing a striptease.

Angela noticed her modern dress and thought about what Blasing had said about Cannon changing. But these were just outward, cosmetic-type changes. Not true change. Peter had lived with the ghosts for nearly a decade and knew the ghosts better than anyone else, hadn't he?

The other spirits moved to Fawn's side, their dresses also changing into sexy and very revealing clothing. Amber was in a red slit skirt and black camisole. Missy wore a pink dress so sheer it might have been a nightgown. The tune changed to " The Entertainer."

"So what do you think?" Fawn asked.

"That you're making it wonderfully difficult for the customers to enjoy our fine cuisine," Blasing managed. "Ladies, do you know anything about a couple of stages arriving?" Each shook her head. "How about any new ghosts?"

"I've seen a new ghost with Marsh," Missy interjected.

"What's he look like?"

"I don't remember. What about us?"

"We didn't mean to interrupt your lunch," Fawn said, glancing at Angela and giving her a sickening sweet smile. " But we couldn't wait to meet Blasing. We'll come visiting again when you're settled. Room 351, right?"

"That won't be necessary," Blasing told her.

"It's no problem," Fawn breathed, her bodice heaving. "Until later, come ladies." She blew Blasing a kiss, then faded away. He was surprised when the sensation coursed hotly through him.

"Remember what I said about ghosts being the same as they were in life?" Angela asked.

Blasing nodded. Did she suspect he'd felt that kiss? HAD he really felt that kiss? And if so, what should he do about it?

"They were all prostitutes when they were alive," she finished. "Undoubtedly, the kind with hearts of gold. I didn't see Jessie or Charity."

"How many are there?"

"Enough for a small harem, if you like that kind of thing," she said tartly. "Five in all; you just met two of the three most visible ones. I've rarely seen Fawn, though." Blasing asked how they died. "I never asked. Probably shot by a jealous lover or five. Let's eat, shall we? Before someone else interrupts?"

After serving themselves, they ate in silence. Blasing was thoughtful and Angela seemed distracted by her own musings. Blasing wondered about the ghosts. To say they were hard to accept was an understatement. If they did exist, hanging around things important to them, then why didn't Jenny haunt him? Their love had been deep and true. And what about Mac? Did he haunt Ghostal Shores?

To keep from going crazy, Blasing decided to people watch— a habit developed long before working security. He found it difficult to believe there were so many different kinds of customers. Blasing thought he could pick out several different accents, including German, French, British, Japanese and Spanish. There were others he didn't even vaguely recognize. There were many unusual styles of glamour fashion, probably by name-designers he'd never recognize, and more expensive jewelry in one place than he'd seen even around Tahoe's high roller rooms.

Blasing took a moment to study Angela. She was beautiful, a mixture of races with her tanned skin, light hair and blue eyes. She appeared a bit sad and maybe a little lonely. When Angela finally noticed he was watching her, she flushed a bit. He had the feeling she was still angry and confused about something.

"Tell me more about Ghostal Shores, please," he asked.

"I don't know where to start," Angela answered. "Actually, I'm confused about the salespeople being here. *It really bothers me.* Why did Heller hire them so fast? The estate has to be settled first. Oh well, an injunction will slow his sales plans."

Blasing felt the hair on the back of his neck stiffen.

"Ghostal Shores is probably finished, as we know it," came a deep-drawled voice from the direction of one of the two empty chairs at their table.

A slight fog appeared, gathering and thickening, before giving form to a tall, well-dressed spirit in a cowboy hat. He had striking red hair that hung to his shoulders, a proud hawk-like nose, and full brows above dark, searching eyes. As though attired for commerce, he was clad in a dark business suit, white shirt and a western tie. He set his hat on the table, then lit a cigar.

The flame was ethereal, and Blasing could see just as easily through it as he could the ghost. " This table is busier than the casinos on New Years Eve."

"I guess the news is out," Angela said, "and they all want to meet the new owner. Peter was beloved by the ghosts."

"A finer man and a shrewder businessman I've never known," the ghost told them. " Hello, Mr. Madera, my name's Roberts, Grant Roberts—financial genius and investment wizard, according to my *LONE STAR* press clippings." He chuckled, then took a puff. Grant looked as if he wanted to lean back, relax, and put his boots up on the table. He was roguishly handsome and appeared to know it.

"What can I do for you, Mr. Roberts?"

"Rumor has it that you're the new owner—excuse me, part owner. If so, I thought I might give you the benefit of some sound financial advice. Mac and I spoke often, and I feel I know these books better than anyone else."

"The Ghostal Shores ledgers?" Angela sounded surprised.

Roberts nodded, giving Angela more than a once-over glance. She swore she could feel his eyes lightly roaming across her body, soft hands caressing her flesh. When she played with her rings, the caressing sensation stopped.

"This place is an endless oil well, my boy, all you have to do is keep pumping. Don't sell the rights to it. That would be foolish. Add more wells if you need to, but don't let someone else reap the benefits of you catching the first train."

"Meaning, don't make this place a timeshare."

"Exactly. Mac didn't want a timeshare. He told me that so many times I grew tired of hearing it. He knew that Ghostal Shores already makes a fantastic return on investment. It has a great location, an internationally renowned reputation and a unique marketing niche. If you sell pieces of it, you'll make a big lump of cash, which means Uncle Sam will take most of it." He was pursing his lips as he continued to eye Angela. "Besides, Peter MacGuire would not want you to sell to Heller, or he would have done so himself. It could be why he was murdered."

"Are you implying Mr. Heller had him killed?" Blasing asked.

Roberts expression was deadpan. "Imply? No. Listen, son. If you sell, you'll probably make a killing and retire, but this place will go downhill. Let some management group run it, or a council of timeshare owners, and it will sink like a stone. I like it here and don't want to see it lose its appeal. If it does, all the fine-looking ladies, like Ms. Angela Starborne here, won't visit us."

Turning back to Angela, he said, "I must say, you are a stunning woman; there would have been more fighting between the white invaders and the natives if all the squaws had looked like you." She glared at him. "Hey, I may be a ghost, but I'm not dead, if you know what I mean. A good looking lady still makes my spirit sing even if my blood can't boil."

"If you'll excuse me, Mr. Madera," Angela said tight-lipped as she rose. "I'll be back in a few minutes, when they've cleared the table of leftovers." She couldn't even wish that something bad would happen to the ghost. He was already dead.

Roberts moved swiftly to peek under Angela's skirt. "I thought so. Alas, not a true blond."

Reacting instinctively, Angela slapped the ghost. She was stunned when there was a loud, wet smack, and fire danced from her hand to her shoulder.

Roberts reeled backwards, surprise etched on his face as he passed through a table and a wide-eyed Japanese couple. They shivered and dropped their wine glasses.

"That serves you right!" Angela barked, then marched off. Her stride was angry, fueled by embarrassment, stereotyping and the burning pain in her hand. How had she hit him?

The music changed from, "Raindrops Keep Falling on My Head" to "Beauty and the Beast." The tune was hauntingly pervasive.

"Wow!" Grant Roberts slowly stood, his hand rubbing his jaw. "That's never happened before! Well, not at least while I've been a ghost. I could get in trouble with that kind of woman—a woman with spunk!" Admiration shone in his eyes. "You lucky bucko!"

Striding stiffly through the maze of tables and looking straight ahead, Angela couldn't believe how complicated things had suddenly gotten at a time when she was trying to simplify her life.

"Hey, Angela! Angela Starborne! EARTH TO ANGEL, THIS IS CANDY WHYTE, COME IN PLEASE."

Angela stopped dead. Sitting at a table was Candy, a fellow student from Cal Berkeley, and her boyfriend.

"What are you doing here, Candykins?" Angela asked. Candy was a too-cute-to-stand native Californian with blue eyes and honey blonde hair. She wore a blue, V-neck sweater, jeans, and lots of gold and amethyst jewelry.

"I could ask you the same, Angel, but since you asked first, I'm here on business and pleasure," she said. "I'm doing research for my paper for Rothstein's class and spending some time with Rod." She gestured to her companion, a nice-looking guy with light brown, curly hair, gray eyes and a close-cropped beard. He adjusted his glasses and smiled crookedly.

"You've met him; he's an accountant who's spiritual. Can you believe it? He's got an affinity for channeling, and he's looking for undiscovered spirits." She smiled. "Actually, I like coming here because I don't feel weird or out of place."

"There are plenty of people who think as we do," Rod added. "Statistics say as high as 80% of the people believe in ghosts. We can talk with them, as well as the ghosts. Even when you filter out the exaggerations, you still get a good sense of history."

"This place will make a great paper," Candy said, " especially if I can come up with a new angle. How about you, Angel? Here on pleasure, I hope? Who're you with? He's a definite twelve out of ten."

"His name's Blasing Madera. He's a client and the new co-partner of this place by inheritance."

"Angel, I haven't seen you this mad since your ex tried to get you in the sack," Candy laughed. "Didn't I tell you to relax around men you find attractive? I mean you are so gorgeous you shouldn't feel this self-conscious. Relax! Have some fun even if it is business. It's not like you have to jump into... anything. Though jumping...."

Angela's gaze was withering. "Is everyone sex-crazed today?"

"I can't help it. Rod and I have animal magnetism, so it becomes a favorite subject. Now you, you're repressed...."

"We do not need to discuss that again. And it's not that." She glanced in Blasing's direction, then dismissed a thought before closing her eyes and saying, "I just have a bad feeling about this place, like there's an accident waiting to happen."

"Maybe an accidental romance? Maybe? It would do you good, Angel. You're not truly a man-hater." When Angela made a face, Candy said, "Well, you're not. Just like you're neither all Oregonian nor Paiute. There's a blend, you know, a middle ground between extremes. I think if you're able to embrace the heritage you once denied, you can find a way to embrace a good man, too. And mmm, mmm, he's a good looking one. Have any brains? Manners? Morals?" Her eyes were dancing; she enjoyed doing this.

"You do go on like a lusty wench, Candy," Rod teased.

"I know, and you like me this way," she laughed.

"I think there's a ghost you should meet," Angela suggested.

"I just want what's right for you, just as Rod and I are right for each other." They smiled and kissed. "Now, what's really bothering you, besides women and ghosts crawling all over your date?" She teased. "And here I thought you'd be more accepting of spirits. The Native American culture is far more spiritual than the White Man's. Didn't your Grandmother Dawnjoy talk with them?"

Angela frowned. "Ancestral spirits are not entertainers; when they pierce the mists they have returned to do something important, like giving us guidance."

Candy's eyes lit up. "You know, I think there's a paper in that!" Angela rolled her eyes. "Besides, what are you worried about? As far as I've seen, all the ghosts are benevolent, unlike some of the Native American spirits."

"Those 'evil' spirits are only used to frighten children. Adults know better; it's part of the maturation process."

"Oh Angel, you're always so serious," Candy responded. " I think you should focus more on living life, like concentrating on that hunk of yours. He's better looking than Brad Pitt or Mel Gibson. Patrick Swayze might be a toss up. But then, I haven't seen him from behind, yet." She cackled, suddenly sounding very much like a wicked witch.

"You know," Candy said when she finally recovered, "I'll be glad to do a tarot reading for you, or both of your astrological charts. It'll tell us if you're compatible."

Angela was going to say something biting when she saw Broderick. As he glided along with his nose in the air, the stiff-backed spirit carried a magnum of champagne on a tray.

"Candy, as always, I've loved getting a few words in edge-wise, but I've got to go."

"Okay, get back to your hunk. We're in Room 320. Let's gossip over a cappuccino, shall we?"

"Bye," Angela said as she left. What would Candy say when she found out they were staying in the same room? Who cared?

Right now she needed to be with Blasing when Broderick took him on tour. Blasing was already unnerved by the presence of one ghost. How would he react when he learned that she'd lied? That not a dozen, but more than thirty ghosts wandered the halls of Ghostal Shores?

FIVE

Angela arrived at the table just as Broderick set the magnum in front of Blasing. "That's so very kind of you, Broderick," Angela said as she slipped into her seat.

"What's the occasion?" Blasing asked the ghost.

"Freedom from tyranny," Broderick said dryly. "The king is dead, long live the king." The ethereal valet began loosening the cork cap.

"Tyranny or slavery?" Blasing asked.

"We work reluctantly under the yoke of a tyrant who has replaced our captain." With a stony expression, Broderick popped the cork. It sailed briefly, then stopped as though snatched.

"But you have nowhere else to go," Angela said.

"You make an astute observation, miss; we are indeed tied—no, better said would be bound—to this place, but there is no way anyone can actually force us to work." Broderick filled their glasses. "And truth to tell, I must admit that I am accustomed to serving Master MacGuire and am very set in my ways."

"Has Mr. Heller ever threatened you with cleansing if you don't work or tow the line?" Blasing asked.

Broderick's gray face rippled, appearing to grow even longer, then became coldly chilling. "Mister Heller made such a barbarous attempt long ago, but Master MacGuire stymied the bloody black-guard, he did!" There was pride and, for the first time, emotion in Broderick's voice. "Now he holds exile as a threat. Which makes little sense, for without us, the resort would not draw as it does now, would it?"

"Of that I am sure," Angela said. Broderick seemed to relax, his eyes losing their frostiness.

"Aren't you toasting with us?" Blasing asked.

"I do not partake of champagne," Broderick said, his left eye-brow raising in surprise. "It does... it used to do queer things to my nose, as well as my noggin."

"But a new captain shouldn't be christened without the participation of his first mate." Blasing flagged down their waitress.

"I am touched and honored, sir," Broderick said, sniffling once before regaining his composure. That was the second time Angela had seen Blasing move one of the ghosts. "That sounds like something my own captain might have said. He was a good man. I cannot drink the champagne, but I can join you in the toast."

"You were in the Navy?" Angela asked.

"The Royal Navy," Broderick stressed, "for over a dozen years before coming to America. I served on the HMS *Queen's Pride* under Captain Andrew John Morris. We fought together in the Crimean War against the Turks. Captain Morris was a good man and thought of me as the son he never had. The captain saw to it that I was properly educated. In return, I was his valet when he retired and traveled the world to view its wonders."

Broderick's eyes brightened. "From Master MacGuire's study, I often watch the vessels sail by. I would so love to cast off in one of the newer ships. They have changed so much." He seemed to daydream for a moment, then stiffened. "Oh dear, I almost forgot myself. Mister Cash has taken it upon himself to guide you on tour. He believes I am incapable of providing... the human touch."

"Cash! Where's the human touch there?" Angela asked.

"You said you worked for me now," Blasing reminded him.

"That is true, sir...."

"Then I want you to take me on a tour," Blasing emphasized, "Angela recommended you, and for the most part, I trust her judgment."

"A smashing decision, sir."

A gust of smoke blew across their table, bringing a question to mind. Blasing turned, waited until the gamblers had finished the hand, then said, "Excuse me, Dirk." The ghost with the patch turned his wild eye on Blasing.

Blasing swallowed, then described the ghosts from the stagecoaches and asked if any of them sounded familiar. The scarred cowboy reminded Samuel of a man he knew long ago, but he couldn't recall a name. Mason just scowled, his expression fearsome as if he remembered something unpleasant.

"I shall continue questioning the staff," Broderick said. "Though I find it indeed odd that Samuel should think he remembered the scarred man. I would expect him to only remember women."

"But Missy thought she saw someone new with Marsh."

"She must have been mistaken," Broderick replied.

Arriving on a wave of garlic, their waitress brought the third glass. Broderick poured a dash of champagne into it.

"Blasing, you know that turning away Mr. Cash won't make Sean Heller very happy," Angela told him.

"I am tired of being at everyone else's beck and call," Blasing said sharply, "including yours. At this point, I plan to take charge of my own due diligence." Angela nodded approvingly.

Broderick asked acidly, "Testy when tired, are we?"

Blasing smiled indulgently and raised his glass. Even if it took all of his willpower, Blasing swore he would conquer his uneasiness around the ghosts. "A toast to making Ghostal Shores the best it can be, a place where ghosts and people mingle in harmony."

"Well said, sir." Broderick tipped his glass toward them. " To the new captain of Ghostal Shores, may his hand be ever steady on the helm." He raised the glass to his lips and hiccuped.

"To boldly stepping toward the future," Angela added.

Broderick gave her a long look, then said, "I do not know if that is possible, miss. I am a ghost, after all."

"But a special one. Give it a try," Angela said. "A new opportunity is presenting itself."

Broderick nodded, his expression a bit dubious. "I must admit that I agree with Lord Falkland. When it is not necessary to change, it is not necessary to change." He sounded very superior and very British.

"Blasing, where did Grant Roberts go?" Angela asked.

"An impudent scoundrel," Broderick muttered.

"He said something about gathering the real books and left," Blasing said. "Speaking of which, I guess we should go before Mr. Cash arrives."

"I'd like to ask him why the timeshare salespeople are here," Angela said, "but he probably wouldn't tell me anything."

"Broderick, how many ghosts reside at Ghostal Shores?"

"Uh, Blasing...." Angela tried to catch Broderick's eye. "I think we should get going. Mr. Cash, you know. He's...."

"Let me think a moment," Broderick began, "there is Barney,

Cannon, David, Janice, of course the five ladies of the evening, Elma, Carrie, the six gamblers...." Blasing paled. "Thirty."

Blasing choked on his champagne, then sputtered, "Thirty!" He gave Angela a long stare. "I thought you said about a dozen."

"I didn't want to unnerve you," she replied.

"So much for trusting my counsel," Blasing said.

Angela started to say something, but Broderick came to her defense. "If I may be so bold, sir, your uncle trusted Ms. Starborne implicitly. If she misled you, she probably felt it was in your best interest. I myself thought about calling together all the ghosts to greet you, but I was afraid such a gathering...might be overwhelming. You must admit, it is a rather imposing number of spirits, especially if you have never before seen a ghost. Have you ever seen a ghost before?" Blasing shook his head. "Then introducing us to you one at a time is conducive to good health."

"I can see when I'm outnumbered," Blasing said, then stood. "After being cramped in a car for over five hours, I'm dying to stretch my legs."

"I do wish you would not say that, sir," Broderick replied. "Dying is no joking matter around here."

"Sorry," Blasing apologized. "So we won't seem rude, I'm going to leave a message for Mr. Cash with Chian."

When Blasing returned, he said, "I'm not up for a long tour today, Broderick. I'm worn out."

"Indeed. Then we shall only visit the 'high' points. Now if you will walk this way." Blasing and Angela followed Broderick out of the restaurant.

The long hallway was carpeted in forest green, bringing out the richness of the dark wood panels along the lower half of the cream-colored walls. Paintings of the coast adorned the corridor, hanging above mahogany tables set with beige and gold lamps. Blasing could tell where cameras had been recently installed; sawdust and flecked paint still remained.

A deeply tanned man wearing a safari outfit and with a colorful parrot riding on his shoulder tipped his hat and wished them a good day. The bird echoed his greeting.

"Broderick, if you're from England, what were you doing in Goldfield?" Blasing asked.

"My captain wanted to visit the west; he had heard the tales of the New World's raging rivers, purple mountain majesty, and seemingly endless expanse of plains. He wanted to see them—and as much of the world as possible—before he died. He passed away the night before I died in that fire at the Goldfield. I was making arrangements to have his body shipped back to England."

"I'd forgotten you died in that fire," Angela said.

"Like so many others," Broderick said as the trio arrived at an intersection with elevators. "Would you like to see the pool, sir?" Broderick asked. "It is quite opulent."

"Sure," Blasing replied. Broderick opened the greenish glass door, then ushered them down the steps.

Blasing was impressed by the size of the pool and was immediately reminded of Roman baths. Along the left side, archway-connected pillars framed a natural looking waterfall, which appeared to feed the pool but had obviously been dry for a while. Golden waves of reflected light rippled lazily along the ceiling, walls and pillars. Below the west-facing windows the deck lounges and chairs were about half full with people reading, sleeping, and basking in the sun. Except for the soft slap of gentle waves, the area was almost sacredly peaceful.

"One of my favorite places," Angela said.

"I wish the waterfall was working," Broderick said as he pointed to a Stonehenge-looking trio of rocks. "It adds such life."

Blasing noticed a long-handled scoop apparently dipping into the pool of its own volition. "What's going on there?"

Broderick squinted. "That is Jonathan; he is cleaning the pool." The ghost valet led them along the sunning deck. "He is the handyman. He worked at the Goldfield for over twenty years."

"He helps the staff perform maintenance," Angela said. "For the longest time I thought he was mute."

When they reached the end of the pool, Blasing could finally make out Jonathan's form. He was less defined than the other ghosts, as if a hazy cloak were draped over him.

"Jonathan, come meet Mister Madera, Master MacGuire's nephew."

The net scoop was put down, then the pale ghost shuffled as much as floated toward them. As Jonathan neared, he became more defined. His gray hair was wild, sticking out on both sides as if he'd been wearing a cap for years, and his eyes were squinty above full cheeks. Below a crooked nose, his mustache was so bushy his mouth was completely obscured.

"Jonathan, this is Mister Madera." The ghost stared intently at Blasing, who felt as though he'd been stripped bare, then the sensation was gone. Jonathan whispered something in Broderick's ear. "You can be assured that I will tell him." Jonathan nodded, looked at Blasing, then went back to work.

"What did he say?" Blasing asked.

"That he is glad to meet you and that you will do well here."

Blasing had the funny feeling that Broderick had left something out. "Did he say anything else?"

Broderick appeared mildly startled. "He wanted me to warn you about the outlaws that just arrived."

Blasing felt a cold chill riffle along his spine, then turned to look at Angela. "They?" Blasing could see she was also thinking about the stagecoaches.

"Have no fear. What Jonathan said is pure rubbish. Although he is a kind soul, Jonathan suffers visions and imagined fears. You see, he was unjustly hanged by a group of besotted miners at the Goldfield; they thought he had stolen from their rooms."

"How terrible," Angela said.

"Even now, he constantly fears their return."

"How sad," Blasing said. He suddenly felt uneasy and couldn't help but wonder if the sensation was his imagination or if a ghost was keeping an eye on them.

"I imagine his fear was sparked by the fact that," Broderick cleared his throat, "you remind him of one of his murderers."

Blasing blinked, taken aback. "Then it's probably better if I keep my contact to a minimum, at least until he gets used to me."

"A very humane idea indeed, sir," Broderick said. He pointed to a pair of doors along the farthest wall where a security guard exited. "Those are the public bathrooms, as you call them. Quite a welcome change from outhouses and chamber pots. They lead to the exercise area and two very odd rooms—one has the air of the desert within, while the other reminds me of our summer travels through America's southern lands. I must admit to being confused about one thing. Why would anyone 'work out' in their spare time?

Do Americans not work enough as it is?"

Angela laughed, and Blasing said, "Quite a place."

"Careful," Angela said with a smile. "You might fall in love with Ghostal Shores, despite its ghostly inhabitants."

As they approached the stairway doors, a trio of women young enough to be between college semesters exited, walking past them. Each was clad in brightly-colored spandex, and their appraisals of Blasing were as bold as their outfits.

"I believe they found you pleasing, sir," Broderick said.

"They're a little young," Blasing replied. "I have kids who'll be their age before I know it." Broderick said he loved kids and asked their names. "Patrick and Kelly," Blasing responded.

"If I may be so bold," Broderick began. Angela tried to slow the ghost, but he continued, "Where is Mrs. Madera?"

"My wife died two years ago of breast cancer."

"Oh dear," Broderick replied. "I have heard talk of this... cancer. I am sorry."

"Thank you, Broderick. It's all right. There's a lot we need to learn about each other."

"Indeed we do," Broderick replied as he ascended the steps.

As they entered the hall, Angela bumped into an old man carrying a cane and dressed in a rich black suit. His hat sparkled as if hiding tiny stars. He glanced up at Angela and smiled, then his expression became blank. "Remember, the ground is your ally, and if you survive the fires, your love will last forever."

"Excuse me?" Angela asked, but the little old man simply blinked several times, then shuffled off despite her calls.

"What was that all about?" Blasing asked as he eyed the two security guards walking past them. One had a pockmarked face. The other wore a cast on his left arm. They nodded to him and walked on.

"I don't know," Angela said, then, "oh, oh, here comes Earl Cash, the day-to-day manager of Ghostal Shores."

"Ah, Ms. Starborne, so lovely to see you again," Cash said. "I'm so glad I found you." His brown hair was cut in a flat-top and his hazel eyes were limpid as if he were having an allergic reaction. His sickly pallor made Blasing think Cash spent most of his time with his aquiline nose in books.

Barely hiding her distaste, Angela made introductions. Cash was the kind of man who looked upon women as being good for only one thing.

"I'm looking forward to working with a reasonable man for a change," Cash said, stiffly extending a hand as he looked down his nose at Blasing.

He developed an immediate dislike of the man, but still shook Cash's hand. "Mr. Heller isn't reasonable?" Blasing asked.

Angela chuckled. Cash stiffened. "That's not what I meant, sir."

"Mr. Cash and Peter clashed frequently," she said.

"What can I do for you, Mr. Cash?" Blasing asked.

"I wanted to see how your tour is going and wished to...."

"Broderick is doing an excellent job," Blasing began. Cash looked nervously at Broderick. "But thanks for your concern. I'm adjusting. You can answer a question, though. Why so much security?"

"Mr. Heller fears another attempt on his life and wishes to minimize any fears our patrons might have."

"They seem better conditioned than I remember," Angela said.

Cash sighed. "We have upgraded the staff."

Blasing stifled a yawn. "If you don't mind, I'd like to continue with my tour, and I'm sure you have more pressing matters to attend to," Blasing told Cash.

Cash seemed to ruffle, but said, "Of course, sir. If you have any questions or need assistance, feel free to contact me."

"Thank you," Blasing said, then motioned Broderick onward.

When they'd left Cash behind, Angela said, "He and Peter fought all the time. Cash looks at the bottom line, while Peter was concerned about the ghosts and customer service. I think the time-share idea is probably Cash's."

Broderick stopped at Room 170 and said, "This is one of our most popular rooms, sir. We call it the Perfume Room."

"Why?" Blasing asked.

"Come see for yourself," Broderick said, then knocked. There was no answer, so he poked his head inside. "Unoccupied. I hope the current guests will not resent our brief intrusion." The ghost reached through the lock, and it clicked loudly. Broderick opened the door, then ushered his companions inside.

A definite security problem, Blasing thought. As soon as he stepped inside, the aroma was overwhelming. "What..." he sneezed, "happened here?" He sneezed again.

"We assume an importer of fine perfumes, oils or lotions died in one of the Goldfield's rooms."

"You sure she didn't suffocate?" Blasing sneezed.

"Are you all right?" Angela asked.

"I'm...." he sneezed. The powerful scent changed from flowery to a heavy, cloying musk. "I'm allergic to...." Blasing sneezed again. Suddenly, the smell was all over him, whirling around as though he were being caressed by women dancing. Sneezing, Blasing fled the room.

Angela handed him a tissue. "Are you all right?"

"I think I am now." Blasing's eyes and nose were red.

"My apologies, sir," Broderick said.

"S'okay," Blasing sniffled. "As I said, we have a lot to learn about each other."

"Indeed," Broderick replied. "There are a few rooms somewhat similar to this, haunted but not by a spirit any have seen. I imagine the Violin Parlor or the Bird Suite might be more to your liking than the Perfume Room."

"The Bird Suite is wonderful in the morning," Angela said.

"Does it smell?" Blasing asked, then sneezed.

"Indeed not, sir," Broderick said testily.

Blasing blew his nose, then said, "I'm not sure I like rooms that are haunted by spirits that other ghosts can't see."

Shortly after they resumed the tour, Blasing pointed down a westward corridor, "What are these?"

The narrow hallway ended in a tall, arched window. The sun was sinking lower to the west and the incoming light ignited the floating dust, turning it golden.

"They are overlook reading rooms for those who can only get eastward facing rooms. As you know, we do not allow television at Ghostal Shores—thank the Queen—except in the bar on special occasions. This encourages people to read more, which is why we have a library. Master MacGuire thought it would be wise if the ghosts had a chance to re-educate themselves. I spend much of my time there, learning about these times. Very confusing. So much information at one's fingertips."

Blasing looked surprised. "Really? No TV's? I thought I saw one in the Perfume Room."

"Yes, sir," Broderick replied. "There are televisions with video cassette recorders in the rooms, but no outside reception. Television and radio broadcasts disrupt the atmosphere of Ghostal Shores, and bother the resident spirits."

"Sounds almost quaint," Blasing said.

"We have video rentals and piped in music if you wish, sir. Unfortunately, Mister Heller has no such qualms. He is putting in that newfangled spying system of lenses. And here my fellow countrymen thought they had made great strides in the name of progress," Broderick said with a distant gaze. "Canals, spinning wheels and steam trains seem just a step above the dark ages compared to televisions, computers and jet airplanes. Richard Arkwright, Josiah Wedgewood and John Wilkinson would be humbled."

"Do electronics bother you, Broderick?"

"Somewhat. Signals; as I believe they are called, make me... itch." Broderick grew thoughtful again, as if pondering something he'd just finished reading. "Americans remind me of the British in the way they believe that if they understand the nature of things, they can control it through science."

"Broderick, do you have an opinion on everything?" Blasing asked.

"Of course, sir. Your uncle consulted with me on everything."

"Whether he wanted to or not," Angela chuckled. Broderick simply raised an eyebrow in response. "Heller originally wanted televisions, VCR's and stereos in each room, but the ghosts objected," Angela continued. "Peter listened to them, so there's no radio or TV reception in the rooms."

"A saint," Broderick said. "I do wish I had told Master MacGuire that when he was alive, but he was always being so damnnably Irish."

That made Blasing laugh, and it felt good; he had to stop himself from patting Broderick on the back. "Can I see one of these rooms without perfume?"

"Certainly," Broderick replied.

As they turned to leave, Blasing still felt the annoying presence, and thought he'd heard the swish of long skirts. "Angela, do you feel anything?"

"Excuse me?"

Blasing stopped walking. "Do you feel watched?" The prickly sensation was strong again, even stronger than before.

"I believe I have discerned the cause of the problem," Broderick said, striding stiffly down the corridor. He stopped and reached into the left wall. As though they were disobedient children, Broderick hauled out two female ghosts. "May I introduce two impudent hussies, Jessie and Charity."

"Friends of Fawn's," Angela said coldly.

"This guttersnipe," Broderick shook his right hand but didn't release the spirit's ear, "is Jessie."

The short, busty ghost with a wealth of golden hair spilling from under her bonnet and down her back gave Blasing a pleading smile. Her young face held so much innocence that Blasing had a difficult time believing she was a prostitute. "Hi," she squeaked. She was dressed in a frilly baby blue dress matching her wide eyes.

"And this scamp is Charity," Broderick said, releasing the Asian beauty dressed in a more contemporary green sun dress. Her dark hair was page cut and only a shade lighter than her eyes. She curtsied and unleashed a sensuous smile.

"A pleasure," she said throatily.

Broderick released them, then said, "What are you... ladies doing, skulking around like the Queen's collectors?" They both spoke quickly, words bubbling. "LADIES, ONE AT A TIME, PLEASE!"

"Amber told us about our new owner," Jessie said, "and we wanted to come see him."

"Heard he was scrumptious," Charity said, licking her lips. Broderick hurrumphed.

"And that Angela didn't like us around," Jessie continued, "so we were just tagging along trying to stay out of sight."

"Until tonight," Charity said with a hungry smile.

"LADIES, PLEASE!" Broderick looked very perturbed.

Blasing just shook his head. "A... mischievous group of ghosts certainly inhabit this place."

"Not all our resident spirits should be judged by these hussies,"

Angela replied.

"We get bored," Charity said.

"Run along," Broderick said, clapping his hands, "or I will have you helping Tess and Margaret clean rooms." Jessie and Charity disappeared in a chilling breeze.

"I am so sorry, sir."

"Just make sure they don't show up in my room," Blasing said. He still felt watched. "If they do, I want them cleaning pots."

"An excellent suggestion, sir." They stopped at an open door with a maid's cart outside. "Juanita, are you here?" Broderick called into the room. There was no response. "Oh dear, I hope she isn't off arguing with Margarite again." Broderick drifted inside.

Blasing followed his ghostly valet into an elegant room with a plush green carpet and drapes, a writing desk, a divan, a massive bureau with an adjoining armoire and a four-poster canopy bed with an ornate chest at its foot.

"An amazing place. I wonder if Patrick and Kelly would like it?" He was quiet as they walked away, then said, "So far I've seen a ghost bellman, waiter, bartender, and maintenance man. No paycheck, no medical benefits and no workers compensation. That must keep the cost of running this place low. Do you receive any compensation?"

"Just the joy of doing our job and a lovely place to reside, which is why so many of us are distressed about Ghostal Shores becoming a 'crimeshare,' as Master MacGuire used to put it."

They reached the end of the corridor. Blasing pushed open the exit door, squinting into the bright sunlight. Straight ahead and down the steps, the northern wing's framework reminded Blasing of some long dead beast's bones. "Where from here?"

"Down the stairs to the garden to meet Sven. There are stairs to the beach if you enjoy sand in your shoes."

They followed the floating valet down a short set of stairs, then a long flight of railed steps where they were buffeted by a gusty, salt-laden wind. Past the railing and far below, the ocean was rough and white-capped, the sea foam looking like steamed milk. The sun was low and painted the water a fiery hue.

"As you know, most of us moved here, though involuntarily, with the brick," Broderick began. "Not true with Sven Ericsson; he lived on

Point Reyes, working at one of the dairies until he died of consumption, which is now called tuberculosis, I believe."

"So he's a local, attached to the area but drawn to the resort?" Blasing asked.

"Exactly, sir."

"I thought Peter and Cannon said all the ghosts came with the place, or rather, with the materials," Angela murmured.

"That's incorrect, miss. Sven, in that sense, is a foreigner."

"Broderick, are you absolutely sure there aren't any new ghosts?" Blasing asked, thinking of the stagecoaches.

"Most definitely. I try to keep abreast of whatever the ghosts are doing, speaking with each and every one of them on a daily basis. I will double-check with Missy. Though she might have been teasing you, hoping you would question her further in private."

"I hadn't thought of that. What about the northern wing?"

"With the construction we were expecting some new ghosts, but none so far, thank the Lord."

"Where did he get the materials?" Blasing asked.

"Master MacGuire would only say that it was a surprise. Although he did mention something about Los Angeles. I just hope we do not have any L.A. odd ghosts. You know the type." Broderick sounded very superior and British. "Punk-rockers, surfer-dudes, gang-bangers and," he shuddered, "sweet transvestites. The things I have read about sometimes make me ill."

They finished descending the long set of steps to a large veranda where an open-ended greenhouse was flourishing. When they walked into the garden, the sound of bubbling water, the sweet fragrance of flowers and sun-drenched warmth greeted them.

"Ah, there is Sven." They met the Swedish spirit, finding him to be what one might expect—tall and husky, as well as blue-eyed and blond. To Blasing's surprise, Sven appeared very healthy.

The Swede told stories about the old days, how Point Reyes was made famous by Sir Francis Drake seeking refuge in a nearby bay. Mexicans first settled the point, later dairy farmers and the rich came after it was purchased by the U.S. He told them how the lighthouse had been built, the lenses hauled up the cliffs by oxen. Even in the worst fog, the light was easy to see from the resort, the horns sounding as though sailing was still the sovereign domain of trade.

"What drew you to this place?" Angela finally asked.

"Ah, ta tell the truth, fine lady, I'm not sure myself," Sven said. "All I remember is bein' lonely and walkin' long the shores, as I 'ave so often done in my days beyond days, if you know my meanin.' When I neared this area, I remember feelin'... kin. I climbed the steps along the cliffs and found this place, and a wonder if I may say. The lights, the runnin' water and all the new inventions I never believed possible."

"It's getting late," Blasing said as he glanced at the waning sun. "But I'd like to talk more later. I'm very interested in this area's history, as well as any tall tales."

"I would be proud ta tell ya." Sven's smile was mammoth. "May Odin watch over ya and keep ya well."

As they ascended the other steps on their way to the southern wing, Blasing said, "Broderick, I thought you said he died of TB."

"You have a fine memory, sir."

"I guess I just thought he might look... less hardy."

"Ah, I see your point, now," Broderick replied. "I believe the explanation you seek is that ghosts do not always appear the same now as when they died, but as they see themselves."

"Really!" Angela exclaimed. Either things had changed or Peter had neglected to mention several things. "Then that's why all the trollops look so young and beautiful." Broderick nodded. "Then you could look younger if you wanted?" Angela teased.

Broderick hurrumphed. "That would be pointless. All masquerading is over when one dies, leaving only the essence of what we were when we were alive. That is why being true to oneself is so important."

A little winded, they paused at the top of the steps just outside the main building's porch. Blasing started to yawn, then noticed the prickly sensation again. Why did it come and go?

"How about visiting the ballroom before Blasing falls asleep?"

"A grand idea, miss," Broderick said. He floated up the short flight of carpeted steps to the main building and was moving to the door when it slammed open, passing through him and clipping Blasing's nose. As he fell backward, all Blasing saw was a fleeing ghost being hotly pursued by a screaming man.

Six

"Melanie, stop this behavior immediately!" Broderick demanded. The gypsy ghost slid to a stop. "And if you would be so kind, you too, sir," Broderick said to the huffing man in the tux.

"Mister Madera, are you well?" Broderick asked as he glided down the steps. "Or should I call Dr. Landrum?" The ghost made it sound as though Blasing simply had a stomachache.

Somehow, Angela had landed sprawled atop him. "Blasing?" She touched his face with cool hands. His eyes were out of focus, and he was wheezing. "Are you all right?" He nodded. "I thought bodyguards couldn't be surprised."

"That's why I work with electronics," Blasing gasped. His vision clearing, Blasing stared into Angela's Caribbean-blue eyes. Her body was soft, firm, and simply too close for comfort.

"Well, you did protect me from that door," she mused. Angela offered him a hand up.

"Who are you, sir? And why are you chasing Melanie? Running in the halls is dangerous," Broderick scolded the short, young man. His expression was desperate, verging on panic. His straw-blond hair was thoroughly mussed, and his brown eyes were large and round like a deer caught in the headlights.

"Uh... sir. I'm g... getting m... mother's wedding ring and the family necklace.... She took off with them."

With an expression somehow more grave than usual, Broderick looked to the gypsy spirit. Melanie was dressed in a billowing outfit the color of a double rainbow. Her numerous rings, earrings and necklaces blazed in the setting sun's light.

"Well, Melanie? I am awaiting an explanation for this chicanery," Broderick told her. "And even my patience has its limits, especially when it comes to draggletailed petulance."

Melanie's red lips formed a pout, then a tear ran down her cheek. She stared at Broderick for a moment, tossed her long, dark locks over her shoulder, then proclaimed, "Broderick, he doesn't love her!

He's just too scared to call off the wedding because of all the people he's invited! How stupid can a man be? I know she wouldn't want to marry someone who doesn't love her! What fool woman would? Time and life are so precious." Melanie began to weep.

"I believe enough has been said—and done." Broderick took the necklace and diamond-baguetted ring from Melanie and returned them to the bewildered man. "Go with my deepest apologies, sir. Is there anything else we can do for you?"

"N... n... no." He looked at the ring, then left dazed.

"Melanie, I want you to apologize to Master MacGuire's nephew," Broderick told the weeping ghost.

"Oh my GOD!" Melanie cried, then threw herself to her knees. "I am so sorry. It's just that when I discovered what was going on... I... I... I couldn't...."

Blasing was embarrassed by her actions. "Broderick, please."

"Certainly, sir. Melanie, we know your wanton nature caused you to intervene," the ghost valet said stiffly but placatingly as he helped Melanie stand. "Go have yourself a good cry. We shall talk later." Misty-eyed, Melanie nodded, looking very much like a lost soul, then she wandered into the southern wing. "She acts as if she is Irish," Broderick shook his head hopelessly.

"She's quite a flirt," Angela said. "I'm not so sure I buy her story."

"She was telling the truth, miss, I can tell."

Blasing nodded in agreement. He felt her regret was sincere. If marriage with someone wonderful was heaven, then a bad union must be hell. "Quite a group of frolicking ghosts we have here at Ghostal Shores," Blasing said. "What's next, a main street parade? Jugglers? Spirits on stilts? Or maybe ghostly camel races?"

Broderick was not disarmed. "I apologize sir, it is not always this bad. In fact, it has never been so."

"I think they miss Peter," Angela said.

"Could very well be, miss. Mister Madera, at tomorrow's meeting, I promise to tell all of the ghosts to shape up or ship out. This wildly improper behavior will not be tolerated. It disturbs the guests." Broderick opened the door, and they went inside where it was considerably warmer.

"Is it my imagination, Broderick, or does everybody, yourself excluded," Angela added quickly, "seem a bit... unstable?"

"I believe you might be correct in attributing that to Master MacGuire's murder. We may be without bodies, but we do have feelings," Broderick replied.

"Could they be stressed because they think they may lose their home?" Blasing asked. He couldn't believe he was discussing ghosts as though they were people.

"Possibly, yes. You are very astute, sir, just as Master MacGuire was but without his excessively annoying stubborn streak."

"I'm not so sure about that," Angela said. Blasing ignored her barb. "But the spirits really shouldn't worry. Mr. Heller wouldn't ever let things get that bad. The ghosts are free labor."

"Some view Heller as being very unstable and untrustworthy," Broderick told her. "Carrie is one. She is simply beside herself."

"That's just Carrie. She's never liked Heller."

"Or much of anyone else," Broderick pointed out. "Sean Heller has always reminded me of Warren Hastings, the first guv'nor of India," Broderick told them, slipping back into London cockney speech for a moment. "'E was impeached for corruption an' misconduct, though it took 'em over 7 years."

"Love your accent, Broderick," Angela teased. It was the first time she'd heard him talk like that.

"I worked diligently to sound as though I had never been born within the sound of Bow Bell. Captain Morris wanted me to speak properly."

"You do, Broderick. You do. What next?" Blasing yawned.

"Well," Broderick began, "there is the library on the second floor; Janice lives there. As I have said, it is my favorite chamber. We have not visited the game room, nor the roof top tennis courts. Pity they are not grass, as is Wimbledon. Then there are numerous shops downstairs, several are run by spirits."

"No shopping, please. I just want to lie down. We can finish the tour tomorrow if you don't mind. I'm not too alert right now."

"How's your head?" Angela asked.

"Could be better, but okay for two shots in one day. I can't really tell if it's spinning because of the blows or because of...." Blasing's gesture encompassed all of Ghostal Shores.

"It takes a wise man to know himself," Broderick said.

"Lead on," Blasing said. The ghost valet straightened his jacket, then floated down the hallway.

As they neared the ballroom, two men—one dressed in the light blue uniform of security and the other the green jumpsuit of maintenance—were working diligently. The one in blue handed tools to his lanky, grim-jawed partner who was installing a bracket for an oscillating camera. Broderick hustled past as if some deadly contagion were present.

Blasing glanced at the Sony box. Their equipment was certainly top of the line, if a bit extreme. Heller must really be worried.

They eventually stopped in front of a large set of ornate, black doors with golden handles. "Step right in, sir, miss." Broderick opened the door, ushering them inside.

"Broderick, I'm tired, where..." Blasing started, but Broderick was already gone. "Damn. You know, Counselor, I'm not sure I can handle dealing with all these ghosts."

"That sounds defeatist, Blasing. Personally, I think you're handling this exceptionally well. Certainly much better than I did. I was always looking around, expecting a ghost to pop out of the wall or up from the floor like a spectral jack-in-the-box."

Blasing laughed whole-heartedly. "That's exactly the way I feel! Are you reading my mind?"

"That would be telling. But I can say you hide it better than most," she replied with a smile.

"I still feel watched, and sometimes I... hear things."

"It's always worse the first day. You seem to be very sensitive."

"Or paranoid."

Angela chuckled, then said seriously, "Are you psychic?"

Blasing's stare was flat.

"Okay, okay. How about intuitive? Do you follow gut feelings? Hunches?" Blasing nodded. "I rest my case. Shall we go in?" Head held high, she smiled and walked gracefully into the cavernous ballroom.

"Wow," Blasing said. "Each time I think I'm becoming used to this place, something changes my mind."

"Funny how life can be like that."

With their footsteps echoing off the wooden floor, they walked into the center of the ballroom to stand under the huge chandelier. Coming in through the tall, westward windows, the dying sun's light set everything afire. The crystals in the chandelier and the mirrors between the two-story drapes burned with the crimson radiance of twilight.

"I really feel watched," Blasing said, then looked up, noticing the balcony along the southern wall. He thought he saw a blur of fading white along the railing, but it quickly disappeared.

A creaking noise sounded as though a door were being opened, and they immediately turned to face the deserted stage. Blasing shivered as if frozen fingers danced down his spine.

The stage was cloaked in shadows, and the only thing visible was a large black piano. One of the stage's lower cabinet doors had swung partly open, revealing a shadowy recess and the first few rows of folded chairs.

The plink of a high-pitched key made Blasing jump, then the piano began to play a slow, ballroom dance. The tune remained an easy rhythm for a time, then changed to something a little faster. Blasing thought he could feel couples whirling about him, their shoes skipping across the floor in time with the music.

"Whoever is playing is very good," Blasing murmured.

The song changed again, this time to something very familiar. It mentally transported Blasing back to a friend's wedding. He danced with Jenny, and he felt a strange mixture of joy and melancholy.

Angela watched Blasing, his expression barely illuminated by the lavender light of the western setting sun. He seemed sad as though he were deeply missing somebody—probably his kids. Angela was surprised by how well she felt she knew Blasing. Their initial meeting had been full of unpleasant shocks, surprises, and commiseration over Peter's death. She'd been amazed such a good-looking man could seem so... vulnerable. Even then, she thought Blaise Madera was too good to be true. She'd like to think her attraction to him was more than animal magnetism.

The music stopped, pulling Angela from her woolgathering. The last chord seemed to linger, reluctant to fade away.

"This place brings back memories," he said in a husky voice. "Being around death reminds one of how quickly things can change."

There was silence between them, then Angela felt she had to break the mood, so she applauded. "Charlie is a wonderful pianist. His music has such feeling."

"Indeed he is and it does," Broderick said, appearing before them in the near darkness, a wavering mist of a man touched by an eldritch glow. "He plays music of every sort. You heard him earlier in the restaurant." Broderick looked intently at Blasing. "Are you all right, sir?"

"Just tired, Broderick. The holidays are hell on security," Blasing sighed wearily. "I would like to go to my room, hear about my uncle, then shower and lie down before dinner."

"Very good, sir. Come with me," Broderick said, turning toward the northern doors. "The lifts are this way."

"Tell Charlie that was... marvelous."

"I will, sir, but I believe he already knows. He has the uncanny knack of being able to play what the audience would like to hear. He calls this afterlife his encore."

Without another word, they walked into the grand entryway. The Cathedral to the Coast was now lit by the floor lamps, their amber glow barely reaching the ceiling. Through the skylight and to the east, the near full moon was visible. The air was tinged with excitement—the hum of voices and laughter, the clink of glasses and soft music coming from the stairway to the Clifftop Bar and Pacific Crest Restaurant.

A pair of couples exited the elevator and headed for the stairway. The first was dressed in matching western outfits. The second pair was formally clad; the man wore a blue satin jacket, and the woman was dressed in a flowing green gown adorned with enough emeralds to drop the market price.

When the elevator stopped at the third floor, Broderick walked to and through the unnumbered door of Mac's suite. They heard the lock unlatch, then the door slowly opened. "Welcome to your home away from home."

"Ghosts are a definite security problem," Blasing muttered.

In some ways—the forest green carpet and the fine antique furnishings—the study lounge was similar to the rest of Ghostal Shores, but its atmosphere seemed special. A wall of one-way mirrored glass overlooked Ghostal Shores's entryway, giving a view of the Cathedral to the Coast. A wall of windows, including a door to the balcony, faced the twilight-caressed Pacific. A fire burned in the white-stone hearth, adding a cheery feel to the spacious room.

"This is some room," Blasing finally said, walking toward the huge mahogany desk and credenza that dominated the room. Two chairs faced them. Despite the wet bar to the right, a coat rack, a couch with end tables, and two bookcases—one with a stereo setup—the room still felt somewhat empty.

"Your room, miss, is the first on the left—the one usually reserved and stocked specifically for guests of your gender...."

"I'm not sure about this," Angela began.

"... while Mister Madera's is the second, where Master MacGuire used to reside. Each has its own bathroom. Let me know if you require anything. Both have cold boxes, I mean refrigerators; my idea, I must admit, since I tired of late night forays to the kitchen for Master MacGuire."

"We used to conduct business here," Angela said quietly.

Blasing walked around studying the lounge. The desktop was crowded, covered by a writing pad, a wooden "in" box, a double-armed lamp with pull chains, and knickknacks from a previous century, including an old Uncle Sam bank and a cherry wood statuette of a Pony Express rider. A simulated derringer lighter lay on a Nevada-shaped ash tray.

Blasing could almost feel Mac here. Smell his cigar. Almost see him at his desk. Blasing wondered if that was an effect of Ghostal Shores, or if it was his imagination. Faint water marks revealed that scotch highballs had rested upon the mahogany surface.

"Broderick, were you with Mac when he was... when he died?" Broderick nodded. "Tell me about it... please."

"It seems so senseless," Broderick began, eyes downcast and his face distraught. Angela thought she could feel his pain; it seemed to fill the room. She wanted to give the ghost a hug, but knew better.

Blasing was stone-faced but his eyes were troubled. "Broderick...."

"I tried to assist Master MacGuire but... he... I... I even pursued the bloody villain, intent on catching the murderous... but...." Broderick shrugged, then in a very human gesture, the ghost valet touched Blasing.

As though he'd grabbed a live wire, Blasing was jolted, then he felt a chill course through him. When he recovered, he couldn't believe his eyes. He wasn't in Uncle Mac's study any longer, but in another office. This one was windowless with numerous mirrors that reflected countless paper constructs,an infestation of origami that covered bookshelves, a large desk, and many cabinet surfaces. Paper birds and planes hung from the ceiling, swaying in front of the vent.

Where was he and how did he get here? Where were Angela and Broderick? The ghost had touched him. What had Cannon said about a ghost touching a person? Strange things could happen?

Blasing was beginning to wonder if the day had been too much for him when a stocky, red-haired man in his late fifties shuffled into the room. "Uncle Mac!" Blasing stammered, "What are you doing here? I... I thought you were...."

Peter MacGuire was a bull-necked man with wide shoulders. He was dressed in a dark green suit that made his hair all the more fiery and his ruddy complexion somewhat pale. Ignoring Blasing, the Irishman stuck an unlit cigar stub into his mouth, set a drink on the desktop, then sat down with a growl.

"Uncle Mac? Can you hear me?" Blasing asked, moving over to the large desk to confront his uncle. What if his Uncle Mac wasn't really here but merely "haunting" this room? "Uncle Mac, please talk to me." Blasing waved his hands in front of his uncle's face but was completely ignored. When Blasing tried to touch his uncle, his fingers pressed through him.

"Can't believe I have to work on a Saturday night when I should be sipping brandy and listening to Bach," Mac muttered as he worked his way through a stack of check-in cards. Next to these was a pile of charge card receipts and a blue bag with Bank of America printed on it. "Damn Heller for blowing a fuse. It's happening all too often, even for him. Affecting his work." Peter MacGuire's accent was a thicker brogue than Blasing remembered.

The pile he was tending suddenly split on its own, then the receipts were riffled. Mac wore a big smile, "Thanks, Broderick."

"Broderick!" Blasing didn't see the English spirit.

"Come to help?" Peter MacGuire asked.

"Of course," the disembodied British voice replied.

"Broderick, you are far too good to me."

"Irrefutably true, Master Pete."

Why do you treat me so well? We should be arguing. Spoiling to fight."

"It's true that only in death would the British serve the Irish, but such is my fate, and I have accepted it. As you once surmised, Master Pete, I come with the place. But in truth, I would say you have mellowed with... time."

"Hmmmm. I'll let that pass, 'cause I certainly could use some help. My eyes are going. I am getting old, dammit."

"Your liver will rot first, sir," Broderick replied.

Mac hurrumphed, then took a drink. "Might as well kill myself before another woman shatters the remaining fragments of my broken heart."

Looking properly stiff, Broderick slowly brightened into sight. "You will live a long time yet, sir, and there will be someone else. The Irish are too stubborn to die gracefully. Sir, may I ask what you are doing here? I thought you had a date?"

"I did. She canceled. What a night! Jason has food poisoning—from our own kitchen no less—and Sean threw such a tirade he almost had a stroke. We called Dr. Reasons, and he ordered bed rest. So here I am making the safe drop."

For a time, they reconciled and audited the evenings check-ins. "You know, Broderick, Blaise is a fine boy; he'll do this place right when I'm gone."

"I do not understand why you expect to die so soon."

Peter MacGuire paused, appeared ready to say something, but took a drink instead. Finally he said, "Just a precaution. I should have done it long ago. You know, I expect you to treat Blaise the same as you have me, with the exception of your highly grating and unsolicited opinions."

"I beg your pardon, sir? Are you referring to my comment that neither a will, nor a potential change in ownership would be required if you had listened to any doctor's advice—even that of a charlatan's—and quit imitating a besotted dragon, sir?"

"Hell man, those are the few pleasures left in my life." He sighed, then said, "I really miss Peggy's visits."

"I know, sir. And I suppose you also miss Ms. Golden and that very nice Miss Juliet Gaylen. Did I leave anyone out, Master Pete?"

"Yes, you did. Are we finished?" he asked. Broderick nodded. "Good," Mac began gathering everything together. "Did you mail the will to Angela Starborne today?"

"Yes sir. It left with the noon pickup."

"Then let's celebrate. Would you get me a fresh cigar?"

"But Mister Heller hates the smell of cigars."

"That's why I want to smoke in here!" Peter MacGuire chortled. Broderick appeared bemused, then disappeared through the wall, hauling a reluctant Blasing out with him as though they were linked.

Everything was a blur as they flew upstairs and into Mac's study. All the while, Blasing was trying to get Broderick's attention. Angela was not in the suite.

Cigar in hand, Broderick and Blasing returned, having to travel conventionally, using doors and elevators this time. "This is the most foul smelling of the lot," Broderick murmured as he pushed the door open to the hallway. "Pardon me, sir, but what...."

A lanky, bearded man dressed in a tux and carrying a gun pushed the office door completely open.

"What' d..." Peter MacGuire began.

The silenced .38 Smith & Wesson coughed fire several times. Peter MacGuire gasped and clutched his chest. He staggered back, striking the wall below the open safe, then slowly slid to the floor. The air around him shimmered, and then something drifted skyward.

Was that Uncle Mac's spirit, Blasing wondered?

"Dear Lord!" Broderick exclaimed as he flew into the office.

As if sensing him, the murderer looked around for unexpected company—his restless, brown eyes peering through Blasing. He got a good look at Mac's tall, skinny murderer. The man's face was pale, gaunt and partly hidden by a crooked mustache and beard. A nervous twitch spasmed along his left eye and ran down his face. With a self-indulgent smile, the intruder closed the door, then moved to the safe, now no longer hidden behind a painting.

Quivering with fury, Blasing launched himself at the man. "Murderer! You'll pay for this! I swear it!" Blasing swung wildly, his fists passing through the killer, then he stumbled and fell.

The murderer picked up the money bag, then kicked Peter MacGuire's body out of the way so he could more easily access the safe. Blasing rose and continued swiping futilely as the murderer removed money and jewelry from the safe.

The murderer dropped something shiny and stooped to pick up a golden ring crafted in the head of a lion. Its small emerald eyes flashed before it disappeared into the sack. With a smile, the killer slipped from the office and down the hall.

Broderick checked his master's pulse, looked about sadly, then flew to the phone, telling the operator to send a doctor and security. "You seem to have passed on, my dear friend. I wish your spirit a safe journey. If I can, I will see justice done." Taking Blasing with him, Broderick raced after the murderer.

They caught sight of the murderer as he descended the stairway below the bayview window. "Stop! Murderer!" Everyone turned.

The man cursed, then sprinted forward, jumping three steps at a time. Broderick and Blasing doggedly pursued. "You will be executed for this foul deed!" Broderick yelled. The murderer glanced over his shoulder, his eyes bulging when he realized an avenging spirit was rapidly closing the distance.

Broderick grabbed the murderer, then recoiled, staggering back. His fingers curled as though they'd been burned, then he collapsed onto the steps.

The murderer stumbled the last few steps to the landing. He tried to catch himself but crash-landed hard. The impact loosened his beard. Shaking a pained right hand and grabbing his elbow, he bounced to his feet and disappeared down the steps.

Blasing tried to follow, but he found he could not. Something held him here. "Broderick, what's wrong?! What's going on?"

"Blasing! Blasing!" Angela yelled, shaking him violently and bringing him to the present. Her beautiful eyes were darkly fiery. "Are you all right? Damn it, Broderick! What did you do to him?"

SEVEN

"I must apologize," Broderick told them, wringing his hands and keeping them close as if they'd misbehaved. "I have broken a rule. I should be reprimanded immediately."

"It's all right, Broderick," Blasing said, his mind grounded in the present once more.

Angela saw the blankness leave Blasing's eyes and was more thrilled than she would have imagined. "You went stiff, then you started mumbling. Then screaming. I was ready to call Dr. Landrum."

"I'm okay," Blasing reassured her.

"You sure?" she asked. He nodded. "What happened?"

Blasing looked at Broderick. "A trip down Broderick's memory lane," he replied. "You touched me?"

The ghost valet nodded. "As I said, I am quite sorry, sir." Broderick repeated, his expression grave. "I should be punished."

Blasing waved him off. "Is that what always happens?"

"I must admit that I do not exactly know. Master MacGuire and I talked of it often. We surmised that several things could happen when a ghost touched a person. I... I was just trying to pass on my thoughts. I regret distressing you both, but I could not adequately describe your uncle's brutal murder, so I...."

"It's all right," Blasing said again. "You know what the killer looks like, right?"

"Yes. I gave my impressions to a sketch artist working with Sheriff Middleton. He did an exceptionally fine rendition, but they have been unable to find such a barbarian."

"I can't believe he just disappeared into thin air," Blasing said. "We're on a peninsula."

"Blasing, will you please tell me exactly what happened?"

He looked at her for a moment, trying to put together everything he'd seen, then explained about 'appearing' in Heller's office. Angela laughed a little when she mentioned Mac wanting to stink up the office, then held her breath during Blasing's gripping account of the murder and subsequent pursuit.

"Did the murderer say anything?" Angela asked. Blasing shook his head. "Nothing to Mac? Nothing at all?" Blasing glared. "He didn't ask him to move? Just shot him?"

"Yes," said Blasing stonily.

"Did he seem satisfied or elated?" Angela pressed.

"No. What are you getting at?"

"I just think it's strange that, if revenge and robbery were motives, the murderer didn't say anything," Angela explained.

"I think I understand," Blasing said. "If he was gunning for Mac, he might've gloated before killing him. And if he was just trying to rob the place, he might have told Uncle Mac to shut up and stand still with his hands up or something. Murder is a far worse sentence than armed robbery."

"But he just shot him—cold blooded murder," Broderick said as if the revelation were just dawning upon him. "Simply ghastly."

"If he was gunning for Heller," Blasing spoke for her as if reading her mind, "he should've been surprised that he'd killed the wrong man." She nodded. "We need to talk with the sheriff."

"I've left a message. What else did you see?"

Blasing explained about the chase.

"What repelled you?" Angela asked the Englishman.

"I have no idea, miss."

"You watched Mac die, right?" Blasing asked Broderick.

"As you saw yourself, sir," Broderick sounded weary. "I saw his spirit depart."

"Do you think Peter haunts Ghostal Shores?" Angela asked pointedly. "He did love the place so."

"I do not know. It is entirely possible," Broderick replied.

"I think we need to determine if my uncle's spirit is still here," Blasing told them. Angela agreed.

"What do you suggest, sir?" Broderick asked.

"Ask Angela," Blasing sighed heavily, then rubbed his eyes. "I don't think my mind can take any more today."

"Personally, sir, I think you are holding up fabulously."

Blasing rubbed his eyes again, then ran his fingers through his hair. "Dinner in about three hours? We can talk financials."

"Sounds good to me," Angela replied.

"Broderick, if you don't mind," Blasing began. Looking a little sheepish, he hesitated at the door to his room, "I'd like you to keep an eye on the suite. Prevent anyone from disturbing me. I don't want to wake up with a ghost in my bed."

"Do not worry, sir. Those cyprians will not bother you. Does your wish not to be disturbed include Mister Heller?"

"Everybody, Broderick. If someone absolutely must bother me in the next two hours, make sure it's you or the counselor here. If it's my kids, just put the phone call through."

"I understand perfectly, sir. It shall be so."

"Rest easy," Angela said.

"Thanks," Blasing said grumpily, then closed the door.

"Thanks for making the... transition easier," Angela told Broderick. "I appreciate it, and Peter would have too."

"You are quite welcome, Miss Starborne. It was my pleasure."

Angela stretched languorously. "I think I'm going to unpack and unwind. I might even soak in a hot bath."

"I shall be ever vigilant, miss. Rest assured, you shall not be disturbed." Broderick's expression was serious; one murder right under his nose was one too many.

"I know I can count on you, Broderick," Angela said, then closed the door. She immediately stepped out of her shoes, then tried to reach Sheriff Middleton by phone again, only to leave another message. She thought about calling her insurance company. That reminded her to write a note to the Ferrari driver—less dangerous than venting herself in person.

Before she could unwind, Angela needed to see if she and her grandmother had forgotten to pack anything. They'd just returned to San Francisco after spending a week at her grandmother's house—a place without modern conveniences—when the phone rang. Her boss had told her about Peter, then ordered her to cut her vacation short. Angela and her grandmother had done laundry and packed in a hurry.

What she didn't expect to find was a note with an old journal in her big bag. She read the attached note; Grandma Dawnjoy was concerned about Angela's privacy. In the journal was a ceremony to protect her room from the spirits' intrusion.

Angela was bemused and curious. Her grandmother often talked about the magic of the earth but rarely went into detail. Even though it sounded absurd in the context of modern times, Angela took a look. A feeling of privacy would make her feel better.

Searching for the implements mentioned in the note, Angela set aside the journal and opened her case containing jewelry and makeup. At the bottom, Angela found plastic bags of sage, salt, crystals and crushed hematite in a leather sack.

When she unwrapped a brightly colored blanket, she found a coyote's jawbone and parts to a ceremonial pipe. She smiled; Blasing would find this very odd, as would many of her business associates. The last year spent with her grandmother had changed her in many ways; she'd learned that animals and their attributes were an important part of the Paiute way of life, and that their bones and feathers added power to ceremonies.

Angela discovered they'd forgotten to pack much of her makeup. Grandma was probably trying once again to make a point about being a painted woman. Angela changed into jeans and sneakers, then thoroughly read the journal; the ceremony was simple and now would be as good a time as any to perform it. Blasing wouldn't interrupt and wonder what she was doing. Broderick could be her guinea pig.

Angela laid everything on the blanket, blessed the tobacco and pipe, then loaded it with the appropriate prayers to the south, west, north and east before smoking a puff in each direction. When she finished, she lit the sage, smudged the jawbone and herself—cleansing them and equalizing their energy—then carried them around the room, driving away spirits and grounding negativity. Angela even climbed on a chair to do the ceiling.

She lined the base of the walls with salt and crushed hematite, then sprinkled some across the doorway. Finally, she laid hematite and quartz stones in every corner and at the cardinal points—north, south, east and west. The last stone she placed in the center of the room. Along with the salt, the crystal grid barred spirits from entering. While she finished giving prayerful thanks with the pipe, she heard a knock at the lounge door, followed by voices—one with a creamy French accent.

"No, miss, I distinctively remember Master Madera saying he

did not want to be disturbed by anyone. He did not exclude you."

"I had an opening in my schedule and just thought he might be interested in having dinner," Eva told the ghost valet.

"Hoping to do some brainwashing?" Angela asked acidly as she walked into the suite's lounge.

"Ah, hello Angela. Did you bore your client to death? Or drive him into hiding?" Eva smiled bitingly. She was dressed for attracting attention. Her dark hair was unbound and her shapely form was hugged by a fine, gold lame´ dress.

"I thought you were busy tonight," Angela reminded her.

"And obviously you are not," Eva said, looking at Angela's attire. "And what is that delightful aroma? Aire de Forest Fire?"

"Eva, what are you doing here?"

"I wanted Blasing to meet some of the salespeople."

"He is definitely too tired to meet with any of the vampires, miss," Broderick said gravely.

Angela nearly burst out laughing.

"Eva, I don't understand why Sean Heller is pushing this. He can't start selling property tomorrow. And I can't believe he's paying anybody to hang around without expecting to have started yesterday."

"Sean just loves to push things, but you know that," Eva said. "I'm sure he has his reasons."

"Well, he sure reacted quickly. He seems... prepared."

"Sean fully believed that sooner or later Mac would give in to the idea, and he wanted to be ready."

"How did Heller take the news that he has a partner?"

"Outrage with lots of ranting, then he began to think things through. Sean believes he can convince Blasing otherwise. I'll be glad to help." Eva smiled wickedly.

"Eva, let Blasing rest and make his own decisions. He's a big boy."

"I can tell." Eva pursed her lips, checking her lipstick.

Angela pushed down a growing urge to slap the French tart. She wouldn't learn anything that way. "Eva, when you broke up with Peter...."

"His mistake," she said coolly, her gaze narrowing.

"... you were furious. Were you ever mad enough to kill him?"

"Angela, haven't you been that mad at least once at every man you've known?" she replied, then turned and saucily walked to the elevator.

Broderick raised his eyes to the heavens and shook his head. "If Master MacGuire had listened to me just once, so much would have been avoided. As usual, the Irish refuse to listen to sound, British reasoning."

Angela stifled her laughter; she'd heard some of the "advice" the English spirit frequently dispensed. "Broderick, I forgot some things. I'm stepping out to shop. I'll be back soon. 'Bye."

She was on the "lift", as Broderick would call it, when she recalled she'd forgotten to have him walk into her room. Would the protection keep out Broderick?

Her companions were a little old lady with a walking cane and a short, elderly man who was humpbacked and stooped. "Hello!" They greeted her cheerily and introduced themselves as the Parkers from Ft. Worth, Texas; they had loved the gunfight in the restaurant. "You know, I just love 'Texas Hold 'Em.' Do you think, if I asked kindly, they'd let me join in for a hand or two?" Mr. Parker asked.

"Ask. They're always looking for new blood," Angela responded.

"Or a patsy," Mrs. Parker laughed.

Did Heller think Blasing was a patsy, Angela wondered? As she mentally stepped back to last night, her thoughts drifted to the handsome heir.

Even with dark, bloodshot eyes, several day's beard growth and an abundance of fatigue lines, Blasing was ruggedly handsome—almost too good-looking to be true. He was tall with wide shoulders, a broad chest and narrow hips. If all bodyguards and security experts looked like Blasing, she thought, more women would claim to be in danger. Angela had been sure he would be a disappointment once he opened his mouth.

"You weren't expecting me?" Angela asked. Just his expression led to a sinking feeling—her new assistant hadn't called. Angela wanted to scream but remained calm despite the sensation that Coyote—an early Paiute predecessor of Murphy's Law—controlled her life. "I hate to be the one to tell you, but.... You see, I represent your uncle and his estate. He was... ah...." She found it difficult, but managed to maintain her professionalism. After a deep breath, she finished, "... murdered last Saturday night."

Blasing's expression changed from fatigue to defeat. Angela was quite surprised; how could a guy this dangerous-looking be vulnerable? She quickly dropped her business facade and empathized. Peter had been her friend, too.

"Who would want to kill him? A jealous husband?"

"No, he was shot while working in his partner's office at Ghostal Shores," Angela replied.

"Ghostal Shores? Is that the hotel Uncle Mac and his partner built on the coast north of the Bay?"

"Have you ever been there?"

Blasing shook his head. "Only heard strange stories about it. Something about it being haunted," he scoffed.

Angela handed him a letter from Peter MacGuire, and he studied it. "It says you must leave immediately and drive with me to Ghostal Shores to claim your estate."

"But he died last Saturday. That's not immediately."

"I was on a retreat," she finished stonily, then tried to look at it from his point of view. Nobody else had wanted to handle the Ghostal Shores account while she was gone, so they'd just waited for her return. "I just found out this morning, Mr. Madera. And Peter MacGuire was more than a business acquaintance; he was my friend. I don't know why neither my office, nor the authorities, informed you. I'm very sorry."

"I'm sorry. I'm very tired. What happened to the body?"

"It's being stored in Petaluma pending completion of some tests. When they're through, Peter will be cremated and his ashes spread from the cliffs behind Ghostal Shores. Peter thought it essential that you arrive at the resort a.s.a.p. ...."

"But I have kids, and a business to run."

"If you come with me, you'll be able to sell your business, send your kids to the best of colleges AND retire a wealthy man."

"Quite a statement." She nodded. After some thought, he called his sitter and convinced Mrs. Wilson to watch the kids.

The next morning, she drove to his house and met his nanny and her charges—Patrick and Kelly. Patrick looked like he'd be tall, dark and handsome one day, while his sister Kelly appeared to be one hundred percent Irish. Although they were somewhat subdued by the news of their uncle's death, Angela found them delightfully charming. Patrick wasn't convinced she was really Uncle Mac's lawyer until Kelly whacked him and told him to quit being dense. Mom used to say Uncle Mac was always in the company of beautiful women.

When the doors to the lobby opened, Angela returned to the present. She hadn't even noticed that a strikingly handsome Brazilian couple looking like royalty had joined them. She wore a backless blue sapphire dress cut low in front and leaving little to the imagination. An abundance of gemstones matched both her dress and her eyes. He was handsome in a crisp, white suit and shirt that contrasted with his ebony hair, dark complexion and opaque eyes. A huge black man was elegantly dressed in a double-breasted suit and fez.

Angela followed everyone out and surveyed the lobby. She loved the blend of customers; they were absolutely amazing, coming from many countries and cultures. Those fascinated by the afterlife and spiritual phenomena came from all walks of life.

As Angela walked toward the shops of Old West Avenue, she glanced over at the old-fashioned newspaper cart. Willy, the youngest of the spirits, was surrounded by customers. He wore clothing much too big for him—mammoth boots, baggy pants, a bulky jacket and a well-worn cap. At eleven, Willy had been run over by a horse while chasing his windblown newspapers in front of the Goldfield.

Willy was such a sweetheart, people offered to take him home. Of course, he didn't want to leave the hubbub and excitement. Peter had been a second father to him; Angela was sure Willy missed him.

Old West Avenue was lined with rustic signs, horse troughs, hitching posts and lamps mimicking yesteryear. Instead of dirt, the "road" was planked. The scent of pine and heavy spices wafted from the shops and drifting along the street.

When Angela walked into the 1880's General Store, she felt as if she'd stepped back in time; the shop was nearly authentic from top to bottom with a worn, wooden floor, rough paneled walls, a wood-burning stove, and shelves crowded with large mason jars. Barrels of all kinds and sizes took up the rest of the floor space. The products appeared contemporary but specially packaged in a fashion reminiscent of early America—made of paper and sized to fit. The computer cash register hid within a podium atop a counter containing candy, cigars and tobacco. The lamps were a mixture of oil and electric.

Angela started searching for cosmetics. When she turned a corner near the wood-burning store, she almost bumped into Carrie sitting in her rocker. Her ghost-cat was startled out of her lap, jumping with limbs akimbo and scrambling for freedom. The elderly spirit caught Angus before the feline could escape.

"Hullo Angela!" Carrie said happily as she stood, then placed Angus in the chair. "Let me have a look at you, child." She took off her glasses. Her clothing was early pioneer—a sturdy blouse and heavy cotton dress—and her hair was knotted atop her head in a no nonsense fashion. "God's blessing, you are so young and pretty, Angela. I'd heard you'd come back ta visit us."

"Not under the best of circumstances," Angela replied. "How is everyone holding up?"

"We miss Mac terribly. Ta say the least, we're all a bit unsettled by the situation. Murder is a touchy subject around here!" Carrie finished angrily. Angela racked her tired brain but couldn't remember why the subject was touchy. "I see you've forgotten, child. Probably thinking about that handsome man you're with, aren't you?" she chuckled. "Well, I don't blame you. You make quite a couple. I was married at fourteen. Can you imagine that?"

"Absolutely not. You've seen Blasing?"

"I sneaked a peak while you two were in the restaurant."

"Spying?"

"Naturally, we're all curious. He's our new owner, and he's Mac's nephew. Sometimes Mac talked about him with longing and regret. That Mr. Madera really shines." Carrie's smile grew brighter.

"What do you mean?"

"You know, dear, it's why you're attracted to him. Though there is also great sadness. Let me give you some advice, ch...."

I mean, dear. All the dead crops must be pulled before new ones can be planted."

Angela didn't understand why the ghosts were being so difficult and obtuse today. Then she remembered the odd man they'd bumped into after leaving the pool. It wasn't just the ghosts.

"Walk with me," Angela said. "I need to pick up some things."

"Certainly, you must look your finest for your dinner date."

"Carrie, why is murder a touchy subject?"

"Many of us—like ole Angus—died in a fire that was purposely set."

"Barney died in that, too, didn't he?" Angela asked.

"Yes, as did many employees, guests, and owners of nearby shops, like me. We think it was because Amos wouldn't pay the money. Back then, the gang bosses were plum powerful. Had their fingers in just about everybody's pie. Amos was an example of what could happen if you didn't pay. We were just unlucky. The fire got outta hand."

"Who's we?"

"Barney, David, Allen, Elma, hmmm, let's see... Lila, Tess, Margaret, Charity, Eddie and Amber. Oh, and Melanie, too."

"I never realized."

"It happened shortly after Jonathan was kilt. Just a few months earlier Grant Roberts was gunned down by that private investigator his wife hired to see if he was cheatin' on her. What an era! Charlie was killed while performing Mozart for the crowd. A stray bullet found him. It was one of those crazy times when the miners had just come ta town. Let's see, I think Dirk and Samuel died in brawls. Missy was thrown off the balcony."

Angela was trying to picture the time. Dusty. Dirty and less civilized. More living off the land. Less government. Fewer people. More space. "The wild, wild west."

"Yes it was, dear. It sure was, and let me be the first ta tell you I don't miss it. Lands sake's, no! I like these civilized times. For one thing, not everybody carries a gun."

"Sometimes I wonder."

"So'll this Mr. Madera do us right?" Carrie asked pointedly.

"I think so. Cannon likes him. And I think Broderick does too."

Carrie nodded, satisfied. "Have you seen Sheriff Middleton?"

"Just after daybreak. You'd think that man was born on a farm! And he was asking more questions!" She frowned as she crossed her arms across her chest. "Even the same ones sometimes like he wants ta see if I'd forgotten what I said."

"Questions? About what?"

"About this place. The other ghosts. Employees. Heller. He's been running around talking ta everybody. You'd think he was a Pinkerton." She smiled. "You know, if he keeps looking he'll find something."

"What makes you think so?"

"Well... a long time ago, I met Merl Heller. He and Sean are a lot alike. Could have been brothers, you know, halves of the same soul. Merl claimed he was a banker, but he really ran the Goldfield gang. Got one of Elva's youngins hooked on opium. Eventually, Jimmy just withered away and died."

"Opium?"

"Yeah, it wasn't illegal back then. Angie, now tell me true like, don't the new men in blue remind you of a gang of crooks?"

"The security guards?" Angela asked. Carrie nodded. Angela remembered seeing one in the lobby and another along the Old West Avenue. "I don't know."

"Like attracts like, you know. The man at the top sets the example ta all, and Mac ain't here no more."

"You think Heller had something to do with Mac's death?"

"Damn well tootin', and I don't care who knows! I ain't afraid of Miss High and Mighty—Madame Zanadane. Nope! She don't scare me none. Not at all!"

"You told Middleton this?"

"Of course!" Several customers glanced in their direction. "You know it's up ta us ta find out the truth. We owe Mac. It'd only be right."

Angela certainly couldn't disagree. After Blasing's experience, she felt compelled. "Peter told me the ghosts could see to the heart of one's spirit, like you did with Blasing. You've looked into Heller's and know that he murdered Peter?"

Carrie fidgeted. "I believe he has murdered, though not directly. And more than once!"

"But you're not sure, are you?"

"Angela dear, his spirit is so twisted and tainted with sin that it's hard ta tell what is what. Besides, what I see wouldn't hold up in front of the judge."

"Then what do you suggest?"

"I don't rightly know. Some investigating on our own? Ghosts can go places people can't."

"Don't get yourself in trouble," Angela said.

"What's somebody gonna do, kill me, dear? Too late," Carrie cackled. Angela mentioned what she'd heard about the murder from Broderick. "You're pretty and smart, child. Maybe this has something ta do with whatever illegal operation Hellraiser's got his fingers inta. Let's talk some more tomorrow."

"Sounds good. Just be tactful and inconspicuous."

Carrie cackled. "I'll be on my best behavior."

"Carrie, are the ghosts united about the timeshare?"

"NO!" Carrie said. Angus jumped away and disappeared. Seeing the cat, Angela remembered to ask about the stagecoaches. "Nope. Why? You think we got visitors?" Carrie asked.

"I don't know, but very possibly," Angela sighed. "Do you ever wonder if Peter's ghost might be hanging around here somewhere?"

"Lord almighty, of course we wondered. But none of us has seen him after his death. We think the fright might have been too much for him. Left him confused."

"Carrie, I'm sorry, but I need to get going. Can you charge these to my room?" Angela showed her what she'd gathered.

"Of course. Have fun tonight, dear. Maybe you won't run inta ole Hellraiser," she cackled.

Angela hadn't taken a half dozen steps toward the lobby when she heard, "Hey, babe! Wait up!" Angela bristled, then turned stiffly toward the voice. A sharply-dressed man, tall and lean with a mustache and roguishly good looks, swaggered toward her.

"Can I help you?" she asked brittlely.

"You sure can, beautiful. My name's Tom Becker from sales. How about joining me for dinner?" With his lascivious smile and the twinkle in his eyes, Tom Becker reminded her of Grant Roberts.

Why did she attract such men? Is this why she was interested in Blasing? Because he didn't seem attracted to her? She sighed. She usually found flexing her intelligence was the best way to drive off casual interest.

"Is this boy botherin' you, Ang?" Eddie Goldman asked as he suddenly appeared next to her. Becker jumped back from the old ghost. The spirit was thin-haired and dapperly dressed in gray pinstripes that made him seem distinguished. His clothing looked newly pressed, his shoes freshly polished, and his hair recently slicked back.

"He was just leaving, weren't you, Mr. Becker?" Angela said. The salesman stammered, then departed quickly. "Thanks, Eddie."

"You weren't going to stop to see me, were you?" Eddie peered across the top of his glasses. "Just hurry on by," he sighed. His short mustache twitched. "You know that's one of today's biggest problems; people being in a hurry. And kids these days. Oy vey! But enough already, I say."

Anyone under forty was a kid to Eddie. "How are you, Eddie?"

"Other than the stiffness in my poor fingers, I'm good. I've got my health," he laughed. "But you, you show up with a man, and I don't see you for the entire day. What am I? Chopped liver?"

Angela couldn't help but smile. "I've been busy guiding him through it all." She chuckled to herself when she thought of Blasing reacting to the gunfight and later knocking her down the steps. Maybe guide wasn't the right word. "Coming to Ghostal Shores the first time is quite an experience, and he's a bit unnerved by it all, especially since Peter was murdered here. To be honest, I am, too."

"I don't blame you. Everybody is disturbed by Mac's murder. Horrible. Simply horrible." Eddie shuddered.

"What do you think happened?"

"Robbery. Pure and simple. To some, gelt is all. The making of it has no reward in and of itself."

"Unfortunately. What do you think of the proposed changes?"

"Fabulous! Business has never been better. The more Ghostal Shores ups its room rates, the more I can charge! This is paradise,

Ang, paradise! All we need now is legalized gambling!"

Angela rolled her eyes, then asked about Sheriff Middleton. Eddie had been questioned, too. She also asked about new ghosts.

"I'm disappointed," the ghost tailor said. "Not a one. The bricks are only good for adding new rooms. If only I had invested!"

"It wouldn't do you any good, Eddie. You're a ghost."

"Only in the flesh. I'm a businessman in spirit."

"I don't understand how you can get so excited about all of this," Angela said as she motioned to their surroundings. "I wouldn't think money means anything anymore."

"It doesn't. It's the challenge—the making of gelt that's interesting. I got it from my father, and he from his. It's been handed down a long way, Ang. Tradition," he smiled. "Go see Elma and Ingrid at the Spirited Woman. They've got a surprise for you."

"I don't know if I like the sound of that."

"Go on! Go on! You'll like it, although you don't need it," he said with an appraising look. "But don't look a gift horse in the mouth, ay? Be well, Ang."

"I'll see you later, Eddie," Angela said. She passed a jewelry store, an antique shop and Quinn's Art Gallery. Some of his landscapes were incredibly realistic with uncanny depth to them.

The Spirited Woman was tastefully crafted from finished wood painted lavender and white. The sign above the storefront depicted two well-dressed women in long skirts and bonnets floating atop a cloud. Angela waited for several fashionable ladies dressed to the hilt to saunter out the door, then walked inside the boutique. The Spirited Woman was bright, colorful and spacious. Mannequins adorned with elegant evening gowns dominated the decor.

Elma walked through a free-standing circular rack of dresses to greet her. Never looking her age, the spirit was a classic ethereal blond beauty with a smooth, creamy face that seemed timeless, although her eyes revealed she'd witnessed much in her passing days. As always, her hair set elegantly high upon her head, making her appear taller. She was dressed in a simple blue dress that accented her slim figure; it had a slit all the way up to the hip—not something worn during Goldfield's days. "Angela, you look wonderful, though a bit tired."

"Hello, Elma. You look irresistible."

"Thank you. You learned a lot at that school for twisting words to your advantage! Ingrid! Angela's here!" Elma called out.

As though being held by invisible hooks, a teal silk gown with spaghetti straps floated out from behind the counter, across the floor and between the racks toward Angela. Several surprised customers jumped out of the dress's flight path. When it stopped in front of Angela, a tall, big-boned but attractive Scandinavian spirit suddenly appeared next to it.

"What is this?" Angela asked suspiciously.

"A gift," Ingrid replied.

"Thank you," Angela said smiling. She set down her sack, then took the dress from Ingrid's ethereal fingers to hold it to her body. "It's beautiful. Your bribe is accepted. I'll do what I can, within reason, to influence Mr. Madera."

They blushed even deeper, although Elma's smile was anything but embarrassed. "You don't need to do anything I wouldn't do," Elma said. "But with a man like that...."

"How do you feel about the proposed changes?" Angela asked, changing the subject. They adamantly shook their heads. "May I ask why?"

"I don't mind change for the better, but..." Ingrid began, then paused, "but my Wolfgang ran his own business, and I learned a few things. I know better than to over-milk the cows."

"Angela, do you think Heller had Mac shot?" Elma asked.

"You've been talking to Carrie, haven't you?" Angela asked. The ghosts nodded. "Why do you think Mr. Heller would do such a thing?"

"For money. Reminds me of a man I knew in Goldfield that made his living hurting people and making money from it," Elma said.

"Well, I think it's that French tart," Ingrid said. "She's still mad at Mac, and with Heller wrapped around her finger, all it took was a word. Though it could have been Cash; he's a vile man."

"Have either of you deduced this information from looking into their spirits?" Angela asked.

"I tried," Elma said. "Something prevents us from seeing their spirits clearly."

"Anyone else like that?" Angela asked.

"We have trouble seeing the spirits of security and some of the salespeople. We have no idea what it could be. Though there have occasionally been customers that seem similarly... protected."

Another mystery, Angela sighed. "What do you think about Peter's ghost still being at Ghostal Shores?"

"That would be nice, but no one has seen him," Elma said.

"I keep telling you, it can take time to pull yourself together," Ingrid countered. "Or even understand that you still exist. I wandered around lost for a long time."

"I would think the trauma of being murdered or dying in a fire would be... difficult to recover from," Angela said.

Elma nodded. Ingrid shook her head, setting her blond braids bouncing. "I wouldn't know. I drowned."

"Where?" Angela asked. There wasn't much water in Nevada, especially in mining towns.

"Close to Tomales Bay, but I lived near here. My husband was a partner in one of the dairies."

"Did you know Sven back then?"

"No. I arrived here after he did, then we got to know each other." She blushed. "Elma was kind enough to teach me about fashion so I could help her with the store... and charm Sven, too." Their expressions were angelic as they hugged.

"And I'm glad she did," Elma said. "You know, I believe fashion hasn't changed all that much with the passage of years. Designers do about the same thing they did in my time with only a few twists. Although," she plucked at her dress, "clothing has gotten a bit more revealing. I love it! It gives me more to work with. Less restrictions, although you have to stay fit and firm. You women of today don't know what it was like back then. We weren't supposed to swear, drink or smoke."

"You hadn't worked in a clothing store before?" Angela asked Ingrid, amazed by what she was learning. Had she misunderstood Peter? Or had he been hiding things from her?

"I used to work at the dairy handling the books and cows."

Angela suddenly realized that what she'd believed—and what she'd told Blasing—was wrong. Ghosts could change!

"Angela, are you all right?" Elma asked. "You look peaked."

"Just a little tired. It's been a long day," Angela admitted.

"What do we do about Mac's murder?" Ingrid asked. "I keep thinking we should do something."

"Not shout it to anyone who'll listen, like Carrie," Elma said. "She's going to get herself cleansed." The spirits shuddered.

"Blasing will have some say on that," Angela told her. "Carrie and I are quietly..." she began and the spirits chortled, "...investigating. She believes Mr. Heller was into something illegal. Want to help?" Angela asked. They nodded. "Then keep your eyes open. We'll talk sometime tomorrow."

They neatly boxed her dress, then sent her on her way. In a daze, Angela rode the elevator, then wandered into her room and collapsed on the bed. She needed that massage to ease her aching shoulder and relax her mind. It was awhirl with questions.

Was Peter wrong and Blasing right? It appeared that ghosts could change, and she wasn't just talking about appearances. Sure, Cannon was familiar with trendy concoctions, and Elma was up to date on the latest fashions, as were Fawn and her fellow harlots. But Ingrid had changed her career and interests. If those could change for a ghost, what else could? Beliefs? Values? Personalities?

EIGHT

Angela was winded by the time she and Candy reached the top of the steps and walked into the walled garden. She tried talking to Candy about Peter's murder and the change in the ghosts, but all she wanted to talk about was Blasing. Candy was disappointed that Angela had let Blasing sleep the night away.

"I think he owes you a fantastic dinner for last night's sleep-a-thon."

"You are a hopeless romantic, Candy. Besides, he needed it."

"I'm a hopeful romantic, Angel," Candy replied. "And I'm just looking for it to happen for the best, as it did for Rod and me. Didn't you say Blasing had kids?" Angela nodded. "Then he probably did need it, but it's still the principle of the thing."

"Candy, I've already told you that I have more important things to think about than romance. Just knowing Peter was targeted for murder—maybe by somebody here—and that the spirits can change, chills me to my soul."

"Angel, nothing is more important than love."

"And could Peter be a new edition to the spirit population?" she continued, ignoring Candy. "And what about those stages?"

Candy sighed. "I don't think Mac's spirit is around, although traumatic deaths and ghosts are closely linked. Changing—or should I say evolving—ghosts; now that has potential. You might be able to use it as a topic for your term paper. I'm working on the Native versus White Man angle."

"Candy."

"Hey, I'll be glad to help you investigate Mac's death. You know me, Angel. I like intrigue. Maybe Heller's running a white slave ring or something. I'll talk to some of the ghosts. We've gotten to know each other quite well, except for Marsh."

"What do you know about Marsh?"

"That he's antisocial. A bitter man who drank himself to death. Hey, if you need help, I'll be glad to investigate Blasing, too." Candy teased. Angela gave her a level stare. "Angel, just let yourself go. Though it sounds as if you already have. The Angela I knew a year ago wouldn't have performed a Native American protection ceremony." Before Angela could reply, Candy asked, "Did it work?"

"I haven't asked Broderick to test it yet."

"See, you are letting yourself go. Go for it with Blasing."

"Candy, women—not that I'm interested—throw themselves at Blasing all the time. It's like... like a sporting event."

"Then don't throw. Listen, I have some ideas," she began as they headed into the lobby.

Carrie stood in front of the 1880's General Store having a heated argument with a tall, willowy woman. She had bushy, black and white-streaked hair swept back as though she were standing in a wind tunnel. Her black and green outfit was pleated and floor length. The mammoth Asian behind her was dressed in black—his double-breasted vest, gloves and boots appeared to be leather.

"What do you think of having a seance?" Candy asked. "It would be a good way to discover whether or not Peter MacGuire's ghost is haunting Ghostal Shores."

"Candy, please," Angela said and motioned her to be quiet.

Whatever the woman said set off Carrie's temper. "I don't need no go-between! Heller can come see me himself if he has something to say, just like Mac did! He respected us! Heller thinks we are his slaves. Well, we ain't! You tell him, missy, that things are about to change!" The woman leaned forward, but Angela couldn't hear her. Carrie snarled, the matronly ghost shook with rage. "You can't threaten me! If you want me out of here, then do your worst! I'll be waiting!" Carrie disappeared.

The woman whirled around. Her large eyes were golden-green and angry. Her face was flushed but smooth and unlined, so that Angela couldn't guess her age. The woman said something to her companion and they glided together, the manservant taking one step to her two while still remaining half a step behind.

"Who was that?" Angela asked.

"That's Madame Zanadane, the new in-house psychic, and her valet, Mr. Chung. She's a big-shot psychic out of Vancouver."

Angela was about to ask more about the Canadian psychic when she spotted Marsh hugging the shadows near a pockmarked-faced security guard. The faded spirit watched Madame Zanadane depart, a look of satisfaction on his ethereal face and a gleam in his pale eyes. Marsh wore a long, dark trenchcoat, and a hat that hid much of his long, lined face. When he caught Angela staring at him, he stepped back into a wall and disappeared.

"Angel, are you okay?"

"I saw Marsh watching."

"So? He's always skulking and spying."

"That's true." Why did she feel it was different this time?

"So what do you think about a séance?" Candy asked again.

"Sounds like a good idea. I'll ask Blasing," Angela replied.

"Broderick?" Blasing asked, then opened the door to find a shiny dome-topped tray waiting for him.

"Good morning, sir. I took the liberty of anticipating your needs. Breakfast is served."

"Morning?" Blasing asked.

"Yes, sir. I see the sleep has done you a world of good, all fifteen hours of it."

"You're kidding, right?"

" I told you earlier that I do not 'kid', joke or even jest."

"I thought you were going to wake me for dinner?"

"Yes sir, I was indeed, but Mrs. Wilson convinced me otherwise." Broderick began rolling the cart through the doorway past Blasing. "She sounded like quite a woman to me."

"Maggie Wilson, my children's nanny?" Blasing asked. "Then my kids called last night?"

"Yes, your children are simply charming. I spoke with them for over an hour," Broderick smiled. "I told them all about yesterday and Ghostal Shores. They were really quite interested, even put me on the speaker phone. Such a marvelous invention. More people can talk at the same time," he sighed. "They are ready to come visit any day now. And I must say that Kelly is very bright. Very bright indeed. I informed them you had fallen asleep early, and Mrs. Wilson implored me to let you sleep. She said you had been working far too hard and needed the rest. I was truly moved."

"How come Angela didn't wake me?"

"I do not know, sir. Ms. Starborne had a massage, dined in, and fell asleep very early."

"Where is she now?"

"Strolling along the beach with Candy Whyte. I expect her back soon. You have a ten o'clock meeting with Mister Heller. Oh joy." His expression was bland, but his eyes gleamed with distaste.

"Then I'd better shower and eat."

"Very good, sir," Broderick said. "Are you feeling better? No ill health from my touch?" Blasing shook his head. "Excellent. I was concerned."

"Don't be. I slept like the... well, you know. No, I guess you wouldn't."

"I do not sleep, but I do rest when I am not exploring the library. Now, you should shower promptly."

As Blasing showered, he hoped his second day at Ghostal Shores was less strange than the first. A few minutes later he was toweling off when Broderick knocked on the bathroom door. "Yes?"

"Mr. Grant Roberts is here to speak with you, sir."

"I'll be right out." The words were barely out of Blasing's mouth when he heard Angela return.

"What are you doing in my room?!"

"Ah, so good to see you again, Angela. I am waiting...."

"Get out! Now!"

"Broderick, bring him into my room!" Blasing yelled.

"Excellent idea, sir. Very diplomatic of you," Broderick replied, then walked through the wall.

Blasing finished toweling, pulled on his shorts, then headed into his room. The financial wizard had lifted the lid off the room service cart and was examining Blasing's breakfast. The steam made the upper half of his body hazy. "You are treated like a king."

I'll try not to act like one," Blasing said.

"That's good. It's not the best way to run a business."

"BLASING?! What's going on in there?" Angela demanded, banging her fist on the door.

"Tell her I'm giving lessons in romantic etiquette," Grant told Blasing.

"Not if you value your life, sir" Broderick said as he exited the wall. "But then we could always squeeze in one more ghost here at Ghostal Shores. You would be welcome," he finished drolly.

Blasing looked hard at the ghost valet, then said, "Angela! He's briefing me on the financial statements. I'm also getting dressed and ready to go."

"Fine," Angela said flatly. Broderick looked perturbed.

"Well?" Blasing asked the Texas Spirit.

Roberts gave Blasing financial figures for the past few years, projections without expansion and with expansion, and what half the resort was worth. "More if you agree to the timeshare route. Look at nearly 300 rooms times fifty weeks at a value of at least thirty thousand a room. That's not including the commercial property. If you sell part of it with each title, then the deeds should be worth more. Or you can sell or rent the commercial space for exorbitant prices."

"Mind boggling," Blasing mumbled through a blueberry muffin. While eating, Blasing finished dressing in gray slacks and a black turtleneck. "I certainly don't feel ready to discuss any business deal with Mr. Heller. I'll just feel him out, say I want to get more familiar with the place," Blasing told the ghost.

"Fine, just fine. I like the way you think, son. Learn what you can. But here are some questions you should keep in mind...."

Twenty minutes later, Blasing stepped into the common room where Angela was waiting. "Did you learn anything interesting?" Her expression was cool, and she was dressed for business—no jewelry, her hair combed back severely, and attired in a dark, power-suit complemented by navy hose.

"I think so, Counselor. Did Sheriff Middleton ever call back?"

"No. Broderick is going to track him down. We should be leaving."

"Lead the way," he said and followed her out the door. "Grant explained the financials to me, and how being a timeshare would affect things. But just because he explained things, doesn't mean I trust him. I'm not going to make any decisions until we talk."

Angela was silent as they waited for the elevator. When it finally arrived, she stepped inside. "Blasing, there are several things that worry me." Angela explained about Elma and realized that what she'd told him earlier wasn't true. The ghosts could change.

"It worries me, too. It means that things once safe could change for some reason," Blasing said. "Who are these ghosts?"

Angela explained about the storekeepers. "All three think

Heller did it, but can't support their accusations. They say his spirit is obscured. They don't trust security, either."

Blasing rolled his eyes. "Let's not jump to conclusions."

Angela also mentioned Carrie's confrontation with Madame Zanadane and Mr. Chung. "And so many of the ghosts don't like Heller, I get the feeling they might rebel."

"So do I."

"Carrie, Elma and Ingrid are going to do some investigating for me. Ghosts can be very sneaky."

"Don't I know it. They could be listening to us right now." Blasing rubbed the back of his neck. It felt as if fingernails had been lightly brushed along his flesh. He breathed deeply, catching the faint whiff of a cigarette. Had Angela sneaked one earlier?

The doors opened to the lobby. "Don't be surprised if Mr. Heller rants and raves," Angela told him. "Your partnership is probably a nasty surprise, and he hates surprises. He probably expected the will to go to probate or something, allowing him time to run the place as he pleases."

Earl Cash noted their arrival at the front desk and left the clerks alone; one loosened her collar, and they both looked relieved that the pencil-thin man had been distracted.

Noticing the man's cast and build, Blasing did a double-take.

"Hello Mr. Cash," Angela said coolly.

"Hello Ms. Starborne. Mr. Madera," Cash said with a perfunctory smile that couldn't hide his disdain. "Come this way. Mr. Heller is waiting for you." He opened a side door, then led them down a hallway lined with doors. He stopped at the last door.

"Are you all right?" Angela whispered, noticing the way Blasing was appraising Cash. He waved her quiet.

Cash stopped at the last door, then knocked. "Mr. Heller, Mr. Madera and Ms. Starborne are here."

"Then send them in, man," replied a harsh, baritone voice with a heavy Irish accent.

Cash opened the door and ushered them into a windowless room of reflective surfaces, crowded bookcases, and hundreds of paper constructs. Hanging from the ceiling and covering every flat surface, the origami always reminded Angela of a horde of colorful insects overwhelming the office. The mirrors made the place seem larger and yet more crammed and chaotic at the same time. The origami's reflections seemed endless. Almost lost in it all were a set of portraits on each side of a painting of an Old West Hotel.

Blasing was mildly stunned. Angela recalled that he'd been here before in Broderick's memories, witnessing Peter being murdered. Was he seeing him killed again?

"Ah, hello, Mr. Madera. I am Sean Heller." He smiled briefly but never looked up, still intent on folding, smoothing and twisting. Behind coke-bottle-thick glasses, the Irishman's ruddy expression was one of concentration. The top of his mottled head could be seen through thin, gray hairs, and his stoutness spread out from the shoulders down. Despite his size, Heller's chair was so large it was a modern throne that nearly swallowed him.

"I do apologize for not being able to meet with you yesterday, but Ms. Starborne's visit was unexpected and my time was already tightly parceled." He sniffed. "Many exciting plans are in motion."

"So I can see. This is a busy place." Blasing appeared annoyed that the man didn't look them in the eye.

"From tragedy, we shall persevere, Mr. Madera. Mac would have wanted it that way." Heller's fingers were amazingly fast. A few more seconds and he was finished, turning a dollar bill into George Washington in a frame. The Irishman set it among his other works, including a horse, dog, a pair of pants and several birds. He immediately started on another piece.

Blasing pulled two plain wooden chairs away from a wall and sat. Angela joined him.

Blasing said, "Mr. Heller, this all comes as a surprise to me. I have questions, and I imagine you do, too."

"You aren't contesting the will?" Angela was surprised.

"Why should I? I knew Mac was working with you. He even mentioned a will, sometimes bemoaning the fact that he had so little family. Personally, I don't care much for family, but then my viewpoint is jaded. That said, what are the terms of the will?"

"In simplest terms, all that was Peter's is now Blasing's."

"That is simple."

"Mr. Heller, how do you feel about my uncle's murder?" Blasing's stare was piercing.

Heller felt it, stopped working on a green paper frog, and looked up. "I am angry."

What else is new, Angela thought. She'd expected a red-faced fireball. Why wasn't he angrier? Blasing couldn't possibly understand the transformation. Heller must have thought that Blasing would be easy to manipulate, or that things were still working for him. There had to be a reason he wasn't yelling and gesturing wildly

"And I am somewhat loathe to admit, I feel lucky. Lucky it wasn't me. Some psycho—probably one I fired—tried to kill me, but he shot Mac instead, and I've lost the only man who can help me run this place smoothly."

"Why do you believe it was an ex-employee?"

"He robbed us on the busiest check-in day, so the most cash was in the safe."

"And few ex-employees have any love for you?" Angela said a bit acidly. She pushed away the urge for a cigarette.

"The burden of management," Heller said, glancing at her sharply, then he went back to working on the paper.

"Is there a reason I wasn't notified about Mac's murder?" Blasing asked. His tone caused Heller to look up again.

"The authorities said they would handle it. I'm sorry. I should have known they'd botch it."

"Was Sheriff Middleton supposed to inform me?" Blasing asked. Heller nodded. "And he is the one following the ex-employee lead?"

"Yes. The man Broderick described doesn't sound familiar, but I don't remember everyone who has worked here." He sniffled, then reached into the drawer and removed a tissue. "Damn cold!"

"Do you believe Mac's ghost is haunting Ghostal Shores?"

Heller started, obviously shaken by Blasing's question. "I haven't seen any signs, but if he were... I would still consider him part owner." He suddenly chuckled. "He might be more qualified than ever to handle the ghosts. I'm sorry. Sounds callous, but Mac would understand. He often said he was a kindred spirit."

"If his spirit was here, he could identify who killed him." Angela closely watched Heller for a reaction.

"I don't see what he could add to Broderick's description, but the spirits aren't as we, are they?" he mused. "No, they certainly aren't. Mac said they could... feel things about people."

"There's a way to find out if he's here," Angela offered.

"How?" Blasing asked.

"A séance."

"What an excellent thought!" Heller exclaimed, then looked at Angela as if seeing her for the first time. "A wonderful idea. I offer the services of Madame Zanadane, our new in-house psychic. In fact, why didn't she think of it?"

"Why did you hire her?"

"Because I'm not comfortable with the ghosts. And from what I can tell, neither is Mr. Madera. You see, Ms. Starborne, time has not diminished my nervousness in dealing with those that have died yet remain, so I hired someone as my liaison. Madame Zanadane already knew the ghosts."

"She's offered her services before, hasn't she?"

Heller nodded. "But they weren't required. Mac was working... with me. Enough of this! To business! If Mac is not with us, we must let him rest by conducting his last requests as he wished."

"But you're continuing with the timeshare idea!" Angela snapped.

"Blasing, if we're to be partners, we must know where each other stands." He finished the frog, then turned around and placed it among the others. Sniffling, he pulled open the central desk drawer and found a handkerchief. After blowing his nose, he removed a brown colored square of paper with white dots and began folding. "Blasing, did you know that people are like paper?"

Blasing thought for a moment, then said, "Blank slates ready to be written upon?"

"That is one," Heller said, glancing up with rheumy eyes. "You are smarter than I was led to believe. I thought a man who did the sort of crazy things you did must be significantly short of a full deck." Heller smiled, a very crooked smile. His fingers never stopped measuring, bending, folding and pressing. "Regardless of our color, we start as a blank sheet waiting to be written upon...." His fingers paused, "... or shaped by outside influences—parents, friends, family, religion, and education, as well as other things. They help us become what we will be," Heller said, holding up a brown paper cow complete with white dots and udders. "The masses."

"Not sheep waiting to be sheared?" Blasing asked.

Heller chuckled, then pulled out a gray piece of paper. "I do like the way you think. Some people can actually craft the paper, while others are at their mercy. With confused desires and little will, they bend to the forces around them." The paper square had been suddenly transformed into a shark.

"Yourself?"

"When it comes to business opportunities, yes." Heller stared at Blasing who seemed unmoved, then leaned back. "Blasing, I think I know a little about you from Mac. If my memory still serves me, at the tender age of six or so, you survived a plane crash that killed your entire family. Mac took care of you until the courts took you away. Mac really loved women. Couldn't resist them."

"I really miss him," Heller sounded sincere. "He put this place together. And I must admit I thought he was crazy. Who would want to stay at a haunted resort? Crazy like a fox, I know that now. Damn the man who killed him! Nothing has run smoothly since!"

Angela didn't believe him for an instant. She'd watched Heller and Peter fight constantly.

"Well, that is the courts and the government for you, isn't it? Break something that's working. And we know how well the state cares for people. If I recall correctly, you went to college but dropped out and moved to Tahoe and became an instructor—a 'hot dog'—I believe the term is," Heller finished.

"I was a thrill-seeker," Blasing replied. "Now they call them extremists."

"Are you an adrenaline junkie, Mr. Madera? If so, running a resort isn't for you. It's work. A bit different from climbing mountains and paragliding. Running a resort is not the rush of skydiving, bungee jumping, back-country skiing, ice climbing, flying ultra lights, or whatever else you did. Instead of dealing with nature, you deal with demanding clientele and mouthy ghosts."

"I'm sure you never did anything young and foolish," Blasing said simply. "I've learned about people. They can be just as deadly as nature. I run a security business, as you probably know."

"If I may ask, why a security business? That is such... an extreme transition."

"I don't recuperate the way I did when I was twenty-five."

"I thought it might be because you got married and had two kids?" he arched a wildly bushy eyebrow. "My sympathies on her passing. I imagine raising children as a single parent is difficult at times. Ties you down, doesn't it?" Blasing nodded. "I am an excellent judge of character, and make no doubt, Blasing, you are still an adventurer at heart. I guarantee that you will grow quickly bored with running a resort."

"I don't know about that," Blasing said. "Maybe with other resorts, but not this one. With the way the ghosts were acting yesterday, my heart was pounding all day."

Heller was quiet for a moment, as if shifting gears. "Have you ever noticed how the past comes back to haunt us—burden us— keeping us from what we really want to do?"

"If you let it," Blasing said.

"True. But money plays a great part in that. Lack of it binds you, while plenty can allow you to escape. It can allow you to spend more time with your kids. Send them to better schools."

Angela wanted to tell Blasing to watch out; Heller was as slippery as a snake and twice as poisonous. Blasing caught her eye, smiled, and then said, "Your point?"

"I'm offering you a chance to get out of the security and resort business. I'm giving you an opportunity to retire right now! I'm offering you twenty million for your half of Ghostal Shores."

Blasing didn't react. Angela said nothing, but knew that was only an opening bid; half of GSR was worth much, much more.

"Shall we celebrate?" Heller asked with a smile. His latest construct, a red sports car, sat on the desk in front of him.

"You know," Blasing said slowly, "I really haven't had an opportunity to see much of Ghostal Shores yet, and I haven't looked at the financial paperwork, either. I plan on faxing it to my accountant before I make a final decision. At this point, I won't even consider selling until I know more about what's going on."

"How about thirty million?" Heller offered casually. "You won't have to get used to the ghosts that way. I write you a check. You cash it. You're free."

Blasing was thoughtful, then he smiled as if realizing he could always sell to someone besides Heller. "Tell me about timeshares?"

Angela thought the Irishman was starting to fume. "Mac would have come around sooner or later. He was a good businessman and had rich... tastes. A trait passed on by his parents. You should be glad you never knew your parents, Mr. Madera," he said, suddenly bitter.

"Often the dream is far better than reality."

"I'd like to hear about your ideas. Would you like to sell me instead of trying to buy me? I might be willing to own my half, and let you manage the day-to-day dealings. But I need to know more about you and your plans. I won't make a decision, let alone a quick one, until I have studied all the pertinent information."

"All right," Heller said. "But I would've thought you'd be the kind to make quick decisions. What do you want to know?"

"As I said, you know my background, I'd like to know yours."

"I'll try not to bore you," Heller groused, then adjusted his thick glasses. "I was born into a lower middle class family in Palo Alto, California." He wasn't staring at them, but off in the distance as though seeing the past. "I was an only child. My mother and father used to work for Stanford in food and beverage until they decided to start their own business.

"They opened a diner not far from campus, and I worked in it after school. The J&M Diner never did very well, but at least it paid the bills. It might have done better if Father hadn't drunk most of the profits. Mother, well, she never said much about it. You see," he said gruffly, looking at Blasing for the first time, "I was serious when I said you might be fortunate to have never known your parents. They can be very disappointing."

"I'll never know."

Heller cleared his throat, then continued, "Well, I swore that I'd work harder, be smarter, and pull myself up to a better life than running a thirty seat diner. I would not be like my mother and father. Live from day to day, hoping that ends would meet."

Angela glanced at Blasing; she'd learned more about Heller in the last ten minutes than in all her previous visits. There was something about Blasing that made people confide in him.

"Well, I worked hard, learning whatever I could from school and out of books and then attended Berkeley. To pay for school, I ran several businesses; the most profitable was running booze to alumni at ball games. We'd take the product directly to their seats. Did you know Mac used to work for me? It was during that time we dreamed of running a resort, a place in the sun where the beautiful and idle rich came to spend time. Of course, we were thinking of women, as well as money, but then Mac was always thinking about women," Heller sighed.

"So where'd the money come from to build Ghostal Shores?"

"I got wealthy the same way you did, Blasing; I inherited it. My father and mother had been dead a year when my grandfather passed on. He willed me this magnificent parcel of land and a fair amount of money. I used to talk to my grandfather about building and managing my own hotel, and he used to chuckle as though they were pipe dreams, but he certainly came through for me. Come to think of it, he and Mac have been the only ones who ever did."

Heller was quiet for a time, and neither Blasing nor Angela spoke. "But to answer your next question, my grandfather made his big fortune late in life—back when transistor radios were a new and exciting product. I invested that money into several up and coming firms in Silicon Valley."

"So, you built your own empire?" Blasing asked.

"Empire? Yes, yes, but I must give Mac some credit, for while I supplied the money, the ghosts were his idea. For my part, I just tried to build a magnificent place that would appeal to jetsetters. I never expected scholars, monks and mystics to study the resort."

Angela stifled a laugh. She was sure those kind of patrons would never have been on Heller's mailing list.

"Ah well, life is full of unexpected changes," Heller stretched. Shall we go for a short walk. Check on the progress of the northern wing?"

"But it's Sunday," Blasing said.

"I'm paying them a bonus to get done by summer," Heller said as he grabbed his cane. "Allow me to stretch my legs while I stretch your imagination." He hobbled down the hall without looking to see if they were following.

"What do you think?" Blasing asked Angela.

"That he's been captured and replaced by aliens. I've never seen him this courteous, let alone calm, with anyone," she whispered. "Still, I think you caught him off guard by asking for information and feigning interest."

"Feigning?" Blasing stated. Before she could react, he shushed her with a smile. She wasn't sure if he was teasing or serious.

The lobby had grown crowded as some checked out, people and carts going in every direction. "You there, man! Clear a path to the door for us!" Heller told a large, green-uniformed bellman. They followed him through a sea of customers. There was a pair of figures in hooded robes coming down from the steps. Behind them was a woman adorned in enough crystal jewelry to open her own store.

"Come this way." Heller tapped his way along the sidewalk heading toward the construction. "I just love a brisk, sunny day in January. It can be nicer now than during the summer, depending on the fog. Do you believe, Mr. Madera, that money is the root of all evil?"

"No. I always thought it was the love of money that was the root. If that's true though, then what's the seed?" Blasing asked. Heller laughed harshly. "Can you tell me a little about how this place came to be? Angela wasn't allowed to tell me much."

"I inherited it from Grandfather Patrick, who inherited it from my great grandfather Thomas, who purchased it with gold in the 1880's from a sheriff. Heh. Would you believe that sheriff sold the same piece of property six times? After a compromise, Thomas got to keep some of it.

"There used to be a country club for the rich at Tomales Bay, but access was difficult back then. While on a college road trip, Mac and I visited the area. It sparked ideas. Years later, when we seriously talked about building a resort, he suggested the haunted angle to draw rich eccentrics. He was crazy like a fox.

"We bought bricks from gold towns—the biggest purchase being the Goldfield Hotel. At first, the Elliots weren't going to sell because they wanted to restore it for the Goldfield Days Celebration," he rolled his eyes, "but after a family argument...."

"Where one brother shot the other?" Angela asked.

Heller snorted, "They finally sold. So did Ella Cain in Aurora. She had tax problems and needed money." He continued on, telling them about the legislative action and delays that spanned years. After being grandfathered, they decided not to rebuild the Goldfield, but improve it, add to it. Cater to the coast.

"And the ghosts came," Angela said.

"Amazingly so," Heller agreed, "and soon thereafter, haunt aficionados. The ghosts love this place, Blasing, and the attention they receive. Don't let their fears influence you. I will not let this place get rundown. It is not good for business, and I run this place to make money. That is done by impressing people with money. I plan to make this place more exclusive, with fewer freeloading eccentrics taking up space."

"Just the rich and famous?" Blasing asked.

"Of course," Heller said. "About four years after opening, we added the southern wing, made mostly from Aurora and some Virginia City brick and stone. None of its historical landmarks, of course, but already disassembled materials. A few new ghosts arrived and blended right in. We were one big happy family, until Mac was murdered. I believe the place has changed since then."

"Often times a business reflects the man at the top. Even as a home reflects those who own it," Angela said pointedly. Heller's glance carried annoyance. He stopped where they could watch the ongoing construction.

"Why are you putting in a camera security system?" Blasing asked.

"After Mac's murder, our guests became worried about their safety. I want them to feel very, very safe here. And I want to prevent a second attempt on my life."

"Won't the signals disturb the ghosts?"

"Not really. Well, certainly not like television and radio reception," Heller replied. "I'm more concerned about whoever killed Mac. They might try for me again."

Blasing felt something odd. He looked toward a stack of old bricks. Was that a ghost? Mac? Could it be Mac's ghost? Blasing suddenly headed for the orange bricks next to a storage hut.

"Blasing?" Angela called. He kept going. What was with him?

"Heller!" a big man wearing a hard-hat and dressed in a windbreaker yelled. "I want to talk with you! Now!" Looking very angry, he walked toward them with long, hurried strides.

"Ah, Mr. Butts. He's the construction site supervisor. A man of limited intelligence."

Blasing felt the hair on the back of his neck rise as he grew nearer the brick. The ghost was gone, and nobody else was around. "Uncle Mac?" Blasing whispered.

Angela was going to follow Blasing, but sensed she shouldn't leave. "I've had it!" Butts yelled. "I'm pulling my men out right now!"

"YOU'RE GOING TO DO WHAT?!" Heller cried. Angela wished Blasing hadn't wandered off. He needed to see Heller in true form. What was he up to?

"You heard me! We're gone! Packing! These working conditions are unsafe!" The hefty supervisor's flushed face. "The ghosts! THE DAMN GHOSTS! Stuff keeps moving about and disappearing, and people are getting hurt because of it. They're even performing their own construction, building things we don't need like that sidewalk they laid last weekend!"

"You're blaming the ghosts for everything, aren't you?!" Heller replied venomously. The men moved closer together, almost nose to nose. "None of the reports I've read mention ghosts! All the accidents are due to incompetence or inattention!"

"If we ain't haunted, we're snakebit. That's bad enough. We're taking a couple of days off. Maybe more. You can talk with my boss tomorrow! Worker's comp is eating our ass!"

"I won't let you leave, coward!" Heller grabbed the man's arm.

"Who are you calling a coward?!" the supervisor whirled around, pulling his arm loose of Heller. The Irishman staggered back, then swung his cane, smacking Butts in the nose.

The supervisor let out a bloodcurdling scream and charged. Butts bowled over Heller, then landed hard atop the Irishman. Heller's face immediately flushed, his eyes bulging. Blasing raced toward the fight.

"Mr. Butts!" Angela stood over the men. "Get off Mr. Heller right now or you'll lose a lawsuit before you can say bankruptcy."

Blasing arrived to help Butts stand. He pulled a handkerchief from his pocket and smothered his pulped nose.

"You should be ashamed of yourself, slipping to his level," Angela finished, her eyes glowering.

"You're right, lady," Butts replied, hands to his nose. "You'll be hearing from my lawyer, you sonuvabitch!" He stormed off.

"That wasn't very smart," Angela said.

"Don't preach to me!" Heller snapped.

"You're welcome," Angela replied. She gave Blasing a look that said this was more like the Heller she knew.

"More and more trouble," Heller muttered. "Mac, I am so sorry you're gone. Damn wimps! I'll find another blasted construction company!" He began stalking back toward the front entrance.

"Better than a loaded gun, the threat of a lawsuit," Blasing said as they followed. "I'm impressed." Angela's look was cool. "Seriously, it was quick thinking and ended the situation without further violence. I thought I might have to restrain Butts."

"I'm sorry I didn't give you a chance to practice any martial arts moves," she said with a small smile. "Truth to tell, I didn't want you to inherit any legal debts."

They overtook Heller while he was speaking with Cash. He seemed to be wilting in the sunlight. "Meg Cassidy is in your office."

"Ah, this should prove interesting. Meg Cassidy has always claimed to be Mac's daughter. Now she wants to press the issue."

"WHAT?!" Angela cried as Blasing asked, "Mac has a daughter?"

"I suspect that she will contest the will." Heller sounded very pleased.

NINE

"Peter never, ever spoke of a daughter," Angela said as they followed Heller and Cash toward the porte-cochere.

"Mac insisted she wasn't his child," Heller said. "Meg insists that she is, but until now, legalities haven't been pursued."

"Who's the supposed mother?" Angela asked.

"Jaclyn Cassidy."

"I recognize that name now. An old flame from his Palm Springs days," Angela said. "I guess blood or DNA tests would resolve the issue."

Blasing was quiet for a while, then asked. "What's she like?"

"Meg Cassidy? Redheaded like Mac with green eyes. She visits occasionally, and Mac avoids..." Heller cleared his throat, "used to avoid her. She's some kind of artist in Los Angeles. Come! You can question her all you like. I'm sure she'll have questions, too."

"This could slow things down quite a bit," Angela whispered. "By the way, what were you doing back there, wandering off? You missed Heller in his prime."

Blasing hesitated, then said, "I saw something... a ghost I thought might've been Uncle Mac's."

"You saw Peter's ghost?" she whispered excitedly.

"I'm not sure," Blasing said. "I saw a familiar, ghostly figure, but it disappeared so quickly. I could have imagined that it was Mac, but I know something was definitely there. I'm not as experienced with ghosts as you are, but I felt something, just as I always do when a ghost is around."

"You are sensitive, aren't you?" Angela's gaze was searching.

"What do you mean by that?" he asked.

Barney smiled at them as they entered the building. The surrounding bustle of the lobby seemed distant, as if they were alone with each other.

"Even if you can't see the ghost, you know it's there, right?" she asked. He nodded. "We should test that theory. Test your range."

"Why?"

She thought for a moment, then said, "If I knew for sure whether a ghost was around or not, and even how close, I'd feel safer. Think of it as a sense of security."

"Sounds like a lawyer talking, all right."

"Well, what do you think?"

"I'm having trouble believing in ghosts, and now you're saying I'm psychic?" He looked very skeptical.

"Everyone is. Think of it as being perceptive."

Cash held open the "employees only" door. The front desk clerks looked extra busy. Heller chugged unsteadily toward his office, his cane tapping rapidly, then he roughly pushed open his door. A thin, balding man clad in pinstripes and a flaming-haired woman dressed in a fashionable green outfit waited for them.

Meg Cassidy was striking, if not quite beautiful, and she certainly resembled Peter. Her fiery red locks were carefully wind-blown, making her seem very tall, and her emerald eyes glittered as though gemstones. They matched her double-breasted suit, wide at the shoulders, cinched at her narrow waist, and cut short to be revealing. "Hello, Mr. Heller. Is this my cousin?"

Before Angela could correct her, Heller said, "Blasing Madera, Mac's nephew, and Angela Starborne, Mac's lawyer."

"I'm Meg Cassidy. This is Mr. Kenneth Donahue, my lawyer. We're here to discuss the passing of my father and his estate."

"My condolences," Donahue said, folding his hands over his briefcase. The bald lawyer reminded Angela of a mortician; and she had the impression he was hiding something, maybe because his eyes were difficult to see behind his thick, round glasses.

"As Mac's lawyer, Angela Starborne knows all about the estate. I only know about my half." Heller said as he moved around to sit in his mammoth chair. "According to her, Blasing is Mac's sole heir." He held up his hands to stall the forthcoming protest. "I'm just an Irishman caught in the middle."

"That's not right!" Meg exploded. Even her anger looked familiar: hands balled on hips, shoulders and jaw set, and green eyes raging.

She was so flushed her freckles became prominent.

"Easy, Meg," Donahue said. He lightly touched her on the arm. "We can work this out."

"We'll just follow the law," Angela said grimly.

Heller sat back watching. When Angela looked his way, he said, "I have no say in this matter, do I?"

"Not really," Angela said.

"We're cousins, after a fashion," Meg told Blasing as she took his hand.

Angela stepped in. "Pardon me, Ms. Cassidy, but I've been Peter MacGuire's lawyer close to six years, and I don't ever remember hearing him mention you."

"I'm not surprised," Meg said bitterly. "He ignored my existence. You see," she bit her lip, "I am my mother's affront to my father's love."

"A poetic fraud, how quaint," Angela said.

Meg looked away, then back to Blasing, tears welling and a ferocity in her eyes. "I used to visit him sometimes, hoping things would change, but it never has—not even after Mom died in November—and now it never will!"

"So you want... what's yours by law." Angela wanted to say a piece of Peter. "Why didn't you prove this before?"

"Ms. Starborne," Donahue started.

"It's all right, Kenneth," Meg said. "Mother still loved Mac. She didn't want me to 'stress' the situation. She kept thinking he might come back. It was probably just a coincidence that she died shortly after visiting here." Her voice was heavy with sarcasm. "But she'd been sick for a long time."

"Ms. Starborne, Mr. Madera, let's discuss this as civilized people," Donahue said placidly. "Under the state of California law, Meg is entitled to a percentage of the estate."

"I don't understand why people think they deserve something they're not given," Angela aired. She looked at Donahue. "You know as well as I, that if you contest the will, the courts could take years to resolve this and suck away much of what Peter left."

"If that's what it takes," Donahue maintained.

"He has an obligation to me," Meg said forcefully. "Both moral and financial. Fathers shouldn't abandon their children."

Blasing spoke softly in Angela's ear. "If you'll get the details from Donahue, I'll take Ms. Cassidy for a walk and see what I can find out." Angela nodded. "Ms. Cassidy, can we leave the lawyers to talk legalities and see what we have in common?"

"Meg, please. That sounds reasonable to me. I'm sure there are things we each know about Dad that the other doesn't."

"Well, isn't this just a peachy day for me," Heller said. "Until the will is clarified and decided, I'm sole owner and will do whatever I wish with MY part of Ghostal Shores. And what I wish, is to start selling my property." His eyes were big above his crooked glasses. "Don't worry, lad, lass. You'll get your share of the profits when it all shakes out."

"I'll file an injunction," Donahue said before Angela could.

"Please, ladies and gentleman," Heller said with a smile. "At least give me a chance. Blasing, you said you wanted to know more about my plans. Well, I've already told you about myself and the history of GSR. Tonight you'll find out about the future! We're having a special sales reception. It'll be quite enlightening."

"How convenient that you already have salespeople on the premises," Angela said tartly.

"We'll be there," Blasing said.

"As we will," Meg Cassidy chimed in.

"I'm still making a phone call to my office to get things rolling," Angela said with a false smile.

Heller still looked surprised by how Angela was reacting, but only said, "By all means, Ms. Starborne. I knew there was another reason Mac kept you around." The Irishman's smile was secretive, knowing something she didn't. It infuriated her.

"Is there an office we can use?" Donahue asked.

With a huge smile, Heller said, "Use mine. I'll be out most of the afternoon trying to get ready for this evening. See you all tonight. It will be an evening to remember. I guarantee it."

Angela watched him leave, then said to Blasing, "I don't trust that man. I don't see how your uncle did, either."

He shrugged, making her a bit angry. "Come, Meg, let's go for a walk." Taking her elbow, Blasing guided her out the door.

Meg had an engaging presence, if a bit dramatic. Blasing could see why Mac might have been stirred by her mother. If what she said was true. If....

Meg said the gardens were her favorite spot, but she wanted to walk the beach. At the bottom of the steps, she took off her heels and carried them. The sand was warm. Blasing noticed a brand new building, its sign proclaiming the coming of sailing to the beaches of Ghostal Shores.

"A beautiful day," Meg said breathing deeply, "but it looks like a storm is coming." The clouds directly overhead were already white and fluffy, ahead of the harbingers of the storm, dark purple cumulus growing taller and larger by the minute.

"I enjoy watching storms," Blasing said. Out here, where he was away from the maddening crowd, the feeling of being watched seemed stronger than ever. He breathed deeply, searching for perfume, but found only the briny tang of sea-salted air.

"Mom always said Ghostal Shores was the place to sit and watch the waves crash against the sands. She loved this place. Saw my father in every aspect of it. Eventually it made her sad to come here."

"What do you think about Mac's murder?"

"To tell the truth, I have mixed feelings," she sighed. "It's hard to feel bad for a man who ignored you, and yet, I'd foolishly hoped we'd resolve things one day. But now...." She shrugged, her expression downcast. "You?"

"I feel like I let my kids down by not letting them get to know their uncle," he said sadly.

"I didn't know you had kids. Actually, I know very little about you. I know about the crash and Mac...."

"I have two wonderful kids. Patrick, age nine and Kelly, age ten. They're in Tahoe with their nanny." He succinctly explained about Jennifer's death.

"I'm sorry. I can be rude sometimes; it comes from living in L.A. My mother died of thyroid cancer. Father didn't even come to the funeral." They were silent for a time before she broke the ice. "Maybe it's for the best your children didn't know Mac. He taught me to distrust men."

"I understand. It can be hard for me to trust, period; but I've tried not to live in the past, nor be consumed by it. If I had been, I'd be bitter and have missed some very wonderful things."

"Your children?" she asked, and he nodded. They were quiet again, walking further along the beach. A lighthouse sat sentinel atop a pinnacle protruding from the cliffs. She pointed to it. "Have you visited there?"

"No."

"It's an interesting place. A great view, but a lot of steps to the lighthouse."

"Been there recently?"

"I go every time I visit. Jason takes me there. I've always wondered if it were haunted."

"Jason?"

"Most call him JJ. He's a bellman on swing shift. He was the first person at Ghostal Shores to befriend me. We've spent a lot of time together, so I know quite a bit about Ghostal Shores. If I wanted, I think I could manage the place."

"What's Jason look like?" Blasing asked. She described him as tall and dark-skinned with wavy chocolate brown hair. Sometimes he sported a mustache. "You know the front desk operations then?"

"Yes. A friend of his showed me quite a bit. What do you think about Ghostal Shores?" Meg asked him.

"It's very... unusual and beautiful. Odd. Unnerving...." He began to list, counting them off with his fingers. Meg laughed throatily. "Well, what do you think?"

"I have mixed feelings. I vividly remember my first time here, the evening of the grand opening, hanging out with ghosts as if they were people."

"What was opening night like?"

"The ghosts' surprise appearance set off celebratory chaos and a storm set a perfect mood. The Hispanic maid was the first to appear. She was as frightened of us as we were of her. I thought that was funny. Why would a ghost be scared of anything? I also remember the one wearing the eye-patch and Samuel, good looking even if he is just a ghost. Maybe a bit too much of a peacock."

She flushed. "I'm embarrassed to say I was more interested in my new boyfriend back home. Here I was, seventeen, out in the middle of nowhere and talking to dead people, when I thought

I should be walking the beach with my beau...." An earring dropped and bounced off her shoulder before tumbling to the sand.

"I'll get that. Was your mother with you?" Blasing asked as he knelt, than handed her the earring.

"Yes, though Father wasn't glad to see us. Mother was in tears most of the time. We'd flown in from Los Angeles." She examined the earring, made a wry face, then slipped it back in her lobe.

"How did Mac and your mother meet?"

"They met in Palm Springs when he was running the Oasis Sands Resort. She was a real estate broker. Mom said he was drinking a lot at that time, and she helped him sober up.

"They were serious, but not committed, which explains how I came to be." She was quiet for a minute, then said, "Earlier Ms. Starborne said she didn't understand why Father trusted Sean Heller. Well, I think I know. Mother said Father often talked about meeting a man who could make his dreams come true — dreams of designing and running his own resort. Well, it appears he found such a man. Heller had the money and Father had the idea. Each helped give the other what he wanted. Mother couldn't give Father what he wanted, I guess. What are you going to do with your... share of GSR?"

Blasing stopped and looked back at the resort sprawling along the clifftops, part of it extending down the cliffs by way of winding steps to the greenhouse veranda, then to the beach sands. "I'm not sure. There is a certain appeal to being part of such an unusual place, but I don't know if my children would be happy here. I might just take the money and run. What about you?"

"Sell it!" she rejoiced. "It would help put him to rest. Split it with me and go chase your own dreams. This is Peter MacGuire's dream. Not ours. We have to forge ahead with our own futures."

"That's a lot of money."

"I don't really have to have the money. It's the principle of the thing. As I said, fathers should not be allowed to abandon their children."

"I can't disagree with that. What would you do with a lump sum child support payment of millions?"

A wistful smile touched her face. "I'd start my own art studio, maybe even a gallery. I've always wanted to display my work, but it's tough to get started. Exposure is so important."

"You don't look like a starving artist."

"I'm not," Meg smiled prettily. She held up hands with artful nails. "I work as a nail technician and make pretty good money. But it's a living, not a passion. My best work probably came from youthful angst. I guess Father was an inspiration. What do you do for a living?" He explained about being a retired thrill-seeker involved with security now. "Why'd you quit all the daredevil stuff?"

"Getting old."

"You don't look old, Ripe might be a better word," she said with an impish smile. "In fact, if we weren't related...." She gasped suddenly and clutched at her chest.

"Are you all right?" Blasing asked.

"Yes! It's nothing! Just my necklace coming apart. That's... odd. As I was saying, you don't look so old." She tried to casually maneuver the necklace so she could remove it under the cover of her jacket.

"Thanks, but sometimes I feel old. And it wasn't just physical, I have responsibilities."

"Hey!" she said, watching her stick pin pop off. It bounced off Blasing. "I'm coming apart," she muttered. She knelt to gather it. "You know, running a security business is not what I would have expected you to turn to."

"Me neither, but it was a good solid opportunity."

"What would you rather be doing?"

"Spending time with my kids."

"And?"

"Photography."

"Photography? Really? You're an artist, too!"

"Yeah, I wanted to be an outdoor sports photographer. I thought I had the skills, but the timing wasn't right. I couldn't afford the cash drought."

"Well, money isn't a problem now, no matter what happens," she said. "Listen Blasing, are you going to fight me on this?"

"I don't know. I'll probably consult my lawyers. And I'm not even sure it's my decision. Angela is still working for Uncle Mac."

"But she works for you," Meg complained, her face tightening.

"Not exactly," he replied.

"You don't believe me!" she snapped, her face flushing.

"What would you think in my shoes?"

"That I was a gold-digging bitch," she said bitterly.

"It's a good thing you're not in my shoes."

"Welcome to the nineties. You'll be apologizing when this is over," Meg said huffily, then spun and walked back toward the resort.

From what Blasing remembered of Mac, she reminded him very much of his uncle. Could her anger and bitterness move her to having Mac murdered? She claimed to know the resort. She had friends here. Half, or even less, of the inheritance would still be a lot. People had killed for much, much less.

He shook his head. Angela had him jumping at ambiguous clues. Were Meg Cassidy and Earl Cash suspects, along with Heller? The investigative process made him think of security. He should visit Ghostal Shores security.

As he neared the cliffway stairs, the winds were stronger and the waves larger, forcing him farther inland on the soft sand. Blasing felt even more watched as he neared the resort.

"Going to be quite a squall," Broderick said as he suddenly appeared.

Blasing jumped. "Broderick, please announce yourself."

"Sorry, sir. Upon my approach, at what distance would you care to be warned?"

"How about fifteen feet?"

"Consider it so, sir."

"I'm sorry, Broderick, I'm just jumpy. Ghosts make me nervous."

"Perfectly understandable. I remember seeing a ghost when I was in the Mediterranean sea. He appeared to be one of the crew who had died in a skirmish. Very, very disturbing."

"Were you looking for me?" Blasing asked.

"Yes, I have finally spoken with all the ghosts, except for Fawn and Marsh. She seems to have disappeared. He sometimes sulks for days. None but Barney saw the stagecoaches, and he did not see anyone exit. No one did, and yet Missy holds fast to her story about seeing a stranger with Marsh. That was several weeks ago. No one knows anything else about any new spirits. I am sorry to say that includes Master MacGuire's spirit, too, sir."

"Thanks."

"What do you think of Megan Cassidy?" Broderick asked.

"I don't know. Do you know her?" Blasing asked. Broderick nodded, his face hinting at sadness. "Did Mac ever say anything to you?"

"I only asked once, and was told never to speak of it—or her—again. He was very boorish about it."

"It?"

"Breaking up with Jaclyn Cassidy."

Blasing asked, "Do you know why it happened?"

"Just that she betrayed his trust, sir. When he was besotted, he'd talk about her, miss her, and quietly curse her for being weak and ruining what they'd had."

"Do you think Meg is Mac's daughter?"

"Master MacGuire rarely asked my opinion."

"But you gave it anyway,"

"I am just a lowly valet, Mister Madera, not a tabloid writer nor a gossip monger," Broderick said, stiffening even more.

"I'm just asking you what you think," Blasing told him. "Cannon said ghosts could usually tell... 'things' about people."

"Ah, I see. I do not know. For some reason, her soul is difficult to assess."

"I'll mention that to Angela. She's very unhappy about this, and if Meg is who she claims, I don't want Angela to be nasty."

"Lawyers hate surprises," Broderick agreed.

As they headed up the steps, Blasing continued to ask questions. "Angela mentioned something about my uncle and Eva breaking up over drugs. Do you know anything about that?"

"No sir, I do not. I know you seek clues to Master MacGuire's murder, but I am not a snoop. If it did happen, it happened behind closed doors. We have rules of decency so the ghosts do not simply wander from room to room during all hours of the day. To anticipate your next question," he said, "Master MacGuire never mentioned it, and unfortunately, he frequently talked to me about women." Broderick rolled his eyes. "He felt she was simply using him. He began to refer to her as a user."

"That could mean several things," Blasing said.

They passed through the gardens and into the lobby. As they

neared the front desk, Broderick asked where they were going. "Security," Blasing replied. "I want to find out what the plans and goals are for Ghostal Shores security and meet some of the personnel."

"Then I shall wait for you outside where the air is only slightly polluted. I find the people and their duties very... distasteful." Frowning, he stopped and waited by the door, obviously resolute that he would go no farther.

Security was bustling as more equipment was being installed. Most of the screens along a wall were dark. "Camera five of the delivery entrance is working," the bull-like man at the console said. The man next to him was tall and sinewy.

"That's a first," someone said.

"We have a visitor, Mr. Chadwick." A large, big-boned man with a beard stopped working and warily watched Blasing.

"Excuse me, sir, but this area is for employees only," the long-limbed man began as he left the console panel and deftly maneuvered through the equipment and boxes. As he neared, the pockmark-faced man asked, "Mr. Madera?" Blasing nodded. "I am Kalvin Chadwick, Assistant Chief of Security. How can I be of service?"

"I was hoping to meet Chief Porter. I work in the security business and wanted to ask some questions."

Chadwick nodded toward a closed door at the end of a short hall. "He's out. Would you like me to page him?"

"Just tell him I would like to see him at his earliest convenience." Blasing nodded to the boxes and equipment. "Sony cameras and Toshiba monitors. Good stuff. And I see you have a Vicon VPS 1200 to coordinate the cameras. Excellent."

"Nothing but the best for Ghostal Shores," Chadwick replied. He had a nervous tick near his left eye, and he toyed with a ring on his left hand.

"How many men do you have?"

"Not including myself and Chief Porter, twenty-five men."

"Nine a shift?" Blasing asked. None of the men appeared typical of what he expected. They were impressively fit and muscle-bound, accustomed to doing more than patrolling and watching screens.

"Wealthy people expect certain things, and we want them to feel safe when they visit. We only had six on shift during Mr. MacGuire's murder. If we'd had more, we might have caught the bastard. We've been hiring new personnel ever since."

"Where do you get your men?"

"Through past employment. Ghostal Shores pays well."

That surprised Blasing. He didn't think Heller would be very free with his money; but if so, he should be able to get some of the best. Blasing planned to get their files from Porter, then speak with Rich Steele. His partner would probably know many of them; he attended all the conventions.

"Well, thank you, Mr. Chadwick. Nice meeting you. Tell Chief Porter I look forward to meeting him." Blasing stepped into the lobby.

He thought now would be a good opportunity to talk with some employees and see what they thought of Ghostal Shores.

"Ah, did you enjoy your visit?" Broderick asked.

"He wasn't in. Since I've got some time before the reception, I'm going to talk with some of the employees. See what they think."

"Excellent idea, sir. Do you require my assistance?"

"I don't think so."

"Then I shall continue with my duties."

"Fine, see you this evening," Blasing replied. "But," he said abruptly, stopping Broderick as he began to drift toward the ceiling, "could you work on your exits?"

"What would you prefer, sir?"

"Uh... that you walk around a corner before you disappear?"

"Of course," Broderick said. Though he appeared annoyed, Broderick did as Blasing requested.

As Blasing headed for the stairs, he still felt a ghostly presence. He tried to ignore it.

When he ascended the stairs, the ghostly presence seemed to move closer. Blasing stopped and said, "Would you either show yourself or quit following me?"

A woman coming down the stairs was startled by his harsh words. "I'm sorry," Blasing apologized. "I'm talking to a ghost." The woman looked around uncertainly then smiled disconcertedly.

Embarrassed enough, Blasing kept quiet and headed for the kitchen to speak with the chef. He wondered if the ghost following him might know something about Mac's murder.

TEN

Restless and dressed in a tux, Blasing waited in the lounge for Angela. "Mr. Heller's presentation should be starting any time now," he told Broderick.

"It would have been appreciated if Mister Heller had included one of us," Broderick said, sounding appropriately offended. "The ghosts are the past, present and future of Ghostal Shores."

"I agree. Join us, please," Blasing said.

"Yes, please," Angela said as she exited her room.

"I need someone...." Blasing didn't finish, his attention seized by his beautiful and formally attired companion.

Angela wore the silk dress Elma and Ingrid had given her. Backless and generously slit up the side, the gown fit Angela's trim form perfectly, magically hugging her curves. The teal hue blended flawlessly with her eyes, making them glisten as tropical waters capturing the sun. Her unbound hair flowed past her shoulders.

"Going to the Prince's Ball?" Blasing finally managed.

Angela smiled, then frowned just as quickly. "Unfortunately no, just a sales pitch." She rubbed the side of her neck.

"You make it sound cheap, miss," Broderick said.

"I'm sure it will be plenty expensive."

"That is too true," Broderick agreed. "Come now, miss. You are going to be late for dinner. Though I believe everyone will stop whatever they are doing when you make a grand entrance. I must say, you spruce up very well."

"Why thank you, Broderick," she said. With Blasing on her arm, she hadn't wanted to look misplaced. "And I am intentionally late. I want to subject Blasing to as few sales people as possible."

"They are a rather... opportunistic lot." Broderick's eyes rolled upward.

"All I said is that I would listen," Blasing told her.

"He'd rather listen to Mr. Heller than me," Angela said, gathering up her purse. "Or that lecherous spirit, Grant Roberts."

"Some men are difficult to fathom, miss," Broderick said. Angela smiled. "As are some women," he finished.

"Come along, Broderick," Blasing said. "Ms. Starborne looks elegant enough to have a pair of escorts."

Angela liked the gleam in Blasing's eyes. Elma's and Ingrid's selection was perfect. "You are surprisingly silver-tongued for a man who works with machines." She grimaced as she craned her neck, then rubbed it.

"Neck bothering you?" Blasing asked. She nodded. "Let me help," he said, moving around behind her. With surprising gentleness, he massaged her shoulders and neck.

"Mmmm," Angela sighed. His touch was just what the doctor ordered. A special warmth and electricity radiated from his hands. "Mmmm." Angela began to melt under his touch, then remembered where she was going. She had to stay alert. "Enough. Thanks Blasing. We're already late."

"Now it is the three of us against the barbarous horde," Broderick said blandly as he opened the door. He was barely visible floating alongside them as they walked to the elevator.

"How did your visit with Meg go?" she asked. He quickly recapped their discussion. "Broderick, how often do you think Meg Cassidy visited?"

"At least twice a year. It is why some of the staff know her so well. I came to my conclusion about her authenticity by watching Master MacGuire, instead of getting a spiritual sense of her."

"I find it odd you can't get a sense of her. Carrie and Elma claimed they couldn't see Heller's spirit clearly."

"Is that unusual?" Blasing asked.

"Yes, sir. I cannot imagine what is causing it."

"Makes me very curious," Angela said. "Does Meg have male friends here?" Blasing explained about the valet and desk clerk. "When was she last here?"

"About ten days ago, I believe," Broderick responded.

"Ten days ago. Hmmm. Just a few days before Peter was murdered. Where's Columbo when you need him?"

"Columbo? Who is this person?" Broderick asked.

"A TV actor," Blasing said. Broderick looked perplexed.

"Thank you for your input, Mr. Madera. In the real world

people do kill people for revenge. There was a case just last year where an embittered son shot his biological parents twenty years after they'd put him up for adoption."

"Sounds like you need Perry Mason." Blasing hit the elevator call button.

"Oh, what a damn mess this could be! A time consuming mess."

"What if I don't want to challenge her claim?" Blasing asked.

Angela's look was dark, but her voice was calm. "The tests will tell us whether there's even any reason to consider it contested." She sighed heavily. "What really bothers me is that until I get an injunction, Heller will be able to do as he pleases. That might be Tuesday or Wednesday."

"Just so you don't think I'm blindly accepting this, I called my office," Blasing said. "They're going to do some investigating."

"Good. I called my office too," Angela said. "Legal action will be in motion tomorrow. I hope I can reach Sheriff Middleton soon. What do you think about Earl Cash?" she asked pointedly.

"His injury is the correct hand and the build is about right. But... I guess he could have been disguised...."

"But I did not recognize his resonance," Broderick told them.

"Is that always a hundred percent accurate?" Angela asked.

"No, as we have mentioned, some people's spirits seem to be concealed."

"Was the murder's?" Blasing asked.

Broderick nodded. "Perhaps. I do not recall, but I believe it to be so. But why would Mr. Cash commit such a heinous act?"

"He and Peter butted heads because Peter became more involved in the resort's management. Some of Cash's compensation is performance based and the timeshare was his idea."

"Money and undermining authority is enough motivation for plenty of people to commit murder. I want to check the medical logs," Blasing told her.

"Because of all the accidents?" she asked.

"And the injuries in security. Do you have any idea why Mac and Jaclyn broke up?"

"I remember Peter talking about Jaclyn Cassidy a few times, usually when he drank too much wine," she replied. "Peter was absolutely crazy about her. Once he said she'd been his sun and moon, but she did something to hurt him deeply—so deeply it continued to affect his life almost thirty years later. He claimed the breakup made it hard to trust people, and I'm assuming he meant women."

"After her, he went through a long, dark spell of consumption," Broderick told him.

"Peter claimed that Heller and their dreams for Ghostal Shores helped pull him together," Angela continued. "Otherwise, he would have been dead long ago. Must be busy." Angela hit the button again. "Prime cocktail hour." Blasing was amused. "What?"

"A few minutes ago you were willing to be late, but now you're in a hurry for the elevator to arrive."

"I want to be late on my own time," Angela told him smugly.

Broderick stuck his upper torso through the doors, then stepped back. "You surmise correctly, miss."

"I'm not sure why Peter spoke to me, but sometimes men say things to women they won't or can't say to other men. I think he brought it up with me because I'd just started my divorce and...."

"You're divorced," Blasing asked, sounding surprised.

She nodded and continued, "...he'd just broken up with another lady love, I can't remember her name. She reminded him of Jaclyn."

"Jasra Micheals indeed took a second lover. That set Master MacGuire drinking again. I must confess that I watered down his drinks whenever possible."

"What made him stop drinking?" Blasing asked.

"I simply pointed out that Marsh died of alcoholism," Broderick told them.

"Oh," Angela said, then laughed. "Thank you, Broderick."

"I wish I could have done more."

"He might not have lived this long if you hadn't done that. The employees loved Peter's increased involvement," Angela said. "This was his home, and in many ways, the employees were his family. His dependency, as he called it, was one of the reasons he couldn't stand Eva using drugs."

"I wish there was some way to confirm this," Blasing mused. "I could speak with Eva and try to feel her out."

"I'm sure she'd enjoy that," Angela said sardonically as she punched the button again.

Blasing stiffened. "It takes more than good looks and puffery to captivate my attention."

"You can afford to be picky."

"Anyone can. And besides, two others very dear to me are important in the mix; and a vixen," he said with a little bit of a smile, "is not a good role model for Kelly."

Angela smiled, then said, "Well, maybe one of the other ghosts knows about Eva. In my book, she's a suspect. Broderick?"

"It is possible, but she is not close to any of the ghosts. She thinks of us as assets, much as Mister Heller does."

"Then possibly another employee? She can't be that good at keeping secrets. She flaunts herself. How did your impromptu visiting go?" she asked Blasing. Angela punched the button again.

He mentioned that Chief Porter wasn't in his office so he'd met the assistant, Chadwick. He told her security was expanding and that their equipment was state of the art.

"I don't recognize anyone anymore. I used to know Max Wells, the security chief, but then he was replaced with Porter and a massive turnover ensued. Carrie mentioned that security reminded her of a gang. She couldn't clearly see their spirits, either."

"They're certainly not typical hotel security," Blasing said thoughtfully. "But I think calling them a gang of crooks is a bit premature. I tried to obtain their personnel files, but the clerk was in the process of reorganizing the files for their new computer system and claimed I needed Heller's permission to browse."

"And your handshaking and kissing babies?" Angela asked.

"I spoke with twelve people in various jobs throughout the resort, from the chef to a maintenance tech. The general consensus is that everyone dearly misses Mac. You were right about them being family. He seemed to be the heart and soul of the place."

"I concur," Broderick added. "He was our emotional and spiritual leader."

"Absolutely nobody—not the chef, valets, maids, room service waiters, clerks nor engineers—is pleased that Mr. Heller is the sole owner. They said Mac used to handle employee relations. Heller thinks relationships are one-way streets. There may be some serious turnover soon. Despite the good pay, almost everybody admitted that they were job hunting."

"If that happens, the guests will surely suffer," Broderick said sadly.

"You know, some of the stories about Heller and his temper almost seem ludicrous."

"You've seen him at his best," Angela said.

An empty elevator arrived and they boarded. It stopped at the second floor and several couples milled in. Broderick faded to near invisibility and stood within the wall so nobody noticed him. One couple conversed in German, while another spoke in French. An Asian couple was dressed to the nines, including corsages to celebrate some happy occasion.

When the elevator stopped on the lobby level, Blasing whispered in Angela's ear, "I feel other ghosts." Everyone exited on the first floor, the rest of the crowd heading for the dining room. Blasing, Angela, and Broderick turned toward the ornate doors of the grand ballroom.

A fog rose before them, slowly building color as it coalesced into four ghostly ladies of the evening. Chastity, Jessie, Missy and Amber gave him large smiles as if they'd just spotted something tasty on the menu. Each was dressed in an elegant gown of their seasonal colors. "We are here to escort you," Missy said, her eyes sultry. She was dressed in white with a necklace of emeralds that mirrored her eyes.

"I have an enchanting escort," Blasing replied more smoothly than he expected.

"Ladies!" Broderick snapped. "Must I shoo away you little guttersnipes again?"

"Again?" Blasing asked.

"Last night I literally threw Fawn out of your room," Broderick informed him. Blasing blanched.

"You need a proper entourage for such a function," Chastity said, her face innocent. She wore a blue-black gown that complimented her short hair and dark eyes.

"One lady is all I can handle," Blasing replied.

"And you will make a spectacle of things," Angela began, "and we may not learn what we want to know. Broderick is joining us to act as your eyes and ears."

"I'd keep Blasing away from Eva," Jessie volunteered.

"Or the other women," Amber agreed. She smiled and patted her wealth of red-gold curls. The crimson of her formal seemed to become brighter.

"More defenders of your virtue," Angela said a bit amused.

"Go find someone who appreciates all this wonderful attention."

"Entertain and entice a few guests," Angela suggested. "Surely there are some handsome men among them."

"Yes, but none affect our fate as Blasing does," Missy said.

"Ah, I see. The truth at last," Blasing said. "Listen. I promise to consult you all before I make a final decision. You have my word. Do you accept it?" They all nodded. "Good, now would you please let us attend the reception?"

"Will we see you later?" Chastity asked.

"Probably tomorrow. I have questions about Ghostal Shores, what you like about it, and what you'd like to see changed."

"I like the sound of that," Amber replied. "Tomorrow, then." She faded. The others wished them a pleasant evening, then disappeared. Before she totally faded, Chastity stuck out her tongue at Angela.

"Come on," Blasing said. He held the door for Angela, and they entered a small foyer where a portable bar had been spread along one side. Through the open doors, the ballroom looked different than yesterday. Beyond a table with an architect's model of Ghostal Shores, carpets had been laid and two dining tables had been elegantly appointed. The silver and crystal glistened in the amber candlelight and gave the setting an enchanting ambiance.

Except for a pair of seats near Eva Dare, the chairs were occupied by Donahue, Meg Cassidy and mostly unfamiliar faces, though they might have seen several yesterday in the bar. Three women were so beautiful Angela wondered if Heller was thinking of running a Western cat house. Then she noticed a pair of men who could easily give Blasing competition. What was going on?

Heller appeared to have quite a production in mind. Two large and now dark TV's waited at the front of the stage, and a screen hung behind the podium where Heller stood. Angela got the impression he'd just started. She couldn't have asked for better timing.

"Now that we have all had a chance to study the model," Heller stressed, "I'd like to go into more detail about the future. We have peaceful residential ghosts, a unique atmosphere, ocean front accommodations, fine dining, a pleasant bar, swimming, a health club, and tennis. What more could anybody want?" The lights began to lower, leaving the spotlight on Heller.

"18 HOLES!" Somebody yelled as Blasing and Angela took their seats. Dressed in a beige outfit designed to titillate, Eva smiled charmingly at Blasing and poisonously at Angela. Meg ignored them.

Heller scowled. "Golf? Why I... That's impossible. But a riding stable is not. Now...."

"Gambling!" someone interrupted again from the other table.

"Ah, not quite so farfetched," Heller smiled. "We can't get gaming, but we appear to be in line to become a poker parlor. Many of our customers and ghosts heartily support this idea."

"It does not take long to figure out which ones," Broderick said acidly.

"Some places outside of San Francisco and Los Angeles are already in operation, so poker appears very possible. It's in our plans, as well as the second restaurant and bar. As you may have noticed, there's a sales brochure next to your plates." Some folks were already leafing through it. Blasing picked up his copy; it was slick with photos of Ghostal Shores and sketches of the future resort.

"The nerve," Angela hissed. "Injunction here we come."

"First, I'd like to start with a series of commercials we've made. Watch the screens." They came on with a static hiss that seemed to fill the ballroom with an eerie blue light. "Mr. Cash."

With his good hand, the thin man pushed the cassette into the VCR, then stood back and folded his arms. The screens flipped once, twice, then were followed by a scene of Ghostal Shores as one drove through the front gate. Abruptly the blue static returned" along with the hissing. The air seemed to vibrate.

"What's going on?!" Heller demanded.

Cash turned off the TV then ejected the video. When he removed the cassette, it was trailing tape.

"The presentation is history," someone at Blasing's table said. Several people chuckled.

Heller stewed but managed to speak calmly, "Then while you get another tape, we'll move on to the slide presentation. Ms. Dare,

if you please." With a backward glance toward Blasing, Eva sauntered to the projector cart.

Heller picked up the remote and pointed it at the projector. The
logo for Ghostal Shores appeared on screen. "As we are now," he
said. A distant drawing of Ghostal Shores came on screen, followed
by one from above, and finally a coastal view.

"After." When Heller hit the button again, the projector jumped
ahead several frames to a sketch of the new poker bar. "Oops.
Let's move back." He worked with the remote, but the carousel
moved back too much, then flipped to the above view again.
"Dammit!" For a minute, the scene hopped back and forth between the sketch of the poker room and the overhead shot.

"Almost makes one think the ghosts don't like him," Angela snickered. Blasing's expression was stern. Angela rolled her eyes, then
said, "Or maybe they just don't like his ideas. I don't see any ghosts
about. Do you feel them?" Angela asked Blasing.

"It's hard to tell with Broderick so close, but I thought I did earlier. Broderick, how about you?"

"I do not see anyone, sir."

Finally, the next slide appeared, a detailed drawing of Ghostal
Shores with the north wing added. The place sprawled along the
tops of the rugged cliffs, then the screen suddenly went dark.

"WHAT THE HELL'S GOING ON HERE!" Heller shouted.

Eva walked over to the projector. "The bulb's dead." She signaled
to one of the staff by the doors. "Get another immediately."

"Well, I won't let technology slow me," Heller said, but his
next words were interrupted by high-pitched squeaks and squawks.
He tapped the microphone attached to his shirt, and it thumped loudly.
Just as he began to speak, rock and roll music came over the speak-
ers. The music grew louder, the bass thundering and the guitars
screaming. Heller staggered back, knocking over the podium. "Turn
off the system!"

The silence was so palpable, then there was a blinding flash of
lightning. Several people gasped, then all other sound was buried by
the harsh crack of thunder. Everything shook and the power died,
leaving them in candlelight. The ice in glasses was still tinkling when
the lightning struck again; but this time the thunder was delayed,
less consuming and farther away.

"Impressive," Angela said with a smile.

"I believe I felt that," Broderick said.

Eva stood up and spoke so everyone could hear, "Everyone, enjoy the bar. Dinner will be served shortly, even if the power does not return." She and Heller left.

"I am going to investigate," Broderick said. Blasing nodded as the English spirit faded into nothingness.

"That could have gone better," a slender man said as he stood and stretched. "But hey, this is a haunted place, spooky things are supposed to happen!" His dark eyes were bright as though he'd already consumed plenty. "But I do hope that wasn't an omen." He wiped at his mustache to hide a smile. "Hi, I'm Tom Becker, the sales manager." Angela recognized him, her expression becoming coldly stony. Blasing stood, and they shook hands.

A nearby woman clad entirely in yellow turned around in her chair. "You're selling something you can't produce again, Tommy?"

"Hey, Alicia, lighten up, babe," Becker said. "I didn't catch your names?" Blasing introduced himself and Angela.

"We've already met," Angela said brittlely.

The salesman ignored her. "So, you're the new partner?" Blasing nodded. "Well, you came along at just the right time. This is a supremely prime piece of real estate. Should be easy to sell for top dollar. We're going to make some big money, aren't we, Harry?"

"Sure we are, Tom," said another mustached man approaching with two drinks. Blasing remembered them from the bar.

"Blasing, this is Harry Poston, the second best salesman at GSR," Becker said.

"First, buddy."

"Excuse me," Eva said, her French accent heavy. "But you... gentlemen please excuse us. I'd like to take Blasing and his lawyer around to meet everyone."

"You go ahead," Angela said coldly. "I'm going to have a glass of wine."

Blasing watched Angela go, sorry she'd left, then looked to Eva who was smiling. "We are at odds, no? Both of us want something different from the same thing. Now come, enjoy the moment. We are at a party, and you are too tense, looking around, studying and judging. Too much. Come, I want you to meet the real sales manager, Walter Bond."

With a smile she took his arm and guided him to a distinguished-looking man with gray temples framing a square face. He caught Eva's eye and came to meet Blasing with a smile and an outstretched hand. "I'm Walter Bond, the sales manager."

Blasing introduced himself, then said, "I thought Tom Becker was the sales manager."

Bond shook his head. "I hope he doesn't start that again. He's a great salesman, but he has delusions of grandeur. But enough about Tom, it's nice to finally meet our second investor."

"I haven't jumped on the bandwagon yet," Blasing said.

"Ah, but the evening is still young. Tomorrow, I'd like to take you through the entire sales process myself."

"Sounds like a wise thing to do."

"Done. This is a can't miss, win-win opportunity. Everybody will be happy."

"Even the ghosts?" Blasing asked.

"The ghosts care?" Bond asked, appearing surprised.

"Yes, very much," Blasing told him.

"I never knew. But I don't see how it can make a difference. Aren't they sort of like employees?"

"You pay employees," Blasing said.

"Blasing thinks it's their home," Eva laughed delightedly.

"Well, maybe if they didn't have a home they'd go to the great beyond," Bond said. "Now, let me tell you about some of our sales approaches and promotions."

Blasing was listening as much to the surrounding conversation as he was to Bond: "I love it when they have an open bar." "Do you think single chicks will buy this place as a way to meet rich guys?" "Step up to the pump, bud. Let's bet on the first sale. First month's top sales!" "I could sell this place in my sleep. I saw our mailing list. Most have been customers already," a woman with a high pitched voice said. "What's the best scam you ever used?" a man asked. "Love the double switch." "They thought the gold card got them free nighttime skiing" Another man laughed. "I only had to sleep with her once to make a sale but it was worth it." "Just need to work a deal with the bartenders...."

"It should go smoothly. These are some of my finest people,"

Walt finished as they reached the group.

"At one time or another, they've all worked for me before," Eva said, waving to the foursome.

Bond introduced Alicia Perez, a native of Mexico. She was slim but very angular as if trying too hard to stay young. Linc Washington was from Boston and introduced himself with a bit of a Northeastern accent. He was a solidly built black gentleman in round glasses and GQ attire. Mary Nguyen was a natural beauty with petite features, dark hair, close-cropped opaque eyes and a creamy golden complexion. The last was Ned Martinez from San Diego, a barrel-chested man casually dressed in light-colored clothing of baggy pants and an open shirt with a jacket.

"We try to have a nice blend so we can speak to all kinds of people," Eva said. "We want them to be comfortable with us."

Cash walked toward them and said, "Ms. Dare, Mr. Bond. Mr. Heller would like to see you right away."

"Of course," Bond said, moving off.

Eva touched his arm and said, "I will be back shortly."

A tall, beautiful woman seemed to appear out of nowhere to take Eva's place. Her short hair was silvery and her eyes were pale green and fathomless. Her long dress was light and airy and the color of sea foam. It enhanced her full figure while giving her an ethereal quality.

"Hello, I am Desiree´ Madison. My condolences on your uncle. He was a good man."

"Thank you. I'm Blasing Madera, You knew Mac?"

"Barely. I've been a guest here several times, which is what convinced me it would be such a great sales opportunity. If you have some time after dinner, I'd like to pass on some... ideas." She glanced at Eva who was returning, then continued her appraisal of Blasing.

"Dinner is served," a waiter announced.

"Let's eat. It will be scrumptious," Eva said, appearing at Blasing's side. "Good evening, Desiree´."

"Later, Mr. Madera," Desiree´ said.

"Good night," Blasing said. "I'll be with you in a minute, Eva. I'd like to speak with Angela for a moment."

"Just remember, Mr. Madera," Eva began with a hot glance and tight expression, "that unique opportunities rarely stay on the market for long." She abruptly turned and stalked off.

Blasing walked toward the window where Angela stared out to sea. Blasing watched flashes of lightning illuminate her face and marvelled at her elemental beauty.

He reached her side as more thunder sounded, but she spoke first during the lull. "Have you met enough salespeople?"

"I believe Cannon and Dr. Landrum were correct in their assessments," Blasing said. "And you, too. I know you're only trying to do what Mac wanted." When Angela turned around, she no longer appeared angry. "Come to dinner and help me sort this out."

"I can only give you advice," Angela said. "You must make the decisions." More lightning flashed, followed by thunder intense enough to rattle the windows. "A candlelight dinner during a storm," Angela said. "How perfectly Ghostal Shores."

Appetizers had been served and champagne poured when Heller spoke up, "A toast!" He held up his glass. "To the new Ghostal Shores. A unique and prosperous property like no other. Long may it excite and entertain."

"Here! Here!" "Amen!" " Well said!"

Glasses were raised. Angela refused. When people drank, they suddenly started choking and gasping. Several spit into their glasses. "This stuff is foul," someone sputtered.

Blasing looked at his glass, then Angela. She just smiled. She hadn't touched her glass. Blasing smelled the wine and wrinkled his nose at the vinegary odor. "Not a good year."

"Champagne!" Heller called.

"No thank you," a woman cried. Heller flushed.

"After dinner," Eva suggested. Heller nodded, the lividness slowly draining from his face.

The soup and salad servings occurred without incident. Angela watched everybody relax—some were too "relaxed." She was growing tired of Eva playing up to Blasing. Why didn't she just say she'd sleep with him to get what she wanted? Meg and her lawyer said little to anybody but Walter Bond.

"So, have you made any decisions yet?" Heller asked Blasing as the table was cleared for the main course.

"Not yet. Maybe after I experience the sales pitch from Mr.

Bond tomorrow," Blasing replied. That seemed to satisfy Heller for the moment.

"And Ms. Starborne, what do you think?" Meg asked.

"I'm trying not to make any decisions," Angela said icily. "I'm just seeking some honest answers."

Starting with her neck, Meg's face went crimson. "Listen...."

Donahue placed a hand on her sleeve. "Meg, please. Blow off steam another way," he said dryly. His expression was bland. "This sort of confrontation won't expedite matters any." Angela nodded.

The entree was served with swift precision; David Madden floated everywhere to insure that everything was perfectish.

"What do the ghosts think about your plans?" Blasing asked.

"Who cares? They are not alive," Meg replied.

"Peter cared," Angela said. "He respected their wishes."

"Is that really a problem?" Walter Bond wanted to know.

"If we're not careful, they might go on strike," Blasing said.

"That's... that's not possible," Heller sputtered, waving his fork about. He knocked over a water glass. Eva jumped up and stumbled over her chair. Blasing caught her before she fell. Eva rewarded him with a quick kiss on the cheek.

Angela tried to contain her anger; she couldn't stand the way Eva threw herself at Blasing. "Mr. Heller, where is the new brick from?" Angela asked pointedly.

"That won't be revealed until after the construction is completed. The mystery will add to sales."

"Is it from a ghost town?" Angela asked.

"I'll say nothing more."

"So, tell me more about your plans without all the flash and technology," Blasing asked Heller.

Dinner finally proceeded smoothly, the thunder rattling windows interrupted Heller several times. The Irishman spoke in detail about the northern wing, its bar, restaurant, and poker hall. He admitted the stables were a stretch, but they were definitely building a putting green. He also mentioned having catamarans and sailboats for rent in the summer.

Angela wasn't sure if it could be stopped, even if Blasing wanted to alter the plans. Unfortunately, she had the feeling he might be taken in by the excitement; but then maybe she was underestimating him.

Blasing excused himself during dessert. While he was gone, Angela heard a soft voice, "Psst. Angela! Down here." She glanced towards Blasing's chair, spotting something wispy wavering underneath the seat. She dropped her napkin, then reached for it.

Under the chair with only her head sticking out of the floor was Carrie. "I've got some important news about Mac and Heller. Blasing is being watched, so come alone." The spirit rippled and sank through the floor.

"Are you all right?" Blasing asked as he sat.

Angela jumped, then gave him a cool look that slowly warmed. "Not really. I think yesterday's accident has finally caught up with me. My back and neck are beginning to ache."

"I could work on it some more," Blasing said.

She was very, very tempted. "No, thank you. I'm going to walk a bit, stretch, then turn in. I may just need rest."

"You sure you trust me around these people?" Blasing asked.

"I may be walking among ghosts, but you're around vampires. You're a big boy now." She glanced at Eva. "Do take care of yourself."

Angela kept her pace measured. She wanted to run. What did Carrie have to say? And who was watching Blasing? And why?

ELEVEN

Angela borrowed a bellman's jacket and walked to the veranda where the wind whistled through the small greenhouse gardens. The courtyard was surprisingly dark between the blanketing sheets of lightning. White, yellow and sometimes even greenish radiance starkly illuminated the rocks, woodland statues and abundance of wintry blooms.

Two violent eruptions of thunder left Angela's ears ringing. She considered leaving, but it was still a few minutes until eleven. She wanted to hear what Carrie had to say. Who was watching Blasing and why? She suddenly wondered how he was doing among the parasites and wished she could have asked him to come along; he effused a protective aura.

Unable to reign in her imagination, Angela kept wondering if the murderer was still on the property. What would he do if he found out they were investigating? Would he come after them?

Despite her uneasiness, Angela didn't feel watched. She had discovered since she'd stopped smoking that she could vaguely sense the ghosts' presence if there was nothing else to distract her; it reminded her of being in a silent woods when something stirred.

The wind continued to rattle and buffet the small trees, bushes, and plants, but the next few minutes passed without any more lightning and little thunder. What was left rumbled in the distance. The clouds slowly parted to reveal a gibbous moon. The silvery light left the shadows fuzzy and indistinct compared to the earlier flashes of lightning. The breeze all but died, and a clearing spread out from the moon across the sky over the Pacific.

Carrie was late, Angela thought. She wondered what could be delaying her. Was she afraid Angela was being watched?

The lobby door opened and the footsteps told her two people came towards her. Angela stepped into the shadows. The sound of high heels moved toward the railing. When they stepped into view, Angela recognized Blasing with a blond from the reception.

In the moonlight, her hair and gown shimmered, and her pale complexion glowed as if silvery light on cream. Only her wide eyes and full lips seemed to define her face. "A beautifully romantic night to be in the gardens with a handsome man."

Angela made a face. She almost interrupted, but then she felt like eavesdropping. Must be the lawyer in her, she mused. Was Blasing like Peter, easy pickings for a beautiful woman?

"You are... persistent, Desireé."

"A mainstay of salesmanship and life. Don't you think one has to persevere to get what one wants?" He nodded. "Are you really the new part owner of Ghostal Shores?" She moved closer to Blasing.

"Yes, but how much is still in dispute," he began, then explained the will was being contested.

"Have you thought about offering a settlement?" Desireé asked as she rubbed her arms, acting as if cold.

"I have to make sure there's a valid case first."

"Are you a lawyer?" She sounded hopeful.

"No, I just have very good counsel."

Angela smiled. She'd try to remember that next time she was mad at him.

"The grim-faced blond who escorted you to the dinner?"

Angela stuck out her tongue.

Blasing chuckled. "She's only that way when Heller is around. She's worked with him before."

"That would explain it. I work for Eva, and fortunately, have little contact with Mr. Heller. Some call him Hellbent."

Blasing chuckled. "I've heard I've only seen him at his best. Desireé, what did you do before selling timeshares?"

"I did some... modeling and photography work. What do you think about Heller's proposals?"

"Quite an undertaking. I like many of the expansion ideas, but I'm not sure I like the timeshare idea."

"Vacation ownership," she countered. "It will support the expansion, providing the funds so a building loan isn't necessary."

"But the ghosts don't want a timeshare."

"Blasing, they're not people, they're just ghosts, a selling point for a magnificent piece of real estate."

"Does everything with you involve... sales?"

"Not everything, but most. I like to think of it as bartering. The best deal is the one where everyone walks away happy," she told him as she leaned against him. Blasing looked around, suddenly uncomfortable and rubbing the back of his neck.

"Oh!" Desiree´ exclaimed as she abruptly reached for her eye. "I lost a contact! Don't move!" She checked herself, then her fingers began searching Blasing. "Wish I had a flashlight."

"I have one." Blasing pulled a pen light from his pocket.

"A boy scout," she said. "What?" Her left earring dropped and bounced off her shoulder, then fell to the paving stones. When she squatted to reach after her fleeing earring, the second one fell free, bouncing off her shoulder and going in the opposite direction. "Hey!" She moved to catch it. Angela heard the crunch and stifled a laugh. "Damn! I found my contact."

Angela's smile widened.

Blasing found her second earring. "Here." They stood together, and Desiree´ used the opportunity to take his hand in hers. "I thought you wanted to tell me about some of your ideas for Ghostal Shores."

"I..." she began, then her watch unlatched and fell to the paving stones. "This is very odd." She pressed against Blasing. Angela was fuming. "Ow!" Desiree´ exclaimed as she backed up quickly as if pinched, then almost fell as one of her heels broke.

"Do you need help?" Blasing asked, reaching out for her.

"Something stuck me! My pin?! I think I'm bleeding." She rubbed herself, then took off her shoes.

Angela could barely contain her laughter as it bubbled around her hands. She doubled over and closed her eyes.

"What's going on here?" Desiree´ asked as she knelt to pick up her broken heel. Her dress ripped, the sound loud and echoing. Screaming, Desiree´ ran for the door.

Angela was laughing so hard she was crying, but she managed to remain silent.

"Well," Blasing began, and Angela thought she'd been discovered, "whoever you are, thank you. She wasn't my type. Do you want to show yourself?"

Angela managed to stop laughing and wiped away the tears. She watched quietly, wondering who might show. Fawn maybe? Or one of the other prostitutes? They seemed very protective of Blasing.

"I know you're here. I can feel you." After a few more requests when nothing happened, he finally went inside.

Angela waited a few minutes and managed to regain her composure. She was sure her face was red-streaked, so when she entered the lobby, she stopped in the bathroom. Fortunately, her makeup barely smeared.

She stopped at the stand and returned the valet's jacket. "Thank you, Jason."

"You're welcome, Ms. Starborne." He was tall, lean and handsome with dark brown curly hair and thick brows. Jason already needed to shave again, giving him a roguish appearance.

"How long have you worked here?"

"For seven years. I've finally worked my way up to assistant bell captain. You visit here often. Do you think this place is different?"

"What do you mean?"

"It seems to be changing. Ever since Mr. MacGuire was murdered, Ghostal Shores feels different." Jason appeared very sad.

"Do you like working here?" she asked.

He hesitated. "Yes."

"But not as much as you did?" she asked. He nodded. "Well, give it time. Maybe things will settle comfortably again."

"You're with the new owner, Mr. Madera, right?" Jason asked. Angela nodded. She wouldn't be surprised if everyone knew. "What do you think of him?"

"He's different than Peter, but he seems to be a good man."

"Oh. Wanna guess what he might do?" he asked tentatively.

"No, we'll all just have to wait and see," Angela replied. She wondered what Meg told him. "What does Meg think will happen?"

Jason appeared a bit surprised, then said, "She isn't sure either. She's even angrier and more bitter than before. I sometimes think she isn't the same woman."

"Well, give her time," Angela suggested. "Goodnight." Blasing could talk with him, but she felt it unlikely he'd been involved with Peter's murder.

Angela walked to the 1880's General Store, stopped at the doors and knocked. It was closed, the doors locked, the blinds pulled and the lights out, but none of that mattered. Carrie lived here. "Carrie, it's Angela. I'd like to talk with you."

She tried several more times, waiting for a response. Angela tried to feel for a ghost, but she hadn't felt the ghost Blasing had sensed on the veranda.

"Is there a problem, miss?" a security guard asked. His pock-marked face was friendly. His keen gaze was interrupted by a tick near his left eye.

"No, Mr. Chadwick," she said, reading his name tag. "I'm looking for Carrie, but she doesn't seem to be home. I'll try again tomorrow. Goodnight."

Where was Carrie? Angela wondered. Why hadn't she met her in the gardens? Did it have something to do with Madame Zanadane? Angela thought she should meet the woman tomorrow; the ghosts were concerned about her.

But for now, she was too tired to go searching for Carrie. If she wanted her, Carrie knew where she was staying.

When Angela opened the door and entered the suite, she was surprised to see Blasing pacing. "Ah, there you are. I was worried. You said you didn't feel well, but hadn't returned."

"I went for a walk and feel much better now." Angela was tempted to tell him she'd gotten fresh air in the gardens.

"Good. I was hoping you'd return soon so I wouldn't have to come looking for you. I don't relish walking around Ghostal Shores at night, especially alone."

"You'll get more comfortable with the ghosts. I promise."

"I feel watched all the time."

Angela tried to sense a ghost but found none. "Now?"

Blasing shook his head. "Have you seen Broderick?" He moved to the bar and began fixing himself a drink.

"No. I'm assuming you haven't either?"

He nodded. A habit she was growing to hate. "Would you like a nightcap?"

"An amaretto, please. I thought you weren't supposed to have anything to drink?"

"Ah, I haven't been mothered in a long time," he said. She flushed. "Angela, I'm past the time suggested by Dr. Landrum, and my head feels fine, although my neck is stiff. How's your shoulder?"

"Much better."

"Knock, knock," came a stiff, heavily British accent.

"Broderick?" Blasing asked, slowly spinning around in a circle.

"You asked me to let you know when I was nearby, sir," Broderick's tone made it sound as if he were enduring a silly request. The English spirit slowly appeared like an image developing on film.

"Thank you," Blasing said. "Where have you been?"

"Where are all the ghosts?" Angela asked at the same time. She hadn't seen any in the lobby.

"There is no reason for concern, miss. After the events at the sales reception, I gathered everyone together to discover if anyone had a hand in the debacle."

"And?" Blasing asked. He brought Angela her drink.

"No one there was involved."

"You're sure?" Blasing said. "Nobody retaliated against Mr. Heller for what he plans to do? The hint wasn't very subtle."

"I concur, but I am quite sure." Broderick sighed. "I suppose I will have to endure scrutiny from Madame Zanadane. Though I must admit I wish my compatriots had done something. Although they are angry at Mister Heller, he has not pushed them far enough. My companions are a weak-hearted lot."

"Who didn't attend?" Angela asked.

"As usual, Marsh, but Fawn, Grant Roberts and Carrie were also absent. Very odd. Grant and Carrie never miss a meeting. They relish the opportunity to air their views, especially if that includes bashing Mr. Heller."

"Carrie was threatened by Madame Zanadane this morning."

"Dear me," Broderick said, folding his long hands behind him.

"Should we call Madame Zanadane?" Blasing asked, looking at his watch. It was after midnight.

"No, I don't think so," Angela said, collapsing onto the couch. "If it's done, it's done."

"With your permission, Mister Madera, I will search for her posthaste," Broderick said. He looked very worried, especially for a ghost who showed little emotion.

"Go ahead," Blasing said. With a quick nod, the spirit dropped through the floor.

"Well, Mr. Madera," Angela began, "now that you've been here for two days, what do you think of Ghostal Shores?"

He sat down on the couch near her. "I love the resort, the layout, the setting, the construction...."

"But...."

"I'm still not comfortable with the ghosts."

"I still think testing your sensitivity will help."

He shrugged. "Like I said earlier, I always feel watched. Sometimes I even hear breathing. Someone is following me."

"The ghosts are justifiably curious about you. Didn't you hear the ... ladies?" She almost choked on the word "ladies." "You hold their fate in your hands." She captured his gaze by lightly touching his arm. Did he feel a spark, too? She admonished herself for having so little control over her imagination. "They are very attached to their home, and the one person they trust is dead. Remember how glad Cannon was to see you?"

"I know. I visited her after a weird occurrence on the balcony."

"Oh?" Angela had to work to keep her face innocent as he explained about Desiree. Soon she was laughing uncontrollably all over again.

"Are you all right?"

She breathed enough to be able to speak. "You describe it so well I can see it clearly. Well, Fawn was missing from the meeting, and she did appear to take... a shine to you."

"Can you feel these ghosts?" Blasing asked.

"Not like you. It has to be a ripple in a calm pool, if you know what I mean."

"Not for me, it's a buzzing noise."

"I doubt Fawn would enjoy that analogy." Angela smiled and took a sip of her drink. She was surprised how at ease, yet vibrant, she felt in his company. "You saw the presentation, or at least part of it, what do you think of the timeshare idea?"

"It has some merit."

"Some merit!" she snapped, jumping to her feet. She couldn't believe he was being so dense. "What merits? Making everyone unhappy except for Heller and some money hungry salespeople?" Blasing tried to get a word in edgewise but didn't have a chance. "None of the ghosts want it! I think you'll find the employees like things just the way they were, and I know Peter didn't want a crimeshare!"

"He felt it would restrict access, drive prices up, and prevent people from getting to meet the ghosts! He thought the ghosts could help people understand things about themselves—that what they'd done in the past affected their future but shouldn't bind them, and that if they let it, if they continued to live that way, then they too would be like ghosts! Sometimes I think he felt such a kinship with the spirits because he felt that way himself," she finished sadly.

"Why didn't you tell me this before?"

"I wanted you to see for yourself! Make your own decision, but I can't just sit back and let Meg and Heller take what he gave you. If he'd wanted Heller to have it, he would have offered him an opportunity to buy it and then just willed you the money!" She paused, regained her composure, then said coolly, "I wish you luck on your morning tour."

"Angela...." he began, but she slammed the door on his words.

Upset and restless, Blasing paced for a while. He didn't understand why Angela couldn't understand. Maybe he needed to do a better job of explaining himself. Or maybe she was just mad because he disagreed with her.

Sometimes he got the feeling they talked to each other but weren't communicating, as though they spoke in different languages. It hadn't helped that she refused to answer his earlier questions.

Still, Angela deserved better. She was trying to help him by providing intelligent counsel. And he liked the fact that she was fiery, standing up for her thoughts and Mac's wishes. He would try to help her see he was measuring what was good for everyone versus what was good for his family—for Kelly and Patrick. He wished they were here to hug; he'd call them first thing in the morning. Blasing suddenly found himself wondering if Angela was missing anyone.

Knowing that train of thought could lead to disaster, Blasing eventually found himself drawn to Mac's desk, silently hoping he could learn something about his estranged uncle. In his searching of the central drawer, he found an old, dog-eared photo of Mac with a striking woman who looked much like Meg, and figured it was Jaclyn Cassidy. Mac looked very content.

Blasing placed the photograph on the desktop and continued searching, wondering what else he might find. Clues to Mac's murder, he wondered? Not surprising, in the lowest left drawer he found a bottle of Johnnie Walker Black, a sticky glass, and a box of cigars.

When Blasing tried to open the right drawers, they gave him difficulty, as if stuck. He reached in, searching and maneuvering until he found a wedged and crumpled envelope. When he removed it, tape still trailed into the drawer. Blasing pulled out the first page, skimmed through the letter to Angela, then flipped through the papers. It was a signed copy of Mac's will! Angela would be thrilled. But why had it been hidden? He carefully tucked it away inside his jacket pocket.

Blasing continued searching, but didn't find anything of interest until he came across a .38 Smith & Wesson in the bottom drawer. He'd never thought of his uncle as the gun-toting type. Blasing examined it, finding the weapon well oiled, then wiped off his prints and put it back.

Inside the central drawer, but on the underside of the desk top, he found something stuck with tape. He worked it free, then pulled away the masking tape to uncover a key. What was this to? He would ask Broderick when he returned.

Even after an hour of searching, Blasing still wasn't sleepy. He paced for a few minutes, then stretched, finally concluding that what he really needed to do was walk. It was just after one; the bar would be open until two. He'd read the will in the lounge.

He didn't relish the idea of wandering around the resort at night, but he didn't want to let his fear of the spirits control him. Besides, they could come by as they pleased; doors and walls meant nothing to them.

Blasing walked to the door, then paused as he began to open it. After a few slow, deep breaths he felt better. He had to quit thinking the ghosts were here, there, and everywhere. With another deep breath, Blasing headed for the elevator.

So which of the female ghosts was following him? He hadn't tried to identify nor match perfumes, although that was an option. But which one smoked? And what about the dark-faced stranger? Was he watching him, too?

Blasing ran a hand through his hair, then along his collar. He didn't feel anything. If he was being watched, they weren't very close, which made him feel less crowded and a bit more comfortable.

Blasing heard the laughter long before the elevator arrived. Leaning on and laughing at each other, a well-dressed couple staggered out of the elevator, waved at him, then weaved their way along the hall.

As the elevator descended, he smelled a delicate but flowery scent, clean and fragrant as if after a spring rain, then the back of his neck itched. "Hello, Fawn," Blasing said, rubbing his neck. "Want to talk?"

A cool draft swirled about with the whisper of silk. He suddenly smelled a second, heavier scent. A tapping noise reminded him of impatient fingers, then he smelled cigarette smoke. Two ghosts? "Ladies?" Silence.

When Blasing exited, he heard a hissing noise and a sudden intake of breath. He whirled around but no ghosts appeared. He thought he felt cool drafts churn, then the doors closed.

A yelp and a soft squeal of pain made him wonder what was going on. As the doors closed, he thought he heard a hushed, "Mine!" Blasing looked around, wondering if anyone else might have heard, and found himself alone in the grand foyer.

When he reached the top of the steps, Blasing wasn't too surprised to see only a few customers in the lounge. The rest were salespeople crowded around two tables. Not wanting to become ensnared, Blasing took the long way to the darker, deserted end of the bar.

"Good evenin' ta ya," Cannon said as Blasing sat at the copper top. He didn't see her but felt the ghost's presence. "I thought maybe ya'd forgotten me."

"Cannon, you are definitely unforgettable."

The invisible spirit laughed uproariously, her joy filling the lounge. Cannon was still chuckling when she slowly appeared, smoke seeming to take on form and focus. "If ya're so silver-tongued, kind sir, why are ya here alone? Where's Angela?"

"Angry and sulking."

"Oh. Well, that happens. Say, are ya all right?" she asked. Blasing explained about being followed by ghosts, the problems Desiree´ had experienced, and what had just happened in the elevator. "Lawdy, dead or alive, ya got women fightin' over ya."

"Fighting?"

"Cat fight, I'll say. Swiping, biting and pulling hair. Maybe two of our resident ladies of the evenin' were fightin' over ya."

"Yes, I guess it did sound like that." He was quiet for a time, then ordered a barley tea with irish creme and Frangelico. "Do any of the prostitutes smoke?"

"All of them, though I think Fawn does the least."

"Seen her recently?" he asked.

Cannon shook her head. "Nor Carrie or Grant." A cup of hot water landed before him, then a tea bag slowly drifted into it. Two dark bottles followed. Cannon didn't seem to be paying much attention, but she never spilled a drop.

"So what do ya think of my home?" Cannon finally asked. Blasing recapped what had happened since he'd seen her last. "Lawdy, ya been busy, Mr...."

"Blasing."

"... Blasing. You ought to sleep just fine." His look caused her to say, "Okay, okay, so ya ain't comfortable with us yet. Ya need somethin' or somebody ta take ya's mind off of everythin'."

"What do you think about Mac's murder?" he asked quietly, then guardedly looked around. The bar cameras weren't operating as of yet.

"From what ya told me, I'd suspect everybody," she chuckled. "Maybe it's a conspiracy. Or maybe," she said, her face scrunching with serious thought, "somebody is moving in on Heller—threatening him."

"What makes you think that?" he asked.

"In the old days, they'd threaten ya first, like they did Thompson at the Goldfield, then hurt somebody. If that didn't persuade ya, then they'd kill somebody before taking final action, like burning down the place."

"Is that what happened to the Goldfield?" Blasing asked.

She nodded. "Whatcha gonna do 'bout bein' a crimeshare?"

"I don't know. Make a slow, informed decision after asking many opinions. You vote no, right?" he asked.

"I'll say, and then some!"

"But you're not angry enough to sabotage the reception?"

"Not yet, but I'm getting there."

"Broderick said none of the ghosts had enough... guts." He'd almost said spirit.

"He's right. They didn't stand up to someone when they were

alive, why should they now that they're dead?"

"Maybe because they don't have to worry about losing their lives," Blasing responded.

"Good point, ya got there. There's more than a handsome head on those shoulders."

"Thanks You'll make me blush," he said. She laughed again, shaking as if partly made of gelatin. "Have you heard anything about the stage or the new ghosts?" Cannon shook her head no. "Well, I've heard what Carrie thinks about security. What about you?"

"Some of 'em remind me of gunslingers," she chuckled, "I'll say, but then so do you! Like I said, ya need someone ta take ya mind offa things. Sometimes the mind works better when it's not being worked so hard. Have ya thought about trying ta make Angela understand, so she wouldn't be so mad at ya?" He nodded.

"Personally, since ya been askin' my opinion anyway, I think ya two make a wonderful couple," she said. Blasing just stared at her. "The kids ya'd have would be beautiful and handsome, indeed." She cocked her head. "So what do ya think? She's beautiful, classy, and as smart as any man. Smarter than most, I'll say."

"I agree with you, but I don't like to mix business with pleasure."

"Ah, that's just an excuse. Ya can't lie to me, I'm a ghost, remember, and I can see ya spirit. Yur interested in her, ya just scared ta admit it ta yourself. Why, I don't know, but think on it. I'll be back." Cannon drifted to help the couple at the far end of the bar. The regular bartender was too busy to do anything but mix drinks for the salespeople.

Blasing suddenly smelled perfume—a very familiar scent. As far as he knew, none of the hookers wore such a fragrance; it was too contemporary. He casually turned around and began searching for his companion. He found her in the server's wait station. "Jenny?"

The spirit of his wife was tall and shapely, her long dark hair swirling about her. Rosy lips, full and glistening, parted in a sad smile. Her green eyes glistened with unwept tears of love. Blasing tried to speak her name again and couldn't, the word catching in his throat. She smiled again, spoke his name, then slowly faded away.

When Cannon returned, she asked, "Are ya all right? Ya look like ya'd seen a ghost. Yes, I'd say so!"

"I thought I saw the ghost of my wife," Blasing said slowly.

Cannon was so surprised her eyebrows jumped to her hairline. "Glory! How can that be?" she finished slowly, then, "Did she give you permission to... pursue Angela?"

"What?!"

"Did she release ya so ya could pursue Angela?"

"What makes you say that?"

"Just a hunch," Cannon said as she shrugged.

"I... I don't need it," Blasing breathed. It took all his willpower not to begin searching everywhere and shouting Jenny's name. "She'd want what's best for me and the children."

"Blasing, I can tell ya really loved yur wife, and if thinking of Angela makes ya think of her, then it must be a good sign."

Blasing glanced back to the dark alcove. He didn't know what to say, but felt it was going to be a very long, sleepless night.

TWELVE

Monday morning, Angela awakened early. As she showered, then dressed in a dark pants suit, she reviewed the things she wanted to accomplish today. Several things had been forgotten yesterday because of the piecemeal selling of Ghostal Shores and the surprise announcement that Peter had a daughter. She would handle those things today, unless something else unforeseen preempted them.

Candy probably would have suggested Angela's mind had drifted to Blasing too much yesterday, which might have some basis. At least he seemed to appreciate her counsel, whether he agreed or disagreed with her—not something many men seemed to do.

She'd heard him late last night, moving and rummaging about the suite. She'd almost peeked out to see what he was doing, but figured she'd already done enough spying last night. She was a lawyer, not a detective, though sometimes the line was ambiguous.

Her first responsibility wasn't the murder investigation, but helping Blasing with the transition. Had Peter foreseen Meg's contesting of the will and failed to mention it? Maybe he just wasn't worried because the claim was baseless. But if Broderick thought Meg was Peter's daughter, then there was a good chance she was speaking the truth. Is that why Peter had been so insistent?

Blasing would be busy most of the day touring the resort with Walter Bond and Eva Dare. That thought made her whole body clench. Blasing might be poisoned, unless she wasn't giving him enough credit. He certainly seemed strong willed and minded.

"Good morning, miss, why such a grim facade, if I may be so bold?" the ghost valet asked.

"Oh, good morning, Broderick," Angela said. "You startled me."

The ghost raised an eyebrow. "Deep in the woods of thought?" She nodded. "Well, I believe I can say with confidence, that Elma would warn you about the ill effects of frowning, claiming it will ruin your beauty."

Angela laughed. "Thank you, Broderick. Yes, it is something she'd say. You know, your advice sounds better than it did for Peter."

"Rubbish," Broderick uttered as he stiffened indignantly. "That is only because he rarely wanted to do anything sensible to preserve his health. There were times I had to resist the urge to wallop him like a child who is not paying attention. I do not understand why, if he insisted on enjoying something unhealthy, he could not use moderation. That would have allowed him to enjoy it even longer."

"Just as you did."

"Of course, madam, but then, as I have heard you Americans say, hindsight is twenty-twenty. Though why you call what you speak English, I will never know. There is certainly nothing proper about it. It is such a mishmash. But as I was saying, as a ghost, I have plenty of time to ponder the past. I have discovered that as with anything else, too much reminiscing is bad for one's mental health."

"I believe Blasing would concur," she said.

"And yet, I believe when I have learned that which I need to learn, I will pass on to a better place."

"Many of the Native Americans believe the same," she said.

"Really?"

"Yes, I have been studying them. I am part Paiute."

"Indeed. Tolerance can produce such astounding results."

Angela laughed lightheartedly. "Oh Broderick, talking with you can be so enlightening. Did you see Carrie or Grant this morning?"

"No madam, neither showed up for the morning meeting, and Fawn is still AWOL."

"What about Marsh?"

"As usual, he was not in attendance; he is not missed."

"Do you believe any of the missing were involved in Heller's presentation problems last night?" Angela asked.

"Their absence is suspicious, but I will withhold judgment. I promise to bring them to you as soon as they are found. Now, would you care for breakfast? Thinking is done better on a full stomach."

"I'll catch something on the run. I have lots to do this morning."

"Not the healthiest of choices, but I do understand."

"Thank you," Angela said dryly. She glanced toward Blasing's door. It was open and the room was silent. She thought she'd gotten an early start. She wished he viewed Heller with the same eyes as she, then they could talk without her getting angry. "Has he already started his tour?"

"I believe he went walking to clear his head."

"Broderick, will you help me with an experiment?"

"Of course. Is it a legal one?"

"Well, it's not illegal. Actually it doesn't involve the law at all," she said, then reached out and touched him.

Broderick's eyebrows shot toward his thin hairline. "I... I do believe I felt that. How odd. What did you do?"

"It must be these hematite rings. Grandma Dawnjoy suggested I wear them for grounding, due to all the unusual... spiritual energies around Ghostal Shores. Saturday I was able to slap Grant Roberts."

Broderick was bemused. "Yes, I heard about that. Two days past and some of the ghosts are still abuzz. I sincerely wish I had been there to witness the event. Among the women, your reputation has been greatly elevated."

Angela chuckled as she removed a simple hematite ring off each finger. When she reached out to touch Broderick, her fingers passed through him, giving her a bit of a chill and the vague mental impression of ghosts gathering. She put the rings back on and touched Broderick without seeing images.

"Simply amazing," Broderick breathed.

"My grandmother seems to know some amazing things. Broderick, this may sound a little strange, but my grandmother suggested I perform a ceremony of protection to keep ghosts out of my room." He raised an eyebrow, looking very skeptical. "Let me explain. When I first visited here, I always felt I was being watched, just as Blasing feels. And the fact that any one of you can just wander into my room didn't leave me with a feeling of privacy."

"I understand, but you understand that we are not voyeurs," he said stiffly.

"I know that—I came to understand that—but that hasn't always been the case. So, in response to that, Grandma Dawnjoy suggested this ritual. I performed it the other night. Would you help me test its... validity? Would you walk into my room?"

"Through the door?" he asked.

"Yes, you might watch your nose, just in case."

He arched an eyebrow again, then walked forward. Part of him passed into the white door, but not much before he abruptly stopped. Broderick was rubbing his nose as he glanced stonily over his shoulder. Still partway phased, the ghost felt left, then right, searching for a way to enter. Soon, he totally disappeared.

About a minute later Broderick returned. "I tried all manner of entry, miss, including the floor and ceiling. I do not know what you have done, but I cannot enter your room."

"Great, my grandma is amazing. Thank you, Broderick."

"I would like to meet her."

"I'll mention it to her."

"Are you sure you do not care for breakfast?"

"I'll get it myself. I want to see if Madame Zanadane is in her office."

"Then I shall continue with my daily duties."

"Fine, and thank you again, Broderick," she said. "Broderick, do you remember if Peter's killer was wearing any type of jewelry?"

"No madam, I do not. I am sorry."

"That's okay. I was just wondering how you were repelled."

"If you discover something, I would like to know."

"You'll be one of the first," Angela promised as she left.

Due to the early hour, Angela encountered no one in the hall nor on the elevator. She rode to the lobby where the staff was reading the paper, drinking coffee and yawning as if it were a contest.

Angela started "tracking" from the front desk, walking along the killer's path to the lower bayview window and down the steps toward the veranda gardens. She paused at the landing where the murderer had fallen. Could he have dropped something? Or would the police have found it already?

Angela searched along the marble and under the carpet. This was where the murderer had pushed Broderick away. How had he done that? Had he come prepared for the ghosts somehow? Could he have been wearing hematite? But how would he know about such a thing?

"Can I help you find something, Ms. Starborne?" Dr. Landrum asked. He appeared ready to go jogging, appropriately dressed in a burgundy and gray warm-up suit.

"Good morning doctor. You are up early," Angela said as she stood. "Coming or going?"

"Going. Want to come along?"

"No, you look tired," she said, noticing the circles around his dark eyes. "Rough night?"

"Two apparent heart attacks. One was just anxiety, the other I believe was angina, though he's never had such an episode before. Did you lose a contact or something?" he motioned to the floor. "You were searching rather diligently, and you don't remind me of the kind of person who would go searching for pennies, lucky or otherwise."

"I lost an earring last night," she lied, not wanting to sound silly telling the truth.

"What does it look like?" he asked with a smile. "Knights in shining armor know no bounds. No task is too daunting."

She thought back, making sure he hadn't seen her last night, then said, "It's a turquoise teardrop."

He nodded and began searching. Just to continue the cover-up, Angela joined him. "How is your shoulder?" he asked.

"Fine."

"And Blasing's head?"

"As good as ever."

"I'm not sure how to take that," Dr. Landrum said, looking at her and adjusting his glasses.

"It's a womanism," Angela responded with a smile.

"I understand. I feel lucky, then, that I hold a more exalted position as a caregiver," he replied. He seemed to have found something in the corner wedged partly underneath the molding.

"Find something?"

"Nothing. Just rock," he said, then showed her his fingertip.

Angela took the chunk with a fingernail, then placed it next to her rings. It certainly appeared to match the hematite. "Oh well. I promised myself this would be the last place I'd look. I'll leave a note at the front desk and hope somebody turns it in."

"You have a lot of faith in people."

"Ghostal Shores was a classy outfit, and the clientele certainly don't need my earring to augment their finances."

"Was?"

"Sorry, I'm having some disagreement with management right now. Which reminds me, I have to get busy on some legal paperwork."

He glanced at his watch. "It's before eight. Here I thought lawyers started late and worked late. Something about being part vampire."

"You must be thinking about my compatriots. Besides, I can't sleep when my mind is whirling."

"I see. My diagnosis is that you need some exercise. Do you play tennis, Ms. Starborne?"

"Call me Angela. But no, I don't play."

"Pity. Oh well, no woman is perfect," he said with a sigh and a smile. "I am Geoff. How about dinner this evening?"

"I would like that, Geoff, but I have to check my schedule. My time isn't always my own while I'm on business."

"I certainly understand that. I eagerly await your call at extension 050. Have a great day, Angela," he said.

"Have a fun run," Angela replied. She ascended to the lobby, where she passed a broad-shouldered security guard, then headed for Old West Avenue. Was that really hematite? And even if it was, what did that prove? Ghostal Shores housed its share of crystal lovers over the years and hematite rings were as common as copper wrist bands.

None of the Old West Avenue shops were open, but Angela wanted to find Carrie, so she visited the 1880's General Store. Angela was surprised to find Angus the cat pacing back and forth, walking in and out through the door and the walls. The beast's movements made no sound, but his meows were loud and forlorn. Every now and then it rubbed against Angela's leg and meowed.

Angela banged her fist several times on the door and called to Carrie, but she didn't respond. A bellman glanced in her direction, but he didn't approach. Neurotic behavior wasn't novel among guests, she supposed.

Angela knelt by the ghost cat. "I don't know what to tell you, Angus. Can you find Carrie? Find Carrie?" The cat just looked at her as if she—not it—was expected to perform the stated miracle. "Well, if you were Lassie's ghost, you'd track her," Angela replied to a caterwaul. Angus moved on stiffly. "Be that way." Angus flicked its tail and disappeared through the door.

The large Asian, Mr. Chung, exited the elevator and walked toward the avenue of shops. The mammoth, black-clad valet carried a tray with a teapot as if it weighed nothing. Due to the size of his meaty hand, the tray looked like a plate. He passed by the general store without so much as a glance.

Angela followed him along the gallery. Mr. Chung appeared to be destined for Madame Z's—Psychic Guidance and Advice. Tarot. Palmistry. Past Life Regressions. The sign wasn't lit, but the lights inside were on, and the door was ajar.

Angela decided now was a good time to visit Madame Zanadane. After witnessing her argument with Carrie, Angela had wanted to learn more about the Canadian psychic. Was she connected with the fiery shopkeeper's disappearance? Angela stopped at the open door and knocked.

Madame Zanadane stared at Angela for long moments, her emerald and golden-flecked eyes large and luminous. With silky smooth skin, the psychic would have looked ageless if it weren't for her knowing, hypnotic eyes. She pushed a stray lock back into place among her windblown tresses of silver-streaked black.

"Good morning...." Madame Zanadane said breathlessly. "May I help you...?" The question was open-ended. "A reading about your future... perhaps.... You seem to be... searching for something or maybe someone?" She finished, though not sounding finished.

"Thanks, but no. I'm Angela Starborne. I thought we should meet."

"You were Peter MacGuire's lawyer...."

"Yes, I am still acting upon his wishes."

"As well as working for his heir?" she asked, still sounding winded. Angela nodded. As the psychic poured herself a cup of coffee, she asked, "Would you care for a cup...?" Her attention still seemed a bit removed from the room.

"No thank you."

Madame Zanadane lit a cigarette, then took two deep drags. Angela fought the urge. "Have a seat." Her gaze regaining focus, Madame Zanadane gestured to the chair in front of her desk.

Angela felt as if she'd stepped into a different realm. The walls were lined with elegantly woven tapestries, each a magnificent replication of a tarot card from the Thoth Deck. The sun blazed above two celebrating angels surrounded by the signs of the Zodiac. The Ace of Cups was a magnificent single cup gushing a radiant rainbow. The third depicted a woman with long hair pouring crystallized matter from two bowls to create the universe.

A single, antique lamp of gold and stained glass sat near the edge of her large L-shaped table. It was covered in deep, purple velvet, and along its edges, amethysts, pink quartz and tourmalines lay. Two crystal balls were predominantly displayed and reflected the lamp's colorful light to create rainbows along the walls. A phone and several other modern conveniences looked odd among the different stacks of cards, a hammered gold bowl containing runestones, and a crystal tree from which a variety of stone fetishes dangled.

"This is Mr. Chung, my companion...." The massive Asian tipped his hat and bowed slightly. Angela nodded. A host of Asian manservants from movies came to mind before she pushed away such nonsense. "What may I do for you, Ms. Starborne?"

"I'm helping Blasing Madera in his due diligence—evaluating the assets and employees of Ghostal Shores. He wanted to meet with you this morning, but the salesmen have him this day."

"I pity him...."

"He wanted me to ask you about Peter MacGuire," Angela continued. Madame Zanadane's eyes narrowed fractionally. "Do you believe his ghost resides at Ghostal Shores?"

Madame Zanadane relaxed. "Eh? Oh, I have not sensed him within the ether surrounding Ghostal Shores."

"Then you don't believe he's here?"

The psychic shook her head. "I believe he has moved to a higher vibrational plane. Many miss him... staff and guests alike, and although he is not a ghost, his spiritual energies linger...."

"Have you tried a séance?" Angela asked.

"I felt no such need...."

"Did you know Peter MacGuire very well?"

"Hardly at all, my dear, though Sean Heller and I have been acquaintances for a long time...."

"How long?"

"I apprenticed with a woman in Palm Springs, quite a change from my native Vancouver... so hot..." she said, even now wiping her brow. "Yet certain truths are found evident in heat...." Madame Zanadane seemed lost in the past for a moment. "Jera Myles was a student of Edgar Cayce, as well as my mentor... while working with her I met a much younger Sean Heller.... We have never been close, but Jera used to read for friends of his...." She paused for a long drag on her cigarette. "Jera and I parted ways after a time... she became interested in making money rather than in helping people...."

"Did you also meet Peter?" Angela asked.

The psychic shook her head. "No... I didn't meet him until Ghostal Shores opened.... By then, the years had changed me—I no longer simply wanted to perform readings in Vancouver, but wished to aid folks all over the world. Troubleshooting. Exploring. Learning... Pushing the boundaries...." Her eyes became lost again, her long fingernails tapping her coffee cup.

"The mysteries of the cosmos are vast.... Most try to study only that which we already know. I wish to delve into that which has defied us... To know about life after death... or is it before? Caught in some duo-dimensional vibratory state of the soul, the ghosts may hold the key to unlocking what's beyond...."

Her eyes returned to Angela. "I am sorry, I digress, eh.... No, I didn't know Peter MacGuire, but I'd heard about Ghostal Shores. The more I heard, the more curious and fascinated I became.... I suddenly realized it was my... destiny to work here...." She was quiet for a moment. "Here, among the thirty-some ghosts, the metaphysical opportunities are limitless. There is no place like this anywhere else in the world...."

"Then this is a prestigious position?"

"Absolutely... my contemporaries in metaphysics are jealous, though most of these are well-wishers, too.... As the case may be, some of them are here this week: the Great Xantini, Dr. Strange, and Julia Zephren will be stopping by this morning... we are having breakfast.... Would you care to join us...?"

Listening to her was making Angela's head spin. "No thank you. When Ghostal Shores first opened, did you apply for a job?"

Madame Zanadane's look was penetrating, instead of distant, as if she was trying to read Angela's mind. "Yes, but they were not interested. But a decade is not too long to wait for destiny...." the psychic said. "I am persistent if nothing else.... As I said, I wanted to work here.... I saw myself working here—desire and expectation are the keys—feeling it... living as if it had happened.... The mysteries to be explored are untold...."

"And the clientele pays well?"

Madame Zanadane continued on, "... There is so much to learn from the ghosts.... We may be on the verge of breaking through an etheric barrier to a higher vibration and a newer, clearer, understanding of how the Universe works... How we work...."

"Then you were willing to give up much to get the job?"

"Of course. I am sorry that Mr. MacGuire's death created my opportunity; I did not wish ill upon him...." She smiled briefly. "The Wheel of Karma turns relentlessly, and I already have enough baggage to dispose of without adding anything."

Angela wasn't mollified, thinking Peter's death meant little more than the removal of another roadblock to Madame Zanadane. "Seems you were still in close enough contact with Heller, so that when Peter died, you were ready to step into the job."

"Are you sure you're not investigating a murder here?" Madame Zanadane asked sharply.

"I'm investigating all the changes that have occurred in the last week. There have been very, very many."

"'Tis true, eh? Life can change quickly.... Peter MacGuire's health was failing rapidly, and he didn't expect to live out the year... That is why I was prepared. I had foreknowledge, and that in itself is power...

"Sean often told me he didn't understand how Mac handled the ghosts.... Sean is unnerved by the spirits and wanted someone to speak their language—so he reconnected with me...."

"That is your official capacity?" Angela asked. She was surprised to hear Peter had been deathly ill. Is that why he had pushed for a will?

"Yes, I am the ghost liaison...." she said with a hint of a self-satisfied smile.

"Then Broderick reports to you?"

"No, this place is not run by the military.... They come to me when they wish to discuss things that involve the living or Ghostal Shores itself.... It's taking time to gain their trust, but that is understandable. One of them—Carrie—and I often clash... she resents my intrusion.... She's angry over the death of Peter MacGuire.... He had a natural affinity for dealing with spirits...."

"So Heller simply wants you to communicate with them?"

"No," she appeared sad, and even a bit concerned. "He wishes more... he wishes me to help... police them, but I believe they police themselves. None seem malicious nor angry, and beyond cleansing them, there is little one can do to a ghost... And that would only happen in extreme measures.... I assure you...."

"Have you had to use such a threat?"

"Ms. Starborne, I do not threaten.... I simply foretell that which will be." Her slight smile failed to touch her eyes.

"Are you having any troublesome ghosts?"

"I do not think so...."

"But Sean Heller does?" Angela asked. The psychic simply smiled, put out her cigarette and folded her hands. "What do you think your job is?"

"To understand the ghosts.... To help them for whatever reason they are still on earth and use this knowledge for those of us who continue to persevere from day to day...."

"Are you to ask their opinions?"

"No, young lady, I am not, but at times I do...."

"And do you attempt to placate them on the timeshare proposal?"

"There are disadvantages to having to work for someone, and my latitude is more strict than I'd like.... If it were my choice, the ghosts would be more integral in running the resort... but.... Ah... my friends have arrived."

Angela turned and studied the odd-looking trio. Between the tall men, the lithe woman seemed sprite-like. Madame Zanadane waved to the broad-chested man dressed all in black, his dark trousers loose and billowy. "Ms. Starborne, may I introduce you to the Great Xantini, Master Mentalist."

His black eyes glittering, the darkly bearded man kissed her hand. "A pleasure," he said, his voice very deep. He was meticulously groomed, and his eyes were knowing, his stare piercing as if he could see what she was thinking. With a bow and a hint of a smile, he stepped back.

"From Boston, Dr. Devlin Strange, expert in mystical objects of power and a collector of such antiquities...." The tall man's face seemed obscured by the heavy shade of his fedora, but the red glow from his pipe hinted at angular features. He simply touched his cap and nodded.

"And last but not least, the lovely and enchanting Julia Zephren."

"Hello. Your name sounds familiar," Angela said.

"I have a magical stage act in Las Vegas, Ms. Starborne," the diminutive blond replied with a perky, southern accent. As though having come from a show, Julie Zephren wore bright blue, green, and gold with a matching cape and tall high heels. "I use sleight of hand and body as well as my other skills...."

"Telekinesis and object teleportation," the Great Xantini finished for her. "For those who believe in such, that is."

"Have ya seen my show, Ms. Starborne?" Julie asked.

"I'm sorry to say I haven't."

"Will you join us for breakfast?" the Great Xantini asked.

"I would but...."

"...You still have much to accomplish this morning," he finished for her, surprising her. That was almost exactly what she was going to say. "Maybe some other time then."

"If the opportunity affords itself," Angela replied. "Thank you for your time, Madame Zanadane. I'm sure Blasing will want to speak with you soon."

"My door is always open...." she said breathlessly.

"Ms. Starborne," Xantini began, "you are searching for something, yes?" She nodded. "May I offer my services?"

"Another knight," she laughed.

"Excuse me?"

She was glad to see he didn't know everything. "The ones in shining armor."

"Ah, I see. Thank you. Do not let your past get in the way of your feelings for the man who occupies your thoughts."

"What?" Angela stuttered. Was Blasing really on her mind that much? Was she that obvious?

"Do not worry. I see much that others don't even suspect," his eyes were cavernous and very knowing. Angela felt a bit uncomfortable. "Let go of the bitterness. Bad memories can become the wound that will not heal if the scab is constantly picked."

"Thank you, Mister...."

"Efrem. Efrem Xantini."

"Efrem, lunch may be in our very near future," Angela said. His smile was dashing in response.

As Angela walked to the elevator, she thought Xantini might be able to tell her quite a bit about Madame Zanadane. Angela didn't trust her; the psychic was too fanatical. Besides, she was curious about what the Master Mentalist had to say about Blasing.

THIRTEEN

Walking the beach had not helped Blasing organize his thoughts, let alone clear them. But then neither had talking to his children, although he felt better centered for it. They were a dose of normality; thanks to Broderick, Patrick and Kelly had to hear all about Ghostal Shores.

Blasing sighed heavily, then headed up the cliffside steps. Angela's observations on Mac's murder had kept him thinking. And thinking. And thinking. Who had murdered Mac and why?

As Blasing passed through the courtyard veranda, Sven waved to him. Blasing smiled back and found himself growing more and more concerned about the ghosts' feelings. He liked Broderick and Cannon, and this was their home. As he passed the landing where the murderer had fallen, Blasing thought of Mac again.

What if the murderer had never left? Was Angela in danger because of their investigation? He shouldn't even be thinking about women, and yet, had he really seen Jennifer's ghost? And if so, why now? To tell him to stay away from Angela? To wish him the best? To give her blessing? Or had Cannon been right? He'd just thought about Jennifer because he'd sensed a kindred spirit in Angela?

When he entered the lobby, Blasing silently chuckled at the couple checking out, sleepy kids in tow and one cradled in its mother's arm. Hit the road before they awaken fully, he thought and smiled. The children moved as automatons, directed and guided by their parents this way and that. Blasing suddenly realized he needed to tell Angela that above all else, he worried about his children and their future. Maybe then she'd better understand him.

A quiet elevator ride and a short walk took him to the suite. It appeared empty and felt the same, although Angela's door was closed. "Broderick! Are you here?"

A knock sounded from the door, and Blasing peered through the spy-hole before opening the door to an unshaven man wearing a long, tan jacket over his sheriff's uniform. "Hello?"

"Morning. I'm Sheriff Middleton of the Marin County Sheriff's department." The big-boned sheriff had long, flat features, and short, gray-streaked brown hair. His large, round glasses couldn't hide his rheumy eyes, nor the bags below them.

"Do you have identification?" Blasing asked. With a grimace, the sheriff displayed his badge. Blasing inspected it, then nodded.

Sheriff Middleton hitched up his pants. "I received Ms. Angela Starborne's message, and since I was close, thought I'd stop by."

"She's out, but my name is Blasing Madera."

"Peter MacGuire's nephew?" he asked. Blasing nodded. "My condolences on your uncle and being the new owner of this place."

"Any reason I wasn't informed of his death last weekend?" Blasing asked briskly.

The sheriff appeared confused. "You weren't?" Blasing shook his head. "Mr. Heller convinced us it'd be best if he informed you."

"Interesting," Blasing said tightly. "Sorry, I'm being rude. Please come in. I'd like to speak with you if you have time."

"Certainly." The sheriff walked inside. "Mind if we speak on the balcony?" He motioned to the glass doors facing the expansive plain of the Pacific. The resort and the cliffs were in shadow, but the sunlight had pierced the fog sparkling atop the waves.

"Not at all," Blasing said.

As soon as they stepped outside, the sheriff lit a cigarette. "Gotta break this habit one day," he muttered. "Seems like a body can't smoke anywhere in California anymore, except outside."

"Sheriff, I know some things in murder cases are restricted information, but what can you tell me about my uncle's murder?"

"Not as much as I would like, I hate to admit. Not damn near enough." He took a deep drag. "Simply put, I and others are frustrated. Having all these ghosts around doesn't help the situation." He paused for another long drag. "I don't even believe in ghosts, but...." He threw up his hands.

"Neither did I," Blasing said understandingly.

"I wish I hadn't mentioned that Doris called the Psychic Hotline."

"Sheriff?"

"Sorry," he let out a sigh. "Your uncle was murdered by an unknown assailant Saturday, January 10 at 11:15 P.M. The assailant incapacitated two security guards by using chloroform. Neither was seriously injured. The murderer robbed the safe of over forty thousand dollars in cash and some jewelry. Besides Broderick the ghost," he paused, obviously having difficulty believing what he'd said, "there weren't any witnesses to the shooting, although several people saw the assailant running down the stairs."

"Did those descriptions match Broderick's?" Blasing asked.

"Yeah, but it's been hard to get my superiors to take a ghost's statement seriously."

"Can you describe the killer?" Blasing asked. Middleton's description fit what Blasing had seen through Broderick's eyes. "And he's still loose?" The sheriff nodded. "Any clues to his identity?" Blasing asked, still trying to match Cash and the murderer in his mind.

"I talked with almost all the employees and most of the ghosts." He grimaced. "We haven't ruled out anyone, we're checking ex-employees files."

"You believe someone with knowledge of Ghostal Shores was involved?" Blasing asked. The sheriff nodded as he took another drag. "Couldn't it have been an inside job?"

"We've checked that possibility. Like I said, I've talked to most of the employees, and I have never ever met a man who was so widely liked, but then maybe it's all relative."

Blasing caught the thinly veiled reference comparing Heller to Mac. "How did the assailant escape?"

"He fled down the steps, then up the stairs from the balcony. He was bleeding, so there was a trail of blood. We lost his tracks along the cliffs near the construction area."

"And your thoughts are?"

"I'm sorry, Mr. Madera, I really am. We still can't figure how the damned guy escaped. I tell you this, I think the slaying was well planned; otherwise, we would have caught the assailant by now. There's only one road off Point Reyes, and we blocked it. Maybe he fled by boat, or if someone really wanted to pay big bucks, they could have used a helicopter. But there aren't any signs to indicate any type of craft landed on the beach."

"Was he disguised, maybe?"

The sheriff rolled his eyes, then took a deep drag. "Possibly. Seems he just disappeared into thin air, almost like a ghost."

"But a ghost would have disappeared directly from the office."

"Yeah, so I've been told. Despite what the laughing boys back at the office say, I'd never convince my superiors a ghost murdered your uncle even if it was true."

"Do you even harbor that thought?" Blasing asked.

"Hell no, like I said, I don't believe in ghosts."

"An open mind might help with this case," Blasing suggested. The sheriff shrugged. "Then you won't believe this, either." Blasing related what had happened when Broderick touched him and what he'd seen, then guardedly expressed his and Angela's concerns.

"Yeow!" the sheriff exclaimed, dropping his cigarette. "Burned myself. Mr. Madera, that's the damndest thing I've ever heard. And if we were anywhere else, I'd think about arresting you for being under the influence. Are you trying to tell me Peter MacGuire wasn't in the wrong place at the wrong time? That someone wasn't gunning for Heller? That somebody had it in for your uncle? I mean, people loved the guy. It's almost unnatural."

"It's a possibility."

"I don't know. I think this place does things to one's brain." The sheriff looked at Blasing for a long moment, then said, "I hate to tell you this, but I'm not convinced this place is safe. We may have to shut it down."

"I think after interviewing customers you'll conclude that people come here to get pleasantly scared," Blasing said, echoing Angela's words. He was surprised to find himself defending the resort. If it hadn't been a problem for over ten years, why would it change now? The arrival of the stagecoaches? Mac's death? "You know, I feel there's a lot you're not telling me."

"Well, you know what they say about intuition. That and three-fifty will get you a mocha latté," he replied stonily.

Blasing thought he'd hit a nerve. "I can't relate how much confidence you inspire."

"I'm sorry, Mr. Madera. Believe it or not, we're talking to some psychics," his mouth twisted as if the word tasted foul, "in the Bay Area. If we can't get a better handle on this soon, we're thinking about... about bringing them in." He sounded defeated.

"Have you talked with the house psychic?"

"She claims it was a simple matter of money, but couldn't help us with who. Just said they were connected with the resort. My wife, Doris, loves this stuff. I ought to let her investigate."

"Where can you be contacted later today?" Blasing asked. "I

know Ms. Starborne would like to speak with you about my uncle's corpse and its handling."

"And you don't?" The sheriff's expression was deadpan.

"I was told it would be held until an autopsy had been completed."

"Yes, it's held in case other tests need to be performed."

"Well, they probably will," Blasing told the confused sheriff, then explained about Meg's claim.

"It just keeps getting weirder, doesn't it? I'm just glad that guy from THE ENQUIRER is long gone. My name would probably get splashed all over the checkout stands!"

"I'll admit I was surprised I hadn't heard about my uncle's murder."

"We're trying to keep it low key. Any hint of ghostly involvement and we'll have amateur investigators impeding the operations," he said, giving Blasing a firm look.

"Why should anyone interfere when you're doing such a fine job?" Blasing asked bitterly.

"Have Ms. Starborne call my office and speak to James Donahue in forensics. He might be able to help," the sheriff said, heading back inside. At the door, he turned around and said, "Mr. Madera, where were you on the night of the 10th of January?"

"Working. Call my partner, Rich Steele, Central Sierra Security in South Lake Tahoe."

"I'll do that. Have a good day," Sheriff Middleton said as he headed for the door.

"Not likely," Blasing said, thinking of the sales tour.

Late in the afternoon, after spending a good portion of the day with Walter Bond and his customers, Blasing headed to security. Bond had been a nonstop talker—a wheeler and dealer, though very suave and professional—and the Spanish couple from Madrid had almost been as verbose. It didn't help that Blasing felt ghost-watched the entire time. Between Everita's cigarettes and Manuel's cologne, he couldn't tell if it was his normal specter or another spirit.

"Bonjour, Blasing," said Eva as she glided elegantly toward him.

"Hello, Eva."

"It must be my lucky day," she continued, lips pursing as she checked her lipstick. The dark Frenchwoman was dressed in a low-cut, beige blouse, wide black belt and tan skirt nearly slit from knee to hip. The black hose made her high heels seem to be a natural extension of her legs, making her as tall as Blasing.

"You look pleased with yourself. Having a good afternoon?" He suddenly felt the familiar tingling and itching.

"Yes, and it just got better," she said, her dark eyes dancing. "I made THE first sale and want to celebrate." Her smile was wide and hungry as her gaze caressed him. "Care to start by sharing a bottle of Dom? Oops," she said suddenly. She managed to catch her falling earring.

Blasing wondered what Rich would say about him turning down a beautiful woman in order to talk with the Chief of Security. "Thank you, but I still have work to do right now."

"Surely you wouldn't prefer someone else's company to mine?"

"Ah, business before pleasure. It's one of the disadvantages of being an adult." A whiff of cigarette smoke came and went.

Eva wrinkled her nose. "But there are other advantages. How about dinner? The dessert I offer is for mature..." she didn't finish, stopping in mid-sentence as her necklace burst, diamonds and opals bouncing off her bosom and bounding across the carpet as if racing for cover. "I...." Her belt suddenly came undone, sliding down her legs. Several men stopped to appreciate the event.

"Enough," Blasing told his ghostly guardian.

"What's happening?!" Eva cried as her skirt slid. She grabbed it, then raced off toward the nearest bathroom. Blasing began to gather the wayward jewels.

"That's one of the last things I expected to see," Dr. Landrum said. The doctor was casually dressed and wearing Ray Bans.

"What's that?"

"A beautiful woman running away from you."

"Actually, it's becoming the norm," Blasing replied.

"Excuse me?" Dr. Landrum appeared very confused. Blasing explained about his ghostly chaperon. "That's definitely a hindrance if you enjoy flirting, not to mention accepting any of the invitations. You can have her."

"Well, then it's a good thing flirting isn't uppermost on my mind right now," Blasing said as he stood.

"And does Ms. Starborne have this problem?"

"What problem?"

"Falling apart around you?"

"No, but that could be because she isn't being seductive nor suggestive," Blasing said, wondering what he'd do if Angela did.

"Really? I ran into her this morning looking for a lost earring. After what you said, I thought, well... Ahem. How are you feeling, Mr. Madera?"

"Call me Blasing, please."

"If you'll call me Geoff."

"You know, so much was going on, I almost forgot about the accident," Blasing said, craning his neck. It made him think of the stagecoaches. What had they brought? Two pairs of drivers, the shadow-faced ghost with cat's eyes, and an emerald-eyed beauty with an air of regal aloofness? "I'm still a bit stiff, but fine."

"Good. I don't like complications when I'm on vacation," he said with a smile.

"For a doctor, you sure make the rounds."

"Yes, as part of my 'job' here, I do make house calls. And with modern technology, I can be found anywhere, so I don't have to be locked up in an office on a beautiful day."

"I carry my pager more than I'd like," Blasing said.

"Well, I don't always like being found, but with emergency medicine, it allows me to roam. My life is usually wait, then rush. Yesterday was the same way. Nothing until after midnight when two guests complained of chest pains."

"Caused by seeing ghosts?"

"No frightening episodes, if that's what you mean," Dr. Landrum replied.

"I did. Is it me, or do there seem to be a lot of problems?"

"Even before I started working here."

"When did you start?" Blasing asked.

"Tuesday after Peter MacGuire died. I'm substituting for Dr. Reasons. He's ill. What are you driving at Blasing?"

"I was just curious if you'd read the medical log prior to your first day?"

"Yes. As a standard practice. I go back about a week or two to see if there are any trends or outbreaks."

"Do you remember if much happened the day after my uncle was murdered?"

"If I remember correctly, it was a crazy day. There were about a dozen incidents, about half of those belonging to staff."

"Such as?"

"One of the valets was clipped by a car out front. Nothing too serious, though he took a couple of days off. Mr. Cash slipped in the shower and broke his wrist. Somebody in security was injured installing equipment. Stitches were required. A cook slipped in the kitchen. Chief Porter cut himself. There's more. Dr. Reasons attributed it to a mass hysteria/group stress sort of situation."

"But since construction has been delayed, there's been a lot less accidents. Been sort of nice." Dr. Landrum smiled. "Now if people can just stay out of car accidents in the front drive, I'll only have to deal with medical emergencies."

Blasing laughed. "We'll try. I promise. I'll drive next time."

"That should go over well. So, what do you think about Ghostal Shores?" Dr. Landrum asked.

"It's a magnificent but strange place, with great employees who love their jobs and ghosts that might as well be people, except they walk through walls and such."

"You sound like you're adjusting."

"That's frightening to consider, but I'm trying."

"If you ever need to talk," he offered, "I have some background in counseling."

"Thanks. Did any of it concern ghosts?"

"No, but losing loved ones is traumatic."

"Yes it is," Blasing said.

"What do you think of your partner?"

"I don't really know him well enough to say. And I may have more than one partner," Blasing began, then explained about Meg. He was finding the doctor a very easy conversationalist.

"At least you have good counsel," Dr. Landrum replied.

"I have confidence in Angela. She's very dedicated to my uncle," he finished, thinking of her anger with him for even considering Heller's proposals. She was certainly beautiful when angry.

"If you don't mind me asking, are you and Angela... involved?"

"No..." Blasing stammered a bit.

"Well, you are staying in the same room...."

"Suite."

"Sorry. It's just you two seemed... comfortable together. I didn't want to step on any toes. Is she Jewish by chance?" the doctor asked. Blasing shook his head. "Do you think she might be interested in someone who is?"

"I don't know. Why don't you ask her yourself?"

"I may do that," he said. "Unless other opportunities avail themselves. Have a nice evening, Blasing."

"Happy hunting," he said, then scratched his neck. Blasing sensed a flurry of action, but didn't see or smell anything. Yet, he felt an air of heaviness—a sense of brooding.

On a white house phone set in an alcove, Blasing called security and asked for Chief Porter. He would be glad to see him right now. As Blasing hung up the phone, he felt anger behind him—a seething, radiating rage.

Blasing turned quickly, feeling hundreds of hot needles rippling along his back, then burning across his chest. In the corner of the alcove, large cat-like eyes blinked quickly. The shadow seemed to quiver as if an animal tensing to spring, then a heartbeat later, nothing was there. Even the anger was gone.

Another threat? Blasing didn't know what to think. As he descended the steps to the lobby, the anger seemed to return. He watched the shadows, but never saw anything, although the tingling and itch were still present. Who was this spirit with the feral eyes? He must have been in that second stage. But why was he angry?

His slit-throat warning was still fresh on Blasing's mind when he reached security. "Hello," Blasing told a bearded and big-boned man working on a piece of equipment. "I'm here to see Chief Porter." The man pointed with a screwdriver toward the manager's office.

Blasing knocked on the frame of the open doorway. "Chief Porter, I'm Blasing Madera."

"Come in, Mr. Madera." As Chief Porter stood, he motioned with his bandaged left hand for Blasing to enter. The head of security was short and built like a bowling ball with very broad shoulders. His office overflowed with stacked electronic equipment, empty boxes, and operating manuals. "Would you like coffee?"

"No thanks," Blasing replied as he sat. "Makes me edgy this late in the day. Ghostal Shores makes me edgy anyway."

"I hear that. I've worked here over a year, and I'm still not totally comfortable."

"I'm sure the spirits pose quite a security problem."

"When you can walk through a wall, you can go anywhere you want," Chief Porter replied. "Our new system won't help much there because ghosts can't be photographed or caught on video."

"At least you'll be able to see what else is going on."

"Exactly."

"How about motion detectors?" Blasing asked.

"Now that's an idea," Porter replied, his eyes brightening.

"I've given it some thought. Sometimes there are... breezes. Are you doing the installation yourself, in-house?" Blasing asked. Chief Porter nodded. "Is that how you hurt your hand?"

"No, I sliced my hand cutting a bagel. But you didn't come here to talk about my kitchen adventures."

"You're right. I wanted to ask some questions about the murder."

"I expected as much. Shoot," he said, then stuck a pen in his mouth. He commenced chewing on the end.

"Two of your men were incapacitated, correct?" Blasing asked. Porter nodded. "How are they doing?"

"For the most part, fine, although Max is still having some trouble remembering the day. When he fell, he hit his head."

"Did either of them see their attacker?"

"No. I wrote them up, but I haven't fired them. I'm expanding and I need experienced men. I can't afford to fire them right now."

"Do you have any clues to the murderer's whereabouts?"

The big man shook his head. "We're helping the sheriff's department. They think it might be an ex-employee. I've heard more than one threaten Mr. Heller."

"Is Heller a hard boss to work for?"

"A little," the security chief hedged.

"I guess I'll find out myself. If you don't mind, I'd like to look at your personnel files."

"Fine by me. Just clear it with Mr. Heller first."

More stonewalling, Blasing thought. "I will. I noticed your men look like pros. Where do you get them?"

"From all over California. Ex-cops. Industrial security." He examined the gnawed pen. "Prison guards. Security companies. I prefer experienced men, and with what Mr. Heller is paying, we can usually draw the right kind of people."

"Some of them look a bit rough."

"You're probably talking about the guys we got from Folsom Prison. You work security, right? Run your own company?" Porter asked. Blasing nodded. "Hey, you coming on board? It might make things easier to have someone with a like mind."

"I haven't decided what I'm going to do. Can you tell me what you're trying to do with security?"

"Make people feel safer. We have a lot of rich patrons and a bad reputation could severely put a crimp in our business." Porter hopped lithely to his feet where he paced. "We're adding about 50 percent more staff and putting in the surveillance systems. All public rooms and hallways will be monitored. Eventually we'll include the elevators. Outside cameras will be installed this summer. Right now we patrol the entire resort on foot, paying particular attention to the delivery entrance and near the front desk. We didn't think robbery was too feasible because of our location, but...." He looked dejected, as if everyone had personally let him down. "We lost a good man and tarnished our reputation. We need people to feel safe again."

While they were talking capabilities and future expansion of the system, a voice interrupted them. "Knock, knock, sir." The voice was full of tedium.

"Broderick?" Blasing asked. The ghost valet appeared to slowly solidify into existence. One glance at Porter told Blasing the security chief was far from comfortable with ghosts.

"Mrs. Wilson called. Kelly is very sick."

"I'd better call," Blasing said. "Chief Porter, thank you for your time."

"You know we'll be turnkey here real soon."

"I'll be there."

Blasing and Broderick departed, the ghost valet looking miffed. "What's wrong?" Blasing asked as he headed for a phone.

"I do not care for those people. They remind me of rogues and ruffians. I simply do not understand why we need a psychic and more of the watch. A ghost did not kill Master MacGuire."

"I know. I'm trying to look into it. I still need to talk with Madame Zanadane."

"I am not sure you should bother, sir. She is very... how do you

Americans say it? Ah yes, 'out there'."

"If it makes you feel any better, Broderick, there's something about security that bothers me, too. Any news about the new ghosts? Or Carrie and Grant Roberts?"

"No, sir."

Blasing stopped at the nearest phone, dialed the operator, then called home. "Yes, Mrs. Wilson. What's wrong? How high? Vomiting too? Yes, take her to the urgent care center. Call me when you know something. Sure. Put her on. Kelly dear, everything is going to be all right, she's taking you to the doctor. Yes. Yes. If you're not better tomorrow, I'll come home. Bring Broderick?" He looked at the ghost valet and received a raised eyebrow in response. "I'll see if he's interested. Yes, I love you, too. Get well, honey-bun." He hung up.

"Is it serious, sir?"

"It might be. Kids can have a fast fever one minute, then be running around laughing the next. Still, one can't be too careful."

At the suite, Blasing checked for signs of surveillance equipment. A thorough search revealed the place was clean. Still restless, Blasing paced for a few minutes. "Broderick, I'm going stir crazy. I need some fresh air."

"What do you have in mind, sir?"

"I don't..." Blasing began. "The construction area."

"Really? If I may be so bold to ask, why sir?"

"I felt a ghost there Saturday and thought it might be Mac. I'd like to find out if I'm right. If nothing else, maybe I can confront the ghost following me without making a fool of myself in front of everybody. I'm tired of being watched and threatened."

FOURTEEN

"You were threatened?" Broderick asked as they left the suite. "When?" The valet sounded shocked and outraged, but his expression changed very little. Only his eyes and jaw hardened.

"The first day I arrived." Blasing described his antagonist, especially his feline eyes. "He was in the second stage." While they waited for the elevator, Blasing related his encounter outside the bathroom.

"Why did you keep this news from us, sir?" Blasing shrugged. The elevator doors opened, and Blasing stepped inside. "The motion he made was an hourglass?" Broderick asked. Blasing repeated the motion. "Something about time. Hmmm."

At the second floor, four couples joined them. All were dressed to impress in lavish evening attire. "Good evening, ladies and gentlemen," Broderick began as he drifted above their heads. "Getting an early start to the evening repast?"

"Cocktails, then dinner," the pretty woman in a pink chiffon dress replied. Unlike the others, the brunette appraisied Blasing instead of looking at Broderick.

"Might I recommend the swordfish. It is absolutely succulent when topped with a sauce of dill seed and dijon mustard."

"Sounds good, thank you," her companion, a darkly-complected and roguishly good-looking man replied. The couples bombarded Broderick with questions, seemingly unaware that the Englishman was a ghost and couldn't taste anything. Blasing found it ludicrous.

Everyone got off at the first floor, stepping into the Cathedral to the Coast. A number of people milled about the foyer, taking in the soon-to-come sunset. Golden light poured through the westward bay window and turned the cathedral into a living flame. With every step, the fiery reflections writhed along the mirrors. Several of the women ah-ed, and their escorts nodded. The sky overhead appeared clear, but scattered dark clouds floated on the horizon, sunlight igniting the fringes of the purple-black masses.

"I apologize, sir," Broderick said as they descended the front steps. "I do get sidetracked sometimes."

"It's all right. Customer Service is number one. So, when was the last time you tasted something?"

"Dinner at the Goldfield the night I died in the fire. It was a 16 ounce prime rib topped with mushrooms and onions, and scalloped potatoes on the side. I wish I had been more hungry." Broderick's face held a rapturous expression. "At least my last meal was a fine one. Now sir, before you sidetrack me further, you said something about threats. Plural. You have only mentioned one."

Blasing told him about the visitation while on the phone with Chief Porter. "Until then I thought the first might have been a hallucination. Are you sure it's not anybody you recognize?"

"Absolutely, but I will continue to investigate. Maybe there is some merit to what Missy claimed she saw. Do you feel watched now?" Broderick was rubbing his temples with his fingers.

"Vaguely," Blasing said.

"Pardon me while I search the grounds for that impudent hussy, Fawn," Broderick said, then suddenly disappeared. Blasing didn't think he'd ever get comfortable with the Englishman's departures. Soon, he didn't sense Broderick or any other spirit.

Upon pushing his way under the caution sign and rope bordering the construction area, Blasing sensed a ghostly presence once again. "Broderick?" His voice echoed through the skeletal structures. Some brick had been laid, as well as stone and concrete foundations to anchor the framing of the northern expansion. The unfinished structure still reminded Blasing of a long dead beast, its ribs standing stripped in the setting sunlight. The shadows were long and thick, covering the yard.

Blasing tried to capture his runaway imagination, then called out several more times. When Broderick didn't respond, Blasing walked to the stack of bricks where he'd felt Mac's ghost yesterday. Blasing was immediately overwhelmed—the itching and biting nearly driving him mad. He stumbled away until the sensation stopped.

"Mac!" Blasing began. Then, "Whoever is here, show yourself!"

"Blaise!" came a voice, then the air shimmered as a stout ghost appeared. "I... Leave! It's dangerous here!" The spirit suddenly faded.

"MAC! Wait! Who killed you? What's going on?"

A movement among the shadows near the door of the foreman's trailer caught Blasing's attention. The darkness quivered and stretched long, then paled as a ghost wearing a long, white jacket appeared. His eyes were yellow-green and shone hatefully from the shadows of his hat brim. The blackness within his open jacket seemed to shift and roll, ready to ooze forth.

"Who are you?" Blasing asked. "What do you want?" The spirit moved forward a few steps, then just as suddenly, disappeared.

"Sir, who are you talking to?" Broderick asked.

"Did you see him? I mean, them?" he amended.

"Who, sir?" the ghost valet asked. Blasing explained. "Master MacGuire and another? Extraordinary. But no, sir. I neither felt nor saw anything."

"Mac was here. The other, the dark spirit, was near the trailer." Blasing walked quickly along the concrete sidewalk to the office trailer.

"Odd that this sidewalk is finished," Broderick noted.

"This must be the one they blamed on you all," Blasing mused.

"I believe you are right. Why would we build a sidewalk?"

"Another one of the mysteries, Broderick. Like why is Mac afraid of the dark spirit?"

The trailer was a mobile office of aluminum siding. Shadows striped the gray walls. Blasing ascended the steps and stopped at the door. It was locked and the curtains closed. When he looked around the site to make sure he was alone, he had a sudden sense of desolation.

Blasing shook it off and tried to feel ahead for ghosts. He didn't sense anything. Or did he? With Broderick nearby, it was difficult to be sure. Maybe Angela was right; he needed to test the extent of his senses. He sighed to himself, almost unable to believe he even considered such thoughts.

"Is everything all right, sir?"

"Just wondering if there was anything inside."

"Did you see... him come from here?"

"Not exactly."

"One moment." Broderick darted through the aluminum sliding into the trailer.

Blasing waited for what seemed a long time, listening to the breeze. He tried stretching out his sense of awareness, but still didn't feel anything, including Broderick. Blasing had just concluded he was only making himself more tense when the spirit returned.

"It is no wonder they were having building problems."

"Why? What's wrong?"

"It is worse than a side street in Liverpool Rubbish is everywhere. No one could plan anything efficiently in such an environment."

"Oh," Blasing said.

"I have unlocked it for you."

"Thank you," Blasing said. "You'd make a great burglar."

"I suppose, if I was so disposed," Broderick said, his nose a bit high in response. "Burgling is not a proper vocation."

Blasing pushed open the door, its crepitation hurting his ears. Except for scattered shards of light, the interior was gray and heavy in shadows. A small gust of wind suddenly whipped through the interior, animating sheets of paper and plastic wrappers into a dervish dance.

Blasing thought about all the horror movies he'd seen over the years, then tried the light switch. The overhead tubes flickered, then starkly illuminated the trailer; it was about as messy as it could be without anything being destroyed. Papers were scattered about in loose stacks, sometimes held down by rulers, other times by tools. Fast food trash overflowed the wastebaskets, and soda cans were everywhere as if the mess were a modern decorative motif.

Blasing took a few steps forward and still didn't itch. "Nothing here. But I think I know why they have accidents." He re-locked the door, and then headed toward the northern entrance. Blasing paused briefly at the pile of brick but no longer felt a ghostly presence. He'd been hoping Mac would return.

Near the northern porch, the silhouette of a woman dark against the red-golden light rose slowly from the earth. The wind and sun caught her hair, creating a swirling, fiery halo around her lithe form. "I think that's Angela coming up the steps."

She gracefully climbed over the stairwell wall, then avoided the ropes blocking off the construction site. As if following a trail along the cliffs, she walked northward until the foundations eventually obscured his sight of her.

"Let's take a short cut," Blasing said, then moved into the unfinished structure. He hopped over a low wall, then dropped into the sunken foundation. The shadow enveloped him and seemed to hang as a heavy cloak. He passed another opening, the horizontal light blinding him for a moment. When Blasing looked for Angela along the coast, he didn't see her. "Where'd she go?"

"There is definitely something odd about this place, sir."

Blasing kept moving toward the coast, light and shadow playing across his body. He jumped a pit, the darkness apparently stretching far below. Coming around a corner, he found Angela squatting along the cliff and examining the grass. "Angela?"

"Oh! Fancy meeting you here, Mr. Madera." Her face was warmly aglow, her expression was slightly amused, much different than when he'd last seen her. "Crawling around getting dirty like one of your kids," she teased as she stood. "Some role model you are."

He looked down; his pants were dirty. "I try."

She laughed. "What are you really doing here, searching for new ghosts?" He nodded. "Are you feeling all right?"

"Yes, of course. What do you mean?"

"I mean if you're looking for ghosts, something must be wrong."

"Oh. Thanks, Counselor. Remember when I felt a ghost out here?" he asked. She nodded. "Well, I came back to see if I still did." He told her what had just happened.

"Then Peter is here, after all, and you think he's afraid of this... dark stranger?" she asked. "But why?" Things were going well until he explained about the pair of warnings. "And you didn't tell me!" Angela flared, no longer looking angelic.

"Angela, one just happened, and I haven't seen you since you slammed the door last night."

"I didn't slam it." She crossed her arms defensively.

"You shut it with resounding firmness," he corrected.

"Damn right I did. You're being led about by the nose."

"You're upset because I'm not letting you lead me around."

"That's not what I meant, and you know it," she replied, flushing furiously.

"I'm listening to everybody. Weighing what I hear. If you have something to say, then say it, but don't grouse. I know habits are hard to break, but don't take wanting a cigarette out on me."

"You know, Mister Madera, you change the subject very well," Angela told him. "Now, what about the first warning?"

He paused. "It was right after your stunt driving, and I thought I might be hallucinating."

She took a deep breath. "My stunt driving, eh?" She stewed for a moment, then said, "I'm worried about this ghost, especially if he's scaring Peter. You say Broderick doesn't know him?"

"No miss, I do not."

"Oh, hi, Broderick," Angela said, startled as he appeared.

"He's guarding me," Blasing said tongue-in-cheek.

"So you work with machines and he handles bodies now?"

"At least you still have a sense of humor."

"Just being near Heller causes it to head south. I'm worried about this dark spirit. If he's threatening you...."

"But nothing's happened."

"If there's nothing to worry about, why is Peter hiding? And why is this spirit bothering you? What motions did he make?" she asked, and Blasing showed her. "An hourglass? How about a woman's figure? I've seen guys make that motion more than once."

"Could have been," Blasing replied, "But why?"

"Maybe he's an admirer of Fawn's, I don't know. Have you been flirting with any spirits?"

"Of course not, unless you count Cannon."

"Anything else you've forgotten to mention?"

"No. Now why are you out here?"

"I'm retracing the murderer's footsteps for a second time. I found hematite fragments on the stairs and some flecks of blood in the dirt leading me to this spot."

"Hematite?" Blasing asked. He peered over the edge.

"It's a grounding stone. With rings made of hematite, I was able to slap Grant," she reminded him. "I think the murderer might have been wearing it to protect him against the ghosts."

"Indeed!" Broderick exclaimed.

"Adds credence to it being an inside job," Angela told him. "Do you think he fell? Or climbed down?"

Blasing replied, "There's not enough damage to the rock. This facade is fragile and would fall away as scree."

"You've climbed before?"

"Many times." he said. "Yosemite is my favorite spot."

"A helicopter?"

"Doubtful. Maybe the ghosts got him," Blasing mused.

"That is not amusing, sir," Broderick said frostily.

Blasing's stomach growled. "Can we discuss this over dinner?"

"Sounds good to me," Angela agreed. Blasing checked his pager. "Expecting a call?" He told her about Kelly. "I'm sorry she's sick." She gently took his arm as if it belonged to her and led him along the cliff's edge toward the resort. "I understand your wanting to race home, but she'll probably be just fine. Children get suddenly sick and recover almost as quickly."

"You're right," Blasing said. "You don't have kids do you?"

"No. They're trying to pass a law that doesn't allow lawyers to mate," she told him, sounding dead serious.

Blasing laughed and suddenly realized he didn't know very much about Angela Starborne. "How has your day been? Anything has to be better than spending it with a real estate agent. Walter Bond can talk the ear off a deaf man." Angela laughed. Blasing smiled, caught by her joy. "Tomorrow we trade."

"Are you sure you want to spend hours talking with lawyers?" she asked. "I thought not. Good news, though. The injunction is rolling. We should have it by Wednesday." He told her of Eva's sale. "Did anyone else?"

"I don't know." He thought about mentioning Eva's disrobing, then decided not to bother. It would only unnerve Angela, or make her paranoid. She wasn't having any problems so far. "Did you mention the contesting of the will?"

She nodded. "They're making plans."

"I spoke with the sheriff and have the name and number of the man you need to speak to in Forensics. It's hard to believe the sheriff couldn't add anything to the case." Blasing briefly summarized the conversation.

When he finished, Angela looked as frustrated as he felt. "At least they could have sent someone open-minded."

"We're talking about county sheriffs," Blasing told her.

"Silly me. Did you talk to Chief Porter about his men?" she asked. Blasing explained about the new system.

"I do not care for the man," Broderick said.

"He's upset because of the increased security and the medium."

"He's not the only one, I'm sure," Angela said.

Blasing nodded. "He feels the ghosts are being blamed for what's going on."

"Did you get access to personnel files?" she said as they reached the construction boundary and ducked under it.

"He wants me to speak with Heller."

"I'll subpoena them if you can't!" She stewed for a minute. "Have you spoken with Madame Zanadane?" Before he could answer, she said, "Damn! I forgot to ask her about Grant Roberts and Carrie. Too much on my mind, I guess."

"What did she have to say?"

"She's a bit of a loony, but says she's not here to threaten the ghosts, but to work with them as a liaison. Heller is frightened of the ghosts, so he wants a go-between. I think you should talk with her."

"I look forward to it," Blasing said, rolling his eyes. "Broderick, you can come with me."

"Oh joy."

As Blasing opened the northern door, he said, "Didn't you say you never got a final copy of the will?"

"That's right. Why?" she asked. Blasing told her about his scavenger hunt, finding the package, gun and key. "It was hidden?" He nodded. "I didn't know he owned a gun."

Blasing pulled out the key. "Broderick, do you know where this goes?"

The Englishman examined it. "Yes, sir. It opens the safe in Mister Heller's office."

"The one concealed behind the painting?" Blasing asked for clarification. Broderick nodded.

"Curiouser and curiouser," Angela said. "I'm tired of piling up questions. It's time to do a séance."

A séance?" Blasing asked with a frown. "Why?"

"To see if we can find Carrie or Grant. I want to..." she almost slipped, saying she wanted to know what they'd intended on telling her last night, "...know why they're missing. It might clear up some things. It would even give you a chance to evaluate Madame Zanadane."

"Must she be involved, miss?" Broderick asked.

"Candy, my friend, can perform it," Angela suggested. "She's very adept." Blasing looked leery. "Don't worry. You can handle it, Blasing, and if it makes you feel better, we'll do it tomorrow.

It'll take a while to organize. Who knows, we might be able to contact Peter. Think what he might tell us!"

FIFTEEN

Announcing the storm's arrival, lightning flashed through the dining room, followed by a glass-rattling crack of thunder. "Wow!" Blasing exclaimed. The lights dimmed, matching the candles on each table, then suddenly returned to full brilliance. Patrons who had been stilled, talked all at once.

"We don't get lightning very often, but it's perfect weather to complement Ghostal Shores," Angela said with a smile over her glass of merlot. The candlelight caught her unbound hair. It shone with a ruddy, golden hue against her deep blue blouse. Despite the crowd, Angela had the sense that they'd been alone during dinner. "You don't get many thunderstorms in Tahoe, do you?"

"No," Blasing replied. "We prefer not to have them. Lightning strikes cause fires. But since I'm not in Tahoe, I think I'll sit back and enjoy the ambiance, as well as your company," he emphasized the last two words, "forgetting that I have a ghost threatening me and a resort full of spirits watching me."

"Not to mention a guardian angel protecting your virtue?"

"Not to mention."

"For a second, I'd hoped you'd forgotten to be cynical. Is being cynical part of the security mentality?" she asked. He nodded. "Well don't worry. I'll protect you from the ghosts."

"That's supposed to be my line," Blasing replied with a hint of a smile. He poured himself another glass of wine.

"Do you use lines?" she asked boldly. Her fingertip absently circled the top of her nearly empty wine glass.

"No. But I have said that before. Would you care for more wine?"

"Are you trying to ply me with liquor?" She held out her glass.

"Never," he replied with a smile.

"You don't even handle the bodies and you say things like that?"

Blasing nodded. "One lovely gal is my favorite," he told Angela as he poured wine into her glass.

"I don't think you need to get them drunk, Blasing."

He smiled. "Those words usually brought a hug and a kiss," he said with a sigh. Lightning flashed, leaving only candlelight. The staff suddenly hustled about to light oil lamps. "But now..." he paused to let the thunder shake the resort, "since watching the Weather Classroom, storms don't bother Kelly anymore."

Picturing Blasing in a comfortable home and fireside, Angela leaned back and stretched as a cat, momentarily wondering what it might feel like with his arms around her. What his lips would taste like. She looked at her glass. Maybe she shouldn't have any more wine.

Angela leaned forward with a lazy smile on her face and bright eyes. "With such a storm, can you see why people enjoy Ghostal Shores? It's a pleasantly spooky resort filled with benevolent ghosts, candlelight dinners...."

"...And a murder mystery with the murdered spirit playing hide and seek. Would you care for dessert?"

"You can be so cynical."

"Angela, you haven't had a ghost threaten to cut off your head. For all I know, it's connected to Mac's murder. If I were smart, I'd just sell and be done with it."

"Would you, now? But I said I'd protect you," she maintained.

"How?" Blasing asked. He rubbed the back of his neck. He saw a brilliant flash of lightning, then heard a peel of thunder. The loudness of the rain drumming against the windows grew to a roar.

"How was everything?" the mammoth maitre'd asked as he developed into sight. Even without all the hair, David reminded Angela of a congenial but fully grown and formally clad teddy bear.

"Wonderful," Angela replied. "Thank you, David."

"How about coffee or dessert?"

"Blueberry cheesecake," Blasing said. "Two plates."

"A very good choice," David agreed. "I will return anon."

"But what if I want something else?" Angela asked, glancing from him to where David had stood and back again.

"You weren't going to order anything."

"How do you know?" A smile tugged at the corners of her mouth.

"I caught one of those thoughts you were talking about. Now, how are you going to protect me from this malevolent ghost?"

"I have my ways," she replied mysteriously, holding his stare.

She wanted to gauge his reaction. "I protected my room with a Paiute ceremony."

Blasing's expression grew skeptical. "A protective ceremony. Sounds like..." he struggled for the right word, "hocus pocus."

"The Paiutes are much more in touch with the spirit world than contemporary White Man. Well, whether you believe me or not, Broderick couldn't enter my room after I'd completed the ceremony?"

"Really?" he asked, still looking skeptical. "You're saying I'd be safe in my room?"

"Actually, my room," she said, then realized the wine had loosened her tongue. "I may be able to protect the whole suite."

"I'll have to see it to believe it. What about when I'm not in my room? Are you my bodyguard then?"

"I have a pendant from my grandmother...."

"Angela. This sounds very... odd." He looked uncomfortable.

"I know. You didn't believe in ghosts, either. Don't you trust me?"

"That's an unfair question. You're a California lawyer," he told her. She put her hands on her hips and mock-frowned. "You haven't always told me everything."

"Same could be said for you."

Blasing sighed. "Well then, it's time to clear the air."

Angela wondered what that entailed. "I believe you're more open-minded than you think." Angela began pulling on the silver chain around her neck. "Wear this and touch Broderick."

Blasing held up a hand to stop her. "Are you sure you're the same woman who came to my office Friday night?" She laughed. "I'll think about wearing this... charm. You know, you're very good at avoiding my question about Mac's ghost and the séance."

She laughed. They'd been discussing it before the thunderstorm had struck. "Lawyers don't avoid questions," she replied. A sharp crack of thunder and lightning caused her to pause and smile, "We just ask nature to intervene."

Blasing buried his face in his hands.

"Well, this is interesting. Dr. Landrum is escorting Eva," she said, tapping a finger on her chin. "Maybe she thinks it will be easier to keep her clothes on around him." Eva was wearing a creamy, shoulderless gown. The good doctor looked handsome in gray pinstripes. Angela refrained from saying anything unpleasant about Dr. Landrum; his company said enough already.

"Angela. It's not that bad," Blasing said.

"True, Chian hasn't had problems, yet." Angela suddenly realized she'd been flirting and had yet to lose any jewelry. "And yet, when has exhibition ever bothered Eva? Sorry, I can't even blame that on the wine," Angela apologized. "I just can't believe she's so cold-blooded about Peter's death. So I applaud your guardian angel."

"You're avoiding the question again," he sighed.

"Blasing, I don't know if we can reach Peter, but it's worth a try. A séance involves a certain amount of compelling. Peter could answer so many questions, and not just about his murder. And we might find Carrie and Grant. May I ask why you are so uncomfortable about it?"

"I don't know, exactly. I could say it just seems... eccentric at best and psycho ward bound at worst, but... it feels like we're disturbing the dead."

"Peter, from what you say, isn't resting. Maybe those murdered can't find peace."

"I can vouch for that," David said with a low-bellied chuckle. He set the cheesecake in front of Blasing, then an empty plate before Angela. "Is there anything else?"

"How did you die?" Blasing asked.

"I slept through a fire," David replied.

"Would you want to be bothered?"

"I would say that if I could help you, why not?"

"You are more than a waiter, David."

"Thank you, madam," he said with a bow. "You are too kind. If I only mentioned it once before, you are radiant this evening—a ray of sunshine casting rainbows through the storm."

Angela began laughing. "Oh, David. You've been flirting with too many of Peter's companions."

"Everyone has to have a hobby," he replied. "Now, would you care for anything else?" Angela shook her head, and he departed.

"It just seems to me... that... you're practicing sorcery or witchcraft or something occultist or arcane."

"Don't get the two confused," Angela told him, watching him become wary. "In Native American culture, sorcery is evil. Witchcraft is protective, a way of working with nature, not twisting it."

Blasing again seemed to be at a loss for words, so he fumbled with serving her a slice of cheesecake.

"Angel! It is wonderful to see you out," Candy Whyte said. She was adorned with amethyst jewelry in her ears, around her neck, and all over her hands. Her indigo jumpsuit seemed almost black and the candlelight made her sparkle as if she were a constellation all her own. Her eyes were so bright and pleased, they might have been blue suns. "And you look fabulous. I don't understand how poring over paperwork can make you look so gorgeous. If it did, I'd try it. Hello," she said to Blasing, "it's a pleasure to meet you, Mr. Madera. This is my soulmate, Rod Thompson."

"And you are?" Blasing asked as he stood.

Candy's glance toward Angela was accusatory. "You're off my Christmas list, dear Angel."

"Candy Whyte, my dearest friend and her beau, Rod," Angela said. She hoped Candy wouldn't embarass her.

"A classmate from Berkeley?" Blasing asked. When she nodded, he said, "That might explain it."

"Ah, a skeptic. Has Angel asked about the seance?"

"She has mentioned it."

"Ah, you have been sticking to business," Candy said, patting Angela's cheek. "Oh well, waste not, want not. What do you think, Mr. Madera?"

"That you ladies will probably do whatever you want."

"There is a spiritual disturbance in this area," Rod said.

"He's very sensitive," Candy told Blasing. "He channels."

"I'm sorry. Didn't mean to be rude." Rod shook Blasing's hand.

"You will find a seance... stimulating," Candy began. "We try to bring everyone to a similar vibratory pattern so we can pierce the veil to a higher plane of existence. It's perfectly safe," Candy told him with an innocent smile.

"Nothing is totally safe," Blasing responded.

Despair in her face, Candy turned to Angela. "I see our arrival has worsened matters. Sorry. Good evening, Mr. Madera. Take good care of Angel, she's a one of a kind keeper. Call me, Angel."

"Goodnight, Candy. Rod."

"You have an... interesting background—a lot of... depth to

fathom," Blasing told Angela. His expression was one of contemplation and befuddlement.

"Thank you," she replied. "You have the makings of a lawyer."

"Angela, I'm not sure what I believe anymore."

"About the ghosts? Or Peter's murder?"

"Both."

"Well, to tell the truth, Blasing, I'm tired of thinking about it. Enough investigating. No more tonight." She rubbed her hands and washed them of it. "For once, I'd like to ask some questions that have answers."

"Wouldn't we all?" Blasing mused.

"Very deep," she laughed. "With that in mind, I'd like to know more about you."

"Me? Why?"

"If I'm going to be your lawyer, I'd like to know more about you. I've been around you three days and feel like I've only scratched the surface." And she wanted to know if this was the real Blasing. Craved it.

"Counselor, you keep stealing the words from my mouth. Are you reading my mind?" he asked.

She shrugged. "As I said, sometimes I think I can pick up a strong thought or two. Think of it as being observant. You want to know more about a lawyer before selecting one?" Her smile was brilliant. Her eyes gleamed as sunlit pools.

"Exactly."

"Well, I am very particular," she said, suddenly haughty. "Clients might choose me, but it's still up to me if I work for them." She patted her mouth with her napkin.

"I guess I could get a new lawyer."

"I wouldn't encourage it," she began, then frowned. "If you so decide, I'd recommend you maintain my firm as advisory counsel, especially if Meg Cassidy has a leg to stand on. Besides, as Peter's executor," she said with a broad smile, "you're stuck with me until the transition is complete. So answer my questions, and remember, you're under oath."

"I am?"

"By having dinner with me, you tacitly took an oath to tell the truth," she smiled smugly. "It's a new law." A strong wind buffeted the windows, then white lightning flashed as a crashing crescendo of thunder assaulted them.

"Even if I'm buying?" he asked. She nodded. "Damn. The nineties have become so complicated."

"Were you an only child?"

"Why do you want to know?" he asked.

"To see if you're used to getting your own way."

"I had an older brother, Carlos, and a younger sister Moira. Both died in the crash with my parents."

Angela almost wished she hadn't asked. His entire demeanor changed, his gaze flattening and his expression downbeat. "Then Peter took you in?"

Blasing nodded. "My mother's parents had passed on the year before, and the Maderas were too old; I would have been too much to handle. Dad was an only child. I stayed with Mac for about three years. I was in counseling most of the time. I was bitter and rebellious, trying to see if I could get myself killed by skateboarding or jumping bicycles, anything."

"Didn't work, I see." Angela considered herself lucky.

"Lord knows I tried," Blasing said, then took a sip of wine. "Do you want a second bottle?"

"Tempting, but probably not a good idea. I rarely drink. My grandmother said my Paiute blood makes me susceptible."

"Cannon told me they can use the porter carts if necessary."

"No, I have a reputation to uphold." She was quiet for a minute, sobering before she said, "Peter never said much, but a neighbor started the problems?"

"One of his ex-girlfriends. She portrayed the MacGuire household as a revolving door for whores. I never noticed."

"You were too busy trying to kill yourself?"

"Just testing the boundaries of my mortality. That went over real well at orphanages. I was escaping all the time," he said with a wan smile, his eyes far away, "so I got bounced around. As a problem child, I wasn't wanted, and to tell the truth, I didn't want to be part of a family. I'd seen what happened to the first one, and the second was taken away by the government."

"That's sad. I'm sorry."

"Don't be," he replied and saw her start. "I don't mean to be rude, it's just that I survived, and it's all right now. I may even be a better person for it." He sighed, then talked about how he was a troublemaker in high school but had good enough grades to get into college. His parents had degrees, so he thought he'd try. After all the counseling, he tried psychology, thinking it would be easy. It had been too easy and he was bored. Footloose and fancy free, he'd had too much unbridled energy.

"So you became a ski instructor?"

Blasing nodded. He looked away, glancing at Eva and Dr. Landrum, then back to Angela who read his lips as the thunder took away his words. "For a while it was fun," he repeated.

"It got old?" she asked, wondering if she always watched his lips so closely. She was thoroughly enjoying it.

"Very quickly. I loved the teaching, especially kids, but I kept getting repeat customers I would have preferred avoiding."

"Fatal attraction problems?" She didn't have to read minds.

"Something like that. They were... expecting me to be something I wasn't. Are you sure you're Angela Starborne? She's usually very business oriented."

Angela colored, looking quickly over to where Candy was sitting; she was watching and winking at her. "I told you I wanted to learn more about a new client. Isn't that business-like enough?"

"Yes, I guess it is," he said a bit sadly. "But don't worry about my virtue, with the current state of things, attracting women might lead to lawsuits instead of love affairs."

"You mean Eva, Meg and Desiree´? Odd that I haven't had such problems," she murmured.

"You aren't interested in me," he said. His gaze was direct, almost challenging, as if looking for a hint.

Angela found herself a bit tongue-tied, thinking there was a way to find out if what he believed about his 'guardian' was true. She chewed on her lip, thinking her rings might protect her. It would be a fun experiment. "Maybe Fawn's just being overprotective. Blasing, what was the riskiest thing you've ever done?"

"Marrying Jennifer," he replied, surprising her.

"Were you afraid it wouldn't work out?"

"It was... difficult to become that close to somebody after building walls. Jennifer said I was probably concerned about losing her to something catastrophic. She was right."

"But you married her anyway."

"And she died." He looked away. "Leaving me blessed and cursed at the same time." When he looked back, his eyes were bright but he was smiling. "Which is why I have to be extra careful in making a decision about Ghostal Shores. I know this is business, but I want you to understand that I'm weighing Mac's dream against my children's future. I get the feeling you want me to be an active partner. Why?"

"You have a good rapport with ghosts and people. You inspire confidence with your interest and compassion."

"Does this mean you no longer object to Mac's choice of me as an heir?" he asked archly, catching her off guard.

Angela hemmed and hawed for a second, then said, "I realize we got off to a rocky start, possibly because of my expectations. You know you share a gift with Peter—your ability to deal with the ghosts. They sense something special about you. As I do."

"Well, I've been wondering if the ghosts sense a kinship because of my numerous brushes with death."

"I hadn't thought of that," she said. Another idea for a paper, Candy would say.

"Blasing, if you don't mind me asking, what caused the rift between you and Peter?"

Blasing was thoughtful for a time, then said, "Women, of course. The first time his womanizing forced the state to take action. A decade later, he tried to reconcile, but I wasn't interested. Family had either died or betrayed me."

"How sad."

Blasing nodded. "Live and learn. Then I met and married Jennifer. We tried to get together again, and for a while it worked, but his drinking problem was really bad. He propositioned my wife." Angela gasped. "He was really sick at the time, I guess. Anyway, Jennifer refused to have anything to do with him."

"Then he showed up for Kelly's birth, and things were all right for a while, but he was always showing up with a different woman. Jenny didn't think it was a good role model for Kelly or Patrick. I agreed, and Mac and I drifted apart, again."

Angela was having trouble believing what she'd heard; it sounded very little like the Peter MacGuire she knew. And yet, she felt Blasing was telling the truth—trusted him to be doing so.

Angela broke eye contact and looked around at the lavish opulence, taking note of the jet-setters and trend-setters worth millions, perhaps even billions, among the eccentrics, priests, and truth-seekers. If they weren't inscrutably studying the surroundings, they seemed either pleased or awed. She recognized Efrem Xantini, who seemed to feel her gaze—or hear her thoughts—and nodded a long distance greeting. "Blasing, what would you do with all the money?"

"To start, find a good financial manager. Then add to college funds. Finally, I'd become a free-lance photographer. I could take Patrick and Kelly with me on my travels. They'd learn things that aren't taught in school."

"Are you a good photographer?"

"It's a God-given talent. I have the eye, the patience, and the luck. Having done a lot of the stunts and such, I also have an understanding of what's dynamic, as well as a few contacts."

"Then why haven't you pursued it? I can see you more as a freelance photographer than a security consultant."

"Pretty simple, really. I had a capital problem. I can starve, but my kids can't. I dream about doing it all the time, just hoping I only put it off for a time. Do you want to have kids someday?"

"Are you offering yours? Or talking in general?"

"In general."

"Yes, though I haven't finished figuring out how I'd juggle things. A real man would treat me like a princess and let servants and maids do much of the work."

Blasing choked a little on his wine. "Sounds like I don't know you as well as I thought. You through grilling me enough to answer some questions?"

"Time to cross-examine?"

"I must admit I've never interrogated anyone under such lavish conditions."

She looked at him speculatively, then said, "I was born Angela Maria Marker of Kalina and Michael Marker. I changed my name to my mother's maiden name—Starborne—after she died. That was a little over a year go. I'm half Pauite and half Oregonian. My mother was a nurse. My father was a programmer. He's retired."

"Pardon me, but you don't look...."

"I know. I know. I foolishly try to disguise my heritage." She flushed. "I originally colored my hair for this purpose, as Grant Roberts so... rudely pointed out." She looked around the room, just daring him to come around.

"Why?"

"For a time, I was embarrassed about my heritage. When my early boyfriends found out I was a 'half-breed', they never spoke to me again. Other kids harassed me unmercifully, so when I graduated to high school, I became a blond to hide within society. Still, being a double 'minority' opened all sorts of difficult doors. I went to UCLA on scholarship, then to UC Berkeley for Law."

"And what do you do for fun?"

"I like the outdoors—hiking, biking, and camping."

"And you ski, right?"

"Some. I'm sure I could use some lessons."

"Hmm. I'll have to think about that. There's always the possibility of legal action when you help a lawyer with anything," he teased. "And you met Candy during law school?"

"No, I'm working on another degree in parapsychology and metaphysics."

"Oh. Your third one?" Blasing appeared uncomfortable again. If this was a problem, she wanted to know up front about it.

"I know, it sounds strange. You see, when my mother died, I felt like I'd missed out, so I went exploring her past to keep her memory alive. Since then, I've been spending a lot of time with my grandmother Dawnjoy—time that brought up many questions. And yet, I have learned much from her, too—about myself, my heritage, and even life in general."

"Pardon me," came a rough voice along with a heavy waft of cigar smoke from the nearby table of gamblers. "Blasing, would ya like to join us fer a couple of hands?"

Blasing turned to Dirk, who smiled, his silver teeth glinting and crooked. "I...." Blasing hesitated.

"We'd be honored," Samuel added with a radiant smile, his perfect teeth brighter than the rest of him.

"Go on," Angela said. "From what you've told me, I agree to work with you, IF you wish to continue this association."

"Excellent, I do."

"Now go play. Peter used to do it to get to know these spirits better. Think of it as good spiritual relations."

"Oh, all right." As he stood, Blasing said, "You're coming too, right?"

"Of course. You don't think I'd miss your debut as the Gambler, do you?"

"Don't worry. My gambling is rarely with cards or checks." He sat between Dirk and Samuel.

"Easy pickin's," Mason said with a bright smile that didn't reach the blacksmith's eyes. He sat across the way, a dark monolith draped in white. When the lightning flashed, it passed through him as well as around him, making him seem more ghostly.

"Too pretty to be playing cards worth spit," Winston said as he rolled his eyes. Samuel glared at the bespectacled banker.

"Go easy on him, he's the owner. We don't wanna be kicked out," one of the block-jawed twins said.

"You're in good hands," Angela joked. "Here, this is for luck." Angela removed her silk scarf belt and draped it over his arm. She rested a hand on his shoulder, prepared to start coming undressed any time now. She felt an inner warmth, then a cold shiver danced between her shoulders and down her back.

Blasing gave her a questioning look as he rubbed the back of his neck. "Thanks."

Had that been Fawn? Or her imagination, Angela wondered? And yet, how could it be, unless she could hide in plain sight from her fellow ghosts? Earlier, Broderick hadn't seen her, and now the gamblers hadn't reacted; but if it wasn't Fawn, then who was it? And why wasn't she having any troubles? Her grandmother's rings? The pendant? If so, she needed to get Blasing to wear the pendant.

"Here you are," Dirk said, pushing several multicolored stacks of chips toward him. "This is your stake."

"I imagine money doesn't mean much to you now," Blasing said.

"Just a measure of who's the best gambler," Samuel told him.

"Or the slickest cheater," the other twin brother added.

"We go as long as the newcomer plays," Mason announced with a blocky smile as he began dealing. One brother sat out. Sweat seemed to shine off Mason's face, making the spirit glow. "Five card, aces high, and sevens wild. Winner deals and calls game."

Blasing picked up his cards to find two pair—twos, threes and a king.

"I'll throw in ten," Winston said coolly. A brother matched it. So did Samuel and Blasing.

"Fifteen," Dirk said with a smile.

"Puttin' the bite on early," Samuel said. He rolled a chip back and forth across the back of his hands from knuckle to knuckle. Eventually, everyone matched the bet. Winston took three and frowned. A brother took two cards. Samuel swept the table, asking for one.

"One," Blasing told the blacksmith, who deftly flicked him a card. Blasing added the three of diamonds to his hand. Dirk and Mason took two cards, neither showing any reaction.

"I'm out," Winston said, then took a drink and fired up a cigar. The brother next to him added ten to the pot. Samuel added fifteen. Blasing went to twenty. Dirk doubled that.

Everyone but Blasing folded, and he thought about it for a long time before he finally matched it. "Call." Dirk had three aces. Blasing swept the pot with a full house.

"Beginners luck," Winston groused.

Mason passed the cards to Blasing, who shuffled and handed the stack to Dirk. He cut the cards masterfully with one ethereal hand. "Five card stud. Bets on each card," Blasing told them and dealt one card down. Everyone stayed in through the third card—the second face up. The bet was fifty a piece.

"I like it!" Dirk said, looking at his fourth card, then slammed a shot of whiskey. The twin playing threw his cards in disgust. Mason appeared to be brooding with no noticeable change. Winston puffed away on his cigar, almost obscuring the ghost and the brothers. Samuel tossed in his four, then waved his hat at the smoke. Blasing dealt himself a second queen. After some gnashing and cursing, Dirk and Mason were left with Blasing and his pair of queens and sevens.

"Fifty more," Mason rumbled.

"Seventy-five." Dirk tossed in his chips. Blasing stared at him for a while, then tossed in an extra twenty-five. Grumbling, Mason and Dirk matched the bet. "Call."

Blasing won again.

"You were right," Mason said to Dirk. "He's a card shark, all right. You said the same thing about that Parker fella from Texas."

"Same game," Blasing said and dealt. This time he got junk and bailed. Samuel won that hand, but Blasing won five of the next eight games. During the play, several people gathered to watch.

"Blasing, I'll be back in a minute," Angela said.

"Ah, now we have a chance." Dirk's metallic smile was supremely confident.

Wondering if Blasing could sense something from the ghosts to help him in his gambling, Angela walked to the restroom. At first, he'd appeared unnerved by sitting with the ghosts, but he'd hidden it well, and adjusted in a short time. Playing, as well as winning, would gain him the respect of the gamblers.

When Angela returned fifteen minutes later, quite a crowd had gathered. A significant female entourage surrounded Blasing. Angela paused to watch as a lovely, young thing with fair skin, long dark hair, and raven-winged brows moved closer, brushing Blasing with her breasts. Angela was irate, then she watched as the bold beauty lost an earring. The diamond bounced off Blasing's shoulder, falling like a star, then bounding into Samuel's whiskey tumbler with a splash.

Blasing looked back over his shoulder and spoke briefly with the woman. She smiled innocently, then backed away, looking disappointed. Samuel was chuckling when he handed her the diamond.

It seemed as if Blasing felt her coming; he turned around just when she needed help getting through the crowd, waving her to his side.

"You've won quite a stack," Angela observed.

"Not this time," he said as he tossed in his cards.

Angela leaned forward, a smile on her lips as she whispered. "Getting any help?" He shook his head. She laid a hand on his shoulder and waited; she felt a spark of excitement, then a chill, but nothing sinister. "Can you tell when a ghost is bluffing?"

He nodded. "I've come very close to guessing every card they hold." She felt a cool chill and saw Blasing rub his neck. Angela felt for another spirit but couldn't tell any difference.

"How's he doing it, pretty lady?" Samuel asked.

Angela found most of them glaring at her. One of the twin spirits had pulled his hat down to hide his disgust. His stacks were almost gone. "He used to deal cards in Tahoe, and he's psychic, so when he deals he knows what cards you have in your hands."

"Wish I could do that!" Samuel said.

"I think he's also reading your auras," Candy Whyte volunteered. She and Rod were watching.

Mason glared. "I think they're having fun at our expense."

"He can't be beating us fair and square," Dirk said. "But keep playing, sooner or later I'll catch 'em at it. I love a challenge!"

Blasing laughed with him, and soon they were all laughing. Angela marveled at how he affected the ghosts. Everything seemed to swirl around him. Could he be right about the close association between them due to his near death experiences?

"Pardon me, child, but I'm sorry I'm a day late," a woman next to her said. Angela recognized the beautiful, raven-tressed female as the one who had flirted with Blasing.

"Excuse me, but do I know you?"

"Meet me in the garden, same time as last night?" The voice and the fire she saw in the young woman's gray-green eyes seemed familiar; but Angela swore she didn't know her. And yet.... Leaning on Blasing's chair, she appeared oddly stooped for her age and apparent health. "Strange things are happening."

"Carrie?" Angela asked with a incredulous whisper.

"Tonight. See ya there, ch... dear."

"Cassie, are you all right?" the woman's friend asked, shaking her. "You sound funny." The brunette blinked several times, then shook her head.

With a quick excuse to Blasing, Angela headed for the veranda. Where had Carrie been? How had she possessed that woman? What was going on?

SIXTEEN

As the lightning flashed through the garden, thunder cracked, ripping the night air. Rumbling echoes overlapped until buried under another ear-rupturing blast. Angela pulled the borrowed bellman's jacket more tightly and moved further underneath the greenhouse roof. All about her glass panes rattled. The wind snatched at her, seeming alive and lashing about wildly.

Had Carrie possessed that woman? Angela wondered. And if so, how had she done that? Could all ghosts possess people? Angela shivered at that thought. Did it have something to do with why Carrie was being so secretive? And who was watching Blasing? Angela closed her eyes, took a deep breath and tried to quiet her racing mind. She wished she had a cigarette, or that Blasing was with her, so that she could wrap herself in his protective aura.

Another blinding bolt cracked jaggedly across the sky, and Angela could suddenly feel a ghost. When her eyes adjusted, she found an image wavering before her, becoming clearer and clearer until a smiling, long-haired ghost wearing an old west business suit and bolo tie stood before her. "Was that slow enough? I didn't want to startle you."

Angela recognized Grant Robert's smile long before he spoke, so her anger had already built a head of steam. "What are you doing here?! Where's Carrie?!"

"Angela, I want to start by apologizing...."

"Not on your life, mister!" Angela snapped. She was so mad she couldn't see straight. "Get away or I'll let you have it again." She swiped at the ghost. When he jumped back, she stalked by him.

"Listen, Angela! I'm sorry. Don't go!" Grant appeared sincere, even taking off his hat. "Carrie will be here in a minute. We have critical information about Mac!"

"Speak your piece!"

Grant Roberts looked nervously left and right. "I would've contacted Blasing, but he's being watched."

"By whom? Quit bringing up more questions without explaining anything!" she snarled. The spirit's eyes were everywhere but on her, which made her wonder if this was really Grant Roberts. She suddenly remembered ghosts could change their appearance.

"Listen, I've important things to say and not very long to say them." He held up his hands to forestall another question. "I've been digging through Heller's files and discovered an agreement signed by Mac that you might not know about."

"WHAT?!" She suddenly thought about the copy of the will Blasing had found. She hadn't read it yet. Damn her for enjoying Blasing's company; it was affecting her work.

"It states that if one of the two partners dies and the estate isn't settled within sixty days, management of the facility reverts to the surviving partner for at least a year, or until all issues are settled." The wind gusted again, catching his hat. It resisted, flapping as if nailed down. "This doesn't change ownership, just management decisions, which will be the power to remake this place if Meg Cassidy contests the will."

"Why would Peter sign something like that?"

The ghost's eyes were busy searching the garden. "Because it makes management sense. After a death, it is very possible for a large business to flounder due to litigation. I've also discovered a third set of accounting books in Cash's suite."

"What!" Angela exclaimed.

"GSR's financials have more layers than IRS regulations. I think these are the originals—the real McCoy's. I thought you should know first, just in case something happens to me," he finished nervously, fingers loosening his tie.

"What could happen to you? You're already dead," Angela said. When she took a moment to study his face, she realized he was frightened of losing his immortal soul. "Where's Carrie?"

"I don't know. She should have been here by now."

"Where were you last night?"

"We were under scrutiny and had to hide out until...."

"So sorry dear," came Carrie's voice. The matronly spirit drifted through the roof to land next to Grant Roberts. She looked even more frazzled than the Texan.

"Where were you?" Angela asked.

"It took me time to recover—whew—from steppin' into that

woman's body, but it was the only way to speak with you unseen."
She leaned on Grant Roberts.

"You took possession of her body?" Angela's skin crawled.

"I was quick about it, dear! She wasn't hurt. To tell the truth, I
wasn't sure if I could, but I had to try. I came up through the floor
and stepped into her, land's sake's, yes I did. So strange. I ... I could
feel again. Looking at Blasing...."

"Carrie! Who is watching you?"

"Mean spirits that're friendly to Hellraiser. Somehow they can
hide from us. I can't see them until they're right next to me." Carrie
scrutinized the greenhouse gardens.

Angela blanched. Other ghosts couldn't see these ghosts? "Are
they watching Blasing?" Angela thought of the dark stranger with
yellow eyes. The spirits nodded. "Where do they come from?"

"From all over...."

"But it started with the new bricks," Carrie interrupted.

"The new bricks are haunted?" she asked. The ghosts nodded.
"Where do they come from?"

"Bodie...." Carrie began, then screamed as her arms and legs were
suddenly pulled in several directions. Grant flew a few feet before
being snatched back. As if roped to wild horses, they stretched in all
directions, their ghostly fabric shredding, then ripping apart.

A brilliant flash seared away their screams and blinded Angela,
sending her to her knees. When she could see again, gossamer wisps
swirled about her, slowly fading to nothing. "Carrie?" Similar to
when she'd slapped Grant but worse, her hands and a spot between
her breasts were afire. Everything else seemed numb, as if she'd
been caught in an explosion.

"Carrie? Grant?" Angela screamed. How could they be dead?
They were already dead. Were they destroyed? Angela suddenly felt
the need to run—to escape the lifeless garden. She hadn't cared for
Grant, but he'd died trying to help Peter and Blasing. Carrie! Poor
Carrie! In many ways, she reminded her of Grandma Dawnjoy, an-
other woman outside of time.

With a sob, Angela raced for the door. She tripped and fell,
sprawling across the brick and banging her chin. Dazed and gasping,
she struggled to her feet, yanked open the doors and ran into the lobby.

"Can I help you, miss?" someone asked, sounding quite concerned. Ignoring his calls, Angela raced for the stairs. She stumbled twice but never free.

Angela ran through the foyer, passing Barney, who noticed her condition and flew alongside her. "Is everything all right, Miss Starborne?" As she ran up the ramp to the lounge, she breathlessly told him she'd seen Grant and Carrie die a second time. "Dear God! The others must be told!"

When she entered the lounge, Angela noticed all the stares and slowed her stride. She kept telling herself to breathe deeply and stay calm. As she passed a vacated table, she snatched up a napkin and wiped away the tears.

"Ms. Starborne?" Chian asked as Angela passed the hostess podium. "Are you all right?"

Angela wasn't sure she could contain herself. She felt ready to burst, to break down—to scream, but she kept going, heading directly for the gamblers. The crowd had increased to encircle the entire table, so she couldn't see who was hanging all over Blasing now, but Broderick was nearby. She could spot the top of the ghost valet's head over the crowd.

Angela worked her way through the throng, curtly managing "excuse me" and mumbling "I'm with the gamblers." She received odd looks but people let her pass. Did they see death in her eyes?

As if sensing her return, Blasing turned around. "There you are! Angela, is something wrong?"

She started to say something, then began to cry, burying her face in her hands. Blasing jumped to his feet and took her in his arms. "Can we have some room, everybody? Angela, what is it? Here, sit," he guided her to the chair but she refused to let go of him.

"I just saw Carrie and Grant Roberts die," she choked.

"W- What?" Blasing stammered, then realized who she was talking about. "But Angela, they're ghosts. They're already dead," he said, looking at Broderick, who was speaking with Barney. The concierge nodded and then disappeared through the floor. The Englishman returned Blasing's look, then spread his hands wide.

"She's serious, can't you see," Candy berated them as she neared. "Men." Rod was right behind her. Candy hugged Angela, who kept one arm on Blasing as if he were a life preserver.

"You... you know how you can... can feel the ghosts?" Angela asked. Blasing nodded. Candy gave him an appraising look. "So can I, but not as well. They were there, then they were... r- ripped apart and I didn't feel them anymore. There was a blinding flash and I was numb, except I felt... sad and empty inside."

Candy felt her forehead. "You're feverish."

"What happened to your chin?" Blasing asked.

"So... confusing. I was on the balcony, in the gardens, talking with the ghosts. Carrie said something about Bodie, then... died in a great flash of light—almost like lightning had struck, but soundless."

"Can I be of assistance?" Dr. Landrum asked.

"Take me to my room. It's safe there," Angela told Blasing, her eyes locked on his.

"She was in the greenhouse watching the storm and thinks lightning struck close by," Blasing told him.

Candy frowned. "She believes she watched two ghosts die horribly," she corrected.

"Vey," Dr. Landrum muttered and moved closer.

"Broderick, could you investigate this?" Blasing asked. The spirit valet nodded gravely, then dropped through the floor.

Dr. Landrum took Angela's wrist and felt her throat. "Yes, very fast. Calm down, Angela. It's Geoff. We're going to take good care of you." He felt her flushed forehead. "Angela, can you tell me what happened?"

"Souls dying. So horrible. So bright."

"Did you fall?" He touched her chin and examined her throat.

"I stumbled over something. My knees and elbows hurt."

"Your chin?" he asked, and she said she didn't feel it. "Lose any consciousness?" He looked inside her mouth, then he examined Angela from head to toe, finding little but bruised elbows and lacerated knees. "Her circulation, sensation and movement seem good, but she sounds confused."

"Are you saying that because she thought she saw two ghosts die?" Blasing asked.

"I did see them die," she snapped angrily between tears.

"That much electricity could easily disorient you, Angela." He checked her forehead. "She seems to have cooled down. Reminds me of an anxiety attack. Ever had these feelings before?"

Her look was cold when she said, "No."

"Can you stand?" Dr. Landrum asked. With Blasing's assistance, she managed to shakily rise. "Can you walk?"

"With Blasing's help." She still had a good grip on him.

"Then I'll examine you here," he said.

"I won't tell you everything until I'm back in my room. Mr. Madera will help me, won't you, kind sir?" she said, sounding dizzily blond. Candy smiled.

"But...." Dr. Landrum began.

"We'll see you there, Geoff," Angela said through a few sniffles, but sounding much better.

"It's not wise...."

"I'll be fine...." Angela began.

Blasing looked at the doctor. "You stop her."

Candy leaned closer to the doctor. "Dr. Landrum, I'm a good friend of Angela's and a parapsychologist. You haven't found any signs of a lightning strike, right?"

"Doubtful."

"Then why don't you consider it stress and anxiety. Isn't she reacting as if she saw a murder?"

He nodded. "All right. A comfortable, safe environment is good. I'll be there in about ten minutes."

"Do I need to keep her awake?" Blasing asked.

"Don't talk about me like I'm not here."

"Not necessarily, just check her pulse every few minutes and make sure she's breathing."

"But I don't want to sleep. Something could happen."

"I'll watch over you," Blasing said with a soft smile. "I'm an expert at keeping away bogeymen."

Angela paused, then said, "You may be, but we aren't dealing with bogeymen." She took a deep, shuddering breath. "I said I'll be fine," Angela told him, pulling away from Blasing. Candy reached for her, but she was waved away. Angela only managed a few steps before she wobbled. Blasing caught her before she fell.

"Are you sure about this, Angel?" Candy asked.

"Of course, Blasing's with me."

"I thought you were going to protect me from the ghosts," he said.

"I guess we'll have to protect each other," she told him.

"Why don't we take off those heels so it's easier to walk?"

"Good idea." She leaned against him as she removed both shoes. "We'd better get going, or I'll have to carry you."

"That doesn't sound too bad," Angela said with a weary smile.

"Tell me what happened again," Candy asked. Rod returned to their table to take care of the check.

"Blasing, we need to read that will."

"Right now?" he asked as they descended the steps.

She nodded, then mentioned the agreement between Heller and Peter. "I asked them who was watching you and he said something about Bodie, then he was torn apart!"

"Watching me, eh," Blasing mused. "Bodie is a ghost town in eastern, central California, north of Bridgeport and southeast of Tahoe. It was supposed to be a dangerous and lawless place."

"Yes, dangerous ghosts. They said they couldn't see them."

"Grant and Carrie couldn't see them?" Candy asked. Angela nodded. "How did Bodie ghosts get here?"

"A stage?" Blasing suggested.

"They said bricks," Angela told them.

"But why?" Candy asked. When the elevator arrived, Candy asked, "You think the strange ghosts, the ones from Bodie, might have done something to Grant and Carrie?" Blasing guided Angela inside.

"I don't know."

"But what could have happened to them?" Blasing asked, still disbelieving. "What can hurt a ghost? Why would anybody want to?"

Angela yawned suddenly, surprising herself. "We need to talk to Heller about the agreement and the third set of books."

"Third set of books?"

Angela leaned even more heavily on Blasing. "Thanks for... your compassion."

"You're very welcome. I was serious about my bogeyman experience and needing a good lawyer. The world needs at least one just to prove it's possible. Now, about that third set of books."

"Said Cash had them. I guess Heller has the second set? We can talk to them tomorrow."

"Angel, are you drunk?" Candy suddenly asked.

"Just a little."

Candy looked at Blasing, then said to Angela, "You are full of surprises today."

"Candy you know me so well. Knew right away Ted and I were star-crossed. Too much karma involved. Do you believe in karma?" she asked Blasing.

"Karma or charisma?" Blasing asked her, looking into her pale blue-green eyes. Her expression was innocent, her eyes guileless.

"Karma."

"I think both good and bad actions have rippling effects, and can affect your well-being."

"How'd you know you had a guardian angel?" Angela asked out of the blue. Blasing cleared his throat. The door to the third floor opened, and he all but carried her toward the suite. "Well?"

"She's come through for me several times," he said. "If you'd like, sometime I'll tell you about a few."

"I would like to hear them sometime... sometime when I was sure I'd remember them," she slurred. "Are you my guardian angel?"

"Why, do you need one?" he asked as they stopped at their suite.

"I'm afraid the ghosts might come for me because of what Grant and Carrie told me," she breathed huskily in his ear. "They must have known something about the new ghosts. And now you know, but you should be able to feel them coming."

He gave his key to Candy, who opened the door for them. "Do you want help?" Candy asked.

"I've got her." Blasing swept her off her feet and carried her inside.

"Just sweep me off my feet. Such service. Are you smiling?" He nodded. "I hate when you do that."

"Sorry. Yes I was smiling."

"Good." Then Angela's mood shifted suddenly. "Blasing, I'm frightened. Are you frightened? You do get frightened, don't you?"

"Certainly. I've been frightened since we first drove through that prospector on the road. Casually interacting with the ghosts is the most difficult thing I've ever done."

"Really? Tougher than bungee-jumping, para-gliding, extreme-skiing and all that dangerous stuff?"

"Yes," he said after nodding.

"Even raising kids alone?"

"Hmmm. Too close to call."

"Well, sorry about that prospector. He scared me, too. That shouldn't have happened. A lot of things that shouldn't be happening are." Blasing gently placed her on the bed.

"Ah," Angela sighed, obviously relaxing. "Safe at last."

"Angel, are you going to be all right?" Candy asked.

Angela nodded. "I may sleep after all."

"Do you want me to wait here?" Candy asked.

"No thanks. But you might warn the ghosts about those that can't be seen, but be careful. If you have any hematite, wear it," she yawned. "That way they won't possess you."

"Possess?!" Candy asked, suddenly alarmed. Nearly drifting off, Angela explained about Carrie taking control of a woman's body at the gamblers table. "Rest easy." Candy kissed her friend on the forehead. "I'll be back later. Take good care of her, Mr. Madera. She's a very special person."

Shortly after Candy had left, Blasing heard a thudding as if someone had collided with something, then a low moan came from the lounge. Angela was startled, then she unbuttoned her blouse. "Blasing, you've got to have this!"

"Angela, it's all right," Blasing said, gently taking her hands in his.

"You are cute," Angela laughed unsteadily, then gently removed her hands from his grasp. She fumbled with her blouse again, immodestly unbuttoning it to remove a blackish-silver pendant. "I'm feeling better," she chuckled throatily. "And take these," she said as she took off her two largest gray-silver rings and put them in Blasing's hand. "Here. See if they fit."

"What are these?" He managed to put one on each pinky.

"They're hematite rings and a pendant from my grandmother. Remember?" She smiled, her head bobbing all too loosely. "I'm safe in here, but you're not. The ghost with the wolf's eyes might be stalking you. Wear these. They will protect you. See, I protect you, and you..." she yawned, "protect me."

"But you're safe here."

"Are you going to spend the whole night watching me sleep?"

"If I need to. I want to hear what Dr. Landrum says."

"You're so sweet. I bet you'd stay all night, too."

"You're not making sense," Blasing said.

"Of course I'm not, I'm a lawyer." She laughed. "I think I'm in trouble. Do you remember when I struck Grant Roberts?" Angela asked. Blasing nodded. "I think it's because I was wearing hematite rings. Poor, poor Grant. Torn apart. Poor, poor Carrie." Angela began crying softly once again.

"Angela, I think maybe we should leave."

"No! We can't leave! We owe it to Peter! Something is wrong. It got those two killed and has Peter's ghost running scared."

Blasing looked at the rings and pendant in his palm. "You're afraid the ghosts may attack and believe these will protect me?"

She nodded. "You can touch the ghosts, except sometimes it burns. Spirit, I am so tired." She suddenly grabbed his arm and pulled him very close—their lips almost touching. "Please watch over me so we can find out what happened to Peter, Carrie and Grant. Please," she appeared as serious as a six year old extracting a 'cross your heart and hope to die' promise. "Wear the rings and pendant, please."

"I can't resist such a plea. I promise," Blasing agreed.

"R... remember to watch out for unfriendly ghosts," Angela whispered. She struggled to open her eyes.

Blasing had to lean close. "Why, Angela?"

"They can look like whoever, whatever, or however it works," she mangled. "You know, look young and pretty like those hookers or healthy like Sigurd. I mean Sven." She curled up next to Blasing. "And people. Watch out for people. Talk to them, make sure they're who they say they are. They could be possessed, but if you concentrate you should be able to feel them if they're part ghost."

"Just be as paranoid as when I first got here?"

"Not quite that bad," she laughed, then said, "Thanks for watching over me. I'm a wreck."

"My pleasure, Counselor. Will you verify and sign my body-guarding certificate? I'll be able to hire out."

"I don't know about that."

"Why not?" he asked.

She smiled as though keeping a secret, then said, "I may just want to keep you for myself." She grew quiet, and Blasing thought she was asleep, "Blasing, how do you avoid all those beautiful women who throw themselves at you?"

"Duck? Often just mentioning my kids sends them running."

"Oh. Blasing, I want to tell you something," she whispered. Blasing leaned closer, and she kissed him on the cheek. "I'm sorry I've been such a bitch." She slipped back to the bed, fast asleep.

Blasing checked her pulse and breathing. When he felt sure she was all right, he covered her with a blanket, then walked over to a comfortable chair and sat. He studied the hematite rings and pendant. He still felt watched. "Broderick, are you here?"

The phone out in the suite rang, and Blasing rose to answer it. He smelled a hint of perfume masking cigarettes. "Hello? You're calling for Dr. Landrum? There's been another emergency? All right. That's fine. Tell him I'll be here."

Blasing hung up the phone and paced a while. He still felt watched. When he went into Angela's room, the sensation lessened. For another test, he placed the rings and pendant on the table. His feelings of being watched grew stronger. "Hello? Hello?"

Blasing stared at the rings, unsure of what to believe, but he'd made a promise. He clasped the chain around his neck, then put on the rings. Remembering what Broderick had said about the signals, Blasing walked over to the stereo cabinet. He didn't care what music played, anything to fill the silence. He just hoped the reception made the ghost as uncomfortable. Maybe then, the unwanted spirit would leave him alone.

SEVENTEEN

Blasing awakened half-dressed and intimately entangled with Angela, who was clad only in an unbuttoned silk shirt. The contact of skin on skin was electric. Her scent was intoxicating. Blasing breathed deeply, wanting to lose himself with her. "So sudden...." Blasing mumbled. He ached for her. His every muscle screamed for release.

As if Angela read his mind, she smiled comfortingly and leaned back to stare into his eyes. Angela traced the contours of his face, running her fingers gently across his lips. Her touch set him aflame. "I've been thinking about this since I first saw you." Her bright eyes grew larger and darker, the teal becoming blue and pulling him in to drown as she neared. She kissed him softly, enticing his tongue, then her hands roamed, hot and as featherlight as fiery butterflies. Her caresses slowly became clever and more insistent, and soon Blasing quivered like a bowstring pulled taut.

Blasing gently kissed his way along her jawline, then down her neck. Angela leaned back with a sigh and stroked the back of his head. He lingered at her breasts, then kissed his way along her rib cage and across her stomach, making her squirm and gasp. Angela seemed aglow, a smoldering soul set aflame in the darkness.

When he moved to kiss her lips, Blasing noticed her eyes were brown, not blue at all, and her blond locks were darkening.

He pulled back. "You're not Angela! Who...."

As she reached for him, the brunette smiled and pulled him to her. Her strength was surprising, and Blasing found he had no will to resist. Something about her eyes, now green instead of brown, held him fast. She kissed him deeply, the sensation so intense he could barely stand it—felt he must leap from his skin if he didn't take her in his arms and love her now!

A flash of lightning and an eruption of building-shaking thunder awakened Blasing. With ears still ringing, he saw a wispy after-image fading as if the woman were a remnant from a dream. Blasing sat up on the couch in the lounge—right where he thought he should be. Mac's will lay nearby.

Despite the staccato flashes of lightning, and the grumble of thunder overlapping itself time and time again, Blasing noticed the stereo was quiet. Rain pattered loudly against the windows and the roof. What happened to the music? To him?

Blasing stood shakily, rubbing his burning chest and the back of his itching neck. When he checked the pendant, it was cool, but his skin was very warm. Based on what Angela said, the burning should signify he'd had a ghostly visit. Could Fawn be using his interest in Angela to take advantage of him?

Blasing's hands felt surprisingly good, and when he looked at them, he discovered why: Angela's rings were gone, leaving only his wedding band. He found one gray metal ring at his feet and the other hematite under the couch. They shouldn't have slipped off.

As he put on the rings, Blasing peeked inside Angela's room. She was fully clothed and sleeping peacefully. Hoping she was all right, Blasing walked to her bed. Each time the lightning flashed, the white light made her beauty seem ethereal, and Blasing imagined he could see beyond skin deep. When he gently touched her forehead to check for a fever, sparks seemed to fly, and he briefly flashed back to his dream: Angela's avid hands and lips were all over him.

Blasing fought his way back to the present. Thinking he needed leashes for his hands, he quickly left. Had there really been a ghost? Or had too many subliminal thoughts bubbled to the surface?

If another ghost touched him, what would be the effect? He hadn't felt quite right since his experience with Broderick. Had his touch somehow... amplified his ability to sense ghosts? And if so, had it done anything else to him?

The phone rang, startling him. "Hello? No, I wasn't, doctor, but she is. Breathing, pulse, and temperature are normal. Yes, I'll keep checking. See you in the morning. Good night."

Blasing glanced at his watch; it was almost three. Where was Broderick? Blasing had grown rather fond of the Englishman and was hoping nothing "fell" had happened to him. Blasing did a double-think: was he beginning to believe Angela's story?

Blasing scratched his neck, then someone behind him cleared their throat. "I am present, Mr. Madera."

"Broderick!" Blasing realized he'd yelled too loudly when he heard Angela stir.

"Sorry to startle you, sir. I am trying to be less... startling, as it were. Should I present myself front and center?"

"No. No. Sorry. I'm just jumpy," Blasing said more quietly. "I'm glad you're back. I was growing concerned."

"My deepest apologies if I have caused you any grief, sir," the ghost valet said gravely. He folded his hands behind his back.

Blasing moved toward the wet bar. "What did you discover?" He poured himself soda and bitters to settle his stomach.

"I found nothing amiss in the greenhouse gardens. Nor any sign of Carrie, Grant, nor a murder, though I admit the place had a... rather queer feeling. I... I cannot describe it."

"Try without touching me this time."

Broderick appeared a bit chagrined. The ghost cleared his throat, then said, "It just seemed... sad."

"Are any of the other ghosts missing?"

"Fawn," he said, rolling his eyes.

"I think she was here."

"Oh dear. I am so sorry, sir. Shall I check the premises?"

"Probably too late. Anyone else missing?"

"I have been unable to find Quinn, but that proves nothing. Sometimes he disappears for days to paint."

"I haven't met him. What is he like?"

"Determined. Very much a perfectionist."

"Was he for or against the timeshare?"

"Devoutly against. Why do you ask? What do you suspect?"

"I don't know," he said, then related what Angela had told him.

"Goodness gracious! Strangers running amok about the premises!"

"Now you know how I initially felt about ghosts," Blasing said wryly. "But this bothers me more. If you can't see them, I...."

"I thought I heard Broderick," Angela said in a sleep-filled voice. She appeared groggy, still dressed in rumpled formal wear. Rubbing her eyes, Angela walked unsteadily to Blasing's side.

She was still lovely, and when he looked at her it rekindled his dream. Angela casually took his arm. "Thank you for listening to me rant and rave. And for watching over me. Blasing, you're shaking. Are you sure you're all right?"

"I'll be fine. How are you?" Her touch had caused another flashback, quickening his pulse.

Angela gave him a concerned look. "Emotionally drained, but I feel better. I'm no longer... stunned, I guess that's what I'd have to call it. Shocked maybe. That flash of light did something to me, though I don't know what."

"You look uncomfortable, sir. Do you feel watched?"

"A ghost was here?" Angela said, moving closer to Blasing.

"I think so."

"One you couldn't see?"

"I don't know, Angela. I... I had a... bad dream. When I awakened, I was confused. I'd fallen asleep on the couch reading Mac's will. Grant was correct about the sixty day agreement."

"And I didn't receive that copy," Angela said with a yawn. "Although you remember mailing it, right Broderick?"

"Indeed I do, miss. As if I had just done it a moment ago."

"Damn!"

"Angela," Blasing said. "You need to rest. We can deal with this in the morning. We can't do anything until then, anyway."

"You're right," she said, fully deflating. "But what are you doing up?" Angela could barely keep her eyes open, yet she continued to study Blasing. "Oh yeah, the nightmare. That's why you're shaking. Want to talk about it?"

"Maybe tomorrow."

"Write it down before you forget," Angela suggested.

"I assure you I won't forget," Blasing replied.

Angela yawned, then stretched, heightening every curve and stealing Blasing's breath. When she finished, she leaned heavily against him. "Has anyone informed Heller?"

"No." Blasing's hands were sweaty but light upon her.

"Not as of yet, miss."

"Well, in the morning we should talk with him and Madame Zanadane. See what she thinks. You can meet her then, Blasing. Maybe a selective cleansing might get rid of whatever's here—whatever came in on the stage or from Bodie," she yawned again.

"What about the séance? Would that work?" Blasing asked. He couldn't believe those words had come out of his mouth.

"It might. Right now, I'm going to fall asleep in your arms."

"Come on." He gently guided her to bed. He felt as if he were running a sprint, his pulse pounding and his breathing heavy. "I wonder if it'd be smarter to do business away from Ghostal Shores."

"Absolutely not! I'm not leaving!" Angela said. "We owe Peter and Carrie and Grant. You're not a chicken," she yawned mightily, "so don't start now. I need your help, Mr. Blasing Madera."

"I could get a more reasonable lawyer," Blasing replied.

"We've already talked about this, but as someone once told me, you can't do anything until morning," she said as he gently laid her to bed. "Hey, are you sure you're all right? You're sweating." She touched his head. "And you're a bit feverish."

"I am warm. I think I'm going for a walk."

"Must have been quite a nightmare," she said sympathetically. "There are ghosts everywhere but here. You could stay with me." Her smile was relaxed, her hand resting lightly on his arm.

"I'm too restless. I'd just keep you awake," he stammered a bit. "I'll check on you when I get back."

She appeared concerned but said, "All right. You're wearing the hematite?"

He showed her. "I'll have Broderick stay and watch over you."

"Take him with you if you want," she mumbled.

Blasing brushed her forehead with his lips, then departed quickly. "Broderick! Please watch these rooms. I'm going for a walk."

"Alone, sir?" Broderick asked, eyebrow raised. "Is that not a bit... adventuresome?"

"Life's an adventure and it appears it may not stop there," Blasing said. Broderick appeared disconcerted by his venture in philosophy. "Don't worry. Angela gave me some protective charms."

"I am not sure...." Broderick began. Blasing touched him with a pinky. "Just as with Miss Starborne, very strange. Suppose I touch you again, sir?"

"Give it a try, but remember what happened last time." Blasing steeled himself for whatever onslaught might be coming.

The Englishman touched his hand gingerly, then gripped it. "Anything, sir?"

"Something vague. I don't know. It seems to work. I'll see you soon," Blasing said. He nearly bolted out the door. Once outside, he took several deep breaths.

Blasing didn't know how long he'd been gone—or where he'd been walking. With two-thirds of the lights dimmed, one corridor looked much like the next. Ghostal Shores was bigger than he remembered, but not big enough. Everywhere he went the sensation of being watched followed him—and that didn't include security, which seemed to be all over the place. Whiffs and wafts of perfume and cigarettes came and went with some unfelt breeze. Was it the same spirit who enticed him earlier?

But why were two unknown ghosts watching him? Or were there more than two? After what Angela told him about Grant and Carrie, Blasing no longer believed it was merely curiosity, or self-preservation by the prostitutes.

"Bon jour, Blasing," Eva said. She seemed to suddenly appear from a shadow. Eva wore the same outfit as earlier but wrapped in a white-fur stole as if the temperature had dropped severely. "This is my lucky evening." Her eyes were bright and shiny, her lips glistening as she flashed a devastating smile. By the way she examined Blasing, Eva looked as if she were choosing between outfits for a special occasion.

"Are you all right?" Blasing asked, remembering Angela's warning about possessed people. Cigarettes and perfume drifted through the air. Blasing fought the urge to scratch.

"Oui, now that you've come to accept my invitation."

A flash of lightning came from a corridor and washed over them, catching Eva's coat. She seemed to glow. Blasing suddenly wondered whether Eva was really here. "Invitation?"

"The one I've been speaking with my entire body. Please don't tell me you haven't noticed."

"I've noticed, I'm just unusually hesitant about mixing business with pleasure."

"You are missing out," she said, moving closer.

"It's very late."

"I'm ready to stay up all night, if you are. Am I that unattractive?" she asked, touching his face.

By the look in her eyes and her comment, Blasing wondered if she were on something, but before he could respond, her necklace slid into her bodice. Eva quickly clutched herself, her eyes widening in shock and panic. Both earrings popped free as if corks from champagne bottles, one shooting across the hallway, the other bouncing off the wall, then rebounding off a table to career across the floor.

"Mon dieu! Not again. What is it about being around you?" She slowly backed away around a corner, out of sight.

Blasing heard a chuckle from behind him. "Who's there?" When the laughter drifted along the hall, he followed it. The perfume and smell of cigarettes came and went. Blasing was determined to resolve this. "Why won't you show yourself?"

The soft laughter took on a deeper, throatier quality. When it moved down a corridor toward a viewing nook, Blasing stopped. Lightning lit the narrow hallway, and for a moment, he saw the diaphanous outline of a woman which faded with the flash. "Because you might be blinded by my beauty."

Against all his better judgment, Blasing entered the corridor. "Tell me more, Miss...."

She chuckled throatily in response, her dim, hazy form moving farther into the nook and deeper into the shadows. Her perfume swept toward him in a wave, its undertow trying to drag him forward. Beneath it was the ash-tang of cigarettes.

"Are you alone?" he asked. She chuckled again. "Are you after my body?"

"Oh my..." the ghost began, leading to laughter full of sensual pleasure. Then it was suddenly cut short, "...hey...."

"What's happening?" Blasing asked, unsure whether to advance or retreat. The back of his neck itched madly.

"Sorry ta be interruptin', Blaise," the spirit said as it appeared, forming the image of a familiar, red-haired Irishman.

"MAC!"

"But this wasn't what she and I agreed upon. You know, women," he continued, his brogue heavy. Mac looked young, much like Blasing remembered him from twenty years ago.

"Mac, what's going on?" Blasing asked.

The ghost looked around nervously. "Blaise, it's dangerous ta stay here! Think of the youngin's, Kelly and Patrick. Leave in the mornin'. Please, donna make me beg."

"Angela won't leave."

"I'm not surprised. She's a b..." he jerked, then coughed.

"Angela's very loyal, but 'tis dangerous ta stay, boyo." He looked about nervously. "Take her away. Use ye charm. Convince her."

"Mac, talk to me! Tell me what's going on! Who shot you?"

"Don't be like me, Blaise. A long time ago, I made a mistake. Take Angela away. She's a fine woman."

"What mistake? Is that why I'm being followed by that... dark stranger with the yellow eyes?"

"He's a vile one, so retched... urk!" Mac's ghost jerked back, disappearing into nothingness.

"Mac?!"

The shadows gathered as though forming a dark robe rising from the floor. The lightning flashed, bleaching the ghost's long jacket and remaining in his yellow-green eyes. His face grew even darker as his eyes narrowed, then he charged at Blasing.

He was caught off guard, but still managed to duck, tripping the spirit as he lunged. The ghost was surprised by the contact and sent sprawling, a string of curses following him as he disappeared into a wall.

"I'll be damned," Blasing said, shaking his hands. They burned and heat emanated from the rings, running up his arms. Just before they'd caught fire, Blasing felt as if struck by a strong gust of wind.

A crack of thunder was the prelude to a harsh voice that sounded as rocks grinding against each other. "You'll pay for this, and I will get back what is mine! Those you hold dearest will suffer before you join us." The jagged, guttural laughter lingered for a while, then slowly faded away into the storm.

EIGHTEEN

When Angela awakened Tuesday morning, Blasing still slept in her reading chair, his head on his arms, continuing to watch over her from dreamland. Again she was surprised by how youthful he appeared. If only she could look so good in the morning. She rose quietly, snagged some clothes, then slipped into the bathroom.

He was still sleeping when she returned, so she gently stroked his face. "Good morning, Blasing."

Eyes snapping wide, Blasing was startled awake. He immediately pulled back, then slowly relaxed. "Good morning, Counselor."

"Thank you for watching over me. How did you sleep?"

"I'm stiff and my hands hurt."

Angela gently took his hands, then carefully removed the hematite rings. "These look burned. What happened?"

Blasing looked at her for a long time, his eyes darkening as if thinking about telling her some secret, then he recounted last night. When he told her about Eva, Angela stifled a chuckle. He continued, telling her about following the spirit. "She briefly revealed herself, claiming I'd be blinded by her beauty."

"Arrogant, isn't she?"

Blasing frowned. "Then Mac appeared, looking young."

"Peter? Again?" she asked. Blasing nodded. "What did he say?"

"To leave. That he'd made a mistake long ago." Blasing explained how Mac was grabbed, then about the cat-eyed spirit attacking him.

"Attacked?" Angela said, sounding strangled.

"Yeah. I ducked, and he stumbled over me. That's when I burned my hands."

"What did he do after he... fell?"

"Threatened me. It's one of the reasons I slept here. Angela, this place is getting stranger and more dangerous. I think we should leave immediately Mac doesn't want us hurt."

"He thinks he can handle it. Stubborn man. Mule-headed ghost."

"You know him better than I. Could he have killed someone?"

"I don't think so, but I can't help but wonder if the mistake he was talking about involved Jaclyn Cassidy."

"I don't know. He just kept emphasizing that we should leave."

Angela surprised him by saying, "I'm beginning to agree with you, Blasing, but I won't leave until we've tried a séance. And we need to talk to Heller about the 60-day agreement."

Blasing sighed resignedly. "And discover if there are other accounting books. I need to review all the financial paperwork to see if what you and Grant gave me match. Then when we talk to Heller, I can sort of feel him out."

"Push buttons and fish for reactions? See if he knows what Mac's horrible mistake might have been?"

"Yes. I'm sure he wants to talk to you about Grant and Carrie."

"What makes you think that?"

"Curiosity, and they're his meal ticket. I also want access to the files—the ones in personnel and held by supervisors, especially Porter's."

"Good ideas. What if the books don't match and Heller won't confess?"

"We snoop. Think Broderick would help?"

"He might."

"Well, it sounds like we're here one more day then," Blasing yawned, "but to tell the truth, I'm more worried about these ghosts that 'can't be seen' than by altered books, crooked contracts and murder conspiracies."

"I am too," she said taking his hand. "The rings and pendant worked, didn't they?"

"They seemed to." He squeezed her hand, then removed his hand to examine it. Both hands required some minor medical attention.

"Would you feel safer if I cleaned and protected your room?" Angela asked, wondering why he seemed so distant today. When they'd first met, he was guarded and formal. Then, last night when she needed it, he'd been kind and compassionate. Had she misunderstood him? Or had something else happened?

Blasing hesitated, then finally said, "Sure. I'm going to be as open-minded as I can be. I just hope the room doesn't go up in flames because too many ghosts try to parade through it."

"I hadn't thought of that," she said. "Are you serious?"

"No. At least I don't think so." He looked very tired.

"What time did you get in?"

"About four," he yawned.

"Then continue sleeping. Here," she said, pulling him to his feet. "Sleep here until I get your room cleansed and sealed."

"But... there's so much to do." He yawned, then looked guilty.

"And you'll do it better after you've slept," she said, almost dragging him to her bed. He was quite a handful. With a sigh, Angela pushed him onto the bed. She bit her lip, tempted to join him, then noticed he was already asleep. The previous three days had really taken their toll. Angela smiled sympathetically, removed his shoes, then left, thinking he looked very good rumpled in her bed.

She had just placed the last crystal for the grid in Blasing's room when somebody knocked on the door. Angela gathered all her stuff, wrapping it in a colorful blanket, then answered the door. "Hello, Candykins."

"Angel! Even in jeans, you look wonderful! Especially after that fright you gave us last night! You must be feeling better! It's amazing what a good man can do for you." Her lascivious smile was lavender, matching her outfit of stretch pants and a flowery blouse.

"Candy, keep your voice down and come in. Blasing's still sleeping," Angela said, moving so Candy could come inside.

"Wear him out?" she asked, then wrinkled her nose. "Nice smell. You smoking again?"

"No! I smudged Blasing's room, then sealed it."

"Oh, how Native. And he slept through it?"

"He's sleeping in my room."

"Oh my. A miracle! It must have been an incredible night! First being buffeted by the spiritual energies from two dying souls, then embraced in passionate romance. Is that what all that thunder and lightning was about?"

"Afraid not. He slept in the chair," Angela replied.

"And you're disappointed? Wonderful! Why didn't you drag him to bed?"

"Be serious and listen to me for a minute," Angela snapped. "Something is wrong with Ghostal Shores." Angela explained what

Blasing told her about his experience.

"Oh dear. We need to get that séance running. Do you think this dark spirit is connected to Peter MacGuire's murder?"

"I don't know. How about doing the séance this evening?"

"Sure," Candy said, walking to the sliding door and staring outside. They appeared to be between storms again—blue sky overhead, but dark thunderheads on the horizon. "I have several people lined up already. Any suggestions?"

"How about Efrem Xantini?"

"The mentalist from Chicago? He's here? You've met him?"

Angela nodded. "But I don't want Madame Zanadane included. Tell him you only have room for one more and I recommended him."

"He's impressive, though a bit mystic-looking for me. You know, Madame Z may show." She turned and examined Angela. "You're sure you're up to this?"

"I feel a bit... drained, even let down, but I'm fine."

"Of course. Such a close proximity to death would affect anybody, Angel." Candy glided across the room and gave her best friend a hug.

"I know. I know. Sometimes just out of the blue, I want to cry, but at least I know I'm only dealing with the psychological aspects now. I feel better physically. Whatever struck me has passed. As for Madame Zanadane, we'll deal with her if she shows."

"Say, you really don't like her, do you?"

"No, I don't. Part of it's because she swooped in like a scavenger after Peter was murdered. Part is intuitive."

"You worried she may disrupt things?"

"I don't know what to think. She's an extension of Heller."

"How about a walk?" Candy gestured toward the balcony. "It's a beautiful day and it might make you feel better."

"Good idea." Angela sneaked into her room and returned with a jacket, gently closing the door behind her. She did the same to Blasing's room. "Let's go."

When they opened the door, they surprised Dr. Landrum. He appeared as if he hadn't slept much, his eyes red and his face scruffy and pinched.

"Good morning, Geoff," Angela said brightly.

"Where do you think you're going?"

Angela stiffened. "I'm going for a walk on the beach. Why, is there a problem?"

"Not without permission from your physician."

"You're not my personal physician, and I feel fine," Angela said, hands on hips. "I want to go outside. Get away from the ghosts."

"I can understand that."

"You understand she wasn't struck by lightning," Candy maintained.

"You slept well?" he asked. "No problems? No confusion?" Angela shook her head. "Light-headedness or loss of balance?"

"No."

"And you remember everything that happened?"

"In excruciating detail," Angela said, seeing the scene again and again in her mind.

"Then you have my permission to go...."

"How *gracious* of you."

"If I can join you, AND you tell me what happened last night." He glanced at Candy. "I'll try to be open-minded."

"Wouldn't you rather spend the day with Eva?"

"I am a doctor first," he replied sternly.

"And he is handsome, well-spoken and wealthy," Candy whispered in Angela's ear.

"Doctor first, eh? All right, you can come along." Angela said, closing the door behind her. "You'll probably think I'm crazy."

"Crazier, Angel," Candy said. "Crazier."

The beach was still saturated. The coastal waters churned dark green and frothy, heavy white waves pounding the shore. Gusty winds carried heavy spray far inland. As they wandered the beach, Angela told her tale, then Blasing's.

Dr. Landrum was having trouble swallowing the story, but Candy shouted, "Not only does a séance make sense now, it's a must! Does Blasing understand that?" Angela nodded. "It might coerce the ghosts—Peter, that woman, and the dark, cat-eyed one—to appear for someone besides him." Candy jumped back from the shore to avoid a large wave.

"As well as resolve whether Grant and Carrie still exist. So many mysteries." Angela wiped her face dry of spray. "I want some answers."

"Tonight!" Candy cried triumphantly.

"I'd like to attend the séance," Dr. Landrum told them. "I've never been to one, and this seems like just the right environment to experience one."

"I don't know if we should, based on your taste for women."

"Mea culpa, Angela. How was I to find out if Eva was what she appeared to be if I didn't spend some time with her?"

"That's an interesting way to put it," Angela replied.

"Is Eva as bad as she seems?" Candy asked.

"Worse," Angela said.

"Not really," Dr. Landrum said. "She's a victim of excess."

"With a heart of gold," Angela snapped.

"Who needs help."

"In the form of a swift kick out the door," Angela growled.

"Angel, let it go," Candy said. "She's a primadonna. Enough said. Remember, we're talking to a man about an attractive woman. You can't expect good judgment."

"Hey!"

"Now, about the séance. I have several people interested in being participants. I'll contact them and set it up. What are you doing today, Angel?"

"Calling the office and meeting with Heller."

"Thrills."

"I also want to visit the library. See what I can find out about Bodie. It would be nice to know what kind of lawless rabble we might be dealing with."

"Angel, you're starting to sound like Broderick."

"But your mind's working well," Dr. Landrum observed. "That makes me feel better. No lasting effects of the strike..." he held up his hands, "whether spiritual or physical lightning."

Angela calmed her glare. "It just seems to be working slowly."

"Well, Angel, you've never been a morning person. In fact, you can almost be as grumpy as Mr. Heller." Angela glared and stuck out her tongue. "See!"

"Has anyone spoken to Mr. Heller?" Dr. Landrum asked.

"I don't know," Angela said. "Broderick might have."

"How do you think he'll take the apparent murdering of two of his ghosts?"

"I don't know, Geoff," Angela said as she brushed her hair from her face. "Usually he's blunt and rough, but he's also unnerved by the ghosts. And when I think about it, I can't prove anything really happened. It just looks like another missing ghost. Marsh and Quinn, who seeks solitude to paint, do it all the time."

"Could that be why Heller's such a bastard?" Candy asked. "He's uptight about the ghosts?"

"He's never really gotten along with Grant Roberts nor Carrie," Angela continued. "He might be ecstatic. They were more adamantly opposed than anybody else to the crimeshare. For all I know, he might wrap events in romance for sales: come unlock the mystery of the missing ghosts."

"How long have you known him?" Dr. Landrum asked.

"About five years, I guess."

"Has he always been so... fiery?"

"You mean foul-tempered? Yes, but he seems to have gotten worse over the last year."

"I think he's a prime candidate for Prozac," Candy joked. "Or maybe he's on uppers. They don't come much more torqued."

"You mean every fold in place and well-creased?" Angela asked. Candy nodded.

"Ever regretted working here?" Dr. Landrum asked.

"Peter, bless his soul, made it worthwhile. Besides, I didn't have a choice. I was assigned here by my firm. They said it was my experience with spiritual phenomenon—Candy and I have been taking classes at Berkeley for years," Angela began, then flushed, "but Peter later admitted it was my legs. He probably was just looking for another... companion."

"But he didn't have any luck, did he?"

Angela smiled wistfully. "Of sorts. We became good friends. There isn't much better luck than that."

"Do you think there's something wrong with Heller?" Candy asked. "Maybe that's why he's in such a hurry to sell."

"Not that I know of. But Madame Zanadane said Heller told her Peter was terminally ill. *IF* we can compel him to come to the séance, we can ask. Did Dr. Reasons say anything about it, Geoff?"

"No. But from what I hear, Mac really knew how to wine and dine. That could have led to several long term problems."

"Well, he certainly had flair. The Irish James Bond of resort owners," Angela sighed wistfully, recalling his imitation of the spy while ordering their wines.

"I guess you have to do something with all that money."

"As if doctors don't have that problem," Candy responded.

"Or lawyers," he said with a smile. "I'd heard from some that Peter MacGuire's greatest achievement was beating the bottle." Angela nodded. "That he and Mr. Heller were old drinking buddies."

"I've rarely seen Heller drink," Angela replied.

"I've always wondered what he spent his money on." Dr. Landrum mused. "Paper isn't that expensive."

"Maybe he just hordes it," Candy said. "So Mr. Heller was old money, and Peter was James Bond?" Candy chuckled. "What a combination. Whatever brought them together?"

"A dream and mutual need," Angela replied, looking out to sea, wondering why Peter's ghost was hiding. Why wasn't he helping them?

"What kept them together?" Candy wondered. "They seem so different."

"Sometimes needs become addictions that are difficult to escape," Dr. Landrum said. "How do you think Blasing will fit in? Though he's not English, I actually think he's more of the James Bond type. Tall, dark and handsome, hardly Irish at all. He attracts women like bees to honey and moves like someone who knows what he's doing and where he's going."

Angela smiled. "This place confused him for a while, but he's adjusting fast. He tries not to let it show that the ghosts unnerve him." They passed the recently constructed boathouse and neared the steps.

"Not a nineties man?" Candy asked.

"I thought that was an eighties man? I get so confused. I can rarely tell the difference. Still the ghosts seem to like him, except for whatever newcomer is haunting him. He's honest and a loving father, not a bad combination."

"Especially with looks like that," Candy said, "although our companion can enter the San Jose buns contest anytime." Instead of flushing, Dr. Landrum smiled.

"What kind of man are you, Geoff?"

He smiled. "The kind and benevolent healer, sort of a Marcus Welby type, but much younger."

"I would say a man who asks a lot of questions, a medical examiner, lawyer, or game show host instead of Marcus Welby," Angela said pointedly.

"Okay, I'll confess," Dr. Landrum said as he ushered them up the steps. "I'm a shameless womanizer who respects women, but I hold myself to the highest standards of care. One of the many nice things about being an emergency room doctor is you don't have to worry about getting involved with your patients. No files to keep. No consultations. No breaches of confidence, trust or etiquette."

"Another one. Angel, you draw them like a magnet."

"I'm flattered Geoff, but I am absolutely, positively not looking for a man. It seems like I just got rid of one."

"That's the best time to find one." His smile was roguish.

"Oh, but you wouldn't like me on my blonde days," she said, then gave him a sample of her blonde-bimbo act. Candy laughed until she hung onto the railing.

Dr. Landrum appeared stunned, then said, "Thought of going into acting?" Angela shook her head. "Well, can you still tell me about yourself over dinner?"

"Shouldn't you be taking care of patients?"

"I'm on vacation!" he protested.

When they reached the garden landing, they almost bumped into a stocky man dressed in a sheriff's uniform. His hat was pulled low and his collar high and tight. Only his cigarette was clearly visible.

"Hello, Sheriff Middleton," Dr. Landrum said.

"Hello, Doc," he tipped back his hat. His face was haggard and heavily lined, including dark-circled eyes.

"Not sleeping well?" Dr. Landrum asked. The sheriff nodded. "Come see me later." The sheriff nodded again, this time taking a long drag on his cigarette.

"Hello, Ms. Starborne. Sorry it took so long for us to meet. This place keeps a man busy. Can I ask you a few questions?" She nodded. "Do you have any idea why anyone would want to kill Peter MacGuire?"

"No. But I can give you at least two hundred reasons why someone would want to kill Sean Heller."

"So can a lot of people. Broderick told me you saw two ghosts 'murdered' last night on the veranda. Heller wants to know what I'm going to do about it." The sheriff rolled his eyes.

"Then he knows. Was he angry?"

"Concerned is more like it. I told him there wasn't any proof. I'd like to hear your story."

She told it succinctly. Twice they had to move so that guests could descend the stairs to the beach. A couple was so well bundled they reminded her of inflatable dolls. The next group appeared to be monks of some indeterminate denomination. The wind made their brown robes flag and snap, their hoods blown back.

The sheriff lit up a second cigarette. Dr. Landrum shook his head and said, "Bad habit."

"Helps calm the nerves," the sheriff said. Angela understood exactly what he meant, thinking she needed to move on before she bummed a smoke. She pacified herself by giving the evil eye to a mouthy salesman and his clients.

"How many times have I told you they'll be the death of you?" Dr. Landrum continued.

Sheriff Middleton was quiet for a moment, as though counting, then said, "Maybe a dozen. Not bad in a week. I hear it more often than that from my wife, Doc. I married her, but I don't listen to her, so why should I listen to you?"

Dr. Landrum laughed. Angela thought they seemed to be birds of a feather.

"Sorry, Ms. Starborne. I don't know what to say about your story, but if there's no body, and nobody missing, then it's sort of difficult for me to do my job."

"You asked. I don't expect you to do anything."

"There's no secular law about killing ghosts," Candy added, sounding as if there should be.

Sheriff Middleton frowned. "I've spoken with my forensics man, James Donahue. He can do what you want about the test, but you'll have to make a formal request. Paperwork, you know."

"Can he also tell me if Peter was terminally ill?"

"I would think so."

"How long will that take? Processing and to get results?"

"A month or so if you're lucky."

"A month!"

"That's fast for government work," Sheriff Middleton said, then took a long drag.

Angela could see where this was headed. It might be tight making the agreement deadline. And they couldn't initiate anything but the tests. They could only respond to Meg Cassidy's claim. Still, showing the judge the time constraint should speed up the proceedings.

A distant sound of thunder flashed Angela back to waiting for Carrie to show up. She felt sorry for her and the lecherous spirit; they'd been trying to help her and Blasing. And probably Peter, too. Could there be lechers with hearts of gold? Grant had mentioned Bodie. Was that the key? Or Peter's mistake, whatever that might be. Regardless, the library would be a good place to start.

"Angela, are you all right?" Dr. Landrum asked, the concern evident on his face.

"I just remembered something, I'll see you later," she said and took off, leaving Dr. Landrum open-mouthed. "Come on, Candy." As Angela headed inside, she couldn't shake the image of the two men standing together.

NINETEEN

"Where to, Angel?" Candy asked as they entered the lobby. It was noisy, busy with salespeople touring customers.

"To the library to find out about Bodie," Angela said. She frowned at Alicia Perez, Walter Bond, and their prospects waiting for the elevator. Each was tastefully, if expensively dressed, with watches that cost more than her car.

"I'm going to finish gathering up the participants," Candy said. "How's eight o' clock sound?"

"Great. See you then." Angela got on the elevator with a security guard and two sales tours. "How's it going, Mr. Bond?"

"A dozen sales yesterday and already two more this morning from people we let think about our offer overnight," he said with an easy ear to ear grin. "I expect the same today and tomorrow."

"Enjoy it while you can," Angela said, surveying their three clients. "And ladies and gentlemen, I suggest you buy fast, because sometime this afternoon there will be an injunction to stop this illegal selling." The trio was shocked for a moment, then bombarded Perez and Bond with questions. Angela smiled when they exited en mass to the foyer. She hummed all the way to the third floor.

The library's twin doors were large and impressive, dark oak relief-cut with trees. When Angela pushed them open, she had the feeling she'd stepped into someone's private coastal study. As if in homage, antique chairs and couches faced the apparently endless Pacific.

"Can I help you?" Janice asked as the spirit drifted from the nearby shelves. Despite her petite loveliness, the ghost had been a school teacher and spinster for all of her days. Today, instead of just timid, she seemed frightened, her wide eyes restless as if expecting trouble at any moment.

"I'm looking for information on Bodie," Angela said.

"The California boomtown?" the spirit asked. Angela nodded. "We have numerous books on the subject in the California section, under ghost towns and mining. Would you like me to show you?"

"Maybe in a minute. What kind of place was it?"

"I've never been there, but I heard it was Hell on Earth. A girl-friend of mine moved there. The last letter I received was just after she'd moved." Janice shuddered, then continued her vigilance.

"A rough place?"

"The roughest. At least a murder a day, and that doesn't include all the accidents." That word reminded Angela of Barney's concerns and the construction difficulties. "Lots of mining, drinking, and gambling. Union gang problems, too. Bodie was one of those overnight developments—mostly bars, banks and whorehouses. Hardly any water anywhere. A miracle to find a blade of grass, let alone a well or stream. But did it deter people?" She shook her head. "Every day there was a fortune to be won or lost. Don't know why, but the place attracted the dregs from the bottom of the barrel. Mark Twain wrote about it in *The Badman of Bodie*."

"Another lawless town of the West," Angela mused.

"Not just another," Janice said, "the worst. It was run by the gang bosses. Anybody threatening came in, they were killed. Lynchings were popular."

"Are you sure you haven't lived there?"

"Oh, I am sorry, I do go on, don't I? Sounds just like I really lived there."

"You didn't?"

"No, Carrie did for a while. Her husband, Melvin, was killed there, so she moved back to Goldfield to run a store with her son. If you have questions, Carrie will probably be more informative than reading any book."

"I'll bet. But Carrie is... missing," Angela gently told her. The pain of their 'deaths' came back to her. She struggled to maintain her composure.

"I heard," Janice replied, looking on the verge of tears. She suddenly became even more fuzzy and diaphanous.

"Janice, have you seen any strange ghosts?" Angela asked.

"N- none have come in here," she stammered, eyes wide.

"And you rarely leave, right?" Angela asked. Janice nodded. "Since Carrie is gone, who else would know about Bodie? Anybody?"

"Try Lila at the apothecary. Her sister lived there."

Angela thanked her and left. The mention of accidents set her mind to working, and she hardly noticed the other passengers on the elevator ride to the lobby.

Angela stopped by the 1880's General Store looking for Carrie. The perky clerk hadn't seen Carrie for two days. Angela headed for the apothecary. Angus walked through a wall and followed her.

When Angela thought she saw Marsh in the entryway shadows, she jogged to the shop, but he was already gone. Lila was also absent; she'd left about a half-hour ago. As Angela walked to the tailor's, she wondered if any of the other storeowners were missing.

Angela's entrance into the men's clothing store drew admiring gazes. Eddie Goldman was busy measuring a tall, thin man with a jeweled ring on every finger. When she asked if he knew about Carrie and Grant, Eddie said, "Don't ask."

"Eddie...."

"Yeah, I heard, but I'm not sure I believe it."

"Eddie...."

"I know. I know what you think you saw," he said, his dark eyes avoiding her, watching measurements he usually performed without thought.

"Felt," Angela replied coldly. With some difficulty, she explained their 'deaths' in detail. Eddie blanched, having to re-measure an arm. "Do you know any reason they would be... killed?"

"All right already with the questions! We both know they didn't agree with Heller." Eddie glared at her. "And you and I both know men with money and power quite often remove people when they can't be bought. Hey, get that damn cat outta here!"

Angela noticed Angus for the first time. The cat lithely leaped into her arms. "Hey!" Surprised, she instinctively caught the ghostly feline. Angus rubbed against her.

"Neat trick. Didn't know you could do that," Eddie said.

"Poor guy." Angela scratched his ears. When she noticed the patrons staring at her, she said, "I know you miss Carrie, Angus, but this is against the rules. We don't want everyone touching the ghosts. Who knows what might come of it." She gently dropped Angus.

"How'd you do that?" Eddie asked.

"Same way I slapped Grant, I imagine. Eddie, what do you know of Bodie?"

"Bodie?" His wrinkled face was scrunched with thought. "Never heard anything good only dreck."

"Anybody missing besides Fawn, Carrie and Grant?"

"Ang, can we speak outside?" he asked. She nodded. "Excuse me for a minute, sir. I'll be right back." Angela stalked out with the spirit on her heels. "Ang, I think you should let things go."

"You mean Peter's murder?" she asked, growing angrier when Eddie Goldman nodded. "You don't think we owe him?!"

"Of course, of course we owe him, Ang!" he agreed, his hands gesturing about wildly, "but I fear for you, you know?"

"I can take care of myself."

"I know, I know you can, but I wouldn't want you to die in a fire. I know what that's like... and it's a horrible way to die. Can't you conduct your legal business away from Ghostal Shores?"

Angela sputtered, then ignoring Eddie's pleas, she turned on her heel and went to visit the barber. Angus followed, his tail held high as if sending a disdainful message to the tailor.

Allen the barber wasn't glad to see Angela. The rotund ghost made sure a customer was between them. Angela wasn't sure if the spirit was edgy because he'd heard about Carrie and Grant, or feared she would slap him for his past behavior. Of course Allen waved to his customers and proclaimed he was very busy, but she stalked him until he answered every question. Allen spoke more civil-tongued than usual, but didn't know anything of interest. She soon left.

Plump and gray Martha flitted about her antique shop, a fake look of bliss on her face. Angela tried to get her to slow down, but she wouldn't, too agitated to stop talking or assisting patrons. Angela attempted to keep up, but after several near misses with customers and numerous apologies, she gave up and headed for the Spirited Woman. Angus still tailed her.

"Hey, Angela, there you are," Blasing called out, his stride confident and purposeful. His appearance turned female heads all along Old West Avenue, and just seeing him lifted Angela's spirits. "Broderick told me I might find you here." Blasing looked terrific—clean-shaven and refreshed, but if she read his eyes right, something still haunted him.

A pair of lovely ladies freshly dressed to kill exited the store, staring speculatively at Blasing. She could almost feel the heat and wondered if they might start dropping jewelry.

"You look better," Angela said. "How are your fingers?" she

asked, taking his hands in hers. She was glad he didn't withdraw this time—no longer skittish as a colt. Yet his gaze still didn't hold hers for long. What had changed?

"They'll be okay. You're looking much better, too."

"Sleep, the magical salve," she said, wanting to tell him his presence did the same for her.

"I couldn't sleep long after you left." The women left in disgust and that also made her smile. "The place smelled odd, so I got up, cleaned up, opened the doors, and studied the financials."

"That was sagebrush." Her smile grew broader, her eyes dancing at his sudden discomfort.

"So my room is... safe?"

She nodded, nearly laughing at his hesitancy, but knowing better. Maybe her heritage frightened him; she hoped not. "Did you find anything interesting?"

"There are numerous discrepancies." He slowly extracted his hands from hers.

"And you're going to confront Mr. Heller and want support?"

"Mr. Heller wants to talk about what happened last night. Have you learned anything?" Angela explained about Bodie, but he already knew that much. "So you think the ghosts are coming from there?"

"Carrie indicated such."

"Why would ghosts take a stage from the bricks to the front door?" Blasing asked. "None of this makes sense."

While they talked, several women loitered around the entrance, modeling striking and sometimes very revealing outfits that would set most credit cards, and even more loins, afire. Would it always be like this, she wondered? "I tried to see Lila at the apothecary, but she's gone out."

"Missing?"

"I don't know yet, but the ghosts are nervous about what happened to Carrie and Grant. Eddie Goldman tried to get me to leave." She could tell Blasing tacitly agreed.

"Company coming," he said as he rubbed his neck.

Elegant as ever and clad in a baby-blue diaphanous dress that hinted but didn't reveal, Elma floated through the frosted doors of the Spirited Woman. "Angela! Mr. Madera! Please come in! Angela, we'd sell more dresses if you'd bring him with you more often." She gave Blasing a dazzling smile that didn't quite reach her lovely, sky-blue eyes.

In multiple braids, Ingrid appeared at her side, less graceful but still warmly gracious. "Greetings lovely lady." The Swedish spirit looked worried, her gaze restlessly wandering.

"Hello, ladies. I came to see if either of you know anything about Bodie?"

Neither knew anything beyond what Angela knew.

Cash passed by, his nose in the air and one arm in a sling. He started to say something, then continued on by. Martha joined the group, floating behind Elma and Ingrid. Soon Willy drifted in their direction. He picked up Angus and began the ritual of petting.

Blasing fidgeted. His breathing grew deeper as he fought his ghostly phobia. Angela took his hand to lend her strength, wondering if the rings would help.

The number of ghosts suddenly increased by four as Missy, Charity, Amber and Jessie arrived. "Hello, Blasing," they said in unison. He jumped. Angela took his arm, afraid he would bolt. Although each spirit appeared to have stepped from the titillating section of the Spirited Woman, the ethereal women seemed dimmer than usual and anxious as if an appointment had gone awry.

"Can you tell us what happened last night?" Missy asked. "We're afraid the same might have happened to Fawn. We haven't seen her since Saturday."

When Angela hesitated, Elma said, "If it is too difficult...."

Angela told of Grant's arrival, though not of his revelations, then about Carrie's tardy appearance amidst the storm. As Angela recounted the tale, Eddie and Allen joined them. Angela made it sound as if she'd met the pair of spirits by accident.

"Just as Carrie was telling me about the invisible ghosts from Bodie, she and Grant seemed to be... grabbed... or roped... or something," Angela said. "I could feel their terror. They were straining. So much pain." Angela suddenly began to weep; she could feel their agony all over again—this time as slow as the drag of a dull knife.

"There, there, dear," Elma said. "You don't have to continue...."

"Then they were pulled apart!" The words lurched from her. "And th... there was a bright flash. I felt them clawing at me, trying to hang on, but they couldn't." She could see it more clearly now that she was less shocked. The pulling. The tearing. Gossamer strips fading. "Then they were gone and I felt so empty." Several ghosts began to cry, too.

Blasing touched Angela on the cheek, pulling her from her reverie. When she continued to sob, he took her into his arms, holding her until she managed to stop. "Oh, Blasing, thank you again. Sorry about your jacket."

"It's all right. Did you... see it again? Experience it again?" he asked anxiously. His gaze searched her blue-green eyes for any sign something was wrong.

She nodded. "It was horrible. Like you reliving Peter's murder." Suddenly Angela looked around; they'd gained quite an audience. "Do you have a handkerchief?" He handed her one.

"It's all right, dear," Elma said. "Broderick told us about it... but not in that way. For the first time in a long time, I am scared—scared of not only what will happen to Ghostal Shores, but what is going to happen to all of us."

"We need to find Marsh," Angela suggested. "See if he knows something."

"We've been looking for him and Fawn," Missy told her.

"Ingrid and I have searched everywhere, but Marsh is impossible to find," Elma complained. "He always has been."

"Evil can hide in plain sight," Eddie said nervously.

"And you haven't seen any transient spirits?" Angela asked. Why did the green-eyed ghost and the dark stranger only appear to Blasing? Or could only he see them? If so, why?

"Where did these ghosts come from!" Allen quivered. "What do they want? Why did they kill Grant and Carrie?"

"Get a hold of yourself, Al," Eddie told him. "Nobody besides Mr. Madera here has even seen these supposed ghosts."

"I believe him," Elma said. "And if you'd look at him closely, Eddie, examine his spirit, you would too."

Eddie looked sheepish. "I'm sorry, Mr. Madera. I see you believe you saw them."

"Eddie...." Elma began.

"He saw Peter's ghost again last night," Angela announced.

"MAC'S GHOST!" several exclaimed. Suddenly, they were all

staring at Blasing.

"Yes, he did," Eddie confessed.

"Why's Mac hiding from us?" Jesse asked.

"We should find him," Charity said. "Help him. Maybe he's confused. Being murdered can do that."

"What about the new spirits? Why can't we see them? Why are they here?" Ingrid asked as she tugged nervously on a braid.

"Maybe they're drawn to Heller," Elma said. "Like attracts like, you know. Maybe he wants his own kind here."

"Do you think this is connected to Mac's murder?" Elma asked Angela. All she could do was shrug.

"What're you going to do, Mr. Blasing?" Willy asked.

"I don't know, son. As far as the resort, things seem to be out of my hands right now. I don't understand about the spirit murders, but Angela and I are determined to find out."

"How would you vote?" Eddie asked.

"As of right now, and I don't have all the information, I'd vote to delay sales. Too many things that might change my mind. Let me ask you: who here is interested in Ghostal Shores becoming a time-share?" Eddie and Allen raised their hands, though the latter reluctantly. Elma scowled at them but kept her tongue.

Jessie didn't show as much restraint, smacking the barber with her purse. "Men!" she huffed. She and Eddie glared at each other.

"As of this afternoon, or tomorrow at the latest, I expect sales to be delayed pending a resolution to the will," Angela informed them. That brought a small cheer.

"Now, let's break things up. We're starting to cause a traffic jam," Blasing said, nodding to all the spectators.

"What about Madame Zanadane?" Amber asked, curling a finger in her coppery hair.

"I haven't spoken with her yet, so I'm reserving my opinion," he told them. Angela scowled at him.

"Before you go," Elma began, "Angela, we've done some investigating. Can't say we found anything. Everything is so busy with all the security changes and installation. Lots of work is being done in the service corridor."

"Anything out of the ordinary?" Angela asked.

"It's all strange to me, dear," Elma said. "Sending pictures over telegraph lines. The service corridor to the employee quarters and storage area is bombarded with them."

"Pardon me?" Blasing said.

"I mean we can hardly visit the area due to all the..." she paused, groping for a word, "static?"

"Makes me itch like I'd been sleeping in poison ivy," Ingrid added.

"When I was interviewing employees, I didn't notice anything out of the ordinary," Blasing said.

"It just seemed..." Elma said, "...that the workers were—I don't know exactly—hiding something."

"In a sense, they are," Blasing said. "That's part of security's job."

"But this seemed..." Elma sighed again, "somehow malicious. I guess not being able to see their spirits clearly like I can with most folks bothers me."

"Oh." Blasing's response was deadpan. "Can you think of any reason why they seem cloaked to you?"

"No, sir, none at all," Elma replied. "Seems so strange. Heller's always been that way. That's one of the reasons Carrie doesn't like him, and we don't trust him."

Angela suddenly recalled a question she wanted to ask. "Did any of you ever sense Peter was sick or dying?"

"I think his liver was killing him," Missy said. "His spirit was dim."

"He hadn't felt right for a while," Chastity agreed.

"All right, what's going on here?!" Heller demanded, using his cane to clear space as he hobbled through the crowd.

"A lawful congress," Angela replied dryly.

"You're blocking traffic," he snorted. His face was red. His breathing was loud and rough.

"And probably stimulating business for the stores," Angela said with a chilly smile.

Heller flushed. "Come to my office. We can talk there."

"About?" Angela asked coolly.

"Grant Roberts and Carrie the shrew," Heller had trouble spitting out their names. Elma returned to the store with Ingrid. The other ghosts began to disperse, many eyeing Heller with veiled contempt. The Irishman didn't seem to notice. "Well?"

"After you," Blasing said. This time he took Angela's arm and guided her towards Heller's office. She placed a hand atop his, and although it seemed to startle him, he didn't remove it. As if he'd adopted new owners, Angus trailed along.

Each time Angela returned to Heller's office, she found the place more disturbing—a brooding nest of paper insects awaiting life. One piece had fallen from a shelf. Angela ground it underfoot. Blasing saw her and smiled. Angus stared at it for a moment, then began batting it around.

"Damn weather," Heller grumbled. He hobbled his way around the massive desk to perch in his large, black leather chair. He sniffed a few times, then blew his nose. Angela thought Heller was more fitful than usual, but when he sat back he simply folded his hands as if determined to look Blasing in the eye. Heller wore several rings made of hematite. Had they been provided by Madame Zanadane? Angela hadn't noticed them before.

"I've heard from Broderick and Madame Zanadane that we may have lost two ghosts," he announced. Angela said nothing. "Would you tell me about it, Ms. Starborne?" He waited. "Ghosts are crucial to Ghostal Shores' success."

"Glad to hear you say that," Angela said. "I was out on the veranda getting some fresh air..." she began, retelling her tale once more. When she began to describe Grant and Carrie being seized, Blasing took her hand. She managed to recount the story without breaking down, but with numerous pauses and long breaths.

"Tragic," Heller murmured, his steepled fingers uncoupling as he reached for an irresistible piece of paper. "What do you think happened to them?" He began folding and smoothing.

"I have no idea," Angela replied. "I didn't know anything like that could happen. Did you?"

"Not in my wildest nightmares," Heller agreed. "They will be missed."

"I didn't think you cared for either one," Angela said.

"You are correct," Heller snapped. "But they will still be missed by the customers." Angela was a bit confused; he sounded angry and pleased at the same time. "We can't lose our ghosts. They're not replaceable like regular help."

Angela's jaw dropped, and she almost collapsed from shock. This didn't sound like the Heller she knew; was he on drugs?

Angus rubbed against her leg for a while, then when the ghost cat looked up at her, he seemed to notice the hanging paper birds and airplanes. A predator now, the cat hunkered low and began stalking, using the furniture for cover.

"Then the ghosts' impressions are correct," Blasing said. "You think of them simply as assets."

Heller sighed. "It's too bad that Madame Zanadane's arrival caused so much concern; it was not my intent to cleanse unruly ghosts. I was hoping she'd build a bridge to better understanding." Heller finished a mouse, then snatched up another piece of paper, seduced by its crisp texture and straight lines.

After a knock and an "enter" from Heller, his secretary brought a message and left it on the desk. She eyed Blasing as she waited. "Ah, Mr. Chapman. Please tell him I'll call him back."

As the secretary closed the door, the hanging origami shifted. Angus launched, bouncing off Blasing's lap then careening skyward. A few quick strikes dropped two paper constructs and entangled several others. Angus landed on the desk, scattering stuff everywhere.

"What?!" Heller shoved his chair back. "What's going on?!" he cried, his eyes wide and his face white. When he finally realized what was happening, color returned to his face. His gaze narrowed as he watched the ghostly cat take apart the inanimate birds.

"I think it's a good idea to know what the ghosts are thinking, and to treat them well," Blasing suggested. "You wouldn't want them turning on you." He glanced at Angus shredding a paper avian.

"I... I want to know what ghosts think," Heller replied, watching the ghost cat with a mixture of horror and fascination. "It was my hope they would air their concerns through Madame Zanadane, but instead of seeing her as a counselor, they believe her to be a threat. I'd like to change that, and I'd like your help, Blasing, since they prefer you as their spokesperson." Although he spoke to them, he was intent on Angus.

"Then you don't mind if I spend some time browsing through files and the books?" Blasing asked innocently.

"Of course not. I thought you had the financial paperwork." Heller still hadn't moved any closer to the desk. Angus quit playing with the downed paper beasts. Now he was eyeing the hanging constructs,

His tail flicked back and forth as though tallying the number he could snag.

"My copies are poor," Blasing explained. Angela contained her smile; she'd have to watch Blasing. He lied too smoothly.

"Oh. Ask my secretary for another set." Heller nervously began folding again. "The personnel files are in a bit of disarray. As you might have heard, we have a new computer system."

"I basically want to look at security personnel records. Porter should have copies in his managerial files."

"Is there a problem with my security?"

"I don't have any idea. What I've seen so far looks good, but the system is only as good as the men running it. Call it professional curiosity. I know which training makes for the best employees, and which areas seem to provide the best recruits. After I do some reviewing, I may be able to offer an opinion."

"Certainly. Certainly, I'd be glad to have it," Heller said. The enthusiasm sounded fake to Angela, but she was already disgusted. "What do the ghosts think?"

"Though none have seen the newcomers, they believe Blasing, and fear there are strangers among them that they can't see."

"New ghosts they can't see? Really? How very interesting."

"If the bricks are from Bodie, they are really worried," Blasing told him.

His gaze narrowing, Heller quickly looked to Blasing. "What do these ghosts look like?" Blasing described them. A bit flushed and damp, Heller finished his masterpiece of paper—a grizzly bear standing on its hind legs. "IF we assume you're correct, I wonder what they want? Why have they come? Any guesses?" Blasing shook his head. "Why do you think only you can see them?"

"Maybe because I've come very close to dying several times."

"Are the bricks from Bodie?" Angela asked pointedly, not being deterred.

"Mac and I swore to secrecy," Heller maintained. "And that will not change until we begin advertising the northern wing."

"I guess I could ask him next time I see Mac's ghost," Blasing began, watching Heller blanch.

"You saw Mac's ghost?"

"Twice."

"Tell him I'd like to talk with him!"

"I would have thought he'd come see you," Angela said. "Maybe he's mad at you. Upset over the sixty day agreement, among other things."

"He shouldn't be. Neither of us wanted Ghostal Shores to drift in the other's absence," Heller snapped. "Mac was afraid he didn't have much time left. Of course, he didn't expect to die the way he did."

"Speaking of which," Blasing said frostily, "Sheriff Middleton told me you convinced them to let you contact me about Mac's death."

"He must've been mistaken."

"Why did Mac think he didn't have much time?"

"Wine, women, and song, but especially the wine."

"His liver?" Blasing asked. Heller nodded.

"So you were preparing for that day so you could sell timeshares?" Angela asked coldly. She found it was getting more and more difficult to tolerate Heller without resorting to violence. Maybe Carrie was right. Looking at the family portraits behind Heller, Angela concluded none of them looked trustworthy.

"Naturally. Mac was contemplating a change of heart. I figured that even if he didn't, his heir might. I wanted to be ready. To seize the moment." As if on cue, Angus sprang airborne, bringing down more origami. Heller went white and began shaking.

"And all the money is in place?" Blasing asked. "There aren't any budget overruns?"

"Just look at the books," Heller replied with an uneasy smile. "And talk to Earl, he's my bean counter. We stick to our budget."

"I will," Blasing said, glancing at Angela.

"Have you made any decisions about the timeshare?"

"I'm still on the fence. There's still so much to weigh that I haven't made a definitive decision."

"Take your time," Heller said with a smooth smile, his eyes only occasionally straying to Angus. "Chief Porter wanted me to let you know the security system comes on line tomorrow."

"Thank you."

"Do you know of any reason ghosts would be wandering to or from Ghostal Shores?" Angela asked.

"Maybe they're attracted to kin or what we're doing here." Angela struggled not to gag. "How did your séance go?"

"It's tonight," Blasing replied. "Would you like to come?"

"No thank you! But please, keep me informed." Heller was sweating profusely. He dabbed himself dry with his handkerchief.

"We will. I think we'll learn something about Peter's murder," Angela told him, wanting to see his reaction.

"Good. I would like this resolved," he told her without looking up. "If Mac appears again, call me. Now if you don't mind, I need to call Mr. Chapman and get the construction under way once more. Oh, and take that... that cat with you!" As they left, Angus followed, appearing very satisfied with his tail high in the air.

"What's wrong?" Blasing asked Angela.

"I'm just confused. I've never seen Mr. Heller so nervous about the ghosts. He was never this bad when Peter was around."

"Maybe he's worried they'll turn on him."

"I guess. A couple of days ago he didn't seem frightened."

"He didn't have one bouncing around on his desk, either," Blasing replied.

"True. But I've never seen him wear hematite before."

Blasing was thoughtful for a time, then said, "Come on, let's talk with Porter and get those files. We have some paperwork to take care of before the séance."

TWENTY

As Blasing, Broderick, Angus and Angela left the elevator, she glanced over her shoulder at Tom Becker and his evening clients. "I almost couldn't resist," she said, her smile dazzling.

"What? Telling him that as of tomorrow all sales stop?" Blasing asked. During dessert of their room service dinner, Angela had received a fax from her office announcing the sales prohibition pending a hearing. "We should inform Heller first."

"Yes, I want to see his expression when I hand it to him," she said. Again, Blasing wondered if Angela was reading his mind.

"I look forward to informing the others that Mister Heller will no longer be selling Ghostal Shores property," Broderick announced. "We may have to make this a resort holiday."

"Don't celebrate yet, Broderick. It's just an injunction—a hold on things until both parties present their case."

"Pardon, sir, but any disruption of Mister Heller's plan is reason to celebrate. By the way, Mister Madera, I am perplexed by how you knew it was me at the door."

"I... I just felt that it was you. Maybe it's because you touched me earlier. I don't know."

"I don't think so," Angela said. "You've always been able to feel ghosts. Maybe the contact just made you more aware. Or able to identify who's who." Angus meowed as if in agreement. "See?"

"I can see you're going to be self-righteously smug and full of yourself for a while," Blasing said.

"And why not? Something's finally going our way. You're just cranky because you didn't get outside today."

"I'm cranky because Sean Heller has been lying to us. I'm glad he isn't coming to the séance; otherwise I might deck him." They'd spent the afternoon matching financial reports.

"I am not surprised that Mister Heller was cheating you, sir."

"He's been cheating Mac," Blasing corrected.

"But then, I must say I would not put it past Grant to incriminate

Mister Heller, either," Broderick told them. "Grant was part scoundrel and part saint. If I may be so bold, is Ghostal Shores in trouble?"

"From what I can tell, it appears financially healthy."

"Thank goodness. What are you going to do, sir?"

"Nothing tonight," Angela said as she stopped at Suite 213.

"I am glad you invited me to the seánce," Broderick said. "I have wanted to attend such an affair."

"Do you think it will work?" Blasing asked the ghost valet.

"If you had asked me in 1886, I would have said no and thought you a madman, but now, I believe differently."

"Well, Broderick, you're probably more comfortable with it than Blasing," Angela said.

"I'm getting better. Broderick and Angus are around and I don't feel like jumping out of my skin." Though he did itch.

"I am so glad to hear that news, sir. I shall make an announcement," the ghost valet said stonily.

Blasing missed the sarcasm. "But I don't make any promises if we have a roomful of ghosts. Earlier today was tough."

"You handled it very well," Angela said as she knocked.

With a smile, Candy opened the door. "Angel, come on in. And you brought Broderick with you! An excellent idea!"

"Is everyone here?" Angela asked.

"You're the last," Candy said. She ushered them into the room.

"Then we can get started right after introductions."

Blasing looked at the trio of ornate candelabra, a half-dozen candles burning on each, "Do we plan on losing power?"

Angela smiled at him. "Flame is more... elemental."

Blasing didn't know what he'd expected, but it wasn't something this simple. The couch, loveseat and table had been pushed to the walls, and thirteen chairs were set around a conference table covered with a green cloth. At the far end, purple silk cloaked a lump the size of a basketball.

"Ah, you have arrived," a tall, bony woman with angular features and dark, short-cropped hair approached. She began waving a feather around Blasing, sweeping him from head to foot. Blasing noticed her lavender, claw-like fingernails and felt he should be armed and ready to protect himself.

"She's smoothing out your energies," Angela said.

"It makes it easier to link our energies," Candy informed him.

"And you need a lot of smoothing," the big woman said with a broad smile.

"Blasing, meet Gwendolyn. She's in my class at Berkeley."

"A pleasure," she said in a husky voice, then moved to Angela and repeated the ritual. When she reached Broderick, she hesitated. The ghost valet looked to Angela.

"Go ahead," she said with a shrug.

When Gwendolyn feathered him, Broderick was typically stoic at first, then he twitched and squirmed. Finally, he chuckled several times before chortling.

"I think you're tickling him," Blasing said. Gwendolyn apologized.

"N- no need, miss. Th- that felt wonderful indeed. Very invigorating." Broderick appeared much brighter than before.

"I hope it works that well for me," Blasing said.

"We should try this on the other ghosts," Candy suggested.

"You can try it on me," Rod said, moving to her side and kissing her.

"You look very composed for all that's going on," Dr. Landrum said. He and Blasing shook hands. "And Ms. Starborne, as always, you are as beautiful as your namesake." Blasing agreed. She was in a body-hugging jumpsuit the color of twilight, and her silver chain belt and jewelry glittered as miniature stars. "I find this all... fascinating. How about you, Blasing?"

"Disconcerting," Blasing replied. "Considering your profession, I'm surprised you believe in it."

"So do some of my colleagues, but I believe there's more to the body than just flesh, that spirit is a major factor in healing. I wanted proof that a spirit exists, and I found it here at Ghostal Shores. Just think of the medical ramifications!"

Angela pointed to Angus, then said, "Investigate all you want. You don't have to worry about animal rights activists." She smiled. "Come on, Blasing." Angela took his arm. He still tingled at her touch, but tried to ignore it, fearing this spark might burst into flames. "Are you all right?"

"Maybe the feathering had some effect after all," he said quietly, then nodded to the man with the fedora. Besides light glinting off his glasses, his face was shadowed. "Who's that?"

"Dr. Devlin Strange, a purveyor of mystical artifacts. Now don't make that face," she chided. "You said you'd be open-minded."

Candy introduced them to Misha Owakai, a petite but doe-eyed Asian who was so excited she hugged them. Misha was also from Rothstein's class on the paranormal.

"Now, the first of our famed mystics, The Great Xantini, Master Mentalist," Candy introduced the darkly clad man.

His face seemed to have a sardonic hint that his baritone voice didn't carry when he said, "A pleasure, Mr. Madera." The Great Xantini's goatee and mustache were meticulously trimmed. His hair was combed so smoothly it appeared to be a skullcap. As usual, he dressed baggily and all in black.

"If you please..." Blasing began.

"...call you, Blasing. I do apologize," Xantini rumbled.

"Um, yes," Blasing said uncomfortably, feeling a bit disconcerted by the man finishing his sentence.

"A pleasure; call me Efrem." The Great Xantini looked to Angela and said, "Now I understand."

Blasing gave Angela a questioning glance. She just shrugged.

Candy introduced Dr. Devlin Strange. As he puffed on his great pipe, the tall man quietly nodded to Blasing, then doffed his cap to Angela, revealing he was bald-crowned. His eyes were deep brown and his angular features were long, accentuated by his sideburns. He wore a golden, eye-shaped amulet outside his dress shirt.

After being introduced to spritely Julie Zephren, who again was lavishly and ostentatiously dressed for show, Blasing said, "Ms. Zephren. I've seen your show. I thoroughly enjoyed it."

"Ya like sleight-of-body?" she drawled, her dark blue eyes glittering as if she knew the answer.

"Don't all men?" Xantini said.

Blasing blushed slightly, then even more so as Julie laughed. "Then the pleasure's all mine." She looked to Angela, then said, "I'll have complimentary tickets sent for two."

"Four," Xantini suggested. "He has two children."

"Four it is!" Julie reached into Blasing's jacket pocket and removed four tickets. "Good any day," she drawled.

Candy finished by introducing friends she'd made during her

stay. Michelle Maynard was an instructor for Neuro-Linguistic Programming in San Francisco. She was in her late fifties with silvery hair and gray-blue eyes. Her robe was dark blue with golden fringing and a great sun on the front. The Patwins, Gloria and Josh, were Universal Life ministers out of Stockton. They were large people with ruddy complexions and reddish hair. Both were dressed as if for dinner in a fine restaurant.

"Has everybody met everybody?" Candy asked. There was agreement among the murmurings. "Good! Then let's get started. Please be seated next to a member of the opposite gender so the energies are better balanced." As they began to sit, a heavy knock sounded from the door.

"That was easy," Dr. Landrum joked.

Candy answered the door. Madame Zanadane stood waiting with her hulking companion, Mr. Chung. The psychic's luminous eyes slowly searched the room as if ready to indict one and all.

"Hello, Madame Zanadane. Would you care to watch?" Candy said.

"You have thirteen already...." Madame Zanadane mentioned breathlessly.

"But we would be interested in any suggestions you provide," Candy said diplomatically.

"Or ya cahn have m'ah place," Julie Zephren offered with the genteelness of a southern hostess.

"No thank you, my friend...." Madame Zanadane said as she entered. The combination of her dark-streaked hair, her black and white striped shirt, and long black skirt made Blasing think of a zebra.

Mr. Chung moved behind her when she sat on the couch. Angus hissed at them several times, then darted under the table. "This should be interesting.... I've never started a séance with a ghost already present.... Good evening, Broderick...."

"Good evening, Madame."

"Let's get started." Candy turned off the lights. The candles blazed with golden-red light, flames flickering and shadows dancing across the walls. Candy sat at the head of the table with Rod on her right and Josh Patwin on her left. Blasing and Dr. Landrum flanked Angela. Before Dr. Strange sat, he removed the cloak from a large crystal ball. The sphere reflected fiery flashes, which swirled across the walls and ceiling as though sunlit reflections drifted across the bottom of a dock.

"It's magnificent," Angela said. "Where did you get it?"

"It, as well as this amulet," Dr. Strange touched the golden amulet, "the Eye of Horus which allows me to access the Akashic records, are gifts from Ta, an immortal being from Atlantis. She gave it to me during a tour of the catacombs miles below the Great Pyramid."

Blasing didn't know whether to take that seriously, but it was delivered earnestly. "I believe Dr. Landrum, and even Blasing, wish guidance as to what they should do," Xantini announced.

"We'll link hands to merge our energies," Candy began, "then focus on one individual—the one we wish to speak to. It is not crucial that you've met the person, as long as one of us has."

"Then what should I expect?" Blasing asked.

"A visitor. A sensation. Maybe nothing at all. We can strongly encourage a visit, but not compel one."

"And the crystal ball?" Blasing asked.

"When you're visualizing—or imaging—use the ball to focus as if you're staring into a flame."

Blasing couldn't believe he was doing this—that these four days had happened at all.

"Now link hands," Candy requested. "We are most interested in contacting Peter Andrew MacGuire. Focus on him. Those of you who know him, pull a moment from time you remember most—when you remember him best. See him before you. With you."

As Blasing stared into the crystal ball, he thought back to the last time he'd seen Mac at Jenny's funeral. That one hurt too much, and he searched for happier times. He remembered Mac at the hospital, beaming over Kelly's birth. As if the crystal ball had bridged time, Blasing could suddenly see Mac very clearly, his uncle's smile reaching his green eyes. His laughter rang in Blasing's ears, wholehearted enough to set his ruddy face aglow.

"Blasing, call out to him. Speak from your spirit."

"Uncle Mac, it's Blasing. I need to speak with you about Patrick and Kelly's future. Please come talk with me."

In the back of Blasing's mind, he wondered what was going to happen. At first he thought he felt something—a presence—but it was difficult to be sure with Broderick nearby. Then a chilling breeze swept around him, swirling about the room. It ruffled his hair and clothing. The candles guttered, a few going out. New shadows appeared.

"Mac?" Blasing whispered. He felt the urge to itch. Another breeze swirled about, blowing out more candles. A mist developed over the table, thickening like a fog atop a lake. Then it began to take the shape of a stout and barrel-chested man. Blasing found himself speechless when the ethereal presence greeted him, then Angela.

"Mac? Mac? What's going on? Who murdered you?!"

"Peter! You're still here," Angela gasped. She gripped Blasing's hand tighter.

"Blaise! Angel!" Mac looked harried. "I can't stay long! Leave! You are in great danger!" Mac glanced over his shoulder, then quickly disappeared.

"Why do you keep running away?!" Blasing yelled. "What are you scared of?!"

"Peter, come back! We need your help! Damn!" Angela cursed.

"He seemed frightened," Xantini observed.

"Let's take a break," Candy suggested. The lights came on.

"I don't understand why he won't talk with us." Blasing looked around, his vision badly blurred.

"Neither do I. Why won't he help us? Hey, are you all right?" Angela asked.

"My vision's distorted."

"Didn't you blink?" Angela asked.

"I don't know." He felt a bit dizzy, unsure whether this was all real or not. It seemed so preposterous. Ludicrous.

Angela passed Blasing a glass of water that seemed to just appear in her hand. "Thank you, Broderick."

"Is there anything else I can get you, sir?" Broderick asked.

"I'll be fine," Blasing replied. "So much... strange going on. I feel... off balance."

"I understand. How about some air?" Angela suggested.

"Sounds good," Blasing said. Dr. Landrum helped him walk onto the balcony. The night air did wonders for Blasing. Broderick hovered about like a nervous hen until Blasing asked him to stop. The ghost valet stepped away but remained vigilant.

After awhile, Angela asked, "Do you feel up to continuing?" She squeezed his hand. He suddenly noticed she'd never let go. He admitted the sensation was becoming more and more comfortable.

"Sure. Let's try to get him to come back," Blasing replied.

When they returned, Madame Zanadane inquired about his health and offered her services if he could not continue. Blasing said he was fine, and this time made sure he blinked, even glancing away now and then. The candles never moved. Never gutted. The air was quiet except for someone's noisy breathing. They waited. And waited. Peter MacGuire did not return.

"I guess he doesn't want to talk to us," Candy said. "Any suggestions?"

"We could try again tomorrow," Gwendolyn suggested.

"Or we could try Carrie," Angela offered. "The 1880's General Store owner is missing. Have all of you met her?" Everyone at the table nodded. "Then let's try her."

Despite their attempts, Carrie didn't appear. Angela then suggested they seek Grant Roberts. Not everyone had met the Texan but most had. Madame Zanadane offered to sit in for Blasing, and after a glance to Angela, he agreed. Nothing stirred, and nothing changed. They tried Quinn and Fawn, but the results were frustratingly the same.

"Very anticlimactic," Dr. Landrum said, rubbing his eyes.

"Nothing to help us learn who murdered Peter," Angela whispered. "Or who the invisible ghosts might be."

"We could try contacting the green-eyed female ghost who came in on the first stage Saturday. If she is the one who has been bothering Blasing, she might deign to visit us," Angela suggested.

Blasing explained what little he knew about the ghost, describing her as best he could, including her smokey perfume. Candy asked if he knew her name. "Lilly, I think. To tell the truth, I'm not even sure that she's green-eyed. Sometimes she...."

"...appears in different guises," Xantini finished for him.

"That sounds like Fawn," Broderick told them. "She likes to act— to pretend to be different... people sometimes. She might just be pretending to be this Lilly."

"This is the first I've heard of this," Madame Zanadane said.

"Anyone you know?" Xantini asked.

"Once she appeared as Fawn, I think," Blasing told them. "Sometimes she changes even as I watch. Sunday night she appeared looking like my deceased wife." Angela made a strangled noise. "It's all right," he said and squeezed her hand. He was glad they didn't ask who else the ghost had mimicked.

"Women drop their clothing and a ghost changes appearances around you," Dr. Landrum said. "You lead an interesting life." Blasing glared at him.

"Fascinating," Dr. Strange said, smoking a pipe. He stood in the open. "A woman who likes to smoke and race stagecoaches. She is reckless. I'll see what I can discover." When he touched his amulet, his dark eyes withdrew to somewhere else.

"If she masquerades as other women, she has low self-esteem," Angela said. Blasing caught the look between her and Candy.

"Let's try ta contact her!" Julie Zephren said. They settled again, focusing on the green-eyed woman. Angela glanced at Blasing and squeezed his hand.

"I learned nothing," Dr. Strange announced as he returned to the circle. "There seems to be some sort of disturbance."

"Call to her," Candy suggested. "Ask her what she wants."

Blasing felt silly but did as requested. "Lilly, what do you want? Why are you here? Where did you come from?" His voice felt strange. The room seemed charged, making him restless. Even the heavy breathing was louder than before. A tingling danced along his neck, and the nape hairs stiffened.

Ever so slowly, an ethereal face appeared above the crystal ball. The woman was beautiful and in her prime with crystal green eyes and high-born features—dark, full brows, elegant cheekbones, and heart-shaped lips quirked in a pout. It was the most regal face he'd ever seen, but there was something in the eyes he hadn't noticed before. Pain. Pain and something else. Fear?

"Is that her?" Angela asked. Blasing nodded.

"She's beautiful," Dr. Landrum said.

"Lilly, what do you want?" Blasing began.

The apparition glanced fearfully behind her, then she was gone as if jerked away. A dark, heavy presence descended upon the room.

"Awww!" came a cry from somewhere along the table.

"Oh my God! Josh!" Mrs. Patwin screamed.

Clutching his chest, Josh Patwin collapsed on the table. Everyone rushed forward, then moved aside for Dr. Landrum. He checked the man's breathing, then his pulse. "Anyone know CPR?" Dr. Landrum asked as he began to lower Josh Patwin to the floor.

"I do," Blasing said. "Please, let me by, Mrs. Patwin."

"Get ready to start compressions." When the doctor gave Josh two breaths, his chest moved. "Still no pulse. Begin compressions. Angela, call security. Tell them we need an ambulance."

Blasing found the proper spot and began pumping. He completed the first set of compressions, and Dr. Landrum gave two breaths. They repeated the process, checked after a minute and discovered a pulse. The minister was breathing again. Broderick returned with Dr. Landrum's emergency bag. Security tagged behind, carrying oxygen and a stretcher.

"Any idea what caused it?" Angela asked.

"His wife said he was a smoker," Dr. Landrum replied. "And he's overweight. My bet's on that and stress." The tension was thick in the air.

"Geoff, did you see Lilly?" Angela asked him.

"Definitely."

"Did you see the other, the dark-faced stranger with yellow, cat-like eyes?" Blasing asked.

Dr. Landrum and Angela shook their heads no.

"I saw a dark, foreboding shadow," Dr. Strange said.

"But why was he here?" Angela asked. "We didn't call him."

"But we called Lilly," Candy said. "Maybe they're connected."

Security and Dr. Landrum moved Josh Patwin downstairs to wait for an ambulance. They debated over whether they should try again tomorrow. They finally concluded to try again tomorrow night.

When they dispersed, Angela spent a minute looking for Angus. The ghost feline had disappeared. "Cats are like that," the Englishman observed.

"Watch out for the dark spirit," Xantini warned Blasing. "He believes you want to steal something from him. And for the moment, that emotion is stronger than the revenge he seeks for betrayal."

"How do you know this?" Blasing asked.

"Thoughts, even from the dead, are like radio waves. One just must be attuned to receive them." His smile was almost mocking.

"We will be careful," Angela said. "We are...."

"...protected. Yes, I know about the hematite; it has interesting properties, don't you think?"

"How do you know about it?" Candy asked.

"Madame Zanadane mentioned it to us at breakfast one morning."

"Well, it's been an interesting evening, in the Chinese sense anyway," Angela said. "Goodnight, Efrem." Xantini bowed. Angela started to leave, then turned around, a question on her lips.

"Yes, I can. And I will see what I can find out," Xantini said, bowing once more.

Flustered, Angela said, "Let's go."

"What was that all about?" Candy asked.

"I wondered if he could read minds, and if so, could he discover who killed Peter," Angela replied.

"He's very..." Blasing began.

"Disconcerting?" Angela asked.

"Don't you start!" Blasing replied.

The elevator doors had just closed when Candy said, "Angela, I'm not really sure about this. But I think I saw Madame Zanadane put something in Josh Patwin's coffee during our first break."

"But you're not sure?" Blasing asked.

"No, it was a quick movement and out of the corner of my eye, so...." Candy shrugged.

"I can't think of any tactful way to suggest to Dr. Landrum that they test for poison," Blasing murmured.

"Damn, I knew I didn't want her with us for a reason. I kept thinking she probably didn't want us to talk with Peter."

"Angela, Candy isn't even sure she saw anything."

"True. I just don't trust her."

"I'll talk to the doctor about looking for foul play," Blasing said.

"Regardless, we should be extra careful and observant tomorrow night," Angela maintained.

"I will keep a close watch on her, miss," Broderick offered.

"Thank you, Broderick. I know you don't care for her either."

By the time Blasing and Angela reached the suite, they were very tired. Angela leaned heavily on Blasing. "Your safe place or mine?" Angela asked. Blasing steered her toward her room.

"What did you feel from the ghosts, Broderick?" Blasing asked.

"From Master MacGuire, confusion. He did not seem himself. From Lilly, a sense of seeking.... Oops," Broderick exclaimed, then staggered back from the doorway. "I keep forgetting I cannot enter."

"Sorry. I should have warned you. At least Blasing sees that it works."

"It is quite all right," Broderick said from the doorway.

"Seeking what? Help? Contact?" Blasing asked as they sat on the bed. Not trusting himself, he started to get up. Angela collapsed against him before he could stand.

"Forgiveness comes to mind," Broderick said. "As does help. And fear. And the feeling of being trapped."

"Did you sense more than one ghost that last time?"

"Yes, I believe I did, but not for very long."

"Can you tell if a ghost did anything to cause Josh Patwin's heart attack?"

"No, sir. I felt an oppressive sense of..." Broderick said, his clear eyes turned inward, "a tight fistedness comes to mind."

"Maybe she's trying to escape him," Angela suggested, "and she thinks Blasing is her knight in shining armor. Probably not the first," she finished dryly, her head resting on his shoulder.

With a tentative touch, Blasing brushed the hair from her face. "But what does this have to do with Mac's murder? Are they from Bodie? What do they want? Clearly Mac is afraid of them. That's three times he's fled just before the dark spirit appeared."

"We can ask them tomorrow," Angela yawned. "Don't know why I'm so tired."

"You probably didn't rest easy last night," Blasing said.

"Broderick, did you notice if Madame Zanadane wore any hematite?" Angela asked.

"No miss."

"I looked, but didn't see any," Blasing said. "It could have been under her clothing, though."

"Broderick, can you feel if someone is wearing it?"

"No miss. There is no change about you or Master Madera."

"Oh well," Angela said. "I can hardly keep my eyes open."

"Sleep," Blasing said, his suggestion narcotic as Angela gently drifted into slumber with a small smile.

"Use of the spirit can be quite wearing on the flesh," Broderick surmised.

Blasing nodded. He watched Angela sleep for a while, then slipped free of her grasp and turned down the sheets. She murmured that she didn't want him to leave, but even with his tired body he thought he knew what would happen if he stayed.

Just after he'd closed Angela's door, a knock sounded from the entrance. Blasing looked at Broderick, who raised an eyebrow in response. "Expecting a guest, sir?"

"No," Blasing said. "I don't feel another ghost."

Broderick stuck his head through the wall. When he returned, his expression was dour. "It is the Frenchwoman."

With a sigh, Blasing opened the door. Eva modeled a revealing white silk gown that was cut low across the bodice and high along her lovely, long legs, now enhanced by stiletto heels. Blasing tried to keep his expression stony; his juices were already flowing from being so close to Angela.

"Bon jour. You like. I see it in your eyes," she said, a smile playing along her lips. "They are like you, blazing." Her eyes were bright and shiny, reminding Blasing of last night.

"Eva, it's late and I'm tired. What can I do for you?" he asked, expecting her to come apart if she tried to get intimate.

"Is there someplace safe we can speak?" Eva asked, then slithered across the front of his body into the room. When she saw Broderick, she tensed.

"Safe? Safe from whom?" Blasing asked, his interest piqued.

"The prying eyes and ears of the spirits," Eva said, nodding toward Broderick.

"What's this about?"

"The new spirits..." she began, then looked around, searching for something. "But I will say no more. They may be listening."

With an indignant expression, Broderick said coolly, "Might I suggest your room, sir." Blasing waved off the ghost, but the Englishman kept speaking. "The French have never been able to keep their heads when around the British, and I, as well as other spirits, are strictly prohibited from going in there."

"Really?" Eva asked, her serious expression brightening. "They can't enter his room?" When Broderick nodded, Eva seized Blasing's arm and guided him toward his door.

"Eva...."

"This is important, Mon ami," she said. Eva closed the door behind them, then moved closer, pressing him against the door.

"We are safe now, Eva. What's going on?"

"I fear that Madame Zanadane is the cause of our ghost problems."

"Oh?"

"Yes," Eva continued as she began fiddling with Blasing's bow tie. After being so close to Angela, Blasing found her attentions unnerving. "She and Sean have been at odds about her position. She wants more power, and of course, Sean being Sean, is reluctant to give it to her. To make herself indispensable, Madame Zanadane has summoned these new spirits and encouraged them to misbehave."

"Why?"

"Simple, Mon ami. She creates the problem, lets it fester, then miraculously solves it. Sean would then reward her, believing that she could handle similar difficulties in the future." She twirled the bow tie around her finger.

Blasing gently took her hand and untangled it from his tie. "And how did you come to this conclusion?"

"Always interrogating me," Eva pouted. "You're spending too much time with lawyers." She glanced in the direction of Angela's room. Blasing frowned sternly at Eva. "All right. I saw Madame Zanadane talking with Marsh and another ghost—a dark one with bright yellow eyes."

Blasing stiffened. "Where?"

"In her office, when I went to speak with her about having a spirit accompany my clients on their tour." Eva's smile was triumphant, her eyes bright. "You will, reward me, no?" She stood on her toes and gave him a kiss. With a shrug, her gown slipped down her body, the silk whispering as it fell to the floor. Her shapely chocolate figure was now adorned only in panties, a garter belt and stockings. "We have both been thinking about this, no?" Her hand slipped inside his shirt.

His eyes narrowing, Blasing captured her hand. "Eva."

"Live a little, mi amour," Eva said, pressing against him.

Blasing slipped an arm around her, quickly swept her off her feet, then turned and opened the door.

Angela had almost drifted to sleep when she heard voices. Was Blasing having visitors? She struggled to her feet, grabbed her robe, then walked to the door. "Broderick?" She opened the door. "Is there something wrong?"

"Oh dear," the English spirit said. "I sense a Shakespearean tragedy in the making."

"What are you doing?" Eva cried. Blasing walked into the suite, carrying a mostly naked form. Angela was stunned.

"Further exposing you," Blasing said as he set her down. She looked wildly about as if expecting an attack.

Blasing stepped back into his room and picked up her dress. As he tossed it to her, he said, "I'm sorry, Eva, but I can't see you 'shackled' with kids."

"But...."

"She's coming," Blasing said as he casually surveyed the room. He blanched when he saw Angela. "Hi, Fawn." With a squeal, Eva ran to the door, yanked it open, and then quickly disappeared into the hall. "Angela, this probably appears... suggestive."

Angela leaned against the doorjamb. "I'm listening." Blasing quickly explained about Eva's arrival; Broderick opening his big, British mouth; and Eva's accusation of Madame Zanadane. "She had to take off her clothes to tell you this?"

Blasing's look of frustration hardened. "No. She wanted to be 'rewarded'."

"I see," Angela said coolly. She wasn't sure what to believe, although she wanted to believe him. And he HAD thrown out Eva, not something most men would have been able to do. "Goodnight, Mr. Madera." Angela closed the door. With Blasing on her mind, she had some trouble falling asleep.

Blasing shook his head, then returned to his room. He could smell Eva's perfume, but Angela graced his thoughts—her sleepy request asking him not to leave haunted him. It came and went, alternating with her standing in the doorway with disappointment in her eyes.

He tried to push away those thoughts. Was Madame Zanadane bringing in ghosts and having them cause trouble? Had Eva been serious? Or was she just trying to get close to him?

Blasing flopped onto the bed, telling himself he'd sleep on it. He hoped he slept dreamlessly, and he did, though fitfully.

TWENTY-ONE

"I'm looking forward to this," Angela said to Blasing. As she walked toward Heller's office with the injunction in hand, Angela struggled not to smile—not to sing.

"Don't gloat," Blasing whispered.

And if it upset Eva, that made her feel even better. Angela tried not to think about last night, but could they believe a word the French tart had said? Eva might have made up the story just to get near Blasing. Or she might be protecting Heller. Angela pushed the scene of Blasing carrying a nearly naked Eva out of his room. Just the thought of her touching him made her jealous. She didn't like these feelings at all.

Angela stopped at the open doorway and knocked. Heller glanced up from his newspaper and coffee with sharp, but somehow rheumy eyes. He coughed, then sniffled before asking, "What can I do for you, Ms. Starborne, so bright and early this A.M.?" The Irishman noticed the paperwork and surprised her by saying, "For me?"

"The injunction I promised, Mr. Heller. Effective today," Angela said, calling forth her lawyerly presence and managing not to sound too triumphant.

Heller blew his nose, then said, "May I see it?"

"You don't look like you slept very well," Blasing observed.

Heller scowled without looking up from the legal document and said, "Damned cold kept me awake all night." As he scanned the paperwork, Heller said, "Heard about your séance. I just received word Mr. Patwin is doing just fine."

"That's good news," Blasing replied.

Heller continued reading, his facial expression stony and studious. Angela kept waiting for an eruption, but she wasn't even rewarded with a frown. "Not only are you prohibited from selling timeshare property, but you're prevented from leasing rooms, too."

"I can read, Miss Starborne," he sniffed. "I was sorry to hear Mac didn't stay long at your séance. I was hoping he could answer questions about his murder and these new ghosts you speak of."

"So did I," Blasing said.

"You understand the injunction?" Angela stammered. This wasn't the reaction she expected. Where was the explosion? The fireworks?

"Of course. I expected something like this, although Ms. Starborne, you are much more clever than Mac ever gave you credit," Heller said, still reading. He didn't see her bristle. "I was hoping to lease some property, but you have wisely foreseen that eventuality. Bravo." He returned the paperwork to her, then handed them the new Ghostal Shores brochures.

It mentioned management couldn't guarantee sales due to on-going estate litigation to be resolved by March 15, but orders could be held with a down payment. "This is...." Angela began.

"Perfectly legal. This, as well as a prospectus, will be given to investors. Sales will continue, as will order taking. Money will be placed in escrow."

"So business continues almost as usual," Blasing said.

Deflated but not defeated, Angela's mouth worked in angry surprise; she should have expected something like this. She could go to court again, and while they might prevent down payments, it was going to be difficult to stop complimentary tours. Angela wanted to throw the brochure in the Irishman's face. Instead, she impassively folded it into an airplane and launched it.

"Sorry to disappoint you," Heller said with a wan smile. "It's simply business." He opened the central drawer, removed a piece of red and blue striped paper and began folding. "Have you thought any more about what you'll do, Blasing?"

"Yes."

"And?"

"I think it's a bit pointless to make a decision that might be rendered irrelevant due to pending litigation."

Heller's frown made Angela smile just a bit.

"We will settle this estate matter before sixty days," Angela proclaimed, sounding hollow even to herself.

"The sooner the better. Eventually, Blasing will come around to my way of thinking." Heller smiled. "Now, if you don't mind, I have things to do."

"Thank you," Blasing said, then guided Angela out the door and down the hall. "Angela? Are you all right?"

She was a bit shocked, having gone from being smug and looking forward to seeing Heller's face to disappointed and angry. "Yes, I'm all right. I... I just never expected such a reaction. He was certainly prepared for this. I keep wondering who that person is and what he did with the real Sean Heller? In the old days, whether he was prepared or not, he'd be irate because someone tried to defy his will." She sighed. "I know I sound like I'm ranting, but you really can't comprehend the change. He must be on drugs."

"I've wondered about that," Blasing murmured.

"What?"

"I'll explain later. Less public."

"Explain now," she said looking around.

Blasing looked to where the cameras were installed, leaned close to her, then whispered, "You remember what you said about Eva and Mac, the reason they broke up?" She nodded. "And what I said about running into her two nights ago?" Angela thought for a moment, then remembered him mentioning Eva's bright eyes and willingness to stay up all night—though there were several possibilities there. "Then there's Heller's cold and his obsession with folding paper."

"Oh. I think I see where you're heading."

"I've had some training and experience with such things," he said, then glanced at his watch. "It's something to think on. Right now, I'm heading to security to watch the system come on line."

"I'm having breakfast with Candy to discuss what we might do differently tonight. She wants to go dancing afterward."

"Dancing? After the séance?"

"Tonight's the first of three nights of dancing in the next four days—Wednesday, Friday and Saturday. Do you dance?"

"Better than I do séances," he replied with a smile. "After security, I'll be in my room looking at files and thinking about that paperwork I'm waiting on," he said with a look telling her more than his words. "I'll see you later."

Angela wanted to talk more with him, but their rooms would be more secure. As she ascended the bayview stairs, Broderick appeared by her side. "Good morning, miss. How was your discussion with Mister Heller?" Angela explained in detail. Broderick appeared perplexed. "Yes, I agree. That is quite odd," the English spirit replied.

They reached the top of the steps and entered the lounge.

"Broderick, we asked you before about drugs. Are you even familiar with them?"

"Only opium. My fellow country fought a war over it. The British government thought we had gained some modicum of control over the importing and exporting of it when Hong Kong became part of the English Trading Company."

"Carrie thought Mr. Heller was into something illegal...."

"She had no proof, miss. Just a feeling that such a man was bound to be committing a crime. You see, she holds a grudge against Sean because of Merl Heller. He ran 'protection' in Goldfield."

"Extortion. Pay or watch your building burn?"

"Yes. But from what I understand of today's world, it is entirely possible to be more underhanded legally than illegally."

"Sad but true," Angela said as she walked past the empty podium looking for Candy. "Blasing would like to talk to you in private about some paperwork he's missing. He's in security."

"Oh dear."

"Anything wrong?"

"Just security." His expression was grave.

"You really don't like them, do you?"

"I find their presence offensive, but I must grin," he gave her a hideous smile, "and bear it."

"You and Blasing should talk some more."

"I will take your advice and wait for him in the lobby."

"Angel! Hey, Angel," came a familiar voice from across the restaurant. Waving at her, Candy sat at a table next to the ghostly gamblers. Angela waved back and headed for her blond-tressed friend. Beneath a beach hat, Candy's face beamed as brightly as a star. Her perfect smile was radiant. One hand held a notebook while the other invited Angela to sit.

"What's the good news?" Angela asked.

"I've seen a new ghost!"

"WHERE?!"

"Right there behind you," Candy nodded toward the gamblers' table. "But he doesn't look like any of the spirits you or Blasing have described."

Because of his height, the new spirit sat farther away from the table than the other ghosts. He appeared to be all elbows and knees. He wore long slicker, jeans, snake-hide boots, and a tall, bent cowboy hat. His long face mirrored the rest of him, including a blunt jaw and a beak nose which had been broken too many times.

"Do you know anything about him?" she whispered.

Candy shook her head. "I just sat down about ten minutes ago. Moments later, this hombre walks through the wall, asks if he can join the game, gets the nod, sits and the game goes on as if he'd always been there." Her voice was hushed and incredulous. "I swear that nobody else noticed."

Angela looked around. Candy was right, no one seemed to care. "Did you ask any questions?" Angela asked. Candy shook her head. "Then you're just eavesdropping?" Candy smiled. "Well, I'm curious and short on time so...." Angela waited until the hand was finished, then asked, "Samuel, can a modern day woman buy you a drink?"

"Sure thing, pretty lady. It's never too early," Samuel said, smiling broadly and tipping back his hat.

"Come to the bar with me. I'll have Cannon whip up a Gin Fizz or an 'Under the Sheets'."

"That's "Between the Sheets'." Samuel floated through the table to join her. "I'm sitting this one out boys, be back in a minute." As they walked off, Samuel spoke over his shoulder, "Women, who can figure 'em. One day they're taking you to task for offering them a flower, the next they're wanting to buy you a drink. Even after death some things never change."

Angela colored. If she hadn't wanted questions answered, she would've slapped him, too.

"Couldn't resist my charms any longer, eh?" Samuel said with the expression of a cat who'd just eaten the goldfish.

Angela's gaze was chilly. "I asked you over here to find out about the new player."

"Not to spend time with me?" Samuel was surprised. "Now I really do need a drink."

"Drinking early this mornin', Ang," Cannon rumbled as she appeared from thin air. "Last night not go so well?" Cans, bottles and spices flew around creating a batch of Bloody Mary's in a huge glass jar.

"That's an understatement."

"Don't give up now. I think he's worth some trouble!"

"Cannon, I'm talking about the man who had the heart attack at the séance," Angela snapped.

"I'm mighty sorry. Can't seem to keep my foot outta my mouth sometimes!"

"Sam, isn't a new ghost joining your game unusual?" Angela asked.

"What about my drink?"

"Can you drink?" she asked. He shook his head. "Then answer the question. Isn't a new ghost joining your game unusual?"

"Not overly."

Angela wanted to throw up her hands in frustration. "Sam, has any ghost joined you for play since Mason?"

Samuel took off his hat and scratched his head. "Come to think of it, no. But others, including Mac and Blasing have played."

"But no ghosts?" She pressed, and he shook his head no. "You don't find that odd?"

"Angela, I'm dead and I'm still getting to gamble and flirt. I find that mighty queer."

"Point taken."

"But Broderick did mention there were strange spirits afoot, and we were to keep an eye out for them, so when this fella stopped by, we thought it only neighborly—and a good idea—to let him join us. The more the merrier."

"Do you know his name? Where he's from? Or why he's here?"

"You know, I'm getting the third degree and we aren't even married," Samuel laughed. "Why do pretty women have sharp tongues?"

"Because they can," Cannon chuckled.

Not for the first time Angela wished she could withhold a tip from Cannon. "Fine," Angela said. "I won't be discreet. I'll go ask him myself." Her voice rose, "I was trying not to interrupt the flow of the game. But when I saw you lose big on that last hand, I thought you might want a break."

"Flattery will get you anywhere, Angela. Women like you make men weak." She stopped and glared. "Let me think for a moment. He ain't said much. You know, since we don't have to worry about being bushwhacked anymore, we just concentrate on the game and keep an eye out for cheating."

"Cheating?" Angela asked.

"Yeah. All of these guys are sharks," Samuel said. "Cheating is a true skill, just like roping, riding, and shooting." He could tell she was surprised. "Angela, we don't get mad over cheating anymore. It's just a game now to see if you can pull the wool over your opponent's eyes or keep him from doing the same to you. You see, cheating keeps your opponent wondering if you're just plumb lucky, playing well, or... agile." A coin was suddenly in his hand, dancing around his fingers, then disappeared. "That's why we were so amazed Blasing was beating us. None of us could spot him cheating. We want a second go round."

"Almost every time a spirit opens his or her mouth, I learn something new," Angela said, shaking her head.

"His name is Bat," Samuel finally volunteered. "He said he'd been wandering around looking for a game."

"Thank you," she sighed. Why was getting some men to answer questions like pulling teeth? "Now where's he from?"

"Said he'd lost big time to the devil and was looking to recoup," Samuel told her with an easy grin.

"Lost big time to the devil?!"

Samuel gave her a long look, then asked, "Does that bother you?" Angela nodded. "It's almost the same thing Dirk used to say when somebody asked him where he was from. He's from Gotohell."

Angela groaned as she laid her head on the copper top. Cannon was laughing hard, shaking the entire bar—glasses dancing and jingling. "Well," Angela managed, "I don't want you to be nosy, for Spirit's sake, but would you try to remember what you hear?"

"Yeah, Sammy," Cannon said, suddenly serious. "Broderick said the newcomers might be ruffians. We can't have that. We're with you, Ang, right Sam?" Cannon emphasized enough to make him nod. "We don't want some unruly sonuvabitch ruinin' a good thing, now do we? Besides, we already have our own S.O.B."

"That's fer God's truth," Samuel said. He looked at Angela a long time, then said, "Angela, because Mac trusted you, and he was good to me, I'll be the master of discretion and find out what I can for you, but I can't go prying too much. It's against the Gambler's Credo."

"But all gamblers do it ta get an edge," Cannon said.

"Don't spread that around," Samuel said. The ghostly bartender rolled her eyes. "See you later, Angela."

"Find out if he has any friends, especially if they're coming here," Cannon blurted. "There's no sheriff around, ya know."

Samuel smiled, "Cannon, we're dead. We don't need a sheriff. I know what Angela thinks she saw, but I just don't believe it. I'm already dead. Good day, ladies."

Angela sat there for a while, then said, "Cannon, I'm going to find Blasing. If you see Broderick, please tell him about Bat."

"I'll spread the word, sure I will. Listen Ang, I'm just as concerned as ya are. I believe ya saw what ya saw," Cannon said. "And please tell that good lookin' man of yours good mornin' fer me. Well, speak of the devil," she said. "Look over there."

Angela turned. Blasing wandered toward Candy's table. He looked good in beige pants and a colorful ski sweater. "He must be psychic. Later, Cannon."

Blasing stopped at Candy's table, and they spoke. She nodded toward the gamblers. The table was crowded now, eight ghosts crammed around the large, round table. Instead of playing, they were dividing chips and shuffling cards.

"Hey, there are two new ghosts," Angela suddenly realized.

Broderick suddenly appeared at her side. He was so surprised by what he'd heard he didn't greet them as cordially as usual. "The short one is certainly a fierce-looking rogue."

"It's going to be all right," Blasing said, sounding confident. Angela knew better; he certainly wasn't comfortable with nine ghosts so close, as exemplified by his toying with the pendant's chain.

"Maybe he is a..." Broderick cleared his throat, "gunslinger."

As with Bat, the short and stocky spirit appeared transparent and virtually colorless. The smoke made him even more difficult to see, and Angela changed her vantage point to get a better view. He was leaning on his elbows, his face inches away from his cards. The brim of his hat, and his abundance of hair hid his expression. When a card slipped through his fingers, he growled, then tried to snatch up the card. His fingers passed through it.

"You'll get the hang of it, stranger," Samuel told the stocky ghost. "Just takes a while."

"Excuse me," Broderick said as he approached. "Who are you... gentlemen?"

"And what are you doing here?!" Heller demanded as he approached, his cane clattering against chairs on his way. Customers frowned at the sweaty and red faced Irishman. He ignored them, cursing between every breath. "Dammit! Who are you?" Now everyone in the restaurant noticed the new ghosts. The murmur grew louder.

"Who's the geezer?" the hairy ghost growled irreverently.

Dirk just smiled and spoke before Heller could explode. "He's King of the Hill, Cogan."

Cogan sniffed the air. "Smells funny," he said jerking a thumb toward Heller. "You're sick. Might want to go see a doctor, bub."

"I've tolerated enough...." Heller began, perspiration appearing across his forehead.

Blasing stepped forward before there was a disaster. "Hi, I'm Blasing Madera. Welcome to Ghostal Shores."

"Who are you?"

"An owner," Blasing said quietly.

"Well, then thanks," the hairy ghost replied. Cogan glanced up briefly, his opaque eyes appraising Blasing. The stunted spirit's nose was flat and his beard, as well as his hair, stuck out in all directions as if he were part bear.

"This is my partner, Sean Heller," Blasing continued.

"Too bad for you. Listen, bub, I don't plan on causin' any trouble, but I will if it comes lookin' for me. I'm just waitin' on my friends. They're checkin' on drinks."

"What? Did you say drinks?" Angela asked.

"I'm not sure I want this ghost here," Heller said, then discovered no one was paying attention to him.

"Interesting accent you have," Angela said. "You from Canada?"

"Yeah, I'm a Canucklehead. That a problem, squaw?"

Angela flushed, but before she could retort, Candy touched her shoulder. "I'm Angela Starborne, and we don't have a problem if you stay on good behavior, Mister Cogan."

"Or what, Missy?"

"We do not deliver threats." Broderick's expression was stern and his glare piercing. "We just do what we must to keep Ghostal

Shores a pleasant place."

"I can appreciate that." Cogan chewed his cigar from one side of his mouth to the other. "I'm just playin' the game and waitin' on my drink."

"A drink? But...." Angela glanced at Samuel and found the pretty-boy spirit just as confused.

"You said you had friends?" Blasing asked. Cogan nodded, then puffed on his cigar. Heller stepped back, waving at the air in front of him.

"In the bar gettin' drinks," Cogan replied.

"But I was just in the bar..." Angela began. She halted when she heard angry shouts, and the sound of breaking glass coming from the bar. Cannon's bellow followed.

"Oh dear, a ruckus," Broderick stated, then raced toward the bar, flying through several tables. Curious, people stood, making it more difficult for Blasing to follow.

"Nice to have met you, Cogan," Angela said, then she and Candy followed Blasing as he dodged around tables and slid between people. "Excuse me! Coming through!" The crowd moved slowly, intent on the disruption, hoping it was another staged haunting.

"Stop this immediately!" Broderick demanded from ahead.

Angela slid to a halt next to Blasing at the entrance to the lounge. The quartet of pale, ethereal strangers didn't notice Broderick as they continued to argue with Cannon. She glowered, standing behind the bar with her arms crossed. Broken glass was scattered across the bar top, the carpet, and the shelves behind the bar. Many of the overhead glasses were missing; the rest looked like teeth hanging over the bar.

"I said stop!" Broderick had almost reached the bar.

"I recognize that mule," Blasing said, nodding to the beast somewhat concealed by the foursome. Lillybell snorted in their direction, then began to pull away, dragging a ghost with her. "Took JP long enough to get here."

"What do you mean you don't have any?!" yelled the tall, bald ghost standing between the two spirits—a towering, shirtless Negro with a sculpted physique and a wizened old man leaning on a walking stick. The threesome was colorless and ill-defined.

"He needs some," the bald spirit said as he pointed to the sickly looking ghost.

With practiced ease, Blasing stepped forward and took charge. Angela stayed at his elbow. "Is there a problem here, Mister...?"

The bald ghost whirled around, his face fuzzy and indistinct, but his anguish obvious. "I just want a drink like I heard, ya know. I prefer not to cause trouble."

"I know you, you're trouble!" JP cried, then returned to struggling with his Lillybell.

"A drink like you heard? Cannon, do we have anything we can serve ghosts?" Blasing asked. As if this was the tenth time she'd answered that same question, she grimly shook her head.

"Did you order something specifically?" Candy asked.

"No, but I heard...."

"Then you've heard wrong, Mister," Blasing said firmly. "Cannon would know. She serves the drinks around here."

Angela was glad to see him defending the ghost, taking some ownership in Ghostal Shores. "You heard from whom?" she asked.

"I demand to know what's going on!" Heller shouted. Puffing and sweating, he'd just arrived.

"Rumors, you know," the bald ghost said, obviously hedging. "Said we could get something here that would really give us a jolt, you know. Like being alive again!"

"Snakeoil salesman," the old ghost wheezed.

"Can you describe him?" Blasing asked.

"I demand to...." Heller cut himself short as a sudden commotion came from the grand entryway where doors banged open. "What in Hell's bells?"

Surprised shouts were drowned by hoots, hollers, yips and yells. The cacophony grew louder, closer, then thunderous, heavy boots racing up the stairs to the lounge.

Several bellowing ghosts came through the walls, phasing out and running through the tables on their way to the bar. The spirits were colorless, ragged, and unkempt with dirty faces and knotted beards. Wide-eyed and licking their chops, others just as earthly and rumpled came running up the stairways.

"So many ghosts," Blasing said, a bit pale.

"Hang in there." Angela touched Blasing to provide support.

"Gonna make a great book," Candy said with a smile.

"Are they friends of yours?" Blasing asked in general, sounding amazingly calm. Angela could feel him quiver.

The old ghost coughed. The other two shook their heads. "I know some of 'em!" JP cried.

Bringing up the rear, a few laggards exited the far wall just as the mass reached the bar. "What'll it be, boys?!" Cannon boomed.

The ghosts smiled broadly. "WOMEN!" several yelled. "BOOZE!" "WOMEN!" "DRINKS ON ME!" one particularly mousy ghost called out.

"Miners," Cannon said disgustedly. "Off shift."

"Get back, dammit!" Heller yelled.

With the twenty-some ghosts jammed around the bar, Angela felt overwhelmed, so she knew what Blasing must be feeling was traumatic. She hoped the rings and pendant were helping, but he appeared to be having trouble breathing. Blasing tried to make room for himself, but every time he moved a ghost, another slipped into that open space.

"Broderick, help!" Angela vigorously threw elbows against the crush. A couple of ghosts grunted, surprised by the contact, but they didn't relent. Getting even angrier, Angela slapped one, making his eyes cross.

"Barbarians!" Broderick yelled. He jostled the miners away from Blasing and Angela. "Make room! Stand back! Give Ms. Starborne and Mister Madera room! Please! Well I.... Did I fail to make myself clear?! You deserve a wallop or two, but this...." With two rabbit punches, Broderick decked two of the mining ghosts. "Should do." The other spirits backed away as the downed ghosts sank through the floor. "Anyone else?"

Grumbling, the ghosts stepped back, acting as a pack of hungry wolves forced away from a kill, then swept around to the far ends of the bar. "WHISKEY!" The rail was quickly crammed shoulder to shoulder with transparent miners. "WHERE'S THE OPIUM!"

"This simply will not do," Broderick said, his expression grave. Angela grabbed a napkin and moved to Blasing's side as Candy helped him sink into a chair. He perspired profusely and mumbled about so many memories.

Looking apoplectic, Heller crashed into a chair. His lips moved but no words could be heard.

"QUIET!!" Cannon boomed. Glasses tinkled, then stone silence followed her shout, even in the dining room. "Now one at a time, what do ya want? This is a civilized bar. Give me any trouble and we'll bounce ya's butts outta here so fast even a polecat wouldn't have time ta stink."

Watching the proceedings, Dirk, Mason and the brothers leaned against the walls of the archway leading into the restaurant. Barney came up the stairs and waited at the top. Assistant Security Director Chadwick arrived right after them. Three guards were behind him; each appeared very confused and concerned.

"Trouble?" Sven asked as he floated up through the floor.

"Not yet," Cannon said. "You there, Chinaman!" she stared at an Asian clad in a baggy shirt, voluminous pants, and circular but pointed hat.

"A drink of nectar, please gentle lady," the slender ghost told her, peeking out from the shadow of his hat.

"What's this with the drinks?" Blasing whispered to Angela.

"I can't serve ghosts," Cannon said, looking at all of them. "It's not that I don't want ta, ya understand, or that I ain't allowed, it's just that I don't have anything. What do ya drink?"

"Don't know. Been so long," a hunched ghost said, licking his parched lips. He coughed dustily.

"But we heard...." someone at the end of the bar started.

"What did you hear?" Cannon asked.

"That there was drink here aplenty, senorita," a Hispanic ghost in the forefront told her. He wore a poncho and his hair was tied back with a bandanna. "You know, something for us. Better than tequila, I hear, put the fire in any hombre's belly again."

"Something that might help my friend," the Negro ghost reminded her. "He's fading. He's my friend."

"I'm sorry, boys," Cannon began, "but I'm being plum honest with ya. There's nothing here. Somebody told ya wrong." Cannon looked to the bald ghost. "I can't help ya. I would if I could."

"She's lying!" a wide-eyed one yelled.

"Yeah, trying to keep it to herself!" another ghost chimed in. Rumblings and grumblings suddenly changed, exploding into curses and more accusations. "Golddiggin' bitch!" "She's just a woman!" "Search the bar!"

The bar started to shake—glasses jingling and shards bouncing about—then it shuddered as the transients rioted. Chairs and tables shuffled across the floor. Another glass shattered. Sven, Barney, Dirk and the twins converged on the bar, ready to fight.

"STOP! Listen to me! NOW!" Blasing hopped up on a chair and shouted. "I am part owner of this establishment," he said, waving to Heller. "I know Cannon is a very honest spirit! And you'll see she's honest if you try. Open your eyes and look! You're spirits now, not flesh, the truth can't be hidden from you if you look! Open your eyes!"

Angela was impressed by the man.

All the ghosts stopped as if struck, their protests dying on their lips. They looked at Cannon and Blasing, then at each other. For a time, they shuffled about, mumbling and grumbling as if children caught doing something wrong.

Finally, the Hispanic spirit smiled broadly and said, "We have seen what you said is true—la verdad, but we are confused. We must talk to Rictor. He seemed to be telling the truth."

"Who is Rictor?" Blasing asked.

"The snakeoil salesman," the wizened one wheezed. "Harsh voice, like falling rocks—wheez—ya know. Never forget it once you've—wheez—heard it."

"Who is Rictor?" Blasing asked again.

"For God's sake, Blasing," Heller whispered hoarsely, "don't anger them."

"He's the boss of Ghostal Shores," one of them cried.

"What do you mean?" Blasing asked.

"Man in a stage claiming to be the boss of Ghostal Shores told us we could find drinks here."

"Told all of you?"

"Some. The word spread, you know."

"He is not an owner," Blasing said.

"You mean there might be more coming?" Candy gasped.

"I think they should leave. Right now!" Heller demanded.

Looking warily at the ghosts, Chadwick and his men joined them. "What would you like us to do, sir?"

"Kicking them out might just lead to more problems," Blasing said.

"Let them stay, see what we can learn," Angela suggested. "Somebody might know more about Rictor and why Mac's afraid of him. That may help us find out why you're being haunted."

"All right. Not that we have a lot of choice," Heller groused.

"You can stay here if you wish, but there are rules that must be followed," Broderick announced. He mentioned the no touching rule and that they must be kind to guests. Fighting was not allowed, and if something was damaged, they must fix it or be expelled. If they upset any guest, they would be bounced. A few laughed, but not for long. Most nodded agreeably.

"We're sorry," the bald ghost said. "We didn't know."

"We got cards if any of ya's a gambler," Dirk said.

"More the merrier," Samuel agreed.

"Ya-hoo," a chubby ghost yelled and moved toward Dirk.

"That does nothing for my thirst," the diminutive Asian ghost said. "I've been looking for so long." He was downcast, his shoulders slumped and head hung low.

"Come, gather round and sit. Let me tell you of this place—of Ghostal Shores...." Broderick began as he led them to a nearby table. The crowd of ghosts drifted with him as though a fog bank.

"Broderick is really amazing," Angela said.

"Yeah, but don't tell him that," Cannon replied as she began cleaning up the glass, the scattered shards gathering together and floating toward a large trash can behind the bar.

"As are you," Angela said to Blasing as she took his hand. "You stood up to a horde of angry ghosts."

"Thank ya fer defending my honor," Cannon told Blasing.

"You're welcome. I didn't know what else to do."

"Well," Cannon said, "Carrie and Broderick always claim that we ghosts reflect the ownership." The alchemist looked toward Heller.

"These new ghosts concern me," the Irishman grumbled as he stood shakily. "They might be bad apples. Madame Zanadane needs to get to work." As he headed for the stairs, he said, "Chadwick, have one of your men keep an eye on them."

"Yes, sir."

"What do you think?" Blasing asked as he surveyed the two crowds—one around Broderick, the other around the card table.

"Must be over twenty," Angela replied. "And I'm afraid there might be more, but we won't know until we question them."

"I'd let them relax," Candy suggested. "Then see if we can find out more about this Rictor. It could help with tonight's seánce."

"I want to know why Rictor lied to them," Angela said. "And why he's here."

TWENTY-TWO

After the failed séance, Blasing suggested going directly to the dance, but Angela insisted on changing into something formal. He'd found a tux in the closet and then changed quickly. While he waited, Blasing turned on the music, poured a B&B and then relaxed on the couch.

The séance had been a bust, he thought. Neither Marsh, Mac nor Lilly had responded to their compellings. Angela thought Lilly was confined by Rictor. She'd suggested calling out to Rictor.

Remembering the dread the dark ghost's presence could evoke, Blasing felt Candy had come to his rescue. Candy thought Lilly was at the dance, where most of the ghosts would be drawn to the vibrant energy of the joyous dancers.

They discussed what they'd learned from the new spirits and discovered that they only spoke to Heller, Blasing and Broderick—the owners and a representative. They ignored Madame Zanadane and Angela. From the transients' comments, it was obvious Rictor had been riding around Nevada and California telling ghosts they could get a drink at Ghostal Shores. But why? Ghosts were supposed to be able to tell if someone was lying. Why did he want them here?

Did they want more life? And if so, why? Dr. Landrum had said they were just repeating old habits. Broderick had denied this, but admitted he didn't feel he could go anywhere else or do anything besides serve as a valet. Ghosts were trapped by their pasts. The good doctor concluded that Rictor was forming the Long Dead Ghost Gang.

The Great Xantini had been little help. He'd been injured, supposedly, in a minor accident, and his mental faculties were diminished. Dr. Strange had been unable to access the Akashic records— some psychic library of all knowledge. Just like a psychic, Blasing mused, when you needed them they fall flat. Well, most psychics, he amended. Julie Zephren wondered if the ghosts were seeking a spiritual fountain of youth—a nectar of life of some kind.

Blasing had described Rictor and recounted the numerous meetings—outside the bathroom, in the phone nook, in the construction yard and the overlook nook. Candy thought Rictor was afraid of Blasing stealing his heart's treasure: Lilly. After everyone created a good mental image, Blasing had tried to call him out. Nothing had happened, so they decided to seek out the spirits in the ballroom.

Blasing sighed again. His mind was overloaded and it didn't all have to do with the ghosts. Earlier today, he had reviewed the security personnel files. Several concerned him; although there weren't any felonious convictions. Rich Steele informed him a few had been accused. Chief Porter had worked at Folsom prison, compiling a spotless record there, but while he was directing security transport for Bank of America in San Francisco, they'd been victimized by the largest heist in the city's history. Although nothing had ever been proven, the security community believed Porter was involved.

Porter's assistant, Kelvin Chadwick, started his career in security in the Military Police. Following in his father's footsteps, he'd advanced to an officer's position. Then he'd been discharged. Rich said it might have been dishonorable if not for Chadwick's father. Numerous guards had worked for Chadwick at Folsom prison.

Blasing sighed. He'd thought they appeared to be more than simple hotel security, and now he understood why the ghosts didn't like them. Their reputations and morals might be questionable, although a gang of thugs might be stretching things. Or was it? Might they be guarding something for Heller? Maybe his reason for doctoring the books? And did it have anything to do with Mac's murder? The more Blasing thought about it, the more he worried. Would their investigation put Angela at risk?

Blasing was just about to knock on Angela's door when she exited. She looked stunning in an ebony jacket and a simple but elegant dress the color of midnight. Her hair was styled to one side, a blond cascade tumbling across her left shoulder. Blasing found himself questioning whether she was real or a vision.

"Are you all right, Blasing?" she said, her blue-green eyes wide. A secretive smile played across her lips.

"You look elegantly fabulous," he managed as he rose. "I will be inspired to dance with you."

"I like the sound of that." She drew close and took his hand. Remembering the dream again, Blasing almost drew back his hand, then forced himself to relax. He cared for this woman and didn't want to hurt her feelings. "I still think we should be leaving instead of going dancing. It's dangerous here. Especially if security is a problem."

"Blasing, you seem undecided about several things." Suddenly, she was very close, somehow managing to slip within his arms. "Sometimes I get the feeling you care for me... and sometimes I think you're afraid of me."

"You read my mind," he breathed, his heart racing.

"You talk about letting go of the past. Of breaking habits. Shall we let go of the past together?" she whispered, her eyes beseeching his. Her lips parted as she moved even closer, ready to be kissed. "Embrace the present."

Blasing kissed her, his entire body breathing a sigh of relief and tensing all at the same time. Angela squirmed closer as if trying to bond flesh through their clothes. The heat threatened to consume him.

After long moments, she broke off their first passionate kiss. "I've been waiting for this." Angela said, then ardently kissed him again, her lips and tongue lively and artful. As they sought each other in delight, Angela slipped out of her jacket.

Blasing's fingers slid the straps from her bare shoulders, then he kissed his way down her throat. "You are so beautiful."

BRRRINGG. BRRRINGG. Totally confused by the phone's ringing, Blasing awakened with a start. He looked around wildly, searching for Angela or a ghost, but finding neither. Then he felt the heat in his hands and across his sternum; Lilly had been here again.

Angela's door opened. "Blasing, are you going to answer that?"

Blasing grabbed the phone. "Hello? Hi Candy. Angela! It's Candy. She's at the ballroom and says the place is packed with spirits, including a couple of ancient mariners."

"I'm ready," Angela said, stepping into the lounge. Blasing experienced a dizzying event of deja-vu: Angela looked stunning in a black jacket and a simple but elegant dress the shade of a moonless night. Her hair was free and combed to one side, a golden cascade tumbling across her left shoulder.

"Are you all right, Blasing?" she asked, her tropical-blue eyes wide. A secretive smile played across her lips.

"You look elegantly fabulous," he said for the second time.

"Thank you. Maybe Lilly will be jealous and show up." She drew close to take his hand. Again he felt wonderfully charged. "Then we can find out something. You know Mr. Madera, I look forward to dancing with you. Candy might be right about dancing."

Blasing hesitated, almost drawing back his hand, then relaxed. Was she real or was he dreaming again? "I'll be rusty."

Suddenly, she was very close, somehow maneuvering within his arms to press lightly against him. Blasing swore there was a magnetizing force pulling him closer, seizing his hands, and making it difficult to breathe. "Sometimes I get the feeling...." she began.

"That we are in danger and should leave?" he blurted.

She took a step back. "Sometimes you are very difficult to understand, Mr. Madera."

"And I swear you read my mind," he replied.

"Did the phone awaken you?" she suddenly asked. He nodded. "You had another nightmare, didn't you?"

"Of sorts."

"And you won't tell me about it?"

"Not yet."

She suddenly smiled, her eyes radiant. "Well, I'll make you a deal. You tell me what's bothering you, and I'll pack."

"Really?"

"Yes. Is it something from your past? Peter's murder? What?"

Blasing started to tell her, then concluded he couldn't. Not this way. "I'll think about it."

"While we dance," she told him. Keeping his hand, she led him out the door. "Where's Broderick?"

"Waiting for us downstairs. He wanted to keep an eye on Madame Zanadane. Did you see her do anything strange in tonight's séance?"

"No."

"Angela, have you ever thought that maybe hematite not only protects you from the ghosts and allows you to touch them, but also allows them to touch you?"

"But if they don't harm you, what else could happen?"

"I... I don't know," Blasing lied.

"Are you worried about all the ghosts in the ballroom?"

"Not all, just one," he said as they got onto the elevator.

They arrived at the foyer with a crowd of formally dressed patrons. Blasing squinted during the ride, almost blinded by the gems, jewelry and perfect smiles. Angela moved closer, and Blasing held her, noticing once more how comfortable this felt.

The large doors along the southern side of the Cathedral Coast were open and a collection of murmuring voices and music poured into the large, open chamber. A few people milled around the foyer, looking at the stars through the skylight or watching the moon descend through the western clouds. Smoker traffic drifted in and out the front door.

"I'm still concerned about security," Blasing whispered. He glanced at a hidden camera.

"Is that your gut feeling talking?"

"Some. I'm not sure I'd be all that suspicious, except the resident ghosts don't like them."

"And you believe them?"

"I don't know what to believe," he said.

"Or what you want, do you?" she asked him pointedly, her gaze seeming to pierce his soul.

"Reading my mind again?" The way she did that unnerved him.

"Body language," she replied. Arm in arm, they walked into the crowded antechamber. Champagne seemed to be the beverage of choice, and the attire of the evening was tuxedos and gowns. Blasing didn't see any ascetics, although numerous eccentrics—their crystals shining and feathers flying—moved about the room.

"There's Broderick," Angela said, nodding to the ethereal figure waiting for them at the doorway to the ballroom.

When the Englishman saw them he drifted toward them. "Good evening, sir. Miss. I must say you look quite dashing tonight."

"I'm trying to make Lilly jealous."

"Then I believe you shall accomplish your heart's desire. Master Madera will be the envy of many suitors." Broderick glanced quizzically at Blasing, then asked, "Are you all right, sir? You feel... off kilter."

"In a way, that's what I said," Angela told him.

Blasing glared, then said, "Not too surprising. I'm walking into a room full of spirits and one of them wants to kill me. See anything out of the ordinary—for Ghostal Shores, I mean?"

"No, sir. If you wish, I shall act as your personal guard," Broderick offered. "I am concerned about this new group of ghosts. They appear to have more than their share of shady characters."

"Bodyguarding's my job," Angela teased.

"Not only is she reading my mind, she's stealing my lines," Blasing tried to joke.

"Let's go dance."

Above the dance floor the twin chandeliers sparkled like miniature suns. A festive air filled the mammoth chamber, spilling out through the antechambers and beyond. Crowded tables ringed the dance floor. A portable bar stood near the coastal windows. Despite the crowd, Blasing thought he heard Cannon's voice, even above Charlie's piano. A host of live musicians joined him, but the ghost was still center stage, his white-gloved hands flying across the Grand's keyboard.

"It reminds me a bit of when Captain Morris took me to the Great Exhibition held at the Crystal Palace in Hyde Park the summer of 1851. Of course, Ghostal Shores has grace and beauty, two of the many qualities that the Crystal Palace did not. All have glass and cast iron. Quite a monstrosity."

Blasing focused on the spirits. Most of the transients gathered around the bar, stringing out on each side and creating a low fog around the coastal windows. Despite their blurred features, the transient spirits were obviously a ragged group and mixture of nationalities from Asians, to Brits and Cossacks. "Have you seen Rictor?" Blasing asked. "Or Lilly?"

"No, sir."

As one song ended and another, slower tune began, the lights dimmed intimately. "Come dance with me," Angela tried again. Blasing allowed her to lead him toward the dance floor. On the way they passed Barney, who gave Angela a sweeping bow that made her laugh. "I'm enjoying myself too much for an investigation."

"I am too," Blasing whispered in her ear.

"Then show it."

With a satisfied smile she slipped into his arms and allowed him to lead. He immediately felt relief from the thousands of watching eyes. "Have you seen Candy and Rod?"

"They're over there, dancing near Samuel and Melanie."

Candy was tight against her companion, unlike the gypsy and the pretty-boy cowboy who grandly cavorted about. Sven and Ingrid danced arm in arm, the stocky ghost couple moving fluidly across the floor as if they'd been dancing together for centuries.

When Blasing and Angela passed a less crowded area of tables, he saw the Berkeley group. A young man tried to get their attention, but they ignored him, pointing to a pair of ghosts that could have doubled for Newman's Butch and Redford's Sundance Kid.

"You dance very well, Mr. Madera."

"Thank you, Ms. Starborne. You are very graceful. I feel as if we've danced many times before." He sounded more eloquent than he felt. Between her nearness and the presence of all the ghosts, he felt as if he were rushing headlong at a dizzying pace.

"Are you all right?"

"Yes," he said. "Madame Zanadane is sitting among her cabinet." The in-house psychic chatted with Dr. Devlin Strange and Julie Zephren. Mr. Chung waited nearby, but the Great Xantini was nowhere in sight. "Do you really think Efrem Xantini is going to help if Madame Zanadane is involved?"

"Since he claims his mental capacities are diminished, and yet shows no signs of it, well... I just wouldn't count on his help."

"They all seem weird to me."

She just smiled. "I can't believe David is dancing with Janice the librarian. Talk about two different spirits," she said, referring not only to the waiter's size, but his confident smile when compared to her timorous one. "Love can make strange attractions."

Blasing pondered a way to tell her how he'd grown to care for her, then wondered how to explain his 'nightmares'. "I'm surprised Lilly hasn't come to bother you."

"Maybe I'm not flirting enough." Angela moved even closer, laying her head on his shoulder. He could feel her heat through his clothes. "Think this will do it?"

"Yes," Blasing replied. He found himself stroking her bare back, the tips of his fingers afire.

"You make quite a handsome couple," Elma said as she and Barney danced past. They appeared stately and graceful, throwbacks to a bygone era of etiquette and modesty.

The music softened, then lingered, and the lights grew brighter. When a more upbeat song came on, Angela moved fractionally backward. "A couple of the newcomers are dancing with the hookers," Angela told him, nodding toward the far part of the floor where Missy, Amber and Charity were being pulled into the circle.

Two of the three transients appeared to be rough ranch hands— just looking at them made Blasing eager to wash the dust from his throat. The third was barefoot, his pants rolled to just below his knees. If he'd had a pipe, he would have been the picture of an old salt, his beard bushy and his sea-cap jauntily askew.

"So many ghosts," Blasing said. He thought he could feel their thirsts and hunger. "All around. So many new ones today. Even more since this afternoon. Miners. Cowboys. Ranchers. And railworkers. Why are they faded? And are there going to be more tomorrow? Might they overrun the place?" Sweat beaded upon his forehead as his imagination shifted into overdrive.

"Are you all right?" Angela asked, squeezing his shoulder.

"You said you'd protect me," Blasing reminded her. "So I'll be just fine, won't I?"

"Of course. With the rings, you're just as safe in my arms as you are in your room."

"Many of the ghosts aren't dancing," Blasing said.

"There are more males than females."

"A few of the spirits appear discontented," he told her.

"Probably because they can't get a drink. A good number seem to be caught up in the music." She smiled. "Even more are amazed by the modern female's attire."

Lust was obvious on even some of the most amorphous faces. A few spirits were on the verge of licking their lips. One wiped his mouth with the back of his sleeve. "I hope there's no trouble."

"Live women don't appeal to ghosts, unless there's some history tying them together."

"That possession by Carrie worries me."

"You can be concerned, not worried," she told him.

"I don't see Rictor or Lilly."

"We could kiss. I'm sure that would draw her out."

Blasing blinked away a flashback from a dream; he'd seen her look this way before. It drew him as iron to a magnet.

"May I cut in?" Dr. Landrum asked, appearing from nowhere.

Angela watched Blasing for a moment, then said, "Think on it, Blasing. I believe it's a surefire bet to work."

"I promise to return her in a dance or five," the doctor said, then they danced away.

Feeling a bit dizzy, Blasing made his way to the door.

"Are you all right, sir?" Broderick asked.

"I'm getting tired of people asking that."

"May I inquire if you are well?" Broderick asked stoically, only arching a brow.

"Marginal, I think."

"I do not believe there is any cause for alarm."

"What are you talking about?" Blasing asked.

"Doctor Landrum is not for her."

"What makes you say that?"

"A ghost can feel... certain things."

"As can people."

Broderick suddenly smiled. "If you choose to, yes."

"Geoff," Angela said, "you are an excellent dancer and a fine doctor. What else are you?"

His smile broadened. "A romantic for the ages."

"I'm sure," she replied, "but that's not what I meant. When you're not doctoring, do you have another profession?"

"Ladies and medicine take up most of my time," he said easily.

"Why do all the men I know seem to be so secretive?"

"I thought men lied and women were secretive," Dr. Landrum said, smiling even more broadly.

She could see her eyes reflected in his round glasses. Her feeling that he was hiding something intensified. "I think you are or were in some kind of law enforcement."

"Why would you think that?" he asked, looking surprised as well as amused.

"You remind me a bit of Blasing—the confident way you carry yourself—and you seem to know Sheriff Middleton very well."

"I'm honored by your comparison."

"And Sheriff Middleton?"

Dr. Landrum shrugged. "I don't know what to say."

"You'd prefer we didn't notice the connection?"

He chuckled. "What an active imagination. Is this part of law-yering?" She just smiled sweetly. "It's nice to know you've been thinking about me. I thought you might be succumbing to Blasing's rugged charm."

"Well, for the most part, he answers direct questions. I can't abide a man who isn't honest with me. Though I did like the way you connected Rictor to the idea of a gang—a lawman's view if I ever heard one."

"Would you believe I worked for the FBI before I became a doc-tor?"

"Not the worked—as in the past—part." She smiled sweetly. "Anything you'd like to tell me? Like if you're here doing the psy-chological study Sheriff Middleton mentioned to Blasing?"

After spending time in the foyer, Blasing and Broderick re-turned to the ballroom. Blasing felt much better and thought he had a way to tell Angela about his 'nightmares'.

"Hello cousin, can I have this dance?" Meg asked. She was dressed in a flowing green gown with white lace along the collar and cuffs. The emerald tiara made her look like a princess.

"Your companion won't mind?" he asked, moving with her to-ward the dance floor.

"JJ won't be off for an hour or so. I've wanted to talk with you for a while."

"What's on your mind?"

"Have you given any more thought to what you'll do with your part of Ghostal Shores?"

"Yes, but I haven't decided anything. The arrival of the new ghosts may affect my decision."

"What do you know about the new spirits?" Meg asked. "The resort is abuzz. Everyone wants to see them." As they slowly whirled across the dance floor, Blasing guardedly told her what he knew. "Wow. I don't believe I feel comfortable here any more."

"I understand that," Blasing said, freeing a hand to rub the back of his neck.

"I'll be leaving tomorrow," Meg told him "I'm sure we'll see each other in court. I hope it doesn't make us enemies."

"It all depends on the test results," Blasing replied. "We may not even need to go to court."

"That sounds wonderful," she replied, emerald eyes aglow. "Then we might still be friends. I don't know about you, but I could use some good family." Blasing just nodded, his mind and occasionally his gaze on Angela. "Mr. Donahue gave Ms. Starborne his number, as well as mine, so if you want, call me."

"Will JJ be going with you?"

"Once things are settled. We've grown closer over the last week I've spent here," she said. "He's been very good to me. He wants to be a writer, and I've read some of his manuscripts. He's very talented. He'll write and I'll produce my art—and I'm not talking about painting nails. I plan to open up a shop."

"I guess Mac wasn't such a bad father after all. He'll be posthumously supporting you for quite a while," Blasing said.

Meg's eyes narrowed. "You know I won't lie to you. I'm glad he's dead, but I didn't kill him, although the thought's crossed my mind several times a day for many years. I'm just glad he didn't come back as a ghost. This place already gives me the creeps," she shivered. "Especially with the new ghosts. I wonder where they came from? Certainly not from the bricks, unlike when they built the southern wing."

"What makes you say that?"

"The bricks are from a warehouse in Los Angeles."

"How do you know this?"

"I remembered reading an article in the *L.A. Times*. The place had been derelict for a long time, first due to claims it was haunted, then from being located in the wrong part of town."

"L.A. bricks? Not Bodie?"

"Yep."

"Excuse me, cheri," Eva Dare interrupted, "but may I cut in?" Chocolate wrapped in vanilla, the Frenchwoman wore a sleek, clinging gown of cream adorned with sequins.

"It might be dangerous," Blasing said and saw her flinch.

"I have watched two women dance with you, no? And they haven't had problems. Cheri?" Her eyes were big and her lips pouty.

"I'll call you," Meg told him.

"Goodnight," Blasing said. Eva slipped as close as Angela had, and while he felt the heat, it didn't affect him in the same way. "How are orders?"

"Excellent! You will be a very rich man."

"I already am a rich man; I have two wonderful children."

"Mmmmm, and what a sexy father you are, Cheri. We should celebrate! Whether you keep your share or sell, you will be free of financial burdens. You will be able to have anything you desire."

"Except for Mac back."

"He is in a better place," she replied, surprising him.

"Why did you two have a falling out?"

Eva leaned close and whispered in his ear, her tongue barely tickling him. "He became boring—so much so, in some ways, he was already dead."

"He wouldn't do drugs for fun?"

Eva gasped in surprise, pulling back for a moment, then she chuckled. "He could no longer be... enticed," she said, running a hand gently upward along the inside of his thigh. "I hope you don't fall into the same pattern."

"I haven't used coke before sex in a long time," he murmured in her ear, playing along and hoping Lilly was close by.

"You've been missing out," she chuckled wickedly, then gasped as an earring sprang free. As she stepped back from Blasing, she promptly broke a heel. Blasing steadied her before she could fall, but she pulled away and fled into the crowd.

"Lilly? Your timing was perfect," he said to the air. No one responded. Blasing walked along the inside of the ring toward the foyer. Angela was still dancing with Dr. Landrum. They seemed to be having a wonderful time. What would Angela think later if she discovered he'd omitted what had happened to Eva and still kissed her 'to discover' Lilly's reaction?

"May I have this dance?" a woman asked as she suddenly stepped from the crowd, her breasts pressing against him. As if born from a dream, she was tall and lithe with long, jet black hair and eyes twice as dark. Her red and gold dress spoke suggestively, outlining her heavenly body. Blasing started to make an excuse, but thought he sensed something familiar about her.

"We wouldn't need to dance here. Anywhere would be fine," she whispered throatily. "Personally, I believe we're overdressed." She began to loosen his bow tie. "If we were alone, I'd undress you slowly, enticing you until you couldn't stand it anymore." Her hand trailed down his chest.

Blasing felt a familiar tingling and seized her hand. His rings caught fire. Flames ran up his arm. "Lilly? Can I help you?"

"Please help me escape! He's horrible!" She began to cry.

"Hey, are you hurting my wife?" a block-jawed man asked.

"No," Blasing replied, letting go of the woman's hand. "Lilly, leave this lady alone, then tell me how I can help!"

"You can't! Nobody can!" she wept.

The large man grabbed Blasing. "What's going on?!"

"Don't hurt him," Lilly cried, slapping the host's husband.

"Debbie!" he said, looking shocked. The woman looked confused, glancing between them, then fainted. A wispy mist flew toward the foyer. Blasing followed.

Twenty-Three

With Broderick close behind, Blasing rushed into the Cathedral to the Coast, looking for Lilly and wondering if she'd possessed anyone else. Blasing figured Lilly would only possess someone very beautiful, and no one appeared up to her standards.

"Do you see any spirits?" Blasing asked.

"No, sir," Broderick replied. They made a circuit of the foyer, Blasing feeling for Lilly or any other spirit. With each passing minute, he grew more frustrated.

"There sir!"

"Where?" Blasing asked.

"Sneaking up the stairs."

"Follow her!" Blasing commanded.

Broderick raised an eyebrow, then pursued. Blasing started to ascend the steps when a shadow stepped from the wall and into his path. The malevolent spirit's jacket was no longer white, now matching his shadowed face. His eyes blazed, an angry cat's glare in the darkness. A sense of things long fouled assaulted Blasing.

"Stay away from my woman, Madera! Stay away from Lilly!" Rictor's voice was gravelly and accented harshly.

"Rictor! I want her to leave me alone!" Blasing snapped, not succumbing to Rictor's presence.

Rictor blinked several times, momentarily taken aback, then he snarled, his guttural accent difficult to understand. "Then quit encouraging her! Leave or else," the ghost finished menacingly, raising a dark fist.

"I own this place," Blasing replied calmly.

"You just think you do," the ghost growled.

"No. I know. And I'm not leaving," Blasing firmly told him. "You're not wanted here! Get out! Now!"

Rictor laughed—a harsh, raspy chuckle. "You don't know shit about what's going on, pretty boy. I'm staying, and if you don't leave my Lilly alone, well, then something might happen to that fine squaw.

Kind of sweet on her, aren't you?"

"Are you holding Lilly against her will?"

"I don't have to answer you," Rictor snarled, rearing back to strike Blasing.

"I believe you do," he replied disdainfully. "I own this place! Now, why are you at Ghostal Shores? Answer me, Rictor!"

With a snarl, Rictor slipped into the wall. "Come back you coward!" Blasing railed.

"No sign of her." Broderick drifted down the steps.

"I just had a visit from Rictor."

"Bloody timing! I have a fistful of topics I would like to discuss with the blackguard," Broderick said tight-lipped.

"There'll be another time, I'm sure. I'm starting to believe Candy is right: Rictor's holding Lilly against her will." Blasing explained the encounter as they walked back to the ballroom.

"I believe you should speak with Miss Starborne."

"Are you reading my mind, too?"

"Not intentionally. An old saying mentions that great minds think alike."

Angela still danced with the good doctor. Neither saw Blasing approach. He heard Angela say, "If you were my client, it would be a matter of legal confidentiality."

"May I cut in?" Blasing asked forcefully.

Angela raised an eyebrow. Blasing appeared a little grim, and that concerned her. "I have been waiting breathlessly," Angela said light-heartedly. She batted her lashed coquettishly.

"I guess so," Dr. Landrum replied. "Maybe you can convince her I'm not hiding something."

Blasing eyed him. "You're not?"

"Don't you start now."

Blasing didn't smile. "Angela, did you feel any ghosts... close by?"

"Do you mean threatening?" she asked. He nodded. "No. Why? Are you all right?" she asked. He glared. "Of course you are. The ghosts aren't bothering you at all. Come dance with me, Blasing. We're blocking traffic." She took his hand. "Happy hunting, doctor," she told Landrum, then stepped close to Blasing.

"I have lots to tell you," Blasing told her.

"Tell me while we dance," she smiled, thoroughly enjoying his nearness. Not only did she feel secure in his arms, but that this was where she belonged.

"Angela, this is serious."

"So is what we were discussing earlier," Angela said. "Did you know that Geoff works for the government?"

"I thought he might. No ghosts have bothered you?"

"No. Why? Is something wrong, Blasing? Please tell me," Angela cajoled. "Don't get all mysterious, too. I can't stand anymore!" He told her about Meg. "The bricks aren't from Bodie but L.A.? That sounds like a scandal in the making. That could be why Heller hasn't announced where the brick came from." She bit her lip, then said, "I've been thinking about subpoenaing the information as being essential to your decision-making process."

"Sounds good to me." Blasing then explained about Eva. Angela couldn't suppress a chuckle, which was quickly quelled by news of Lilly possessing a woman and Rictor's threat. Blasing finished with, "If I don't leave, you may be in danger."

"You're already dangerous," she replied with a smile as she moved closer. She could feel his body respond, which made her decision for her. "I guess we'll just have to stay close to each other."

"Lilly wants to be rescued."

"So do I," Angela said, unclasping her hands from behind his neck and sliding one through his hair, delighting in the intimate touch.

As she moved to kiss him, Blasing said, "Angela, about the nightmares."

"One minute," she replied, then her lips melted to his. Angela felt wonderfully buoyant, almost light-headed. Then her body responded to his hands, igniting a warm wave that washed through her. When she reluctantly broke away, she was breathing heavily, amazed at how "right" the kiss had felt. Even better than she'd dreamed.

"Just like I... imagined," Blasing whispered, his dark eyes luminous. He caressed her cheek.

Angela wanted to laugh—to sing. She suddenly felt young and foolish. His voice sang in her ears, and for the moment, it was only the two of them. "I have dreamed of kissing you. From our first meeting, I was drawn to you, but I didn't want to get involved. Stupid me."

"I understand."

"Well, I'm not coming apart at the seams, anyway. It seems my hypothesis is correct. Lilly can't bother me because of the hematite."

"Angela, uh... the night you saw Grant and Carrie die.... Um." She could tell he was holding back. "Your spirit has been sort of haunting my dreams," Blasing finally said.

"Haunting? What are you trying to tell me?"

"You said you'd leave if I told you about my... dreams."

"I'll pack right after you tell me if you want. Be honest with me, Blasing. What's bothering you? I am... concerned."

"I've dreamed of kissing you..." he told her, his intense gaze pinning her. "There was a reason I asked you about wearing the hematite being a two way street—touching and being touched?"

Angela felt a cold stab of irrational fear. "Y- yes."

"When I was asleep on the couch the other night, you came to me dressed only in a shirt," he began, then explained. She could see them brazenly exploring each other's body—touching, caressing, enticing suppleness to firmness. When Blasing was through, Angela felt her control slipping. "Something seemed wrong. The color of your eyes. The way you spoke to me."

"What are you trying to say?"

"Then 'you' became Fawn—large brown eyes and all, then... then her eyes were emerald, certainly not the lovely Caribbean blue of your eyes."

"Did you...?"

"No," he replied.

She sighed, trying to release the delicious tension within her, but it didn't work. "Good. My people believe personal power can be given over or stolen during sex."

"Meaning?"

"When you experience ecstasy, you give a part of yourself. Some people use sex to steal—sort of like vampires—hoarding the feeling of power. Others want to control your personal power. I find them in court quite frequently. The Paiutes believe there are spirits that do much the same—stealing one's power through fear." She smiled. "I'm glad nothing happened, Blasing. She might have damaged you. Was this before I gave you the pendant and rings?"

"The rings were removed, but not the pendant. This afternoon while I waited for you to finish dressing, you stepped from the room like a vision and kissed me, just like now."

His words sounded her thoughts. "Was it Lilly again?"

"I think so. The rings and pendant were burning."

"What happened?" she asked, her mouth dry.

"You slowly undressed me, and I undressed you, kissing...." he explained what he remembered—the look in her eyes, her scent, the feel of her—ending with the ringing of the phone.

"I think we should leave before I make a scene by tearing your clothes off and ravishing you right here."

Blasing was breathing heavily. She could feel him hard against her, but he still said, "You're in danger. We should just leave."

"There's tomorrow." She almost couldn't believe what she was saying, but she couldn't help herself. "Come guard my nights," she said, then sensed reluctance. "Something wrong?"

"I feel... I don't know... I guess... tainted."

"Blasing, I'm glad you dream of me," she told him gently, holding his gaze. "And that you can... tell the difference. Come with me, I'll show you where dreams and reality differ. The truth will set you free." Angela took Blasing's hand and led him toward the exit. Candy winked at her as if knowing exactly what was going on. They passed close to the Great Xantini. He simply nodded to them.

While they waited for the elevator, Angela thought she would leap from her skin as her impatience grew. An old, worried inner voice warned her about mixing business with pleasure, but she ignored it, believing this to be the man she'd been waiting for. She'd been trying to deny it, but fortunately she'd failed. Blasing had felt right for her from the beginning.

"We should be finding a hotel," Blasing said as the elevator started to rise. "One without ghosts."

"Who knows," Angela said, kissing him. "They might follow. We are safer in my room. Worry about Rictor and Lilly tomorrow. If I keep you occupied," Angela said with a sly smile, "maybe Lilly will stay at home, wherever that is."

Although the elevator didn't stop, it seemed to take forever to reach the third floor. Blasing's hand burned into her's. The heat from his body made her want to shed her clothing.

When Blasing reached the door, he paused to sense for spirits. Then he ushered her grandly inside, kicked the door shut, and lifted her into his arms. On the way to her room, they stopped, consumed in a heated kiss that stole away each other's breath. When they paused, he began walking again. She finished undoing his tie.

"You are so beautiful," he whispered.

"But am I mom material?"

"Kelly thought you had potential," Blasing replied. "As do I."

"Really?" she asked. "Then I meet an early criteria." He nodded, and she laughingly rained kisses all over his face. He laughed, then returned her ardor.

A paperweight suddenly sailed off Mac's desk and slammed into Blasing's back. "Hey!" Next came an ashtray, then the derringer lighter. Blasing ducked the first, then set down Angela so he could deflect the second. The whirlwind shifted, carrying papers as it swirled toward the bar. Glasses and bottles began to shake as if enraged.

"Come on!" Angela cried, pulling him toward her open door. A shot glass smashed off the door frame, spraying shards everywhere.

Blasing slammed the door, and they waited in each other's arms. Glasses smashed against the door, then the pounding began in earnest, shaking even the frame, but the door did not open.

"Sanctuary. Thank you, Grandma Dawnjoy."

Blasing put a chair under the knob. "Just in case...."

"I think the lounge might be trashed in the morning."

"Then we should severely rumple this one," Blasing told her, his eyes large and hypnotic. He began by kissing her forehead, then her eyes and cheeks—little burning butterflies racing throughout her body—before he found her mouth. While tongues intertwined to entice each other to near painful expectation, she unbuttoned his shirt, letting her fingers dance across his chest. With a touch that made her squirm delightfully, he slid the straps off her shoulders. She let the dress fall, proud of the way she looked, and thrilled by the way he responded to her.

"You are so beautiful," he breathed as he joined her on the bed. His lips followed his fingers removing her lingerie. She squirmed and called out his name. He lingered among her thighs, teasing and pleasing. Time became a heated blur, lost in the haze of passion as she leaped from one peak to the next.

"You are so sexy," she gasped. Then she pushed him away to finish undressing him. Her hands ignited him. She delighted in watching him quiver and sigh under her ministrations. For a long time there was movement and delicious friction—the intoxicating smell and feel of him—as the heat and pressure built to excruciating tension, then she suddenly clasped herself around him. A white wave of light and warmth washed over her, making her glow as if her spirit was no longer confined to flesh.

Blasing groaned and held her close, languishing in the afterglow. "Much better than any dream."

"Our spirits sing with each other." After a warm, comfortable silence, she asked, "Do you feel... tainted any more?"

"No, I feel renewed! And younger," he laughed. "Much younger."

"Did all your worldly wisdom leave, too?"

"No," he whispered. "I know I'm blessed."

She felt him shift, then laughed. "You recover like a younger man."

"Ah, make fun of my years, will you? I'll show you."

"I hope so," she said, then kissed him, fanning the embers into an inferno once more. This time their lovemaking was languid, and they didn't finish until long after midnight.

Angela surprised herself by waking up sometime during predawn. Unable to control herself, she kissed him awake until he was ready for her again. When they finished, he said, "I may sleep the day away in your arms."

"Sounds like a marvelous idea," she replied, then fell asleep again.

The ringing of the phone awakened Blasing, who gave the phone to Angela. "Hello? Oh, absolutely wonderful! What time is it? Eight-thirty!" She might have been asleep two hours at most.

"Who is it?" Blasing groaned.

"Candy," she answered. "What?! What did you say?! All the ghosts are missing!?" She couldn't believe it. Where could the ghosts go? "No? Just the residents. Are you sure?"

Blasing hopped out of bed and walked to the lounge. One look told him the Englishman was missing; the lounge was a total wreck—everything overturned, broken or smashed.

"You're sure? Then just the transients? That bothers me. No, we haven't seen Broderick since last night. Yes, it was wonderful. Is wonderful. But I'm concerned about the ghosts. Where have they gone? What about Madame Zanadane? I'm not surprised. Okay, I'll see you in a minute." She hung up the phone, then said, "Broderick and the others seem to be missing. Only the newcomers are left."

"That is suspicious. We have... physical dangers to worry about as well. You should be leaving."

"You want me to leave? Now? When the ghosts need us?"

"You said you'd leave if...."

"I said I'd pack."

"Lawyers twisting words!" he snapped. "Is that what you meant? To trick me!? And here I thought you were different." He headed for the door. "I'm going for a walk!"

TWENTY-FOUR

"Blasing, wait!" Angela yelled. She didn't want to lose him after coming so far. "Do you really expect me to desert Broderick, Elma, Willy and the others?"

"They're dead. How can a ghost be in trouble?"

"I don't know. But they are and they need us," Angela implored. Unable to speak, Blasing raised his hands in a helpless fashion. "Can you abandon Broderick when he needs you?"

"No, I now think of him as a friend."

"And you want to help?" she asked. He nodded. "But you don't think I should?"

"That's not what I said."

"You think you can do this all by yourself, don't you?" she asked. He hesitated. "Well, listen here, my arrogant lover. It'll take both of us. You take care of the bodies, I'll take care of the spirits. What do you say?" she asked. "I can't leave a friend in trouble, and neither can you. Peace," she said smiling now, her arms open wide. "Hug on it."

Blasing took her in his arms. They kissed on it as well.

"Wow, you two really got into it," Candy said as Angela let her into the devastated suite. "You surprise me, Angel. I never knew you were such an animal."

"Candy," Angela sighed.

Candy reached into her purse, then put on her sunglasses. "I should have worn my sun block. You are radiant. I like it!"

"Tell me about the ghosts."

"What's to tell? The resident ghosts have disappeared. Nobody has seen them this morning." She shrugged. "Tell me about last night." Her blue eyes sparkled deviously.

"Too much to tell," Angela replied with a shy smile. "And I don't want to ruin the magic."

"Where's Blasing?"

"He's on the phone with his office. Now have a seat and quit stalling."

"Where?" Candy gestured to the overturned chairs, then the broken picture and glass shards covering the couch.

Angela turned over the couch cushions and shook them clean. Then she walked into her room, returning with a blanket to cover the cushions. "Sit and tell me what you know, even if it's not much."

Candy plopped down in frustration. "I'm serious. Nobody knows anything. Not the guests, the staff, nor Madame Zanadane."

Blasing's door opened. "Hello, Candy. Discover anything yet?"

"Neither of you look as concerned as you might," she said, referring to their smug expressions. "I think I understand why Lilly was so upset. Many others will be, too, Angel."

As Blasing sat on the end of the couch, Angela garnered his hand. "Lilly has no claim on me, except that she needs help," Blasing said.

"Oh?" she said speculatively. Blasing explained about his encounter with Lilly and Rictor last night. "Then I was right!"

"I told you she was gifted," Angela told Blasing.

"And eccentric, not to mention lascivious," Blasing said dryly. Candy burst out laughing. "I've kept calling for Broderick, but he hasn't appeared. I'm wor... concerned about him." Not only did he suddenly fear for Broderick's spirit, but they'd planned on slipping into Cash's room to search for his ledgers.

"I think you should go ghost hunting," Candy suggested. "Maybe they'd respond to you as an owner."

"I doubt it will do any good since Broderick's not responding, but let's try anyway," Blasing agreed.

The library was closest, so the trio stopped there first. As Blasing slowly pushed open the heavy doors, he called out to Janice. His voice was swallowed by the large chamber. Silence reigned.

"She rarely leaves—one of the reasons I was surprised to see her dancing with David. Try sensing her," Angela suggested.

After a minute of walking about the library, Blasing returned with his hands spread wide. "Nothing," he yawned.

Angela hugged him. "Let's try somewhere else. Hey, are you carrying a gun?"

He nodded. "Just in case. I'm licensed."

"Your body isn't a lethal weapon?" Candy asked.

"Not a registered one," he yawned.

"What did Rich Steele tell you this morning?" Angela asked incredulously. "More about security?"

"Rich has a friend with the IRS who has been reviewing Mr. Heller's returns. It appears he didn't inherit as much money as he claimed and only posted modest gains on his Silicon Valley investments. It doesn't add up to enough to build this place without investors."

"So he's either lying to us or the government."

"Or both," Blasing agreed. "And you were right about security. Some of his men are borderline. I'm all for a chance to reform, but they probably won't do it as a group."

"A crook is running the place and has hired protection?" Angela asked.

"It's beginning to look that way."

"Sounds a lot like the Wild West," Candy said.

"Doesn't it," Blasing agreed.

"Should you talk to Sheriff Middleton?" Angela asked.

"Rich is going to do it for me. Less conspicuous that way."

Next they visited the avenue of shops; they had yet to open and felt abandoned. The green-uniformed staff lounged about, drinking coffee, reading the paper, and trying to look attentive.

"Willy's not selling papers," Angela said, growing very concerned. "It's not like him." She called out to the young spirit, but he didn't respond.

They walked to the storefronts where Blasing called for Elma, Ingrid, Eddie and the others. He didn't feel any ghosts, and locked doors frustrated him. It was high time he had his own set of keys! His ownership wasn't in doubt, just his percentage of it.

"Can't you pick them?" Candy asked.

Blasing's response was deadpan. "I'll get keys from the front desk." He took several steps, then stopped, looking around slowly.

"Feel something?" Angela asked.

Blasing nodded. The feeling—the itching—grew stronger with every step taken toward the barbershop. "In the shadows," the ghost was very difficult to see, colorless and more a patch of fog than form.

As they neared, Blasing picked out a few features; the ghost stood with wild hair, a huge nose, and a bushy beard like one of Kelly's gnomes. "Hello, I'm Blasing Madera, owner of Ghostal Shores." He was surprised at how easily that rolled off his tongue.

"Pickens," the ghost responded. "Carl Jackson Pickens."

"And what can we do for you, Mr. Pickens?" Blasing asked.

"I'm lost. Just felt drawn here." The ghost shrugged.

"Where are you from?" Angela asked.

"Gold Hills, Nevada. Where am I?"

"Point Reyes, California, north of the San Francisco Bay."

"Do you know a Rictor, from a stagecoach?" Blasing asked.

"Rictor?" the ghost's voice quavered. "Lon Rictor? Got a voice like an avalanche?" Blasing described the spirit. Without a word, Carl Pickens turned and walked through a wall.

"How queer," Candy said. "I couldn't exactly see his expression, but I thought I sensed... fear."

"Now I am worried," Blasing said. "Candy, you said that only the residents were missing."

"Yes."

"Then let's go talk with the newcomers. I'll bet most of them are in the bar. If anyone would know, those ghosts might."

On the way, Blasing stopped by the front desk. "Is Mr. Heller or Mr. Cash here?"

"No, sir. Mr. Heller is with Madame Zanadane, and Mr. Cash is at breakfast."

They visited security. After pleasantries, Blasing told Chief Porter what he wanted. The stocky man was very hesitant, then said, "Why don't we talk to Mr. Heller first?"

"You have been informed that I am an owner here," Blasing emphasized the last few words. "Correct?"

"Yes sir."

"Have you been informed not to give me keys?"

"No sir."

"Or prohibit me from anything?"

Porter hesitated, then said, "No sir, Mr. Madera."

"Then give me my set of keys." Porter hesitated. "Chief Porter, I know security. It would be a cost savings not to have a second chief on the payroll," Blasing said in a low, angry voice louder than any shout. Blanching, Chief Porter handed him the keys. "Thank you.

When something is held back from me without reason, I get the impression something is being hidden from me." Blasing thought he saw confirmation in the man's eyes.

As they left, Angela said, "You certainly asserted yourself as an owner. I thought I could feel it ring throughout the resort."

"Seems I have to if I want anything done," Blasing replied sharply.

"Mr. Madera, sir," someone called out from behind him.

"What can I do for you, Mr. Cash?" Blasing asked the pallid man. Blasing got the impression Cash would be wringing his hands if one wasn't in a sling.

"Mr. Heller and Madame Zanadane would like to see you right away. There is much concern over the missing spirits." Cash didn't sound as if he shared such a sentiment.

"I'll meet you in the restaurant when you're through," Candy told Angela, then departed.

"Do you believe they've gone on strike?" Mr. Cash asked Blasing as they walked toward the front desk.

"No. I think Broderick would've informed me."

"I see. What if the guests find out? They—they could be wanting their money back."

"Don't put the cart before the horse," Angela said.

Cash sniffed, then stopped at the front desk as if resuming his position. "Please take this to Mr. Heller," he told Angela as he handed her a stack of envelopes and papers.

Angela started to respond angrily, then snapped her mouth shut. As they approached Heller's office, she was grumbling. "I'm not his secretary. Let alone the mail boy." She was squeezing the pile so hard she noticed the top package contained a tape. It didn't have a return address.

As usual, the Irishman sat in his black leather throne, his paper subjects surrounding him, and Madame Zanadane sitting as counsel. The Psychic was dressed in bright purple and wearing an amethyst necklace. Mr. Chung stood just behind her.

"Hello, Blasing," Heller said.

"Sean."

Heller raised an eyebrow, then asked, "Did you hear about the missing ghosts?" Blasing nodded. "Helluva way to start the day," Heller complained, then blew his nose. "And I just had a meeting with them all last night."

"You did? What did you tell them?" Blasing asked. He wished he'd been there, but then, he'd been completely occupied by Angela last night.

"We were trying to get a consensus about what to do about the spiritual transients...."

"And?"

"The ghosts said they'd discuss it among themselves, but they leaned toward making friendly offers and training those who wanted to stay," Heller said. "I like the idea."

"More ghosts though," Angela said.

"New ghosts are money," Heller told her. "The press are even coming to cover the event."

"Event?"

"A Second Coming, so to speak. The publicity's just what we are looking for, but now... I don't want them to visit only to find our spirits missing. We have to do something!"

"When does the press arrive?" Blasing figured Heller must really be worried. He hadn't touched a piece of paper.

"Tonight. Do you think you can help?" Heller asked, sounding a bit desperate. "My in-house psychic can't seem to help," he glared at Madame Zanadane, "so I was hoping you might. For the good of the resort, you know."

"Again, they wouldn't speak with me...." Zanadane breathed.

"Do you think they're refusing to work?" Heller asked.

Blasing couldn't resist when he said, "It's possible. Some are upset because they're not being consulted about the changes."

"But I just consulted them last night!" Heller exploded.

"As I said, I don't know. I was just going to talk to some of the transient spirits. See what they knew," Blasing said. "Would you like to come? They might talk to us since we own the place."

"N—no thank you," Heller replied, then he stood, pacing as if possessed.

"You're sure?" Blasing asked. Heller nodded. "I stopped by security. I have a set of keys."

"I know. Chief Porter called me."

"Is there a problem?"

"Of course not! You should have had a set a long time ago. In fact, I sent a set to your room."

"They never arrived," Blasing said coolly.

"What?!" Heller hit the intercom button and yelled at his secretary.

"Did Broderick or any of the others mention being afraid of the new ghosts?" Blasing asked Madame Zanadane.

"Why, no.... Why do you ask...?"

"Broderick told me he thought the newcomers reminded him of a gang," Blasing said. So had security.

"They never mentioned it, but then I am not as close to them as you...." She sounded bitter.

"Would you care to join us?" Blasing asked. She nodded stiffly and rose.

As they walked toward the steps, Blasing saw Meg storm her way toward the front desk. "Problem?" he asked.

"My damn car won't start!"

"Going to have to stay a while longer?" Angela asked sweetly.

Meg glared at her, then turned her anger on the front desk clerk, who assured her he'd call security.

When the trio ascended the steps to the bar, the back of Blasing's neck itched maddeningly. He wasn't surprised to find a small horde of faded ghosts clustered around the bar—about double the number present yesterday. Cannon was nowhere in sight, but Blasing knew better than to trust vision when dealing with a ghost.

"How come I feel nervous?" Angela asked.

"Because you think they had something to do with the spirits' disappearance?"

"Could be. Are you sure you're up to this?" she asked.

Blasing nodded stiffly, then headed for the bar. With each step, the prickling grew worse. Something about the transients bothered him more than the residents. When Angela took his hand; the nagging sensation lessened. Madame Zanadane and Mr. Chung were right behind them.

"Excuse me, sir. I'm Blasing Madera..." he began, speaking to a lean ghost he didn't recognize.

"So. Who cares who the hell you are, sonny?" the gnarled ghost asked rudely. He didn't have any eyebrows, and along with being bald, his face seemed featureless.

Another spirit Blasing knew as Isaiah tapped the ghost on the shoulder and said, "He's an owner. Be polite or get out."

"Damnation! Sorry, Mr. Madera," the ghost apologized. Blasing asked his name. "Gus Minden."

"And where did you come from, Mr. Minden?"

"I... I'm not sure. I sort of woke up and wandered into the nearest bar."

"Did you come from next door?"

"Yeah, I think so," the spirit nodded. A few of his companions moved in a little closer, making Blasing uneasy. A squeeze of the hand from Angela helped him fight the urge to bolt.

"Do you mean the bricks...?" Madame Zanadane asked breathlessly, leaving the question hanging as if there were more to be said.

"He doesn't look like he's from L.A.," Angela mentioned. Madame Zanadane looked confused.

"Madame, do you know where the bricks are from?"

"I haven't been informed... but after checking their psychic emanation, I believe they originate from Bodie... and this spirit just confirmed it."

Blasing just nodded, wondering who was right, Meg or Madame Zanadane? And why was Heller still secretive if marketing was the only reason? "Do you know Lon Rictor?" he asked Gus Minden. When Blasing received a blank expression, he described the ghost and the stage. Gus still wasn't familiar with either. "How about you, Isaiah?"

"I heard about this place from Lucius. He saw the stage and this Rictor fellow told him about this place," the pear-shaped spirit responded. His droopy hat hung down on each side as if it had weathered too many rainstorms.

"Where is Lucius from?"

"Hangtown, California, I think."

"Any of you know where the bartender is?" Blasing asked.

"Been wondering myself," Isaiah replied.

"Anybody know where Cannon is?" Blasing asked loudly.

There was a lot of murmuring, but nobody knew. By the dejected looks, Blasing thought they were telling the truth. "How many of you arrived after yesterday afternoon?" Blasing asked. Including Minden, a dozen others raised their hands. "Tell me your name, where you're from, how you got here, and why you're here."

There was Newt Chilcut, a very faded ghost from Genoa. He'd felt drawn and walked to Ghostal Shores. A hefty and dark ghost named Washington Smith came from Virginia City. A man in a stage had encouraged him to drink and feel closer to the world. Tai Chen, a diminutive Asian, was drawn from San Francisco. He expected a place to rest.

Blasing asked the rest and received similar answers from the Nevadans and the Californians. Few had met Rictor, most just heard of him. "Well, gentlemen, you're welcome to stay IF you behave yourself. If you don't, we'll throw you out," Blasing told them. "A representative of the resort will be with you later today to explain how things work at Ghostal Shores."

"I think they're holding back," Angela said as they walked into the restaurant.

"Let's see if any of the poker players know anything."

"Do you believe the bricks to be the cause of the disappearances..." Madame Zanadane asked. "Or this Lon Rictor? By the way, when did you first learn his first name...?"

"Late last night," he said, then told her what they knew of Rictor and Lilly's relationship.

"Then we should help her...."

"My first priority is the locals," Blasing said as he approached the gamblers. Candy joined them, but said nothing.

Dirk, Mason, Samuel and the gang were missing, so instead of two tables, only one game was in progress. Bat and Cogan sat at the table with four ragged spirits Blasing vaguely recognized. Cogan and Bat were skilled at handling the cards. The others were still having some trouble.

"Evenin', bub," Cogan said with a puff of smoke.

"How's your luck?" Blasing asked.

"All right, but Mason told me yours was better."

"That man can moan," one of the ghosts said.

"Beginner's luck. When was the last time you saw him?"

"Couple a hours ago, I think."

"Have any idea where he went?" Blasing asked. Though he was talking to Cogan, he watched Bat. The ghost emanated a sly, devious air—in the way he glanced from under his hat as he absently chewed on a toothpick.

"Said somethin' bout having a meeting, I believe," Cogan said. "They all went."

"A meeting?" Blasing mused.

"Staff meeting, I think Dirk said."

"That stiff Englishman came and got them," another said.

"Just a staff meeting?" Candy said incredulously. "Then they're not in danger?"

"We don't know whether to believe these spirits...."

Blasing studied Cogan for a while, trying to perceive the truth from impressions, just as he had during the poker game. "Well, I think I'll give them until noon to finish their meeting. If they're not done by then, I'll worry."

Housekeeping was hard at work cleaning the lounge area. Despite the noise, Blasing and Angela didn't have any trouble falling asleep in each other's arms.

When they awakened, they showered together, then ordered breakfast. Angela was on the phone, and Blasing was going through financials when he felt a familiar ghostly presence. "Broderick?"

The Englishman slowly appeared. "You are getting very good at sensing my arrival, Master Madera."

"Where have you been?"

"Well, when you and Miss Starborne seemed enamored with each other, I did not want to intrude. Madame Zanadane called a meeting and we gathered with Mister Heller to discuss the transients. Some pleaded to have the newcomers removed, but Heller was not interested, so we had a meeting with each other. Arguments! Arguments! One after another! We still have not decided. Some want to kick them out; others, remembering the lonely feeling of wandering this land, felt more compassion."

"I see. What do you think?"

"I believe we should be selective. There are some tolerable spirits sprinkled among the rabble. Carrie always said that like attracts like, and I agree. I believe they are here because Heller is in charge. If we just accept anybody, I fear for the quality of our service. And there are some I simply do not trust. Jonathan claims one was involved in his murder."

"Hmm. Well, I told them they could stay IF they behaved, and that you'd explain the rules to them," Blasing said.

"As you wish, sir."

"Broderick! I thought that was you. I was so worried," Angela said, surprising the spirit with a hug. He glowed.

"I am so sorry. Time slipped away."

"Happens to me sometimes," Angela said.

"I believe it is even easier for a spirit to wander."

"Broderick, do you remember what we discussed earlier?"

"Of course, sir, that is why I am here."

"What are you two talking about?"

"You'd prefer to know after the fact," Blasing told her.

"I would?" she asked, moving into his arms.

"Yes, for legal reasons. We'll show you when we get back. Then there'll be lots of paperwork to do." He kissed her for a long time, then reluctantly moved away. "Let's go, Broderick. See you soon, Angela."

TWENTY-FIVE

When Blasing confirmed no one was in the area, Broderick reached through the wall and loosened a wire on the security camera. "Done, sir." Broderick walked through the wall.

Now Blasing only worried about someone leaving their room at the wrong moment. He still felt watched, but if that ghost was working for Heller, there wasn't anything they could do.

When Broderick opened Cash's door from inside, Blasing was waiting for him. "Quicker than a key," Blasing said with a smile as he slipped inside and closed the door.

For a few quick moments, he studied the single bedroom. It was a bit crowded with a desk added to the usual bed, armoire, and a chest of drawers. Cash must spend a good amount of time out of his room.

"I loathe to think I have slipped to a roguish level."

"You didn't have to do this, Broderick. I could have disabled the camera and picked the lock. But thank you. It lessened the chance of being seen. Now, see if you can find any hidden books, ledgers or papers. Check the wall spaces first, then the closet.

"Well, I feel it's only justified due to what Mister Heller has done to you and Master MacGuire." Broderick walked halfway into the wall, then began a circuit of the room. "And I must say I am glad you confirmed my feelings about the security staff."

"You haven't told any of the others, have you? I don't want to start trouble until there's concrete proof." Blasing thoroughly searched the desk but didn't find a ledger.

"I understand we have no proof, sir. But I must say I am not concerned with myself, for there is nothing they can do to us. We are already dead. I worry about you and Miss Starborne."

"Thanks. Damn," Blasing said as he came across a Powerbook laptop computer in the drawer. He opened, then powered up the laptop computer which promptly requested a password to continue.

"Sir, is there a problem?"

"Instead of looking just for books, look for diskettes, too. Do you...."

"Yes sir, I am somewhat familiar with computer jargon—though why must it be so complicated...." he sighed.

"Was Grant?"

"I do not know. Oh dear, I have found something, but not what we expected."

"What is it?" Blasing asked.

"I have found a camera—something like the ones people carry to 'tape' people—hidden in the wall."

"What?!" Blasing exclaimed. "Is it on?"

"No sir, that is why I did not feel it."

"I wonder if Cash knows? A lack of trust between thieves? And if so, where are other illegal cameras hidden? Show me where, exactly." Broderick pointed out the camera, and Blasing taped paper over the view port, just in case. "Now, let's find what we're looking for and get out of here."

Broderick didn't find anything else in the walls, so the spirit moved to the closet. When neither of them had found anything after fifteen more minutes of searching, Blasing said, "Let's go. We'll have to hope what we want is on the computer. Feel anything?"

"No sir."

Blasing removed the taped paper, then listened at the door. Although he didn't feel anything, Blasing still thought he was being watched.

"Are you sure that camera's not operating?"

"Absolutely, sir." Broderick sounded annoyed.

"Good. Check the hall in all directions and let me know if it's clear," Blasing said. Broderick slipped through the wall, then returned moments later with the good news. Blasing left Cash's room unseen. As they passed the hallway camera, Broderick re-attached the loose wire.

Upon returning to the suite, Blasing searched for cameras and audio bugs. Where he could, Broderick helped by walking through the walls. "I apologize for not being able to do the walls of your rooms."

"What are you doing?" Angela asked as she exited her room.

"In Cash's room we found a portable computer," he pointed to Mac's desk where it lay, "and a hidden camera."

"Honor among thieves," Angela said. "I have one of these. I carry it with me." She opened the Powerbook, turned it on, and then frowned at the password prompt. "We should call Candy. She's a computer whiz."

"You're kidding."

Angela shook her head. "Hard to believe, I know, but she is very, very talented. And Rod works for Apple."

"Sounds like a good idea."

Thinking how odd, Angela paused at the giant bayview window, watching another Pacific storm engulf the coast. They usually didn't get these types of storms. Lightning flashed down from black, boiling clouds, and lights throughout the resort flickered. Several more times, the scene repeated itself, giving Angela the impression everything was blinking—a perfect reason for a camera to malfunction. She hoped Blasing and Broderick were having as much luck returning the computer as they had expropriating it.

Candy had proven Angela right by accessing the main menu and transferring Cash's files into Angela's Powerbook. Upon examination they were perplexed; there were ledgers on file, but they made no sense. Candy thought they might be in some sort of code. She was using the resort's facilities to send the files to Rich Steele.

Blasing had suggested leaving immediately and presenting the information to the authorities. Angela had maintained they still didn't know who had killed Peter. She felt that the mystery of the ghosts was somehow connected to Peter's murder. Besides, if Carrie was right and like attracted like, then Blasing's presence was needed to counter Heller's.

Lightning flashed greenish-white causing the lights to blink again. The resounding thunder drowned out the buzz of voices coming from the stairwell. There might be too much ambiance tonight. When raindrops began splattering against the glass, she headed up the steps, hoping Blasing was already at the bar.

Lightning struck again, knocking out the power for good this time. Candlelight and lanterns added a golden tint to the heavy haze and lengthened the shadows of the Clifftop Bar, turning it into a haunted study disguised as a bar. Or might have, she thought, if the place hadn't been jam-packed with people and ghosts.

A bluish-white flash and a crack of thunder filled the lounge, and a hush came over the bar. Despite the storm, the customers seemed to be enjoying the ambiance. A friendly frightening, she'd heard it called. Spooked but not scared. Let's go "California Ghosting." It'll be fun.

Cannon's antics certainly seemed to minimize the haunting chill. Laughing and mixing drinks with the flair of a stage magician and enough invisible arms to be an octopus, the bombastic alchemist thoroughly entertained the crowd. The reflection of the dozen whirling bottles in the mirrors made it seem as if she juggled more than twelve.

Angela didn't see a place to sit, except for an open seat at the bar historically reserved for Peter. That much hadn't changed. She took some solace from it. Luck was with her as she passed a table by the window. A young couple left hand-in-hand, smiles on their faces and eyes riveted on each other. Angela dropped next to the open table as if playing musical chairs.

To keep her mind off Blasing and if anything bad had happened, Angela people and ghost watched. She had never seen the bar this crowded, except for special occasions, and figured news of the recently arrived spirits must have spread like wildfire. She sighed. Only Californians would take all this so easily in stride, enjoying the blackout, the thunderstorm, and eerie excitement of being surrounded by ghosts.

When she counted the spirits, Angela found at least forty milling among the masses, and that didn't include Cannon at the bar or David waiting tables. She wasn't sure if that was all of the new spirits. Even without the crowd, counting the ghosts was difficult; too many were little more than ill-defined mist.

"Hello, beautiful," Blasing said as he sat down, surprising Angela. "Did you charm someone's table away from them?"

"Just lucky. How about you, handsome?" She was relieved he'd returned safely.

"Very. Though luckier if I could convince someone to leave, or at least talk with Sheriff Middleton."

"Blasing, we *have* to stay. We have to make sense of things. Something is wrong here—physically and spiritually."

"And you think they're connected?"

"Just look around. As I said earlier, maybe Carrie is right. Maybe these ghosts are drawn by Heller and Rictor. If that's true, your presence might counter them."

"You have a lot of faith in my presence," Blasing said wryly.

"I do."

"I feel like I've walked into a western movie tonight."

"I can see that," Angela laughed. "That cowboy hat-wearing foursome—the large, heavyset spirit accompanying the two skinny phantoms and an old-seeming ghost, remind me of the Cartwrights. And that one there limps, making me think of Chester from Gunsmoke. And there," she nodded at a bear of a spirit leaning unsteadily against the bar, "he could be the inspiration for Rooster Cogburn."

"An Indian who likes westerns?"

She laughed and blushed. "See that ghost carrying something? He might be Chuck Conner's brother."

"The Rifleman?"

She nodded. "And those...." If she hadn't been staring at a trio of ghosts, Angela might not have noticed the pinpoints of light shining behind them in a shadowy recess. "Do you see that in the cocktail server's station?" she whispered. The twin points grew slowly brighter—from dull amber to a yellowish-green—and larger into orbs, then began to shift as though a pair of eyes.

"That must be Rictor," Blasing said, beginning to rise.

Angela's heart skipped a beat. "Wait! Let's see what he does!" She was suddenly frightened for Blasing.

The shadows in the niche shifted and overlapped as if the surface of a roiling oil slick. Then a tall, big-boned spirit clad in a long dark jacket and black cowboy hat with a red band stepped out of the shadows. His block-jawed face was dark as a starless night with baleful twin moons.

"He looks a little different," Blasing said. "Darker. Richer." Rictor stepped among an ethereal trio, placing his hands on two of their shoulders.

"What's he doing?" Blasing asked.

The spirits suddenly seemed to crystallize—their misty forms, features and even surprised expressions becoming sharp. One was a rough-looking spirit with a pinched, unshaven face and shifty-eyes the color of pitch. The ghostly miner touched his face, then smiled, the light flashing off a golden tooth. His flat-faced companion also looked very surprised. Rictor touched the third, and he came into focus, revealing a bald and scarred spirit.

"I want to know," Blasing said, again starting to rise.

"A little longer," Angela said, wondering if Rictor had somehow fortified the ghosts.

The gold-toothed miner poked his scarred companion, astonishing the spirit. He elbowed the last of the trio, and they suddenly began poking each other harder and harder, their crazy laughter drawing people's attention.

"What did he do?" Blasing asked. "They sound drunk."

"I don't know, but he's doing it again."

Rictor appeared to be walking from ghost to ghost, a spiritual Johnny Appleseed, each time sowing change, making the ghosts he visited clearly visible. Whispering and pointing, the customers were certainly aware of Rictor's handiwork. Every ghost was male and dressed in the worn clothing of a ranch hand, railman, miner or prospector. They appeared to be hard men with varied backgrounds from all over the world.

"I don't think I like this," Blasing said. Angela suddenly agreed. Geoff's words about Rictor putting together a gang suddenly seemed to make more sense.

Rictor moved among the Cartwrights, and they assumed more the image of men and less of mist. The heavy-set ghost laughed as he ran his transparent hands across his ethereal frame. The tallest took off his stetson and whooped. The others joined him, their laughter wild and raucous.

The portly spirit suddenly shoved one of his companions. Arms waving and yelling, the skinniest ghost tumbled backwards through a red-haired young man at a table surrounded by several clean-cut men. The redhead appeared confused; his three friends laughing at him didn't help.

Cursing angrily, the fallen spirit jumped to his feet, then shadowboxed as he issued a challenge. The table full of guys was too amazed to duck, and they were touched by the enraged spirit. Anger flared in their faces, their eyes wild as they cursed each other.

"Oh, oh. I've seen this scene played out before."

"I thought you didn't handle bodies," Angela said.

"Call Madame Zanadane or Xantini! I'm calling security!"

Blasing said as he left the table. Angela tried to follow, but couldn't, morbidly fascinated by what was happening.

At the inflamed table of young men, one punched his nearby companion. He retaliated, landing such a mighty blow his friend collapsed onto the table, overturning it and smashing the glassware. Another of the afflicted simply looked around, chose a target, and then slugged a man at a nearby table. His ladyfriend screamed as her date crumpled to the floor.

"STOP THIS!" Cannon yelled.

The playful altercation between the misnamed Cartwrights escalated, and the shoving became a wild slugfest. The portly spirit took a good one on the chin and stumbled into another of the transients. The miner gave a Cartwright a shove, sending him into another group of ghosts. The brawl swelled. Several patrons tried to escape but encountered two ghosts chasing each other and quickly changed their minds, throwing themselves into the melee with wild abandon.

Cannon flew from behind the bar to grab a couple of spirits, but she couldn't corral enough. David tried to help, but was knocked down. "HELP!" Cannon screamed.

At first, the patrons' fight consisted mostly of punching and wrestling, but as the spiritual conflict regressed to a no-holds-barred brawl full of kicking, head-butting, and even biting, the customers grabbed chairs and began swinging. Tables crumpled, glass shattered and chairs splintered, leaving people wounded and dazed.

Wishing she'd left with Blasing, Angela crawled under the table. Pieces of broken chairs rained down about her, joining a sea of glass shards on the carpet. She was shocked, unable to believe people dressed so elegantly could fight so violently. The men seemed rabid; the cat fights were vicious. Fabulous dresses, extravagant hairdos and expensive makeovers were ruined in moments.

Suddenly, Barney, Sven, Broderick and the gamblers came flying through the walls, ceiling, and floor to subdue the spiritual combatants. When words of wisdom didn't work, the ghost butler decked several of the rapscallions. Cannon picked up two troublemakers and slammed them face-first into each other.

Blasing, Chadwick, and ten men and women from security arrived. Blasing restrained a man wielding a chair, then pushed him into a charging opponent, sending them both sprawling. He took the moment's respite to shout at the ghosts to stop—to calm down! A few guards were rougher than Angela would have expected, landing solid blows or aggressively restraining brawlers.

Cannon and the other spirits surrounded the transients. Broderick was grimly stern as he expressed his opinion. When he paused, Cannon erupted, shouting about how to behave in her bar.

As the spirits were forcibly settled, the customers suddenly snapped out of their battle frenzy, looking confused and wondering aloud what had happened. Why were they being restrained? Many were battered, torn and bleeding. Geoff had more work coming.

"Angela? Are you all right?" Blasing asked as he moved broken chairs out of the way.

"Yes," she replied. He helped her to her feet and hugged her. "You're hurt," she said, wiping blood from his brow.

"Just a scratch. Another magically enchanting evening at Ghostal Shores. I wonder how many customers we'll lose to this?"

"And how many lawsuits. But don't be surprised if this brings in more customers, too. People are strange." He was quiet, so she said, "Let's go back to the suite, call room service, and discuss our... options."

"Sounds like a great idea. We'll let Porter and his crew explain things to Heller."

At the top of the steps, they encountered a pair of very damp reporters. One carried a video camera. The other was strikingly attractive with page-cut, white-blond hair and diamond shaped eyes that seemed to see everything.

"Blasing Madera," she said. "What a wonderful surprise."

"Hello, Tawny. You don't look as if you had a pleasant trip."

"It was great for ducks. There's already flooding, and water is nearing the road in several areas. Just out of Inverness a mud slide covered part of the road. It's a stay at home by the fire night," she said with a smile. "But I'm dedicated to my job."

"A fire. Sounds like she has the right idea," Angela said, squeezing Blasing's arm.

"Tawny Lane, I'd like you to meet my lady, Angela Starborne."

"Hello, Angela," Tawny said, looking as if she'd swallowed something bitter. Angela smiled graciously. "And this is Al Murly, my cameraman and Channel 22 comrade."

For the first time, Tawny glanced past Blasing at the devastation. Several customers were hurt. Even more were upset, the crying and yelling just gaining momentum. Dr. Landrum joined security, who were taking statements.

"W- what happened here?" Tawny asked.

"I'm going to get some footage," Al said moving past Blasing.

"Blasing, is that...."

"It's all right. Just part of re-living the west."

Tawny's gaze narrowed. "Want to tell me about it?"

"You can talk to me anytime. As an ace reporter, don't you want to interview people while they're still dazed and reeling?"

Tawny's lips thinned to a line. "You have a sharper edge than I remember. Something interesting must be going on here. How about meeting me for a drink later? You two can fill in the gaps." Blasing laughed abruptly. Tawny reddened. "Did I say something funny?"

"It's just that we can't fill in the gaps ourselves. And I think you'll have plenty to prey on and spark the ratings."

"How's ten sound?" Angela asked. "They should have the lounge cleaned up and open again by then."

"Excellent," Tawny said. "See you then."

Blasing took a long look at the injured people and the devastation, then said, "You know, Ghostal Shores doesn't seem so benignly frightening anymore."

TWENTY-SIX

Angela had called room service and now sat at the desk looking over Cash's computer files on her laptop. They still didn't make any sense.

"Sheriff Middleton was right; Ghostal Shores isn't safe," Blasing told her as he continued to pace. "At least a dozen people were injured. If we don't close, something worse might happen."

"From a legal standpoint, a temporary shut down is our smartest move. It shows we're being responsible. But good luck getting Heller to close. He'll probably just buy off the injured, saying the barroom brawl is just part of the charm of the Old West, like you did to Tawny." Blasing snorted. "Madame Zanadane will attempt a cleansing before he even considers closing."

A knock came from the door. Blasing peeked through the spyhole, then he let the room service waiter inside. All the while, Blasing carefully watched the young man. After he left, Angela teased Blasing, "Do you think it's poisoned?"

He glared at her. "I'm being paranoid, remember? There's already been one murder, and we are upsetting the status quo. Don't forget, some rooms come with cameras. The phones might be tapped, too." Blasing glanced at his watch. "I wonder where Broderick is?"

"Probably lecturing those unruly and uncouth ruffians," she replied, then investigated dinner. "And trying to make things right. He probably feels the brawl has tarnished his reputation. Blasing, I'm sorry. I should've let you stop Rictor."

"You're assuming I could've. How do you stop a ghost?"

"Maybe Broderick would consent to some tests. I'm sure he doesn't want to see Ghostal Shores closed, but then he doesn't want to see it trashed, either. Now, come sit and eat."

"I don't understand how you can take this all so calmly!"

"I'm surprised a barroom brawl has you so upset," Angela told him. "Or does it? What's really bothering you? That I agreed to meet with Tawny? Maybe I just want to meet a woman from your past."

"Angela, we had dinner once. If you want to find out what I don't like in a woman, have a nice long chat with Tawny Lane."

"I'm sorry, Blasing. I just don't want you to snub a reporter. Good PR might be important."

"I know. I'm sorry too. Whatever Rictor did to make those ghosts... clearer concerns me. They even felt stronger."

"More alive?" she asked. Blasing shrugged. "Let's talk about what we know. See what we can unravel. We know Peter was intentionally murdered. That the murderer was well-prepared for ghosts, strengthening the case that it was an inside job. Suspects are Meg, Eva, Cash, Madame Zanadane and of course, Heller."

They discussed the suspects. Meg hated Peter very much, possibly enough to murder him. Feeling she was entitled, her heart was set on the inheritance.

Cash had his reasons. Peter was always stopping him from doing questionable things to improve profits. Performance bonuses were part of his compensation, and the Crimeshare had been his idea. And yet, Blasing noted, the murderer hadn't been frightened of ghosts. Cash was obviously unnerved. They could see it in his eyes.

Peter fired Eva, depriving her of a six figure salary. That didn't include Crimeshare sales. People killed for less.

Angela's intuition pointed toward Madame Zanadane. She could have hired somebody to murder Peter. Madame Zanadane had coveted the in-house psychic job for a long time, and she was the most likely to know about the hematite.

Angela was thoughtful. "Heller could have learned about hematite from her, then hired someone. If the murderer hadn't been wearing the grounding stone, Broderick could have harassed him until he was caught. But why would he have Peter killed? He was already dying. Heller didn't have long to wait to sell timeshares."

"And Mac already had drafted his will."

"True, but I never received a finalized copy, remember? I think someone diverted it. Don't you think Heller seems the obvious choice here? Maybe too obvious. A set-up, maybe? But why? If you hadn't found a copy of the will in the desk, we wouldn't know about the sixty day window. We already know Cash is doctoring the books. But why? Just plain extortion?"

"If so, why do the files seem to be in some kind of code? What if the two aren't related?" Blasing supposed. "Maybe whoever hired our murderer has nothing to do with Heller, and he and Cash are just extortionists. That is a very different crime than murder."

"Maybe Peter threatened to expose him. But why is Rictor here? And what mistake was Peter referring to? Could Rictor have possessed someone—like Carrie did—and used him to kill Peter? I doubt Rictor could have scared him. Peter was comfortable around the ghosts."

"Lots of questions," Blasing agreed. "Like why didn't Mac leave a note along with the will? Why has Heller hired questionable security? The only thing to implicate them is their past and a hidden camera in Cash's room. And I still want to know how the murderer escaped."

"And whether he was working on his own, for somebody or being used. I remember Carrie claiming that Heller was involved in something illegal. How about drug-trafficking?"

"I believe Eva uses drugs."

"As do half the salespeople, I'd wager," Angela surmised.

"And I think Heller does, too. His cold is a ruse."

"A ruse?" she said, very amused. "So how come nobody else thinks anything illegal is going on?"

"Good question, unless almost everyone is involved."

"The ghosts would notice," Angela said.

"Would they? I wonder. I'm not sure they would."

"They'd feel it. Hey, maybe that's why Broderick can't clearly view Heller's spirit! Could drug use obscure it?"

"A very interesting observation, Counselor. Do you remember what Elma said about the service corridor?"

"All that static?"

He nodded. "I think I should go investigating."

"How about we go investigating?"

"That would look suspicious, but I am curious about backup systems and the generator."

"Oh. What about the ghosts?" she asked.

"I'll take Broderick with me. He can handle himself."

"You're not heading out to rescue Lilly, are you?"

"Angela, I don't know what to do. If I took your advice, I'd just gather all the ghosts, tell them I'm the owner, and to shape up or ship out!"

"That might work, except Rictor seems to be a galvanizing force."

"I believe Angela has quite an excellent idea, Master Madera," Broderick said. He clarified to visibility just inside the door.

"There you are," Blasing said. "I was beginning to worry."

"My deepest apologies if I have caused you any grief, sir," the ghost butler said gravely as he folded his hands behind him. "I must say it has been a very trying day. Not long after we finished emphasizing proper conduct. I was accosted by several 'varmints'—each of which had participated in the bar brawl and wished to privately disagree with me while numbers favored them.

"I was beginning to fear I was overwhelmed when Sven, Ingrid—my that woman has a mighty right cross—and Barney arrived. Well," he smiled, "we routed them and held them until enough of us had gathered, then we exiled them and warned them never to come back." He rubbed his hands as if washing them of the trouble. "I only wish we could have tarred and feathered them."

"What did they want?" Blasing asked.

"Revenge for impeding their 'fun'."

"No sign of Rictor?"

"No, sir. Please stop worrying. Everything is under control. It just takes time. As we are making our rounds, we are talking with the transients, and I believe they understand the rules more clearly now—what is expected of them and the consequences of improper behavior. I do not expect similar violence, although we are prepared for it."

Blasing recalled what Heller said about the ghosts being unable to police themselves.

"You know, a cleansing might not be a bad idea," Angela said. Broderick appeared seriously insulted. "I'm sorry, Broderick, I must be tired. I don't think I've ever agreed with Heller before, but a selective cleansing might get rid of the unwanted spirits."

"I think Heller's right to be concerned," Blasing said. "Hell, I know I am. Very. Can we guarantee our customers' safety?"

"Not beyond a shadow of a doubt."

"Broderick, I hate to say it, but he's right from a legal point of view. It would be the next logical step to protect ourselves in case of a lawsuit. It's that or close down for a while."

Broderick paled.

Broderick, do you have any idea why some of the new ghosts have become... sharper?" Blasing asked.

"No, sir, though I did notice it. We asked them, but none of them admitted any knowledge. Maybe it has something to do with being at Ghostal Shores," Broderick suggested. "None of us appeared then as we do today. There is something... invigorating about this place."

"I think we should leave in the morning, present our case...."

"We should try the cleansing first," Angela suggested.

"I'm not only worried about ghosts. Someone murdered Mac . They might not stop at one."

"I can take care of myself."

"I should have sold that first day," Blasing groaned.

"You're too responsible for that," she said. He glared at her. "You care for people. Just convince Sheriff Middleton—or maybe Dr. Landrum to close the place for a couple of days. Besides, you don't want to desert Broderick and the others, do you?"

"And we thank you, sir. We believe matters would be far worse if you were not present. You even inspired several of the locals to stand up to the offenders. A laudable precedent indeed."

"Broderick, I think of you as a friend, but as you said, you're a ghost. What can happen to you?"

"The same as Carrie and Grant," Angela said.

Blasing ran his hands through his hair, then jumped up to pace some more. "Why are all these spirits here? And what does Rictor want? What did he mean by I didn't know what was going on here?"

"You seem to affect him the least," Broderick said. "Almost as if he did not respect you."

"Well, the deal was, Counselor, that I would take care of the physical, if you'd take care of the spirits."

She nodded. "If we can handle one group, I believe we'll take care of the other."

"Then I should investigate the service corridor. See what I can find. Then maybe we won't have to worry about Heller's presence. Why don't you see if Candy and Rod can come over?"

"Safety in numbers?" she asked. He nodded. "Are you mad at me for refusing to leave?"

"Yes," he replied, then kissed her. "But conscientious moms

often make people mad."

Although he didn't always get it, Anthony preferred swing shift. Needs for a valet were infrequent, so the night was usually slow, allowing time to study. But tonight was different. It might be the weather or the power outage, but he'd worked stormy evenings before, and they hadn't felt like this. Anthony shivered as a swirling gust of wind whipped into the valet booth. Damned if it didn't feel like someone was walking over his grave.

Anthony had heard about the barroom brawl, but he wasn't overly concerned. He'd been working here for nearly five years and seen plenty of strange things, so he wasn't frightened when he heard the clink-clink of spurs against concrete. Lightning flashed, starkly unmasking the front entrance but revealing nothing.

Now the sound seemed to be less crisp, as though several had joined the first's measured pace—an entire troop of gunslingers slowly approaching, each step in time with the others. The cadence suddenly changed, growing discordant and louder, as if they were ascending the stairs.

Unable to shut off his mind, Sheriff Middleton wandered the lantern-lit halls, illegally chain-smoking as he drifted. He couldn't get over this place and what had happened in the last week or so. If life was going to be this weird, he didn't want to live to ninety. Maybe he should recommend a raid, just to shut down the place for a while, but nobody higher up liked the idea. There were other forces at work here; he could smell it.

The sheriff neared the ballroom and passed a side corridor when he heard a woman sobbing. "Please... d... don't h... hurt me." Stepping against the wall, Middleton pulled his gun.

"Ah don't want ta hurt ya honey, but if ya scream, I'll cut ya. Now...."

"Please..." she gasped. Middleton could picture a crazed man yanking a woman's head back by the hair and exposing her throat to a knife. Ripping cloth and a flurry of movements painted enough of a picture for the detective.

"Thatta way. Just like that," he said, and the woman gasped.

Unable to wait any longer, Middleton leaned around the corner, a gun aimed to where he thought the perp might be. "Hands in the air!" he shouted to an empty hall. Where were they? Perplexed, he walked warily to the end of the corridor. The flash of lightning revealed nobody was in the reading nook.

Barroom brawls, he sighed. How much worse were things going to get, Chief Warren Porter wondered? He followed his flashlight beam as he ambled along the corridor from the kitchen to the loading dock. His heavy footsteps echoed lonely along the dark employee hallway. It spooked Porter that he'd been helpless to stop the ghosts from running wild.

Before he'd taken the job from Mr. MacGuire and Mr. Heller, he'd asked about the chances of the ghosts getting out of control. Sean Heller had been a bit concerned, but not Peter MacGuire; confidence had oozed from him. It was obvious he'd been more vital to the operation than anyone expected.

Now MacGuire's calm self-assurance was gone. Porter felt circumstances poised on the edge of getting nasty. If he hadn't been in so deep, he would've just given notice and left. But he had too much invested to run away.

The rotund chief of security stopped at the doors and peered through a deliquescent window. He couldn't see much, but everything seemed normal—if anything could be described as normal at Ghostal Shores. Porter had just hitched up his pants and was reaching for his walkie-talkie when he heard voices. "Heh, heh, Virgil, will ya lookee here?"

"Wow! It's as big as my fist! Must be worth a fortune!"

Porter whirled around to see if he had "real" company. More ghosts, he cursed quietly. Hopefully, they weren't in the mood to cause trouble.

"C'mon how'd ya sneak it past Carlson?"

"I got my ways."

"Ah c'mon. Please. I'm desperate and almost outta opium."

"Well, I guess. You don't look good, not good at all, Virgil. You need to lay off the opium."

"C'mon Bart," Virgil pleaded.

There was a tapping sound, hard wood against the floor. "Sounds solid, don't it? Well, it ain't. I just pack the handle of my pick with dirt on the way in, and gold on the way out. Half the take goes to my foreman, though."

"That's a lot."

"Don't worry. I know someone that'll take care of 'em and take less."

Not liking the sound of that, Porter slipped away. If he didn't hear something from Heller soon, he might leave anyway. Money was no good to a dead man.

Eva awoke with a start that splashed water in her face. She relaxed when she realized she'd fallen asleep in the tub. The water was still warm, but two of the three candles on the counter were out, leaving the lower half of the bathroom in thick shadow.

As though a window opened, a sudden chill gusted through the bathroom. Eva goose-bumped and slid into the water. "Hello?!" There was no sound in her bedroom, but she sensed someone was here.

Eva listened intently for a long time. Finally, after not hearing anything, she forced herself to relax and think of something else; Blasing was magnifico. She ran her hands along her svelte body and thought what he might do to her, and she for him.

Stopping in mid-caress, she realized she'd never get to sleep if she kept torturing herself. Tomorrow was going to be another glorious day. The barroom brawl shouldn't hurt sales orders if handled right. Ah, the smell of money; it was even more intoxicating than a man ready and waiting.

Another gust suddenly whipped through the bathroom. Darkness descended as if collapsing on unsuspecting prey. The smoke from the dying candle caught her in the face and smelled foul, reminding her of... a cigar!

Eva scrambled to her feet and out of the tub. When she reached for her towel, her hand scraped a rough paneled wall. Who had moved it? Someone burped, startling her. Eva frantically felt around for her towel. A bar of soap sat atop it. After quickly wrapping herself in her towel, she sniffed the soap. It smelled like lye!

Eva suddenly realized she was in an old-fashioned wash basin. Someone coughed. She panicked, frantically searching for her lighter. After knocking over a candle, she managed to light two tapers. In the haze surrounding her she spotted several basins along the floor. Water slopped over the side of the nearest one and a huge shadowy figure rose.

Eva screamed and dove for the light switch near the sink. She stumbled over something and almost fell. Wet feet smacked heavily against the floor. Eva fumbled for the switch. Where was it?!

Eva slapped at the wall, hoping that the power had returned. Bright, electric light flashed off the white decor and marble tile, nearly blinding Eva, but her brief glimpse revealed she was alone.

Awakening with a frenzied start, Earl Cash immediately sat up, face to face with an old, faded ghost. Cash tried to scream but only croaked hoarsely. Lightning flashed and the ghost disappeared, only to return when it grew dark once more. The thin, grizzled spirit with deep set eyes stood next to Cash, eye-balling the assistant manager from head to toe.

What was a ghost doing in his room? He'd never seen this ghost before! He hated the ghosts! They made him crazy! He could feel them! Sometimes hear them! Why had he stayed? Why? Because he didn't dare leave! But if he stayed, they would drive him crazy before he could retire to a tropical paradise.

The ghost had stepped back, then positioned his transparent hands to frame Cash. The spirit nodded suddenly, then walked toward a supply of long planks leaning against the wall. Gathering several, the mortician set to making a coffin.

Meg paced back and forth across the room, the flickering light of the lamp causing her shadow to writhe as it moved with her. She couldn't believe they couldn't fix her car! Someone had to have some damned automotive know how!

She hated this place! Hated the ghosts! If it wasn't for the inheritance, she never would have come back to Ghostal Shores. Never! The idea that the ghosts could go wherever they wanted—wandering from room to room and watching the guests—made her more than a little uneasy. And these new ghosts! They frightened her badly; they looked at her hungrily.

Meg felt a breeze; she shivered as cool fingers caressed her back. She whirled about, quickly looking over the room. It was empty. Or was it?

When she finally sat on the bed and reached for a book, the caressing came again. She whirled about. Alone, again. Or was she? How could she know?

After his tense meeting with all the ghosts, Sean Heller returned to his room. How he hated the ghosts! Just being around them twisted him into knots, and his abdomen burned as though having a meltdown. Rushing to the bathroom through a dark room, he yanked down his shorts, sat on the toilet and sighed.

After a moment, he felt a strange draft. Then he noticed the dry heat and overwhelming stench as if the plumbing had backed up. Heller tried to breath through his mouth, but his nose was burning and his eyes were watering.

A buzzing noise summoned the image of a fly, then Heller thought he felt the insect circling him. He swatted at it, but the pest wouldn't leave him alone. A second joined the first, then a third and fourth gathered to torture him. Heller grabbed for the toilet paper and found a large book on a shelf.

Confused, he stood and leaned over the sink to flip on the light switch. The lights came on, and he was blinded for a moment, but the silence told him that the flies were gone, although the smell lingered.

When he opened his eyes, he found nothing wrong with the toilet or sink. What in the Hell was going on? This wasn't part of the deal. Not part of it at all!

As Candy exited the elevator and walked toward Angela's room, her mind was awhirl with ideas. The arrival of the transient ghosts had added a whole new aspect to the scene. Would the population fluctuate? Would it become overcrowded? And if ghosts did wander and travel from place to place, were there other spirit hangouts? Could another one be built? Many assumed that Peter MacGuire and Sean Heller were lucky—maybe lucky enough to hit upon the formula for success. She had more than enough ideas for a paper. Now if only she had some answers to help Angela resolve her questions.

Just before she reached Angela's room, Candy noticed the heat. It intensified, getting hotter by the second. A searing gust of wind carrying acrid smoke suddenly staggered her, making her choke and cough. A fire? Angela! Candy rushed to Angela's room and pounded on the door. "Angela!"

Flames abruptly exploded about her, erupting from the carpet and running along the walls to lick at the ceiling. She could feel the heat but didn't hear the fire. What was going on?

The roar of the inferno suddenly sounded as though the volume had been cranked. "Angela!" Although Candy felt her clothes could burst aflame any moment, she noticed that neither the walls nor the ceiling were being burned. Neither was the carpet. She touched the door, finding it cool. What was going on?

Candy remembered something she'd read. This wasn't real; only a few senses were engaged and physical objects appeared unharmed. It must be a psychic emanation--maybe something a ghost had experienced long ago.

Candy quit pounding on the door and closed her eyes. The heat slowly faded as if a memory had slipped away. Candy opened her eyes. Everything appeared unchanged. Maybe the increased number of ghosts caused this etheric event.

When the door opened, Candy said, "Angela, you won't believe what just happened to me!"

"I cannot advance any farther," Broderick said dejectedly.

"You sure?" Blasing asked. They stood just inside the doors to the service corridor.

"Yes, sir. I believe I could stand the biting sensation." Broderick scratched. "But with each step I grow more dizzy."

"Then wait here," Blasing said. Broderick began to object. "Broderick, if you can't stand it, none of the other ghosts can either."

"Yes, Master Madera. And thank you for your confidence," Broderick bowed slightly, then turned and left.

Blasing headed down the starkly lit hallway. Besides being in his or Angela's room, this was the first time he hadn't felt spied upon. Having the power back on would mean he would be on camera, but he didn't care. He was nearly out of patience and hoped his investigation would tip someone's hand. He just prayed they didn't go after Angela.

Blasing stopped at a long string of Toshiba, Sony and RCA

boxes lining the corridor. Most had been opened, but a few were still taped closed. He contemplated checking them—wondering if the best place to hide something was in plain sight—then decided to make a quick round of the entire area.

After a short walk, he came across a spare furniture storage room, then a supply room where a ramp led out of sight. Blasing followed it to the loading dock, then returned to the service corridor. He met the maintenance supervisor exiting a fenced area. "Are we prepared for another outage, George?"

"Definitely, sir. This time of year we frequently have blackouts due to the wind."

Blasing thanked him, then moved on to the more populated areas, passing a closed uniform room, a bustling laundry, and walking into the employee breakroom. He doubted he'd find what he was looking for here.

On the way back, he checked several cameras and found signal boosters. He couldn't think of any reason they'd be necessary, except for upsetting the ghosts. Why didn't they want ghosts in this area?

Blasing examined the supply room, discovering dust outlining where boxes and cabinets had been recently. Broderick would have really come in handy now. Why had so much been moved? Re-organizing? Making room for equipment? Hiding something?

On his way out, Blasing checked the equipment boxes. "Can I help you, Mr. Madera?" Chadwick asked, his pockmarked face stony, although his left eye twitched. He carried a flashlight the size of a club. His bearded companion looked as if he'd just finished working out, muscles ready to burst from his shirt.

"Not really. At Sean's request, I'm doing an audit and study of the equipment, since I'm familiar with it," Blasing replied, briefly glancing at the pair as if unconcerned.

"Does he think there's a problem?" Chadwick asked.

"Doesn't he always?" Blasing asked. Chadwick frowned. His companion nodded as if to say "that's the truth." "Why don't you ask him? Then he can climb your back."

The bearded man laughed harshly. Chadwick's glance cut him short. "Let us know if we can help," Chadwick replied.

After they departed, Blasing continued looking through the boxes, then walked toward the lobby. "Broderick?!" Blasing called as he exited onto Old West Avenue. The Englishman didn't respond. Had he gotten tired of waiting? Blasing doubted it.

As Blasing walked past the shops, he heard his name. He whirled around in time to see Lilly dart into a corridor between shops. A rumble of thunder began, the sound growing louder, threatening to deafen him. The wood-floored avenue trembled, lamps shaking and swaying, storefronts quivering and doors rattling as if ready to burst open. Earthquake?! Blasing dropped to his knees.

At first, it appeared a brown cloud was devouring the shops, then Blasing noticed horses bunched at the front of the dust ball. The mustangs' eyes were wild, showing white, and their teeth were bared so tightly their lips appeared pinned to their ears. As they raced toward him, they seemed to be hauling the wake of dirt with them, their long manes disappearing with the rest of their bodies in the earthen haze.

"Come on!" Lilly screamed at him from the corridor. Blasing hurtled toward her, then rolled until he was safe.

As the cluster of ghostly mustangs raced closer, Blasing saw they weren't alone. Behind them were rows upon rows of ghostly horses driving the others forward. When the first horse passed, the wall of dirt hit him hard. Blasing couldn't see anything, but he listened for a stagecoach among the pounding hooves and the wild neighing of the mavericks. The stampede seemed endless, but finally the last spirit flew past, and the dust settled.

Blasing wasn't surprised when everything returned to normal. What did that tell him about himself? He felt for the ghostly presence, but Lilly was long gone, having arrived just in time to save him.

TWENTY-SEVEN

As Angela and Candy ascended the stairs, they could hear the happy drone of a busy bar just ahead. "Doesn't sound as if the brawl or those...phantasms affected business any," Candy said.

"What you told me about the fiery haunting is frightening but... it probably helped business. You know how weird people are."

"I resemble that remark," Candy replied, to which they both burst out laughing. "You know, the more I think about it, the more I wonder if Mac was murdered by someone possessed."

Angela bit her lip. "Blasing and I have talked about it. Might Rictor have killed him? I doubt Peter would've been frightened by a ghost, even one as disturbing as Rictor. Face it, we're still a long way from figuring out what's going on."

Changing the subject, Candy said, "Angel, I don't understand why you're meeting with this reporter who's hot for Blasing's bod."

"Courtesy?" Angela replied. Candy snickered. "Curiosity?"

Candy just frowned slightly this time. "Finding out more about his past? Or do you want to be there for the reunion?"

Angela's glare was icy when she replied, "If I didn't trust him, Candace, I wouldn't be bothering."

Candy sobered. "Sorry. My mouth's running again. I just thought, well, last night when you saw him with Eva."

"Candy, he threw her out. Just be polite when you meet Tawny Lane," Angela sternly told her. "Let me be catty if it's called for. All right?" Laughing again, Candy agreed.

Despite what had happened, Angela couldn't tell any difference in the barroom crowd. The patrons were a fascinating mixture where formally dressed people sat near a couple clad in tie-dye. The attire was so varied from table to table that Angela might have walked into a costume party. A good number of people wore colorful gypsy-ish clothing. There were men and women draped in bright robes, a trio cast from a jungle safari, and a couple clad as though time-travelling from the late eighteen hundreds.

Not appearing quite so odd, foreigners in clothing from their homelands seemed to be part of the show. A dark man was proudly dressed in an all white suit and turban. Angela thought he could have stepped out of Casablanca. An English professor-type in tweeds was smoking a pipe and wiping clean his glasses.

"Hey, more new ghosts," Candy said. As usual, the spirits were clustered around the bar, vultures waiting for something to die. The newcomers looked pale but very well defined. The nattily attired spirits reminded Angela of bankers and businessmen. She thought of Geoff's gang comment.

"And those two look like gunslingers," Candy continued. Instead of just hard faces, there was a steeliness about them—a presence that indicated they would cause trouble at the drop of a hat.

"I wonder if Broderick or Cannon has spoken to them?"

"I don't see Cannon, but we're being waved at," Candy nodded toward the table where Tawny sat waiting.

Angela sighed. Where was Cannon? The new spirits concerned her. Could they be the cause of the phantasms? Angela would like to question the newcomers, but she would wait until Blasing was with her. They talked to him.

"Hello, ladies," Tawny greeted them. "Quite a place." She looked around at the crowd and the montage of spirits. "After earlier this evening, I would have expected a diminished crowd."

"This is California," Candy reminded her.

"Yes, of course. How silly of me."

"And we survived," Angela said.

"But then Blasing was with you," Tawny said. "He is a very, very lucky man."

"Tawny Lane, this is my friend, Candy Whyte."

"A pleasure. I believe I've heard of you Ms. Whyte. Didn't you help the police with the E-street murders several years ago?" Candy beamed. "Are you here working on the Peter MacGuire murder?"

"No, I'm just a friend. I'm doing a paper on Ghostal Shores for a class at Berkeley. Angela's representing the new partner of the resort."

"Please, sit. I want to hear all about it."

Angela glared at Candy, then sat. "How much do you know?"

"A fair amount. I know Peter MacGuire was murdered, but

until recently, I didn't know Blasing Madera was his nephew."

"Otherwise you might have visited earlier?" Angela asked archly.

"Most likely. I enjoy mixing business and pleasure, but alas, I'm too late. I can tell by the way he looks at you."

"I thought you wanted to know about Ghostal Shores?"

"I do, and he's an integral part, isn't he? Besides, I can't talk about him this way if he's around, can I?" Tawny bit her lip, then said, "If I may be so bold, how did you interest him?"

"I'm not really sure," Angela said. "When we first met, I was not interested in becoming involved."

"But you changed your mind."

"I tried to keep my distance, but he changed my mind for me."

"So resisting him was the secret," Tawny said wistfully.

"I don't think she resisted him," Candy chuckled. "She was just in denial." All of them laughed together. "How do you know him?"

As the reporter told her tale, Angela became particularly interested in a trio of vagrant spirits, especially when the big, burly ghost with arms the size of railroad ties and his two Latino companions approached three young women. Each was dressed to the hilt in mildly revealing clothing and lavish jewelry. Angela guessed the attractive trio were college co-eds pretending to be worldly and mature.

By everyone's smiling reactions, the flirting began immediately and in earnest. The redhead dressed in a clingy, emerald and shoulderless gown seemed to be the boldest. The spirits leaned closer, then the biggest one stood straight, grabbed his crotch, and said brashly, "A motherlode of gold right here, honey! Feel free to mine it!" The women's reactions combined horror and outrage.

"Did you hear that?" Angela asked, interrupting Tawny. By her expression, the reporter had heard.

"Hey, it's what you want, honey. Nobody dead or alive is better than Dan Crane! Nobody! And you don't have to worry about the pox!"

The livid redhead tried to slap the ghost but struck nothing, losing her balance and falling out of her chair. Crane began chortling, then rumbled to back-slapping laughter with his companions. When several surrounding spirits joined in, the sound grew ugly and degrading.

"That bastard," Candy snapped.

Angela was suddenly very worried. Where was Cannon? What had happened to the local ghosts? "Are you wearing your hematite?" Candy nodded. Angela stood a little and looked into the restaurant, seeking the gamblers. Where had they gone? She wished Broderick had a beeper. Instead, she quickly removed her cell phone from her purse and paged Blasing.

"Damn you!" the short brunette yelled as she grabbed her purse and stood. "Come on, Desiree´! Penny! Let's get out of here!"

"But that's all we're asking for," a Latino ghost pleaded, dropping to one knee. He began singing a song about a midnight romance and roll. The women paused in their departure, captured for a moment until his lyrics became particularly bawdy.

"I'm not listening to this," Candy said, starting to rise.

"You're being very rude," a scholarly-looking man at a nearby table told the ghosts. They quickly sobered, their pallid and transparent expressions twisted as if they'd bitten into something sour. Appearing nervous, his much younger lady friend tried to shush him, but he continued on. "Well it is, dear." She whispered to him, then he said, "All right. If you insist. But I would do the same for you." They quickly departed. As if something were catching, several couples joined them. Others were mesmerized by the scene.

"Hey, I bathe," the shortest Latino sounded upset.

"You tell them, Paco," the other encouraged.

"What am I? No good?"

"Got me, amigo," Crane chuckled, his belly shaking. "But I'm bored. I think it's time for a little entertainment. These momma's boys might be afraid of getting bounced outta here," he motioned to all the other ghosts, "but not me."

"I think we should leave," Angela said. Some of the ghosts appeared angered by the challenge to their manhood.

"No, this is news!" Tawny replied, clicking on her recorder. Then she dug into her purse and removed her cellular phone.

"We can't let them run over us," Candy said.

"Wait, see if Blasing gets here."

"Hey, honey, come here," Crane yelled to a petite, Asian woman sitting with two lady friends. When the big ghost pointed to her, her chair shook for a moment, then scooted across the carpet toward him. The screaming woman jumped from the chair, tumbling across the floor until she crashed into a deserted table.

The ghostly stooges slapped their knees, then each other on the back. Many of the other transients helped to fill the lounge with derisive laughter.

Candy helped the terrified Asian lady stand, then she and her companions fled. With a head of steam, Candy headed for the trouble-maker's table. Angela's fear rooted her to the spot.

"Hey, everybody's leaving, Tito," Paco said.

"Can't have that, can we, Crane?" Tito asked.

The burly spirit tilted back his hat and shook his head. He appeared to ignore Candy as he said, "Gonna have to do something."

Several men were seized as if by invisible hands and roughly tossed down the stairs. Indignant, outraged, and injured cries filled the air as they tumbled toward the foyer.

"Stop it!" Candy cried.

The women trying to flee were dragged back into the lounge, then their clothes fell apart, bursting free as seams parted and straps snapped. Buttons exploded like bullets, ricocheting off walls and tables, shattering glasses and cracking mirrors. Zippers undid themselves, and skirts fell to the floor, leaving some women dressed as if for a strip show with stocking-clad legs, frilly garters, and lingerie wrapped bottoms. A long-legged woman with jet-black hair and pink undergarments tried to grab her clothing, but it twisted free, slipping from her grasp as though composed of snakes.

"Stop it!" Candy cried again, moving closer for a face to face confrontation. Paco suddenly grabbed her, yanking her forward, then slapped her hard. Candy reeled, staggering several feet before collapsing.

"Candy!" Angela rushed to her. Could this be what Blasing meant by being able to be touched because of the hematite? She checked her friend and found an ugly welt swelling on her cheek. Then she realized Candy wasn't breathing!

Several scantily clad women fled, but two couldn't escape: a willowy woman with long, white-blond tresses and a busty brunette with a round face and big brown eyes. The dark-haired woman was too frightened to move. The blond lay on the floor, stunned from falling hard when her dress had slipped to bind her ankles. A table slid next to them, and Paco yelled, "Dance!"

Neither of the women moved, so the shorter Latino ghost drifted toward them. As he did, the blond slowly floated off the floor, spinning around in a circle for all to see before landing atop the table. She lost her battle with her clothing when the straps on her camisole popped, sliding to her waist and exposing her breasts. Then her panties suddenly flew off, leaving her clad only in heels, stockings and a garter belt.

"Dance!" several of the ghosts yelled. "Dance!" The chant grew louder as more spirits caught the fever.

The frightened woman was paralyzed in a covering pose, then the table began to tilt underneath her. With her high heels skittering across the top, she threw her arms and legs akimbo, trying to regain her balance. She never managed, thrashing about, her breasts bouncing about as her hips and buttocks gyrated.

"Muy bueno!" Paco yelled. "You're next," he said to the frightened brunette.

Angela gave a sigh of relief when Candy started to breathe. Rage overwhelmed her. Angela walked slowly toward the raucous spirits. She wished Blasing was here but refused to live in fear.

"Hey, another one wants to play," Paco said, pointing to Angela. "Dance!" When nothing happened, he was dumbfounded. "Hey!"

"No more! This is not how things are done at Ghostal Shores!" Angela snapped.

"Slap this bitch!" Crane chuckled.

"Stop it! This isn't why we are here!" a voice rang out. The ghosts suddenly stood still. When the table quit moving, the brunette and blond fled.

Vivid and sharper than any other ghost, yet also dark and brooding, Rictor stepped from the shadows. Below the brim of his black hat and inside his dark, floor-sweeping jacket, the shadows appeared to shift and writhe. "We need to talk." His voice was low and guttural, commanding one to listen. "There's a better way to get what you want."

"You again! Who are you?" Crane asked.

"The new boss of Ghostal Shores," he said quietly, but Angela could feel it ring through the resort.

The ghosts suddenly cheered as they moved to surround Rictor. Several of them gained color and clarity. Angela didn't like what she was seeing.

"Angel?"

"Shush, Candace. You'll be all right, but be quiet for now."

Rictor parted the crowd and walked toward her. "You are becoming a problem, Miss Starborne," Rictor growled. "For the last time, I suggest you and Blasing Madera leave."

Angela rose slowly, mustering every ounce of dignity she could gather. "What do you want?" Blasing was right about Rictor's presence—she felt she stood on the edge of disaster. His voice called forth images of a wagon carrying corpses along a graveled road.

"Just to do my job, and for Blasing to leave," he told her. She thought his accent was Germanic. "He'll leave if you go. He asks you all the time. He's concerned about you, and well he should be!" Rictor snapped open a switchblade.

"What does Lilly want?!" Angela demanded. "Lilly! What do you want?!" Would she help her?

Everything suddenly shook as though an earthquake had struck, bottles rattling against each other. Hanging glasses crashed to the bar. Tables bounced across the floor. Angela tried to stand, then gave up, dropping to her knees.

The shaking didn't seem to bother the dark ghost. "Answer her, Lilly darlin'," Rictor growled. "LILLY?! Answer her!" Rictor yelled. He began looking around wildly. "Damn it woman!" the dark spirit cried, then suddenly disappeared. The host of spirits murmured almost as one, then several drifted into the shadows. More moved to follow.

"I suggest you and your associates leave, Mr. Crane," Angela said. "Or you will be forced to leave. I hear cleansings are very painful."

The Latinos shot the burly ghost worried looks, then the threesome faded from sight.

"Whew," Angela said. The bar was deserted except for her, Candy and Tawny.

"That was either the bravest thing I've ever seen," Tawny said, "or the dumbest. Makes for a great story though!"

"This isn't about a story!" Angela snapped. "This is really happening, and people are getting hurt. You might get hurt."

"I'm willing to take that risk."

"Others may not," Angela snapped. "And they'd rather not be in your story!"

"Angel, baby, I think we can thank your beau for the save," Candy murmured.

"Wha... why?"

"Where else would Lilly be?"

"I hope he's all right," Angela said, suddenly concerned. If Rictor arrived in a rage....

"Hey, don't look so worried. If Rictor could hurt Blasing, he would have done so long before now. Besides, I'm the one who's hurt."

"Well, your jaw doesn't sound broken. How's the rest of you?"

"Dizzy... I know, what else is new, right?" Candy winced as she tried to sit up. "I have a headache, too."

"Lie still, I'm going to call Geoff," Angela said, then moved to the house phone.

As soon as she hung up, Blasing arrived. He took one look at the state of the lounge—furniture overturned, scraps of clothing littering the carpet and buttons scattered as though a kid had spilled a bag of M&M's—then quickly moved to Angela, taking her in his arms.

"Thank God you're all right!"

"I'm fine," she said, and kissed him, reveling in his touch—in his presence.

"When I called and you weren't in the suite, I tried Candy's. Then I decided to come here, thinking you might have arrived early. I knew something was wrong when I saw a broken chair and tattered garments scattered all over the foyer. I feared the worst."

"It's all right, for now." Angela told him.

"How's Candy?" he finally asked.

"I'll be all right," Candy replied.

"Glad to hear it. Have you seen Broderick?"

"No," Angela replied. "And there's been no sign of Cannon or the gamblers. I'm sure they would've been here to help if they could."

"I'm worried about them."

"I know. I'm worried, too."

"The ghosts need us now, wherever Broderick and the others are," he told her. "You were right not to desert them. I don't think they'd desert us."

Chadwick and security finally arrived with Heller hot on their heels. The Irishman appeared sickly, his eyes glazed and his skin pale despite being flushed. "What happened here?" Before Angela could respond, Heller exploded, "I knew the god-damned ghosts couldn't control themselves. I told him! I told him a thousand god-damned times! Where are they anyway?" He suddenly shuddered, then groped for a chair and sat.

Chief Porter arrived shortly, checked on Heller, then walked over to Blasing. Dr. Landrum wasn't far behind. Both wanted to know what had happened. As Angela explained, Dr. Landrum examined Candy, then Heller. "Rest for both of you."

"We must shut down the resort," Blasing said.

"WHAT?!" Heller exploded again. "WHY?!"

"Sounds like a good idea to me," Dr. Landrum said.

"It's just a minor problem," Heller sputtered. "Madame Zanadane will take care of it. Whenever she gets here, that is! We'll purge this place, damnit we will!"

"Rest!" Dr. Landrum repeated. "Or you'll have a heart attack."

"I think we should discuss this in a civilized manner, behind closed doors," Blasing suggested. Tawny frowned at him.

"In the morning," Dr. Landrum suggested. "Mr. Heller's in no condition to be discussing a stressful subject. He needs to rest."

"Most of the problems seem to surround the bar," Dr. Landrum began. "Just close it."

Chief Porter looked at Blasing who nodded. "Done," the head of security said, then began organizing his men.

"I hope that works," Blasing said. "If there are more hauntings, there's no telling what might happen."

"They've already been going on," Porter said, then gave him a brief run down on the calls security had already received.

"I don't like the sound of that."

"Candy experienced one," Angela said. She explained about her friend's fiery experience.

"And I almost got run over by a stampede."

"That's what that rumbling noise was," Angela said.

Blasing nodded. "What should we do?"

Angela shrugged resignedly. "I'm tired and can't think straight."

"We should be glad no one has been seriously injured," Dr. Landrum told them. "I think everyone should rest the best they can." He motioned to a guard to help the Irishman to his room.

"Blasing, I can't go to bed without helping the ghosts," Angela told him. "They may need us, and some of them are my friends."

"What do you suggest?"

"Hunting for them. Combing every inch of this place until we find them or discover what's happened to them."

TWENTY-EIGHT

Tawny wanted to tag along, but Blasing said no, telling her it might be dangerous. When Tawny argued, Blasing asked Porter if they had the authority to house arrest someone. Porter smiled and nodded. Tawny sputtered but Blasing's gaze was granite steady. Angela smiled; she knew better. They left without being followed.

"You sure you're up to this?" Blasing asked Angela as they descended the stairs to the foyer.

"I refuse to cower in my room," she replied. "Though if you're there with me the idea has some merit."

His smile was fleeting. "I wish we didn't have to do this. Walking around Ghostal Shores at night gives me the creeps."

"I know, there's something beyond maliciousness about these new ghosts. Malevolence, maybe. But as an owner, the GSR ghosts are your friends. You have a moral obligation to them, the staff and the guests, in providing a safe environment."

"Too true," he said wearily, "but unless things change, Ghostal Shores may not be much of an inheritance. When news of the brawl and the stripping gets out, we may be ruined."

"I'm not so sure," Angela replied. "Remember, we are in California, and these incidents are morbidly sensational. Still, I hope you're not as prophetic as my grandmother."

A loud crack of thunder struck, seemingly just outside the overlook window, and the lights went out. Brightness returned with another flash of nature's pyrotechnics, then all was dark.

"Just great," Angela said. She dug into her purse.

"I have a flashlight," Blasing said, pulling a pen light from his jacket pocket.

"Boy Scout, meet Girl Scout," Angela said, removing the squeezable light from her key chain.

"I was never a Boy Scout, but I did take a survivalist course."

"Well, this is less dangerous than carrying around a firebrand," she replied. "Where do you think all the ghosts have gone? Do you think they left in fear?" she asked. He shook his head. "I hope they're not dead. More dead. Do you feel watched right now?" she asked, rambling a bit nervously.

"No." Blasing paused at the Pacific Overlook to check on the storm. Rain pelted the window in bursts, driven by a lashing wind. Lightning struck again, turning the glass white, then it seemed to fade, giving way to the grumbling thunder.

"All this rain is going to cause problems. This is the golden state, after all," Angela said as they started down the dimly illuminated steps. They didn't need their lights. Several lanterns sat in niches along the stairs.

They stopped at the 1880's General Store, but Blasing still didn't sense a ghostly presence. "Let's keep checking," Angela suggested. They "felt" around the entire area, but neither sensed any spiritual presence.

"It doesn't look good," Blasing said grimly.

"Let's wander and see what we can find," Angela said, then pointed to a stairwell door next to the apothecary. "That will take us up to the first floor."

"A great suggestion for a romantic evening," Blasing said wryly, then held the door open for Angela. The stairwell was pitch dark. "Something's wrong with the emergency lighting. That should never happen."

"When it rains, it pours," she said.

"Very funny."

When Blasing pushed open the door to the first floor, the sounds of the storm became clearer, thunder rumbling through the walls and rolling down the overlook corridors. Blasing felt strange about searching the resort by feel. Not only was he accepting ghosts and Native magic, but also extra-sensory perception. Had he lost his rational mind—or simply concluded that science didn't know it all?

They were heading for the ballroom when he scratched the back of his neck. "I feel something." Blasing stared at a guest room door. "But it doesn't feel... quite right," Blasing said.

"Maybe the door's screening it."

"I hear noises, too." Blasing frowned, then leaned closer to the door, placing one hand on it.

Suddenly, the door was yanked open. "I'll be back in a minute, dear... oof!" Blasing stumbled forward a step. The thin, balding man sat down quickly, holding his stomach and gasping for breath.

"Albert?" the woman in the room asked.

"We're so sorry," Angela apologized. Blasing put out his hand, but the man refused to accept it.

"This damn place is crazy! First those damn ghost birds go wild! Then the power blacks out! And now I'm bowled over by a damned peeping tom!" Behind them, the birds screeched, making an ear-splitting racquet.

"I'm so sorry," Blasing began again.

"Yes we are," Angela said. "My fault. Forgot my room number," she tittered, then assumed her best blank-eyed blond expression. "Key wouldn't work. Silly me. Must have had too much to drink."

"Quite all right," the man stammered.

"Albert!"

"Wrong room dear," he replied, accepting Blasing's help to stand this time.

"We'll be going. Sorry again," Angela replied, then guided Blasing away. When they were out of ear-shot, she said, "I'm not surprised we felt something. That was the Bird Room. I should've remembered. Funny, I thought Peter told me they didn't make any noise after sunset."

"I believe the brochure says the same," Blasing replied, then scratched the back of his neck. It was a moment before he realized he felt a ghost. "There's one near." He pointed to the dark doors.

They swung open easily to reveal an elegant but deserted foyer with couches and chairs around tables of exquisite Backgammon, Chess, and Mah-jong sets. "Still feel it?" she asked. Blasing nodded. As they approached the ballroom, thunder echoed behind the double doors, making the chamber sound cavernous. He reached for the handle, then stopped and turned to Angela. "Something wrong?"

Blasing nodded to the closet door, then taking a deep breath, he opened it. "Elma, is that you?"

The beautiful, elderly spirit slowly appeared, growing slightly brighter. Elma's once lavish and fashionable clothing was tattered, and her face worn with worry. Dark, hollow eyes stared fearfully at them. "Quickly! Come inside!" she whispered.

"What's this all about?" Angela whispered as she gently shoved

Blasing inside, then followed him and closed the door.

"They're killers! And they're hunting us down!" Elma tried to whisper, but her voice reverberated throughout the spacious closet.

"The transients?" Blasing asked.

Elma nodded vigorously. "I've even seen my killer. I swear the devil has come to town."

"You mean the spirit of the man who killed you long ago?" Angela asked. Elma nodded gravely. "You're sure?"

"Absolutely. He's the one that set the fire at the Goldfield. Tall, slim, almost anemic looking with the shifty, dark eyes of a weasel." She shivered.

"How do you know this?" Blasing asked.

"I was so angry about the fire stealing everything from me, that it took a while to realize I'd died, so I chased after the man. I flailed away, shouting at him, but it didn't do any good. When I realized I couldn't touch him, I followed him for a time, cursing him with every step. His name was Chafe Tomlin."

"Why are they hunting you?"

"I don't know!" Her eyes suddenly widened. "I've got to hide!"

"Wait!" Angela cried. "What's going on?"

"What can we do to help?" Blasing asked, but the spirit had already disappeared.

"That wasn't much help," Angela said dejectedly.

"Why are the transients hunting our ghosts?"

"Let's keep searching. Since we found one ghost, we may find more. Maybe we'll get lucky and locate Broderick."

Anthony climbed into the Jaguar and started the car, enjoying the smooth purr of its engine. He usually loved working valet parking, driving fancy cars and hobnobbing with the well-to-do, but he wasn't enjoying it tonight. People were demanding; they were ready to leave NOW. He could see the fear in their eyes. Hear it in their voices. Something bad was going down. Did it have anything to do with the noises he'd heard earlier?

There had already been several near accidents because valet parking was trying to please everyone. When they realized they couldn't, or even when they did, that they weren't tipped, all the valets slowed down. Cars no longer whipped out of parking places, around corners, or zoomed out of the garage, screeching to a halt under the portico.

Anthony checked the mirror, then backed the XJS and headed for the exit. He'd certainly miss driving these amazing automobiles and eye-balling those incredible women if he went back to his father's laundry business in Jersey. He would just have to ride it out.

As he came around the last turn and neared the exit, Anthony thought he saw an old truck back into his path. He spun the wheel to avoid it, and surprised a man walking to his car. Anthony yanked the wheel right this time, but overcompensated, slamming into a Lexus, then rebounding into the path of an oncoming Ferrari. They slammed together at the entrance to the garage, jamming the exit full of expensive scrap metal.

Tom Becker had chuckled when the lights went out again. Who needed 'em anyway, he was driving while blind. Unfortunately, none of his sales buds felt in the mood to party, so he'd gone searching for the ghosts he'd partied with last night. As he neared the ballroom doors, he thought he heard laughter. And wasn't that a piano playing a happy, upbeat tune?

Tom opened the door to reveal an Old West tavern. The smoke was heavy, so everything seemed fuzzy. The walls were swathed in elegant reds and greens, and the chandeliers shone brightly overhead. The tables had been pushed to the side, and people danced with abandon. His timing, as always, was impeccable.

A lean blond ghost with a wicked smile and a billowy red dress took one arm, while a brunette in deep, purple velvet took the other. As they guided him to the center of the dance floor, their perfume enveloped, then overwhelmed him.

Their touch made him dizzy. Wild scenes danced through Tom's head; he was here, there, everywhere, partying all over the Old West. The bars were sometimes fancy and sometimes dirty, dusty dives. One had a pool. Oops. He was soaking in a horse trough. Several had gambling, and he was playing cards for high stakes. All the stops had booze and women, some worth sipping, but most were shooters. Funny how booze and women were a lot alike.

The perfume thickened, heady and intoxicating, and he felt as if he floated. A shapely red-haired spirit, her green eyes bright as lanterns, stepped into his arms and they began dancing. Tom tried to flirt, but all she did was laugh or sigh. All the while, Tom wondered if he could lay a ghost.

In mid-stride he changed partners to a cute, jet-haired ghost with curls and a musk perfume. The tune became fast, they raced laughing and gasping across the floor, spinning and whirling. When the music ended, Tom was exhausted. "Hey babe, I'm pooped. Let's take a break." He tried to step back, but she held on, forcing him to continue dancing. Tom tried dragging his feet, but they seemed too light to do any good. "This isn't funny," he panted. "My spirit's willing, but my flesh is weak."

She spun him into the hands of another spirit, and his head whirled. He developed a pounding headache. Another one grabbed him, and they danced awkwardly across the wooden floor, spinning, galloping, and cavorting. "Hey, let me go! I'm tired, damn you!" Her nails were getting longer, digging deep into his back. "Hey!" he groaned. "You're killing me." His feet refused to obey him, following the ghost's every move.

She laughed at him as they continued to glide across the floor. Tom screamed for release until he was hoarse and his lips cracked, the tears stinging them until he had no more tears to cry. Finally, the ghost let him go. Exhausted and dizzy, Tom spun away from her, landing awkwardly on the floor.

When Earl Cash awakened to the last distant ring of the phone, he heard intermittent rain, but it sounded close—immediately overhead. THUMP. Thump?

It was pitch black, and despite hearing the thunder, GSR's assistant manager didn't see any flashes of lightning. The abrupt thrumming inconsistent heavy patterings of rain against the window... or on a roof. Was it warm in here, or was it him? He'd always been a bit claustrophobic. Earl tried to push off the covers and discovered there weren't any. Feeling around, his hands immediately bumped into rough, wooden walls.

THUMP.

Earl ran his fingers along the sides, then a few inches above his face. He was encased! The bursting sound of rain came again, landing just in front of his nose. He recalled the dream he'd had earlier of an undertaker building a pine box. THUMP, then the thrumming—trailing dirt upon board above him—came again, and he realized he was being buried alive.

Choking and gasping, Cash clawed at the lid. He tried to scream, but only managed a hoarse croak. As the walls closed in, he pounded on the lid. "Help! Help! For God's sake, I'm alive! I'M ALIVE!" Why would Heller do this? He'd been loyal!

The darkness continued to shrink, pulling tighter and closer until it felt skintight. Spots danced before the accountant's eyes. "Help me!"

THUMP. Earl felt as if the dirt landed directly on him, burying him and filling up his nose. He suddenly found breathing impossible. As all went dark, dirt landing atop the coffin was the last sound Earl Cash heard.

Chief Porter hid in his office, feeling helpless and afraid it was going to get worse. Anyone with any common sense would leave, which still left plenty of customers and staff at Ghostal Shores. He wished he could muster the nerve to face Hellraiser; the old goat would bust a gut when he tendered his resignation.

Leaning back and lighting a cigarette, Porter put his feet on the desk, spilling his whiskey and water. His head lolled onto the back of the chair and against the cork message board behind him. The security scanner and walkie-talkies had been turned low; he didn't want to hear any more. He'd had enough strangeness.

He shivered. "Damn drafty in...." Something slammed into the wall near his right ear. Wide-eyed, Porter searched the room. When he glanced to his right, he spotted an almost invisible dagger quivering in the wall.

"I'll bet you two bits I can come closer than that," a raspy voice said.

"Oh shit!" Porter cried. He tried to rise, but his legs were lifeless. A knife hit the wall with a loud 'THOCK', just a little over an inch from his left ear. The security chief tried to rise again, but even though his arms worked, they weren't enough to lift his bulk.

"Not impressed. Two bits says I can come closer without drawing blood."

"N... NO!" Porter cried. He felt a swift breeze cut across the top of his head, then another knife hit the cork board behind him. A push pin hit him, followed by a falling Post-It note.

"Bet I pinned a hair!"

"But not from his ears!"

Double THUDS near each ear resounded as the knives hit the wall. "YEOW!" Porter cried, his hand going to his left ear.

"Damn," one muttered.

"Games over. You lose."

"New game. Bet I can hit him between the eyes."

Porter screamed as he bolted from his chair. He stumbled on the chair's rollers, falling and hitting the corner of the desk chin first.

What a night so far, Tawny thought; there had already been two barroom incidents—one so spicy it was sure to draw plenty of attention. She concluded that even if Blasing wouldn't tell her anything, she'd uncover enough strange stories to keep viewers captivated and boost the ratings.

Tawny vaguely remembered when Ghostal Shores first opened; it had been a "circus" media event. People had always been fascinated by haunted places. "Al, let's do a little roving reporting and see what we can find out from the people who are staying."

As they wandered the halls, they passed magnificent candelabra which gave the place the timeless ambiance of a grand ole' castle. "Storm sure makes this place spookier. Do you think people are hiding in their rooms?" Murly asked. He was using the light on his camera to illuminate the halls.

"Maybe we should knock on..." Tawny paused. She hadn't heard any thunder, but the hallway was shaking. "Did you feel that?"

"What?"

"The shaking?" she asked. Murly shook his head.

As they walked around the corner and headed down a long corridor, the shaking grew stronger, the paintings on the walls rattling. "I feel it now!" A picture suddenly fell to the floor and bounced. A lamp joined it, cavorting across the corridor. Tawny lost her balance and slipped to the floor.

"Hey! Look at that!" Murly pointed ahead. Tawny looked up.

A bright light was coming toward them, piercing a swirling fog that filled the hall. A cloud puffed across the ceiling, then disappeared.

A second followed, then the quaking grew thunderous. A piercing whistle deafened them, shattering the lens on his camera.

"It's a god-damned train!" Murly yelled over the breathless chugging of the approaching locomotive. "Let's get out of here!" As he helped Tawny stand, the headlight brightened, blinding them. Steam engulfed them, making it difficult to breathe.

"Start filming!" Tawny yelled.

"Are you crazy? Run!" Murly took off at a sprint, but Tawny paused, glancing behind them and wishing she had a camera. When she saw the cowcatcher and the light barreling down on her, she put on a burst of speed.

"Tawny?!" Murly glanced over his shoulder just in time to see his compatriot disappear in the roiling steam. "TAWNY!"

"I paid you, now I expect to get my money's worth," the tall, lanky ghost told Meg. The spirit was neatly dressed in black and wore a red scarf around his neck, not quite covering a scar. His dark outfit matched his face, completely hidden by the shadow of his hat.

Meg tried to find her voice, but it was frozen in her chest.

With a movement so quick she could barely follow it, he tossed his hat onto a nearby chair. His face was craggy and unshaven, and his eyes were dark with a wild glint to them whenever the light found them. He smiled, and his eyes went flat with the pitch darkness of a mine shaft.

Meg shakily rose to her feet. "Get out of my room! I mean it! Get out!" she finished with a shout.

The spirit suddenly appeared next to Meg, pushing her back onto the bed. He undid his belt quickly, his gun making a heavy *thud* when it hit the floor; the sound seemed to echo beyond the bedroom as though some bell had tolled. "Ellis hasn't had himself a woman in a long time." His breath smelled of whiskey and old cigarettes.

Meg gagged several times before she could scream, "Help me! Help!" When he reached for her shirt, she batted away his hands, but he managed to get hold of her. She kicked him and he staggered backwards, tearing her night shirt wide open.

Meg tried to run, but he recovered quickly, kicking her feet out from under her. She was stunned for a moment, giving him time to flip her onto her stomach and hold her down by the neck. With an appreciative chuckle, he pushed aside the remnants of her shirt tail to reveal her buttocks.

"Stop! Please stop! Help meeee!"

"I paid you, whore bitch!"

"No! This isn't real!" She felt him maneuver himself between her legs. "NO!"

Meg bolted upright in bed, wildly looking around the room. There didn't appear to be any ghosts in the swaths of moonlight, but she wasn't so sure about the shadows.

She took several deep breaths, telling herself it had just been a nightmare—very real, but just a nightmare! Meg took her face in her hands and sobbed. Staying here was driving her crazy. And maybe someone wanted it that way, because it was more than a coincidence that Donahue's car wasn't working either. Meg vowed to hitch a ride tomorrow.

Meg wiped her eyes. When she looked around again, she realized she wasn't in her hotel room. This room was much smaller with bare wooden floors and walls that had been poorly papered. Instead of the fine furnishings a worn chair, a freestanding closet and a cloth covered night stand filled the bedroom.

When the window rattled, she shuddered. Where was she? How did she get here? What was going on?

In the distance, Meg thought she heard a piano, then laughter, followed by hoots and hollers. Footsteps grew louder as they neared her door.

"Now isn't that a fine lookin' filly," a burly ghost said as he opened the door and waved toward Meg.

"Sure is, Pike," the tallest of his three companions agreed. Like dogs led to a bone, they followed Pike into the room. Each of the four spirits appeared pale as if they'd been bleached, yet seemed to glow with a witchy, inner light.

Meg couldn't believe this! She was still asleep, jumping from one nightmare to the next! This couldn't be happening! She tried to scream but couldn't find her voice.

"I'll bet she'll ride just fine," Pike said as he walked toward Meg's bed. The others followed, fanning out to surround the bed.

With a strangled scream, Meg jumped from her bed. The ghosts

California Ghosting | 379

set themselves to catch her, but she raced for the window. Without slowing she hurtled through it, the glass tearing flesh and dress alike. Meg slammed into something and nearly blacked out, almost losing her balance and toppling over the railing. Everything was slick... and wet. Was it raining?

Pike stuck his head out the window, leering when he saw her. "Come on boys." He began climbing out the window. "Hey, purdy whore. Come back here! We paid for you! And we don't mind a little blood or a little pain! Trev likes to bite, don't ya Trev?"

Meg glanced over the railing. Light and music spilled from the bar below, illuminating the muddy street. Hoping she wouldn't break an ankle, she slid over the railing and dropped.

Sheriff Middleton was dog-tired. To say the least, it had been a very long week. He didn't understand why they hadn't closed this place. It was more than a health hazard; it was down right dangerous. At least no one had been killed. Yet. He was going to have a heart-to-heart talk with Heller.

At the front desk, Middleton flashed his badge to a clerk, then pushed open the door to the office hallway. He was halfway to Heller's office when a wall of mist appeared, wavering before taking the shape of a young female spirit. He tried to remember her name? Fawn was it? Or Misty?

"Are you really a sheriff?"

"Sort of."

"Mac said you were."

"Peter MacGuire? Is...."

"If you wish to talk with him, come with me." Her long dress trailed behind her as she passed through the door to the lobby.

Middleton smoked three cigarettes as he trudged after her to the first floor, past the restaurant, and along the corridor. All the while he wished he'd never, ever, mentioned his wife calling the Psychic Hotline.

The ghost glanced back at him, then slipped through the greenish glass door to the pool. With a sigh, Middleton followed. Why was Mac waiting for him in the pool? Why hadn't he come to him? When he reached the bottom of the steps, the sheriff was surrounded by at least a dozen, rough-looking ghosts. Beyond them, several tied a rope between a pair of pillars. A bench had been pushed against one of the columns.

"So, you the Law?" a tall, dark ghost asked as he drifted forward. Rictor's voice was harsh and deep—a biting whisper. His coat fell long and dragged the ground. His black stetson shadowed his face, but not his cat-like eyes. "I don't like The Law. Caused me lots of trouble." Rictor fingered several holes in his jacket. "None of my boys like The Law either." He motioned to the ghosts beside him. "Especially Kindrick."

A scruffy spirit wearing an eye patch and tossing a dagger grinned, revealing several missing teeth. "Nor Delgado." The other had once been a bull of a man with wide shoulders, no neck, and a blunt nose to go along with his flat face.

Middleton couldn't see behind him, but the ghosts on his left and the right closed in. One was missing two fingers on his right hand, while the other was Mexican, his sombrero hanging across his back. "Hora de muertre, gringo. Grab'em, Chafe."

When the gang seized Middleton, he was paralyzed by a flood of sensations and images. He was in a dozen fights, sometimes shooting, sometimes brawling. He killed, raped and rode with the wind in his face and The Law at his back. He'd set fires, and laughed as first the hotel, then the entire block went up in flames. In a dark alley, he stabbed a man in the back and enjoyed it.

Middleton had the vague sense of being hauled along the pool's edge toward the makeshift gallows. "Why are you doing this?!"

"I told you. I don't like The Law. Had many a run-in with marshals, sheriffs and deputies. And you smell just like them."

"Why are you doing all of this?! Terrorizing Ghostal Shores?!" Middleton screamed, his eyes open wide and tears running down his face. He'd just experienced riding down a young boy. "At least tell me that before I die!"

They lifted Middleton atop a bench, then positioned the noose around his neck and tightened it, the rope digging into his flesh. "I don't tell The Law nothin.' I should let you suffer, but I have more important things to attend to. Delgado," Rictor said, then made a cutting motion across his throat. The massive ghost kicked the bench out from under Middleton and left him swinging.

"Now you can talk with Mac for eternity," Rictor laughed harshly.

Twenty-Nine

As Blasing and Angela walked the deserted halls hunting for ghosts, they travelled through pools of darkness nestled between table-top lanterns. Lightning flashed along the overlook corridors, followed by thunder rolling along the hallways. Except for security personnel, the resort seemed deserted. That made concentrating easier, but after a couple of hours, Blasing's head throbbed.

They hadn't seen any spirits since Elma, and Blasing worried they wouldn't see another. Several times he'd gotten a fix on a presence only to discover he'd been confused—as with the bird room—or that the ghost had just departed. Were they avoiding him? But if so, why? "You know, a week ago I didn't believe in ghosts or psychic abilities."

"Blasing, you're extremely psychic. Following your instincts and intuition may be the reason you survived thrill-seeking."

"Could be, I guess. Angela, I'm worried about Broderick and the others. We've covered all of the resort, except for the service corridor and the garage." He'd even stood at the northern exit, reaching out into the muddy construction yard. Maybe it had just been too far. With the treacherous nature of the construction area, they'd decided not to venture out in the dark.

"You know, I think it's time for a break. A snack and something to drink would go a long way in reviving our flagging effort. On the way, let's stop at Dr. Strange's room. Maybe they have news," Angela said.

"I hope they're having better luck," Blasing told her, then snapped his fingers. "You know, we should get Walkie-Talkies from security and pass them out. Not everyone has a cellular phone."

"Good idea."

"I'm still concerned that the backup generator didn't kick in. George told me it was working fine." Lightning flashed, then thunder cracked in staccato-fashion. "Damn!"

"What?!"

"I forgot to call Patrick and Kelly earlier today."

"You can use my phone," Angela said.

Blasing glanced at his watch. "It's too late now. Boy, am I going to hear it."

Angela laughed. "I'll speak on your behalf."

"Thanks."

"Well, surprise," Angela said. "Here comes Nate Tucker, the maintenance manager." Tucker was a rangy man dressed in faded green overalls, a GSR baseball cap, and a full belt of tools that clanked with each step.

"Evening, Nate."

"Ms. Starborne." Tucker tipped his hat. "Mr. Madera."

"What's wrong with the generator?" Blasing asked.

"Don't know yet, I'm heading there now."

"Good luck," Blasing said. He started to walk away, then stopped and turned to watch Tucker.

"Something wrong?" Angela asked.

"I thought I felt a ghost."

Angela was alarmed. "Do you think he's possessed?"

"Let's find out." As they grew closer, Blasing once again felt the presence. They followed Tucker into the dark service corridor and caught up with him near a tall green-metal fence. The sign above the gate read "Electrical KEEP OUT."

"Mind if we tag along?" Angela asked a surprised Tucker.

"I want to see all the operation," Blasing told him.

"Even the back-up generator?" he eyed Blasing uncertainly. Blasing nodded. "Gonna be a new age of management all right," Tucker muttered as he unlocked the gate. "This way." His halogen beam illuminating their way, Tucker led them along a breezy passage where rain and thunder could be clearly heard once more.

"Still feel it?" Angela asked. Blasing nodded. "Me too."

"Almost brand new," Tucker said, motioning to the generator. "Just bought it in October. It's diesel-powered, so we gotta have ventilation."

Blasing and Angela watched as he laid out his tools. "Nate, does a ghost reside down here?"

"Jonathan used to. But since they installed the cameras, I haven't seen him."

"Jonathan, please speak with us," Blasing called out. Tucker shook his head as if thinking he worked for crazy people.

"Please," Angela echoed. "We want to help."

While Tucker worked on the generator, a mist rose from the maintenance manager's back. He didn't notice. "If only you could," the ghost replied.

"What are you doing?" She motioned to Tucker.

"Whoa," Tucker muttered as he leaned against the generator. "Dizzy all of a sudden." Blasing steadied him.

"Hiding from the hunting posses," Jonathan replied. "They're rounding up everyone. Staying near a person confuses them."

"Are they hurting you?" Angela asked.

"I don't know for sure, but I think I've felt some of the others die. Barney, and maybe Janice."

"But you're already dead," Blasing stammered.

"I know. I can't explain it. I just feel it."

"Do you know this Lon Rictor?" Blasing asked.

"An evil spirit," Jonathan replied, looking warily all around. "He's the boss now. They all work for him. I didn't think they could follow me down here; then the generator went out, too."

"Possessing Nate would usually make it easier to handle being down here?" Blasing asked.

"Yup, usually there's so many insects I can't stand to be down here, and neither can any of the other spirits."

"Do you know anything else about Rictor or the other ghosts?"

Tucker moaned again, slumped a little more, then screamed as he jerked upright. After a quivering moment, Tucker collapsed. Jonathan leapt free and raced for the ceiling where he disappeared.

Blasing jerked back, his head spinning. When Angela moved to help Tucker, Blasing cried out, "Don't touch him! The generator's shorted-out! He might be conducting!"

"He's fallen clear," she said.

Still groggy, Blasing moved to Tucker's side and checked for breathing and a pulse. When he found neither, he began CPR, tilting Tucker's head and performing rescue breathing interspersed with chest compressions. "Fourteen, fifteen,... Angela, call somebody on his Walkie-Talkie," Blasing said, then breathed twice for Tucker, his chest slowly rising. "One, two, three...."

Angela grabbed the Walkie-Talkie. "Security! We need a doctor! What?! Oh?! He's there! Wait... Geoff! Geoff, we're in the generator room. Nate Tucker was electrocuted! He's on his way," she told Blasing.

"Ah!" he exclaimed. "We've got a pulse! And he's breathing!" While they waited, Blasing covered Tucker with his jacket and monitored his condition.

"What do you think happened to Jonathan?" Angela asked.

"I'm not sure. I was so focused on Tucker, I lost track of him," Blasing mused.

"Well, at least he wasn't torn apart like Grant and Carrie. I hope Jonathan's found another place to hide. You look exhausted."

"Could be why I missed the presence of another ghost."

"It could have been an accident." They stared at each other for several seconds before she agreed. "I don't think so either."

"What do we do about the ghosts?" Blasing asked, then took her hand. "This is worse than a nightmare."

"It appears we'll have to drive them out," she said.

"Look at what's happened, Angela, and you still won't leave."

"I know, you have children..." she began as she moved closer.

"ANGELA!" came Dr. Landrum's call.

"Over here, Geoff! He's breathing!"

A flashlight was the second sign, then Dr. Landrum and two security guards came jogging breathlessly toward them. One was carrying an oxygen tank, while the other had a backboard. "How's he doing?" Dr. Landrum asked. He knelt by Tucker and checked his vital signs.

"Breathing's steady, but his pulse is a little fast."

"You look tired," Angela said. "Is anything else wrong?"

"Been busy already," Dr. Landrum said as he adjusted his glasses. "He's stable. In through his hands and out through his feet." He motioned to Tucker's melted sneakers. "The best thing we can do is give him oxygen, load 'em and give him someplace comfortable to rest while we wait for an ambulance." He motioned to the guys. They set down the backboard and began carefully loading the unconscious man. Dr. Landrum checked the oxygen, turned on the tank, then attached the mask to Tucker's face.

"Geoff, what's going on?"

"Lots of things. First, there was a crash in the garage." He explained about the accident. Nobody had been seriously hurt, though they had to extricate one of the drivers. The biggest stink was over the main exit being blocked. The other exit was closed because of the power outage. Tawny Lane was in shock and kept mumbling about a locomotive.

"But those... images are just psychic emanations. They're not real," Angela said.

"Tell that to Chief Porter and Mr. Cash. They've both had strokes," Dr. Landrum told them. A bellhop on an errand from Heller had found Cash. I don't expect him to survive the night. A security guard found Porter dead on his office floor."

Angela looked at Blasing. Both wondered if it was murder. "Anything else?" Angela asked.

Dr. Landrum sighed and told them about the drunk salesman; he'd broken his neck in the ballroom. Earlier a drunken woman had fallen down the steps. She was supposedly chasing jewelry. Fortunately, she'd only broken an arm. "That's two dead and seven injured, not counting the barroom incidents. Blasing, I implore you to help me shut down this place. Please talk with Heller."

"Maybe tonight will convince him."

"I spoke with him a while ago, and he seems to think this is all very coincidental. Two accidents involved drunks, and as I said, Porter is overweight. Add to that, valet parking admitted they were hurrying."

"I think we'll go talk with Heller, now," Blasing said.

"Last I saw him, he was in Cash's room."

Angela and Blasing exchanged glances, thinking they knew what the Irishman was doing. "Geoff, please keep me posted."

"Sure thing."

"Kerry, give Angela your Walkie-Talkie," Blasing told one guard. "I'm going to keep Tucker's. Geoff, be at Heller's office in the morning. Eight o'clock sharp."

"I'll be there."

They were walking along Old West Avenue when Blasing felt a tremor. "Oh, oh."

"What's wrong?" Angela asked.

"Didn't you feel that?"

"Wasn't that thunder?" she asked. Blasing shook his head, then dropped to all fours, putting an ear to the floor. "Stampede?"

"Sounds like it," he replied tersely as he stood. The quaking grew more prominent, the doors shaking and rattling as the lamp posts rocked from side to side. A pounding as if a massive drum were being beaten faster and faster grew ever closer.

"Which direction?"

"Ahead of us, coming toward us," Blasing said, then shivered as a cool breeze passed him. "Did you feel that?"

"A ghost?"

"I think so. Angela, let's find cover!" Blasing suggested as he grabbed her hand and headed away from the thundering herd. It didn't seem to help; enraged, wailing moos grew louder and louder. "Stampeding bulls this time!"

"Why run? They're just images." Angela asked, expecting to have to drag her feet, but he stopped and looked around.

"What happened to the hallway?" The corridor had disappeared. They stood in a long canyon of reddish rock. "That's incredible." Angela touched the wall. "I know the apothecary is here. I'm sure of it!" She closed her eyes, feeling for the door.

The ground shook, and the sound travelled along the rock walls, feeling as if dueling locomotives charged toward them. Small rocks fell, bounding down the cliffs and bouncing across the floor of the narrow canyon.

"Come on," Blasing said, barely audible over the rumbling.

"But Blasing, I almost...." Her fingers slipped from the door handle as he dragged her away. "Dammit!"

"I'm trying to save your life!"

"I'm not scared! I'd found the door to the apothecary! Blasing, these canyon walls aren't real! The stampede isn't real!" She glanced over her shoulder to see a herd of ghostly bulls rampaging forward. The dust swirling about them obscured their numbers. Bloodied and jagged horns sliced the dirty cloud. The lead one staggered, then fell.

"Sorry," Blasing apologized.

Angela moved to the wall and searched again. Blasing joined her, frantically looking into shadowy niches for cover, but they were all shallow. The walls were smooth and impossible to climb. "We're stuck."

"Blasing, none of this is real!"

"We have to outrun them!"

"NO!" she cried, continuing to search for the doorway. If she could open it, then she could prove what she'd been telling him; this wasn't real.

"You may not be scared, but I am." He was ready to run.

"That's because they're ghostly images! The spirits spook you, maybe even on a subconscious level, because you're sensitive!" She felt along the storefront, following the window frame.

"Are your last words to me going to be psycho-babble?" he said harshly.

"They're not my last words!" She felt the door jamb, then found the door again. "Ah!" She grabbed the handle and yanked on it. It didn't open. "Damn! It's locked. Blasing, do you remember what Candy said about the phantasms? They're just memories. If you don't give them life, they won't have any."

"I'm still not sure I believe that ghosts telling each other stories is causing this," he snapped.

"Maybe that's not the cause, but they aren't any more real than what you saw when Broderick touched you!" The thundering herd was deafeningly close. "Don't you see? This type of thing could cause heart attacks and shock! Look at you!"

"So, I just stand here and let them run over me saying it's just an illusion! It's just an illusion?!"

"Say it's not real!" she told him, squeezing his hands. "If it helps, don't watch! FOCUS ON SOMETHING! PRETEND YOU'RE SKIING SOMEWHERE! YOU KNOW, VISUAL IMAGING! ARE YOU FAMILIAR WITH THAT?"

He nodded, but she could tell he wasn't doing very well. As the stampede grew closer, it was hard to stand. The desperate calls of the bellowing herd were loud even over the deafening sound of their pounding hoofs. Blasing kept glancing at the oncoming mass, and Angela knew she had to do something, so she kissed him.

At first, she could hear, almost feel the rampaging herd, then it blended with the roaring in her ears. She parted her lips and kissed him passionately, her tongue intertwining with his. His hands kneaded her back, and they strained against each other as if trying to start a fire.

They were still kissing when she finally noticed that the stampede was long gone and Old West Avenue had returned. She gave him one last kiss, then gently pulled away. "It's all clear."

"Too bad," he replied, still holding her gaze.

"Now, Mr. Madera," Angela began sternly, pointing at him scoldingly, "next time I'm onto something, don't grab me and haul me off. I have ideas, you know. I CAN think for myself. I made it through law school, DESPITE male assistance, and I was taking care of myself just fine before you came along!"

"I'm sorry, Angela. My first instinct was to run."

"Just remember, we're partners, and I have an opinion."

"That goes without saying, but it doesn't always have to be served hot, Counselor," he said.

"Point well taken," Angela agreed, cutting the tension. "Fight or flight," she sighed, letting her anger drain away. "It's all right, Blasing. It's that damned security mentality. It forces knee jerk reactions and inhibits creativity. What did your intuition say?"

Blasing was thoughtful. "I'm not sure."

"The ghost's interfere with it?"

"Either that, or my... fear of them does."

"They still frighten you?"

"Don't they you?" Blasing asked.

Angela nodded, then smiled. "Certainly. You've come quite a long way in dealing with them. Now I suspect you're hungry."

"Very. But let's stop by security first. I want to leave Candy a Walkie-Talkie."

"She grows on you, doesn't she?"

"Like a kooky relative," Blasing said.

Angela laughed, then said, "Hey, this gives me an idea."

"What?"

"Something I want to try. I have some crushed hematite. I wonder what it would do to phantoms?"

"More hocus pocus," Blasing groaned.

When they reached security, they discovered the offices were dark and deserted, the black monitors staring at them with vacant eyes. All the equipment was quiet, except for a Walkie-Talkie. Voices came and went—many concerned and some scared, Ghostal Shores sounding as if it were under siege. Blasing searched the area and a cache of Walkie-Talkies in a metal cabinet. He expropriated three. Blasing started to leave, then paused, caught by a nagging idea. "I want to check Porter's office." It was locked, but after trying a dozen keys on his ring, Blasing found the one that opened it. A visual inspection didn't reveal anything amiss, although they found a packed duffel bag under the desk.

"Looks like he was planning to leave." Angela unzipped it and began digging.

"What are you doing?"

"Playing detective. Why would he be leaving right now?"

"Why would anyone want to stay?" Blasing countered.

Angela stuck out her tongue. After a little more searching, she pulled a video tape from the bag. "I wonder what's on this?"

"*Ghost* with Swayze and Moore?" he chuckled. She groaned. "Well, we won't know until the power comes back on."

While Angela continued rifling through the bag, Blasing carefully scoured the office. "Hey, I may have found something," he said, loosening a panel along a wall to reveal a VCR. "Think there's a connection?"

"Yes. Something very interesting must be on this tape."

"Let's get out of here before someone comes back." Blasing returned the panel to its proper place.

"Well, well," Angela said. "Look what I found." She opened a small silver case and found a plastic bag containing white powder.

"Wipe your prints off and leave it," Blasing said. "We'll get Sheriff Middleton to stop by."

The lights flickered, then came on. With whirring and clicks as though a great colossus coming to life, all the equipment began to function once more. "Guess they got things back on line," Blasing said. "Let's get out of here." They quickly re-arranged things, then departed before any of the guards returned.

On the way to the elevator, they called the sheriff's room but didn't get an answer. "He might be out investigating the deaths Geoff mentioned," Angela said. "Blasing, I'm tired."

"I am too. Just a few quick stops, then to the suite."

They stopped at Candy and Rod's room, leaving a Walkie-Talkie. At Dr. Strange's room, everyone had left but Madame Zanadane and Mr. Chung. "What is your take on all of this, Madame?"

"Obviously, there is a plethora of spirits and such a gathering is magnifying etheric manifestation... meaning their thoughts and day-dreams are becoming near real...."

"Very real," Blasing murmured.

"... hence the odd visions many have experienced.... It's incredible.... I was just stepping out to try and encounter one to study it.... Would you care to join me...?"

"No thanks," Blasing replied. "We've seen them."

"You'll get a full sensory experience." Angela said.

"Elma and Jonathan mentioned something about being rounded up by posses. Claimed some had been... killed... further," Blasing told the hypnotic-eyed psychic.

"I've never heard of such a thing..." the psychic gasped. "I shall ponder it.... Let's meet in the morning...."

"A good idea," Angela said. "Maybe we can figure out some sort of strategy."

"There'll probably be a mass exodus in the morning."

"People fear the unknown, giving it power where otherwise it has none." Madame Zanadane told Blasing, her hypnotic eyes locked on him. "Don't be fooled, Mr. Madera.... Come along Mr. Chung...." The mammoth valet and Dr. Strange joined her.

"Going outside?" Angela asked the psychic. Dr. Strange was dressed for foul weather.

"Yes. All this spiritual energy is wreaking havoc with my abilities," Dr. Strange replied around his pipe.

"Then you haven't been able to access the Akashic Records?"

"That's correct. It's as if a wall has been erected."

"Do you think it's intentional?" Blasing asked.

"No. I spoke incorrectly and with irritation," he said, sounding very Bostonian. "Static is a more appropriate term. I intend to walk as far away from the resort as necessary to escape it."

"Maybe one of us will discover something...." Madame Zanadane breathed.

"Well, be careful," Blasing said.

"Indeed. We have been informed much has gone awry. But fear not, I wear the Talisman of Yaegy," Dr. Strange told them. With a nod, he closed the door behind him, then the threesome departed.

"Too weird," Blasing said. "What are the Akashic Records?"

"The memories and records of the human race—it's history so to speak, although since time isn't linear, its past, present and future are available," she said. Blasing's expression was disbelief. "It's a psychic skill to be able to access it."

Blasing didn't say another word until after they'd reached the Great Xantini's room. With dark bags under his eyes and mussed hair, the Master Mentalist looked exhausted. Angela almost felt sad about asking him if he'd discovered anything, until he finished her sentence. "Yes. I am feeling better, and have been doing some scanning. What strikes me oddest, is that security is hiding something. I bumped into Chief Porter earlier today. I hate to be the one to inform you, Blasing, but your security chief has a drug problem."

"Thanks. But he doesn't have one anymore. He's...."

"Dead? Oh dear. He'll never be able to run his blackmail scam then."

"Interesting that you can read their minds, but the ghosts can't read their spirits," Angela murmured.

"Do you know who he was blackmailing?" Blasing asked. Xantini shook his head. "Have you...."

"Scanned Mr. Heller? No, I'm afraid not. He seems to be successfully avoiding me. But now, Mr. Cash is a different story. He is afraid something is about to be discovered, though I'm not sure what. Oh, he's near death from a stroke. Porter and Cash. Hmmm. Seems like a conspiracy, doesn't it?"

"Anything involving Peter's murder?" Angela asked.

"I don't know. But my comrade seems to be concerned that I'm investigating," he told them.

"Why is Madame Zanadane worried?" Angela asked.

"I don't know. Her mind is closed to me. What did you say about the ghosts being unable to read their spirits?" Xantini asked. Angela explained what Broderick, Ingrid and Elma had told her. "That is odd," Xantini replied. "Security and some of the salespeople. Hmmm. I, too, am at a loss."

"Well, thanks for your help," Angela began.

"But you are tired, as am I. Goodnight then," Xantini started to close the door. Before Angela could speak, he said, "Oh, certainly. I would be glad to meet with everyone in the morning to discuss strategy. Eight? At Mr. Heller's office?"

"Goodnight Efrem," Blasing said, taking Angela's arm. The way he read their minds really bothered him.

"Not as strange as you might think, Blasing," Xantini called after him. "No more odd than sensing ghosts and 'reading' people at a glance."

"GOOD NIGHT!" Angela emphasized, dragging Blasing along

"Too damn strange," Blasing said. "I'm surrounded by kooks."

"Even me?"

"And a beautiful eccentric," he amended.

"You're surprisingly eloquent," Angela said and squeezed his hand. "You know, I'm becoming more and more concerned about Madame Zanadane. Although we didn't see her do anything odd during the second séance, she knew about the hematite. Efrem thinks she's hiding something."

Blasing waited outside their suite, sensing for ghosts. At first he didn't feel anything, then, "Hey, there's one here!"

"Where?!" Angela asked. Less than a yard away, a misty column appeared, widening as it thickened, taking the form of a stout man. "Peter!" "I'm so glad to see you!" She wanted to hug him, but something kept her from it, despite his broad, warm smile.

"I'm sorry I've stayed away from ye, Angela, me lovely counselor. I wish it t'were otherwise."

"Mac, what's going on?" Blasing asked.

"Why aren't ya listenin' ta me, Blaise? Not that ye ever did." His green eyes radiated sadness. "I fear for ye, son. And you, Angela. Ya must both leave as soon as ye ken! Now! Rictor is evil and 'tis dangerous ta stay, even in your protected room."

"Why are you scared of him? How can we help?" Angela asked.

"Leave, so I won't be aworryin' bout ye. He holds ya safety over me head, and I dona want ye ta join me. Don't ye worry. I can handle 'em." Mac's spirit glanced over his shoulder. "I must be goin'! Quickly, into your room, now!" He faded away.

"Peter!" Angela cried.

"Don't give him away," Blasing whispered as he opened the door, then quickly pulled Angela inside. "I guess we should pack." He held her close, staring into her eyes. She appeared troubled.

Angela frowned. "I don't know. Peter can be too stubborn to ask for help. Let me think on it. Something doesn't seem right."

"All right," Blasing sighed. "But he's not the only one who's stubborn." She glared. "Okay, we need to watch the tape, anyway. I'm surprised Xantini didn't mention we had one in our possession, just expropriated from the bag of a recently deceased coke-snorting chief of security. Maybe he was just being tactful," Blasing said.

"Not again," Angela said. The lounge was trashed, lamps smashed, furniture overturned, and drawers and closets emptied, their contents scattered across the floor. "Lilly," Angela cursed as she walked to her room. All her drawers were emptied, clothes everywhere. A trail of cosmetics led to the bathroom. "Damn! It looks like she got in here, too! Check your room!"

Blasing did. "It's trashed."

Angela moved about her room, checking the crystal grid. "Blasing, the grid is in place. She couldn't have been the one."

"Then what do you think?"

"That whoever did this is looking for something and thought that by trashing the place, they'd lay the blame on the ghosts."

Blasing whistled. "Could be. Do you think it was security?"

"I don't know, but since Porter appeared to be blackmailing Heller, it seems logical."

Blasing returned to the door and put a chair under the knob, then set a planter in it. "Just in case."

"Your room is less trashed." Angela walked into his room.

As he joined her, heading directly for the entertainment center, Blasing said, "At least the power is on." While she removed her shoes and bra, Blasing set up the VCR. "Ready to go."

"Come here," Angela said, her arms wide open.

Blasing pressed 'play' and joined her on the bed. After several long, languid kisses, Blasing said, "Do you think we should inform the others about Mac's ghost and his warning?"

"Why? You don't think they would believe you, do you? To tell the truth, I really don't understand why Peter appeared just now. He didn't tell us anything new."

"He's right to be concerned. People are dying."

"Why now? Why not earlier? You know, it might not have really been Peter. Remember, the ghosts can change shape." Angela glanced at the screen. "Hey, that's Heller's office."

"Think Porter was blackmailing Heller?"

"That's what the Master Mentalist implied."

They watched for a while, the tape running, showing: Heller at work—on the phone, yelling at someone, doing origami. Eventually they fell asleep.

THIRTY

Heading down the stairs, Blasing and Angela were running a bit late. The power failed again, so the elevators were paralyzed. With the emergency lighting on the blink, the stairwell was pitch black. Blasing used his penlight to illuminate their way.

"You have the tape, right?" Angela asked.

"Yes." Blasing patted his jacket. After last night, he didn't trust leaving it in the room.

"Hey!" Angela said, stopping suddenly on the stairs. "I must have been really tired last night. The other day Cash gave me mail to deliver to Heller. The package felt like it had a video tape in it. Maybe Heller has a clip off this tape!"

"Not much we can do until the power returns."

"Search Heller's office," Angela suggested.

When they couldn't exit at the lobby level because of the crush of people, they backtracked to the first floor and descended through a crowd to the landing above the lobby. "Chaos," Angela breathed.

"They must have cleared the parking garage exit, so everyone wants to leave right now," Blasing said.

The lobby was gray, a few battery powered lanterns adding to the faded light coming in the front entrance. Security had tried to rope off areas and keep things organized, but there were too many people jammed around overloaded carts. Valets pleaded for people to move, but there wasn't any place to go. The crush had spilled over onto Old West Avenue for as far as they could see. Some patrons even waited outside, getting soaked by the blowing rain.

Except for the front desk staff, everybody was dressed for stormy travel. Umbrellas were brandished, sometimes used to poke and prod, causing tempers to flare and harsh words to be exchanged. Exclamations, encouragement, and impatience blended incongruously into a cacophonic roar. Each time the doors opened, letting in damp gusts of wind, people looked up expectantly.

"Mr. Megellan, your car is ready!" a bellman yelled. One couple cheered. Others groaned, complained, or cursed, eyes angrily alight and faces etched with frustration. One impatient patron shoved another; the confrontation threatened to escalate beyond face to face shouting, but cooler heads prevailed, and the pair were restrained.

Angela was concerned by the anxiety and barely curtailed fear obvious in so many faces. Their eyes told her they didn't care what they had to do to leave; big money flashed as if dollars were pesos. When they saw this wasn't working, violence came to mind. "This is not good at all. Where's Heller?"

With Chadwick nearby, Heller stood on a stool near the front desk. "A free night's lodging and dinner if you'll stay with us one more day! This is a memorable experience! Nothing like it may ever happen again!"

Many waved him off. Others jeered and cursed him. "I hope to Hell not!" "Too dangerous!" "How many people have been hurt already?!" "I was crazy to come here." "Damn you to Hell, I'm suing!"

Heller looked hopelessly at his customers, then glared at the reporters. Looking frazzled, Tawny Lane and Al Murly were still hard at work, recording the mass exodus. Not everyone wanted to be interviewed, but most had nothing else to do, and this might be their fleeting moment of fame.

"I wonder why Tawny's mad at Heller?" Blasing wondered aloud, noticing that each time the reporter glanced at the Irishman, her expression tightened and her eyes narrowed.

"She can join the crowd. I wonder if anybody's staying?" Angela asked. "Ow, what an elbow shot. That man may need to see a dentist. You know, I think that was a salesman. Hey! I see several of them trying to get to Heller."

"I'm not surprised. We won't need to shut down operations if everyone leaves," Blasing said

"IF we can convince Heller to let the employees leave, too. We'll need help, and I don't see the sheriff, Geoff, or any of the psychics. Let's move closer. Follow me."

As they jostled their way through the throng toward Heller, Angela heard snatches of conversation. "I'm glad I'm getting out of here. My room was on fire, I'm telling you, then it just flamed-out." "Don't worry dear, we'll call our lawyer as soon as we get home." "Inexcusable." "She just appeared on my bed and started stripping. What a body! Oh baby, if she were only flesh!" "Felt like the Old West." "It sounded just like there was a blacksmith in the hall. Too weird for me, Deb." "Scared the bejesus out of me." "They stampeded down the hallway. I swore they were coming into my room!"

Somebody stepped on her foot. Angela almost lost a shoe. She grabbed at Blasing's jacket to keep from falling.

"I don't know why I got so angry. I'm sorry I hit you," a young man with a bruised face said. Several in the group appeared to be nursing injuries. "Said my arm was broken." "I have five God-damned stitches." "You know, I've always wanted to be in a barroom brawl, but now...."

"How're you doing?!" Blasing yelled back to her. He bumped into somebody, who whirled about, fists poised and ready. "What in the hell do ya think you're doing?!"

"Undercover security," Blasing responded. "This woman is highly contagious and we need to get her to the front desk and out of the crowd as soon as possible."

"Highly contagious," the man stammered. Blasing nodded. The man immediately stepped back, whispering the words. They spread quickly.

"Great response," Angela chuckled.

"Lawyeritis."

After that, they experienced little trouble reaching Heller and the salespeople crowding around him. "This is ridiculous!" Heller yelled. "Eva, talk some sense into them! This is the opportunity of a lifetime!" The Frenchwoman simply stared longingly toward the front exit.

"A little trouble and you want to leave!" Heller shouted. "You were told there would be ghosts! You haven't even been here a week! If this is your mettle, then I fire you! You're all fired!"

"Screw you, Heller, and the horse you rode in on," a well-dressed man with lank hair and butchered nose said. "Tom's dead."

"Now listen here...." Heller began. Chadwick stepped next to Heller.

The rest of security became alert and wary.

"Dead?" a woman near Blasing asked. Her face paled.

"Did someone die?" someone behind her asked.

"Die?" The word spread quickly, seizing everyone's attention. Their reactions were the same: fear slowly growing into panic. Their expressions asked, would they be next? All eyes turned to Heller.

"You listen!" the enraged salesman surged forward.

Two salespeople grabbed him. "Come on Harry, it isn't worth the trouble, and you know it," Alicia Perez told him. Harry yanked his arm away and pushed himself through the crowd, setting off a chain reaction of shoves and skirmishes.

"Someone died!" "He was murdered by the ghosts!" "We could be next!" "Have to get out of here!" The shoves became harder, some people driven to the floor. Fists and elbows flew, the crowd surging toward the front door.

"People! People please!" Heller yelled. "Please be calm! We're doing the best we can, as fast as we can!" The mass surged forward.

Blasing fought his way to Heller. "Get down! Let me try!"

"But what...." Heller began. Not waiting, Blasing pulled the Irishman from the box and climbed up.

Blasing foresaw seconds before the crowd would trample the valets and each other. Wishing there was another way, he drew Mac's gun and fired several times into the wall. As the echo reverberated, Blasing yelled out, "NOW THAT I HAVE YOUR ATTENTION, LISTEN TO ME! THIS IS FOR YOUR OWN SAFETY!"

Just like everyone else, Angela was astonished, her attention riveted to Blasing and the smoking gun. He appeared larger than life, a heroic figure here to prevent disaster and lead them to safety. Well, she could dream, Angela mused.

"I'm sorry to get your attention in such a jarring fashion, but it seemed necessary! I am not a danger to you, but you were becoming a danger to yourselves. First, let me say there were heart attacks last night and accidents, but there isn't any proof that a ghost killed anyone." That announcement led to a lot of murmuring, but there were plenty of relieved faces.

"Second, Ghostal Shores is very concerned about your welfare and wishes your departure to proceed in a safe, orderly manner. Effective immediately, we are expediting cars based on lowest to highest claim check numbers. Politely turn in your claim check to the closest valet. If you're not in the top twenty, I recommend you adjourn to the restaurant or upstairs foyer. You'll be paged. In the meantime enjoy a complimentary buffet breakfast."

Angela watched the crowd carefully. Although some responded negatively, probably from those with very high numbers, most seemed to relax. Many approved of the orderly approach. Others were simply intimidated by Blasing's firearm.

"I didn't agree to any of this!" Heller grabbed Blasing's jacket.

With a cool look, Blasing slapped the Irishman's hand away. "For your information, it's never wise to grab a man with a gun, especially when he isn't afraid to use it." Heller stammered. Chadwick carefully watched him. "I'm saving you money in goodwill and preventing violence. Besides, you were offering free dinners anyway. Now let the kitchen staff know immediately."

Heller shouted to the front desk. A young man took off running.

"Why don't we close for a couple of days?" Blasing asked. "Let things die... calm down some."

"It might save us some legal problems if we show we tried to be responsible," Angela told him. "Proving accepted risk won't be hard if we react to the changes."

Heller puffed up as if ready to explode, then seemed to gain control of himself. After some thought, he said, "You sound like that damned doctor and that empty-headed sheriff. Like them, none of you have any authority here."

"I'm talking about common sense," Blasing said.

"There are people here who don't want to leave," Heller countered. "I've spoken with them. Go to the restaurant if you don't believe me. Talk with them. They loved last night's events so much they've booked more time. Even more would be coming if it wasn't for this shitty weather. The problem is those who want to leave," he waved to the crowd, "want to leave this instant!"

Heller was thoughtful for a moment, then continued, "Tell you what, Ms. Starborne. Any staff that wants to leave today, can go. We can probably manage understaffed considering the current conditions, but I'll offer bonuses to stay."

"That's fine," Blasing said.

"Bravo, Blasing, that was inspired," Dr. Landrum said as he approached. "I was afraid they were going to trample each other. Now things will go much more smoothly, unless the ghosts act up again."

"They appear to be more active at night," Angela said.

"Well, maybe by then, Madame Zanadane can cleanse this place," Heller said.

"I'd like to discuss that, as well as what happened last night, and what might happen tonight," Dr. Landrum said.

"YOU WANT ME TO CLOSE, TOO!" Heller immediately flushed.

Dr. Landrum motioned to the offices. "In private, please."

"All right," Heller grumbled. He led them down the hallway to his lantern-lit office.

"What happened to your wall?" Blasing asked, nodding to the hole. The drywall near the ceiling had been ripped open. In the shadows of the recess, wires splayed in every direction.

"Damned ghosts nearly tore apart my office," Heller groused.

Angela looked around. The place was a mess, but it looked more like sloppy construction work. "Same thing happened to us," she said. Blasing gave her a look, and she immediately thought of Porter's video tape.

"Sit where you can," Heller said, dropping heavily into his throne-like leather chair.

Angela sat, but Blasing and Dr. Landrum remained standing. "These are the facts. We've had three deaths...."

"Earl died about an hour ago," Heller informed them.

"My point," Dr. Landrum continued. "Three dead and a dozen injuries last night—not including either bar incident, which led to another twenty-some injured. Some are directly attributable to the ghosts, some only speculatively."

"You said Porter and Cash suffered heart attacks...."

"But what was the cause? What caused Mr. Tucker's electrocution, the collision in the garage...."

"... accidents...."

"... the woman falling down the stairs? The man breaking his neck in the ballroom?"

"Tom Becker was a lousy drunk."

"The woman claimed she followed her stolen jewelry which was floating down the stairs."

"She'd been drinking!"

"Wake up, Heller!" Angela snapped. "Or you'll lose everything!"

"Another man swore he was robbed and knifed by a ghost," Dr. Landrum continued.

"Impossible!"

"After what I saw happen in the barroom yesterday," Candy said as she entered the office, "I'd say almost anything is possible."

"Who invited you?!"

"We should've known something was wrong with the arrival of the stagecoaches," Candy finished calmly.

"Part of the charm of Ghostal Shores," Heller rebutted. "I just held a meeting with the ghosts yesterday evening and...."

"Rictor claims he's the boss of Ghostal Shores," Angela interrupted.

Heller blanched. "Preposterous! A ghost can't run things!"

"And I fear he's doing something to make the transients—the outlaws— even... stronger," Angela told him. "Fear could do that. It's a way to steal power."

"Ridiculous!" Heller pounded his fist on the desk. His eyes were wild and his face red. "You're not experts!"

"I believe she is right...." Madame Zanadane glided into the office. "I feel the ghosts with every fiber of my being, and they are certainly stronger than before.... Can't you feel it...? It charges the very air itself...." Mr. Chung was behind her, eyes looking everywhere as if expecting a ghostly attack.

Behind them waited Julie Zephren clad in black stirrup pants and a gold jacket, the Great Xantini in his usual baggy, black attire, and Dr. Strange dressed as if for outdoors in his hat and long jacket. "Now the gang's all here," Angela said.

"Rictor is evil, just as he was in life," Dr. Strange began.

"...and he will stop at nothing to make this place his," Xantini finished, looking very grave.

"You've discovered something?" Angela asked.

"Unfortunately no. Just a flash of intuition," the Bostonian psychic replied. "Something's disrupting all of my artifacts, even from the main road." Dr. Strange lit his pipe and puffed, which elicited a glare from Heller.

"M'ah tarot readin' agrees with 'em," Julie drawled.

"Hokum!" Heller spat.

"But why?" Angela asked.

"A hideout for his gang?" Dr. Landrum suggested.

"A decidedly authoritarian point of view," Xantini observed, eyeing the doctor with a speculative expression.

"I read ah gatherin' of forces," Julie agreed.

"I concur, though the motive escapes me...."

"Hauntings usually involve the past," Candy pointed out.

"Then we keep digging," Xantini said. "All will be revealed in time."

"True," Madame Zanadane breathed, but if we cannot clear this place of the malevolent spirits by evening, I believe it wisest to close as soon as possible... by morning at the latest."

"Hurray," Dr. Landrum responded. Heller sputtered.

"We agree," Blasing said, nodding to Angela.

"We'll lose too much money!" Heller protested.

"A drop in the bucket," Angela said. "Ghostal Shores' reputation is more important than a few days' profits."

"Madame Zanadane," Heller began, "this place is my livelihood. I must show my customers and the world Ghostal Shores is safe! The reporters are getting this tragedy on video, and soon the world will know. Help me!"

The eerie-eyed psychic was silent for a moment, then said, "The abundance of spirits gathered in one place, especially such vile and malicious ones, creates an etheric field which manifests phantasms based upon the spirit's thoughts.... I believe this field will grow stronger, causing even more problems over time.... Soon, they may be more than just visions, just as they are now more than thoughts...." Blasing and Angela exchanged glances. "But how they are growing stronger...? I can only speculate, but I suspect Ms. Starborne is right.... Fear steals energy from us..."

"Mr. Heller, where are the bricks from?" Dr. Strange asked.

"Yes," Angela said. "That might explain something."

"I need to know, Sean.... Knowing names and origins are essential to cleansing...." Madame Zanadane's hypnotic eyes appeared to make the Irishman nervous.

"Bodie, California, by way of Los Angeles," Heller finally answered, giving Angela the evil eye. "After World War II, Ella Cain— the owner of Bodie and several other ghost towns—was having tax problems, so she sold some of the buildings. The brick was used to build a warehouse in L.A. in 1946. It was used sporadically because the owner and tenants believed it was haunted. Mac discovered this and convinced me to buy the place and ship the materials here."

"That was his second mistake," Angela murmured. Heller glared at her. "We saw Peter's ghost last night."

"Both of you?" Candy asked. Angela nodded. "What did he say?"

"That matters would get worse, and that there's a struggle between ghosts. To leave ASAP," Angela summarized. "I'm not sure it was him. Ghosts can change their appearance."

"But why would someone imitate Peter MacGuire?" Dr. Strange asked.

"To get them to leave," Xantini offered. Angela nodded.

"They're reacting just like outlaws of the Old West, having that peculiar brand of fun robbing, stampeding, and performing malicious acts," Dr. Strange agreed.

"Times haven't really changed," Angela muttered.

"But why was Rictor recruiting?" Xantini mused.

"Because it's his nature.... All ghosts stay on earth for one particular reason... Rictor's is to lord over others.... If he passes beyond the veil, he won't be able to do that...."

"He's hunting down the ghosts to force them to join the gang?" Angela asked. That didn't feel right to her. Something else was going on, but she couldn't figure out what. Candy's mention of history rang truer.

"I should never have let them stay," Heller said.

"A cleansing will be difficult, but with help from all of you, I believe Rictor can be expunged.... Then the others will follow...."

"When?" Blasing asked.

"I need some time... just after noon would be best, when the daylight is strongest and the spirits are weakest...."

"During twilight, certain etheric portals open," Dr. Strange said.

"I'd recommend the cleansing be performed near the bricks," Candy added.

"A good idea, child.... It is their home.... Making them aware of the white light and portal to the Great Beyond might be enough to send some home.... Others we may have to push...."

"That's all well and good, if it works," Dr. Landrum began, "but

I'm concerned about the Ghostal Shores' patrons, right now. Some might be injured, even dead, behind closed doors, unable to call for help, and we'd never know."

"What in Hell's name do you want, man?!" Heller snapped.

"I think we should consider searching rooms where we don't get a response to very loud knocking. I need your permission to start searching the resort. Lives are at stake."

"That's against the law," Heller stammered. "And I don't believe I have that kind of authority. By the way, where is Sheriff Middleton? With the chaos in the lobby, I expected to see him this morning. For once, I could've used his help directing traffic."

"That's another reason I'm worried. He might be a victim," Dr. Landrum continued. "I'll take the responsibility for the search."

"You're not the police."

Dr. Landrum flashed his badge. "Actually, Sheriff Middleton and I have been working together." Though she wanted to scream "YES" in triumph, Angela simply nodded. Neither Blasing nor Xantini appeared surprised. Heller and the others were stunned and shocked. "Now, do I have your permission?"

"You don't need it, but you have it!" Heller yelled. Flustered and beginning to sweat, he punched the intercom button, then yelled, "Decker! Get in here." He punched it again before remembering the power was out. "Damn!" He moved to the door, then yelled down the hall. "DECKER! BRING CHADWICK IMMEDIATELY!"

"Is Kelvin Chadwick the head of security now?" Landrum asked.

"Yes, work through him."

"Mr. Heller?" a stern young man wearing "Lennon" glasses tried to get the Irishman's attention. "He's already here."

Chadwick arrived moments later, his pockmarked expression grim and his eyes steely. His twitch was worse, his jaw tight, and his hands restless as if ready to strangle something.

"Is there a problem?" the Irishman asked.

"I have bad news, sir. Guests are arriving," Decker told him.

"What?! That's good, man!"

"What he means to say," Chadwick interrupted gruffly, "is that guests are returning. The roads are blocked. Mudslides outside of Inverness have made them impassable, so people are coming back. They have nowhere else to go. I don't see any other viable option but to house them."

"We're trapped," Julie drawled nervously.

"According to the weather report, the storm's supposed to last another day. We could be stuck for a while," Chadwick told them.

"I guess that answers our question about being responsible and closing," Heller told everyone. "We can't very well turn people out into the rain, can we?"

"Absolutely not," Chadwick agreed. "Customer and employee safety is job one."

Angela wondered what job two was. Or better yet, if Chadwick ranked jobs by tenths or other fractions.

"I think we should distribute a list of Do's and Dont's..." Madame Zanadane suggested. "It might minimize guest contact...."

"The ranger station should be contacted," Dr. Landrum suggested. "If we can't purge the resort, we need a safe haven. People can't sleep in their cars, and we don't want any more dead."

"Why the ranger station?" Blasing asked.

"There's government housing. It, the gift shop and the lighthouse could provide shelter. It has to be safer than being trapped here overnight."

"Don't worry, officer, I believe we can take care of this...." Madame Zanadane breathed.

"Don't be insulted if I prepare, just in case," Dr. Landrum replied. "Now, if you'll excuse me, I have rooms to search."

THIRTY-ONE

"Oh, oh," Angela said. The lobby was packed again, although not quite as jammed. This time everyone crammed around the front desk. "I have a feeling they've heard the bad news."

"What are we supposed to do?!" "Goddamn weather!" "We're trapped with these crazy ghosts!" "Doomed!" people railed, fright deeply etching their faces, eyes wild and worried. Women wept, and their clinging children bawled loudly. Men sullenly eyed each other as if the wrong word or look would start a fight.

"Time to soothe the savage beasts again with your mellifluous voice," Angela told him.

Blasing gave her a wry glance. "I'll try it without the gun this time." Blasing stepped on the box.

The crowd quickly quieted, except for whispers of "It's him!"

"Excuse me, everyone! As you've heard, the roads are closed due to mudslides. I understand you want to leave, but don't have any choice except to stay with us or sleep in your car. We feel your discomfort and trepidation and are sympathetic to your plight. I urge you to stay calm. Children are present, and they need your guidance. In light of the circumstances, you'll get the same rooms as before at no charge. Cold breakfast is also on the house."

"But I want to leave," someone whined.

"We are attempting to restore power and hope to do so at any moment. Until such time as we do, use the oil lanterns stored in the closets of your rooms. They're safe; the oil won't ignite even if spilled. Since the phones are inoperative, announcement flyers will be placed on your doors—a list of do's and dont's in dealing with the ghosts.

"I repeat, please try to stay calm. Powerful emotions only attract the ghosts. Anger makes them more mischievous. We hope to have the situation under control by evening. I know it may not seem like it, but we are doing the best we can. Like you, we are only human. Any constructive ideas will be appreciated and accepted at the front desk.

Address them to Blasing Madera."

Again, the crowd seemed somewhat mollified. People grumbled, but they had no choice unless they wanted to walk to town or sleep in their vehicles.

Blasing stepped down. "Let's go have breakfast."

"You're hungry?" Angela blurted, instead of telling him how proud she was of him. Whether he realized it, or not, he was making Ghostal Shores his own.

"Of course! The possibility of getting lynched by an angry mob twice in the same morning has stimulated my appetite."

Angela laughed and kissed him. "I don't understand you, but it's going to be fun learning."

"Want company, Angel?" Candy asked. Rod stood protectively behind her.

"Sure! Come along."

People nodded respectfully and cleared space as the foursome passed. Several patrons asked questions, and Blasing stopped, taking the time to address each one. Even for those he couldn't answer, the people were understanding when he apologized. Just his presence and attention seemed to comfort them.

"He's amazing," Candy whispered to Angela. "Grace under pressure. Even his voice puts people at ease."

Eventually, they made it to the stairway. As they ascended, a dull roar barely noticeable at first grew louder. "The restaurant sounds packed," Candy mentioned.

"Good thing the bar is closed. Despite what's happened, it would be packed, too. I can't believe we've finally gotten Heller to agree to close the place, and now we can't," Angela sighed.

They stopped at the Clifftop bar, then ducked under the taped barrier reading "under construction." Chairs and tables lay overturned, and glass and wreckage were strewn everywhere. Porter had figured the devastation would prevent people from wandering in and left things accordingly. Stretching his senses, Blasing walked around feeling for ghosts. Angela remained quietly at his side. "Anything?" she finally asked.

"No. They must be waiting for this evening. Let's eat."

Angela sighed as the foursome walked over to Chian at the podium. The lovely Asian looked a bit ruffled. "Any tables?"

"Just a moment, Ms. Starborne."

"Blasing, are you all right?" Angela asked. Blasing looked as if he'd sensed something, his gaze far away.

"There's a familiar presence I can't quite identify yet. Let's walk around."

"Wait here," Angela told Candy. "We don't want to look too suspicious."

"Sure thing, Angel."

Angela nodded to Chian, then followed Blasing as he wandered between the crowded tables.

Some of the customers were damp, having just returned from the road. Wary and wondering where disaster would strike next, few watched what they ate. Their fear was barely contained, churning under a thin veneer of calmness. In contrast, several tables of people obviously enjoyed themselves, looking forward to the next encounter. A trio of "Deadheads" clad in tie-die and skeleton-adorned apparel burned incense and ate with gusto.

"Any luck?" Angela asked Blasing.

"It seems to be moving. You know I'd like to get into Heller's office and check out the safe."

"You think he might be keeping that video tape there?"

"Maybe even the ledger. He doesn't know we have a key to his safe. And I'd bet my life that wall wasn't damaged by ghosts. Looked more like a camera had been ripped out."

"I thought so, too."

"Here," Blasing said, stopping at a table where Tawny Lane and Al Murly sat. "Broderick?" Blasing whispered incredulously.

"Fancy meeting you here," Tawny Lane said. "Interesting and newsworthy times. Wish we could broadcast them. Any idea who sabotaged our truck?"

"What?" Angela asked. Blasing wasn't paying attention to Tawny, but she didn't seem to notice.

"Someone broke into our truck and damaged our equipment, so we can't broadcast. Now we have to report what's happening by cellphone and shoot video for when we can escape."

"Blame it on the ghosts," Angela told her. "They don't like the signals."

"Right. We're trapped aren't we?" Tawny said. Angela nodded.

"I figured this might happen. That's all right, danger is my business." The reporter grew serious, leaning forward just a bit. "Want to explain what happened in that private meeting?"

"We discussed shutting down the resort," Angela said. She waved to Candy and Rod, and they joined them, crowding around the table usually set for four.

"But you can't because of the roads? So what's next, BLASING?" Tawny emphasized, finally noticing he hadn't said a word. He appeared distracted, his expression distant as if listening to far away voices.

"We are going to attempt a cleansing later," Angela said.

"Will that get rid of trains?" Tawny asked.

"What trains are you talking about?" Angela asked.

"Tawny, excuse me for being abrupt. Broderick, are you here?" Blasing asked.

"You have found me, sir!" Broderick whispered loudly. Tawny jumped, then looked around wildly.

"Broderick!" Blasing susurated, trying to curtail his surprise and excitement. "Thank God you're all right!"

"Is the coast clear?" the disembodied Englishman asked.

"I don't feel any other ghosts."

"I trust your instincts, sir. Would you open a menu, please?" Blasing did as Broderick's head rose through the table to float between the menu's open pages. "I am sincerely sorry, madams and sirs, but under the circumstances, I believe it is best to remain hidden," Broderick sounded different. Blasing had never seen him anything but stiffly formal or slightly agitated until now.

"What's going on?" Blasing asked.

"Sir, you must take Ms. Starborne away! Ghostal Shores is lost."

"That doesn't sound like you," Angela said.

"Take her far away! Quickly! Do you not feel it in the air?"

"We won't leave you in the lurch," Blasing began. As Broderick started to protest, Blasing continued, "And besides, we can't." He explained about the slides covering the roads.

"Oh dear. Then I fear for us all. Very much. Yes, indeed."

"Peter, if it was his spirit, said he'd help," Angela told the ghost. "Have you seen him?"

"Master MacGuire? He is here?" Broderick looked confused.

Angela nodded. "No, miss. I have not. Maybe he has been appre-hended along with so many of the others by those bloody blackguards."

"Broderick, what's going on?" Blasing asked firmly.

"We are being rounded up for some fell purpose of which I have yet to ascertain, but I will. You have my word on it." His expression was grimly concerned. "As you have discovered, the transients are uncouth and amoral, and more than a little dangerous. We should have evicted the blokes immediately. As far as I can deduce, Rictor was a crime boss in Bodie. The blackguard has rounded up his gang, like attracting like, you know, and seized Ghostal Shores." Nose first, Broderick peeked through the menu at the crowded restaurant. Fear radiated from his ethereal eyes.

"We know that," Angela said.

"You have deduced more than I had hoped, but then you have spo-ken to Master MacGuire."

"He hasn't been very enlightening," Angela said.

"Oh dear."

"Rictor," Blasing prompted.

"I know little of said villain's agenda, but whatever it may be, from what I have seen, it is certainly dastardly. He has captured most of the ghosts, but despite wracking my brain, I cannot comprehend why."

"Why would he be holding them hostage?" Tawny asked.

"Broderick, is there something you might know about the ghosts or Ghostal Shores, something important that you don't realize is im-portant?" Blasing asked.

"I cannot think of anything, sir."

"Could they be preventing you from doing something?" Candy asked.

"Or learning something?" Blasing mused.

Angela thought this question struck a chord, but she wasn't sure why. "Broderick, how can we help?"

"I heard you mention a cleansing and my hopes soared."

"What about the local spirits?" Candy asked Broderick. "Would it adversely affect them?"

"Even if misfortune befalls us, it is worthwhile if it expunges the villains from Ghostal Shores. What they have done is simply ghastly."

"Have you seen Carrie or Grant?" Angela asked.

"I believe they were murdered as an example of what could happen. It reminds me of the days when cutthroats demanded money to leave a shopkeeper alone; otherwise, they would set fire to his shop."

"Like the Goldfield? The fire you died in?" Angela asked. Broderick nodded.

"Deja vu," Candy said. "Could history be repeating itself?"

"I do not see how, miss. Ghosts would have no interest in money," Broderick said. Angela thought of Eddie and the challenge of making money.

"What would they want?" Blasing asked.

"To live their lives again?" Candy asked. Broderick shook his head. "To slip back into the familiar?" He arched a brow.

"We know Rictor is a control freak," Angela said. "Just look at Lilly."

"And control is power," Candy said.

"Blasing, remember when we talked about stealing power?"

"Using sex or fear to usurp personal power? Spiritual power?" Blasing asked. Tawny eyed him speculatively. Angela nodded. "That still doesn't tell me much. Will Rictor gain life if he steals enough power?"

"A semblance of life—a life he remembers," Candy said.

"But why did he come here?" Blasing sighed in exasperation. "This is getting us nowhere. Broderick, Jonathan mentioned that you could confuse the hunting posse by staying close to someone—you know, a living person."

"Jonathan is not all there, even more so for one disembodied."

"Broderick, we've touched before," Blasing said, Mac's murder briefly flashing through his thoughts. "You could share this body."

"Sir. We have no idea what ill effects there might be."

"You could hide in our suite," Angela suggested. "I can open one side for you. You'll be safe there."

"Miss, the British do not cower before any threat! I want to drive this gang of blackguards from the resort, regardless of the consequences. If you cannot leave, then please conduct a massive housecleansing. There are lives at stake."

"But the locals..." Blasing began.

"It must be done, sir. Start with the bricks. If they cannot be cleansed, then purge the resort."

"Broderick," Candy began, "for the cleansing to be effective, we need as many names as you can remember. And if you can recall where they're from, that's even better."

Broderick had only given them names and origins of several transients when he suddenly stammered, "They're near!"

Casually strolling in as if they owned the place, a quartet of spirits entered the restaurant. The transients held more than a hint of color now, seeming less ethereal and more substantial. Their walk was loose, but their expressions alert and wary.

"I recognize them," Angela hissed. "Three are from last night's debacle in the bar. The one called Crane is flanked by Paco and Tito."

"And Bat's leading them," Blasing said, gritting his teeth. The long, lanky spirit with the hook nose was a few steps ahead of the trio. "Broderick, stay very, very close to me. If you bolt, they'll notice you. Stay put."

The foursome stopped and slowly scanned the restaurant. The nearest table was immediately abandoned, the patrons leaving in such a rush they stumbled, almost falling. The ghosts laughed, a degrading sound intending to embarrass.

"I should demand they leave," Blasing said.

"Blasing, don't."

"Angela, you stopped me last time."

"I know, but if you leave, they may notice Broderick."

"Do what you must, sir. I am quite capable of taking care of myself."

The transients sat and started to gamble, but then Bat said something to them, and they suddenly stood, each assuming a sentinel's stance. After a minute, Crane nudged Tito, who nodded, then the bully said something to Bat. The lean spirit immediately began walking toward their table.

"Merge, Broderick," Blasing said without moving his lips. He quickly removed his pendant and rings, handing them to Angela. When Broderick protested, Blasing hissed, "Do it! You work for me, remember?" He suddenly felt a sliding motion as if sinking into soft water, then Blasing suffered dizziness and surprising weakness. His vision doubled as if he were drunk, and he had to grab onto the table for balance.

"Blasing?" Angela steadied him.

"Do not be concerned, miss," Blasing said. "I am just dizzy. I... I need to eat," Blasing finished as the quartet stopped at their table, looming over them like dark thunderheads.

Angela noticed they carried guns and thought of gunslingers. Would her rings be a help or hinderance? "What do you want?"

"Aw, the feisty bitch," Crane said. "I'd love to pork you."

Her face livid and remembering what had happened last night, Candy jumped to her feet and slapped the barrel-chested spirit. His head rocked, and he reeled back a few steps, shocked by the contact. "I haven't forgotten last night," Candy hissed. Rod grabbed her arm so she couldn't stalk the backpedaling spirit. "Come on you bastard, I have a surprise for you."

Bat appeared amused. "A ghost was just here. Who was it?"

"I do not have to answer to your kind. I own this place," Blasing said. "Depart immediately or suffer the consequences."

"You don't run this place, Rictor does," Paco sneered.

Controlling Broderick's anger, Blasing slowly rose from his chair. "Leave or your forced departure will be very, very painful."

The trio laughed. Bat did not. "I don't believe you are the kind of man to bluff. But we're not interested in you. We only want the ghost who was just with you."

"All Ghostal Shores ghosts are my employees," Blasing said steely. "As well as my friends."

Angela also stood. "This place doesn't belong to you. Leave."

"These bitches remind me of my old lady," Crane snarled. "I'll fix 'em like I did her." The mammoth spirit drew his gun and fired.

"Angela!" Blasing shoved her aside, then felt a sharp, burning pain in his shoulder. It blossomed into his arm and chest.

"Blasing? Why'd you do that? It isn't.... Blasing!" Angela cried as he collapsed onto the table.

Screaming swarmed the restaurant as people fled, knocking each other down and overturning chairs in their frenzied flight. "They're shooting!" "Not a show!" "That man was shot!"

Laughing, Crane aimed once more.

"I'll see you driven from here," Blasing snarled and threw his pendant, smacking the shootist. Crane screamed, dropping his gun to clutch at his eye.

Tito and Paco drew their weapons, ready to fire. Bat charged with a knife in each hand. "Rictor will thank us for this!"

"BLACKGUARDS!" Broderick roared as the spirit erupted from Blasing. The valet struck Bat in the face, knocking him backward, then charged the Latinos. Paco and Tito fired, but Broderick kept attacking. He slammed a fist into one's eye, then dropped the other with a vicious upper cut.

"Get him!" Bat wheezed. Broderick kicked the lanky spirit, then Crane. With the triumphant yell of, "God Save the Queen," Broderick raced off, drawing the ghosts with him.

"Get him or Rictor will have our hides!"

"Blasing! Blasing! Are you all right?" Angela maneuvered him back into the chair.

He was ashen and his eyes were unfocused. "I thought you were going to take care of the spirits," he said, his eyes rolling back.

THIRTY-TWO

Working his way through the onlookers, Dr. Landrum arrived on the scene. He gently moved a clinging and red-faced Angela away from Blasing, who was hunched over in obvious pain. "What's wrong?"

"H- he was shot by a ghost," Angela managed.

"I see," Dr. Landrum replied stoically. "Where does it hurt?"

"My left shoulder," Blasing managed through gritting teeth, his face pale, and his eyes clenched shut.

Dr. Landrum gingerly straightened him, then said, "I'm going to remove your jacket." Blasing nodded, then winced during the process. "Looks good so far. No blood. How are you feeling?"

"Dizzy."

"As if a loss of blood," Dr. Landrum said quietly as he checked Blasing's vital signs.

"Angela, are you all right?" Blasing asked.

"I'm here." Her voice quavered. She moved to his good side and took his hand. Candy stood next to her, keeping a motherly watch.

"Are you all right?" Blasing asked again.

"Y- yes."

"You don't sound all right. Hey! Where's Broderick?!"

"Whoa! Calm down!" Dr. Landrum put a restraining hand on Blasing's chest. "I mean it. Whatever it is can wait." Before Blasing could protest, Dr. Landrum said, "It can wait. From your pulse, I'd surmise your system has undergone quite a shock. I'm going to remove your shirt." Angela helped this time. "My, my. I don't know if you were shot, but you have quite a contusion." Blasing's shoulder was swollen and bruised, sickly purple and green streaking outward from the point of impact. Dr. Landrum gently palpitated around the shoulder and scapula.

Blasing winced. "With your touch, you ought to play the drums."

"Angela, you say he was shot?" Dr. Landrum asked. She nodded.

"By a ghost with a ghost gun?"

"Yes," Angela said. "It was my fault."

"No it wasn't," Blasing replied. "It all happened so fast."

"Nothing should have happened," Candy said. "If this continues, the next time someone is shot it will be bloody."

"Hmmm. Well, whatever hit you, I don't believe it broke the bone, but without an x-ray I can't be sure. You should keep this shoulder immobilized. I can give you something for the pain."

"I don't want anything! It'll make me stupid. Angela, where's Broderick? Hey, are you all right?" Angela looked away. She was red-eyed, her cheeks streaked, and she looked ready to cry again. "Angela, I'm going to be all right."

"I'm so sorry you were shot. None of this should have happened. A ghost shouldn't have been able to strike Candy, and it certainly shouldn't have been able to shoot you!" Her voice carried an edge of hysteria.

"Angela...."

"You could've been killed!" She smacked him lightly with her purse on his good shoulder. "Damn it, you shouldn't have pushed me out of the way! Grandma Dawnjoy's rings would've protected me!"

"You don't know that."

"Blasing, did you think Angela was going to get hurt?" Candy asked. He nodded. "That might be why you were hurt."

"He believed in it and that made it real," Angela mused. "Damn it, Blasing! Think about Kelly and Patrick! Think about...."

"Angela." Blasing pulled her into a one-armed hug. "It's not your fault." He kissed her forehead. "Besides, we wouldn't have met if I hadn't come to Ghostal Shores."

"And gotten shot. Blasing, disaster relationships don't last." She sounded fatalistic.

"How do you know?"

"My tumultuous marriage was a result of a quake in San Francisco. I met my ex when part of my apartment collapsed. Don't worry. It's not a complex. Oh Spirit, I'm prattling and starting to sound like I was born in California."

"Even with all this, meeting you is the best thing that ever happened to me," he told Angela, then they kissed.

"This frightens me," Candy said. "If believing in the bullet, even the possibility, made it real, what else might happen? And is it just belief, or have they changed? Become more real?"

"Real?" Blasing asked.

"More in phase with our reality. More substantial. More grounded," Candy continued. "Science has proven thoughts and emotions have shapes and energy patterns. Maybe the ghosts vibratory pattern is becoming more in sync with our dimension. Everything's just light moving at different speeds, anyway."

Blasing couldn't believe the first words out of his mouth were, "But how?" instead of "ridiculous!" He looked to Angela. She didn't even appear skeptical. Neither did Rod.

"I have no idea," Candy replied.

"I can't believe you people buy into this," Tawny told them.

"Small, closed minds," Angela sighed. She and Tawny glared at each other, sparks ready to fly. "Maybe this has something to do with the missing ghosts. Could Rictor and the transients be stealing the local's... essence? Their power? Their... light?"

"How?" Candy asked. "And what good would that do?"

"What're we going to do?" Blasing asked. "We have to do something. I have a feeling time is running out."

"As unbelievable as it sounds, it makes for a salable story," Tawny said as she moved closer. "Ever been shot before, Blasing?"

"Go prey on someone else's miseries."

"I'll take that as a no. Ghostal Shores is a place for firsts. First ghost resort. First ghost rebellion. First ghostly shooting."

"Quit being so cold, bitch," Angela told her, her glare taking Tawny aback. Angela turned to Blasing and said, "After what happened the first time, I couldn't believe you offered Broderick a place to hide. You must care for him very much."

"I keep asking, but nobody tells me. Has something happened to him? Where is he?"

"After you were shot, he attacked, surprising the ghosts. Then he ran off, drawing them away," Candy told him.

"Damn!"

"He thought he was doing the right thing," Angela said.

Blasing leaned back, then winced as the doctor wrapped his shoulder. "I hope nothing's happened to him."

"Don't give up," Candy said.

"I'm just discouraged. Have you found anybody in your behind-closed-doors search?" Blasing asked Dr. Landrum.

"Two so far. One paralyzed and another unconscious."

"Any proof the ghosts are the cause?"

"None, but is there much doubt?"

"Put these on," Angela said, handing Blasing the hematite rings, then helping him don the pendant. "That's better. If you'd been wearing them, you might not have been hurt."

Murmuring swelled around them, then the onlookers parted. Huffing and puffing, Heller arrived, his face flushed and his eyes wild. "Doctor, I mean, detective...." Heller suddenly noticed Blasing's condition. "What happened to you?"

"He was shot," Angela said coldly.

"Shot? By whom?!" Heller exclaimed.

"One of the ghosts."

Heller's jaw dropped. He managed to grab a chair before he collapsed. "Wha... What are we going to do?"

"What do you want, Mr. Heller?" Dr. Landrum asked.

"Uh? Oh. Security called. They've found Sheriff Middleton at the pool."

"In the pool? Did he drown?"

Heller shook his head. "They said to come see for yourself. You too, Blasing, if you can."

"What do you say, Geoff?" Blasing asked.

"Normally, I'd tell you to rest. But this isn't normal, and I don't think you'd listen to me anyway." Blasing just smiled. "So I might as well keep you near, where I can keep an eye on you." With a slight tug, Dr. Landrum finished applying the sling.

"I'm going to talk with Madame Zanadane and Efrem Xantini, inform them about the shooting," Candy said.

"See you soon," Angela said.

When Heller exited the stairs to enter the pool, he stopped cold. "Oh my God!" Heller gasped.

Blasing, Angela and Dr. Landrum were right behind him. "Oh Don," the detective whispered, then ran alongside the pool. Blasing and Angela followed with the reporters close behind.

Near the defunct waterfall, Chadwick and two guards looked up at the grotesque figure strung between two pillars. The sheriff's face was bloated and blue with his purple tongue sticking out. Lank hair almost covered his wide eyes, and his badge had been pinned through his nose. Blood and urine stained his clothing and the tiles below. Written in blood on the Stonehenge-like stones behind the body was "We fought The Law and The Law lost."

"Spirit help us," Angela whispered. "It's... it's," she struggled with a word to describe the atrocity, "...horrible." Blasing pulled her close, and she buried her head in his chest.

"Cut the rope and lower him! NOW!" Dr. Landrum shouted. One guard ran to a storage cabinet near the workout rooms, then returned with a ladder.

"Al, start shooting," Tawny said.

"Don't," Blasing said. "There's no need."

"But it's news!"

"Don't be insensitive," he snapped.

"It's my job to be objective. Keep filming Al."

"We're ready, sir." A guard climbed the ladder and cut the rope. Dr. Landrum and Chadwick lowered the body. The doctor cut the noose, freed the sheriff's hands, then performed a quick examination. Middleton was long dead. As Dr. Landrum removed the badge and pinned it to the sheriff's chest, he was stone-faced.

"I'm so sorry, Geoff," Angela told him.

"Why did they do this, this way? Why?"

"They're evil spirits of evil men." Blasing said, recalling what Broderick had said.

"They hate the Law," Angela said. "They hated the Law in Bodie in the 1880's, and they still hate it now."

"I'll get them for this," Dr. Landrum said brittlely. "Don suffered a long time. His neck didn't break, so he suffocated. I'm afraid he may have just been one of the first. By morning, there may be more. We have to do something!"

Angela touched Dr. Landrum gently. "To get them, you'll have to be smart and stay alive, Geoff. Save what lives you can. Do what you do best."

"This place is insane! Even if the roads are closed, we've got to get out of here before it's too late, or we'll join him!" He fought to maintain control. "As soon as I can, I'm driving out to the point to check the ranger's station. It should be safe. People might be able to stay there until the roads clear."

"We'll go," Angela volunteered. "You need to keep checking

for injured. Somebody might need your help."

"But Blasing's in no condition...."

"I'll drive."

"And I won't let her go alone, even if I am scared of her driving," Blasing said. Angela laughed and hugged him. She was sick at heart, but being with him eased her pain.

A guard in a rain slicker approached Chadwick, then they moved to Heller. "What?!" Heller exploded.

"What's going on, Sean?" Blasing asked.

"They just found Meg's body in the veranda gardens." Heller looked totally stunned, as if he'd lost something important.

"She fell from her balcony," Chadwick told him. "We're checking her room right now."

"I guess this takes care of the sixty day nonsense," Angela said coldly. Before Blasing could say anything, Angela said, "I'm sorry, but she tried to steal something from you and Peter."

Heller's expression changed, narrowing. "Where were you last night, Blasing? You have the most to profit from this."

Angela felt Blasing stiffen. "He was with me."

Dr. Landrum stepped between them. "I'm going to look at the body. Angela. Blasing. Drive out to the guard station. Now, Mr. Chadwick, we have rooms to search. Let's find out if anyone needs our help. Then we'll worry about how people died."

"But he shouldn't leave!" Heller cried. "He's a suspect!"

"He can't go anywhere! None of us can!" Dr. Landrum replied.

"Let's get going, Blasing," Angela said, taking his arm and steering him away from the Irishman.

"I have bad memories about your driving," Blasing said.

"We're not in my car," Angela replied. She drove Earl Cash's company vehicle—a forest green Jeep Cherokee.

Lightning flashed repeatedly and the deliquesce landscape became starkly lit in flickering snatches. Tree copses and clusters of bushes lashed back and forth, the wind threatening to tear them loose. Angela held the wheel tightly, driving slowly around the sharp curves.

The Action! Channel 22 van followed behind them, Lane and Murly determined to stay with them. Scavengers, Blasing thought, just waiting to feed. He couldn't prevent them from following, but the wind might. The powerful gusts were pushing the boxy vehicle all over the road. Murly's face was pallid, and his knuckles were white atop the wheel. Water washed over the road, in several low-lying gullies between hills, but never more than a few inches.

"Blasing, I'm really worried about you getting shot."

"And I worried about what happened to Meg. Was it the ghost? Or someone... alive?"

"Blasing, I don't want to talk about her."

"I'm all right. You can be concerned, but please don't worry."

"I deserve that," she said in exasperation. "But there wasn't any gun."

"Just like there weren't any stampeding horses or cows."

"That was different."

"Was it?"

"I think so. The others were just memories, phantoms like what you saw when Broderick touched you. They had no substance. Dreams visible, but not made real...."

"This wasn't?"

"Didn't Bat and the others remind you of Ghostal Shores spirits? More colorful. Less transparent. More... there."

"Angela."

"Well, it's the only explanation that makes any sense. Why else would you have been hurt? I'm disappointed Peter isn't helping us. But I have an idea from watching Crane's reaction to being struck by the pendant. At first I thought it might just work against the phantoms, but now I think it'll work against the ghosts, too."

"What will?" Blasing asked. Angela reached into her jacket pocket, then stopped, quickly putting that hand back on the steering wheel. "Something wrong?"

"Probably just the wind. Hey! There's a glow coming from over the rise," Angela pointed out. The top of the forthcoming knoll shone with an amber light. "And I think I see smoke!"

"Damn. It could be a fire."

"Carrie said the gangs liked fire."

They drove past the sign announcing the Point Reyes Lighthouse into a parking lot crowded with whirlwinds of smoke, then by a placard posting "No Admittance—Employees Only." At the cliff's edge, a blaze was devouring the top of a two story building. The wind snatched at it, and the flames guttered, roaring as they burned hotter and hotter. Windows on the first floor exploded, and fire leapt out, running up the outside of the brown and green building. A hundred feet away, the gift shop and information center at the top of the long lighthouse stairway were also afire. A wall of flaming debris blew free of the building, causing a firestorm to blast through the parking lot and over their car.

"Stop here. I'm going to check for survivors." Blasing threw open the door. It tried to slam closed, as he fought his way out of the car.

"Be careful!" Angela yelled.

"Incredible footage," Blasing heard Murly say. "The wind is causing that place to burn like it's soaked with gasoline."

Ducking and dodging a cloud of burning debris, Blasing moved closer. The rain stung his face, and in moments he was drenched. Blasing yelled out, then realized no one could hear him over the wind, let alone the thunderous roar of the inferno. Flames licked out every window, and already the roof had been consumed. At any moment, he expected the place to collapse as if a fiery house of cards.

Anyone inside was surely dead, Blasing thought as he circled the building. But had someone escaped? If so, maybe they could shed light on the fire's origin. The thought that ghosts might be the arsonists frightened him.

Blasing darted to the cliffside and paused to concentrate. Had he felt a ghost? The wind and chill of the rain made it difficult to be sure. Trying to ignore the storm, he stretched out his senses and found nothing. If spirits had been here, they were gone. He made a quick but thorough check of the area, then returned to the car.

"Anybody?" Tawny asked. She looked like a drowned cat, her white-blond hair plastered across her face.

"No," Blasing replied curtly.

"Do you think it was an accident? Or the ghosts?"

"I have no idea. But nobody will be staying here. Let's go back to Ghostal Shores." Blasing climbed back into the car.

"There's a towel in the back," Angela said as she put the car in gear. Blasing found it and dried off, then tilted back the seat to rest. "You all right?" She steered the Jeep onto the main road.

"My shoulder feels ready to fall off."

"Damn!"

Blasing snapped the seat upright. "What's wrong?" he asked as they screeched around a turn, then raced into another.

"The brakes aren't working!"

"Tap them! They may be wet!"

"I'm trying!"

"Drop into low!"

Angela did, but it was too late. They flew over the top of a low hill, then landed hard. The Jeep skipped across the road and through a ditch, sending them airborne again.

"Spirit, please!" Angela muttered a prayer.

Metal screeched as they tore through barbed wire, then the front struck hard, jarring them and splattering mud across the windshield. The second impact whipped Angela's head back. She almost blacked out

Blasing grabbed the wheel, righting them as they began to slide. The plowing effect slowed them briefly, but now they rumbled downhill, picking up speed and bouncing toward the cliffs surrounding Drake's Bay.

As Blasing reached for the gear shift to throw it into reverse, a front tire suddenly ruptured. The Cherokee spun around, now bounding downhill backwards. "Let's get out of here!" Blasing undid his safety belt.

The Jeep hit a hummock and flipped onto its side. They bumped heads as Blasing fell atop Angela. Muddy water blinded them as a window erupted.

The Jeep hit another bump and flipped over, awkwardly rolling from door to door as it tumbled downhill. Blasing bounced about, smashing into the ceiling, floor, windows and Angela. Blasing slapped at the dash around the radio, trying to hit the rear liftdoor release and hoping they could bounce out the back.

"We're going to die!" Angela cried. "I love you!"

The Jeep suddenly crashed. Shuddering, it slowly rebounded like a drunk having run into a wall, then stopped. To Angela and Blasing it seemed as if they were still moving.

"Blasing? What happened?" Angela asked, shaking him.

"We stopped. Must have hit something...." He groaned, "Are you all right?"

Feeling relieved, she said, "Yes."

He groaned again and opened his eyes, staring through the shattered windshield at the dark blue waters of Drake's Bay. He had no idea what had stopped them, but he gave silent thanks to his guardian angel, then said, "Never a dull moment with you...."

She smiled.

With every move hurting, Blasing climbed out through the open window on the passenger side. He dropped down, landing next to a huge stump. The Jeep rested on the stump, the bumper crushed inward. The front wheels spun freely at least three feet off the ground. He helped Angela wiggle free of the twisted wreck.

"That's what saved us," Blasing said, nodding to the stump. "That and my guardian angel."

He looked around—left and right. There wasn't anything else in sight to stop them from plummeting over the edge into the bay and to certain death. "

"If we hadn't swerved...." Angela shuddered.

"Right," Blasing agreed. "Not to complain too much, but it would have been nice if she'd warned me. I wouldn't have unbelted."

For awhile they just stood in the rain holding each other, never more grateful for life, the guardian angel, and each other.

"But was it meant for Cash? Or for us?" Blasing asked.

He suddenly began patting his pockets, then pulled the tape from his jacket pocket.

"Damn!" It was badly cracked.

THIRTY-THREE

Standing in the shadows behind a tall plant across from the front desk, Blasing shifted uncomfortably as he waited for Heller and Madame Zanadane to leave the Irishman's office. Blasing knew he shouldn't complain about his aches and pains; they could've been far worse—he and Angela might have died in the wreck. Once again, Blasing thanked his guardian angel.

The attempt on their lives and the ransacking must mean they were close to solving something. He hoped his curiosity and Angela's dedication didn't get them killed. Especially Angela. He never thought he'd feel love again for anyone after Jenny, but with Angela, it burned just as strong.

While Blasing waited, his thoughts drifted back an hour. Muddy and battered, he and Angela supported each other as they walked with Tawny and Al to the Action! Channel 22 van. Angela's neck bothered her, and his shoulder felt dislocated.

During the ride and after getting a written agreement not to disclose certain information until he'd authorized it, Blasing told Tawny all he knew about what was happening at Ghostal Shores. Angela didn't trust her, but Blasing said that if something happened to them, somebody had to know the truth.

Upon their arrival, Heller seemed shocked. Blasing could tell it was an act. Madame Zanadane wondered if they were capable of attending the cleansing. Blasing assured her they would be there—after a shower.

While washing each other by candlelight, they laughed, glad to be alive and amazed at where they found mud. Angela's touch was soothing. Some of his aches faded away. She rubbed an herbal liniment on his pains, and he felt even better, though not a new man by any means.

They were toweling off when Geoff arrived. While the doctor examined them, they told him about the wreck. Then Blasing repeated what he'd told Tawny. The doctor wasn't nearly as surprised. He rebound Blasing's shoulder and told Angela she had a strained neck. Then he asked to see the tape. Blasing showed it to him but refused to turn it over.

A baggage accident pulled Blasing's attention to the present, but neither Heller nor Madame Zanadane were in sight. Too bad he and Angela couldn't have just stayed in the shower, Blasing thought, but Ghostal Shores' problems—his problems—wouldn't go away by wishing them gone. If he just left, what would he tell Kelly and Patrick? In a world embracing irresponsibility, he wanted them to learn to accept responsibility. People were in danger, and although it wasn't his fault, he was responsible for their safety.

The clattering of Heller's cane caught Blasing's attention. In long slickers, boots and hats, Heller and Madame Zanadane were dressed for foul weather. Mr. Chung carried an umbrella like a weapon.

Blasing waited awhile, then crossed the lobby. Angela was going to explain his delayed arrival by claiming Lilly had appeared, and, for whatever reason, the spirit refused to speak in Angela's presence. Blasing didn't think it would take long to rifle Heller's office. He knew where the safe was located, and, according to Broderick, had a key to it.

No one stopped Blasing when he opened the "EMPLOYEES ONLY" door and crept down the dark, deserted hallway. Pausing for a moment, he listened at Heller's door, then tried to open it. It was locked. He quickly tried every key on his set. None of them worked.

Blasing silently cursed and removed his lockpicking tools from his jacket. Despite practicing, he'd never been very good at this. After a few minutes he worried someone would discover him, or that he'd never get it open. Then the lock suddenly clicked. Blasing quickly stepped inside and pushed the door closed, locking it behind him. A cold breeze made him shiver. Was a ghost present?

Pushing away his paranoia, Blasing walked around the desk to the painting of the Goldfield Hotel. It hung among the photographs of Heller's ancestors—Merl, Thomas and Patrick. Blasing was amazed at the striking family resemblance; they appeared to be the same persons photographed in different costumes and backgrounds to suit the era.

The safe hid behind the painting—right where he remembered it from Broderick's memories. With a silent prayer, Blasing slipped the key into the lock. It turned easily, and he heard a welcomed click. A perfume scent masking the smell of cigarettes wafted by him. "Lilly?"

Blasing heard footsteps approaching Heller's door. "Thought I saw Blasing come in here." Someone tried the knob, but it didn't turn.

"It's not him I'm worried about."

"Mr. Heller told us to watch his office and that no one was to enter. I'm assuming that includes his new partner."

"But it's still locked."

"Macon, you've got shit for brains. He could've locked it from the inside. Let's check it out."

Lilly suddenly appeared, blew Blasing a kiss, then slipped through the door. "Hey, what the Hell's that?"

"It's a ghost! Hey, what're you doing?"

"She's kissing you, Macon. Man, you are an idiot!"

Blasing suddenly felt another presence and ducked behind Heller's mammoth chair.

"She likes us!" Macon replied. "Can you screw a ghost?"

A hiss so loud it seemed to cut right through the door. "Get away from my woman!"

"OH MY GOD!" was followed by two thuds.

"Lilly! Why are you... Lilly! Come back here!" Rictor shouted, his voice cracking like a barbed whip.

Blasing no longer felt either of the ghosts. Lilly must have drawn Rictor away.

Opening the safe, Blasing found a ledger, a manila envelope containing a VHS tape and a small purple velvet box. Within it, a lionhead ring of gold with emerald eyes seemed naggingly familiar. Mac's murder flashed through Blasing's memories, then he saw the murderer empty the safe, placing money and jewels, including the lionhead ring, into his bag. Was this the same ring? It had to be! Heller couldn't have had time to replace it. The ring was too ornate and unique. How had Heller recovered it?

Blasing was now certain Heller was somehow involved with Mac's murder. Maybe he had even orchestrated it. Blasing stifled the urge to find Heller and throttle the truth from him. He left the ring but stuck the ledger in his waistband along his back and put the tape in his jacket, hoping it would fare better than the other one. Angela carried it in her purse for safekeeping.

Blasing re-locked the safe, then left the office, stepping over the prone bodies of the security guards. A quick check told him they were still alive. "Thank you, Lilly." He peeked out the door, then exited, jogging up the steps to the foyer. He walked quickly through the restaurant, then ran along the halls toward the northern exit. His body screamed at him to rest.

When Blasing opened the door, he was greeted by a flash of lightning. Thunder and a powerful wind lambasted him, the rain stinging his face. "Just perfect," he mumbled. Pulling up his collar and donning a hat, he rushed out into the storm.

Blasing followed the muddy footprints to the construction yard, noting the border tape had either been pulled down or blown away. As he walked around a foundation wall, he looked for the gathering. When he didn't see anybody near the bricks, his heart clutched. Where were they? Had something happened to Angela?

After a rumble of thunder, Blasing thought he heard his name. It came a second time, Angela waved at him from the open door of the construction foreman's trailer. Smiling broadly, Blasing waved back. Angela motioned to someone inside the trailer, then descended the steps.

Dr. Landrum, Candy, Rod, and the Great Xantini followed her. After a moment's delay, Julie Zephren, Heller, and Dr. Strange, with his pipe turned upside down, joined the parade slogging through the mud. Just behind Tawny and Murly, came Madame Zanadane with Mr. Chung at her side. Except for the in-house psychic and the cameraman, each person carried an umbrella and struggled to keep it from flying away. Lightning flashed repeatedly, igniting the gray gloom. The rain came in bursts, quickly changing intensity and direction—sometimes driven horizontally.

As Blasing neared the bricks, he felt his hackles rise. The ghosts swirled invisibly about him, their energies angry and rampant—a storm all their own. Now he barely noticed the winds and the rain. Did the spirits sense what was coming? Could they resist?

Angela reached him first, giving him a very wet hug. "How...

are you all right?"

"Yes. Just a bit overwhelmed."

"They are here..." Madame Zanadane breathed. The others gathered around her, their umbrellas clustered together creating a shaky and porous shelter. "Do you feel them...?"

"All over," Blasing replied.

Almost everyone felt them, except for Dr. Landrum and Heller, who was scowling. Curses contorted his lips as he wiped his face with a soggy handkerchief. The wind tugged at everyone, their umbrellas violently colliding. Blasing thought it was a ridiculous sight. But then why not? They attempted something ludicrous.

"Let's get on with it!" Heller demanded.

"What did Lilly tell you...?" Madame Zanadane asked.

"She implored me to free her. When I told her what we were doing, she blew me a kiss and said she'd do what she could to help," Blasing lied. The Great Xantini appeared about to say something but refrained. "She also warned me that Rictor would not give up easily."

"That he might try to stop us," Xantini finished for him. His nod was slight, but seemed to be one of approval.

"That is unpleasant news..." Madame Zanadane breathed.

"But not totally unexpected," Xantini added. He snagged his black hat just as a wind gust lifted it.

"What should I do?" Blasing asked, the last of his words snatched away by the wind.

"Ah yes, you missed our orientation.... Essentially, the ghosts are lost.... We shall show them the way home..." Madame Zanadane told him.

"Home?" Blasing asked.

"The Great Beyond," Candy told him.

"The realm beyond the veil," Dr. Strange murmured.

"A plane of higher vibration," Xantini explained.

"Don't worry... you may not consciously remember the way, but we have all made the journey more than once already...."

Dr. Landrum let out a long breath, and Blasing saw he didn't believe in previous lives either. But then, so much he never believed had already occurred. Angela believed, and he believed in her. He would just have to take it on faith.

"I, as the focal point and most experienced, will link the buried memories and present the resonance to the ghosts...."

"Visualization helps," Candy coached Blasing. "I'm sure you've heard the recounts of near death experiences. Picture a great white light as bright as the sun but not painful to view. The light is a shaft leading to the Great Beyond."

"Some hear music," Dr. Strange murmured, absently fondling his amulet.

"Remind them of the light.... Make them feel its siren song sing through their soul..." Madame Zanadane told him. Blasing rubbed his neck, the itching increasing. "They're gathering...."

"That might make it easier," Dr. Strange said.

"This is crazy," Heller grumbled. "Let's get on with it!"

Blasing glanced at Heller, stifling his seething anger. "So we link hands, then visualize this... shaft of light?"

Madame Zanadane's gaze was luminescent and piercing. "We must be confident.... You two as owners have a large role to play.... You must demand the unwanted spirits depart.... Tell them they are no longer welcome here—to go home.... To the Great Beyond.... The most recent newcomers will be the weakest, having spent the least amount of time here.... Start with them...."

"What about the locals? The GSR ghosts?" Blasing asked.

"They have been bound here for a time.... The transients and those without purpose will be the easiest to guide away. Those with purpose and tenure will be well rooted.... Now, we must begin...."

As they had at the séance, they formed a circle around the stack of bricks, then linked hands. "Reach out with your energies!" Candy cried over the winds. Blasing squeezed Angela's hand, then closed his eyes, concentrating—seeing—creating—a bright light. In his mind's eye, it started as a pinprick coming through the dark clouds, then it broke through the roiling mass, slowly widening into a column.

"I will link us.... Do you see the light...? You must see the light.... It is waiting for them... calling to them...."

The column of light became a shaft. Blasing could sense a shift in... something he couldn't explain. Despite the chill of the wind and rain, he suddenly felt warmer—a wave washing over him from head to toe. The lashing storm seemed distant, the thunder muted as though the foul weather cleared.

"Incredible," Tawny whispered, caught speechless for once.

"Can you all see it...?" Madame Zanadane breathed excitedly.

"Not very well through the camera," Murly moaned, taking his eye away from the eyepiece to check the scene. "But I can see it."

"That can't be!" Angela said.

"YES! I can see it!" Dr. Strange cried, then several shouted at once as a tunnel of light broke through the clouds to surround them. A different, gentler wind swirled within the column.

"Wrap it around you for protection," Angela instructed. Blasing imagined the light flowing over him as though it were a waterfall. He immediately felt very safe. Was that music or singing he'd heard?"

"The resonance is building! Expanding!" Madame Zanadane cried. "Spirits, your home awaits you! Your place of rest, joy and wonder! The answers you seek and who you are await you! Your friends and loved ones are ready to see you again! THE GATE IS OPEN! WALK TO THE LIGHT! STEP INTO THE LIGHT!"

"DO NOT BE AFRAID!" Candy cried.

Blasing felt a swirling, and yet it was not the wind. Then he felt a totally unexpected presence. "Jenny?" She'd given him a hug! He could smell her! Feel her here! And yet, it wasn't like earlier in the bar. Who had that been? Fawn? Lilly? Who?

"Peter?" Angela whispered. "Peter! He's here! Peter, please help us with this! What?! You haven't been with us!"

"Sean! Blasing! Speak to them!" Madame Zanadane said firmly. "Demand the transients leave! Send them on their way!"

"You aren't wanted here! Go home!" Blasing yelled, then he called names: Bat, Rictor, Crane, Paco, Tito, Gus, Cogan, Lucius, Newt, JP, Isaiah, Tai and on and on—down the list of transients.

"Rictor! I own the damn place!" Heller shouted. "LEAVE NOW! You and the others aren't welcome here! Get the Hell out of here! IMMEDIATELY!"

"Gabriel calls," Julie added.

"Seek the kingdom...."

"WE, THE OWNERS, RESCIND OUR HOSPITALITY AND SEND YOU ON YOUR WAY!" Blasing suddenly felt a ghost very close by.

Cogan, the wild-haired stub of a ghost, floated before him. "You're doing the right thing, bub. Thanks!" The spirit tipped his hat, then became mist drifting skyward. The clouds majestically parted and a shaft of golden sunlight burst through to surround them. "Come on, old-timer," Cogan said. JP Johnson appeared, a rapturous expression on his usually taciturn face as he rose.

"Amazing!" Dr. Landrum gasped.

"Damn, I wish this wasn't so hazy," Murly complained.

"It's working!" Candy cried.

"About damned time something did!" Heller groused. "GO ON! GET OUT OF HERE!"

When a third ghost appeared, Blasing recognized the elderly, infirmed spirit who had wanted a drink so badly. His expression was one of relief, and it filled Blasing with joy. That spirit was joined by his tall friend, and the huge, African ghost. They waved good-bye, their eyes reflecting the golden sunlight. Soon, they'd merged with the brightness where the light met the clouds.

"Keep seeing the light!" Madame Zanadane cried, her head back, eyes wild as her zebra-striped hair flew in the wind.

"GO HOME!" Heller shouted. "YOU'RE NOT WANTED!"

The shy Asian appeared next. Tai bowed, then he too was skyward bound. A crowd suddenly materialized behind him, spirits Blasing and Angela had spoken to when they'd arrived en masse. They'd been the friendly ones—those confused as to why they were here. They were thrilled, hugging and laughing.

"Thank you! Thank you so much! We have waited so long!" Isaiah cried.

The energy suddenly changed, a biting chill whipping through the circle. A group of rogues appeared, their expressions grim and fearful. Their eyes darted about, looking for a way to escape. They waved Colt .45s menacingly at Blasing and the others. "Stop or we'll shoot!" one demanded.

"LEAVE!" Blasing yelled. He ignored their firearms this time; they weren't real.

"LEAVE!" Heller agreed. "NOW!"

"No! Our place is here!" the one with the lazy eye shouted. One of his companions fired, the gun sounding as muffled thunder. Madame Zanadane laughed at them.

"You don't belong here!" Candy shouted.

"YOU'RE DEAD!" Angela cried. "Go meet your ancestors!"

"But I will have to pay..." a scarred rogue wept.

"Great Spirit will understand," Angela said gently, surprising herself and the ghost. He tentatively looked around at the others, then let go, drifting into nothingness. The lazy-eyed one followed, but the rest of the quintet stayed, confusion and indecision shaping their expressions.

Next to Angela, Rod suddenly shuddered. "Are you all right?" Angela asked. He blinked rapidly several times, and his mouth worked silently. Then his face seemed to take on new character.

"He's channeling," Candy said.

A gleam in his eye and a devil-may-care smile spread across his face as Rod said, "Hello, Angie, you good-lookin' squaw."

"G—Grant! What're you doing here? Aren't you dead?"

Rod nodded. "Even more so than before, but I had to come back to help. Had to screw ole Hellraiser." His smile was radiant.

"What's going on! How's Carrie?"

"No time to explain! Just tell the ghosts a great adventure awaits them, and much excitement. More than they've ever dreamed."

"W—why?"

"That's how Rictor holds them! That and the weakness of my compatriots. This might not've happened if they'd had any backbone. And arrest Heller. It'll help loads. Wish you the best, Angie. Farewell," Grant said, then Rod returned. "What happened?"

"Later," Candy replied.

"Listen to me and know it to be the truth!" Angela yelled. At least she hoped Grant was telling the truth. A grand adventure awaits you in the Great Beyond, and more excitement than Rictor can promise, let alone deliver. He's lying, while this is truth!"

The ghosts stared at her, then at each other. One nodded, then slowly but inexorably, they were drawn into the light leading to the Great Beyond. When seven more despicable spirits materialized, Angela repeated her message. Blasing reinforced it.

"Keep at it," Madame Zanadane cried, her face flushed.

Lila of the apothecary appeared, yelling, "I'm free! Free! Here I come Thaddius!" Allen the barber materialized next, waving happily as he departed. He called Eddie to join him but the ghost didn't show. Allen was followed by Martha from antiques, then Juanita and Tess from housekeeping.

"Go in peace," Angela said.

"THIS MUST STOP!" came Rictor's voice. The energy changed, seeming to slow and cool as a shadow stretched over them.

"There's resistance!" Madame Zanadane cried. "Stay strong!"

A darkness gathered before Heller, then Rictor appeared, his baleful eyes bright. "STOP THIS NOW!" In the shadow of his hat, his scarred face was twisted. "YOU WANTED ME HERE! BEGGED ME TO HELP YOU! AND THIS IS HOW YOU REPAY ME!" Rictor's voice dripped venomously with hate. "YOU'RE JUST LIKE MERL! LIAR! TURNCOAT!"

"LEAVE! NOW!" Heller shouted.

"I WILL NOT! I BELONG HERE! THIS TIME I'LL STEAL WHAT'S YOURS." Fighting against a spiraling maelstrom, Rictor swam closer and closer toward Madame Zanadane.

"I'm not afraid of you!" she defied him.

Rictor's eyes widened, then a slow, oily smile crawled along his face. He suddenly lunged at the Canadian psychic but fell short. "NO!" He began drifting upward. "KINDRICK! BAT! CRANE! Help me! LILLY!" Rictor continued to struggle, staring at Madame Zanadane, his eyes boring into her.

Madame Zanadane smiled, then suddenly wilted, her eyes rolling back as her face and body went slack. Dr. Strange and Heller tried to hold her aloft, but she slumped to the muddy ground.

"YES!" Rictor cried. The echo of his cry seemed to linger as darkness returned with the fury of the storm.

THIRTY-FOUR

"Take her to First Aid!" Dr. Landrum told the pair of security guards carrying the stretcher.

When they entered through the northern doors, the first thing everyone noticed was the lights. "All right! The power's back!" Angela cheered.

"What am I going to do?!" Heller moaned as he wrung his hands. "Everything I've worked for is ruined!"

"What did Rictor mean by 'you invited him'?" Angela asked. She pushed the wet hair from her face, unveiling a piercing stare.

Heller wore the look of someone hunted. "What do you mean?"

"He said you'd invited him," Angela repeated. "Everyone heard it, so don't try to deny it."

"Fool woman, he wasn't talking just to me, but to Blasing as well. Remember, against MY better judgment, we granted them permission to stay. I wanted to be done with them right away!"

"That's a lie! You hoped to have more free labor!" Angela snapped. "Now see where your greed has brought you!"

"Hah! This coming from a lawyer! Isn't that like the pot calling the kettle black?" he snapped.

"Answer Angela's question truthfully," Blasing said in a low, menacing voice. Since finding the lionhead ring, he'd fought to control a growing rage. He consciously unclenched his hands.

"I did speak the truth. We are in this together, Blasing."

"Yes we are," he replied coldly. "And I plan to solve it. And in doing so, the truth will be revealed."

Heller's eyes narrowed. "What do you mean by that?"

"You'll see. Though only the consequences will surprise you."

Heller stammered a bit. "Then solve it with my blessings!"

"Mr. Heller, did you have any dealings with Rictor before last week?" Xantini asked.

"Of course not!"

Xantini cocked an eyebrow. "I've never understood why people believe that lying is more believable if done with vehemence."

Heller glared, his face growing livid. "I don't care if you believe me. What're we going to do?"

"Just reverse whatever you did earlier," Xantini suggested.

Heller's eyes bulged, but before he could explode, Candy said, "Angela, I know you protected your room. Do you think you could protect a larger place?" Her question caught everyone's attention.

"I might, if I had the proper supplies," Angela replied.

"You can keep out ghosts?" Xantini asked, greatly interested. Angela nodded. "Fascinating. How?"

"I thought you could read minds."

Xantini sighed. "For everyone please." Angela explained about her grandmother and the protection ceremony.

"What do you need?" Dr. Strange asked.

"Salt, sage, hematites and quartz. I have the rest."

"There are plenty of psychics he'ah," Julie Zephren said. "Who knows what they might've brought with 'em."

"I have some sage," Dr. Strange told her.

"After I change into dry clothes, I'll start asking people," Candy said. The others agreed to do the same.

Heller appeared skeptical. "Then what?"

"We create a safe haven until we can figure out something else or can leave," Angela told him.

"The generator should be high on the list of places to protect," Blasing suggested. Everyone nodded. "I'd feel more comfortable with power at my fingertips. We might be able...."

"...to use it as a weapon," Xantini said. "I see. Broadcast signals bother them. With enough power, we might drive them away."

"Maybe even the televisions, if they could be rigged right," Blasing continued.

"Once we've located Angela's components, we should meet again to discuss our options," Dr. Strange said. "I've the feeling time's running out."

"Just in case the power goes again, does everyone still have their Walkie-Talkies?" Blasing asked. Candy and Xantini nodded. "I'll have some delivered to the rest of you. Use channel 6. See you all soon."

As Blasing and Angela finished changing clothes, there was a knock on the door. "Who is it?" Angela asked.

"Rod and me, Angel."

Angela peeked through the spyhole, then opened the door.

"Hi, Angel. Just wanted to stop by before making the rounds. See if there's anything else you need."

"We're surviving. Come in." Angela closed the door behind them.

"Still decorating in modern trashed style?" Candy said, surveying the shambled lounge.

"Yep. No reason to have it cleaned up. Last time our rooms were ransacked, too."

"Did your protection fail?" Candy asked.

"We don't think it was a ghost," Angela replied.

"Then why?" Candy asked. Angela ushered her toward Blasing's room. "Hello Blasing," Candy said. He was setting the VCR. "Getting ready to watch a movie? How to deal with unruly ghosts, maybe?"

"It's a tape from Heller's safe," Angela replied.

"Oh?" Candy appeared confused, until Angela told them about searching Porter's bag, the recorder in his office, the hole in Heller's wall, and Blasing breaking and entering.

"Angel, I always knew you were attracted to the roguish type."

"You're sure it was the same ring?" Rod asked.

"Positive," Blasing replied. "That entire... memory is burned into my mind. I'm hoping this is the proof we need to arrest Heller." Angela took his hand and squeezed it reassuringly.

"So Heller had Peter killed," Candy mused. "Just as you thought all along, Angel. But why? Do you think it has something to do with Peter's 'mistake'?"

"Maybe the tape will tell us," Blasing said. When he hit play, the screen flipped, then displayed Heller's office. Slumped in his mammoth chair with his face hovering over his hands, the Irishman worked paper. All the lights were on, eliminating almost every shadow as if Heller were afraid of the dark. The floor around his chair and the top of the desk were covered with unfinished origami— twisted, mangled or torn in two.

"Why's this happening to me?" Heller snapped, then tore the paper prop-plane-to-be in half. "I've planned everything so carefully, but nothing's going right." He tossed the scraps on the desk, adding to the heap. "I can't even fold paper, and I can do that in my sleep." Heller furtively glanced at the door, then rose to lock it. When he returned to his chair, he opened the middle desk drawer and removed a wooden box of pencils. The Irishman dug through them to remove a miniature silver spoon, then unscrewed the bottom of the ink well. "This should steady my nerves," he muttered as he dipped into the small plastic bag. He stuck the spoon into a nostril and inhaled. After re-loading, he repeated the action. He sniffed for a while and rubbed his eyes, then snatched up the paper with a smile and renewed vigor.

"His cold," Blasing commented.

The heap of warped origami blew onto the floor, and the hanging constructs swung wildly, then a shadowy figure stepped through the door. The tall stranger wore a long, dark coat, and a black stetson with a red band. His eyes shone bright yellow, but his face was dark until he took off his hat.

"MMM... MMM... Mac?" Heller's eyes bulged.

"Yes, 'tis me, Sean," the ghost said, his brogue thick. Heller's jaw slackened, his mouth open as wide as his unbelieving eyes. He tried to speak, but could not.

"I don't believe it! Mac is Rictor!" Blasing gasped. He hit the pause button on the remote. The ghost looked like a much younger version of Mac—tall and lean before the wine and rich food had made him soft. His hair was full and the color of orange flame. As usual, his nose was red, and his eyes housed green fire.

"Or has Rictor been masquerading as Peter?" Angela asked. "He hasn't been very helpful, just telling us to leave."

"I didn't think the ghosts could be filmed," Rod noticed.

"Proves my point; they're becoming more in tune with this dimension's vibration," Candy said.

Blasing hit the play button. "You... look younger, M... Mac," Heller finally managed.

"I can look as I please now, Sean," Mac said as he unbuttoned his coat. "And I know more than ever before. Aye, I know ye had me murdered! Murdered because of yuir drugs! At least I never would've killed ye over a woman or a case of wine!"

"YES!" Angela shouted triumphantly, her face aglow. Then she pointed at the screen. "We're going to nail you, you bastard!"

"Then Mac has been pretending to be Rictor," Blasing said. "But why?"

"MMM... Mac...." Heller stammered.

The ghost slowly strode toward the desk, crushing half-finished origami under his boots. "But you, my friend, used my weakness against me because I thought Earl's timeshare idea was a lousy one. Ya thought it was a lifesaver since ye needed the money to support yuir filthy habit. Ya even began running drugs, although small time, but it wasn't enough for you and Eva, eh? Ya got yuirself in too deep, didn't ye? Had ta get bigger. Had ta hire Porter. Did ye snort too much of the product? Ye know, you're weak just like yuir father, and it's turned ye black inside."

"I'm not like my father!" Heller raged. "I... I was afraid you'd turn us in because of what happened with Jaclyn. If only you hadn't gotten involved with the operation again."

"I know Porter and Madame Zanadane are in on it too, boyo. He hired the murderer, she set him up with the rings, then Porter, Chadwick and friends killed him, didn't they? Got hurt in the process, didn't they? Yuir man was good with a knife, eh? I guess they won't find him in that sidewalk in the northern wing."

Mac pushed back his coat and sat. He was packing a shiny Colt .45 on each hip. "But even if they do find the body, they won't be able to prove anything. Ye are sneaky, Sean. Have me sign that 60-day agreement, then muck up things by bringing in a ringer. Meg ain't my daughter. Finding out Jaclyn was pregnant with her by someone else was the reason we broke up." Mac's stare narrowed. "She's yuir daughter, isn't she?" Heller started, obviously surprised by the revelation. "Ya turned Jaclyn onto drugs, took 'er from me, didn't ye?!"

"I... I..." Heller stammered.

"I knew it!" Angela shouted. "Meg's a fake!"

"Now what should I do about it? What would you do? Kill you?" Mac's hand was a blur as he threw something, the knife snagging the Irishman's collar, pinning him to the chair.

With a laugh, Mac struck a match on the bottom of his boot to light a huge cigar. "Like shooting fish in a barrel, it is. I wonder if I should bother." He drew a six-shooter so quickly it simply appeared in his hand, spinning around before resting to point at Heller's face. "You know, I don't think I'll do anything yet." Mac chuckled as he donned his hat.

Mac's face slowly transformed, his eyes radiating a sickly yellow glow that hinted at a broad, bony face. "Not at least for a while."

"Rictor! What in the Hell are you doing?! You scared me half to death!"

"Half is better than all the way," Rictor chuckled, his voice once again harsh and heavily accented.

"Answer me!" Heller demanded.

"Practicing to be Peter MacGuire. Fooled you, didn't I?" he laughed harshly.

"I'm confused," Candy said.

"Shhh!" Angela susurated.

Heller was pale as he blustered, "This isn't what I hired you for! I hired you to control the ghosts so they wouldn't rat on me when I expand the operation. Say... were any of your ghosts involved in interrupting my sales presentation?"

"No." Rictor was stone faced.

Heller's expression was disbelief, but he just said, "All right. Tell me why you're stalking Blasing."

"That's my business."

"You work for me!" Heller slammed a fist on the table. "So that makes it my business!"

Rictor's gaze narrowed, his lips compressing to a white line before saying, "Don't worry. It's taken care of." His voice was quiet, but everyone watching shivered.

"What is it?" Heller asked.

"I was hoping to drive him into selling."

"I didn't ask you to do that. No, I think there's more to it than that. I won't let THIS lie pass."

Rictor's gaze became hooded. "Just a wayward woman. Lilly's sweet on him."

"Women," Heller hurrumphed. "What a pain. What did you do with the shrew and Grant Roberts?"

"We killed them as an example to others."

Heller's eyes shot up. "Didn't know you could kill a ghost! And put out that cigar!"

"It's not real."

"It still stinks. Now, about Carrie and Grant."

"A lot of things you don't know," Rictor said, his voice quietly menacing. "You just think you do, just like Merl. You're a lot like him. You even wear his ring."

Heller blanched, looked at his hand, then back at Rictor. "You knew Merl?"

"In passing," his harsh voice somehow hardened even more.

"What was he like?"

"Like I said, you two could have been twin brothers."

Heller beamed. "Thank you. Now, did you really have to kill Carrie and Grant? They were important assets."

"As was Mac, but he became expendable, didn't he? Listen, Mister Heller, my men and I have been doing as you asked. The ghosts fear us. Soon, they won't do anything without our approval— I mean your approval."

"So what're you doing here, Rictor, besides pissing me off?"

"I think the English butler is going to be a problem."

"Broderick? He's always a problem."

"I gathered. He and Cannon, maybe Dirk too, are the only strong-willed spirits left. The rest are a weak-hearted lot."

"What do you intend to do?"

"Round 'em up and put a scare into them, so don't worry if they disappear for a while. Broderick won't return, but the others will, unless they grow a backbone," He laughed raggedly.

"I don't care what you do as long as you don't interrupt business. Listen to me. We can lose a few ghosts but not too many. It's what attracts people."

"Don't worry, they'll be replaced. I'm at least thirty strong now and growing."

"Uh... speaking of stronger. You look more colorful. What's going on?"

"Let's just say I have plenty of support."

Candy and Angela exchanged glances.

"Fine," Heller said. "Just do as I say and we'll get along fine. Remember, I own this place. I'm the boss of Ghostal Shores."

"Sure. I remember. I know how that is. I was a boss once before. Merl worked for me.... You know, you're an inspiration to me and my men. Your evil shines like a beacon," he chuckled. "And I'm your right hand man. Your... ghost manager." He laughed. "Don't worry. I'll take care of business as if I owned the place. After all, we're birds of a feather." With that, Rictor turned and walked through the door.

"Damn it all!" Heller railed, then began to cry. "Mac, I am so sorry. So very sorry. I wish you were here today." Much quieter, he said, "I wish I hadn't had you killed." The Irishman wiped his eyes, blew his nose, then did another silver spoon of cocaine.

"That should be all we need to nail the bastard," Blasing said grimly. "And now we know Mac is really gone—has been gone."

"I knew Heller had murdered Peter. Felt it in my heart," Angela said. "Poor Carrie, I wish she were here to celebrate."

"We should copy it," Rod said.

"I'm hoping we already have the original. We'll find out soon, if it plays." Blasing loaded the cracked tape. There came a knocking, and he stopped. Drawing Mac's gun, he approached the door, then peeked through the spyhole. "It's Geoff."

"Does he always carry a gun?" Candy asked.

"Just recently," Angela said. "He's worried about security."

"I guess I don't blame him, but I thought he was in electronics," Candy said.

"I could sure use a cigarette right now," Angela said.

"Don't start," Candy said.

"Come in, Geoff. Your timing is perfect," Blasing said.

Dr. Landrum looked around at everyone, seeing the relief in their faces. He still wore his damp clothes and his hair was slicked back. "Glad something is. Have you watched the tape?"

"Yes. It was very enlightening. Come in," Blasing said.

"Have a seat," Angela said.

Blasing ejected Porter's tape and replaced it with Heller's. When the tape finished rewinding, Blasing hit play. As it rolled, Dr. Landrum was astonished, then grimly pleased. "This is from Porter, right?" Blasing explained about his adventure in breaking and entering. "From Heller, eh? Too bad this was obtained illegally."

"This wasn't." Blasing put in Chief Porter's tape. "But we haven't tried it again to see if it'll play." The screen flipped and the cracked tape squeaked but still played. They fast forwarded through a lot, but none was surprised when the same scene played out.

Holding out his hand, Dr. Landrum said, "I'd like the original."

Blasing ejected the tape, then gave it to him.

"You don't seem surprised, Geoff," Angela said.

Dr. Landrum chuckled. "Not as surprised as when you identified me as an undercover cop." Angela beamed. "Like you, I suspected this, I was just afraid we'd never prove it. And actually, I'm not local law enforcement. I'm DEA."

"Really?!" Angela exclaimed. "Then the plot thickens."

"Blasing, you don't look surprised," Dr. Landrum said.

"My surprise level is very high right now."

"And he said women and medicine were his only interests," Candy said wryly. "Typical male. Simply can't tell the truth."

"How long has your investigation been underway?" Blasing asked.

"For about a month before Peter MacGuire was murdered."

"Are agents still here?" Angela asked.

"Yes, and from what I've seen, we may need their help. You think all of security's involved in this, don't you?"

"I don't know about all, but we should suspect anybody Porter's hired," Blasing said.

"According to the files, that's all of them."

"What made you suspicious?" Candy asked.

"The department has been watching Eva Dare for a long time."

"Figures," Candy said. "Men can't help but."

"The last place she worked, the Marquis in Paris, was the site of a major drug bust about four months ago. She was incriminated, but there wasn't enough proof to arrest her. Some investigative undercover work led to busts in other resorts where Eva previously worked. Everything seemed to indicate she was involved in dealing, but we lack concrete evidence. She travels quite a bit internationally, so we're very concerned."

"So do the salespeople," Angela said. "They're almost like migrant workers, moving from resort to resort. They could carry drugs, couldn't they? Is Eva the organizing factor?"

"We think so. About a month back, DEA agents began investigating, but they haven't been able to find anything here. Not a scrap of evidence. We were thinking of pulling out when Peter MacGuire was murdered."

"Will you shut down the resort?" Blasing asked.

"Yes, but we'll have to wait until reinforcements arrive. Even if I make a cellular call, they wouldn't be able to get here."

"I wish they could," Angela said gleefully. "I'd like to see Heller arrested."

"We have to solve the ghost problem first," Blasing reminded her. "It's only four hours until dark."

"I think taking Heller out of the mix would help—and so did Grant Roberts," Angela said.

"What?!" Blasing exclaimed.

She explained about Rod's channeling. "Just another reason I'd like to see him arrested. If you remember, the ghosts often said like attracts like, so if Heller was gone...."

"I'm concerned Heller might get wind," Blasing began, "from a listening device, a ghost, or who knows what, and slip away."

"I'll order the roads blocked. Have the Coast Guard patrol, just in case. I'm tempted to even call in a chopper."

"I wish they could come right now," Angela said. "I fear we may not last 'til morning."

"Do you really think we're in that much trouble?" Rod asked.

"It's not just the ghosts." Blasing reminded him about their car "accident."

A deafening alarm suddenly sounded, shaking the hallway walls. "The fire alarm!" Dr. Landrum exclaimed.

Blasing grabbed his Walkie-Talkie. "Security, this is Blasing. What's going on? Fire in the kitchen, come on!" He put the tape in his jacket and rushed out the door with Dr. Landrum close behind him. Angela, Candy and Rod followed.

Blasing and Dr. Landrum pushed open the stairwell door and bounded down the steps. When they arrived at the foyer, the alarm still blared. Frightened people milled about with pained expressions, their hands over their ears. Others moved hesitantly toward the front doors, buttoning their coats and readying their umbrellas. A small group gathered around the entryway to the Clifftop Bar. Security guards suddenly appeared from the bayview stairs. Pushing their way through the throng, they ran up the ramp. Blasing and the others followed.

As he entered the bar, Blasing smelled an acrid plastic-wood stench. Smoke roiled along the ceiling, coming out of the restaurant. Blasing and Dr. Landrum sprinted to the Pacific Crest dining room.

The restaurant appeared to be enshrouded in fog with rain drizzling on their tables. Smoke billowed from the doors to the kitchen. A group of servers, security, and onlookers anxiously waited nearby. The sprinklers appeared to be working sporadically, spraying some of the restaurant. Tawny Lane and her camera man had found a dry spot and were reporting and taping.

Two men in blue wielding fire-extinguishers moved closer to spray the base of the doorway. A stout security guard carrying a man with blackened clothing suddenly burst through the double doors. She staggered several steps, then passed him to those waiting. Dr. Landrum rushed forward. After a quick check, he began resuscitation on the red-haired man. The woman guard collapsed to her knees and coughed violently.

The pair with fire extinguishers opened the doors and slowly moved into the kitchen. "Holy...!!" one cried as flame belched from the entryway as if dragon's breath, driving them back outside. Their clothing caught fire. They pointed the extinguishers at each other, letting loose and dousing the flames.

"What's going on?" Blasing asked a waitress.

"Kitchen fire! We haven't seen Pietro!"

"The head chef," Angela told him.

One of the kitchen doors swung open with a belch, but this time steam instead of smoke poured from the charred maw. Warm moistness wafted over them. Water streamed out under the door.

"I think the sprinklers are working. Something's going right for once," Blasing said.

"Don't go in yet," Angela said, gently grabbing his good arm. "Wait until it clears some more. Feel any ghosts?" she asked. Blasing shook his head no.

The power abruptly failed. The room dimmed to a foggy grayness, weak light filtering in from the coastal windows. "Par for the course." Blasing pulled out his penlight. "Stay here." He moved to the door. Rod joined him.

"Let's go in," a security guard behind Blasing said.

"You lead, Chet," Blasing said, not trusting security. The beefy guard motioned to another large man named Bruce. Flashlights in one hand, and an extinguisher in another, they entered the dark kitchen.

"Be careful," Angela yelled, then began pacing. As she neared the cordoned-off Clifftop Bar, Angela saw a shadowy figure. Was it Marsh? She rushed toward it.

"Marsh! Talk to me, dammit! Did you start this fire? Where is everybody?!" The shadowy figure turned, his broad, mocking smile almost as bright as his yellow eyes peering from the shadows of his black hat.

"That's not Marsh! It's Rictor, the sonuvabitch! Do I have a surprise for him!" Candy sprinted in pursuit. Rictor ducked through a wall. Screaming, "Coward!" Candy rounded the corner, chasing him.

"Candy, wait! You can't catch him!" Worried about her friend, Angela followed.

As Angela rounded the corner, Rictor slipped through the mirrors behind the bar. "Face me, you coward!" Candy cried. She raced behind the bar, heading for the door to the storage room.

"Candy wait! He wants you to follow!" Angela yelled. Her friend hit the door hard, slamming it open and disappearing into the dark storage room. Angela followed, pausing at the dark, open door. "Candy, are you all right?"

"He's in here, I can feel him, mocking me—taunting me!"

Angela peered inside. Suddenly, the door swung shut. Thinking he wanted them separated, Angela jumped inside. The storeroom was pitch dark. "Damn you, Candy!" Angela reached into her purse for her squeeze flashlight. "Candy?"

"I'm here, and so is he."

"Are you all right?"

"I... I don't know. It's almost as if...."

A creaking sounded above them. Angela sensed motion and flashed her light upward. "It's a trap!" Heavy cabinets full of supplies fell toward them, bottles slipping out ahead of the brunt of the avalanche. Candy dove toward Angela, knocking her down and landing atop her friend. They were pummeled for a moment, then a mammoth shadow slammed them to the floor.

Waves of cool and warm air swirled around Blasing as he and the others searched the kitchen. Between the steam and the stench of burning flesh it was hard to breathe. Blasing paused to tie a handkerchief over his nose and mouth.

"Anything?" Chet asked, wiping his glasses with a sleeve. Illuminating the steam, four beams of light scoured the dark kitchen. Water poured from everything—over tables, from counter tops and out of and down the cabinets. Frozen foods, lettuce and vegetables drifted in the current toward the exits. Along with the produce, Blasing spotted a charred spatula and a blackened chef's hat. A man in a burnt, once-white kitchen uniform floated near a sunken fire extinguisher.

"Check him, Bruce," Chet said to his partner. Bruce carefully checked the body for lifesigns, then shook his head.

Blasing was wary, keeping one eye on the pair. They reminded him of enforcers; Chet looked like he'd once been a defensive lineman, his shoulders wide and his legs the size of treetrunks. Bruce could have been a marine, lean and stoic with a flattop.

Blasing felt a slight tingle as if ghosts were near, then it was gone. "It started over there." Blasing pointed with his light to the grill area. The walls were blackened, and the chef's serving window was scorched, the paint blistered and bubbled. The scent of fried wiring and flesh was overwhelming. A crumpled body lay near the stove. For just a moment, Blasing saw Angela's body in its place. He shivered and pushed away the unpleasant thought.

Chet walked toward the downed figure. "Poor Pietro." The head chef appeared to have collapsed atop a frying pan. Broken wine and rum bottles were everywhere, and it appeared a shelf had collapsed.

"Poor soul," Blasing said. Again he thought of Angela—knew she was in trouble. "Rod, Angela's in trouble." The hair on his neck stood.

"Are you sure? Candy was with her," Rod asked.

"Then come on," Blasing said, ignoring the presence of ghosts. The security guards jumped him, driving him back against a metal cabinet. Pain lanced down his arm and up his neck, making his head spin. Bruce swung him back toward Chet.

"What's going on?!" Rod cried as he spun around, blinding one with his flashlight.

"Go find Angela!" Blasing cried. Why were they trying to kill him now? Rod was a witness!

With glazed eyes but smiling, Chet swung his flashlight. Blasing twisted, taking a glancing blow, then brought up his knee. With a gasp of pain, Chet collapsed. A mist rose from his body as if he'd overheated.

Blasing head-butted the guard holding him. Chet screamed as his nose erupted. Before he could follow-up, there was a CLANG, and the guard pitched forward, out cold before he hit the floor.

"Come on," Rod said. He dropped the frying pan and ran from the kitchen with Blasing on his heels.

They frantically searched the restaurant but didn't see either of them. "Something's very wrong," Blasing said. Where would Angela have gone? He closed his eyes, trying to feel for her. He found himself drifting toward the Clifftop Bar.

"I don't see them," Rod said. Blasing followed his feelings to the bar, then around behind it to the storeroom door. "In there?" Rod tried to open the door. "Something's blocking it!"

"Keep trying," Blasing said, then ran around to the restaurant side of the horse-shaped copper bar. The other storeroom door opened easily. "Rod, get Dr. Landrum!" Blasing yelled, his light dancing across the jumbled pile of cabinets, boxes and bottles atop the women's bodies. With strength he didn't know he possessed, Blasing cleared the pile, lifting one shelf, then the other, and shoving them aside. "Oh, Lord! No!"

Blood seeping from her ear and with her neck lying at an awkward angle, Candy lay atop Angela. Her blond hair was stained, blood welling from a wound to her head.

THIRTY-FIVE

Blasing immediately began mouth-to-mouth, watching Angela's chest expand. He checked her pulse again; it was weak and thready. "Dammit, Angela! Don't leave! Fight!"

"How's she doing?" Dr. Landrum asked as he entered the storeroom. Rod was right behind him.

"Her pulse is weak, and her breathing is rapid and shallow."

"And Candy?" Rod asked, worry heavy in his voice.

"There was nothing I could do for her," Blasing said.

Dr. Landrum examined Candy. "A broken neck. She died instantly." He looked to Rod. "Painlessly. I'm sorry."

"Oh no, Candy." Rod knelt by her body, gently cradling her.

"She was atop Angela, probably tried to save her life," Blasing said.

Dr. Landrum moved to Angela, checking her vital signs. "She's in shock, and I'm afraid there's probably intracranial bleeding. She needs oxygen."

"I've already called security," Blasing said. "If I'd been thinking clearly, I would've called you on the Walkie-Talkie."

"I'm sorry, Blasing," Dr. Landrum said when he finished examining Angela. "We need a miracle."

All Blasing could think was that it couldn't end like this. Was this all there was? If so, it was a cruel joke at best. Blasing took Angela's hand and squeezed. She looked pale as a ghost, and he feared she was about to become one. "Angela, come on! Fight! Stay with me! I love you! You've said the spirit is stronger than the flesh—can mend the flesh, now prove it to me!"

"Blasing?" came a questing, tentative voice. Blasing rubbed the back of his neck and prayed the ghost wasn't Angela's.

"Candy?!" Rod exclaimed as he jerked upright. "She's...." he stopped, paralyzed by astonishment as a swirling mist exited Candy's form. The spirit hovered above Candy's body, where it assumed a vaguely human shape. "Candy?" Rod managed.

"I... I think so. Yes! This is so incredible! I... I... even in my wildest imaginings I never dreamed."

"Candy, I love you," Rod said, his voice breaking.

"Darling, the light is so bright. So warm and welcoming.... Rod, I love you too, but it's time." The spirit's face clarified, and Candy's expression radiated love and compassion. Her eyes were incandescent, suns aborning in them.

"Candy, is... Angela w- with you?" Blasing asked.

"Angel, why... oh, no! Angel!" Candy's ghost drifted to Angela. "Wait! She's not with me yet! There's still hope!"

"How can I help?!" Blasing demanded.

"First, take off her pendant and rings," Candy told him. Blasing did. "Now take her in your arms and surround her with your love. I'll help as much as I can."

Blasing let his love wash over Angela. As tears rolled down his cheeks, he kept cajoling her to return to him—to look to the future. She looked serene, ready to accept death and whatever came afterward.

Candy's spirit sank into her friends motionless body. Angela shivered twice but showed no signs of improvement. After a few moments, Candy's ghost sat up in Angela's body. "It's not working. You love her as much as any man can, Blasing, but you're untrained."

"Tell me what to do?!" Blasing cried out in frustration.

"I'm too new in this... form. Certain... things elude my understanding."

"I'll help," came a new voice. "It's the least I can do."

"Who?" Blasing asked, feeling a second ghost. "Lilly?"

The female spirit slowly became visible, her sad, green eyes appearing first, then her beautiful face—her expression a mixture of compassion and longing. The cold aloofness Blasing remembered was long gone. She wore a frilly, shoulderless gown of emerald that billowed to the floor as if a weeping willow.

"What're you doing here?" Blasing asked. "And where's Rictor?!"

"Occupied. As to why I'm here, for all my existence, I've searched for such love as you and Angela have."

"You mustn't search for your other haf—not the one that makes you whole," Candy said, "but one who complements your wholeness already."

"I know that now. Blasing, you and Angela have shown me this. And Candy, your selfless love embarrasses me. I couldn't stop Rictor—stop this, but I think I can help Angela. I want to help."

"Please," Blasing told Lilly. "Please help us."

Lilly sank into Angela's body.

Blasing and Dr. Landrum watched in amazement as the wound on Angela's head magically mended. Angela took a deep, shuddering breath, then her eyes fluttered open. "Blasing?" she asked. He hugged her, then they kissed.

When they separated, Angela said, "Thank you. That was worth it," in a strange voice, then Lilly drifted from Angela's body.

"Angela?" Blasing asked, looking from Lilly to his love. "Lilly, what did you do?"

"Added my spirit to hers. She is right. We are only limited by what we believe."

Angela blinked quickly several times. "Blasing? What happened? I feel so weak." Blasing hugged her, not wanting to let go, but Dr. Landrum insisted on examining her.

"Rictor tried to kill you. Candy and Lilly saved your life."

"Candy? Yes, I remember. Candy said good-bye. Said not to cry," Angela said. Tears rimmed in her eyes. "And I remember... Rod, she said she'd be waiting for you, preparing a warm welcome, and that she would be near to comfort you." Angela's eyes were out of focus. "But some of her will always be with me."

With a choked cry, Rod huddled over Candy.

"Incredible. Simply incredible. Her vitals are normal," Dr. Landrum said. "Angela, watch my fingers." He moved them back and forth before her eyes.

"I feel fine, except I'm tired and heartsick for...." Her sigh was shuddering. "Blasing, my love! My heart! You brought me back! I came back for you!" She smiled, wonder illuminating her eyes and expression when she said, "I could hear my ancestors chanting, and I wanted to embrace the light, then I heard you. I could feel your love healing me, making me whole and knew it wasn't my time." She gently touched his face. After long moments of drinking in the sight of him, she looked over to Lilly. "And thank you, Lilly."

The spirit smiled, her green eyes aglow. Brighter than before, the ghost effused a light from deep within.

"Angela?" She slumped in his arms.

"Just sleeping," Dr. Landrum said, calming Blasing. "It's incredible. I can't find any sign of an injury. I knew there had to be other ways of healing. Of practicing medicine. The meaning of this is... is...." He groped for the word.

"Profound," Blasing finished for him.

When security arrived, they looked at Rod huddled over Candy's body, then at Dr. Landrum. "She's gone," he told them as he nodded toward Candy. "Lay her in the refrigerator with the others."

"I want to go with them," Rod said. Dr. Landrum simply nodded.

"I'm taking Angela back to our room," Blasing said. "You should check on the guards in the kitchen." Blasing briefly explained about the strangely-timed attack and his suspicions about the ghosts.

"I'll see to them, then come check on Angela."

"We must hurry," Lilly urged. "There's little time before darkness, and Rictor is very angry with you. Many have deserted him for the Great Beyond." Her smile was broad, then faded just as fast. "Right now he's rallying those who remain, but very soon he'll vent his anger on this place and these people."

Ignoring the pain in his shoulder, Blasing gently carried Angela through the crowd toward the stairs. Heller rushed, brandishing his cane causing people to dance out of his path. "Blasing! What in hell's name is going on?!"

With a cold, fierce stare, Blasing walked wordlessly by him. Heller didn't ask any more questions, but followed Dr. Landrum when he motioned toward the kitchen.

Lilly re-appeared when the elevator doors closed. "I didn't want that man to see me."

"Because he and Rictor are in cahoots?"

"Not any longer. Lon has his own plans. Always has."

"Oh, where is Rictor now?"

"Gathering his scattered forces. That's why I can roam free. He doesn't have time to concentrate on keeping me under his thumb. Blasing, will you keep me from Lon? I have been his possession for a long time."

Blasing nodded. "If I can. If we drive Rictor from Ghostal Shores, will you be free?"

"I believe so."

"But how do we do that?" Blasing asked as the elevator opened.

"I'm not quite sure."

They walked in silence to the suite, where Blasing sensed for other ghosts. When he didn't feel any, he opened the door. "Do you know what happened to Broderick and the others?"

"They are being held captive in the bricks. There is something special about them."

"I don't understand. The bricks?"

"Neither do I. Nor why they are still prisoners. There are enough of your friends to escape, since they outnumber their captors, but they lack heart. I fear they'll remain prisoners until Lon is driven from here." Lilly looked around at the devastated lounge. "What happened here?"

"We thought you might have done it," Blasing replied.

"No. You cleaned up after I tore it apart in a fit of pique."

"Angela thought as much," Blasing sighed. "If only Mac was here to help us."

"Blasing, I have a confession. It was me near the bricks, looking like Mac."

"And in the overlook?" Blasing asked. Lilly nodded. "And outside our rooms?"

"No. It must have been someone else."

When Blasing set Angela on her bed, she mumbled, "Rictor convinced you to do it because he wasn't scaring away Blasing?"

"Yes. I thought it was a good idea at the time. It seemed the safest way to get you to leave—I didn't want Blasing hurt—but it backfired. Afterward, you seemed even more determined to stay."

"Then you've always been following me?" Blasing asked as he sat on the bed. "Did you also take my wife's—Jennifer's—form?"

"Yes, I'm sorry. I drew on powerful memories and..." she shrugged defeatedly. "I am so sorry."

Angela squeezed Blasing's arm. "It's all right." he told her. "I thought as much. Lilly, what happened to Fawn?"

"We both followed you at first. I was jealous and tried chasing her away. When she wouldn't leave you alone, I hauled her to the bricks for a spirit-to-spirit talk. For some reason, she became stuck there. It gave Lon his idea to hold the ghosts hostage. I'm so sorry."

It's all my fault. What are we going to do?"

"I have an idea," Angela said. "When I was dying, I received a different perspective. It seemed to confirm what I thought."

"You need rest," Blasing tried to soothe her.

"I can rest when Rictor is gone. Broderick was right."

"About?"

"Like attracting like. There is an...ambiance about Ghostal Shores that holds Rictor here. His presence also contributes to it. Remember how I told you it seemed Ghostal Shores had changed?" she asked. Blasing nodded. "Well, they were probably planning Peter's murder. That drew malevolent spirits."

"Yes, it awakened him," Lilly said. "He met Marsh first, who put him in contact with Sean Heller. Things worked out just as Rictor planned. Heller wanted more ghosts—more free entertainers, and someone to control the other ghosts. Rictor knew this before he ever met Heller and manipulated him."

"With Peter gone, the entire atmosphere changed."

"It mirrors Heller, a place of greed and selfishness."

"And Lon," Lilly added. "They are two of a kind."

"As long as Heller remains an owner, Rictor will have power. We must change the resonance of Ghostal Shores," Angela said.

"How do we do that?" Blasing asked.

"Lon thrives on the permission he received from Heller," Lilly agreed. "He wanted Lon to recruit a gang to keep the ghosts in line, so they wouldn't expose his outlaw activities." Blasing felt his fury build, no longer a hot fire, but a cold, calculating hate. "Don't let your hate guide you as it did Lon."

Blasing flushed. "But Heller renounced his invitation."

"It must've been too late," Angela said. "They're birds of a feather. Rictor is just doing what Heller did in hiring security."

"But why can't the Ghostal Shores spirits see you? See Rictor and his gang?" Blasing asked.

"I don't know." Lilly appeared thoughtful. "But the local spirits are very different than us, and I'm not just talking about being more colorful or better defined. There's something about being at Ghostal Shores, maybe because they've been interacting intimately with people, that makes them different. I remember when we first arrived, Lon told us to stay in shadows—to be invisible. The locals never saw us, and soon the gang thought they were invisible. He tells them that all the time. Be invisible."

"Candy might suggest that because you're spirit, your thoughts affect your ethereal form more quickly than if you had a body," Angela said. "Or maybe you're just operating at a different level—a higher vibration—than the Ghostal Shores spirits. Contact with humans could change that. Who knows? I'm not sure it matters," she sighed. "Lilly, what can you tell us about Rictor?"

"More than I wish I knew. Lon Rictor was born in Austria. When he was a young man, he heard the stories of fame and fortune in the West. He came over by boat, then travelled across the country until he found a job in Bodie working for the Morrison Mining Company. As with many of the miners, he saw nothing wrong with stealing. Soon killing anybody that got in his way was easy."

"He worked his way through the fledgling union ranks until he was its right hand man, but in truth, he ran things with Marlbro as a figurehead. As part of their extortion, several times they almost burned down Bodie. Resistance was eventually worn away and his gang was running the town. Lon even branched out into other towns, like Goldfield, where Merl Heller ran the operation."

"Sean's ancestor?!" Blasing asked.

"Why am I not surprised?" Angela asked rhetorically. "Candy claimed it had something to do with the past."

"One night when Merl was in Bodie, he paid men to jam shut all the doors and set the Golddust Hotel on fire. They shot anyone who tried to escape. Many of us died that night. Fitting justice, I guess, considering how many people Lon killed that way." She shuddered, then hugged herself. "I thought I was finally free of him, but I remember Lon yelling he would never rest."

"You think he's going to torch Ghostal Shores tonight?" Angela asked. Lilly nodded. "Why didn't he do this earlier?"

"He was building his gang and waiting for the right moment."

"No amount of hematite will protect us," Angela said.

"We can't let all these people die," Blasing gnashed. "We've got to do something!" He began pacing.

"If we demonstrate we can handle evil on the physical plane," Angela began, "it might give us an edge in dealing with the malevolent spirits. At least weaken them. Usually it works the other way, spirit to flesh, but this is an unusual case."

"So Geoff must arrest Heller?" Blasing asked.

"And you have to proclaim yourself sole owner of Ghostal Shores. You're no longer in doubt of your ownership. Meg is a fraud. Your assumption of control might tip the scales," Angela said. "It doesn't sound like much, but...."

"If you do that," Lilly said, "the outlaws will respect Blasing. They may see that the adventure Lon promised was bright and shiny, but simply fool's gold. Demand they leave, and I believe few, if any, will stay with Lon. And for all his bravado, he is a coward. I don't believe he'll stand alone."

"That seems so simple," Blasing said.

"The physical is tied to the spiritual, and vice-versa. As above, so below," Angela said wearily. "Please try it, my love." He nodded. "Lilly, how did you become involved with Rictor?"

"My family was poor and didn't need another mouth to feed. His wedding presents helped save my family from starvation. At least he helped me pursue my love, the stage and theater."

"He bought you!" Angela raged. Lilly bowed her head, "So he still thinks of you as property."

"Yes, I go where Lon goes, and we go where the bricks go. That warehouse in L.A. was a depressing place. We have an affinity for the brick," Lilly began. "Maybe when we burned to death, our spirits sought something material and latched onto them."

"Could we trap Lon inside the bricks? Haul them inside, then do the reverse of what I've done to our rooms?" Angela wondered.

"Then what?" Blasing asked.

"I don't know love, but maybe it would buy us time until the roads are clear, and we can evacuate this place."

"If only there was some way to disband his gang," Lilly said.

"We tried that," Blasing said, then answered the knocking at the door. After checking to be sure it was safe, he let in Dr. Landrum. He moved immediately to Angela's side.

"Amazing," he told her. "You're as healthy as ever."

"Thank you, I feel that way, too."

"How many died in the fire?" Blasing asked the doctor.

"Three. The fire started near the griddle. We found broken bottles of alcohol. High proof, extremely flammable stuff."

"Ghosts, do you think?" Angela asked.

"Probably. We just don't know for sure," Dr. Landrum replied.

"What did Bruce and Chet have to say?" Blasing asked.

"They seem to be suffering from amnesia; the last thing they remember is running up the stairs to respond to the alarm. You must have hit them hard. Are you going to press charges?"

Angela hadn't heard about this, so Blasing thoroughly explained about the attacks in the kitchen. "They were possessed," Angela said. "Since they can't affect us directly, they tried indirectly. You with possessed people, me with falling objects."

"Suggestions on what to do?" Dr. Landrum asked. Angela explained why they should arrest Heller. Lilly re-affirmed it. "Why should we trust you?" he asked the spirit.

"She saved my life, Geoff," Angela replied for Lilly.

He sighed, then contacted his fellow agents on his cellular phone. "They'll be ready in five minutes," Dr. Landrum said. "I'd like to do this as smoothly and quietly as possible."

"I don't think that's possible," Angela said. "Heller will rant, rave, and scream so loudly everyone will hear it."

"Good," Lilly said. "All the ghosts should hear him, too."

Dr. Landrum sighed. "Angela, I wish you'd reconsider."

"And miss Heller getting arrested? I wouldn't miss this for the world! I'd crawl from my death bed, maybe even the grave to see Heller arrested for Peter's murder. Besides, you're just afraid it might be dangerous, right?" she said pointedly. He nodded.

"I'm not sure she'd be safe here, either," Blasing said. "Lilly says she didn't cause this and look what happened in the kitchen. What if they start possessing people?"

"They won't try it very often," Lilly said. "It's very tiring. Those two spirits won't be able to do much until tomorrow."

"And last time I strayed away from Blasing, I almost got killed," Angela said. "He's my good luck charm."

"My guardian angel works diligently," he said with a smile.

Lilly laughed. They stared at her. "Sorry. I can't tell you. You must discover certain things on your own."

"I told you I didn't trust her," Dr. Landrum growled. "Besides, won't she draw Rictor to us?"

"No," Angela said. "Lilly?" The spirit drifted toward Angela, who opened her arms and embraced her. Ever so slowly, the two merged, Angela absorbing the century-old spirit. "Now we're ready."

THIRTY-SIX

After Blasing was deputized, they descended the stairs to the lobby. Angela was excited, hoping she'd finally get to see justice done. One of her promises fulfilled.

Even with lanterns, the lobby seemed dimly lit, and the shadows heavily cloaked. The tension was thick. Staff members looked nervous. Caged animals awaiting slaughter came to Angela's mind. Nobody understood why the power was out, and everyone felt the after affects of the kitchen fire. What would happen next time if there weren't any sprinklers to stop it? There wasn't any place to go.

Angela was glad the lobby was virtually empty. Blasing and Geoff carried guns, just in case security attempted to prevent the arrest. She tried to identify Geoff's fellow DEA agents, and only spotted one—a woman with a linebacker's build—because she nodded to Landrum.

"We're set," he said. "Now's as good a time as any."

"With the power out, this should make things easier," Blasing said. "Security won't be able to use camera surveillance."

"Never thought of this blackout as a blessing," Angela murmured as they neared the door to the management offices. The new assistant manager, Decker, looked curiously at them. Blasing nodded. The bespectacled young man went back to work.

"Feeling any ghosts?" Angela asked.

Blasing shook his head. When he opened the door they could hear Eva's demanding voice. "Enough, Sean! Cheri´, please tell me, what did that ghost, Rictor, mean when he said you'd invited him?!"

"Eva, I did no such...."

"I heard it from the Great Xantini!"

"Eva, shut the door or lower...."

"You did, didn't you? I can see it in your face! You invited that ghost here! Why?!"

"I don't have to stand for this, woman! I own this place!"

"We had a deal! We're partners, and YOU promised to consult

with me on anything as important as employing strongarm ghosts! They're your spirit enforcers, aren't they?!"

"Get out, bitch! Get the hell out of my life!" Heller raged, his chair creaking as he rose.

"I'd leave immediately if I could, but we're trapped here! Trapped with those damned ghosts! First the brawl, then the stripping at the bar, then... then these... visions, or whatever they are. People are dropping like flies. Cash, Becker, Porter, and now Madame Zanadane. They were in this with us. Am I next?" Her laugh was tinged with hysteria. "They're going to kill us, aren't they? You've lost control, and they're going to kill us all!"

"You forgot to mention Mac," Blasing said as he walked into the room.

"A ghost didn't kill Mac!" Heller blurted, then noticed the trio. "What're you three doing skulking around?!"

"Who's skulking?" Angela replied icily.

"I see you're obviously all right, Ms. Starborne. Care to explain what's going on?" Heller asked.

"No. Although it involves legalities, it's not my department," she told him, then smiled frostily at Eva, thinking, "you're finally getting what you deserve, bitch."

"Sean Heller, you're under arrest for the murder of Peter MacGuire," Dr. Landrum told him. "You have the right to remain silent."

"WHAT?!" Heller exploded, his eyes as wide as golfballs and his face as colorless as a transient spirit's.

"Anything you say can and will be used against you in a court of law. You have the right to an attorney," Dr. Landrum continued.

"This is outrageous!" Heller roared; the veins in his forehead stood out prominently. Dr. Landrum continued advising the Irishman of his rights. "Ludicrous! Mac and I were partners! Witnesses saw his killer escape!"

Angela was watching Eva; she tried to hide her dread, but her dull gaze told the tale. Slowly, she sank into a chair.

"You put him up to this, didn't you, Blasing?" Heller shouted.

"We provided him with the proof," Blasing admitted.

"There's no proof! You're lying!" Like a hobbled bull, Heller charged Blasing. When the Irishman swung his cane, Blasing caught it easily, then yanked it from Heller's grasp, throwing him off balance. As he fell forward, Blasing grabbed him by his collar.

"We have your confession on video tape," Blasing said coldly, now nose to nose with Heller. "I got it from Porter."

The color drained from Heller's face. "I... I don't know w- what you're talking about."

"But I do, and that's all that counts," Dr. Landrum said. He pulled the Irishman's arms around behind him, then handcuffed Heller to the chair.

"I—want to talk to my lawyer."

"Certainly," Dr. Landrum said, "when the phones are working."

"Eva..." Heller began.

"I had nothing to do with this!"

"In exchange for information, we would be willing to provide immunity," Dr. Landrum told her. "But we want to know about all the places you've worked. About all your contacts in the states and abroad. Otherwise, there might be extradition proceedings. Foreign prisons can be so... uncivilized, especially for a woman of your breeding."

Eva's dark face paled. Her mouth worked silently for several seconds before she said, "Geoff, I... I thought we had something going."

"We did. A narcotics investigation. Would you like to talk?"

"Eva, don't say a word!" Heller shouted. Dr. Landrum gagged him.

Eva's beautiful face twisted hatefully. "Not until I've spoken to my lawyer."

"Fine," Dr. Landrum said. He moved a chair flush against the back of Heller's, then handcuffed Eva to Heller's cuffs. When Dr. Landrum finished reading Eva her rights, he said, "Let's shut down security. Angela, call us if they try to leave."

"Why don't you just leave me a gun? I could blow off his kneecaps if he tries to escape," Angela said wickedly. "But my aim is poor and I might misfire high." Heller looked apoplectic.

"Come on, Blasing."

"Be careful, love," Angela told him.

Blasing kissed her, then followed Dr. Landrum to the lobby. Blasing looked around to see if anyone had noticed Heller's shouting.

From the clerks' reactions—heads down and studiously busy despite the computers being off line—they had, but were ignoring it, fearing his wrath would spread to them.

When the duo reached the door to security, Dr. Landrum nodded imperceptibly to his partners. Then he opened the door and followed Blasing into the lantern-lit offices. Only one guard was present, and he manned dispatch. Behind the guard, the monitors were as dark as empty eye sockets in a skull. Only the radio's red and green battery-powered lights were bright in the dimness.

"Marlin?" Blasing thought he remembered the man's name.

The blonde-haired man sat up straighter. "Yes sir, Mr. Madera?"

"Sean Heller has just suffered a minor stroke," Blasing gestured to Dr. Landrum, who nodded. "So I'm running the resort."

"Yes, sir."

"How many men are working right now?"

"A dozen. Instead of three shifts, we're working two twelves."

"You can contact everybody by Walkie-Talkie, right?" Blasing asked. Marlin nodded. "Good. Call everybody. We're having a meeting right here in fifteen minutes."

"But sir...."

"Fifteen minutes!" Blasing snapped, doing his best Sean Heller imitation. "And whoever can't make it will be terminated immediately! They can walk out of here, for all I care!"

"Yes sir! Right away, sir!"

Blasing hovered over the big-boned man as Marlin made the general call. He received a lot of flack until Blasing snapped, "Whoever doesn't show in fifteen minutes is gonna get their ass fired." Marlin passed on the message, which eliminated all balking.

"I'm going to look in on Heller, see how he's doing," Dr. Landrum said.

Blasing nodded, then sat on a desk below Porter's office window and waited. Blue-uniformed guards trickled in, sometimes in groups, but mostly one by one. Almost everybody looked tired. Most were worried, wondering what else had gone wrong. Blasing recognized Kerry, who'd helped Chadwick and Dr. Landrum transport Nate Zucker, and the two who had been attacked by Rictor outside Heller's office—Macon and a square-jawed man with a scar. Sharon looked sick from pulling the young man from the burning kitchen. Max, the man who had been on duty near the front desk when Mac was murdered, still didn't appear any more alert than when Blasing had interviewed him.

Bruce and Chet, moving as if still dizzy from being possessed, approached him. "Mr. Madera. We don't remember it, but we heard about what we did and want to apologize," Chet said. Bruce nodded. "We don't know what came over us."

"I think I do. Sit. I'll explain everything soon."

A few hard faces with shifty eyes looked at Blasing suspiciously, and from time to time, they eyed the door as though contemplating escape. When they asked questions, Blasing responded brusquely with, "You'll know when everyone gets here!"

Marlin whispered to a flaming red-haired woman, and news of Heller's condition quickly spread. The whispering sounded like the back of a classroom. It was constantly interjected with the same question. "Where's Chadwick?"

Blasing wondered the same thing. He thought he heard someone whisper, "Could be a set-up." About the time a few guards shifted, looking ready to leave, Dr. Landrum walked in. "He's stable." That seemed to settle those preparing for flight. He moved to stand behind those leaning against the wall in the short entryway hall.

"Good," Blasing said, then glanced at his watch. A quick count numbered nineteen guards. "Well, times up," Blasing said. "I guess I'll need to promote a new chief of security." Where was Chadwick?

"I'm interested," someone said.

"Dixon, you cannibal."

"That's right, babe."

"People," Blasing began, then two more guards walked in, making the number twenty-one. Three to go, but Blasing knew he couldn't wait. "As you've heard, Mr. Heller suffered a minor stroke. Doctor." Blasing gestured to Landrum.

"We don't know the extent of the damage, and won't until we get him to the hospital. Currently, he has limited movements in two of his limbs, but he can't speak sensibly."

"What else is new?" someone snickered. The dangerous tension left as if air whooshing from a balloon.

"Knew he'd bust a gut or something one day," Max said. A few people laughed.

"Got what he deserved," Bruce added.

Blasing drew Mac's .38 from his jacket and laid it across his legs. "Ladies and gentleman, these are dangerous times, with numerous people dead or injured over the past few days." Every eye was on him and the gun, which he raised for affect. "You're probably wondering what good this will do against a ghost, and I tell you, nothing." A few that might have been reaching for hidden weapons paused, giving Dr. Landrum time to identify them. "There isn't much physically we can do to the ghosts, but I have an idea. Who knows about the signal boosters on the cameras?"

Almost everyone raised their hands. "Good. Were they installed to test the ghosts' sensitivity? Work like an electric fence?" Several guards nodded; they appeared relaxed again. "And how well did it work?"

The large, flat-faced man called Dixon spoke up. "Worked great. Keeps them out of the service corridor."

"Good. We may be able to use that against them," Blasing mused. He could see hope in their faces. "Is there any reason they couldn't be transferred to other cameras?"

"None," Dixon said with a smile, obviously thinking of his promotion. "You work in security electronics, don't you?" Blasing nodded. Dixon proceeded to tell him what needed to be done.

When he was through, Blasing said, "Now I have some bad news. Dr. Landrum." Blasing waved to the DEA agent, then stood up on the desk, ready for trouble.

Dr. Landrum presented his badge and aimed his gun. "I suggest you folks move into the room," Dr. Landrum told those nearest him. They reluctantly shuffled forward. Blasing watched for hostile responses. "Thank you. I'm Special Agent Landrum with the DEA. Sean Heller has been arrested for orchestrating the murder of Peter MacGuire and for running narcotics from this resort. Eva has been arrested on the latter charge. A video tape in my possession reveals Chief Porter was also involved, and he incriminated all of you."

"I don't have any idea what you're talking about!" Dixon cried. Numerous others proclaimed their innocence.

"You're all under arrest for the intent to sell drugs," Dr. Landrum told them, then began reading them their rights.

A large, bald man with arms as big as railroad ties suddenly grabbed the young, red-haired woman, putting a knife to her throat.

"Let me out of here, or I kill the bitch!"

"D—Dylan. What are you doing?"

"She ain't one of us," Dylan said. "Porter hired her because she has big tits." He started edging toward Landrum, using the redhead as a human shield.

"There's no where to go," Dr. Landrum said coolly.

"Besides," Blasing snapped, "according to Eva, Vikki's not innocent!" Dylan's mouth dropped open. The woman's eyes widened. "Go ahead Dylan, cut her! Give her what she deserves. As far as I'm concerned, she's just as guilty as the rest of you for killing Mac!" Blasing leveled his gun at Dylan.

"You're bluffing. You ain't DEA."

"I've been deputized."

"Thanks to Eva," Dr. Landrum told them, "we've been investigating you for over a month."

"That bitch!" Dixon snapped. "I told you she was mouthy!" Drawing a gun, he jumped to his feet, bringing others with him as if on cue.

Blasing lashed out, kicking Dixon in the face and sending him reeling. As he stumbled away, Dixon shot wildly, the thunderous roar deafening. Marlin grabbed his chest and slumped back to his knees. Blasing dropped to a crouch and returned fire, grazing Dixon. He gasped and spun around, ready to return fire. Blasing snapped off a second shot. The guard collapsed, falling against the legs of two others and knocking them to the floor.

Gunfire erupted again, and the wall next to Blasing exploded. Drywall flak swirled about him like snow. Blasing sprang onto another desk, pulling down a stack of equipment atop Chet and crushing him.

As Dylan fired again, Vikki stomped on his foot, then head-butted her captor. Dylan screamed, staggering back as his nose gushed. Dr. Landrum fired twice. Dylan's arms flew wide as he slammed against a wall, then slid to the floor.

The door suddenly burst open and a scrawny man from valet carrying a gun dove into the room. "Tally! Watch out!" Dr. Landrum cried.

Macon shot at the doctor, tearing a hole in the corner of the wall and driving him back a step into the short hallway. Blasing fired, hitting the guard high in the chest. As several scrambled for the fallen weapon, Blasing squeezed off another shot, gouging the floor near the gun. "HOLD IT!" They froze.

Agent Tally fired and Max dropped his knife, collapsing a few steps away from Blasing. Seeing a third of their companions down, no one moved. The reverberations echoed for a time, then slowly died, leaving only the moaning of the injured.

"Hand me that gun by the butt, Sharon," Blasing said to the blond-haired woman with wide eyes. He gestured a second time before Sharon hesitantly complied.

"Now, one at a time as I point to you, toss your weapons to my feet," Dr. Landrum told them. "A wrong flinch and Agent Tally will shoot." One by one they followed instructions. Most had been armed with at least a knife or a baton looking like an oversized flashlight. "You keep watching 'em Tally. Blasing and I'll search 'em."

No one moved. Some seemed to have quit breathing, but if looks could kill, Blasing and Dr. Landrum would've been very dead. The doctor found spools of cable and began binding everybody. After he finished, he tended to the wounded. Three lay dead.

"I'm going to bring Heller and Eva in here."

"Let's put everyone in the breakroom in the employee wing," Agent Tally suggested. "We can pull some spare beds from storage."

"Sounds good," Dr. Landrum replied.

"But we'll need Heller in the conference room," Blasing said.

"We can move him later. For now, I'd like to have them all in one spot. Easier to watch that way. Tally, make sure you strip them clean. Some of the men have worked with prisoners, and may have learned to hide things from the experts."

"Yes, sir."

"I wish we'd caught Chadwick," Blasing said.

"So do I. But it could have been worse," Dr. Landrum said, then left. He returned in a few minutes with Heller and Eva being led by the two front desk clerks, JJ and a woman named Martina. Each wore a smile, their eyes aglow as if a dream had come true.

The security crew cursed Eva and Heller. The defiant Irishman spat back profanities. Dr. Landrum bound Heller to a table next to one of the wounded, then led a downcast Eva and the three other women into Porter's office where Martina searched them even more thoroughly. While Agent Tally removed Heller's rings and an amulet of hematite, he begged and pleaded. "I have to wear them! Rictor will kill me otherwise! Please!"

"We'll protect you," a security guard chuckled menacingly.

Blasing stopped the clerks as they moved to leave. "JJ, Martina. Gather the staff in the lobby. I'll make an announcement in forty-five minutes." JJ nodded, then took off as if his pants were on fire.

THIRTY-SEVEN

After a meeting of the minds with the Great Xantini, Julie Zephren and Dr. Strange, Blasing and Angela returned to the lobby. It was crammed full with expectant employees. Even a few curious patrons attended.

Blasing's appearance caused whispering and excitement to ripple through the crowd, and when he stood on the front desk counter, they applauded exuberantly. "Hello. Most of you know me, but for those of you who don't, my name is Blasing Madera. I'm Peter MacGuire's nephew and, in accordance with his last wishes, the new owner of Ghostal Shores. As you might have heard, Sean Heller is being held in the custody of law enforcement officials as a suspect in the murder of Peter MacGuire."

There were gasps as though several people had been stabbed. The whispering grew louder until Blasing raised his hands for silence. "All of security is also under arrest and being held in the employee breakroom, now off limits to everyone.

"Until you hear otherwise, I'm in charge of Ghostal Shores." Many of the employees had already met Blasing, and the response was a thunderous roar of approval. They laughed, hugged and slapped each other on the back. The whole resort was shaken as though there'd been a tremor.

Many from the staff moved forward to shake Blasing's hand, and he obliged them for a few minutes, then announced, "All right everybody! I know you have lots of questions, but we're short on time. There's a group of new ghosts—the transients that you have heard about—that are trying to steal Ghostal Shores away from us. To scare us and drive us out. Possibly even kill us." The hush was so profound that any nervous movement seemed a shout.

"I believe they also might've been associated with Heller and contributed to Mac's death."

"Murderers!" an elderly woman whispered loudly.

"Not only are we threatened, but so are our friends—Broderick,

Cannon, Elma and so many others you have come to know and love. They make our jobs easier, our days brighter, and the resort a very special place. I was frightened of them at first, but now that I know them, they are my friends.

"We believe part of our problem with the transient spirits stems from the bricks used in the northern wing expansion. The ghosts seem to be intimately tied to them. I'm asking for volunteers to haul the bricks to the conference room where we will attempt to reverse our situation."

Almost everyone raised a hand. "I'll do it!" "Be glad to help!" "When can I start!" "Show me the way!"

"Thank you for your outpouring. Dress for the weather and meet at the northern entrance. If I'm not there, you are to follow the orders of these people as if they were my own." He motioned to the nearby psychics, "Julie Zephren, Dr. Devlin Strange, Efrem Xantini the Master Mentalist, or Angela Starborne. They are experts in the paranormal and psychic fields. Follow their instructions implicitly. Your safety might be at stake."

"Blasing, I'd like to say a brief word," Xantini said, then the Master Mentalist rose with a grand flourish of his cape. The crowd reacted as if expecting some miraculous feat of magic. "In the past few days, many of you have seen strange visions—even stranger than usual—or had disturbing encounters."

"Despite their apparent ethereal nature, unlike the ghosts, they are simply psychic projections—in other words, phantoms. These phantoms have no substance, though your belief in them can cause you harm. If you ignore them, they'll be as harmless as the dragons you see in the clouds, or a nightmare upon awakening. If you believe in them, the fear and stress can cause serious harm."

He started to step down, then looked to a young Hispanic woman. "Yes, there is something you can do to protect yourself from the ghosts. Besides staying calm and confident, wear hematite. It has grounding properties."

Blasing stood again. "Lastly, we expect outbreaks of fire, just like in the kitchen. With all of security under arrest and the sprinkler system unreliable, we need a volunteer crew of firefighters to work with maintenance. See George Thomasson immediately."

"We can get to know each other better in the near future, but for now, we have problems to resolve...." As if on cue, the power returned. Everyone cheered and the smiles broadened. "I expect the best you can give. Let's pitch in together and do whatever's necessary to make Ghostal Shores a wondrous place once more." He started to step down, then paused. "Oh, one last thing. If you have a portable radio or a boom box, please bring it to Dr. Strange in the conference room. Thank you."

Angela was amazed as the staff, unsettled earlier, now hurried off to get their boots and jackets. What was it about Blasing that inspired people? His respect for them? His compassion? She hugged him as he climbed down. "Another rousing speech. And without holding a gun on them this time," she teased.

Blasing kissed her. "They knew I had a lawyer at hand, much more threatening than any firearm."

"Efrem, if you will handle people in the yard, Julie will guide them to the conference room. Doctor, will you oversee the placement of the bricks?" The trio nodded. "Keep your senses alert for the ghosts, and if you can, call Angela or I before confronting them."

"If you encounter Chadwick or the others, don't engage them," Xantini finished for him. "Call Agent Landrum or Tally on our Walkie-Talkies. Channel 6."

"Everyone prepared?" Blasing asked. They nodded. Each was adorned in plenty of hematite. Xantini wore blackish-silver rings, Julie earrings and a necklace with diamond-shaped stones, and Dr. Strange a star amulet to go along with the rest of his collection.

"Dr. Strange, are you sure you have everything you need?"

"Yes, I've double-checked, Angela. Thank you for sharing the protection ceremony with me. It's very interesting, but then often times there's power in simplicity. Rest assured, I'll have things ready when you arrive."

"Let's go, gentlemen," Julie said, grabbing Xantini and Dr. Strange by their arms and leading them toward the stairs. "We're not doin' any good just standin' he'ah yakkin'."

"Good luck!" Blasing called to them, then met with the acting in-charge maintenance supervisor, George Thomasson, warning him about the fires and expressing the urgent need to move the signal boosters to the cameras closest to the ballroom.

"Sure we can. No problem. A few of my men helped security

install them." Thomasson wore a constant scowl as if his face were stuck in that expression. "If I put everyone on it, we'll get it done in about two hours, depending on what emergencies crop up. I'll have some of my men removing amplifiers while others get the upstairs cameras ready."

"Excellent," Blasing told him. "Any idea why the emergency lights aren't working?"

"None. One of my men is working on it. He thinks there's some kind of remote switch controlling them."

"Isn't that illegal?" Blasing asked. Thomasson nodded. "Well, keep working on both problems. I'm headed to the generator now. Call me on the Walkie-Talkie if you need me. Angela, do you have what you need?" She nodded. "Then let's go. Good luck, George."

Just as they started off, the fire alarm sounded. Thomasson hurried behind the front desk and checked a console. "The fire's in the library."

"Are the sprinklers working?"

"I think so. Wish I knew why they were on the fritz."

"The ghosts," Angela guessed.

"We should make sure things aren't going up in flames," Blasing said, starting to lead the way.

"No," Angela said. "Let George handle the fire. This could be a diversion, especially if Rictor was listening to your speech."

"I didn't feel any ghosts."

"I felt your talk shake the resort," Angela said firmly. "We must protect the generator before the ghosts do something to it."

"George, take whatever volunteers you can find and check it out. Call me as soon as you get there." The supervisor nodded and sprinted off, calling for his people.

"Worried about Chadwick?" Angela asked. They passed the row of SANYO, RCA and TOSHIBA boxes stacked in the service corridor.

Alert and tense, Blasing carried Mac's .38 Smith & Wesson. "Yes. I almost lost you once today. Kelly and Patrick should have the pleasure of getting to know you."

"That's sweet." She squeezed his arm, her touch supportive.

As they neared the generator room, Blasing's name was called over the Walkie-Talkie. "Blasing here. Yes? Excellent. See you soon. So far, so good. The sprinklers are working."

"Maybe the ghosts are too busy to mess with them," Angela said hopefully. "Aren't they separate from the electrical systems?"

"Yes, but so are the emergency lights," Blasing said.

"Hey, look who's coming," Angela said, nodding toward Dr. Landrum. "Feel any ghosts nearby?"

"Hard to tell with Lilly near, but I don't think so," Blasing replied.

"Well, keep your senses keen, darling. Remember, the spirits can possess people."

"What's the good word, Geoff?" Blasing asked.

"Good and bad. We haven't found Chadwick, nor the other two guards, but everything's secure in the breakroom. Tally, McMicheals, and the two I deputized are watching over the prisoners. What about you? I thought I heard a fire alarm."

"There was a fire in the library. The sprinklers handled it."

"I'll bet that frustrates the ghosts," Dr. Landrum replied. "They didn't have sprinkler systems in the 1880's."

Two maintenance men reminding Blasing of Mutt and Jeff exited the fence gate of the generator room and walked toward them. The shorter one, Volkov, carried a ladder. "How's it going, gentlemen?"

"Fine, sir. We're to start work on the signal amplifiers?" asked Parkinson, the older and taller of the two. Blasing confirmed it. "What about a work order?"

Dr. Landrum flashed his badge. "Consider it a direct order. And get more help! Immediately!"

"Yes sir!" They moved to the nearest camera and set up the ladder.

"Thanks," Blasing said as he opened the gate.

"No problem. I don't want you to get off on the wrong foot with your employees. They might think you're a tyrant," Dr. Landrum chuckled. "Wait here a moment." He stepped inside. "It's clear."

"As far as you can see," Blasing said. Stretching his senses, he walked quickly throughout the chamber. "It's clear, all right."

"Then I'll get to work," Angela said. She set her bag on the floor and began preparations. Chanting prayers, Angela drifted about the room, smoke trailing from the sage burning in the jawbone of a coyote. The smoke shifted and coiled as if threatening to take shape.

Dr. Landrum wrinkled his nose. Except for wiping his eyes dry, he stayed alert, his gaze constantly looking for trouble.

While he watched Angela, Blasing called Zephren, Xantini and Dr. Strange. "How's it going?" Angela asked when he was through.

"They have a three by eight stack of brick almost built."

"Wow! Everybody must be working."

"After learning what was happening, a large number of guests joined in," Blasing informed her. "Over two hundred people are carrying bricks."

"Excellent," Angela said. She set down the jawbone, then picked up the bag of salt. She trailed it around the edges of the room.

"How's this going to affect... you know who?" Dr. Landrum asked, motioning toward Angela.

"As long as Lilly's with me, she should be fine," Angela replied. She continued her ritual chanting until they heard Blasing's name spoken frantically over the Walkie-Talkie.

"I'll be right there! Geoff, will you guard Angela?"

"Of course!"

"Where are you going?!" Angela asked.

"They're starting to see phantoms in the hallway. People are getting skittish. Julie believes their courage will be bolstered by my presence. I'll be back as quickly as I can."

"I don't want you to go," she said.

"I don't want to leave, but you have to finish what you're doing. It's important."

"I know," she pouted. They kissed for a long moment. "Come back safe. Here, take some of this." She gave him a plastic bag. "It's crushed hematite. Throw it at a phantom. I think it'll make it disappear, but I haven't had a chance to test that theory."

"Thanks!"

"Remember what I said about possessions!" she reminded him.

As Blasing passed the deserted ladder, he wondered where maintenance had gone. Wires hung from the camera, and parts lay on the floor next to a tool box. The fire alarm jolted him, then Julie yelled for him over the Walkie-Talkie. Blasing started running again. He was going to warn Angela about the missing workers when Parkinson, Volkov, and another with a ladder stepped from the storage room.

"Got some help, sir," Parkinson said.

"Excellent," Blasing said as he ran past.

Thomasson's voice came over the radio, "Mr. Madera, it's in the southern wing this time. The sprinklers are working spottily, but we have hoses on it. So far, so good. Unless something weird happens, heaven forbid, it should be out soon."

"Great! Keep me posted."

Dodging grim-faced people as they streamed through the Cathedral to the Coast toward the ballroom, Blasing raced up the steps, reaching the bar quickly. A heavy, coiling fog stretched in every direction, becoming thicker as he raced through the restaurant. Tight-lipped and wary volunteers carried bricks down the stairs, then returned northward, trudging along a mud-beaten path in the green carpet.

"You're doing a great job," Blasing told them. A young woman dropped her bricks, and Blasing helped her re-gather them, getting quite muddy in the process. "Keep the faith." Faces around them brightened. "We'll get through this."

Blasing found the Great Xantini and Julie Zephren in the elevator intersection near the pool entrance. A little farther along the hall, Tawny Lane spoke with people while Murly taped.

"Ah, here he comes," Xantini said without turning. The Mentalist was sopped and stood in a puddle of his own making.

"Everyone looks grim. What have you seen?" Blasing asked.

"At first, just shadows and faces. Then just ah few minutes ago, ah stagecoach whipped through he'ah, the horses neighen' shrilly and a man laughin' madly. One of the drivers fired ah shotgun into the air. Gave me chills." Julie shuddered.

"Describe the occupant, if you can." She did; it was Rictor. "Was anyone hurt?" Blasing asked. He'd been sensing for ghosts, but hadn't felt any so far.

"No, but it upset everyone," Xantini said. "There's a definite feeling of dread in the air."

Blasing nodded. The impression he always received from Rictor—that something bad had happened and you just didn't know it yet—was heavy, hanging in the air with the fog. He described the earlier stagecoach.

"That's the one all right," Julie drawled.

"Rictor's trying to scare us."

"It's workin'," Julie replied.

"Maybe we have enough bricks," Blasing suggested.

"Maybe. But I think we should go until it's...." Julie was interrupted by a low rumbling that shook everything as it rolled along the hall toward them. "What's that?! An earthquake!?"

The rumbling grew. A nearby table shuffled across the floor, the lamp falling when it reached the end of its cord. Blasing tried to steady himself against the wall. Yelling and screaming came from the northern end of the hallway, then people staggered toward them. The floor betrayed them, and they bounced off the walls, colliding with each other like human pinballs. Those who fell, if not pulled quickly to their feet, were trampled, tripping those in blind flight. "Run!! It's coming!"

"What's coming?!" Blasing asked as people raced past. He looked down the hall, but all he could see beyond the crush of muddied volunteers was a rolling cloud of fog. Despite Tawny tugging on him, Murly continued to film the chaos. Blasing grabbed a fleeing man. "What's coming?!"

"I... I don't know!" His eyes stared nearly blank with fear.

"You're just running because everyone else is?" Blasing asked. The man nodded dumbly. "Damn! Wait here!" Blasing charged forward into the panicked throng.

"I'm coming with you," Xantini yelled. Julie followed them.

"Stay calm!" Blasing yelled repeatedly as he waded through the fleeing masses. He could understand their fright; he'd experienced something like this before. Even now he still wanted to run.

The rumbling grew louder, drowning out the screams. The shaking intensified, the walls quaking as if alive. Pictures jumped off the walls and tables overturned, tripping people in flight. Others fell over them, scrambling and clawing to rise. Some were crushed by their companions. Light flickered ahead, sometimes flashing blindingly down the hall.

Each time Blasing bumped into someone or pulled them to their feet, he imparted his message. "THERE'S NOTHING TO FEAR!"

"IT'S AN ILLUSION!" Xantini told them.

"BLASING! THE TRAIN IS COMING AGAIN!" Tawny cried. She nearly tackled him. Her face was pale, and her eyes wide with fright. She tried to say something else, but couldn't.

"DON'T WORRY! I'LL TAKE CARE OF IT! STAY HERE!" Blasing told her. He pulled free and continued through the crowd.

"BLASING!" Tawny screamed.

"BLASING! WHERE?" someone cried.

"WHAT'S HE DOING?!" another yelled.

Struggling through the crush of people, Blasing could finally see what the cloud harbored. A whistle pierced the air, threatening to rupture his ears. A bright, spearing light washed over them. The ghostly train was a juggernaut of iron and steel, its cowcatcher dented and bent as if its sole purpose was to catch and destroy. Ahead of the locomotive, he could see clouds of low, rolling dirt mingling with the steam. Large, horned creatures barreled toward them, buffalo stampeding ahead of the locomotive.

Blasing remembered what Angela and the psychics had said: it wasn't real. Or was it? He touched his shoulder where he'd been shot. That wasn't supposed to be real either, but the pain was very real. But this time he wore Angela's rings and the pendant. Did that mean he'd be run over? Or through? Blasing shoved aside his fear. "I'LL SHOW YOU IT'S NOT REAL!"

"HE'S MAD!" a man yelled.

"LET HIM BY!" Xantini ordered. People staggered aside, clinging to the walls and creating a clear path to the oncoming locomotive and stampeding buffalo.

"IT CAN'T HURT YOU!" Blasing yelled. Despite every nerve screaming to run away, he kept advancing toward the onrushing locomotive. He had to trust his instincts. It was just like the stampede of bulls in the canyon. He hoped.

When Blasing cleared the last of the crowd, he stopped, firmly planting himself between the ghostly rails. It was difficult to stand, the floor thrashing about as if ready to break loose. All the tables were overturned, their lamps joining the paintings cavorting across the floor. Doors banged back and forth, slamming repeatedly.

Xantini and Julie joined him, the threesome stretching across the hall. Murly followed a few feet behind, dogging their every step.

"THERE'S NOTHIN' TA FEAR!" Julie reminded them.

Blasing was having second thoughts about hurling the hematite when he thought he heard Xantini say, "Let it run through us. Show them there's nothing to fear." He sounded calm, then Blasing noticed he never saw the mentalist move his lips,

Blasing held the hematite in one hand and Angela's pendant in the other, repeating to himself, "It's an illusion. Be brave."

Julie took Blasing's hand. He thought he saw a hint of doubt. Had he just crossed the line from bravery to foolhardiness? It wouldn't be the first time—but the first in a long while. When he glanced over his shoulder, he saw many people stop to watch. A few hesitantly moved forward to join them, creating a human barricade across the tracks.

The whistle screamed shrilly again, then was buried under the rumble of thundering hooves. The rails shook and sang. Light flashed across them, cutting through the swirling dust and steam. The buffalo grew closer and clearer, bloodied horns cutting swathes in the dust. Many of the beasts bled, some partially skinned as if they had just escaped the hunt.

Blasing clamped his jaw tight to keep his teeth from rattling. Then he closed his eyes and concentrated on being with Angela. Remembering the last stampede, he stepped back in his mind to kissing Angela. This had to work, he told himself. "Kiss me!" Angela demanded, and he did, trying to lose himself in memory. There was a biting breeze as the air swirled past him, then a coldness rushed through him.

"IT WORKED!" Julie cried happily.

"Of course," Xantini said calmly.

Blasing opened his eyes just in time to see the coal car race toward him. What was that?!, he wondered. Something dark rushed toward him. He hurled the powdered hematite just before he saw stars and collapsed.

"Something's wrong," Angela said. She was setting the crystals for the grid.

"It hasn't been that long," Dr. Landrum said.

"I can feel it." Angela said. She tried not to hurry—not to skimp on the ceremony—but it was difficult. "Blasing's in trouble." He wouldn't want her to leave, she kept telling herself, but if something terrible had happened to him, and she could have prevented it....

The gate swung open. Dr. Landrum whirled, his gun trained on Parkinson who dropped his tool box and raised his hands. "S-sorry! I- I'm supposed to check the fuses."

Dr. Landrum lowered his gun. As the maintenance worker sighed, another man stepped into the door and fired. The doctor clasped his right arm as his gun fell from numb fingers.

"I wouldn't!" Chadwick told him. He was flanked by two others dressed in green jumpsuits. "I don't need you both alive!"

"You sonuvabitch!" Angela yelled.

"You're going to try and free the others," Dr. Landrum muttered.

"You got that right. Then we're taking over this place."

THIRTY-EIGHT

"Blasing! Blasing!" Julie patted his face. "Are ya all right?"

"I think so," Blasing moaned. His head pounded.

"We did it! You did it! The train and the buffalo are gone! And everyone has seen that the phantoms are nothing!"

Blasing heard the hustle and bustle of many people moving around him. "Uh... What hit me?"

"A ghost with a shovel," Xantini told him. "You drove him and the phantom away when you hit them with whatever you threw."

"So the phantoms aren't real, but watch out for the ghosts," Blasing moaned, gingerly touching the side of his head. His fingers came away bloodied. "Anybody else hurt?"

"Only those who trampled each other," Xantini said. "But none too seriously." Blasing tried to stand. The mentalist helped him to his feet. People cheered and applauded, feeling victorious.

As his head cleared, Blasing asked, "Is that the fire alarm?"

"Yes, it's been going on for a while," Xantini told him.

Blasing reached Thomasson through the Walkie-Talkie. "It's in the employee quarters," Blasing told them. Suddenly, he thought—felt—Angela was in danger.

"That's wher'ah everyone's bein' held," Julie drawled.

Everything went dark, but the alarm kept sounding.

"Damn!" Blasing cursed. "Angela! Angela! What's going on down there?!" He waited for her reply, but none came. "Angela! Geoff! The employee quarters are on fire!" After several more tries, the dull ache in his heart strengthened. "Something's wrong! Efrem, keep bringing in those bricks. Make sure Dr. Strange is ready for visitors!" Blasing yelled as he sprinted for the foyer. The terrible feeling that the ghost train had been a distraction grew stronger; Rictor wanted him away from Angela.

Gun ready and his flashlight guiding him along the service corridor, Blasing raced toward the generator room. His beam illuminated two ladders—one standing, the other laying on its side. A quick glance told him no further work had been performed on the cameras. That the extra man with Parkinson and Volkov wasn't with maintenance. Damn! He could be so stupid sometimes!

Turning off the flashlight, Blasing quietly approached the generator room. The service corridor was silent, except for the distant murmur of voices. Blasing reached out into the darkness, sensing for ghosts. He didn't feel any. "Angela? Geoff?" His soft call echoed along the hallway.

Blasing felt Angela was in danger, but not dead. They seemed to be linked somehow—spirit connected to spirit. Blasing knew he'd feel a stab through his heart if she'd died. He'd do everything in his power to ensure that didn't happen.

Holding his flashlight above his head and ducking low into the doorway with his gun ready, Blasing clicked on the beam as he entered the generator room. He was greeted by undesired silence. With just a moment's searching, he found Angela's bag on the floor. Crystals lay scattered around it and across the floor. Someone or something attacked her before she'd finished her ceremony.

Upon closer examination, he found drops of blood. He prayed they weren't Angela's. The generator sustained extensive damage by human hands, not a ghost's. Chadwick and his men had been here. Now that they held hostages, they'd try to free their companions.

Turning off his flashlight, Blasing snuck along the dark corridor toward the employee quarters. In the distance he saw a dim, hazy light. He hadn't been walking long when a sudden crack of gunfire ripped the air.

Blasing dropped prone, waiting for a second shot. When no further rounds were fired, he moved forward in a crouch toward the garbled voices. Soon, an acrid, smoky smell burned his nose.

As he moved closer to the employee breakroom, the voices sounded less jumbled. "I'll give you ten minutes, Tally, then I'll start killing the hostages! I don't need all of them!" A trio of shadows shifted behind a barrier of folding tables set on their sides. Blasing thought he knew which one was Chadwick. Several more people appeared to sit on the floor, probably Angela and the hostages.

"What kind of guarantees do we have?" Tally asked.

"He'll just kill...." Dr. Landrum gasped, then grew silent.

"What else are you going to do, Tally?!" Chadwick asked. "Burn to death?! There's a fire in the kitchen. You can't get out that way, and there's another behind you. You're trapped, Tally! And you know, if you burn to death, that'll work for us. We'll just add four more bodies to the bonfire. Now, you have eight minutes left before one dies."

"DAMN MAN! DO WHAT HE WANTS!" Heller shouted. "WE'RE GOING TO BE BURNED ALIVE! AND IF WE DON'T, THE GHOSTS WILL KILL US. GIVE ME BACK MY RINGS! DON'T YOU UNDERSTAND? HE'S GOING TO KILL ME!"

"IIE'S LYING," Eva cried. "THEY HELP HIM CONTROL THE GHOSTS!!"

"YOU BITCH! SHE'S LYING! GIVE ME BACK MY RINGS!"

Blasing looked up at the ceiling. Oily, black smoke roiled along it like thunderclouds rolling ashore. Blasing didn't see how he could do anything from here.

A flashlight suddenly swept over him. He held still, not breathing as it passed. Blasing expected to be fired upon, but nothing happened. Maybe the smoke worked in his favor.

What could he do? Even if he backtracked and left through the loading dock, running through the rain to the employees' kitchen entrance, it wouldn't do him any good. There was already a fire there. He'd just end up where Tally and McMicheals were already held at bay.

It was the only time in his life he wished he were a ghost. Then he could save Angela.

Angela tugged at the wires binding her wrists; soon she wouldn't be able to feel anything, which might be a blessing. She looked at Geoff and wished she could do something for him. Bleeding from his mouth, a gash along his face and the gunshot wound in his arm, Dr. Landrum slumped against the wall. She silently cursed Chadwick for not letting her help the doctor.

Behind several overturned tables, the two DEA agents discussed their options. Few, if any, Angela thought. She prayed again to Great Spirit. Was there something she could have done differently—something that would have changed things? She thought back over the last half-hour.

The trio had bound them, beaten Geoff, then dragged the four of them to the breakroom. Chadwick and his goons had tried to free their companions with a surprise shoot-out, but it was short-lived, injuring one of the deputized employees and the woman agent, McMicheals. Both sides assembled cover from furniture pushed against the walls, becoming quickly entrenched in their positions. Then the fire alarm sounded. Shortly thereafter, the power died.

Smoke drifted up the corridor, slowly filling the breakroom. Dodging gun fire, Tally raced to the kitchen door, only to find it jammed, for there was no lock. Each time Tally tried to reach the counter, he was fired upon, driving him back to cover. Soon it didn't matter; smoke spewed from the archways leading into the kitchen.

None of them had much longer if the fires continued to spread. Soon Rictor would set a fire in the hallway, blocking their last path of escape. She'd told Chadwick, but he wouldn't listen to her. He didn't believe that the Bodie ghosts were taking over Ghostal Shores.

Rictor would get what he wanted, Angela thought. Heller and his "gang" burned to death in a hotel fire, just as Rictor had died over a hundred years ago. Frustrated, Angela wanted to cry but held back her tears. Crying was pointless; she wouldn't give up.

Angela peeked through a gap in the folded tables. The smoke hung thick in the breakroom, hovering just above the prisoners who were bound to beds, and getting lower by the minute. Continuing to rage and shout, Heller was red-faced, straining against his bonds. Eva sat nearby, a mocking expression on her face as she watched Heller thrash about.

A gun was suddenly shoved in her face. "Einny, meanie, mienie, mo, which one's the first to go?" A guard's .45 rested on Parkinson, who blanched and nearly passed out. "You got five minutes, old man. You better start praying."

Angela saw sudden movement out of the corner of her eye as agent Tally jumped to his feet. "Do with them what you want!" he yelled, his voice sounding gravelly. "I don't care! I already got what I want!" His laugh was harsh and guttural as he fired at them.

Angela rolled over to face the floor and hoped she lay low enough not to get hit. Dr. Landrum cracked an eye. "Rictor has possessed him!" she said.

"From fire to under fire," Dr. Landrum grimaced.

"The idiots!" Chadwick cried, his expression incredulous as he crouched behind the tables. "What're they doing?" Pressed wood shards flew about in puffs and metal pinged as bullets ricocheted off the tables and concrete walls. Parkinson gasped, then suddenly slumped on his side, eyes staring lifelessly.

During a momentary lull the possessed DEA agents reloaded. Angela jumped to her feet. "Lon, help me! Please! I'm stuck in this body!" Lilly cried out through Angela. Slowly, the lovely ghost seeped from her host, rising until half of her form visibily wavered. Lilly struggled as if trying to escape but unable to get free. "They'll kill me again! HELP ME!"

"I'll be damned," Chadwick muttered. "What're you doing!" He pistol-whipped Angela. Lilly screamed as they crumpled.

Dark mists quickly arose from Tally, then Rictor charged, his long black coat trailing behind him. "GONNA KILL YOU BOY!" His yellow eyes burned angrily. "Get 'em Kindrick!" A spirit with a patch over his right eye left McMicheals' body to join the dark ghost's charge.

"SHOOT THEM!" Chadwick fired repeatedly.

Rictor flew through the table and grabbed Chadwick's head. The pockmarked man shook and shuddered, then screamed, "OH GOD! I'M ON FIRE!" Chadwick began to pat himself as if trying to extinguish invisible flames. "GOD HELP ME! I'M ON FIRE!"

Kindrick snagged a guard, and he also screamed. The other guard hesitated, then ran. As he cleared the table, Blasing smashed Mac's .38 across his face, sending the man crashing to the floor. "Angela, come on!" Blasing cried.

"Thank you, Great Spirit." Angela struggled to her knees, reaching for his hand with her bound ones. He pulled her to her feet and lifted her over the tables in one smooth motion. "What about Geoff?"

"Run! They don't really care about me! RUN!"

"But you're the LAW!" Angela reminded him.

"Run dammit. He'll chase Lilly!"

"Can you run?" Blasing asked, concerned by the blood seeping from the jagged wound on Angela's cheek. She nodded. "Head for the conference room!" Blasing ran, pulling her along as if she were a tail to his kite. "Dr. Strange should have completed the ceremony by now."

"He doesn't have a prayer pipe!"

"But he does have a pipe," Blasing said.

They hadn't run far when they heard an enraged scream. "LILLY!"

"Faster!" Lilly urged. Watching behind them, the ghost now protruded from Angela's back.

"How fast can a ghost run?" Blasing breathed. In the smoky darkness, the corridor seemed to stretch on forever.

"I have no idea," Angela replied, breathing heavily between words. "But we aren't going to make it." If Blasing hadn't been pulling her along, she would have collapsed by now.

"LILLY!! DAMN YOU, BLASING! WHEN I CATCH YOU, YOU'RE GOING TO WISH YOU WERE ALREADY DEAD!"

"They're getting closer! Can we duck inside the generator room?" Blasing asked.

"Wouldn't do any good," Angela panted. Faster than her footsteps, her heart thundered in her ears. "One of those idiots had a good time kicking around the crystals, so the room isn't protected."

"Then we're as good as caught!" Blasing gnashed bitterly. Gunfire rang out and something pinged off a nearby wall. "Run! Keep low!" The first ghostly bullet was followed by a second and third; Blasing heard the air sing and felt the ethereal slugs whiz by his head.

"DON'T SHOOT!" Rictor roared. He stopped, then wheeled to strike Kindrick across the face. "You might hit Lilly." After Kindrick nodded, his one good eye wide with surprise, Rictor continued to give chase, cursing all the way.

The tingling grew worse, becoming an itch along Blasing's back. They're getting close."

Angela glanced over her shoulder. Rictor's cat-like eyes grew larger and larger, his feral teeth bright against his dark form. "If only my hands were free, I've got something that might...."

"I smell fire!" Blasing sniffed as they passed the fenced gate to the generator room. Not far ahead, an orangish-red glow danced among the smoke roiling across the ceiling.

"BLASING, YOUR KIND STOLE MY LIFE! YOU WON'T STEAL MY WOMAN!"

"I thought Heller's kind stole his life," Angela wheezed.

"Oh, Lon! Save me!" Lilly pleaded, her arms imploring.

"Lilly, what're you doing?!" Blasing asked.

"I'M COMING!" Rictor shouted. As the dark spirit closed the distance, Blasing thought he could feel Rictor's rage wash over him. Blasing stumbled over something. The ladder spun around, tripping Angela, too. Blasing tried to recover, but Angela dragged him to the floor with her. Blasing landed hard but shook it off, immediately springing to his feet and hauling Angela upright with him. Rictor bore down on them, his harsh laughter mocking.

"We aren't going to make it," Blasing huffed.

"Keep running," Lilly said quietly through Angela. "Lon darling," Lilly sighed, "Save me!"

Ahead, a section of ceiling crashed to the floor in a fiery geyser. Sparks flew as fireflies, then part of the wall tumbled forward, blocking the corridor with a wall of fire. The flames wavered, then three spirits astride ghostly horses burst through the fiery tendrils. The ethereal beasts' eyes were wide, their teeth bared, and their flanks lathered with white froth. The beasts landed gracefully, then charged, pulling the flames with them as if each wore a comet's tail.

The ghost leveled six-shooters, ready to fire, when Rictor screamed. "DON'T SHOOT! YOU MIGHT HIT LILLY!"

"He doesn't want anyone to hit me but him," Lilly said.

"Blasing, don't worry about the horses," Angela told him.

"But JP Johnson's mule and Angus...." Blasing began.

"I know," Angela said. She glanced over her shoulder.

Rictor's eyes were huge, his hands reaching for her, only a foot away. "No where to go, squaw bitch!"

"Lon, thank heavens!" Lilly reached out as if to embrace the dark spirit, then roundly slapped him. Rictor reeled, colliding with Kindrick. They tumbled in a heap.

"Thanks!" Angela cried.

"That won't hold him for long!" Lilly said.

As they raced around the corner and into the storage room, they could hear Rictor shout, his harsh voice shaking the walls, "LILLY, WHEN I GET MY HANDS ON YOU, YOU'RE GOING TO WISH YOU'D DIED AND GONE TO HELL!"

"I've already been in Hell," she muttered.

The clatter of hooves on concrete grew louder. As they sprinted up the loading dock stairs toward the outside door, the trio of horsemen exited the walls just behind them. "I'll meet you upstairs!" Lilly cried.

"Where are you going?" Angela asked.

"To lead him on a wild goose chase. Don't worry, I've had lots of practice," Lilly laughed wildly. The female spirit whirled about and charged the horses. The first two were surprised and reared back. As Lilly passed by, she yanked the riders from their saddles. With sounds of delight, the two ghost stallions bolted. Lilly caught hold of one and climbed astride, riding off.

The third rider fought to control his spirited Appaloosa, riding around in a circle and yelling, "Whoa, Reignfire!"

"Come on!" Blasing cried. They shoved the door open, bursting outside into the storm. The wind and rain lashed at them, nearly driving them backwards. Lightning flashed. They stumbled forward, blinded for just a moment.

"We may not have long," Blasing said, quickly unwinding the wire imprisoning Angela's hands.

"We aren't supposed to have storms like this," Angela said. "Maybe it's connected to the spirits." Blasing unwound the last of the wire from her wrists. Angela wept as blood rushed into her hands.

"Oh, Lord," Blasing whispered. "Look at the resort. It's going up in flames."

Through the rain, they could see Ghostal Shores afire. To the south the roof smoldered. Flames spat from broken windows. Smoke billowed from the nearby kitchen entrance, orange flames trying to crawl up the outside wall but beaten back by the rain. Somewhere toward the northern end, another fire was underway, suddenly rupturing a window and spewing fiery debris into the storm.

"Come on," Blasing said, snapping her from her morbid entrancement. "That horseman might be right behind us."

"Hopefully, he'll be chasing Lilly," Angela said.

With the rain in her face, she could barely see. The ground was soggy and footing treacherous. Angela slipped several times, but Blasing kept her standing. Any other time she would have marveled at his balance, but just now she was glad they were alive.

They were nearing the front entrance when they heard a neighing behind them. A quick glance told them the horse and rider were closing fast.

Lightning flashed, almost blinding her. Angela thought she saw something large to her right. "Blasing, look...." she began, but the area was deserted.

Her legs were leaden by the time they reached the driveway. She stumbled across it toward the porte-cochere. Close behind they heard the hurried clop of hooves on pavement, growing rapidly louder and closer. Angela could feel the beast right behind her, its breath cold on her back. She fought not to believe in it; it wasn't real. Glancing over her shoulder, she stared into the horse's wild eyes.

Just as she whirled to throw the crushed hematite, a riderless mustang bolted from the topiary. It reared high, calling to its companion. The Appaloosa missed a step, its head snapping toward its playmate. "Whoa! Dammit Reignfire!" the horseman yelled as he yanked on the reigns. The Appaloosa's head whipped around, snapping at its rider. When he slapped Reignfire's nose, the stallion started bucking.

"Thank you, Great Spirit. Thank you, so much." Angela threw the shards. The hail of hematite struck the rider; screaming, he covered his face with both hands. One more buck, and Reignfire sent him flying.

"Good shot!" Blasing breathed. They sprinted ahead.

When they reached the front steps, Angela gasped, "Blasing, hold on just a second."

"But...."

"I can't keep running. Besides, we're taken care of," she said, pointing to Reignfire. The ghostly horse circled the fallen rider and nipped at him, driving him to the ground.

"I see. Must have wanted to do that for a while."

"Thank you, Great Spirit. Feel any other ghosts?" she asked. Blasing closed his eyes. If they hadn't been in such dire straights, she would have laughed. He looked like a drowned rat, water streaming down his face from lank hair and his clothing saturated and sagging. She could just imagine what she looked like.

"No, but someone's coming," Blasing said, pointing back to where they'd come from.

"A ghost?"

"I don't think so."

"Can you see who?" she asked after a flash of lightning and a crack of thunder.

"No, but I don't think we should wait to find out. You rested enough?" Blasing asked. Angela nodded. Hand in hand, they jogged up the steps. Blasing paused for a moment at the front door, feeling for ghosts once again. "So far so good."

As they entered the Cathedral to the Coast, the lightning flashed, reflecting off the mirrors and blinding them. When Blasing could see again, he said, "Where is everybody?" A heavy mud track led from the stairs to the open doors of the ballroom, but the foyer was deserted.

"Off fighting fires, maybe."

"I don't like this," Blasing muttered. He reached for his Walkie-Talkie, but he'd lost it somewhere.

"What choice do we have?"

"Dr. Strange!" Blasing yelled several times as they cautiously approached the open ballroom doors. His voice echoed hollowly.

He thought he heard voices downstairs, then from across the ballroom came, "Blasing! Angela! In the conference room! Come on! All is ready!"

"We're on our way!" Blasing yelled. Heading for the conference room, they rushed across the mammoth chamber. Lightning flashed, darkening the shadows along the tall curtains. "Angela, do you think...."

"He's possessed? I don't know. He was wearing plenty of hematite last time I saw him."

As they began to cross the ballroom, the back of Blasing's neck suddenly began to tingle. "Ghosts!"

"Angela!" Lilly cried. Riding the ethereal stallion, she burst from a wall. "He's right behind me!"

"Come on!" Angela yelled. They sprinted across the floor. Lilly caught them quickly, then leapt from the horse into Angela.

Blasing glanced over his shoulder. He could feel ghosts nearby but didn't see them. About halfway across the room, an overpowering sensation struck Blasing. He stopped in mid-stride.

"Blasing, what's wrong?" Angela asked.

Creaking and rumbling, a ghostly stagecoach erupted from the curtains along the far wall and raced toward them. "Keep running! We can beat them!"

The stage driver shouted and lashed the gaunt beasts with a whip.

Whooping and hollering, his companion fired a shotgun into the air. The horses hooves sounded heavy on the floor as the beasts raced toward them, then turned abruptly at the last instant. The stage swung across their path, cutting them off. Blasing jumped back, barely getting out of the way of a skidding wheel.

The driver yelled, "WHOA!" The train of horses slid to a stop.

"Welcome!" Rictor cried, then jumped from the stage to stand before them. His smile was crooked and his eyes as bright as lanterns shining from a coal shaft.

When the dark spirit gestured to their surroundings, a fog arose from the floor, surrounding them and filling much of the chamber. Lightning flashed, illuminating the mist as it quickly separated, taking the forms of gunslingers and rogues. Kindrick, Crane, Bat and Marsh stood among them.

"We've been waiting for you," Rictor finished, pointing to the rope hanging from the balcony. "Heller's dead," he said quietly. "Now it's time for you to hang. Then Lilly will be mine again. And Ghostal Shores will be ours!"

THIRTY-NINE

"Get them!" Rictor screamed. As though curtains collapsed, the spirits fell upon Blasing and Angela. They were immediately overwhelmed and driven apart.

Xantini, the pair of reporters and the rest of the psychics charged toward the ballroom. The doors slammed shut, halting their headlong rush. Even though there weren't any locks, it wouldn't budge no matter how hard they pushed and shoved. "Get those open!" Tawny cried. "We don't want to miss any of this!"

"Yeah, especially now that the ghosts can be videotaped. If only the equipment in our van hadn't been damaged. I'd go live," Murly finished mournfully.

"Live? Hmmm... Yes, broadcasts!" Xantini murmured, then ran back to the conference room.

Angela desperately fought back against the ghosts, sending Paco reeling with a roundhouse slap. Angela didn't know how she could touch the ghosts; she wasn't wearing hematite. Was it Lilly's doing?

Angela slugged another spirit in the throat. He fell back, but it didn't matter; there were too many of them. Where one spirit fell, two surged forward, grabbing her and pinning her arms. "Great Spirit, help me!" Angela kicked Tito in the knee. He crumpled, but the others kept after her. Some were more interested in grabbing her breasts than holding her.

"She's a hellcat!" Paco protested.

"Don't let go!" Bat cried. Using his hat, he slapped Paco. "Get in there! Quit grabbing her tits and hold her!"

Lilly also fought back, striking Marsh and another spirit holding Angela. The ethereal outlaws laughed at Lilly and yanked her from her human host. As if presenting a king with a gift, they carried Lilly to Rictor.

"Blasing!" Angela screamed. "Blasing!" She struggled against the dark spirits, but they held her fast.

Blasing felt their anger and their glee—the sensation of so many ghosts, so close, nearly driving him crazy. He kept fighting, striking one ghost, then kicking another, the rings burning each time he landed a blow. The tingling along his skin intensified, a horrible feeling of being bitten a thousand times over.

"Get those rings off 'em!" Rictor shouted.

Kindrick and half a dozen outlaws surged forward, overwhelming Blasing and forcing him to the floor. Even though every blow hurt, the ghosts kept hitting Blasing again and again. Those that couldn't reach him, kicked him instead. "Damn that hurts so good!" Pike laughed, then kicked Blasing some more. Each blow struck more than flesh. Blasing felt as if he were separating from his body, slowly sinking into the darkness.

The ghosts yanked on his fingers, crying out in pain when they touched the rings. One was finally removed and tossed, sending it bouncing across the floor. Then the other followed it. "But he still burns!" Delgado cried, his ugly face contorted in pain.

"Be a man!" Rictor shouted.

With a strained cheer, the ghosts yanked Blasing to his feet, then lifted him high, carrying him as a sacrifice toward the noose.

"NO!" Angela cried. It couldn't end like this. "CANDY! PETER! HELP US!" Where was Blasing's guardian angel?

"They ain't around, Miss High n' Mighty," Bat told her.

"Lon, don't do this!" Lilly cried. "You're just repeating the past! Remember what happened! If you hadn't hung Merl's partner, Jeremiah, for making eyes at me, Merl might not have killed us! Do you expect it to turn out any better this time?!"

"Shut up, you traitorous bitch! You'll get yours soon enough," Rictor snapped harshly. With a final glare at Lilly, he turned to Blasing and said, "I warned you. If you'd left that first day, or listened to Mac's ghost...."

"Mac was never here."

Rictor slapped him, snapping back Blasing's head. "...you'd still be alive come tomorrow,"

Blasing's head lolled, then he recovered. "This is our place! My uncle built it! Now leave! You don't belong here, Rictor! Ghostal Shores is ours! Mine and the ghosts who stay here!"

Rictor laughed. "It was never yours. You didn't have any authority before Heller died, and you don't now. Hang him! Make it slow and painful."

"Gladly," Crane said. He wore a patch over the eye where Blasing had hit him with the pendant. "I owe 'em."

"This guy's a pain." Kindrick smiled his toothless grin as the one-eyed ghost looped the noose around Blasing's neck, then cinched it. "Ready," Kindrick told them.

"Listen to me, all of you!" Lilly yelled. "Rictor's lying to you! Using you, just like he's using the Ghostal Shores' spirits!"

"What?!" Marsh cried with a high-pitched screech.

"What's she saying?" Delgado asked, his bullish form shifting nervously.

"Don't listen to her," Rictor said. "She's just a woman!"

"You've fed off the fears of those here at Ghostal Shores, haven't you?!" Lilly asked. The ghosts nodded, listening intently to her. "Fed off their submissiveness? Stolen their spirit! Their will! Their power!"

"LILLY!" Rictor roared. "NO MORE!" He whirled about and struck her hard.

She dropped to her knees, then determinedly, she rose. "I don't fear you anymore! I refuse to give you my... soul any longer! I'm taking it back!" Rictor slapped her again. Lilly laughed wildly. "Didn't any of you learn anything the first time you followed the Great Lon Rictor? Back then, he led you to your deaths. Now he will steal your very souls."

"LILLY!" Rictor couldn't believe she was defying him.

"Now that you're stronger, he's feeding off of each and every one of you. Stealing your spirit! Your soul! Notice how he's...."

"SHE'S A DESPERATE, LYING, BITCH!" Rictor struck Lilly again and again—harder and harder, silencing her.

The outlaws appeared restless, looking questioningly at each other, then back and forth between Rictor and Lilly. Some of the spirits' luster and vividness slowly faded.

"Hey, what's wrong Pike? You don't look so good," Marsh whined.

With a strength Lilly didn't know she possessed, she grabbed Rictor's wrists. "He's a leech!" Lilly spat at Rictor. "Look at him!" The dark spirit struggled to free himself. "You're feeding him! Be free! There are greater things...."

Rictor wrenched his hands free and started choking her. "Bitch! I gave you everything!"

"See what everything is to him!" Lilly gasped. "Soon you'll be wandering around—soulless. He doesn't want you to be part of his gang," Lilly gurgled, but it could be heard by all. "He wants you to be part of him...."

"Hey! Am I too late?!" Dr. Landrum shouted as he shoved the handcuffed Irishman ahead of him.

"Doctor, you must give me back my hematite!" Heller pleaded. "For the love of God, Rictor'll kill me. Please, doctor!"

"HELLER!" Rictor chewed on the words, having trouble spitting them out. The spirit's pale face was beet red with rage.

"Hey, it's another Lawman to hang," Kindrick laughed.

"Yeah, I bet he doesn't burn when we touch him," Delgado laughed.

Angela cursed. The spell had been broken by a unifying sight—The Law. They hated The Law.

Discarding Lilly like a rag, Rictor pointed at Heller and bit off each word. "You should have burned!"

"None of them died," Dr. Landrum told him. Drenched and bleeding from several places, he could barely stand, but the doctor grabbed Heller by the hair and jerked his head upward. "Sean Heller is under arrest for killing Peter MacGuire...."

"I told you he was like us," Marsh laughed.

"Inspirational," Crane chuckled.

"...and will be executed by the State of California for said crime!" Dr. Landrum continued.

"You can't do that!" Rictor shouted. "He's mine to kill. I owe Merl! I owe you Merl!" The dark cowboy pointed at Heller.

"He's no longer THE owner of Ghostal Shores!" Angela yelled. "Blasing Madera has total authority!"

The spirits looked at each other as if wondering what that might mean to them.

"You don't belong here!" Blasing wheezed. "Free MY friends and get out! Get out! Broderick! Cannon! Dirk! Come take back what's yours! Fight back!"

In the conference room among the bricks, close and yet very

far away, Broderick was ready to pull out what little was left of his hair. His ghostly companions gathered around, ashamed of themselves but listening all the same. What must he say to convince his companions to rebel—to fight for themselves? To help Master Madera and Miss Starborne? "Has death not been enough? They callously murdered us! Do you also wish to hand them your souls?"

"He could kill us like he did Carrie and Grant," Janice whimpered.

"He didn't kill them! They were already deceased. Rictor just released them from... here. Maybe they finally went to Heaven." Someone snickered. "Would that be so bad? Or would you rather serve Rictor?" Broderick asked.

"Maybe we're still here because we've never broken free of their kind's power!" Cannon boomed. "I say it's our fear that holds us here!"

"You are free spirits!" Broderick told them. "You know the truth! He cannot hold us! All he can steal now is your desire and will!" The Englishman scrutinized the spirits' faces, seeing they still cowed.

"Did you feel that?" Fawn asked.

"What?" Eddie asked.

A smile spread across Fawn's lovely features. "Blasing said this place was ours! That we are owners, too!"

"This place isn't ours," Janice said meekly.

"Why?" Mason said. "We're what attracts people. We ain't slaves or nothin'."

Fawn stared at Janice. "And he said we were his friends."

"Yes, I thought I felt that," Elma said.

"But Heller's an owner, too. I'm not sure I can stand working with him," Barney said. "I'd prefer to leave."

"Don't leave! Fight!" Dirk said. "I ain't had a home since my daddy threw me outta the house when I was twelve! This place is worth fightin' for!"

"Listen!" Elma said. The ghosts could hear agent Landrum's pronouncement of Heller's arrest for Mac's murder. "They caught him! We have to help bring him to justice!"

Suddenly, they could all hear Blasing. "Broderick! Cannon! Dirk! Come take back what's yours! Fight back!"

"I'll be damned," Eddie murmured.

"He does consider us his partners!" Cannon boomed.

"We have to help them!" Elma demanded of everyone, her eyes blazing as they searched each soul.

"We must help," Broderick began, "not only for Blasing and Angela, but for Mac, God rest his soul, and for ourselves. We must free ourselves from this fear. What say you, Jonathan?" The hazy spirit nodded hesitantly at first, then decisively. Broderick looked to the others. "What say you all?"

With a resounding cheer, they charged their captors.

"He'll suck you dry!" Lilly hissed. "Why do you think you don't see Red McClennon and Derrick Turner following him? He murdered them because they looked at me sweetly!"

"Lilly, don't..." Rictor muttered menacingly, once again turning on her. "I loved you!"

"You only love yourself! I understand what true love is now. I've seen it!"

"Look with your own eyes!" Angela yelled to the ghosts. "You're spirits! There's no flesh to hide the truth! Just look!"

"Don't listen to them! We can have vengeance on the man who killed us! Sean Heller is Merl come back to life! Just look at him! Killing him will free you from the past! We can make this place ours!"

Murly grabbed a chair from the conference room and smashed it against the door.

"Ah don't believe that's workin'," Julie said.

They suddenly, they heard music from behind them. "What's going on?" Tawny asked.

"All those musical devices," Dr. Strange said. "Efrem is turning them on." The psychic ran back to the conference room. Curious, Tawny and the others followed.

The Great Xantini moved quickly from boom box to Walkman, raising antennas, turning on the power and selecting radio reception. "Excellent idea," Dr. Strange said. He joined the Master Mentalist.

After they turned on several, Julie said, "Do ya notice somethin'? The air...."

"...seems abuzz. Curious," Xantini said. "Let's keep going.

Yes! The Ghostal Shores spirits are here, I can hear them!" Xantini cried. "This is helping! Turn them all on! Quickly!"

"I don't care what she says!" Kindrick cried. "I'm with you Lon!"

"Yeah, me too!" Delgado yelled.

Before the echo of their cries died, the Latino spirits holding the doors were bulled over by Broderick, Cannon, and the rest of the local spirits as they charged into the ballroom. Despite appearing gray and faded, the air around the local ghosts sparkled as if a mist afire. Their expressions were angrily alight, their eyes burning with an unfamiliar conviction.

Cannon bristled and shook like a bull ready to charge. Their eyes gleaming dangerously, the sextet of gamblers stood with their arms crossed. Eddie looked ready to spit nails. Even Jonathan appeared flushed and ready to fight.

"As young Master Madera proclaimed, this is our home!" Broderick announced. "And we shall defend it!"

"Let's show 'em we ain't slaves!" Mason shouted as he led the charge, plowing into the transients and sending several sprawling.

Elma, Chastity, Melainie and even Janice raced forward with fists balled and a head of steam. "And we ain't your women!" Chastity declared. She jumped on the back of an outlaw and bit him.

"This is our place!" Elma yelled as she joined in.

"And we want it back!" Dirk decked an outlaw, ducked a blow, then slammed his fist into Pike's gut.

"FIGHT BACK, YOU DAMNED COWARDS!" Rictor screamed. "Oww!" he cried, then kicked at Willy who had bitten him. Angus landed on Rictor's back and began clawing. Lilly cheered, and as the dark spirit spun around in an attempt to dislodge the cat, she struck him with her fist. The blow landed flush on his jaw, making his yellow eyes roll back. Before Rictor could retaliate, he was bowled over by David with a perfectish tackle.

"Leave...." Blasing started, then choked when Kindrick and Crane yanked on the rope, hauling him upward.

"BRODERICK!" Angela screamed. "HELP BLASING!" She slammed an elbow into Tito's face, then they were bowled over by Winston the banker and the block-jawed gambling brothers.

Another charge led by Cannon and Ingrid crashed into Kindrick and Crane. The pair let loose of the rope. Blasing crashed to the floor.

Fawn, Missy and Amber joined the female ghosts, jumping into the fray. Kicking, scratching, and biting, the ghostly women ripped the outlaws apart piece by piece. "Leave and never come back!" Cannon demanded.

"BITCHES!" Crane cried.

As Blasing slowly regained his sensibilities, his vision cleared, and he smiled wryly. The Ghostal Shores ghosts were rebelling, actually standing up for themselves. His smile broadened; the transient spirits started to look more than a little washed out.

"We ain't won yet, sonny boy," Cannon snapped.

"We're on our way!" Blasing cried. "Some are leaving!" Several of the hazy and insubstantial spirits fled.

"Go home!" Cannon boomed.

With an angry snarl Rictor kneed, then elbowed David, escaping the large spirit's grasp. When Rictor stood, he looked around in disbelief. Much of his gang had deserted him, leaving less than a dozen members.

"You're finished, Rictor!" Blasing yelled.

Rictor's color had faded, the rich blacks of his outfit looking bland and washed out. Even his face had paled, his cat-like eyes dulling to a sallow hue. "If I can't have this place, no one can!" Rictor announced. "Burn!" he shouted as he pointed to the nearby curtains. They smoldered a bit, smoke swirling around them. "BURN!" he commanded again. There was a puff of smoke, then nothing.

"I don't understand," he stammered.

"You don't have it anymore, Lon!" Lilly yelled.

Bewildered, Rictor abruptly dropped through the floor, appearing just as suddenly next to Heller. "You can't live if I can't! For what Merl did to me—you did to us—that night at the Gold Dust!" He reached out for Heller.

"Doctor! The hematite!" the Irishman cried, but it was too late. Rictor touched him, and in his mind's eye he burned. "I'm on fire!" Heller screamed. "Oh God, help me! I'm on fire!" Dr. Landrum tried to grab Heller's hands and put the rings on his fingers, but the Irishman flailed about too much, desperately patting at himself as he thrashed about in a macabre dance.

"You always were a poor loser!" Lilly yelled, then she jumped upon Rictor's back. The dark spirit spun around, flinging her to the ground.

"You're coming with me!" Rictor shouted. He grabbed Lilly by the hair.

As Rictor turned to leave, Angela confronted him. "You can leave," she said in a low, menacing tone, "but you're not taking Lilly."

Rictor laughed. "You can't stop me. No woman can!"

"Oh, is that so?" Angela asked. With a flick of the wrist, she threw a fistful of hematite shards into Rictor's face. He screamed in agony, his form wavering as if threatening to disappear.

Now free, Lilly dropped through the floor.

"If it is quite all right with you, miss," Broderick said as he moved to Angela's side, "I will finish here."

"Ha! You!" Rictor started. "You serve a queen! A woman!"

Broderick stiffened momentarily, then stepped gracefully forward. Angela didn't see the jab the Englishman threw, but Rictor's head jerked back. Broderick followed with a blow to the stomach, then landed several combinations. With each impact, Rictor seemed less vivid, his grayed darkness fading further. Broderick connected with a roundhouse, and the spirit gang's leader dropped to the floor like a sack of oats.

"Be so kind as to get up, you blackguard, so that I might do it all over again," Broderick said, sounding quite pleased.

"Great to see you again," Angela said to Broderick.

"Thank you, miss," Broderick replied. "When they heard Dr. Landrum's and Master Madera's pronouncements, the staff was inspired. The guards were so busy scratching that we had little trouble handling them."

"Angela!" Blasing limped toward her. Angela threw herself into his arms. They hugged fiercely.

The Englishman smiled. "If Master Madera can accept us, then what other miracles might be in store?"

"I ain't finished yet," Rictor muttered. "Are we boys!" The once dark spirit tried to get to his feet but could not. A few of the outlaw spirits—Bat, Crane, Delgado and Kindrick—still fought to free themselves, but most of the others simply watched Rictor struggle to stand.

Suddenly, a very ragged and faded spirit rose from the floor. "Caleb?!" Marsh cried. "Is that you? Where you been?" The mousy spirit couldn't believe his eyes.

"Can't be Caleb," Delgado replied. "Rictor told me Caleb deserted us!"

"Finally free," the ghost whispered, then coughed several times. "Rictor's been holding me prisoner. I just..." Caleb coughed again, "... escaped."

"Aye," a second spirit agreed as he appeared next to Caleb. Both ghosts were ill-defined and appeared sickly. Angela couldn't identify any features and wondered how the ghosts could recognize either one.

"Bean?!" Pike cried suddenly.

"Don't trust Rictor! He's been, I don't know... feeding off of me like some kind of leech. Lord, I'm so damn tired."

"They're lying! I haven't..." Rictor began to deny.

"Look! Can't you see the truth?" Caleb cried.

"If they're too dumb to see, then damn 'em!" Bean faded away. Caleb remained a little longer, giving the transients time to see the truth.

"They're telling the truth!" Pike cried.

"You bastard! You used us!" Kindrick cried. Together, he and Crane surged free of Ingrid and the others. Kindrick elbowed his way free of Cannon's grasp, then charged Rictor. The rest of the GSR spirits were just as surprised by the gangs' ferocity and couldn't restrain the remaining outlaws.

"STOP!" Rictor cried imperiously. "You work for me!"

As lanky Bat barreled by Broderick, he was already swinging. His roundhouse blow laid Rictor flat. Bat followed with a vicious kick to the gang leader's ribs.

Shocked by the viscousness of Bat's attack, Broderick stepped back into Pike's way. The ghost shoved the Englishman aside, then pulled his knife.

Rictor grabbed Bat's leg, yanking the lanky spirit off his feet. "You're not man enough to take me," Rictor snarled. With a smile, Pike dove in, headbutting the once dark spirit. Rictor staggered backward, barely retaining his balance.

"You owe us!" Delgado roared. The bullish spirit and the slovenly

Crane charged from behind, each driving a fist into Rictor's back. With an agonized gasp, the gang leader crumpled to one knee.

"You work for me!" Rictor cried defiantly, but his eyes were so pale they were almost white. Delgado and Crane slammed their fists into his back again, flattening the ever fading spirit. "I made you," he moaned, his voice growing hoarse.

"You turncoat!" Kindrick accused as he joined the others. Bat made room for the one-eyed ghost, who also pummeled Rictor. With fists balled and angry white faces, a half-dozen other gang spirits waited to get a piece of their former boss.

"Stop! Please!" Rictor whimpered, his voice now a harsh whine. Another ghost crowded in, and five spirits pounded away.

The GSR ghosts moved to encircle the beating, but none of them stepped in to stop it. Angela noticed Broderick wringing his hands as if wondering whether he should do something or not. "He deserves it, Broderick," Angela told the Englishman.

"I know. It is just difficult to watch."

When Rictor quit screaming, the outlaws stepped back. They had lost all color, but Rictor was in even worse shape. The once dark spirit was hazy and appeared gray, mostly a cloud of mist except for the features of his face.

"I want back what's mine," Kindrick said. He pulled his knife, then rushed forward, slashing and tearing at Rictor. Crane shouted out in agreement and joined him.

"No!" Rictor wheezed, his voice almost gone. Like a pack of wild animals, the others closed in, tearing at and shredding the ethereal spirit. Long tendrils and wisps of fog flew from the massacre as if fur from a cat fight. At first the wisps were pale, almost translucent before fading in a brief shower of sparks, then they darkened.

The polluted haze grew heavier and heavier, and finally Rictor's hoarse cries grew silent. Suddenly, there was a loud tearing sound. A bitterly cold wind swirled, gathering and growing in strength. Rictor let out a piercing final scream that was quickly lost in the howling whirlwind.

Angela shivered. Blasing pulled her closer. Curtains were caught in the maelstrom and torn from the walls, whirling about the room in a circle. The door below the stage jerked open and chairs were yanked from their storage space. They clanked and cavorted about like metal tumbleweeds caught in a twister.

None of this bothered the ghosts, the curtains and chairs passing through them, but Angela and Blasing were endangered. After getting clipped by a spinning chair, they dove away from the gathering and pressed themselves against the floor. Curtains fluttered by and several tumbling chairs bounced over them.

A sudden burst of brilliance bleached everything white, and the incandescence seemed to paralyze everyone. The howling died, and the air seemed cleaner—the scent of a lightning strike pungent in the air. When the brightness faded, the outlaws stepped back from each other. All that remained of Rictor was a dark smudge on the floor.

"What now, boys?" Cannon asked.

"You ain't got nothin' ta fear from us," Delgado said. "We been foolin' ourselves. We'll be leavin' now." Kindrick nodded.

"Never show your face around here again," Blasing told them.

Cannon, Mason, Dirk and the others stepped back, letting the outlaws pass. As if they'd lost the will to be, the washed out spirits meandered away. Angela thought she saw them fading further with each step. When they departed through the walls, there was almost nothing left of them.

"I hope that ends it," Angela said.

"We'll be ready for them if there is a next time," Dirk assured her.

"You bet!" Cannon agreed, chortled at her own play on words.

"We showed 'em what we're made of. Yes we did!" Mason agreed.

"What about Heller?" Blasing asked Dr. Landrum. The Irishman's face was frozen in contorted agony, his eyes wide and his lips snarled back in pain.

Dr. Landrum checked for breathing and a pulse. "None," he said, then began CPR.

"Do not bother, sir," Broderick said. "I saw his spirit depart, for Hell, if there is such a place."

Dr. Landrum paused for a moment, then said, "I have to try...." He continued his resuscitation attempt.

Blasing moved to help, but Broderick stopped him with a light touch. "There is no hope, sir. None at all."

Lilly drifted from the floor. "There you are!" Angela exclaimed.

"I was beginning to worry about you!"

Next to Lilly, Fawn also drifted up from the floor. "Meet Bean," Lilly said with a impish smile when she motioned to Fawn.

The female spirit grew hazy and ill-defined for a moment, then returned to her usual form. "I think acting is such a natural part of a lady's wiles."

"And you were Caleb?" Angela said, realization suddenly dawning. Lilly nodded. "Why didn't they see through your disguises?"

"Maybe because we're great actors," Lilly laughed, "or maybe they were looking to see if Rictor had been leeching from us, and he had been, off both of us," Lilly replied. Fawn nodded.

"Excellently played! Bravo!" Broderick applauded.

"Thank you, ladies," Blasing said. Fawn smiled and bowed.

"I owed you all, and I owed it to myself," Lilly told him. "Fawn, I'm so sorry," Lilly apologized, "can you forgive me for being such a witch?"

Fawn looked at Angela, then said, "Ah, he was already spoken for anyway." Laughing, the two spirits hugged.

"Simply amazing." Murly wore a huge smile as he taped it all. "We're going to be famous."

Angela kissed Blasing, then said, "You need to see a doctor."

He gently touched her wounded cheek. "So do... Hey! What about the fires!" Blasing suddenly remembered. "We could still be in danger!"

Xantini handed Blasing a Walkie-Talkie, and everyone waited breathlessly as he spoke with Thomasson. They could tell by Blasing's half of the conversation that things were going well, and when he finally said, "Everything's under control—for once. The sprinklers are working just fine." Everyone cheered and hugged, spirits and people mingling freely. "I think this is cause for celebration!" Blasing announced.

"Heller?" Blasing quietly asked Dr. Landrum. He shook his head. "Just like Meg. Rictor got his revenge before his gang turned the tables on him. What happened to your people?"

"They took the prisoners back to the security office. After inhaling all that smoke, they weren't in any condition to cause trouble. We'll look around and find someplace else to put them."

"Before we celebrate, let's take a count and make sure everyone's all right," Blasing said.

"We can spread the news quickly," Broderick offered.

"Don't scare anyone," Angela cautioned him. "Let them know everything is normal."

Blasing laughed good-naturedly at the absurdity of her statement, then added, "And when you do that, invite them to the celebration."

"A grand idea, sir, but where?"

"How about the lobby and Old West Avenue? A street party, so to speak." Angela suggested.

"I'll let the staff know they can join in, too. They deserve it," Blasing said.

"A grand gesture, sir!"

"Let's get moving!" Blasing said. "Just do the best you can. A little food, plenty of wine, music—hey, where's Charlie?" The piano began to play a jaunty, upbeat tune. Charlie appeared on the bench, his fingers dancing across the ebony and ivory.

"How about an exclusive interview?" Tawny asked Blasing.

"Later. Interview a ghost! They regained something important tonight!"

"Yeah!" Murly agreed. "We can have an exclusive! The first to interview the spirits of Ghostal Shores! Famous is as famous does!"

"If we have permission to release what we know," Tawny said, directing her comment toward Blasing. He nodded. "All right!"

On the way down the steps to where the resort staff waited, Blasing leaned against Angela. "I hope you're not too exhausted. I have a private celebration in mind for later," she said with a lascivious smile.

"I'll muster some energy," Blasing said, then hugged her. Stopping on the landing, they kissed.

"You know, somewhere, I think Peter is smiling," Angela said. Her smile seemed to light up the night.

FORTY

The phone rang just before dawn, pulling Blasing from Angela's warm embrace. "Okay, I'll be right down," Blasing replied.

"Who was it?" Angela asked around a yawn.

"Doctor DEA," Blasing said. He grabbed his clothes from a chair and began dressing. "The road is open, and things are hopping. Ambulances have arrived and law enforcement officials are shutting down the resort." He yawned. "Coming?"

Angela groaned. "I'll be down in a few minutes."

"Right. See you downstairs." Blasing kissed her, then departed.

Angela found Blasing and Dr. Landrum standing on the front porch talking to a tall man dressed in a dark suit and sunglasses. Wringing his hands, Broderick hovered alongside Blasing.

Not wanting to interrupt, Angela waited, taking in the scene. The crimson sun was just peeking through the eastward trees, casting a lurid red glow across the grounds and almost matching the flashing lights of the emergency vehicles. Officials had apparently designated Ghostal Shores a disaster area; triage was being employed.

The entryway drive had been blocked off, allowing only official vehicles to enter. As one ambulance departed, another took its place. A trio of police vans lined up, and under the direction of agent Tally, they had almost finished loading the security personnel.

Guests departed quietly, being evacuated in an orderly fashion, their cars pulled to the curb and loaded for them. Each customer was briefly questioned by special agents dressed like the man next to Blasing and Dr. Landrum. Angela gathered they were writing down names, addresses and phone numbers, just in case more questioning was needed or their investigation revealed something.

"All's well that ends well," Broderick said.

"Not quite," Angela replied. "Candy's gone."

"But she's gone to a better place, Miss."

"I know," Angela said, then began to cry. "Better than haunting someplace." She started, realizing what she'd said. "Oh, Broderick! I'm sorry, I didn't mean...."

"Quite all right, miss. I know what you meant, and I quite agree. Why stay on earth when you can go to heaven? I am not sure why I am still here, but I do know that if I had not come to Ghostal Shores, I would not have met you or Master Madera."

"Thank you, Broderick. You are very special," Angela said, wiping away a tear, then she gave the ghost a hug.

"Oh dear." Broderick stiffened.

"Let yourself go, Broderick," Angela sniffled. Finally, the English spirit returned her hug. "You won't hurt me, and sometimes it's okay to bend the rules. It's the intent that's important, not the rule itself."

"It seems that times are changing. Miss, do you have any idea what will happen to us? The ghosts and I are very concerned."

"Let's find out." As they approached Blasing and Dr. Landrum, the agent left, heading down the steps. "Good morning, Geoff. How are things going?" Angela asked. She slipped under Blasing's arm.

"Very well, considering."

"We should be closed by noon," Blasing told her. "Including employees. After all the guests have departed, they'll be evacuated."

"I'm impressed," Angela replied.

"We aren't sure that all the employees are innocent bystanders, so we're making sure we know where to find them," Dr. Landrum said.

The front doors opened, and Eva was led out by two agents. Although a bit haggard, the Frenchwoman appeared surprisingly calm. She glanced in their direction, glaring at Angela but smiling at Blasing. Eva appeared as if she wanted to speak, but said nothing.

"Some things never change," Angela sighed. Women were going to be staring hungrily at Blasing all the time, but she could handle it, because he'd be looking at her. "What's going to happen to her?" Angela said, hoping Eva would rot in jail.

"I think she's going to turn evidence to reduce her sentence," Dr. Landrum replied.

"Oh dear," Broderick said, looking very sad.

Dr. Landrum glanced askance at the ghost. "It'll depend on how the investigation progresses. They'll be tearing up the sidewalk in the northern wing. Then, after the resort has been thoroughly searched, I imagine you'll be free to remodel and re-open."

"I just love dealing with insurance companies," Angela sighed. "What did you decide about Tawny Lane?"

"She left a couple of hours ago. We aren't allowing any reporters on the estate, but I suspect a guest or two will go straight to the media. Hell, some who seek the limelight or some extra cash have probably pulled over outside the front gate and are granting interviews as we speak. It was only fair that since Ms. Lane survived the last two days, she get first crack at the story."

"The media was bound to find out sooner or later," Angela agreed. "Besides, she probably called it in last night."

"Could be why there's so many media types waiting outside the front gate."

"Maybe we'll get lucky, and she'll put a positive spin on it," Blasing said.

An elderly man dressed in a San Francisco 49ers slicker ascended the steps to approach them. "Excuse me. Mr. Madera?"

"Yes, what can I do for you?"

"My name's Trace Oliver. My wife and I wanted you to know that this was the most exciting vacation we've ever had, and we'll come again as soon as you re-open! And don't worry, I've heard the same from many other people. We can't wait to see the changes. This place is better than Disneyland!"

"We look forward to having you back, Mr. Oliver," Blasing said as he shook the man's hand. "Drive safely." Oliver nodded, then returned to his wife near their car.

"I told you Californians were an odd lot," Angela said.

"We do live with the ground shifting beneath our feet," Blasing replied.

"There is that. Geoff, what's going to happen to the ghosts?" Angela asked.

"Nothing. They can stay of course. We can't make them leave."

"Besides, someone needs to watch over the place," Blasing said. "Keep away the vandals."

"If you'll excuse me," Dr. Landrum said. "I have some things to take care of."

"Certainly," Angela said. "I guess it's all wrapped up nice and neat. I wish Heller and Meg had lived to go on trial."

"Chadwick and the others will," Blasing said. "And some would say Meg and Heller received their just desserts. Besides, Candy wouldn't want you to insist on your pound of flesh."

"You don't think so?" Angela said quizzically. She looked to the east, the sun peeking over the tops of the trees, washing the grounds in a lovely pink light. It reminded her of Candy. "I think you're right. It's time for healing and going forward." Angela hugged Blasing. "She'd want me to look to the future. And I think we have good times ahead, Mr. Madera. She'd want me to focus on that, not on mourning her. I feel she'll always be with me—an inspiration to keep going."

"You know, earlier I thought I'd seen Jenny, and that she'd given me her blessing—for us to be together...."

"But that turned out to be Lilly," Angela said softly.

"Yes, but when we were trying to cleanse the bricks, I know I felt her. When she hugged me, I knew that it was all right to move on. To be with you."

Angela smiled, her eyes brightly aglow. "I look forward to helping you rebuild.

"You will be joining us?" Broderick asked hopefully.

"Most definitely," Blasing said.

"If I pass the kid test," Angela said. Broderick appeared perplexed.

"She's going to take some vacation time and visit Tahoe," Blasing told him.

"An excellent idea, Miss," Broderick said.

"Glad you approve," Blasing said wryly.

"They owe me after interrupting my last vacation, and Blasing and I need some peaceful time when events aren't throwing us together, making us wonder if we'll be alive tomorrow. We want to make sure we're not doing anything hasty. We've known each other just over a week now. And disaster relationships... Well...."

Broderick's gaze seemed penetrating. "You are not doing anything hasty. Trust one who can see your spirits. But I must say, it's going to be very lonely around here for a while."

Blasing smiled. "Angela and I talked about that. How about coming with us to Tahoe?"

Broderick stammered and stuttered like Angela had never seen him before. "I... I cannot. I am tied here. And very busy."

"The children would love to meet you," Blasing said, "especially Kelly, and since we'll be living here someday soon, I'd like to gradually introduce them to ghosts, unlike what happened to me. I don't want them frightened of you all."

"Perish the thought," Angela said.

Broderick loosened his collar. "A... good idea, sir, but...."

"Broderick. You're never too old to change. Let go of the past. There won't be anything to do around here for a while, come join us," Angela cajoled. "So many other things have changed, and you saw what happened to Rictor when he clung to the past. Live a little."

"But who would watch over the ghosts?" Broderick asked. "What if the ruffians return?"

"Cannon and Mason can handle it, along with Dirk. And Lilly has offered to stay and help. I accepted," Blasing said. "She's earned it."

"Indeed, but...."

"Do the ghosts really have to be watched?" Angela asked. "They seem to have grown some during our stay."

"Indeed. They did show heart, standing up for themselves. A change for sure, and a very impressive one at that, I must say." Broderick pondered the idea for a time, then said, "I shall do it! I would so love to meet your children!"

"Great!" Blasing said. "You're part of the family. I'll help you adjust, just as you helped me."

"I will do my best, Master Madera."

While she still held on to Blasing, Angela hugged Broderick once more. "Glad to have you with us, Broderick. One thing though. When his kids are around, don't call Blasing, Master Madera, he'll get an even bigger head than he already has from all those women fawning over him."

With an arched eyebrow, Broderick said, "Hmm. I see your point, Miss. And yet, having respect should never change. And to tell you the simple truth, I do not..." he closed his eyes for a moment as if concentrating, "...I don't know if I can change that much, but I will... I'll certainly try."

"He used a contraction!" Angela gasped. "Two even! What's the world coming to?"

"I guess there's hope any of us can change for the better," Blasing mused. "What next, Broderick? A smile?"

"Could be Sir, after all, we are Blasing new trails," Broderick chortled.

Excerpts from

The Magic Bicycle
and
Vampire Hunters

by William Hill

Otter Creek Press
www.otterpress.com
whill73528@aol.com,

THE MAGIC BICYCLE

FIRST RIDE

As the bicycle raced faster and faster, the world around them blurred into a whirlwind of colors. Danny felt lighter and was sure the bicycle had lost contact with the road. But he still felt safe.

A roaring sound like a thousand charging lions was followed by a tremendous clap of thunder. Bright, almost blinding sparks surrounded them, then the world went white for a moment, then turned into a hazy grayness as if they were riding through engulfing clouds. Danny suddenly noticed it was quiet. Where was the sound of the wind?

Clouds parted. They were riding atop a gleaming rainbow. Below were brilliant streaks of red, orange, yellow, green and blue. Forming walls along each side of them was an electric purple. It was so bright that when Danny looked at himself, everything he wore, even his skin, glowed brilliant violet.

Murg meowed loud and long. Danny looked over his shoulder. The calico was standing on his shoulder staring skyward. Danny followed Murg's gaze and found sparkling stars in the darkness above. They were riding across the sky to South Carolina!!

The world suddenly went white, then flashed brightly as if they rode directly into a star. The lions roared once more. The thunder cracked as if a giant hole were being ripped in the sky. Danny was disoriented for a moment, then he realized they had done it! In less than a minute, they had ridden from Texas to the east coast near Myrtle Beach, South Carolina.

ALIEN ENCOUNTER

Danny tumbled head over heels as he crashed down the stairs, each step biting into him as he bounced. He covered his head as best he could and hoped he survived. His feet rebounded off the bannister and sent him cartwheeling over the edge of the stairway.

Danny landed on an old tattered mattress that cushioned his

impact. Something warm brushed against his leg. "I'll live, Murg," Danny groaned. He opened his eyes and was shocked to be staring at himself. Crimson and azure light flashed through the boarded windows of the basement and splayed about the room, illuminating his double.

Jumping to his feet to flee, Danny conked his head on the edge of the steps. Stars seemed to fill his vision, falling across his double's face. Its expression had changed from imitating his surprise to capturing his pain. "Who... what are you?" Danny whispered.

Words sounded inside Danny's head. "Greetings, I am Kahlaye-dee, a stranger to your planet." Danny was amazed. Not a word had touched his ears. The aliens' lips had never moved.

Danny watched slack-jawed as the wondrous transformation took place before his eyes. His double's features changed, no longer mimicking Danny. The shape-shifter's form shrunk, becoming thinner, although its head stayed the same size. Its flaming red curls disappeared, now replaced by short blue hair that stood straight up, reminding Danny of a classmate. Its skin had lost its fleshy color and now gleamed with a bronzed hue. The stranger's nose had lengthened, flattened and spread wide. Its— or maybe—his eyes were still blue, but now glowed from deep within the tall, recessed sockets of his elongated face. Thin lips curled as the skinny being smiled, then reached out to touch him.

THE VAMPIRE HUNTERS

THE INITIATION

"Ahhh..." the barn door opened slowly, allowing a faint light to be cast across the barn yard. Scooter jumped at least a foot and almost screamed, barely managing to swallow.

Chandler's shadow was crisp, his form distinctly outlined against the light. With a bottle in each hand, he stepped outside and began to guzzle from one bottle, then the other.

Shakily raising the camera, Scooter tried to get a good look at Marcus Chandler. Even the darkness couldn't totally conceal his pale complexion. It seemed to have a gleaming quality that reminded Scooter of the house's eerie luminescence.

Scooter took a deep breath, crossed his fingers, then jumped in front of the author. With quivering hands, he snapped picture after picture, the flash illuminating the night as though flickering lightning.

"AWWW!" Chandler screamed. He dropped the bottles, clenching his empty hands. In the flashing white light, Scooter could see Chandler's gaunt face. It had been transformed into something horrible, contorted and twisted as if he were in sheer agony. His flesh appeared to take on an unholy illumination. His eyes were amazingly bright, blazing embers within black holes.

"Who's there? Damn you! Damn the Press! Why won't you leave me alone?" Chandler suddenly swung at Scooter, who stumbled backwards to avoid the blow.

Almost dropping the camera, Scooter turned and ran toward the Armadillos. "You're dead meat!" Chandler cried as he blindly pursued the young redhead.

"Hear me? Dead meat! You're not in Hollywood anymore! You're in TEXAS! Hear me?! Texas! And you're trespassing on my property!"

Kristie and Russell looked at each other, their thoughts the same: RUN!

Straining against his collar, Flash barked. Scooter raced past them, not even pausing as he tossed Garrett the camera and the Polaroid prints. The golden Lab jerked free and joined his friend in flight. Russell and Kristie bolted together, following in Scooter's wake.

"Nothing to worry about, Chaquita," Garrett told them.

"Race ya to the wheels," CJ suggested eagerly.

"Yeah!" BJ agreed. Holding their hats, the brothers fled. Jo was just a few slow steps behind.

Garrett knelt to pick up a fallen photo, then sneered, looking from the completely gray picture to Chandler. As Garrett watched, the infamous director sprinted through the grass, unerringly heading toward the truck they hid behind as if guided by radar. Racquel's fingernails dug painfully into Garrett's arm. "Let go!" he whispered.

Garrett's sneer was short-lived, his expression slowly becoming doubtful. He wasn't afraid of anything... unless this guy really was a vampire. Could that be? Impossible. But... he looked like a vampire! And the way he moved....

"Come on, Chaquita," Garrett breathed, scared for the first time in a long time. As Chandler hurdled the fence, Garrett grabbed Racquel and ran as fast as he could, dragging her along with him.

"Please! So help me, God, I'll never do this again!" Russell gasped as he ran, holding his arms in front of his face as protection from the ripping branches. He could barely see Scooter and Flash ahead of him, darting in and out of the trees with surprising agility.

Russell knew nobody could outrun Scooter. He'd reach the bicycles first. But what about the rest of them? If he got caught and his dad found out.... Russell sprinted as if slavering Dobermans were breathing hot on his heels.

Huffing and grunting, Jo ran as fast as she could, rumbling through the woods. She wanted to be far away from here. Jo liked to believe she was like her three brothers——one tough gringa. But now, all she wanted was to cruise the back roads on her Harley, the wind in her face blowing away her fear and sweat.

Something grabbed at her feet. Jo stumbled. Unable to recover, she fell forward.

When she looked up, she said, "Hey, what are you doing here?! You following me?"

Darkness swept forward from the figure, engulfing her. Jo felt a biting pain, then the last thing she heard was a haunting chuckle.

Nearby, Kristie came to a halt. Was that a scream? She strained to listen but couldn't hear anything besides the thundering of her heart and the gasping of her ragged breath. She couldn't see anything either. What if something had happened to one of them? She was unexplainably afraid for Scooter. Should she use her flashlight? Or would it give her away? She wished she had never come along, wished she were elsewhere.

Unable to control her fear, Kristie fled. The boys would take care of themselves. Boys always did. In the distance, she heard a dog bark and wondered about Scooter.

Still running, Russell thought he heard something fall, then the silence was heavy as the rapidly thickening fog muffled all sound. The mists were pervasive and almost waist deep in some places. He couldn't see where he was running and was worried he might step in a hole.

Somewhere, Flash began barking. Russell paused, struck by the feeling that something bad had happened to Scooter. Should he look for him? He heard a soft swishing noise. Then a slow intake of breath, followed by a much sharper gasp. Russell's fear threw him into over-drive. Hoping Scooter would forgive him for being a coward and a deserter, Russell sprinted toward the abandoned cabin.

Somewhere behind everyone else, Garrett and Racquel moved through the woods. "Here's a shortcut!" Garrett exclaimed. "We'll beat everybody to the wheels!"

"What about Russell?" Racquel asked.

"He'll be fine." Garrett replied. She looked doubtful, so he kissed her on the cheek and said, "Trust me, Babe." Racquel didn't smile, so he said, "Come on, or I'm gonna leave ya." Racquel hesitated only a moment before following.

Elsewhere in the woods, BJ grabbed CJ by the arm. "The bicycles are this way."

"No way, Jose´" CJ disagreed, but BJ dragged him along anyway. They moved quickly toward a thicket where a fallen tree was draped so heavily in fog it might have been poured on. There was the hooting of an owl, but no other movements or sounds.

"We're lost!" CJ cried. Sweat ran down his nose, making his glasses slide. He shoved them higher onto his nose. They kept fogging, so he finally took them off to dry. "Your sense of direction sucks the big one." BJ ignored him and kept moving. "Hey, I thought I saw something."

"Bull. Ya don't even have...." BJ started, then he too saw a cloud of dark fog drifting toward them, reshaping and almost taking on a human form. The brothers thought they heard a low chuckle and ran. They stumbled along, missing trees but tripping over rocks, stumps and fire ant mounds. All around the fog was rising as though a pool were filling up to its rim.

"Wish you hadn't dropped the flashlight," BJ said. "All you ever do is complain," CJ reported. "Moan and groan. Moan and groan." They had come to a rail fence that should have stretched left and right but was truncated, immediately disappearing into the mist.

"Hey, I don't remember this."

"I don't either." Suddenly, as though a breeze touched the mist, the fog billowed and something appeared to slide along the fence rails. The boys bolted.

"Man, oh man, oh man..." Scooter breathed, running even faster than earlier and easily outdistancing the others. He barely noticed Flash running smoothly alongside. Scooter ran through a low branch that nearly decapitated him and barely noticed. He had only one thought in mind—ESCAPE! Unless he was lost, the fence should be coming up soon, and then he'd be at the deserted house and on his bicycle.

Scooter thought he heard the crack of a stick behind him. Worried about his friend, Scooter glanced over his shoulder. "Russell!!?" As he turned around, Scooter's world abruptly crashed to black. Flash began barking wildly.

The brothers paused, their breathing harsh. Both bent over, hands on knees with sweat dripping from their soaked shirts. They hoped to have outraced whatever was pursuing them. "I'm exhausted," CJ gasped. BJ nodded.

Something suddenly appeared in the fog, darting among the trees ahead of them, quickly moving in and out of the tall grasses. The Mochrie brothers fled at a dead run.

Shortly, BJ and CJ arrived at a creek bed where the fog was worse, heavier and opaque. CJ paused, but BJ said, "Keep going this way." Then he saw the fog swirl and puff, signaling that something massive approached. BJ thought he saw something out of the corner of his eye. "Somebody's trying to scare us. Stand and fight!" He shakily pulled out his .38. Both were sure they heard the quiet, mocking laughter this time. BJ hesitated, unnerved and unsure of where to fire.

They looked at each other and ran again. CJ was behind his brother when he tripped, falling head over heels, arms outstretched. "YEAAOK!" Something snapped. Pain rocketed up his arm. Writhing in agony, CJ grasped his left wrist and moaned, tears streaming down his cheeks.

"CJ?" BJ called, stopping, then retracing his steps. Where was he? He could hear him but couldn't see him! "What's wrong?! COME ON!"

Not far away, the white mist whirled and roiled. A cold breeze rippled past him as something dark took shape within the fog. Red pinpoints, like eyes of a rabid wolf, held him frozen for a moment, then BJ raised his .38 and fired. KABLAMM! KABLAMM! KABLAMM! The darkness swept forward, shoving the mist aside. The .38 clicked emptily. BJ turned and ran.

CJ heard his brother flee. "BJ! Don't...." A coldness suddenly reached him, sweeping across him and chilling his sweat-drenched body. Panic surged through him. He tried to clamber to his feet but slipped and fell. The fog around him seemed to dissipate, but the darkness grew even larger, heavier.

A tall, long limbed figure abruptly loomed over CJ. "Help me BJ!! Help me"

OTTER CREEK PRESS
P. O. BOX 416
DOCTORS INLET, FL 32030-0416

Telephone: 904 264-0465
Toll Free : 1-800-326-4809
Web Site : www.otterpress.com
Email   : Whill73528@aol.com

ORDER FORM

$ 15.95 each U.S.
$ 19.95 each Canada
$ 24.95 each U.S (Hardback)
$ 28.95 each Canada (Hardback)

Please include $4 for S&H

Copies _____   Amount $ _____

Book Title(s)   _____

_____

_____

_____

Address   _____

City _____ St. _____ Zip _____

Otter Creek Press accepts checks and money orders.

ABOUT THE AUTHOR

William Hill is a native of Indianapolis, Indiana, and first learned to read through comic books, and adventure and science fiction novels.

He has lived in Kansas (Shawnee Mission), Tennessee (Nashville and Bristol—setting of *Dawn of the Vampire*), and Texas (Denton, Dallas, Richardson, and Cedar Creek—setting of *Vampire's Kiss*). He has "serious" degrees from Vanderbilt University in Economics and an MBA from the University of North Texas.

Since realizing that the corporate world often stifles creative thought and discourages personal imagination, Bill has been employed as an alchemist in South Lake Tahoe, and an EMT/Ski Patroller at a North Lake Tahoe resort.

Although his first writing love is magic-oriented fantasy, Hill's first and second novels—*Dawn of the Vampire* and *Vampire's Kiss*—are supernatural thrillers published by Pinnacle. *The Magic Bicycle* is published by Otter Creek Press.

Bill and his lovely and supportive wife, Kat, who injected felineness into Murg and femininity into Angela, currently reside in Lake Tahoe, Nevada. Bill intends to write imaginative fiction and fantasy until dirt is shoveled upon his coffin.